Growing up r[...] of time observ[...] research! Now she spends her days fantasising about gorgeous men and their love lives. Annie has been a reader all her life. She also loves travel, long walks, good company and great food. You can contact her at annie@annie-west.com or via PO Box 1041, Warners Bay, NSW 2282, Australia.

**Angela Bissell** lives with her husband and one crazy Ragdoll cat in the vibrant harbourside city of Wellington, New Zealand. In her twenties, with a wad of savings and a few meagre possessions, she took off for Europe, backpacking through Egypt, Israel, Turkey and the Greek Islands before finding her way to London, where she settled and worked in a glamorous hotel for several years. Clearly the perfect grounding for her love of Mills & Boon Modern Romance! Visit her at www.angelabissell.com.

A RITA® Award-nominated author, **Elle Kennedy** grew up in the suburbs of Toronto, Ontario, and holds a B.A. in English from York University. From an early age she knew she wanted to be a writer, and actively began pursuing that dream when she was a teenager. She loves strong heroines and sexy alpha heroes, and just enough h[...] to keep things interesting.

Elle loves to [...] website, www.elleke[...] to send her a note.

D1332912

# Ruthless Revenge

## COLLECTION

July 2018

August 2018

September 2018

October 2018

November 2018

December 2018

# Ruthless Revenge: Sweet Surrender

ANNIE WEST

ANGELA BISSELL

ELLE KENNEDY

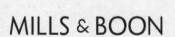

MILLS & BOON

Published in Great Britain 2018
by Mills & Boon, an imprint of HarperCollins*Publishers*
1 London Bridge Street, London, SE1 9GF

Ruthless Revenge: Sweet Surrender © 2018 Harlequin Books S.A.

*Seducing His Enemy's Daughter* © 2015 Annie West
*Surrendering to the Vengeful Italian* © 2016 Angela Bissell
*Soldier under Siege* © 2013 Leeanne Kenedy

ISBN: 978-0-263-26828-7

09-1118

**MIX**
Paper from
responsible sources
FSC™ C007454

# SEDUCING HIS ENEMY'S DAUGHTER

**ANNIE WEST**

# CHAPTER ONE

'OF COURSE YOU'LL do it. You know you will.' Reg Sanderson paused in the act of pouring a double whisky to fix his gimlet stare on his daughter. As if he could bend her to his will, like he had years ago.

Ella shook her head, wondering how any man got to be so caught up in his own importance that he didn't notice the world had altered. *She'd* changed in the years since she'd walked out. Even Fuzz and Rob had changed lately, but their father hadn't realised.

He was too focused on his business machinations. Except they were no longer just business. His latest scheme was an outrageous mix of commercial and personal.

No wonder Fuzz had run. Felicity Sanderson might be flighty and spoiled, as only the favourite child of a very rich man could be, but she was no fool.

'Don't be absurd.' Ella stared her father down, ignoring his razor-sharp glare. It had taken years of practice to stand tall against his brutal behaviour but it came naturally now. 'This is nothing to do with me. You'll have to sort it out yourself.'

Who'd have thought Reg Sanderson would come cap in hand to his forgotten middle child, the one he'd ignored for so long?

Except there'd been nothing cap in hand about his bellowing phone call, demanding she come to his harbourside home instantly because her sister Felicity was about to destroy her life.

'Of course you're involved,' he roared, then caught himself, pausing to swallow a slug of alcohol. 'You're my only hope, Ella.' This time his tone was conciliatory, almost conspiratorial.

Ella's hackles rose, tension clamping her belly. Her father shouted whenever he didn't instantly get his way. But it was when he pretended to be on your side that you really needed to beware.

'I'm sorry.' She bit her lip, reminding herself there was no need for her to apologise. Yet ancient habits died hard. She lifted her chin. 'It's a crazy idea and even if it weren't I couldn't fill in for Felicity. I'm not—'

'Pah! Of course you can't hold a candle to your sister. But with a makeover and some coaching you'll do.'

Ella stood tall. Once upon a time his constant references to the many ways she didn't measure up to her older sister—in looks, grace, vivacity, charm, the ability to throw on anything and look like a million dollars—had been the bane of her life. Now she knew life held more important things than trying, fruitlessly, to live up to his expectations.

'I was going to say I'm not interested in getting to know any of your business cronies, much less *marrying* one.'

Ella shuddered. She'd escaped her awful father in her teens and never looked back. This man her father so wanted to do business with would be in the same mould: grasping, selfish, dishonest. She'd met his associates before.

'I'm sure if you explain the situation he'll understand.' She got up from the white leather lounge, retrieved her shoulder bag and turned towards the door.

'Understand?' Her father's voice cracked on the word, transfixing Ella. Despite his volatile temperament, she'd swear it was the closest he'd come to real emotion in years. Even when her mother died he'd shed only crocodile tears.

'Donato Salazar isn't the sort to *understand*. You don't realise how badly I need him. I suggested marriage to cement our business ties and he agreed to consider it.' Her father's tone made it clear what an honour that was. This from a man who viewed himself as the acme of Sydney business and society.

'I need Salazar's money. Without it I'll go under and soon. Even with his money…' He looked every bit his age despite the work he'd had to keep the lines and sags of good living at bay. 'I need a *personal* tie to keep me safe. A family tie.' His tone was grim, his expression ugly, a familiar scheming look in his eye.

The idea of her father's massive wealth at risk should have shocked her. But somehow it didn't. He was an inveterate risk-taker.

'You don't trust him.' Ella stared in revulsion. 'Yet you want your daughter to marry him.'

'Oh, don't be such a prude. You remind me of your mother.' His lip curled. 'Salazar can give a woman everything money can buy. You'll be set for life.'

Ella said nothing. *She* knew her mother's worth, and that money couldn't buy the important things in life. But the discussion was academic. Fuzz had run rather than meet this Salazar person and Ella had no intention of sacrificing herself to her father's schemes. Besides, this paragon of corporate success wouldn't be interested in having Reg Sanderson's *other* daughter foisted on him. The dull, uninteresting one who actually worked for a living.

She was ordinary, a nurse who spent her days home-visiting the sick. She had nothing in common with a corporate high-flyer. Ella turned towards the door again.

'Without Salazar's money I lose everything. The business, this house. Everything. And if I go belly up, what do you think happens to your siblings?' He paused long enough for foreboding to trickle down Ella's spine.

'What about the money for your brother's new venture?' No mistaking the venom in his tone. 'The one Rob's so wrapped up in now he's left the family business. The one supporting your sister, Felicity, and her *boyfriend*.' He all but spat the word.

Ella swung around, her pulse fluttering in her throat.

'*Rob's* money, not yours.'

He shrugged, his gaze sliding sideways. 'I…accessed some of it to tide me over.' He must have sensed her outrage, cutting her off before she could speak. 'If I go down, so do they. How do you think they'll cope when the cash to finish refurbishing their fine resort disappears?' Triumph lit her father's pale eyes.

Impotent fury blindsided her. He'd *stolen* from Rob but still expected her to help him!

Trust him to realise her feelings for her siblings was a weakness he could exploit.

She'd felt profound relief that Fuzz and Rob had finally broken from their father's slimy influence. He'd poisoned their lives too long. If they lost this chance to build something for themselves… Ella shrank inside. Rob *might* be okay; he'd shown unexpected steel in walking away from all their father offered. But Fuzz had done so little for herself. Despite her sister's air of casual unconcern Ella knew she had deep-seated self-doubts. A setback like this—

Ella stiffened her shoulders like a prisoner facing a firing squad even as everything inside screamed in protest.

'All right,' she bit out. 'I'll meet him.'

But only to explain that her sister, Felicity, was no longer part of the business deal.

It would be straightforward. What sane man expected marriage to cement a business deal?

'Here she is at last.' Her father's voice vibrated with bonhomie. 'I'd like you to meet my daughter Ella.'

For a moment longer she stood, watching the dying sun turn Sydney Harbour to a mirror of peach and copper. Then with a swift, sustaining breath she made herself turn.

'Ella, my dear.' Her father's greeting made her blink. It was the first endearment he'd ever given her. She stared blankly. Once she'd have given anything to hear him address her with approval and pleasure.

The realisation made something long-forgotten crumple inside.

He spoke again. Ella heard the name Donato Salazar and pasted on a smile. She turned to the man beside him, looking up, then up again.

Something jabbed hard at her insides, a blow that all but rocked Ella back on her feet after the shock of her father's words.

The man before her didn't belong at one of her father's parties. That was her first thought.

These events teetered on the borderline between trendy and louche. This man was too...*definite* to be either. *Elemental* was the word hovering in her head. He was like a force of nature, a leader, not one of the led.

*Beautiful* was her second thought.

Even the thin scar running up one cheek emphasised rather than detracted from the powerful beauty of that face.

It was beautiful in the way a remote mountain crag was, its icy peak compelling to climbers yet treacherous. In the way a storm at sea was beautiful in its lethal magnificence.

Which led to her third thought: *dangerous*.

It wasn't just his utter stillness, his total focus as he scrutinised her like an amoeba under a microscope. Or that his spare, gorgeous face was hewn of slashing strokes and planes, not a curve to be seen. Except for that thin, perfectly defined mouth that drew her gaze.

In her profession she'd seen lips curved in smiles of joy or relief, drawn tight or stretched in pain or grief. She'd never seen one like this, hinting at both sensuality and cruelty, the grooves around it all about control.

Danger. It was in the air around him, the way it thickened, alive with his presence, enveloping her, drawing her.

That beautiful hard mouth moved, articulating words Ella couldn't catch as her brain blurred. Then it curved in a smile and everything sped up, her pulse, her thoughts, her breathing.

'I'm sorry, I missed that.'

'I said it's a pleasure to meet you, Ms Sanderson.' Once more those lips curved up, but Ella knew with absolute certainty it wasn't pleasure Donato Salazar felt.

That was confirmed when she met his eyes, dark denim-blue beneath sleek black eyebrows that winged upwards. His look was assessing and…annoyed?

'It's good to meet you too, Mr Salazar.'

'Mister, Ms, there's no need to be so formal.' Her father spoke and Ella had never been so grateful for his presence. He seemed almost benign by comparison with the man beside him. 'Call her Ella, Donato. We don't stand on ceremony here.'

The tall man nodded and she told herself the perfect fall of his smooth, dark hair did *not* shine with the blue-black gloss of a raven's wing. Just as that wasn't the hint of a cleft in his chin. Or a flare of understanding in those deep-set, remarkable eyes holding hers.

The idea of being read and understood by one of her father's associates was too extraordinary to consider. She'd never fitted into Reg Sanderson's world. She'd been the cuckoo in the nest, unfathomable and uninteresting.

'Ella.' Donato Salazar's voice was deep, with a resonance that trawled through her insides, leaving her strangely empty. 'And you must call me Donato.'

Perhaps it was the gleam in his eyes, the satisfied twitch of those lips, or the fact she'd finally got over his shocking first impact on her, but suddenly Ella was herself again.

'That's kind of you… Donato.' Something in his eyes

flickered and Ella felt a throb of satisfaction. He was human after all. For one stunned moment he'd seemed larger than life.

'I understand you're from Melbourne. Are you staying in Sydney long?'

'That depends—' a look flashed between him and her father '—on a number of things. For the moment I have no definite plans to return.'

Ella nodded easily, as if those plans didn't include marriage to Reg Sanderson's daughter.

That was *not* going to happen.

'Let's hope the weather stays fine for your visit. Sydney is a city to be enjoyed in the sunshine.' As if she spent her days lolling on her father's motor cruiser, quaffing champagne or indulging in long lunches.

Ella pressed a hand to her empty stomach. Fuzz had left mere hours before this party to honour the man their father wanted her to marry and Reg had summoned Ella straight from work. Typically, while there was plenty of alcohol flowing, food had yet to make an appearance.

'Ah, the weather.' Donato's tone was unreadable, his eyes serious, yet she detected a flicker of superior amusement at one corner of his mouth. 'A polite and predictable conversation starter. Will you tell me how much better it is here than in wet, windy Melbourne?'

'It hadn't occurred to me.' Ella feigned surprise to hide her annoyance. She'd had her fill of being a source of amusement for her father's sophisticated friends. Years as the ugly duckling made her prickly when patronised. 'Are Melbournians really so touchy about their weather? I thought they were more robust.' She ignored her father's glowering frown. 'But do, please, feel free to choose another conversation starter, polite for preference.'

Something glinted in Donato's appraising eyes and Ella drew herself up.

'Really, Ella—' her father began.

'No, no. The weather it is, Ella.' Donato said her name slowly as if tasting it. Absurdly, since his accent was as Australian as her own, she caught a hint of exotic foreignness, an unexpected sliver of something unfamiliar and alluring in her simple little name.

The hairs at her nape and along her arms stood to attention.

She firmed her lips at such a flight of fancy. If hearing him say her name with that appealing lilt made her giddy, how would she cope when she finally saved enough for her long-awaited holiday to South America?

'Tell me—' he leaned in and Ella caught an enticing hint of coffee and warm male skin '—since you're interested in the weather. Do you think we can expect a summer storm later? Lightning and thunder, perhaps?'

Ella looked from her father, his expression icy with warning, to the clear sky, then back to Donato Salazar with his glinting, unreadable eyes. He knew how her father was sweating on this meeting and he didn't give a damn. Ella was torn between admiration and anger.

'Anything is possible, given the right atmospheric conditions.'

He nodded. 'I find the prospect surprisingly…invigorating.' He didn't move but suddenly he seemed to loom closer, towering over her despite her borrowed heels. The air around her seemed to snap and tighten. Or was that her nerves?

Ella told herself that squiggle of response deep inside was because, at five feet ten, she wasn't used to men dwarfing her. It had nothing to do with the idea of this dark, challenging, vibrant man being *invigorated*.

The image that word conjured made her catch her breath. Since when had her imagination been so flagrantly erotic?

She had an awful suspicion he read her thoughts. Heat

seeped under her skin, spread across her chest and up her throat.

Maybe she'd been working with elderly patients too long. How long since she'd been close to a virile man in his prime? One whose gaze challenged her not to react to him, even as she felt that telltale melting at her core.

'Tell me more,' he murmured, his voice like dark, rich syrup. 'What atmospheric conditions would lead to electricity in the air?'

He was toying with her.

He'd sensed her instantaneous, deeply feminine response to him—that tremor in her belly, that lush softening, and it amused him. His face was as close to bland as such a strong, remarkable face could be. Yet she *knew*. Something she couldn't name connected them.

'I have no idea,' she snapped. 'I'm no meteorologist.'

'You disappoint me.' His words were silky, his gaze fixed unwaveringly on her as if she were some curious specimen. 'Most people I meet like to talk about things they know well.'

'To show off their knowledge, you mean?'

He shrugged. The implication was clear. People tried to attract his attention. Her father was about to do it, clearing his throat ready to interrupt this conversation that wasn't going as he'd planned.

'You think I should try to impress you?' Stupid question. This man could make or break her father and, by association, her siblings. She might not need to impress him but common sense dictated she shouldn't antagonise him either.

Yet it was antagonism she felt, swirling in her blood. That and attraction. And something like fear. It was a dangerous combination.

'I can tell you—' she spoke as her father opened his mouth '—that our weather often comes from the south.'

'From the direction of Melbourne, you mean?' Donato's eyes narrowed.

'Precisely.' She angled her chin higher, refusing to look away from that intent stare. 'So if there's an abrupt change in the atmosphere from the south, a big blustery wind, for instance. Or a sudden influx of hot air…' She shrugged. 'Who knows what bad weather might result?'

'Ella—' Her father's voice promised retribution but was drowned by a sharp crack of laughter.

It reverberated around her, deep and appealing. Ella's skin prickled and shivered as if in response to the elemental rumble of thunder.

Donato Salazar had a surprisingly attractive laugh for a man who looked like he could play the Prince of Darkness with no effort at all. The trouble was laughter, the humour in his eyes and that unlooked-for smile turned him into someone far more approachable.

Her fingers tingled. She wanted—so badly she wanted— to cup his face and discover how that sharply defined jaw, that rich olive skin felt beneath her hand.

Ella swung her hands behind her back, clasping them tight together like a schoolgirl.

She shivered. Her response to this man was anything but childish. Her heart pounded against her ribs, her mouth sagging till she realised and snapped it shut. And that melting sensation had spread. Between her legs felt soft like warm butter.

Horror filled her and she stumbled back, only stopping when his laughter cut off and his gaze meshed with hers.

There it was again. That certainty he *knew* what she felt. The realisation should have mortified her. Instead it felt almost…liberating.

Ella blinked. Her imagination was working overtime. Lack of food had made her woolly-headed.

She did *not* turn into a puddle of pure lust after five minutes' acquaintance with any man.

She did *not* have some psychic connection with this stranger.

'I apologise for my daughter.' Her father skewered her with a glacial look. 'She—'

'There is no need to apologise.' Still Donato didn't shift his gaze from her. That steady look was unnerving. 'Your daughter is charming.'

'Charming?' Reg spluttered before quickly gathering himself. 'Of course, yes. She's certainly *unusual*.'

Ella might have felt grim amusement at her father's description of his cuckoo-in-the-nest daughter if she weren't so flabbergasted.

*Charming?*

Never in her life had she been described that way. But never had she set out to be deliberately rude either.

It was a night of firsts. Her father needing her. Her visceral response to this tall, dark, enigmatic stranger.

If there were going to be many more surprises maybe she should grab a drink to steady her nerves.

'You must be proud of such an intelligent, forthright daughter.'

Ella froze in the act of scanning the landscaped terraces for a waiter.

'Proud? Yes, yes, of course I am.' Her father needed to improve his acting skills. He was usually an expert liar but Ella had never seen him so ill at ease. So desperate.

'And pretty too.'

Ella swung her head round to meet that probing gaze.

This had gone far enough. She'd done her best, rifling her sister's abandoned wardrobe to find something suitable. She wouldn't face a crowd of glittering socialites in work clothes and rubber-soled lace-up shoes. But she had no illusions. Fuzz was the one who turned heads. Never Ella.

'There's no need to butter me up. And I prefer not to be talked about as if I'm not here.'

'Ella!' Her father looked like he might have a stroke. His colour was too high and his pale eyes bulged before narrowing to needle-sharp fury. He really did need to change his lifestyle if he was going to make it into old age. As if he'd listen to her!

'My apologies, Ella.' That low velvety voice made her shiver. 'No insult was intended.'

'It's not you who should apologise, Donato.' Her father closed in, his grip biting her arm. 'I think—'

'*I* think,' Donato interrupted smoothly, 'it's time you left the pair of us to get better acquainted.'

For an instant her father stared. Usually he was smooth as oil, charming and quick with a comeback. Seeing him so patently at a loss was a new experience. Once it would have delighted Ella. Now a chill clamped her spine.

Who *was* this man with the power to frighten him so?

'Of course, of course.' Her father pasted on a toothy smile. 'You two need to get better acquainted. I'll let you do just that.' With one last warning pinch of her arm he released her and sauntered off as if he hadn't a care.

Ella watched him go. Ridiculously, she wanted to call him back. As if she hadn't spent most of her life avoiding him. As if he were the sort of father to protect her.

For the absolute conviction stiffening her sinews warned she really did need protection.

Abruptly she swung around, her gaze lifting until— there it was again—that jangle across her senses, that taut feeling of suspense as her gaze locked with Donato Salazar's.

His mouth tipped up in a smile that tugged at her heart, dragging it hard against her ribs, making it thrash like a landed fish. Her breath quickened as everything in her that was female responded to his ultra-male charisma.

Yet his eyes showed no softening. That stare probed her very being and found her wanting.

# CHAPTER TWO

DONATO LOOKED DOWN into those clear eyes and felt the impact like the ripple of a stone plunging into deep, still water.

They weren't ordinary eyes. Oh, no, not Ms Ella Sanderson's. He'd yet to discover anything ordinary about her. He'd come here expecting her father's daughter and instead found...

What, exactly?

He didn't know yet but he intended to find out.

He disliked being caught out.

Years ago, in prison, being caught off guard could have cost his life. It had almost cost him an eye. He'd made it his life's work to be in control, the one pulling the strings, never again reacting to forces he couldn't handle.

It had been a long time since anyone took him by surprise. He didn't like it.

Even though he liked what he saw. Too much.

Those eyes, for a start. Mercurial. Some indefinable shade between blue and grey that turned to silvery hoar frost when he riled her. He'd felt her disapproval like the jab from a shard of ice, straight to his belly.

Yet his overwhelming response was to wonder how her eyes would look when rapture overtook her. With him buried deep inside, feeling her shudder around him.

Was it any wonder he felt annoyed? She'd hijacked his thoughts, momentarily interfering with his plans.

She wasn't what he'd expected, or wanted. No man wanted that sudden sensation that he was no longer master of his destiny. That perfidious fate still had a few nasty surprises in store.

Fate be damned. Donato had stopped being its victim years ago.

'Alone at last,' he murmured, watching her mouth tighten.

So, she didn't like this thing sparking and snarling between them either. But as well as her caution and disapproval he sensed puzzlement. As if she didn't recognise the syrupy thickening of the atmosphere for what it was—carnal attraction.

Instant. Absolute. Undeniable.

'There's no need for us to be alone. Your business is with my father.' Her jaw angled belligerently.

Donato felt a quickening in his belly.

How long since a woman had reacted to him like that? Not with disdain because of his origins, but defiantly. The last few years had been littered with women eager to grab what they could—sex, money, status, even the thrill of being with a man with his dark reputation. How long since a woman he wanted had been difficult to attain?

For he found he wanted Ms Ella Sanderson with a primal hunger that would probably shock her. It disturbed him and he'd thought himself unshockable.

'But tonight is about socialising. This is a party, Ella.' He slowed on her name, enjoying the taste of it almost as much as he enjoyed the flicker of response in those bright eyes.

Oh, yes. Ms Sanderson wanted him as much as he did her. The way she swiped her lips with the tip of her tongue. The telltale tremble of the diamond drop earrings beside her slender throat. The way her eyelids drooped as if anticipating sexual pleasure. The quick rise of her lovely breasts against the azure satin of that tight dress.

Her nipples pebbled, thrusting towards him. It was all he could do not to reach out and anchor his palms against her breasts. He wanted their weight in his hands. He wanted more than he could take here, on one of the terraces leading down to the harbour from her father's mansion.

Donato shoved his hands into his trouser pockets and saw her eyes narrow to slits as if daring him to stare at her body.

'Do I disturb you, Ella?'

If she didn't want him to admire the view she should have worn something else, not a dress that clung to her curves like plastic wrap. In that at least she hadn't surprised him. He'd expected Sanderson's daughter to be like her father, show rather than substance. Till she'd turned to face him and he'd known with absolute certainty she was different.

'Of course not.' He liked her low, confident voice, so totally unlike the high-pitched giggles of the women by the pool, already shedding their inhibitions. 'Are you in the habit of...*disturbing* people?' Her tone wasn't arch with flirtation but serious, as if trying to fathom him.

That made two of them.

He shrugged, noting the way her gaze darted to his shoulders. Had he ever met a woman so primed and physically aware of him?

It made him want to take what he desired straight up, then worry about deciphering her later.

He took a step closer and she stilled. Even her breath seemed to stop. Her nostrils dilated. Did she breathe in his scent just as he found himself discovering she smelled of...sweet peas? The perfume of an old-fashioned garden.

Memory blindsided him. Of a garden in sunshine. Of his mother's all too rare laugh and Jack's patient tone as he taught them the difference between weeds and the precious vegetable seedlings.

How long since he'd thought of that?

It belonged in another lifetime.

'Donato?'

He stiffened, registering her hand, lifted as if reaching for him. Then it dropped to her side. He didn't know if he felt relief or regret.

He wanted to touch her, badly. But not here. Once they touched there would be no holding back.

'Some people find me disturbing.'

It would be comforting to believe he had this impact on everyone. Yet to Ella her response seemed utterly personal, as if something linked the pair of them.

'Why is that?'

Those jet eyebrows shot up. What? Surely not everyone was bowled over by those dark, fallen-angel looks? There must be some, heterosexual men and the blind, who were unaffected.

'What do you know about me?'

She shrugged. 'Just that my father wants to do business with you. Ergo you're rich and powerful.' She snapped her mouth shut before adding something uncomplimentary. She'd already shot her mouth off when she should have been smoothing the way for the news that her sister wouldn't be playing happy families.

It was remarkable how he'd provoked her into lashing out. Her profession required discretion.

'I know you're from Melbourne, visiting Sydney for a major project.'

'That's all?' His look penetrated, as if peering past the gloss of her sister's clothes and jewellery to the plain, no-frills woman beneath. Her traitorous body heated and she had to lock her knees.

'That's all.' She'd had no time for an Internet search. She'd barely had time after meeting her father to find suitable clothes to wear.

'You take so little interest in your father's business?'

'Yes.' She didn't elaborate. What her father did was no

longer any concern of hers. Except when it threatened Rob and Fuzz. 'That is—'

His raised hand silenced her. 'Don't explain. It's refreshing to meet someone honest enough to admit they're only interested in money, rather than how it's made.'

'You've got me wrong.' He made her sound like a leech.

'Have I? How?'

Belatedly she shook her head, caution stirring. 'Never mind. It's not relevant.'

They'd never meet again. It was a sign of weakness to worry about what he thought of her. Besides, she baulked at Donato Salazar knowing anything about her. Knowledge was power and he looked the sort to wield his power mercilessly.

'And what *is* relevant?'

'The reason you're here tonight. Felicity.'

'I came here expecting to meet her.' His gaze drifted over the crowd on the upper terraces.

'She's unavailable. She couldn't be here.'

'So your father mentioned.'

Ella wondered what else her father had said. She'd bet her whole savings account he hadn't admitted Fuzz had done a runner to north Queensland rather than face this man.

The idea of Fuzz anywhere without cold champagne on tap, working spa baths and an adoring audience was unbelievable. Yet Rob said they were camped in a couple of rooms at the old motel, making do with a primus stove and cold showers while the renovations were underway.

For the first time Fuzz was in love. Matthew, Rob's friend, now business partner, was decent, honest and hard-working, a rarity in her family's social circle. It gave Ella hope that Fuzz had fallen for him rather than the smarmy powerbrokers she'd dated before. Matthew's decision to turn the rundown motel he'd inherited into an upmarket resort had been the catalyst Rob and Fuzz needed to break from Sydney and their father.

'So you're standing in for your sister.' Donato's dark voice trawled like pure alcohol in Ella's veins, making her blood tingle. 'What could be more pleasant?'

His expression changed, lines deepening, gaze piercing. He looked...predatory.

Instantly heat bloomed.

'Not in the way you think!' Ella blurted.

'You know my thoughts?' Again that rise of slashing ebony eyebrows. It made him look like a haughty Spanish grandee of old.

'Of course not.' How did he throw her off balance so easily? She'd spent years learning to keep her thoughts to herself and her emotions under control. She always had both feet on the ground.

Yet around Donato Salazar she felt different.

He looked intent and assessing and his stare sent anxiety spidering across her flesh, drawing it tight. Ella wasn't used to such close masculine attention. Not from men like him. She felt out of her depth and that made her bristle. She decided to change the subject.

'I'm sure you'll enjoy yourself tonight. My father's parties are renowned.'

A shrill cry split the air, followed by a splash in the pool. There was laughter then another splash.

'So I gather.' His expression didn't change but there was steel in his tone that told her he had no time for party games. 'But I'm here to become acquainted with your family. With *you*, Ella.'

There it was again, that tremor of excitement as he said her name. Ella rubbed her hands up her bare arms to smooth sudden goose bumps. Too late she saw her mistake, when his gaze zeroed in on the movement. It wasn't cold. The night was balmy. He knew she was reacting to *him*.

Ella shouldn't have let pride tempt her into raiding her sister's wardrobe. Years as the frump of the family, the one with puppy fat and boring brown hair instead of glorious golden locks, had made her determined to look good. Now, wedged into her sister's dress, perched in glittery shoes, she craved her sensible trousers and flats.

She turned to lean on the waist-high terrace wall, pretending to look at the harbour view.

Donato stood over a metre away. Yet she *felt* him as if they touched. How was it possible?

'I didn't know until tonight that your father had three children. I'd only heard of two.'

That was no surprise. Reg Sanderson never boasted about his boring middle child as he did about his clever son or gorgeous older daughter. Until tonight Ella had been *persona non grata*.

'Felicity and Rob are closer to him. Rob even worked for him.' Until too-close exposure to their father's business soured his enthusiasm. Rob was a corporate lawyer and Ella suspected he'd seen too much of their father's business tactics.

'Yet I haven't seen photos of you with your sister in the press.'

Ella blinked. 'You read the social pages?' He looked the kind of man who only read finance and politics.

'You'd be surprised what I read.'

She frowned. 'It matters to you, does it? Who's seen at high-profile parties?'

'It matters that I understand people when I'm about to do business with them.'

Ella stiffened. 'Your business is with my father, not me or Felicity.'

His regard was enigmatic and unblinking. Challenging.

'You were checking up on her?'

He shrugged. 'Isn't it natural that I take an interest in your family?'

*Since he planned to marry into it.* Her stomach clenched.

'Did you hire investigators too?' She whipped around to face him full on.

'Why would that bother you?'

'Because it would be an invasion of privacy. It would be—' she shuddered '—intrusive.'

Had there been cameras trained on her sister when she partied? When she and Matthew were together? Ella frowned. Fuzz mightn't be the best sister in the world but she was the only one Ella had.

'Did you *spy* on my sister?' Ella stepped up to Donato, her hands finding her hips, her bottom lip jutting.

'Your sister? No.' He was staring at her mouth.

Crazily, she felt her lips go dry. She swallowed and he watched the movement. How could it feel as if he trailed a finger down her throat when he hadn't lifted a hand?

Hormones. They danced riotously, making her heart drum against her ribcage and her insides clench needily.

Ella swiped her parched lips with her tongue and wished she hadn't. His look *seared*. She wanted to back up a step but he'd know why. She was stuck there, her neck arched to meet his intense scrutiny, her body taut as a spinnaker billowing and snapping in a sudden gale.

She didn't imagine the turbulence in the air. It was real and it emanated from *him*.

'You didn't hire investigators?' she pressed.

He shook his head, eyes never leaving hers. 'No one investigated you or your siblings. Otherwise I'd have known about you before tonight, wouldn't I?'

Ella drew in a deep breath, searching for calm. Trying to ignore the way her bra scraped her over-sensitive breasts and budding nipples. Trying to concentrate on the conversation, not how this man made her feel.

It took a moment to realise what he *hadn't* said.

He'd said nothing about whether he'd had her father investigated.

A sound made her turn. It was a waiter with a laden tray, coming down the stairs. Ella moved towards him. Her throat was dry but more, she craved something to distract her from the sensation of being cut off alone with Donato.

'Drink, sir? Ma'am?'

'Champagne, Ella?' Donato was right behind her. Had she really thought to escape so easily?

'Water, please.'

'Sensible choice.' He took two glasses of sparkling water and nodded his thanks to the waiter, who headed back to the higher terraces. Ella watched him go, wondering what would happen if she simply followed.

That wouldn't work. She needed to sort this out here, in private, away from curious eyes.

'Sensible?' Did he think she'd drink too much then lose her inhibitions?

Donato held out a drink, touching only the bottom of the glass, as if careful of any glancing contact.

Ella was inordinately grateful. Since they'd met she'd felt his presence like a touch—on her lips, her skin, her breasts. She suspected the real thing—his skin against hers—might be her undoing.

Carefully she took the glass. 'Thanks.'

'Sometimes it's wise to keep a clear head. Tonight is one of those times.'

She'd lifted the glass to her lips but paused. Was he talking about her father's idea that he marry Fuzz? Or did he refer to the swirl of attraction enveloping them?

'About my father's proposal…'

'Which one?'

Ella stared. There was more than one?

Of course there was. The old man no doubt had a whole

raft of business proposals for Donato. He'd be looking to screw every dollar he could out of him.

'About Felicity.'

'Yes?' Damn the man. He just stood there waiting, making her feel appallingly awkward.

Ella sipped her water, grateful for the cool fizz on her palate, easing the constriction in her throat. 'She's away long term. She has a commitment interstate.'

Donato nodded and Ella drew a relieved breath.

*Of course* he wasn't interested in her father's suggestion that they marry. Donato Salazar would pick his own woman. He'd just been too polite to tell her father his idea was old-fashioned and unnecessary.

'She won't be coming back to Sydney.'

'So I understand.' He paused. 'Am I permitted to ask what keeps her away, or would that fall under the category of an invasion of privacy?'

Was he laughing at her?

'It's no secret. She's working in Queensland, managing a large interior-design project.'

'Really?' One eyebrow cocked up. 'I wasn't aware your sister actually worked.'

Ella felt a slow burn radiate out from her belly. Not sexual arousal this time but shame on Fuzz's behalf.

It was true. Her twenty-seven-year-old sister had never done a day's paid work. The closest she'd come were charity modelling gigs. But that was changing. Fuzz was committed to this project. If she stuck at it this would be the making of her. Once she was away from their father—

'As you say, Donato—' Ella halted, thrown for a second by how much she enjoyed saying his name. She was like a teenager stricken by lust for the first time! 'You don't know us.' She drew herself up, standing as tall as she could. 'Fuzz… Felicity is part of the design team for a major Queensland resort.' Well, it would be a major resort once it was finished.

'This is the resort your brother has invested in?'

'You know about that?'

'Your father said he'd left the family firm in order to strike out on his own. Still in the same field though, entertainment and hospitality.'

'Not quite the same. My father's wealth is built on gambling, poker machines and casinos.'

'Not just gambling.' The riposte came quickly and Ella tried to read that crisp tone. There was something adamantine in his voice, something new that sent anxiety skidding down her backbone. Instinct twanged in warning. She took another long sip of iced water, grounding herself.

'Your father has had diverse interests.' Ella thought she saw his lip curl. Then the impression was gone. He looked back blandly.

'Felicity has another reason for being in Queensland.' She needed to make it clear her father's scheme was impractical. 'She's living with her partner. They're working together.'

'A permanent relationship, then?'

'Absolutely.' More permanent, at least, than any of her sister's previous relationships. 'I know my father suggested you get to know Felicity better.' She couldn't bring herself to use the word *marry*. 'But in the circumstances that's not possible.'

'I understand completely.' Donato's lips curved in a smile that did the strangest things to her internal organs.

The man was devastating. Totally mind-blowingly gorgeous. He looked like some lethally enthralling anti-hero bent on breaking every rule, perhaps even ravishing a few virgins along the way.

Ella blinked and stared. What had got into her head? Flights of fancy were *so* not her.

Donato moved in, blocking her view of the other terraces and instantly her nerves jangled. She tightened her grip on the water glass, slippery with condensation.

'Your father thought our business partnership would be enhanced by a family tie. He suggested marriage.'

Ella waited for his derision at the idea. Instead she met only speculation in Donato's gaze.

'That's not an option. Felicity is spoken for,' she reiterated.

'I hope she'll be very happy.' Donato raised his glass in salute. 'And may I say how lucky I am that your father has another charming daughter to take her place?'

# CHAPTER THREE

ELLA STARED INTO eyes that held not a whit of humour.

The hairs at her nape rose at the weight of that heavy-lidded regard.

*Her, as her sister's replacement.*

For a split second Ella felt triumph, elation at the prospect of being *his*. Of experiencing all that intensity, not as a curious specimen to be studied but as a lover.

Her gaze slewed to the breadth of those shoulders, the lean strength of the man beneath the exquisite tailoring. What would it feel like being held in those arms?

She reared back, water spilling from her glass.

'I'm not my sister's stand-in.' The words jerked out from her constricting throat.

'Of course not. You're a unique individual.' His smile was all smooth charm. If you didn't look into those eyes, calculating and *aware*.

'Don't patronise me.'

'My apologies. I assumed you'd prefer me to be frank.'

'Of course I do.' She gripped her glass in both hands.

He watched assessingly. 'Then let me say nothing appeals more than the prospect of knowing you better.'

There was nothing salacious in his tone, or his expression, yet those words—*knowing you*—held hidden depth. Knowing as in sexually knowing.

It should have horrified her yet it didn't.

She wanted him. Here. Now. With an immediacy that overrode every cautious, pragmatic, sensible bone in her body. With a raw hunger that totally disregarded the fact he was caviar and champagne in a crystal flute or perhaps arctic vodka, strong and lethal, while she was brown bread and tea in a good, sturdy pot.

'Don't be absurd. We have nothing in common.'

'I suspect we have a great deal in common, Ella.' He paused, as if savouring her name. 'Your father and his business, for instance.'

She spun away, stalking half a dozen steps before turning to face him. He was just as imposing, and smug, from here.

Then, to her dismay, he closed the gap with a couple of easy strides. Annoyance fizzed in her belly.

'You're not interested in getting to know *me*.' A man like Donato Salazar would want a high-profile trophy wife. Not a plain Jane woman whose feet ached at the end of a long day.

'I thought we'd already established that you don't know what goes on inside my head?'

He didn't look annoyed. Instead he looked…engaged. His tall body canted towards her as if drawn by the same force she felt urging her closer to him.

She stepped back, ignoring the knowing uptilt of those slashing eyebrows.

She understood attraction. Even understood the lure of the dangerous, though she'd always chosen a safer, more prosaic route through life.

Yet she'd never experienced this heat of desire. It saturated her, made her imagine impossible things. Like grabbing Donato's collar and yanking that proud, scarred face down to hers. She wanted to savour him, lose herself in the passion she knew was hiding below that veneer of polite calm.

His nostrils flared, his chest rising sharp and sudden, as if he'd intercepted her thoughts. His gaze dropped to her mouth.

The night air zapped and thickened.

'I don't know anything about you.'

'But that doesn't matter, does it?' His deep voice wove around her. 'It doesn't stop what you're feeling.'

Ella opened her mouth to snap that she felt *nothing*.

But he was watching keenly, waiting for her to flutter and fuss and deny this *awareness* between them. She wouldn't play coy. It would be an admission of fear and showing fear to this man would only invite trouble.

Ella jerked her chin up. 'I don't know what sort of women you usually mix with, Donato. But know this. I'm not about to act on impulse with a stranger.'

'No matter how tempting.' He gave voice to her thoughts, making her start.

'What?' he drawled, his voice like honey and gravel. 'You think I'm not tempted? You think my hands aren't itching to slide over your luscious body? To pull you tight against me and feel how well we fit? To taste you?'

The sudden change from amused outsider to consummate seducer slammed her heart against her ribs.

'You think I'm not tempted to make you acknowledge exactly how much you want me?'

Ella's breath disintegrated. His gaze flickered to her heaving breasts and fire exploded within. She was burning up and nothing, she suspected, could put out the conflagration except Donato.

The idea appalled as much as it excited her.

She looked at the glass shaking in her too-tight grip. Had her drink been spiked? How she wished she had such an easy excuse.

'It doesn't matter what you want, Donato.' She lifted her head to meet his stare. 'It's not going to happen.'

His gaze sharpened and anxiety feathered through her. Too late she pondered the wisdom of declaring an outright challenge. She had a disturbing feeling Donato Salazar thrived on smashing challenges.

'Never say never, Ella.'

The intensity of his look scared her. Suddenly she felt out of her depth. She wanted to be in her flat, curled up in her pyjamas with a movie and the block of chocolate she'd been saving all week.

'I want to know you, Ella.'

'How? Sexually?' She put her glass down on a nearby table before she dropped it.

'I like that you say exactly what you think, Ella. It's refreshing.'

She stuck her hands on her hips and this time she did give in to impulse, stalking a step closer till she realised her mistake and shuddered to a halt. But she refused to backtrack, even though she stood near enough to inhale his heady masculine scent.

'You're a slow learner, Donato. I told you not to patronise me.'

He shook his head. 'I'm just telling you the truth.' His mouth widened in a smile that drew her belly tight. 'Do I want your body? Absolutely.' His gaze dipped then rose again. 'We'll be magnificent together.'

No *if*, just absolute certainty. Where did this man get off, assuming she was his for the taking?

'But I want more. I want to understand you.'

Of all the things he could have said, of all the things he *had* said, this was the one that cut her defences off at the knees.

No man had ever wanted to understand her. Not her father, who'd wanted her to be pretty and frivolous and pander to his ego. Not the guys she'd met at long-ago society parties, nor the men she'd dated since.

Longing coursed through her. He was clever, this man, too clever. He really did know what women wanted.

'Why?' She tilted her head to one side, wishing she could read him. 'We're strangers. And don't tell me it's because you think my father's idea of marrying into this family is a good one. I want the truth.'

Ella held herself tall, ready for Donato's blast of outrage, conditioned to it after a lifetime dealing with her father's volatile temperament.

'You think I'd lie?'

'Men usually do when they want something.'

'You don't have a high opinion of men.' He looked curious rather than offended. 'But I applaud your caution.'

'You do?'

He nodded. 'It pays not to accept everything at face value. Too many people put themselves at risk then find themselves in situations they can't control or escape.' His voice rang with a depth of feeling that surprised her.

She couldn't imagine anyone taking advantage of Donato.

'Did that ever happen to you?'

Long moments passed, then he surprised her. 'Of course. But once was enough. It won't happen again.' His words held absolute certainty.

Ella wished she possessed such conviction. She should walk away from Donato Salazar and the danger he represented. He made her want things that scared the daylights out of her.

She imagined giving in to him. There'd be no fumbling, no awkwardness. She guessed with him sex would be far too easy and utterly devastating.

'Why me?' She set her jaw. 'There are plenty of glamorous women here. Quite a few would give you sex if you asked.'

'You don't think you're glamorous?'

How had he latched onto that? On the fact she felt like an imposter even dressed in silk and diamonds.

'I know my limitations.'

'And you think your looks are one of them?'

'The way I look doesn't matter.' She ignored the tension clamping her stomach.

He put down his drink beside hers and she wondered, frantically, if he'd reach for her. Instead he shoved his hands into his trouser pockets. The movement emphasised the power in both his broad shoulders and muscular thighs.

'I think it matters very much, *to you.*'

Ella wiped clammy hands down her dress. Her sister's dress. Fuzz would look delicate and gorgeous in it. On Ella it strained at the seams and the skirt rode too high.

'I was wrong when I called you pretty.'

She froze. She'd asked for the truth, hadn't she? What did it matter if these last few years she'd begun to believe she was attractive in her own quiet way? His admission shouldn't feel like such a blow.

'Pretty is for little girls. And you're all woman, Ella.' She saw his hands bunch in his pockets, drawing the fabric of his trousers tight. 'You're the only woman here that I want in my bed.'

Her breath was an audible gasp.

'You're stunning. The fire in your eyes, that sassy mouth of yours, all that lovely lush bounty of hips and breasts and long, long legs. I want—'

'That's enough!'

Ella pressed a palm to her pounding chest. Her heart hammered up high as if it had broken free. 'We're not discussing my looks or who you want in your bed.'

'We're not?' His mouth kicked up at the corner in a tiny smile that was far more devastating than the one he'd given her before. It was the sort of smile a friend or lover might give, a shared intimacy.

Ella tugged the silk dress further down her thighs. 'No.

We're discussing the fact that you marrying into the Sanderson family is totally unnecessary.'

'Unnecessary? Yes.'

At last! She felt as if a huge stone lifted off her chest. Finally some of the tension drained from her body.

'But definitely appealing.' His eyes traced a sinuous line down her tall frame and it was a wonder Ella didn't self-combust. If any other man had ogled her like that she'd have slapped him. Instead her shoulders tightened, pushing out her breasts as if she revelled in that proprietorial look.

'I beg your pardon?' Pity the words sounded breathy rather than outraged.

'You heard me, Ella. Don't play coy.'

'I'm not playing anything!' Had the world gone mad? Had lust addled her brain? 'You can't seriously tell me you think my father's plan makes sense.'

'Actually—' his eyes locked with hers '—I think it's an excellent idea.'

'You've got to be kidding.' She stared into that steady blue gaze, waiting for some sign that Donato was joking.

No sign came. Ella folded her hands over her chest then wished she hadn't when his gaze flickered to her breasts, pushed up under the tight silk. She hated how that split-second glance flustered her.

'It's not going to happen. Felicity won't marry you.'

'So you said.' He leaned forward, holding her gaze. 'You're repeating yourself. Do I make you nervous?'

'Nervous? No.' Casually she reached for her discarded glass and took a slow sip.

'Something else then?' His voice was a dark purr. Instead of reassuring, it primed her fight-or-flight response. Donato was no tame cat. He was about as safe as a panther eyeing its next meal.

'Several things spring to mind, Donato, but I'm too polite to spell them out.'

His chuckle was warm treacle spilling through her veins. 'It's been an absolute pleasure meeting you tonight, Ella. I hadn't expected to enjoy myself so much.'

'I amuse you?' Her jaw firmed, her look dared him to laugh at her.

'That's not the word I'd use.' Abruptly his laughter died. His expression was sombre and intent.

'I don't want to know.'

His eyebrows arched. 'You don't? I hadn't pegged you for a coward, Ella.'

She shook her head. 'I'm not afraid of you.' She was too busy being terrified of the stranger she'd become while she was with him.

'Good, that will make things so much more enjoyable.'

'What things?'

He rocked back on his heels. 'Our relationship.'

'We don't *have* a relationship. I'm going to leave and you'll spend the rest of the evening enjoying the party.' It was a test of willpower not to look at the pool terrace, where the laughter had escalated to riotous. He'd be welcomed with open arms. 'We won't see each other again.'

The realisation was like a rock plummeting inside her stomach. Despite all tonight's negatives, Ella felt invigorated, more energised than she had in ages.

'Why? Do you have a man waiting up for you?' Donato dragged his hands out of his pockets, his stance widening as he folded his arms across his chest. The movement transformed him from lazy spectator to belligerent adversary. Or maybe it was the way he scowled.

'There's no one waiting up for me.' Ella could have bitten her tongue. He brought out the reckless, unthinking side she usually managed to squash.

'Excellent. I won't be stepping on anyone's toes.'

Ella read his smug expression and her fingers slipped

on the damp glass. There was a crash. Water sprayed her
bare leg as the glass shattered on the flagstones.

'Are you okay?' He stepped forward, so close he stole
her air. His hand lifted as if to touch her and something
engulfed her—a warmth, a frisson, an unseen shimmer of
electrical charge.

'Fine! I'm fine.' Ella assumed it was water trickling
down her calf, not blood from a tiny cut. She'd look later.

She stepped back, coming up against the stone wall. She
swallowed down panic. 'It's been a very long day and I'm
tired.' With an effort she kept her words even. 'Find someone else to play your games.'

Piercing eyes scrutinised her, then Donato nodded and
stepped aside to let her pass. Relief stirred.

'You underestimate me, Ella. I'm not playing games. I'll
call for you in the morning.'

'Why? There's no point.'

There was no smile on his features when he answered.
'To get to know you before the wedding, of course.'

'Cut it out, Donato. The joke's over.' Was that a wobble
in her voice? Great. Just great. Ella stalked past.

To her horror he turned, his long stride fitting to hers,
his hand hovering at the small of her back. She *felt* it as
surely as if he'd pressed his palm to her spine.

'I'll walk you to the house.'

'I can get there alone.'

'You're tired. I'll keep you company.'

Ella slammed to a halt and a whisper of sensation
glanced down her back as his hand skimmed her dress.
An instant later he'd stepped back.

It was more than tiredness bothering her. Being back
in her father's house, she had that awful sensation she'd
known in her teens, that she was dressing up, pretending
to be someone she wasn't. She'd even grown klutzy again,
though she worked with her hands all the time.

Worse, being watched by Donato unnerved her. As for his pretence that he wanted to marry her! That made her burn from the soles of her feet to the tips of her ears.

'Now you listen!' She swung around and lifted a hand to jab her index finger into that imposing chest.

To her surprise Donato stepped back before she made contact.

'Don't.' The single word was terse. His face hardened, grew still but for the tic of a pulse at his temple.

'What?' He didn't like her invading his personal space? Tough. She didn't like being the butt of his joke. She planted her hands on her hips and moved even closer.

'Not a good idea, Ella.'

'Why not? You can dish it out but you can't cope with a woman who stands up to your cruel little games?' Silly to taste disappointment. For a while there she'd almost believed there was more to Donato.

That proved it. She *was* tired.

His lips thinned, curling up in a smile unlike either of the ones she'd seen before. This one held no warmth or humour. It was a hunter's assessing look and it was full of satisfaction. It brought her up sharply, her heart thrumming frantically.

'On the contrary, Ella.' His voice slowed to syrup on her name. 'I can't tell you how much I'm looking forward to you *standing up against me.*'

Dazed, Ella wondered if he too pictured them locked together, she held high in his embrace, her legs around his waist. She swallowed, willing the fiery blush away.

Then she read the tension in his neck and shoulders, in his clenched hands. 'Don't try to con me, Donato. You don't like me being this close to you.'

'Brave but foolish, Ella.' He unfurled his hands, stretching his long fingers, and abruptly Ella felt far too close for comfort. 'I don't want you *near* me. I want you *against* me, skin to skin, with nothing between us. I want to watch you blush, not just with arousal—' his gaze trawled her heated face '—but with ecstasy.'

Her gasp was loud in the throbbing silence.

He breathed deep, his chest rising so high Ella could swear she felt a disturbance in the air, brushing her breasts and drawing her nipples to tight buds. Her body blazed with the fire he'd ignited.

'I drew back,' he murmured, 'because when we *do* touch, I want us to be alone. So we can finish what we start.' His eyes were heavy-lidded yet there was nothing lazy about his scrutiny. She felt it in the jangle of her nerves. That only made her angrier.

'You expect me to believe one touch from me and you wouldn't be able to control yourself?' Her eyebrows arched. She wasn't that naïve, despite the foolish way her body responded. She was no siren, to make men forget themselves.

'I know neither of us would want to pull back once we… connected.' He let his words sink in. 'I also suspect your desire for privacy might be even stronger than mine. Anyone could walk down here and interrupt us.'

He looked around as if searching for a suitable spot for them to get naked together.

'I don't believe you.'

His gaze collided with hers. 'You want to test it?' His nostrils flared, his eyes gleaming slits. He looked primitive, dangerous, like a warrior daring her to combat.

Her brain screamed a warning and Ella stepped back. The scrape of her heel on the flagstone was unnaturally loud. Even her breathing was amplified, and her pulse, beating that quick tattoo.

'No, I don't want to touch you. Not now, not ever.' Just as well there was no summer thunderstorm tonight or she might have been struck down for the enormity of that lie. 'I won't be seeing you again, Donato. Goodbye.'

Squaring her shoulders, half expecting him to stop her, Ella turned and strode along the terrace back towards the bright lights and people.

He let her go. See, it had been easy after all. She'd called Donato's bluff and that was the end of it.

That was *not* disappointment she felt. It was relief that she'd never have to see him again.

# CHAPTER FOUR

DONATO WATCHED ELLA march away. He'd thought nothing about Reg Sanderson could surprise him. Yet Sanderson's daughter had stopped him in his tracks.

*Ella.* He savoured her name.

Perhaps it had been a mistake pulling away from her. Maybe if he hadn't kept his distance he'd have shattered this illusion that she was different.

Except it would take more than a quickie up against the garden wall to quench what was inside him.

Which, he assured himself, fitted his plans perfectly.

That was what he had to concentrate on. Revenge. He'd always known it would be sweet. With Ella as an added bonus it would be delicious.

He sauntered to the house. There was no one here he wanted to spend time with. Only Ella. Despite her bravado he'd read her fear. Sensible woman. But he'd allay those fears and ensure she enjoyed their time together.

He'd stopped to tell a waiter about the broken glass on the lower level when Sanderson appeared. His pale eyes looked almost febrile, belying his casual stance. Satisfaction stirred. This had been a long time coming. Too long. He intended to enjoy every moment of Sanderson's descent into ruin.

'All alone, Donato?' He scowled. 'Where's that girl of mine? Don't tell me she's left you alone?'

'Ella was tired.'

'Tired? I'll give her tired!' he roared. 'I—'

'It's better she gets her sleep tonight.' Donato kept his

voice bland though he wanted to grab Sanderson by the scruff of his neck and shake him till his teeth rattled.

Because Donato hated him with every fibre of his being? Or because of the way he spoke of Ella? Didn't the man realise how precious family was? Had he no concept of protecting his child against a man whom everyone knew was as implacable and dangerous as they came?

What sort of man sold his daughter to a stranger?

Donato already knew the answer. Reg Sanderson. The bastard had already destroyed too many lives.

It would be a public service as well as a pleasure to see he got his just deserts.

Darkness engulfed him. No, Donato wouldn't see him dead, which was what he deserved. Donato had come close to killing once and he'd learned a lot since then. This way was better. Sanderson's suffering would be drawn out.

'She should have stayed here, with you. I apologise.'

Donato raised his hand. 'It doesn't matter. I'll see her tomorrow.'

'You will?' The older man's expression stilled. 'So, you're interested? In *Ella*?' Was that barely concealed shock in his voice? Sanderson had no notion what a gem his daughter was. The man was blind as well as deplorable.

Donato had seen the photos of Ella's sister, a golden girl with obvious allure. Yet if he really sought a bride he wouldn't choose Felicity Sanderson. If reports were accurate, she hadn't a loyal bone in her body.

Did Ella really believe her sister would stick with this new lover, or did she merely try to protect her from the danger he, Donato, represented?

The idea of her protecting anyone from him was ludicrous, given his far superior power and resources. Yet the notion stuck and he filed it away for future consideration.

'It was a delight meeting someone so refreshing and intelligent.' Forthright and clever enough to be suspicious, Ella had intrigued from the instant she'd looked at him.

Sanderson didn't quite hide his satisfaction. His smile was hungry. 'It's wonderful you hit it off so well. I'd hoped you would. There's no telling with Ella; sometimes she can be a little...'

'A little...?'

Sanderson shrugged and took a swig of his drink. 'To be frank, she can be a little outspoken sometimes. But in a good way, of course. Refreshing, as you say.'

He smiled that conspiratorial smile as if they were good buddies and Donato had to repress the compulsion to slam his fist into the other man's whiter than white capped teeth. He'd done a lot of things in his time, some of them society had labelled reprehensible. But nothing that sickened him like playing Sanderson's temporary friend.

'I prefer honesty to polite platitudes.' Especially when those platitudes hid murky secrets.

'Don't we all?'

'Meeting your daughter has helped me feel I know you better. That's important if we're to work together.'

'I thought you'd see it that way.' Sanderson paused, then said carefully, 'So, you want to proceed with the partnership and the loan?' His absolute stillness gave him away. He was strung tight.

Grim satisfaction filled Donato. 'Definitely. This is too good an opportunity to miss.'

It had taken years of preparation to reach this point, and now he was poised to destroy Sanderson financially and socially. If he couldn't put him behind bars for his crimes, Donato would at least see he lost what he cared for most. 'My staff are ready to meet at ten tomorrow to discuss the details.'

'You won't be there?' Concern flared in Sanderson's

eyes. Excellent. It was time he discovered he couldn't keep running from the consequences of his actions.

'My staff are competent to handle the meeting. I plan to be with Ella, getting to know her better.'

'I'm sure she'll love that.'

Not initially, Donato knew, but he'd change her mind. He looked forward to it.

'Does that mean you liked my notion of a Salazar-Sanderson marriage?' Sanderson looked urbane and relaxed, yet the ripple on the surface of his whisky betrayed him.

Donato scrutinised him, from his deep tan and perennially gold hair to the gloss only close acquaintance with serious money could buy. That didn't hide the mean lines around his mouth, the avaricious gleam in those pale blue eyes or the pugnacious angle of that thick jaw.

He knew what Sanderson was. Imagine him as a father. No wonder his eldest daughter was a beautiful waste of space. Which made his younger daughter...what, exactly?

'Donato?' Sanderson didn't sound quite so smug now.

'The marriage idea?' Donato took his time, relishing the other man's unease. 'I think it's an excellent one.'

Sanderson's eyes widened momentarily before his face eased into a calculating look. 'Ella is a special girl, and lucky.' His toothy smile reminded Donato of a crocodile. Or maybe it was just that he knew Sanderson to be as cold-blooded as any reptile.

Despite the money he'd made, Donato had no illusions that he was love's young dream. Not with his criminal record. He was the sort of man parents prayed their daughter would never bring home.

Yet here was Sanderson thrusting his unsuspecting daughter into Donato's arms. Was there anything Sanderson wouldn't do for money?

'And Ella agreed?' Pale eyes fixed on him.

'Ella understands what I want. We'll sort out the details soon.'

'It will be a pleasure welcoming you to the family.' Sanderson made to shake hands but Donato pretended not to notice, turning to snag a wine glass from a passing waiter.

'Here's to the wedding that will make us family.' Sanderson raised his glass.

Donato suppressed a wave of nausea at the notion of being so intimately linked with this man. Sanderson had destroyed the one person Donato had ever loved. The only one who'd ever loved him. Sanderson had destroyed countless others too and didn't give a damn. But Donato did, and he'd make sure Sanderson paid in full.

'To the wedding,' he murmured. 'Soon, don't you think?'

'Definitely.' Sanderson nodded. 'Though Ella might—'

'I'm sure I can persuade her to an early date.' The thought of persuading Ella made his blood hum. He was counting the hours till he saw her again. That was a first.

His host nodded. 'I knew you'd be the man for her. A lovely girl, but she needs a firm hand.'

Was that how Sanderson had managed his family? Donato's investigators had concentrated on Sanderson's business activities, especially any nasty little financial secrets, not on his family. Sympathy flickered, even for party girl Felicity. But most of all for Ella. Ella, with the wary eyes, who didn't believe she was beautiful.

'Don't worry. You can leave Ella to me.'

'Good man.' Sanderson waved his whisky glass. 'I suppose you'd prefer to marry in Melbourne so I suggest—'

'No, I couldn't do that. I know the bride's family organises the wedding. You'll want to give Ella a big society event.' Donato smiled, genuine amusement surfacing at Sanderson's dismay. Obviously, in his scheming to snare Donato's support, and money, he hadn't reckoned with footing the bill for a lavish celebration.

'That's kind, Donato. But you're a very private man. Ella will understand if you want to tie the knot quietly.'

Donato shook his head. 'I wouldn't dream of depriving her. The bigger the celebration the better. It will signal the beginning of our partnership.' There, that made him smile. 'Let's make it the society event of the decade.'

Donato watched his host turn a pasty shade of green. 'I realise it's a huge task organising such an event at short notice so I'll give you some assistance.'

'That's very good of you, Donato. I won't say no.'

'Good. I'll lend you someone to help with the preparations. I know just the person. She's got an eye for quality and understands we'll want no expense spared.' He put up his hand when Sanderson would have interrupted. 'Don't thank me. It's the least I can do.'

Sanderson bit back a response, his expression for a moment ugly, though quickly masked.

'Now, if you'll just give me Ella's mobile number? I forgot to get it earlier.'

Interestingly, for a man who thought his daughter so 'special', Sanderson didn't have the number programmed into his phone. He had to go inside to get it, leaving Donato to consider the outcome of tonight's events.

Sanderson was on the hook.

As for his absurd proposal that Donato marry his daughter…that was the bid of a desperate man.

But Donato would play along. It would be the icing on the cake to know his enemy had spent his last credit on a huge public wedding that would never take place. Not only would Sanderson be ruined beyond redemption, the farce of the non-wedding would make him a social pariah.

Even if Donato had to come in quietly later and pay the bills so no suppliers were out of pocket, the expense would be worth it. Sanderson would be in the gutter, ashamed and ostracised, bankrupt and unable to start again. He deserved far worse but it would do.

Only one thing niggled. When Sanderson had first suggested marriage, Donato had had no qualms about agreeing. From what he'd learned, Felicity had a Teflon-coated heart. She'd thrive on the notoriety and the monetary compensation Donato would provide when the wedding was cancelled.

But Ella was different. He didn't yet have her measure and that gave him pause. He never went into negotiations without knowing his opponent. Or in this case his partner.

His lips tilted in a satisfied smile. No, it didn't matter if this once he winged it. He'd work out a way to compensate her. But he had no intention of walking away. Not merely because this dovetailed so nicely with his plans for revenge. But because he wanted Ella.

He intended to enjoy her, and their courtship, to the full.

# CHAPTER FIVE

'Lo...?' ELLA DRAGGED the phone to her ear, burrowing deeper into her bed. It was far too early on a Saturday morning for anyone to call.

'Not a morning person, Ella?' The deep voice poured through the phone to ripple like soft suede over her bare skin. Instantly she was alert, her eyes popping open to survey the morning light sneaking around the edges of her bedroom curtains.

'Who is this?' Her voice sounded prim, almost schoolmarmish, but it was her best effort. She'd gone to sleep with the sound of Donato's voice in her ears; she'd even dreamt of it when she eventually managed to snatch some sleep. It was unfair to be confronted with it now when she hadn't had time to gather herself.

'As if you don't know, sweet Ella. Did I wake you?' The words worked like a caress, drawing her skin taut, jerking her free of the last traces of sleep. That voice should be outlawed. It was too decadent, too delicious to be unleashed on an unsuspecting woman.

'Yes. No!' She rolled her eyes in frustration. 'Who's speaking?'

'Forgotten your fiancé already?' His voice plumbed new depths, curling heat right down inside her. 'I can see I'll have to try harder.'

'Donato.' No point pretending. 'What do you want?' She wouldn't dignify that fiancé joke with a response.

'I told you last night want I wanted.'

*Her.* That was what he'd said. And her body had gone into libido overdrive at the look in his sultry eyes.

'But for now just tell me, are you still in bed?'

'What if I am?' Ella frowned. Why? Was he somewhere nearby? Had her father given him her address? Surely not. Donato Salazar wouldn't venture into the working-class suburbs in search of her. Though, after what she'd learned about him on the Web when she got home, he wasn't a stranger to poor neighbourhoods. She still found it hard to believe what she'd discovered.

'Tell me what you're wearing.' The words raked her skin, drawing it tight over a belly that clenched needily.

Just at the sound of his voice?

Ella bit back a moan. This couldn't be happening to her.

'Tell me, Ella. Pyjamas?' He paused. 'A nightie?' Another pause, longer this time. 'Silk and lace?'

She firmed her lips, not letting herself rise to the bait.

'Or do you sleep naked?'

The gasp escaped her lips before she could stop it. Weirdly, it felt as if, just by saying it, he must know.

And now he did. She'd given herself away with that intake of breath. She heard it in his voice. 'Give me your address and I'll be straight over.'

'No!' Her voice hit top register. Her heart was pounding as she heard his dark-chocolate chuckle against her ear.

She wanted to tell him she didn't usually sleep naked. It had just been so hot last night and she couldn't get comfortable, even after a cold shower. But she knew he'd put two and two together and realise it wasn't the summer heat that had kept her from sleep, but thoughts of him. His ego was big enough already.

'Why are you ringing, Donato?'

'It's not enough that I want to hear your voice?'

That sounded like a parody of her own feelings. She tried to despise this man who was a crony of her father's, who'd toyed with her last night. Yet she kept the phone pressed to her ear, luxuriating in the soft rumble of his voice. As if she *wanted* that flurry of desire rippling through her.

Ella shuffled up in the bed, yanking the pillows up behind her so she could sit. Lying naked in bed with Donato's voice in her ear was wrong on so many levels.

'Get to the point, Donato. Why did you call?'

'Do you usually sleep so late?'

Ella peered at the time, stunned to find it was after nine. 'No.' Usually she was up at six to fit in Pilates or a swim before work.

'So you had a disturbed night? Were you dreaming about me?' That thread of satisfaction in his voice grew stronger.

'Is there a point to this call?' She sighed ostentatiously as if she hadn't indeed spent half the night taunted by dreams of him. 'Or do I hang up now?'

'Give me your address so I can collect you. We're having lunch together.'

Ella scowled. She told herself it was because of his assumption she'd go along with what he wanted. But what unnerved her was the little jiggle of excitement that skipped through her.

'Ella?'

'If you'd invited me to lunch I'd be obliged to thank you for the invitation before I declined. But as there was no invitation that's unnecessary.'

'Absolutely,' he said smoothly. 'Because we *will* be lunching together.'

Ella shifted against the pillows. She shouldn't enjoy this fruitless argument. Yet she couldn't bring herself to end the call. Not when basking in the sound of Donato's voice was the closest she'd come to enjoying a man's company in a long, long time.

What did that say about the state of her love life?

Pathetic! That was it.

'What's your address, Ella?'

'I'm surprised a man with your resources doesn't already have it.' Her father would have given it to him in an instant, if he'd been able to find it. 'Don't tell me your dossier on the Sanderson family doesn't include something so basic.'

'I don't have a dossier on your family.'

'I thought you'd be a better liar, Donato.'

Instead of taking offence he chuckled again, the sound like warm water lapping through her veins. Ella's hand on the phone grew clammy and her bare nipples budded. Frowning, she snatched the sheet and dragged it up, anchoring it under her arms. As if that would protect her from whatever this magic was he wove around her.

'I have a dossier on your father's business and on his private…interests.' Ella winced, not liking the sound of that. There were some things she didn't need to know about her father. 'And some information on your sister.'

'You told me you didn't set your investigators onto her!'

'I didn't need to. A quick trawl through the social pages was more than ample.'

Ella hated the way he dismissed Fuzz as if she were nothing. Her sister might be flawed but she wasn't as bad as all that. She just needed purpose, and freedom from their father's influence.

'Really?' Her voice dripped disapproval.

'It seemed a sensible precaution since your father suggested I marry her.'

*And now Fuzz was out of the picture that left Ella.*

Ella glanced around the bedroom with its Monet print on the wall and her pride and joy, the nineteen-twenties tub chair she'd rescued from a garage sale and reconditioned with the help of a night class. The wooden legs glowed with polish and the sage-green upholstery was restful as well as pretty.

The idea of strangers nosing into her world, ordinary

as it was, picking through the details of her life, set her teeth on edge.

'I don't make it into the social pages. How much have you found out about me?'

'Not nearly enough.' The skin at Ella's nape drew tight at the sultry note in that deep voice.

'Your investigators only work business hours? You disappoint me, Donato. I'd have thought they'd scurry to do the bidding of a man with your reputation even late last night.'

'You've been doing some digging of your own.' He didn't sound fazed.

'Don't tell me you're offended?'

'On the contrary, I'm pleased. It proves that, despite your rather emphatic goodbye, you anticipated meeting me again.'

Ella scowled. He was right. Why bother finding out about him if she'd cut him from her life? She'd had an insidious certainty it wasn't so easy to get rid of Donato Salazar.

No, it was more than that. She'd wanted to know everything she could about him. No man had ever made such an impact on her.

'And as for hiring investigators to work through the night...'

'Yes?' She shifted uneasily. Was someone even now interviewing her neighbours or accessing her records?

'You made it clear you believed that an unforgivable breach of privacy.'

'So?'

'So I'm not going to do it to you.'

'Sorry?'

'You heard me, Ella. I'm not in the habit of saying things I don't mean.'

For a moment words eluded her. 'Just like that? Because I said so?'

'Just like that.'

Ella's pulse faltered then tripped to an unfamiliar beat. He was serious. Yet she couldn't quite believe he'd renege on using the power his money could buy just because it offended her.

*Why would he do that?*

She shoved her hair back from her face. To her amazement her fingers were ever so slightly unsteady.

*What did he want from her?*

Surely he'd been lying last night, saying he wanted to know her. As for that nonsense about them marrying—

'I want to know everything about you.' His deep voice burred in her ear. 'But I want to find out from you.'

She'd known Donato Salazar was dangerous, but still she wasn't prepared for the way he devastated her defences. It took precious seconds to find her voice. 'I'm afraid you're going to be disappointed.'

'Nothing about you is disappointing, believe me, *Ella*.' There it was again, that caress when he said her name. As if those two simple syllables were an endearment.

'I meant—' she set her jaw '—you'll be disappointed because we're not going to meet again.'

He was silent and stupidly something like anxiety feathered through her. At the idea this was the last time she'd speak with him? Impossible!

'Are you scared of me, Ella?'

'Scared? No.' Strangely enough, it was true. She was scared of what he made her feel, of the urgent, restless woman she'd become in the short time since they'd met. But not scared of him.

'Not even after what you discovered in your research on me?' The banter was gone from his voice. He sounded deadly serious.

Deadly. Now there was a word. Last night she'd thought he looked dangerous. Then, at home, sitting with her computer, she'd discovered how right she'd been. How many people had she known personally who'd been to prison for assault?

None.

Was it naïve of her to believe that, despite his teenage criminal record, Donato Salazar wouldn't hurt her?

She'd been stunned to read about his crime and his prison term. At the same time it went some way to explaining the sense she'd had last night that he was a man apart from everyone else.

As a nurse she'd worked with a huge range of people, from the frail aged to the bloodied survivors of brawls to the drug-addicted and downright dangerous. She was cautious, methodical, never taking unnecessary risks, especially doing home visits. But the only alarm she felt now was at her own avid response to Donato.

'I'm not afraid of you because you've got a criminal record, Donato.' In the intervening years he'd built a reputation for ruthlessness in business but there'd never been a hint he was anything but a model citizen. He'd been lauded for his work supporting inner-city youth centres and legislation to assist victims of abuse.

'Then you're unique.' Was that bitterness she heard? She hitched herself higher against the pillows.

'Are you saying I should be? That you're violent?'

'No.' His voice was flat. 'I'm not that person any more. I've learned to restrain my impulses. Instead I channel them into something more productive.'

He said nothing for a moment and she wondered what was going through his mind. 'So, you're not frightened. But you *are* curious.'

'You're not the average Australian business tycoon.'

His laugh was sharp but appealing and despite herself Ella's lips twitched. How could she feel at ease with this man? His past and his dealings with her father should warn her off, yet she felt incredibly drawn to him. It wasn't just desire; she was fascinated by the way his mind worked. She enjoyed their verbal sparring.

'You've met lots of tycoons, have you?'

'A few.'

'And you weren't impressed.'

By the men with whom her father did business? 'Not usually.'

'But still you want to know me better. Here's the chance to satisfy your curiosity, Ella. Over lunch. We have a table reserved at the Opera House restaurant. I'm assured the food is excellent.'

But it wasn't food on his mind, or even conversation. The low pitch of his voice was pure seduction. Ella pressed her thighs together, pretending she didn't feel that tiny pulse of awareness awakening between them.

'No, thank you.'

There was a pause. 'Has anyone ever told you you're stubborn?'

'Yes.'

'You know you want to. You're denying yourself as well as me.'

'Don't presume to know my mind, Donato.'

He sighed. 'Don't make me force you, Ella.'

She tucked the sheet more securely under her arms and sat straighter. 'You can't force me.'

'What if I told you your father's financial viability is totally dependent on my support? And that support is dependent on the wedding he's organising for us.'

'You're lying. You don't want to marry me. We discussed it last night.'

What sort of bizarre game was he playing?

'*You* discussed it, Ella, but you wouldn't listen to my response.' He paused and the silence thickened around her.

'Ask your father if you don't believe me. He'll confirm it. The wedding goes ahead or there's no deal. And if there's no deal…'

# CHAPTER SIX

DONATO WAS WAITING for her, standing in the doorway of a white, two-storey art deco gem of a mansion that made Ella's mouth water with envy. In the forecourt sat a gleaming convertible in dark red. Not a modern supercar but a vintage model with running boards that made her think of champagne picnics and romantic escapes to the country.

She choked down annoyance. It was easier to loathe the man before she realised they shared the same tastes.

But this wasn't his home. Donato lived in Melbourne. Maybe he was a guest here. He probably lived in a soulless box of a house and had a chauffeur drive him in a stretch limo.

The thought soothed her. She didn't like the notion they had anything in common. Anything other than that disconcerting stir of attraction. And the suspicion she'd got last night that he wasn't a fan of her father. Clearly that was pure imagination, since he proposed to link himself with Reg Sanderson's family.

Ella stopped her little car, telling herself it was the house that quickened her pulse. Not the man.

With huge streamlined windows and a curved end like the prow of a ship, the old house was stunning. The glimpse of dark blue ocean glittering beyond it enhanced its beauty, as did the lush garden that hid it from the security gates. Gates that opened as soon as she'd nosed her car off the street.

Had Donato been watching for her, or his security staff?

She'd seen no one on the long drive from the street to the clifftop house.

Now there he was under the huge circular portico, his expression unreadable. Against the bright beaten copper of the doors he looked severe. She told herself it was because he wore black trousers and shirt, the sleeves rolled casually up his arms. Yet the contrast between the man and the bright metal behind him reminded her again of that fallen-angel image.

There was nothing casual about his wide stance. Or the way he watched her. Through the windscreen Ella felt the sizzle of his dark eyes. Her skin tingled, her blood a rush of adrenalin as she stared back.

The scary thing about Donato Salazar was the way he saw beyond the surface to the woman she was inside. To the woman she'd never dared let herself be.

Ella had never felt so *naked* as with him. It was as if he saw through a lifetime's defences. He challenged her in a way no man ever had. Donato called to a reckless side she'd never let loose.

For a moment fear pinned her to her seat. Then she thrust open her door and got out, to be instantly enveloped by the summer heat.

Over the car roof their gazes collided and meshed. Ella's pulse racketed and her insides clenched in a way that wasn't about fear but anticipation.

*How could she want a man who'd calmly decreed she had to marry him or watch her father ruined?*

Setting her shoulders, Ella slammed the door and stalked across the terrace.

He didn't move towards her, just stood: tall, brooding and enigmatic. His hands were shoved deep into his pockets, making him look nonchalant. That only spiked her annoyance.

Even worse, he looked every bit as stunning as he had

last night. The muted lighting at the party hadn't exaggerated the wide set of his shoulders or the lean strength of his body. Her gaze skittered over corded forearms, dusted with dark hair, and heavy thigh muscles. For a shaky moment she wondered how it would feel to be held against that hard masculine frame.

Fear skidded down her spine. She didn't do lust. Not like this. And not with a man like Donato Salazar.

He smiled as she approached and the pale scar on one side of his face disappeared into the groove running up his cheek. Just like that white heat shimmered through her feminine core. She blinked, stumbling a little on an uneven flagstone, and reminded herself she was too furious to feel attraction.

Nevertheless, she wished she'd taken time to hunt out a pair of heels so she didn't have to tilt her chin to look at him.

'Ella, you're looking particularly vibrant today.'

'Vibrant?' She shook her head. 'The word is *angry*.'

'It suits you.' His smile didn't falter. If anything he looked satisfied. But despite the smile there was something guarded about his expression. His eyes held secrets.

Not surprising, given the games he played. She'd give an awful lot to know what they were.

What made him tick? What was he after? For the life of her she couldn't believe a man like Donato Salazar really wanted to marry one of Reg Sanderson's daughters. Especially her, the prosaic, sensible, not-a-glamorous-bone-in-her-body one.

She stiffened. This wasn't about her. It was about saving Fuzz and Rob.

'We need to talk.'

'Of course. Come through.' He stepped back and gestured for her to enter.

She strode past him into a wide circular foyer. Her staccato steps petered out as her gaze caught on the perfect curving lines of the staircase to the upper floor. Delicate wrought iron formed a balustrade featuring wood nymphs and fauns dancing up the steps. Pure art deco whimsy.

Ella took a step closer, entranced despite her fury.

Then from behind came the thud of the heavy front doors closing her in. The hairs on her nape stood up and a frisson of anxiety resonated through her.

Ridiculous. She was here because she needed to have this out with him, face to face.

'This way.' Donato was beside her, leading the way towards a sitting room that featured views across a terrace and in-ground pool to the Pacific Ocean beyond.

Ella didn't budge. 'This won't take long.' She planted her feet.

He swung around, eyebrows silently rising. 'You look very combative.'

'You're not surprised.'

He shrugged and walked back to where she stood in the centre of the circular foyer. 'I know you're a volatile woman.'

Ella snorted. Volatile? She was the stable one of the family. The one who never had tantrums. The one who quietly got on with whatever needed to be done. Before she left home it had been she, not her father or older sister, who made sure the housekeeper and gardener received their instructions and their pay.

'I'm not volatile. I'm justifiably annoyed. There's a difference.' She breathed deep, feeling indignation well. 'Or will you decide my reaction is due to the fact I'm female?' That had always been one of her father's favourite put-downs.

Donato raised his hands as if in surrender. Yet the spark in those dark blue eyes told her he was enjoying himself too much to give in.

'I'm a lot of things, Ella. But not sexist.'

He was far closer than she liked. Too close. Her stomach gave a betraying wobble.

She swallowed hard as the aroma of rich coffee and warm male skin enveloped her. It was as if her body was absorbed in a different conversation than the one coming out of her mouth. A conversation that was about heat and desire and that phantom ache down deep in her womb.

She didn't know how to combat it. Creating distance between them was the obvious option but she wouldn't let him see even a hint of fear. She'd learned young that revealing weakness only made things worse.

'I want to know what's going on.'

'Well, since you opted to come here rather than to Bennelong Point, I've arranged for us to share lunch on the terrace.'

Had she ever met anyone so coolly sure of himself? So infuriating? He cast even her father into the shade with his supreme self-confidence.

Yet, despite her annoyance, Ella didn't get the same feeling from Donato as she did from her father, who so blatantly exulted in triumphing over others. Donato was manipulating her yet she didn't feel bullied. More...*challenged*.

Which showed how dangerous was this undercurrent of attraction humming in her veins. It tempted her to put a pretty gloss on Donato's outrageous demands.

Ella crossed her arms, glaring. 'I didn't come here for lunch.'

'You need to look after yourself. You didn't stop for breakfast, did you?' Donato took a step closer and suddenly the spacious two-storey room shrank around them. Ella breathed deeper, needing oxygen. 'You were still in bed when I rang.' The glint in his dark eyes reminded her of his teasing as she lay naked in bed, and heat drilled down through her belly.

Ella stiffened, ignoring the telltale flush rising in her throat and cheeks.

'I want the truth. You don't *need* to marry Reg Sanderson's daughter. The idea of marriage to cement closer business ties doesn't wash. You're the one my father needs, not the other way around. Why are you playing along with the idea?'

For a millisecond Donato's eyes widened, giving her a glimpse of surprise in a flash of indigo that rivalled the ocean's brilliance. Then his eyelids lowered and his gaze became unreadable.

Ella's breathing quickened. There was something there. Something she'd said, something he didn't expect her to know. But what? She racked her brain but she'd only stated the obvious. She could find no significance there.

Yet she couldn't shake the feeling she'd inadvertently hit on something important.

'Things aren't always as clear-cut as they seem.' Donato paused. 'Your father's proposal has definite advantages.'

Ella jammed her hands on her hips. 'What advantages? Name one.'

In answer Donato's eyes skated down, past the warm blush in her throat, over her loose-fitting top, lightweight trousers and flat sandals.

She'd dressed for comfort rather than sophistication. Her floaty aqua and silver top was a favourite. Now, under Donato's trawling stare, Ella had a qualm that it had somehow suddenly become transparent. Surely his gaze grazed her skin, following every curve the material should have hidden. As if he already knew her intimately.

*Already.* The word was a promise she couldn't dislodge from her brain.

Ella's body came alive, just as it had last night. She'd told herself that had been an illusion created by tiredness and stress. But she didn't feel tired now. She felt wired, waves of energy ripping through her, awakening every nerve ending.

She jutted her jaw. 'You don't have to marry me to get sex.'

'Why, Ella—' his eyes gleamed with a banked heat and his mouth curved in a slow smile that turned her insides to mush '—that's quite an offer. I'm charmed and delighted.'

For one insane moment she almost smiled back, till her brain processed his words.

'I'm offering nothing.' Her head snapped back, her pulse thrumming at the look in his eyes. 'I'm just stating the obvious. Even if you wanted to go to bed with me, marriage isn't necessary.' Unfortunately her explanation came out in an unsteady rush as he leaned closer.

'Such a tempting idea,' he murmured. 'I'm glad you suggested it.'

'Stop it, Donato. You know I'm not suggesting anything.' But now she couldn't banish the idea of them, together.

'You're thinking about it, aren't you?' His voice dropped an octave to a warm rumble she felt deep inside. 'I am too, Ella. I find the idea intoxicating.'

He lifted his hand to cup her cheek and sensation juddered through her. Ella shot back a step, her breath snagging. Instead of releasing her, Donato followed, his broad callused palm hot on her skin.

She felt crowded, surrounded.

*Excited.*

Silence thickened. The saw of her breathing seemed loud, as did the quickened patter of her pulse. But it was the sensations detonating through her body that panicked Ella.

Donato had sabotaged all her erogenous zones, attuning them to his touch. Her lips tingled as his gaze dropped to her mouth. Her nipples budded against the sensible bra she wore, as if mocking her determination *not* to dress up for Donato. Her silky top stirred as she hauled in deeper breaths, the touch of fabric a barely there caress. And between her legs…

Ella swallowed hard, drowning in the slumberous heat of those searing eyes.

'Let me go, Donato.' Her voice was as shaky as she felt. Not with fear, but because her body came alive so instantly, so completely, at his touch.

With every atom of her being she was aware of his big frame mere inches from her own. It was as if he projected a force-field that sent shock waves across her skin and deeper, heating her core.

'No.' He shook his head. 'I've waited too long.' His palm slid down her cheek to caress her jaw then thrust back into her hair. Ella's neck arched and she bit down a sigh at the luxurious feel of his fingers against her scalp. Tiny little shivers coursed down her back and shoulders.

'Rubbish.' Her voice was far too soft. She cleared her throat and tried to summon the energy to move away. Her knees had grown wobbly. 'We haven't known each other a day.'

Remarkable to think it was less than twenty-four hours since they met.

Donato bent his head even closer and Ella's breath hitched. He held her captive with that remarkable dark blue gaze. 'It's still been too long. I've wanted you since the moment I saw you.' The words were pure seduction, low and tantalising.

Ella told herself it was just a line he tossed out, but even then she couldn't dredge up the power to move. Stunned, she teetered on the brink of losing herself. She swallowed, her mouth drying at what she read in his stare.

'Don't take me for a fool, Donato.' Despite her indignation her tongue slowed on his name, savouring it. She looked up into that austere, scarred, compelling face and wished, for once in her life, that she really *was* the beauty in the family. The sort to turn even this man's head. 'You came to the party expecting my sister, not me.'

'And how pleased I was that she couldn't make it.' The words were a caress.

'No!' She jerked back, finally breaking from his hold. 'Don't pretend you were bowled over by my looks or my glittering personality. It won't work.' Ella had learned long ago, growing up in her sister's shadow, that she wasn't the sort to turn male heads. Pain twisted, razor-sharp, in her chest.

'You don't believe me, sweet Ella?'

Damn the man. Even that easy endearment sent her heart tumbling. Was she really that needy? So ready to be seduced by a show of attention?

Yet even as she lashed up indignation she knew she was fooling herself. Despite her protests that sense of connection between them was as real as it was inexplicable. It had slammed through her the moment she'd turned to find Donato's eyes on her at the party. It had sung in her veins as she'd sparred with him under her father's horrified gaze. It had turned her on as she lay naked in bed, wishing he was there with her instead of taunting her with that sultry deep voice over the phone.

'Don't toy with me, Donato.' She pressed her lips together.

'You don't trust me, do you?'

Her chin hiked up. 'Not an inch.'

'Maybe this will convince you.' He grabbed her hand and, before she could yank it free, placed it on his chest.

Instantly she stilled. The hard staccato beat of his heart pounded beneath her palm. It wasn't the steady pulse of a man in control. It was the rapid pulse of a man on the brink. Her eyes widened.

Runnels of fire traced across Ella's skin as she met eyes

the colour of twilight. His gaze bored into her, challenging yet, incredibly it seemed, honest.

'I want you, Ella.' His gaze pinioned her. 'And you want me.'

Before she could form a reply his big hand lifted to the upper slope of her breast, palm down. 'See? We match.'

It was true. Her heartbeat careered just as fast as his. And all she could think about was how it would feel if he slid his hand just a little lower, to cup her breast.

A hot chill raced through her and desire spiked. Her breath grew ragged.

As if reading her mind, Donato slipped his hand down to cover her breast. Ella bit her lip to shut in a gasp of delight. But she couldn't stop herself from pressing nearer, eyes closing as his hand moulded her soft flesh. Something like relief welled.

He moved and her eyes snapped open. Gripping her arm, he stepped in against her, powering her back until her spine collided with something solid.

They stood toe to toe, hip to thigh, torso to torso and she shivered at how good that felt. Even the scent of him in her nostrils was delicious. The sheer potency of his big body was a promise and, she realised belatedly, a threat.

'No!' She lifted her hands to his shoulders and pushed. He didn't budge. He was as immovable as the Harbour Bridge. 'I don't care what deal you and my father have sewn up. You can't *force* me. Let me go!'

His jaw set and she watched that pulse throb at his temple. He breathed deep, his nostrils flaring. Then, to her surprise, he stepped back. He stood just inches away, his breath hot on her face, the force-field of his body making her flesh prickle and spark.

'This isn't about any deal, Ella. This is about us.'

'There is no *us*.'

'Of course there is. You feel it too, the awareness between us. The desire.'

She felt it all right. It scared her as nothing else ever had that she could recall.

'You think having sex will convince me to marry you?' Her chest rose and fell with her choppy breathing. 'You think you're that good in bed? Or are you relying on blackmail to force me since my sister is out of reach?'

'Don't be a coward, Ella.'

She stiffened. One thing she'd stopped being long ago was a coward. After the life she'd had to endure with her father, the continual battle for respect since love was denied her, she'd earned the right to hold her head high.

'I'm no coward.' It came out through clenched teeth.

'You're looking for excuses.' Donato raised his hands. 'Forget your father. Forget the wedding and the business deal. Forget your sister. I was never interested in her.'

Ella scrutinised his face but his look was sincere. His gaze zeroed in on her mouth and she swallowed hard.

'This is about you and me. I'm telling you I want you. The question is, are you woman enough to admit you want me too?'

'With you holding my father's potential bankruptcy over our heads?'

Donato shook his head. 'There are two separate issues here.' He spoke slowly, his eyes never leaving hers. 'There's my business deal with your father, and yes, the proposal for a wedding is tied to that. But,' he continued when she would have interrupted, 'that's not what we're discussing right now. No one is forcing you into anything. Believe me, I would *never* force a woman into my bed.'

Ella stared into his face, noting how those dark features set in stern lines of rigid control. There was hauteur in the flash of his eyes and pride in the set of his shoulders.

*She believed him.* The realisation rocked her.

'What we're discussing now is sex.' His voice turned deep and liquid on the word, matching the slow-burning need inside Ella. 'You and me. Uncomplicated, satisfying, scorching.'

'Scorching?' Ella didn't know how the word escaped. It wasn't what she'd meant to say. Clearly the look in his eyes had incinerated part of her brain. 'You assume a lot.'

He shook his head. 'I assume nothing. I *know*, Ella. Can't you feel it?' Again he reached for her, but this time he only clasped her hand lightly. Fire sparked from the point of contact and she had to work to suppress shivers of delight.

How had she come to this? She'd raced halfway across Sydney to confront Donato, filled with righteous indignation and—

But there'd been more, hadn't there? No matter what she pretended, it hadn't just been indignation. She'd been almost *relieved* for the excuse to see him again, despite her fine talk about them never meeting again. She was angry, for sure. But she was also…enthralled.

She swallowed, her throat scratchy as she confronted the truth. She wanted Donato Salazar as she'd never wanted any man. Her skin felt too tight, her chest too full.

Donato stroked one finger along her palm and she gasped as pleasure rocketed through her.

'Tell me you feel it too,' he purred.

Ella bit back a groan of despair. She was out of her depth. She'd never been good at flirtation. Suddenly she didn't care about pride or keeping up an image. This was about survival—and she felt like she was going under for the third time.

'What do you want from me, Donato? I don't play these games.'

'I don't play games either. Not about this.' His face was grim, the hint of teasing erased from features that looked pared back and intense. He swallowed, his Adam's apple bobbing hard, and something within her eased at that visible sign that he wasn't totally in control.

Suddenly he stepped back, releasing her hand, and cool air wafted between them.

'What happens next is up to you.' His heavy-lidded look was a challenge and an invitation.

# CHAPTER SEVEN

DONATO LOOKED DOWN into stunning blue-grey eyes, grown huge and wary. He felt the doubt radiating from Ella, just as he felt the heat of her sexual arousal.

His body was taut, humming with need. He couldn't quite believe the effort it took not to step closer and persuade her into surrender as he knew he could. The attraction dragging at his belly, arcing between them, was powerful.

But there'd been something about the way she'd mentioned her sister, on top of her talk of being forced, that held him back. He'd seen the quickly veiled hint of fragility in Ella's expression.

He didn't have her measure yet but one thing he knew. He needed Ella to come to him.

The moment of silence grew to two pulse beats, three, four, more. His nerves and his patience stretched. He forced himself to stand there unmoving, as if he wasn't strung out.

Then, with what sounded like a muffled oath, Ella launched herself forward. She cannoned into him, soft and curvaceous, warm and delectably feminine. Automatically he grabbed her to him, catching her in a tight hold. Her arms looped over his shoulders, her hands burrowing up through his hair, pulling his head down.

He had a moment to register that fresh-as-a-garden-after-rain scent then their mouths collided and his brain shorted.

So good. She felt even better than he'd expected. And she tasted—

Donato plunged deep into her mouth, forcing her head

back, swallowing her sigh of response. Ribbons of heat unfurled through him as he savoured Ella, so delicious, so right. Her soft lips, her demanding tongue, the way she melted into him even as she challenged him to give more. He angled his head, hauling her even closer, lost in a kiss that was so much more than he'd expected, despite his anticipation.

He couldn't get enough. Her lush body cushioning his instant erection. Her hot, eager mouth that tasted of peach nectar. Her thigh, sliding restlessly against his leg as their tongues tangled and lips fused.

Donato grabbed her thigh and hauled it up, swallowing her gasp of shocked approval. There. He wanted her there. He bent his knees, angling his hips so he rubbed against the softest, most secret part of her.

To his delight Ella's hands tightened against his scalp, not pushing him away but clutching as if she couldn't get close enough.

Dimly he wondered what had happened to slow seduction. To years of expertise at pleasing a woman. To caution and taking things one step at a time.

With Ella there were no steps. There was just a head-long plunge into riotous need.

With his other hand he grabbed her backside, lifting her into him, and she purred her approval. That throaty sound incited, inviting more. She nipped his bottom lip and angled her head to taste him better and his head spun.

Yes! He'd known Ella wouldn't be a shrinking violet. Not the way passion had sparked and simmered in her, a conflagration waiting to be ignited. Yet he hadn't expected—

Thought died as she rolled her pelvis against him.

Hell! He was shaking all over. If he wasn't careful he might drop her.

No, he couldn't drop her. His hands were welded to her. But they might collapse together on the marble floor if his legs gave way. He was pretty sure he could still enjoy Ella, even with a concussion. In fact a concussion would be worth it to experience Ella coming apart around him.

But she might get hurt.

With a desperate effort he dragged his eyelids up. He couldn't remember shutting his eyes. All he remembered was the sensual assault as she launched herself at him and his body going into meltdown.

Lips still locked with hers, Donato scanned the foyer, instantly discounting the stairs to the upper floor and the bedrooms. They'd never make it that far. At this rate he wasn't sure they'd make it out of their clothes.

The sideboard. It sat between two doors, a collector's piece of exquisite workmanship. Perfect.

Lifting Ella against him, he stumbled across the foyer. Her eyes snapped open, the blaze hitting like a punch to the solar plexus.

'What?' She tugged her head away and instantly Donato wanted her back, her mouth surrendering to his.

Then she must have felt the solid furniture behind her because understanding flickered in her eyes. Donato lifted her so she sat on the sideboard, then he stepped in, pushing her knees wide.

For the merest of moments there was stillness between them, a waiting awareness, a final chance to break apart. Then Ella's eyes drifted shut as he lightly touched her breast. It was high and plump enough to fill his hand. Delectable. Just like her shuddering sigh of approval and the way she arched into his touch, eager for more.

Donato smiled grimly. She was so responsive. He wanted to tease and pleasure her, but he wasn't sure he could manage anything like his usual finesse.

Then Ella's hand closed over him and his vision blurred, his groin tightening. All the blood in his body rushed south.

Need rocked him and dimly he wondered if he'd have time to get free of his trousers before he came.

Instinct took over from thought as their mouths met and fused. She tugged his head down again, as if afraid he might pull back. Donato ravaged her mouth, forgetting all about control in the need to crush her close.

Between them hands scrabbled at clothes, fumbling and tangling.

Ella's fingers against his erection almost destroyed Donato. He grabbed her hand and planted it against his chest, over his thundering heart. Then he was wrenching at her trousers, hauling down the zip as she wriggled, helping him. His hands were unsteady but soon there was warm silken skin beneath his touch. Seconds later he was free of his own constraining trousers and pulling her to him.

*Carajo!* Had anything, ever, felt so good?

Donato lifted his head to drag in oxygen, his lungs already overloaded. Her eyes opened and he was lost in the silvery dazzle of her stare.

Then he touched her with one finger, circling, probing, and her eyes slitted to diamond-bright shards, her throat arching back as if her head was too heavy. Ella was soft, warm, wet, shifting restlessly as one finger became two and—

'Condom.' The word was a wisp of sound he almost missed. Then Ella straightened, her eyes locking with his. 'I don't have one.' Delicate colour climbed her throat, a contrast to the pure silver of her eyes. 'I didn't think…'

Donato was fascinated by the suspicion that Ella was embarrassed, this woman who'd launched herself at him without reservation, so for a moment the implication didn't hit. When it did he jerked back, stunned.

How had he, of all people, forgotten anything so basic? Such thoughtlessness wasn't part of his DNA. Not now, not ever.

It was the work of seconds to grab the foil packet from his trouser pocket and rip it open. See? What seemed a lifetime ago he'd had foresight. He just hadn't been prepared for the cataclysm that was Ella Sanderson in his arms.

There was something unbelievably arousing about holding Ella's gaze as he sheathed himself. The soft pink rose to streak her fine cheekbones. For a fraction of a second the word *endearing* flashed into Donato's brain, before higher thought became impossible and he gave in to primitive instinct.

Hands to her smooth bare hips, he pulled her close then with one sure movement pushed home.

A sound halfway between a sigh and a sob escaped Ella's reddened lips and he made himself still, though the tight embrace of her slick heat almost made him lose himself.

Had he hurt her? He tried to unlock his jaw to ask but if he moved a muscle he mightn't be able to hold back from the inevitable.

Then Ella shifted, her legs lifting over his hips, locking around his waist, making him sink deeper into beckoning warmth. She clung to his shoulders and suddenly there was nothing stopping him. That was invitation in her eyes, not pain. And the feel of her moving against him...

Donato succumbed, taking her fast and hard, revelling in her beautiful body that accepted him so eagerly. Each tilt of her pelvis, each softly indrawn breath was an incitement to pleasure. He couldn't get enough. He couldn't manage finesse. There was nothing but the compulsion to make her his in the most primitive, satisfying way possible.

The world was already blurring when Donato felt the ripples of her arousal quicken around him. The sensation was too much and he braced one arm on the wall behind her, bucking high and hard with a desperation that was more animal than civilised man.

He needed her, and this exquisite pleasure.

'Ella!' Her name was a husky roar, surprising him as it emerged from his mouth.

Her body stiffened then jerked around him. Her eyes sprang wide open and he fell into pools of burnished moonlight.

There was a flash of heat, a surge of energy and he spilled himself, collapsing into her as the world exploded. Chest and shoulders heaving, head bowed against her fragrant neck, Donato experienced pure rapture as Ella clutched him close.

He'd expected passion and pleasure. But nothing like this. When had he ever called out a lover's name like that? When had he ever forgotten protection?

Donato gathered her in, relishing her soft womanly body, so lax in his arms.

The world had contracted to the living pulse beating through her, through him, filling the air around them and the darkness behind her closed lids. Ella wasn't sure she was still alive after that cataclysmic orgasm.

*Had it ever been like that before?*

Of course it hadn't. If it had she'd never have let her love life sink without a trace.

Donato moved, pulling gently away, murmuring something she couldn't hear over her rocketing pulse and harsh breathing. Soon she'd open her eyes but for now she slumped back against the wall that at this moment felt as comfortable as any feather bed.

Her bones had melted. She wasn't sure she could move her legs. But it didn't matter. She never wanted to move again. She felt blissfully, utterly wonderful.

She felt… Words faded in the afterglow of rapture.

Finally, the awkward angle of her head against the wall and the hard surface beneath her penetrated her dazed brain. She should move. She had…surely there was something she had to do?

Gingerly Ella sat up, hands braced on the seat beneath her, only to find it wasn't a seat. It was hard and bumpy. With a huge effort she pried open heavy eyelids and looked down. She was sitting on a carving of a chariot. It was pulled by horses with wide nostrils and, as she shifted, she saw a couple of naked men, maybe gods, riding behind.

Ella blinked, her hands stroking the satiny polished wood beyond the carved plaque. Her gaze strayed to the delicate, obviously hand-carved garlands of fruit and flowers that grew fancifully out of the top of the sideboard to trail decoratively down the front.

Her throat closed. If she wasn't mistaken she'd just had mind-blowing sex on top of a piece of furniture worth more than she earned in a year. A museum piece that some collector had no doubt lovingly restored.

Her fingers tightened on the edge of the brilliantly polished wood. Her eyes closed.

*Forget the furniture, Ella. How about the fact you had wild sex with a stranger? A man you've known less than a day? And you barely made it past his front door?*

She swallowed hard, her throat constricting as her body hummed with the resonance of the climax they'd shared.

*Who was this woman and what had she done with Ella Sanderson?*

A footstep sounded and her eyes popped open. Relief made her sag, her hand to her racing heart. 'It's you.'

'You were expecting someone else?' Donato looked as debonair and dangerous as ever. More so, with his thick black hair deliciously rumpled. A shiver spread out from her womb and she kept her eyes off his face, not ready to meet that intense scrutiny.

He was fully clothed. Ella tugged her long top lower. But that voice in her head drawled that it was too late for modesty. That didn't stop the blood rushing to her face as she registered her bare legs and the fact she still wore her shoes. Her pants lay in a heap a few steps away.

She swallowed, reminding herself that embarrassment couldn't kill her. It never had in all those years facing her father's superior friends. Even this, the pinnacle of mortification, would pass.

'I wondered if you have staff.'

'Not today. I gave them the day off.' He paced closer and her head jerked up. The gleam in his eyes was pure carnal invitation, as was the half smile flirting at the corners of his mouth. Heat blasted her, turning the marrow in her bones molten.

How could she feel so needy again? Surely it had only been minutes since they'd— Ella slammed a door on that train of thought.

He was before her now, his palms resting lightly on her bare thighs. His hands were broad, hard with calluses, and the feel of them on her skin made her pulse skitter. She remembered him touching her intimately and the breath sighed out of her lungs.

Then his words penetrated.

'You gave them the day off? Why? Because you were so sure we'd…' Ella swallowed hard. 'So sure of *me*?'

His expression was still, giving nothing away, except for that banked heat.

'I was sure that, whatever happened, I wanted complete privacy. No distractions.'

She angled her jaw. 'In case I ravished you before I even got past the foyer?' Her bravado hid a world of discomfort. She wanted to scurry away and hide, not brazen out her inexplicable behaviour. She'd acted like a tart instead of her cautious, reserved self.

'I've discovered I adore being ravished in the foyer.' His

fingers touched her chin, tilting it towards him. 'And it was a mutual ravishment, Ella.'

Did he say that to make her feel better? It didn't.

She'd known from the first that he was Trouble with a capital T. She just hadn't reckoned on her own body betraying her. In twenty-six years it had never done so before. Sex, in her admittedly limited experience, had been carefully planned, horizontal and...nice. Not a blaze of out-of-control libidos.

Something flared in Donato's eyes and she just knew he was thinking about it too. Sex. The scent of it hung in the air and, despite her lassitude mere minutes ago, Ella's body was ripe and ready for him again.

She shifted back on the sideboard, yanking her chin from his touch.

'I need to get dressed.'

For an answer his hand slid slowly up her thigh, creating waves of tingling pleasure. 'No need for that. Let's go somewhere more comfortable.' His eyes had that heavy-lidded look that made her pulse race. His voice had dropped to a low burr of temptation.

Insidious longing filled Ella and she slapped her hand on his to stop him reaching up under her top. She didn't trust herself to resist if he touched her *there*.

'No!' She breathed deep. 'I want to get dressed.'

His fingers splayed wide on her thighs, curling around them, sending awareness rippling through her. The tension in her belly notched higher.

'This isn't over, Ella.' His head lowered towards hers, his breath hazing her lips. 'Don't pretend it is.'

Was that a threat or a promise? It stiffened her spine, giving her the strength to shove him back with the flat of her hand. For a moment she thought he wouldn't move, then his fingers trailed down her thighs and away as he took a pace back.

Ella shimmied to the edge of the sideboard and onto the floor. Her knees wobbled for a perilous moment but she forced herself to stand tall. Just as if she paraded half naked before men on a regular basis.

'Don't hide from the truth, Ella. Amazing as it was, that barely touched the surface, for either of us.' His swift, all-encompassing survey left her blood singing.

Looking him in the face was far harder than facing her stressed manager in a foul mood, or her father in full flight. 'I'd prefer to have this conversation with my clothes on. You have the advantage over me there.'

The slow curve of his lips did devastating things to her and the devilish glint in his eyes was even worse. She sank back against the sideboard, needing support.

'You want me naked?' His hand went to the top button of his shirt and Ella swallowed hard. Of course she wanted him naked. He was right. She hadn't had nearly enough of him.

'I want my clothes.' Her voice was too strident but it was the best she could do. Dragging her gaze from his to the discarded heap of fabric on the floor, she moved forward.

'If you must.' Before she could get there Donato had scooped up not only her trousers, but her cotton undies too. They dangled from his fingers—plain and ordinary, just like her. She'd challenged herself this morning *not* to dig out her sexy lace knickers and bra, bought on a whim and worn once. To do so would have been an admission that she fancied him. That she wanted him to think of her as alluring. Well, the laugh was on her. Instead of black lace, he had his hands on beige cotton.

Ella met his eyes and refused to blush. She held out her hand.

'They're still warm from your body.' Just like that he cut her off at the knees, swiping away the last tatters of her hard-won dignity. He sounded pleased. He didn't sound like a man taking no for an answer.

She grabbed them from him and, following the direction he gestured, strode across the marble floor to the sanctuary of a bathroom.

Donato watched her stride across to the cloakroom, enjoying every step. He shifted, erect just at the sight of those beautiful long legs and the tantalising glimpses of her pale bare backside as her long top swayed from side to side. Her head was up and her shoulders back as if she owned the world. Such a contrast to the blushing woman who'd found it hard to meet his eyes a minute before.

Ella Sanderson was a conundrum. She was the hottest woman he'd ever had. Just talking to her turned him on. And she was so passionate. Yet there was a reserve about her, and there'd been no mistaking the shock in her eyes at what they'd done.

He ploughed his hand back through his hair. He was shocked too. Not because they'd had sex. That had been inevitable. But that it had been so earth-shattering. And that it left him needy, desperate to have her again.

There was something else about Ella too. A hint of vulnerability despite her sassy mouth. In fact that mouth of hers deserved close study over a long period. It gave her away, he realised. Any man could see it was the mouth of a temptress. But it trembled just a little when she was unsure of herself. And she *had* been unsure.

More than once that suggestion of a tremor had made him stop and rethink. He'd bet Ella would hate that, if she knew.

She challenged him more effectively than anyone he knew. He loved sparring with her, waiting to see what she came out with. She was a delight. That moment when she'd stood there, half naked, gnawing her lip and patently regretting what they'd done, Ella had still had the sass to imply she'd been the sexual aggressor.

As if he hadn't been the one forcing her to confront her own desire!

Donato's lips quirked. Had she worn that ugly underwear to keep him at bay? He found himself curious to see what her bra was like. She had a voluptuous body, no matter how she tried to hide it with that shapeless top. Her rounded hips were made to entice a man. She was slim and lithe but she had the sort of curves that made a man glad he was male. He looked forward to having her naked in his bed.

There was a click and the door opened. She stepped out, fully dressed and in control. The wanton woman hidden beneath her shapeless top; even her hair was yanked back in a ponytail. But the skylight above allowed diffused sunlight to catch the tones of honey and caramel in her soft brown hair. Her chin was up, ready for confrontation, and Donato stepped forward, his pulse quickening.

This time she met his gaze head-on. Instantly he felt that crackle, as electricity splintered the air.

It took him a moment to realise her eyes were once more that intriguing shade of blue-grey. For a few moments, when she'd shattered around him, her eyes had been pure molten silver.

Donato began calculating how long it would be before he saw that precious shimmer again.

# CHAPTER EIGHT

THEY SAT AT a glass-topped table on the shady pool terrace. Ella didn't know whether it was the luxury of her deeply upholstered chair, the glass of chilled Semillon Donato had poured or his air of ease but, remarkably, she began to relax.

Almost as if that hectic interlude in the foyer had never happened.

No, not that. She was hyper-aware of him—every move, every look. The shimmering excitement in her belly had eased a little, but not vanished.

Yet something had shifted. The challenge was no longer overt but overlaid with what felt curiously like understanding. Or a truce.

There'd been no provocative comments since she emerged from the bathroom. No double entendres. No confrontation and definitely no smirking from Donato.

He'd ushered her out here, chatting easily as if they hadn't just imploded in each other's arms. Maybe that should have insulted her, but Ella was relieved, feeling some of her jittery tension drain away.

She'd settled at the table, relieved to be off her unsteady legs, and watched him uncover a feast. The sort that took hours, and professional chefs, to prepare.

She should be critically analysing every nuance of the situation, working out how to counter the threat Donato posed.

It was a measure of the strangeness of the day, and of his easy charm, that Ella simply gave in to hunger and ate.

The food was delicious. There were tiny melt-in-the-mouth lobster patties, crispbread bites with prawns and aioli, a colourful salad decorated with fresh mango, and an array of other delicacies.

Had Donato snapped his fingers and ordered a banquet? Did he offer such feasts to all the women he seduced?

Her breath shortened. He hadn't needed to seduce anyone today, had he? She'd been primed and ready for him.

He refilled their glasses and Ella's gaze fixed on his well-shaped hands and sinewy forearms, strong and dusted with dark hair. He was so blatantly enticing. Something dropped hard in her belly.

Fantastic sex as an antidote to life's problems? If only it were that simple.

'Are we going to talk about it?' She pushed her plate away. 'Or are we going to ignore the elephant in the room?'

A long dimple carved Donato's cheek and a chord in her chest tweaked hard. So much for burning off the passion he'd aroused. Instead her susceptibility had increased.

Ella blinked, stunned but somehow not surprised. She'd never been into casual sex. And for her there'd been nothing casual about today, though she wouldn't examine just what that meant.

'You think of sex as an elephant?' he murmured.

Her lips twitched despite her resolve.

'Don't be obtuse.' She reached for her glass and took a sip. The crisp wine was delicious against her suddenly dry throat. 'We've resolved nothing. I—'

'Of course we have.' His smile grew and he gave her *that* look. The one that made her feel as if she didn't know her own body any more. 'We've confirmed that you and I are every bit as good together as we'd assumed.'

His eyes didn't leave her face but heat licked her in all sorts of hidden places. He lifted his glass in silent salute and drank. Ella was left wondering how the sight of that tanned throat working as he swallowed could create a squall of such hectic need in her.

She shook her head.

'Don't play coy, Ella. You wondered right from the start how we'd be together.'

Ella firmed her lips. 'Don't try to distract me, Donato. It won't work.'

The glint in his dark eyes and the quizzically raised eyebrow told her he disagreed. She put her glass down with a click and sat straighter.

'You said this morning you still want this marriage.' She couldn't bring herself to say *marry me*. It was just too far-fetched. 'Why? There's nothing you'd gain by it.'

His raised eyebrow shot even higher.

Ella put up her hand. 'We've already demonstrated you don't need marriage for sex.'

Would he make a quip about that? She'd laid herself open to it. But no, he merely sipped his wine.

'How about an introduction to Sydney society?' He tilted his head to one side as if sharing a confidence. She didn't believe it.

'You hardly need that.'

'Don't I?' He leaned back further, lounging casually as if they discussed nothing more important than the ship passing far out to sea, or the rainbow lorikeets clustering in the ancient Port Jackson fig tree at the bottom of the garden.

Ella wanted to grab him by the collar and shake him till he lost that complacent look. Or kiss him. She shoved the thought aside. She was already in enough strife.

'Of course not. You've got the money and influence to open any door.' Just look at this house. Whether he owned or rented it, it cost a bomb.

'But you know I also have a criminal record. I served time in juvenile detention, then prison.' Did she imagine his mouth thinned on the words? Though his expression remained unreadable, his face looked somehow more severe.

'So?'

'It hasn't occurred to you that someone with my background might find doors still closed to him? That some people are uncomfortable mixing with an ex-con? A *dangerous* ex-con.'

Dangerous. There was that word again.

Yet would a truly dangerous man have treated her as he had?

She'd disintegrated at his touch, thrown herself at him, behaved with a reckless carnality that even now took her breath away. Yet not once had he tried to force her, though it was obvious he wielded power as easily as she did a thermometer. Though he'd challenged her from the moment they'd met, she'd never relinquished the right to choose. If anything, he'd emphasised that, leaving it to her to bridge the gap between them.

Nor had he made her feel cheap. He'd reminded her it had been a *mutual* seduction.

Ella thought of Donato's hand at her back as she'd walked out here on legs that threatened to give way, how he'd given her time to come back to herself after their tumultuous lovemaking.

Donato Salazar, ruthless tycoon, the man who held her father in the palm of his hand, had been *kind*.

And not because he wanted something. She'd already given him what he wanted back in the foyer, with her legs around his waist and her hands clutching him close.

He was far more than the dangerous predator she'd first imagined.

Ella remembered something she'd read on the Net last night. About how there'd been virtually no turnover in his personal staff, about the loyalty he inspired. She'd assumed he paid well. Now she wondered if it was more complex, more to do with the man himself.

Ella stared, mesmerised by the hint of tension in Donato's shoulders.

Was it true? Were there really doors still barred to him?

She couldn't believe he let the opinions of others matter. There was something so *sure* about him, so adamantine.

'You're saying you want to marry into my family to gain respectability?' She frowned. Her father had been part of elite Sydney society for years but his position had slipped. There were some who disapproved of him and his flashy ways.

'Is that so unbelievable?'

'Frankly? Yes.'

He said nothing. Impatience rose.

'So you're not going to tell me what's going on?'

Eyes the colour of twilight held hers. Their colour seemed to darken as she watched. It must be a trick of the light. But there was no mistaking the subtle change in his expression. It grew shuttered.

Moments ago she'd flirted with the idea Donato wasn't nearly as scary as imagination had painted him. That illusion vanished now. He looked as unsentimental as the worst corporate raider.

Except there was more. Ella felt again the heat of his possession. That current of electricity. That *connection*. She couldn't believe, after a lifetime dealing with her self-serving, merciless father, that she'd respond this way to a man who was just the same. Her sixth sense told her there was a lot more to Donato.

Briskly she rubbed her hands over her arms, trying to smooth her prickling flesh.

'Why don't you tell me the truth? Why insist on this farce of a marriage?' Her voice rose as disappointment vied with frustration. Had she really hoped things had changed because they'd been intimate?

Heat streaked Ella's cheeks and she turned, staring across the lush garden to the sea beyond. She wasn't used to these games. She wasn't used to casual sex and its aftermath. Donato had provoked her and she'd let anger and desire lead her out of her depth.

She should be home now, washing clothes for work next week. Or scouting the sales and second-hand furniture stores for another lost treasure to restore.

Donato leaned forward and involuntarily her gaze slewed to his. Something kicked in her chest as the air thickened.

*It's too late. The damage is done. You can't turn back the clock. He fascinates you and you still want him.*

Ella reached for her wine glass then let her hand drop. It wasn't alcohol she needed. Her head was fuzzy enough without it.

'The truth is rarely simple, *cariño*. And not always desirable.'

Was it the unexpected lilting endearment that caught at Ella's throat? Or the expression on Donato's face? That fleeting hint of emotion stilled Ella's heart. She stared, wondering if she'd imagined it. But there'd been no mistaking the stark pain she'd glimpsed. It stunned her.

'You want the truth?' He shook his head, muttering something that might be Spanish. It had those fluid cadences. Then he sat forward, his elbows on his knees as he filled her personal space. 'The truth is—I want this wedding your father is planning.'

She should have been insulted. Despite their sexual attraction, he didn't want marriage for the sake of marrying *her*. He'd been just as willing to marry Fuzz. Instead Ella was intrigued. There was something there. Something she couldn't put her finger on, that would explain everything if only she understood.

He wanted the wedding.

Not *her*, but the wedding.

Ella frowned, testing the notion that Donato would marry a stranger, a total stranger, just to secure a place in society. It didn't make sense.

'Stop scowling, Ella. You'll give yourself a headache.'

'You don't think the idea of being forced into marriage is enough to make my head hurt?' She couldn't believe he'd do it. It was too preposterous.

To Ella's surprise, Donato reached out and took her hand, clasping it loosely. 'It will be all right.' His voice was low and reassuring, like a wave of soft warmth. 'All you need to know is that while the wedding plans go ahead so does my support for your father.'

For a heady moment she wanted to sink against him, trust that it really would be all right. But how could that be?

'Except you're threatening him.' And, as a result, the rest of her family.

'You care so much about his money? You're dependent on it?'

Her eyebrows arched. She hadn't been dependent on Reg Sanderson's money since the day she turned seventeen and walked out of the door to pursue her own life. It didn't matter that her dreams were mundane by her father's standards. Becoming a nurse, doing something concrete and practical to help people. Being financially independent. Choosing her own friends. All those things had been important milestones.

'I care that you think you can blackmail me into marriage. It's not ethical.' She speared him with a look and tugged to free her hand from his grip. It didn't work and she shot to her feet.

Donato rose at the same time, looming close. 'You want ethics from me? From an ex-crim?' His jaw set.

'Why not?' Ella should be intimidated by the glint in his

eyes and by the way he crowded her, his wide shoulders hemming her in. Instead she felt a delicious thrill as she arched her neck to hold his gaze. With Donato she'd never felt more starkly the divide between male and female. She revelled in his size, his brooding presence and the unfamiliar sensation of being almost petite.

*Was she insane?*

'You're not a thug, Donato.' There was too much intense thought behind his alert gaze for that to be true. And too much control—it was stamped on his features. Then there was the way he'd made love to her...

For the first time it seemed words eluded him. He stared as if he'd never seen her like before.

What? Had he really thought she'd have given herself to a man she feared?

'You don't say,' he said at last. 'And you're an expert on thugs? Growing up in a north-shore mansion and attending a posh private school?' His words were a silky taunt and she wondered at the anger she'd inadvertently stirred. Because she refused to think the worst of him? Had she questioned too closely?

'You *did* check on me.' Ella blinked, amazed at how betrayed she felt. She tasted disappointment, a bitter tang on her tongue.

Donato frowned. 'I said I hadn't. It doesn't take an investigator to know your father wouldn't send his darling daughter anywhere she'd mix with the wrong sort.'

Ella's stomach swooped in relief. She hadn't wanted to believe Donato had lied.

She huffed a mirthless laugh. She'd never been Reg's 'darling daughter'. If only Donato knew, her school had had its share of bullies. Maybe if she'd been pretty or pert or less studious they wouldn't have targeted her.

'I've met some thugs in my time.' Her father being one.

'They bully those who seem weaker. But really they're cowards, scared of anyone stronger.'

'Yet you don't think of me as a bully?'

Ella drew a deep breath, then wished she hadn't as she dragged in his spicy warm scent. It made her want to kiss that hard beautiful mouth. She dragged her hand free and stepped back, her chair grating across the flagstones.

'No, I don't.' Donato was demanding, arrogant, clever and ruthless. But he'd been considerate, reassuring and almost...tender. He'd kept his word, refusing to have her investigated because he knew the idea revolted her. He'd been honest, up to a point.

'Tell me about the man you attacked.'

Donato's head reared back. 'What makes you think I want to talk about that?'

She shrugged. 'Why wouldn't you? Don't tell me you're scared I'll judge you?'

Instead of bridling at the taunt, Donato surveyed her with a thoroughness that brought all that reckless awareness straight to the surface in a blaze like wildfire.

Ignoring the flare of arousal, she stared straight back. She needed to understand him.

'Why did you fight with him?'

He shrugged, his expression closed. 'He deserved it. He hurt someone.'

Ella frowned. She hadn't read about anyone else in the fight, just the teenage Donato and a forty-year-old man. Yet it had been the older man carted off to hospital after the police intervened.

'So you were protecting someone?' Her chest contracted at the idea of a teenager taking on a grown man to save someone else.

She'd never had a protector in her life, had always fought her own battles, but the idea held huge appeal. Perhaps *be-*

*cause* no one had ever stood up for her. It made his actions more understandable, more forgivable.

Ella counted one breath, two, three, before finally he shook his head.

'It wasn't that simple. Don't imagine I'm some hero.' His mouth twisted harshly. 'I'm not.'

Her thoughts stalled at his tone, and at that flash of dark emotion. He looked…tortured. And she'd swear she heard desolation in his stark words. Then, even as the impression formed, his expression was wiped clear.

But that split second had been enough to set Ella's thoughts whirling.

Did he blame himself for not protecting this other person? Clearly *something* still ate at him, despite the passage of time. Donato was in his mid-thirties, yet long-ago hurt was buried beneath all that surface sangfroid.

Whatever he felt in that carefully guarded soul, it ran deep and strong.

Instead of frightening her, the knowledge drew her. She wanted to smooth her hands over his set shoulders, press herself against him and learn all there was to know about Donato Salazar.

Fear jolted through her. Fear of how much she wanted to break down that wall of superior calm and find the man behind it.

*You haven't known him a day and already you want so much!*

Alarm made her voice abrupt. 'Is that the only time you've been violent?'

'What is this, an interview?'

Ella notched her chin high. '*You're* the one talking about marriage.'

'I've never been violent towards a woman. It's not something you have to worry about.'

'Because you say so?' She crossed her arms over her chest.

'It's not something I'd ever do.' Indignation flashed in his eyes, but it was the proud set of his chin, the distaste in his flared nostrils and flat mouth that told her she'd struck a nerve. 'I was brought up to respect women. You have nothing to fear from me.'

Scary how easy it was for her to believe him.

'What about men?'

'If you were a man we wouldn't be having this conversation.' His voice dropped to the deep, resonant pitch that made her want to do something crazy, like drag his head down to hers and kiss him till he told her all his secrets.

She made herself take a single step back from him. His jaw tightened.

'You haven't answered my question.'

'Am I physically dangerous?' He sighed and shook his head. 'It was all a long time ago. I told you on the phone. I learned to think before I act. Prison is a great teacher.'

He lifted one finger to follow the line of that narrow scar bisecting his cheek. 'I thought I was tough as a kid but I had a lot to learn.'

Ella's heart lurched. Imagine going behind bars as a teenager and emerging a man. Imagine who he'd mixed with there. No wonder Donato had a hard, impenetrable edge.

That scar, though silvered now, scored perilously close to the corner of his eye. It was faint enough to give him a rakish hint of the buccaneer, but she'd dealt with knife wounds when she'd worked in Emergency. She knew what sliced flesh looked like.

'Ella?' His breath feathered her face, warm and coffee-scented. 'You're feeling *sorry* for me?' His brows knitted as he leaned over her, astonishment clear in those brilliant eyes.

'No, I...'

Her words dissolved as his lips brushed hers, soft and almost tentative.

That was all it took. One kiss. Not even a kiss but the merest whisper of a caress, and she ignited, falling against him as he tugged her in. He wrapped his arms around her, not hard, but to her disordered mind it seemed protectively, tenderly. That just fuelled her response, like petrol poured on open flames.

He pulled his head back to stare down at her, his gaze darkening to midnight.

'I don't need your pity.' She felt the rumble of his voice through their bodies, where she pressed against him. 'I was found guilty, remember?'

'Who said anything about pity?' Yet there was a knot in her throat at the idea of him as a kid, coming of age in prison because he'd tried to defend someone.

His look sharpened. 'Women want me because I'm rich. Because I'm powerful. Or for a thrill because I'm big and bad and dangerous.' That unblinking gaze pinioned her. '*Never* because they feel sorry for me.'

It was a warning, as clear as a flashing red light. Yet he hadn't mentioned the most obvious reason any woman would want him. Because he was the single most fascinating, sexy, infuriatingly charismatic man on the planet.

Ella had finally found a weak spot in his aura of omniscient authority. When she had more time, when she wasn't pressed up against him from thigh to breast, she'd think about that.

Now, though, her thoughts frayed. Logical Ella was unravelling. That new bold Ella stirred again, the woman who dared to act on impulse, regardless of consequences. She shuddered as desire rose like a blast of hot summer air.

'Good, then you won't expect sentiment from me.' She

rose on her toes and anchored her hands in his thick soft hair, pulling him down to her level.

She was confused by this man, alternately irritated and fascinated. But she *needed* him. More now than before, as if what they'd shared earlier had given her a taste of something deliciously addictive.

'Kiss me, Donato.' It was new Ella speaking, her voice an unfamiliar throaty purr. 'And make it good.'

Ella had never said anything like that to a man. But the fingers threading his hair were hers, as were the breasts straining against his hard torso, and the hips circling needily as he clamped her against him. The mouth was definitely hers, fusing with his demanding lips, sighing her pleasure as he forgot about conversation and gave her what she needed.

By the time they made it to a large canopied day bed near the pool, she was in her underwear and he'd lost his shirt and shoes.

Ella lay back, enjoying the view of his bronzed torso, powerful and dusted with dark hair across the chest. Even the couple of scars, pale on his ribs, didn't mar his perfection. Muscles bunched and twisted as he reached for a condom then shoved down his pants.

A gasp escaped and he looked up.

It would be too naïve of her to blurt out that he was the most imposing man she'd ever seen. Just the sight of him made her heart hammer.

'You're well prepared.' Was that her voice, that husky drawl of invitation? 'Do you usually carry so many condoms?'

His mouth curved in a tight smile at odds with the blaze in his eyes. 'I was expecting you.'

He reached out, dispensing with her underwear with casual efficiency. His eyes like lasers, so hot she felt her skin shiver. Then his mouth was on her breast, his hand between her legs, and there was nothing but Donato and pleasure so intense it saturated her, from her bones to her brain and everywhere in between.

He licked her nipple and her breath caught. He sucked it inside his hot mouth and her hands on the back of his head turned to claws, dragging him closer.

His hand moved and she bucked against him. Impossibly she felt a trembling begin deep inside. A trembling that grew and spread.

'Now! I need you now.' Desperately she groped down between them. He was thick and solid against her palm, twitching at her touch.

Heat suffused her, intensified at the slide of his hard body against hers. The tickle of chest hair against her breasts, the haze of his breath on her neck. His fingers covered hers, guiding, till he was right where she needed him.

Their eyes locked as Donato dragged her hands above her head, holding them high against the cushions as he thrust home with one hungry glide that brought them colliding together.

Ella arched up, stunned by the sheer intimacy of him there, at the heart of her, his eyes holding hers as surely as he claimed her body. The air locked in her lungs as sensation rocked her. Not physical sensation but something she couldn't name, a sense of rightness, of belonging.

Donato's eyes widened. Did he feel it too?

Ella remembered how it had felt coming apart in his arms, drowning in his gaze. She felt it again, fierce pleasure and more too, the powerful connection, the sense she gave up part of her soul, not just her body. It had scared the life out of her.

She squeezed her eyes shut, focusing on the crescendo of physical rapture. The climax that was upon her before she knew it, throwing her high to the stars. She bit her tongue, desperate not to cry his name as ecstasy took over, needing not to give in completely.

Donato jerked hard, spilling himself, his voice a guttural, seductive slur of Spanish, and her eyes opened of their own volition.

Instantly she was lost in indigo heat, in the heady, terrifying tumble into unfamiliar territory that wasn't merely about eager bodies and erotic caresses. Into a place where she was no longer Ella but part of him, part of Donato, and he was part of her.

He held her gaze for what seemed minutes, their breathing ragged, chests heaving, bodies twitching in the aftershock of that momentous eruption of delight.

Ella told herself it was okay. She'd be fine. She was just unused to sex. To giving herself to any man. This was purely physical.

Then he bent his head and touched his lips to hers in a delicate feather of a kiss and something huge and inexplicable welled up inside. Ella choked back a lump in her throat, blinking furiously as heat glazed her eyes and a tear spilled down her cheek.

# CHAPTER NINE

'If you stay the night, who knows,' Donato murmured hours later, languidly tracing Ella's back, 'we might make it to a bed.'

It was the first time he'd invited a woman to stay overnight but he'd passed the stage of being surprised at his need for Ella. Whatever this was between them, he'd enjoy it to the utmost.

A rich chuckle shivered through her, tickling his hand and tugging at something in his belly. She had a warm, sexy laugh. 'That would be a novelty.'

He smiled. That was better. The sight of her silver eyes awash with tears had disturbed him, even if it had been in the aftermath of a stunning climax.

He'd gathered her close, ignoring the upsurge of desire as she settled across him. The shadows had lengthened and she'd slept, making him wonder at her exhaustion. Perhaps she hadn't slept last night either.

Ella Sanderson wasn't what he'd expected. From her plain cotton bra and knickers, as if she'd deliberately dressed *not* to entice him, to the look in her eyes when she'd probed about his past.

Donato's chest clenched. No one since his mother had ever been completely on his side, not even his lawyer. He wasn't used to it. That explained the weird, full sensation when Ella had looked at him with such sympathy, her mouth a pout of distress.

He shook off a sense of disquiet. Deliberately he pulled her against his erection, enjoying her gasp. He enjoyed holding a woman who was all sweet curves and hollows. He looked forward to exploring every centimetre.

A phone pierced the silence and Ella moved. Donato was surprised at the strength of his urge to tug her back.

'That's mine.' She scrambled across the day bed, breasts swaying, her peach of a backside making his mouth dry as he imagined taking her from behind.

'It can wait.' He propped himself on one elbow for a better view. How could a woman who looked as good as Ella doubt her attractiveness? He'd put the pieces together now—her discomfort when he'd called her attractive, her haughtiness that defied him to find fault and the surprise in her silvery eyes when he'd pulled back to admire her.

'It might be important.' She scooped up her phone and, before he could stop her, stood.

'On a Saturday?' What could be so vital? Another lover? The idea punched his gut. Instinct, or maybe pride, told him Ella wasn't promiscuous, despite the rampant sex they'd shared. He'd seen her shock when they came together so spectacularly and her dazed disbelief when rapture claimed her.

He guessed her bravado hid a deep reserve.

His gaze lingered on her hourglass figure, slightly broader at the hips and deliciously narrow at the waist. Long shapely legs and hair like dark honey. She wrapped a nearby towel around herself and scowled at the phone.

'Hello, Dad.' Her voice was wary. More than wary.

Donato's interest stirred.

Ella shot a harried glance at him then moved away. But the curve of the building improved the acoustics so he caught part of the conversation.

'No, it's not all settled! We'll find another way.' She hunched the phone against her ear and pulled back her shoulder-length hair in a gesture that screamed frustration.

'You wouldn't! That's Rob's money. You have to repay

that before you do anything else.' Another look over her shoulder before she walked to the end of the pool.

Donato watched her long-legged stride. She couldn't keep still. One hand slashed the air and her mouth turned down as if she'd swallowed something sour.

Talking to Reg Sanderson had that effect on him too.

So there was a rift between father and daughter. He'd guessed that, seeing the lack of affection between them. Plus there was outrage in Ella's voice when she spoke of Rob's money. Rob, her brother? Had Sanderson got his claws into his kids' assets?

Donato shouldn't have promised not to investigate her and, by extension, her siblings. It tied his hands. There was far more he wanted to know, but having given her his word—

She strode back, her features taut. Something clenched hard inside him.

'Come here.' Donato put out his hand. 'You need someone to help you feel better. I'm just the man.'

His invitation wasn't entirely selfish. He didn't like her troubled expression, knowing Sanderson had caused it. Another reason to hate the man.

Ella lifted her hand as if to take his, then stopped.

'No.' Her hand dropped and Donato was surprised at the strength of his disappointment. 'Thank you. But...' She shook her head and the afternoon sun caught the sheen of honey gilt. 'I need to go.'

Donato was about to insist she remain when he read the strain around her mouth. He knew he could have her in his bed all night, enjoying what his body urged him to take. He could weasel the information he wanted after breaking down her defences.

He let his arm fall. He wanted Ella's passion and her sweet body. He wanted to understand her and her relationship with her father. But he wouldn't seduce the details from her.

His belly churned in a moment of unfamiliar disquiet. He was already taking advantage, pretending to want marriage. It wasn't just Sanderson pressuring her, putting the shadows beneath her bright eyes.

Amazingly, for the first time in years, doubt shivered through what passed for his conscience. More than doubt, it was guilt, its sharp blade scraping.

Donato sat up, his jaw setting as Ella gathered her clothes. She might be vulnerable and sassy, sexy and funny and, he suspected, brave, but he couldn't allow her to stand in the way of justice.

Nothing would save Reg Sanderson from his deserts. Not even the fact his daughter was the most appealing, fascinating woman Donato could recall knowing.

He stood, retrieving her floaty top that had landed on the day bed's high canopy.

'Thank you.' Her eyes didn't meet his and he caught again that hint of embarrassment.

Their hands brushed and sensation jolted. *Maldición!* Need was like an electric current running through him.

'I'll see you tomorrow.'

She shook her head and he had to restrain himself from catching those honey-brown tresses and hauling her close again.

'I'm busy.'

'Be ready at nine. I'll collect you.'

'You don't know where I live. And you promised not to set your investigators onto me.'

Donato suppressed a smile. That was better. Her eyes shone with challenge and her chin notched high.

'I didn't promise not to follow you home.' He let that sink in. 'I'll just toss on some clothes.' He reached for his shirt, absently noting a couple of missing buttons.

Her deep sigh drew his attention. Despite her defiant air, she clutched her clothes close, hiding herself. As if he couldn't perfectly recall those enticing curves.

'Okay. I'll meet you tomorrow. I'll come here at midday.'

'Nine.'

'Eleven.'

'Nine.' He brushed her hair off her cheek. 'And I promise not to ring you after midnight.' She shivered and he moved closer, inhaling her skin's delicate perfume, like sweet peas and sunshine.

'Nine-thirty, then. And you won't call me at all.'

Donato didn't say anything. If she thought he'd pass up a chance to hear her voice, husky and delicious, when he couldn't have her in his bed…well, she didn't know him yet.

'That's it. You've got the hang of it now.' Donato's voice was warm with approval and encouragement and Ella felt emotion flare. Pleasure? Pride? Or excitement at being so close to him?

No time to work it out now. She had to concentrate.

'Shift your left hand.'

She watched as Donato demonstrated. Like her, he was suspended on a rope, halfway down a rock face. Except, unlike her, he was perfectly at ease. His eyes danced with pleasure and she'd seen his exhilaration earlier as he'd abseiled down the cliff then swarmed back up with an efficiency that left her in breathless awe.

She knew he was strong. It was two weeks since she'd become intimately acquainted with his body. But seeing him now she realised how carefully he leashed that power when they made love.

'Ella? Are you okay?'

'Fine.' She wrenched her gaze to the rock and made herself concentrate on his instructions. Carefully she stepped backwards, feeling the rope play out in her gloved hand.

'Perfect. You've got it.'

Delight filled her. It was partly the thrill of abseiling and partly the effect of his approval.

Since when had she wanted Donato's approval?

She froze, her throat catching.

'You're doing well, Ella. Just keep moving.' His voice was encouraging but businesslike enough to focus her. The perfect teacher.

Who'd have thought it? She remembered that first night when he'd seemed so daunting with his saturnine looks and air of despotic authority.

But the Donato she'd begun to know had surprising depths. He got his own way too much and there was a shut-off side to him she couldn't penetrate, yet he was unexpectedly thoughtful and...kind.

He moved close but not close enough to crowd her. 'Try bending your knees and pushing off. Just a little bounce. You know you're safe.'

Ella nodded. She'd inspected the equipment, learning all she could before she'd agreed to try this. And their professional guide was at the top, watching out for her.

Tentatively she bent her legs, pushing off from the rock. For a dizzying instant fear hit her, then the thrill of it kicked in. She did it again, this time releasing the rope a little so she moved out and down in an arc.

'I did it!' A grin split her face.

'Of course you did, since you set your mind to it.'

Ella turned and found Donato smiling as if he was as thrilled as she was. The warmth of his smile lit her inside.

'Come on, let's get to the bottom.'

Ella turned back to the rock, concentrating on each movement. Yet as she descended, thrilled by the fun of it, she was aware of him beside her, matching his pace to hers.

Finally she stood on shaky legs, breathing hard, adrenalin coursing through her body.

'Good?' Donato pulled her close, his hands on her hips, and a different sort of thrill shot through her.

'Marvellous.'

'Glad you agreed to try something different this weekend?'

'Absolutely.' She braced her hands on his shoulders when he would have pulled her closer. 'When did you learn to climb?'

He waited before replying, as if assessing her curiosity. 'In my early twenties. I discovered a taste for wide-open spaces.' His mouth curled at the corner. 'Not surprising after being penned in. When I could, which wasn't often, given I was building a business from scratch, I'd get out of the city. Windsurfing, climbing, hang-gliding.'

'They sound challenging.' And dangerous.

'I like the wind in my hair. The feeling of not being hemmed in.'

Ella thought of his Sydney house. Set at the top of a cliff with a commanding view of the Pacific, it was as un-hemmed-in as you could get in such a metropolis.

'What about you, Ella?' He tilted up her chin so his words brushed her face. 'What do you do to unwind?'

*Make love with a breathtakingly gorgeous, enigmatic tycoon.*

This fortnight there'd been no time for anything but work and Donato. If she wasn't with him in the evening, he was flirting with her over the phone, his espresso-dark voice a constant reminder of what she missed by refusing to stay with him.

But the need to keep part of her life private remained strong. Donato had stormed into her world like a cyclone flattening every defence. He dominated her thoughts and even her dreams.

'How do I unwind? You'll find out soon enough.' Their weekend in the Blue Mountains west of the city was in two parts. Donato had suggested they spend half the time doing something he enjoyed and the other half was her choice.

As if he wanted to share his private life with her, not just his bed. As if he wanted to know more about her too. It was a beguiling idea. After two weeks of toe-curling orgasms and carefully light banter, this signalled a shift in their relationship.

Ella had tried telling herself they didn't have a relationship. They had sex. Stunning, all-eclipsing sex.

And they had this farcical engagement. Her father insisted they were marrying and went ahead with preparations despite her protests. But it would take more than his demands to make her marry a man she didn't love.

Meanwhile she needed to help her siblings. Her father had misappropriated Rob's inheritance from their grandfather, the money he needed to finish the resort's refurbishment. Reg had promised to repay it when his business with Donato was sorted.

Ella felt trapped, by her attraction to Donato and the situation with her father.

She'd told Donato repeatedly there'd be no wedding. Every time he'd shrugged and said it would all work out.

It was like a game, one where only he knew the rules. When she tried to press for a resolution he distracted her, usually with some outrageous provocation that led to verbal sparring and, most often, sex.

Now he wrapped his arms around her and her heart gave a familiar leap. 'Don't I get a kiss for introducing you to abseiling?'

She shook her head, teasing. 'It was our guide who did the work, organising the equipment and—'

'If you think you're kissing anyone but me,' Donato growled, a light in his eyes, 'you're sadly mistaken.'

Instantly she was all quivering anticipation. That hint of possessiveness was too appealing.

She wanted Donato. Not just his kisses but his attention, his time. Warning bells clanged.

Ella needed to remind him, and herself, she was her own woman. He was so overwhelming it was a constant battle not to be swept up, simply giving in to him.

She put a hand on Donato's broad chest, pushing. 'That's for me to choose. You don't *own* me, Donato. You haven't bought me.'

She'd anticipated a mock scowl, or that lethally slow smile that stirred all her senses.

What she got was sudden stillness and a look that made the hairs on her nape stand on end. Not a look of anger. She couldn't read his expression, but she knew he'd gone somewhere she didn't want to be.

His hold tightened, his fingers digging too hard. Then suddenly she was free. Donato stepped back, hands flexing. His chest rose as he sucked oxygen, like a swimmer too long underwater.

'Donato? What is it?' His stark expression made the blood curdle in her veins. Shivers ran down her arms and disquiet stirred.

His eyes were fixed on the distance.

'Donato?'

His gaze swung down to her. She read turmoil and strong emotion. What was going on? One minute he was laughing and intimate. The next he'd totally withdrawn.

'Of course.' The last vestiges of tension vanished as she watched. He looked the same as ever, confident and in control. But Ella knew something had happened, as it had when he'd spoken of his past.

What was he hiding? Everyone had secrets, but she sensed Donato's cast very long shadows.

Ella gripped his arms, needing the physical connection. Needing, if possible, to help. His taut biceps were hard as the rock they'd just traversed. She loved his strength. Being with Donato made her feel almost petite and dainty.

Deliberately she stood on her toes and brushed her mouth against his. Instantly he responded with a slow, bone-melting thoroughness that made her wish their guide wasn't waiting above.

Finally Donato pulled back.

'Come on, Ella. It's time you learned how to climb back up.' His lips curled in that devastating smile and she found herself smiling back.

But she was silent as he busied himself with their gear. For his smile had been wrong. It hadn't reached his eyes.

Ella told herself that just because they were lovers didn't give her the right to pry into things he obviously didn't want to share. She too kept part of her life off-limits to Donato.

Yet the need to understand him gnawed. She wanted to know so she could help. Because she never wanted to see that blank shadow on his face again.

Was that the reaction of a short-term lover?

Or was it the reaction of a woman sinking deep over her head?

# CHAPTER TEN

'RETAIL THERAPY!' Donato groaned. 'I knew it was a mistake to let you choose our activity for the day.'

Yet it was a token protest. After spending a whole night with Ella, waking with her in his arms for the first time, it would take more than a little shopping to spoil his mood.

Last night, after their day of climbing and abseiling, there'd been an intensity to her passion he couldn't get enough of. Given their history of instant attraction and explosive loving, that was saying something.

The sooner she moved in with him the better.

Donato ignored the voice reminding him he'd never shared his home with any woman.

This was different. Ella wasn't a clinging vine, grasping for the material things he could provide.

Hard to believe that she was Sanderson's daughter. The more he knew her, the less like her father she was.

'If you haven't got the stamina for it, Donato, go back to the hotel.' She flashed him a look of pure challenge.

'Stamina?' He stared down into those stunning eyes with mock indignation. 'I defy you to find a man with more stamina.'

For a moment Ella's eyes looked more pewter than blue, just like when she lost herself in his arms. Instantly his heart beat faster.

'We'll see how you fare after a few hours hunting for lost treasure.' Then she turned to bend over an ancient motheaten chair, dismissing him.

Donato smiled. Perversely, he loved the fact Ella made

a point of not kowtowing to him. For years, since his phenomenal burst of commercial success, people had fallen over themselves to agree with him. No one dismissed him.

He liked that Ella treated him like an ordinary man. Neither a commercially astute businessman whose every pronouncement was gold, nor a sinister outsider to polite society who could never be completely trusted because of his murky past.

And he liked knowing that no matter how pointedly she stood up to him, he just had to touch her and she went up in flames.

'Treasure? Hunting through junk, don't you mean?'

She shrugged. 'If you can't cope I'll see you later.'

But Donato wasn't going anywhere. He was fascinated, watching Ella's assessing eye as she prowled the antiques centre. He'd developed an interest in antiques himself, drawn by the idea of a bygone world of grace and beauty that was everything his early life hadn't been.

Ella moved through the place, her sharp eyes spotting the same mantel clock he did. It belonged not in a dusty bric-a-brac emporium, but in a collector's home. Then she paused by a tiny damaged table. He hadn't noticed it. Now he realised how finely it was made. With restoration it would be beautiful.

Ella had a good eye. It intrigued him to think they shared an interest in beautiful old things.

But what kept him at her side, helping her shift a lumpy chair to get to an old trunk, was more than an interest in antiques. She almost hummed with happiness as she explored. Her enthusiasm drew him.

She was appealing when she challenged him, standing so haughtily, refusing to cave in despite her father's pushing. But when she was happy... Donato was surprised at the cliché that sprang to mind. But it was true. When Ella was happy she *glowed*.

He wanted to bask in that radiance. Her lips curved in

an excited smile as she ran her hands over the trunk. Donato wanted to be part of what made her happy. He wanted to make her smile.

How long since he'd wanted to do that for anyone?

It was a relief to see her like this. Yesterday, with a few casual words, she'd unleashed a wave of bitter remembrance. More than that, she'd evoked guilt.

*You don't own me.*

*You haven't bought me.*

Even now his blood iced at the words. At the implication he was stripping away her control of her own life by agreeing to this sham engagement.

Did she really feel disempowered?

Acid swirled in his belly and rose, filling his mouth.

His fight wasn't with Ella. It was with her father. He'd imagined Sanderson's daughter would be as shallow and selfish as him, eager to triumph in the role of high-profile fiancée to a rich entrepreneur. Instead he'd found a woman whose idea of a good time was hunting for old wares.

*You haven't bought me.*

Donato's jaw clamped so hard pain radiated through his skull.

He knew, exactly, what it meant to buy someone. To own someone.

The words, so casual, so meaningless to most, were honed knives. They sliced into the darkness that was his past and his very essence. He felt the ice-hot slash, not to his face or his ribs this time, but to his heart. It heaved as the blackness of the past rose up.

'Donato.' A hand touched his and he looked down. Ella's eyes met his. Stunned, he felt again that spark of connection he'd told himself he'd imagined. This time it was a welcome sizzle of heat, cracking the ice in his veins. 'Come and look at this.'

Did she know? Had she seen the murky shadows engulf him?

Donato straightened. Of course she hadn't. No one did. They were his to bear alone.

'What have you found now? Jewellery?' He forced a smile to his face and watched her blink. That was better. He preferred Ella distracted rather than questioning. 'It has to be something glittery to make a woman so excited.'

'Don't pretend to be a sexist beast. We both know you're not.'

'Not sexist?'

Their gazes locked and, extraordinarily, Donato felt as if her assessing gaze saw too much. 'Not either.'

Which showed how little Ella knew about him.

Because of his prison record most women viewed him with trepidation, even if mingled with a good dollop of excitement. They fantasised about the bad boy, especially one who had wealth to smooth his way. If they knew the full details of his past they'd shun him. That had never mattered. He didn't care about the approval of pampered society women.

Yet with Ella, for the first time, he almost wished he were a different man. Except that would mean denying his past and he would never do that.

She linked her fingers with his and tugged. Donato was surprised at how good that felt. 'Come on. I want your opinion on this. It reminds me of something you have in that mansion of yours.'

Despite his teasing grumbles, Donato was good company. Better company than Ella had expected.

This was the second day they'd spent together doing something other than fall into bed. Not that they'd ever needed a bed. Heat danced through Ella's veins. It had taken two visits to Donato's house to make it as far as his bedroom. Even then they hadn't made it to the mattress.

When he'd suggested a weekend together she'd thought they'd be naked. Instead she'd found something even more distracting.

A man who switched off his phone to spend time in the wilderness, introducing her to some of the extreme sports he enjoyed.

A man with patience and humour, who took time to ensure she enjoyed herself.

Donato didn't care about keeping up appearances like her father. All morning he'd helped her fossick amongst collectables and downright junk. He hadn't blinked when he'd got dust on those exquisite casual clothes or she'd asked him to heave furniture out of the way.

Ella wondered what he'd make of her choice for the afternoon. She led him through the gate of the National Trust property and into the garden.

'More antiques?' He looked around with interest.

'You haven't been here?'

'I'm from Melbourne, remember.'

Ella felt a fillip of pleasure at introducing him to one of her favourite places.

'It's a heritage house and garden.' Said like that it sounded boring and she'd thought hard about bringing Donato here.

But the Everglades was special. When she'd first visited she'd been young enough to wonder if there were fairies in the wide sweep of bluebells that clustered here in spring. Later she'd been enchanted by the peace and beauty of the rambling gardens. After the fraught atmosphere at home, this had seemed like Paradise.

'You'll enjoy the house. I know you like art deco.'

'I sense a theme. It seems a favourite of yours too.' Ella

heard his smile but didn't look up. Already she spent too much time under Donato's spell.

Ella shrugged. 'My mother's aunt lived in a nineteen-thirties house. I loved it.' Actually, she'd loved the peace and sense of acceptance, so different from her own home. Eventually that had translated into an appreciation of the house and its style.

Her great-aunt had brought Ella on trips here. She hadn't worried that her niece preferred to celebrate her birthday quietly instead of at a catered party for a hundred. Ella's father had thought her mad. Aunt Bea had encouraged her.

'She was important to you.'

Ella swung round. 'How did you know?'

'You sounded wistful.' His fingers brushed her cheek in a gesture that felt alarmingly tender. Ella was used to passion or provocation. Tenderness was usually reserved for the bedroom.

But this weekend there'd been more. His expression made her throat tighten.

'She *was* important,' Ella said eventually. 'My mother died when I was young and Aunt Bea was…special.' Ella had felt closer to the old lady than to her father. It didn't matter if Ella had puppy fat or a boring penchant for books. Or that she didn't sparkle in company. Aunt Bea had loved her, and through her Ella had learned to respect herself. 'She brought me here.'

'In that case I'm glad you chose to share it with me.' He threaded his fingers through hers in a gesture that seemed as intimate as the sex they'd shared this morning. Her tight throat constricted further.

Ella reminded herself that Donato was clever and perceptive. It was obvious the place was important to her.

Yet not even logic shattered the sensation of closeness, of *understanding*.

As if she understood Donato! He still wouldn't stop her father's nonsense about a wedding.

'Come on, there's a lot to see.' Ella stepped forward, under the spreading boughs of the ornamental trees. But she didn't shake off Donato's grip. There was something comfortable about simply holding hands, something...appealing.

They explored the garden theatre, the landscaped terraces and the lookout across the cliffs to the wilderness beyond. It was as they meandered back, past the house and a section where plants were being propagated, that she noticed Donato's abstraction.

He paused, surveying a bed of freshly turned soil and tiny plants. To Ella's inexperienced eye the scene wasn't as interesting as the rest of the grounds.

'Are you a gardener?' Why hadn't she thought of that? She'd been explaining what she knew of the garden design. Maybe he knew more than her, given his choice to live in a home with beautiful grounds rather than an easy-care apartment. 'You should have stopped me. It didn't occur to me—'

'I'm no expert,' he said, eyes still fixed on the garden bed. 'It just reminded me of something.'

'Really?' Ella moved closer. 'What does it remind you of?'

'Smell that? Fresh turned soil and compost.'

Ella inhaled. 'It's...earthy.'

'Good, rich soil. Someone has put in a lot of effort here.' 'What does it remind you of?'

He bent to pluck a couple of tiny weeds out of the carefully tended bed. 'When I was a kid we had a big vegetable garden. It smelled like this. Of earth and growing things.'

He straightened and turned, moving briskly away. Ella hastened after him. 'You enjoyed gardening?' It was the first glimpse he'd given of his past except for the few bare answers to her probing about his prison sentence.

Donato shrugged. 'It was a chore, that's all.'

Yet he'd taken time to pull out the weeds amongst the tiny seedlings. 'You didn't like it?'

Again that lift of broad shoulders. 'It had to be done. It supplied a lot of our food.'

'Whose garden was it? Your mother's or your father's?' Ella knew nothing about his family and suddenly the need to know more about him was overwhelming.

'You're curious all of a sudden.'

'Why not? You've got nothing to hide, have you?'

Donato stopped beneath the shade of an overhanging tree. 'Everyone has something to hide.' In the relative gloom he looked bigger than ever, his broad chest and shoulders imposing. But it was his voice that sent a ripple of warning through her. There was steel in that tone, telling her she'd trespassed too far.

This from the man who'd upended her calm, orderly life! So much for believing they'd begun to build something new this weekend.

'You're scared to tell me even that?' She shook her head. 'Is it so secret?'

He folded his arms. It made him look more impressively masculine and annoyingly attractive.

'Says the woman who refuses to mention she works in case I find out too much about her.' At her stare he nodded. 'Of course I know. You're never available during the week before six at night. I may be busy with my own business but I notice these things.'

Heat rushed up Ella's throat and into her cheeks. He was right. She'd avoided talking about herself, except at the most superficial level—food, music, books, sex. Nothing about her family or career. Nothing emotionally intimate. Until today when she'd told him about Aunt Bea. It had seemed such a huge concession—revealing even that tiny snippet.

She'd understood from the first that Donato was dangerous. Instinct had warned not to let him close. When she'd been unable to resist him physically, she'd worked to isolate him from the rest of her life. He didn't even know where she lived.

But he'd been no more forthcoming. She refused to feel guilty.

'I hardly think talking about your childhood chores constitutes an invasion of privacy.' She crossed her arms, imitating his challenging stance. All it got her was a heavy-lidded glance at her plumped-up breasts that sent traceries of fire through her belly.

Ella's instantaneous response to Donato was so predictable and so profound it unnerved her. She was torn between wanting more and wanting nothing to do with him. Because above all she wanted to discover what made him tick.

With a huff of self-disgust Ella spun away. The game he played was too deep. She'd begun to believe they shared something more profound than incendiary sex. Clearly she'd fooled herself.

'Wait!' A hand on her arm halted her.

Ella looked at his fingers loosely circling her flesh. Even that was enough to send a zing of anticipation through her. Her body had never got the message that Donato wasn't to be trusted.

'I'll make a deal with you.' His hand slid up her arm in a caress. She swallowed. She wouldn't let him seduce her again. 'I'll answer your question if you answer one of mine. Truthfully.'

'I don't lie.' She drew herself up.

'But there are things you'd rather not discuss.'

He was going to ask about her father and his business.

It had to be that because that was Donato's real focus, the reason he'd taken an interest in her.

Hurt blossomed. But Ella was a big girl. She could cope. She could juggle the need to protect her family and her attraction to Donato.

Still holding her arm, he moved to lean back against the trunk of a massive tree. Before she could protest he pulled her against him, his arms wrapped around her waist from behind, her bottom tucked between his legs.

'No, don't move.' His voice was a soft burr, feathering her ear. 'Just relax.'

Being held felt so good, the solidity of Donato's body at her back, his arms holding her. Ella gave up and let her head sink against his collarbone. She stared out at the greenery screening them from the rest of the garden.

'The garden didn't belong to my mother,' Donato said. 'She knew as little about growing things as I did. It was Jack's.'

'Your father's?'

Donato didn't move. His heart beat steadily behind her. Yet something stirred—a change in his breathing? A feeling of wariness?

'I didn't know my father. Jack became my mother's partner when I was six.'

'Your stepfather then.'

Donato slid his fingers through hers and stroked the palm of her hand. 'No. He never thought of himself as my stepfather.'

Ella frowned. There was something so…guarded about the way he spoke.

Of course there was! He was the most self-contained person she knew. Yet something niggled. She'd expected more warmth in his voice over a childhood reminiscence. But then, most of her childhood memories were less than happy. Had it been like that for Donato too?

'He was abusive?'

'Jack was decent in his own way. He just wasn't interested in kids. All he cared about was my mother.' *Now* there was a shift in his voice, a depth of feeling he didn't bother to hide. 'He put me to work as soon as we moved in with him—set me to weeding while he began extending the vegetable patch since it had to feed three instead of one.'

A muffled laugh rumbled up from behind her. She felt as well as heard it.

'What's so funny?' Being dependent on the food you grew was no laughing matter.

'I was determined to do a good job, impress him so he wouldn't kick us out. By the time he'd turned back to check on me I'd ripped out half his precious seedlings and he treated me to some curses even I hadn't heard before.'

Ella watched a pair of crimson rosellas land in the tree before them, quietly chattering. But her thoughts were on Donato at six, convinced he had to work hard so as not to be kicked out. A child surprised to hear swearing that was new. What sort of life had he led?

Her hands tightened on his. 'Is that all he did?'

'He made me replant everything I'd pulled out. Then he gave us both a lesson in plant recognition. Neither of us knew a tomato plant from a potato or a bean.'

'So your mother was city bred too?'

'That's more than one question.' He sounded relaxed but, pressed against him, Ella felt the infinitesimal tightening of his muscles. 'It's my turn.'

'Okay.' She braced herself for a probing question about her father's business or ethics. That was what he'd want to know. That was why he'd demanded honesty.

'Tell me about your job.'

'Sorry?' She turned her head but the curve of his shoulder and encircling arm stopped her seeing his face.

'I want to know what work you do. It's no use pretending you're like your sister, living off Daddy's money and drifting from one amusement to another.'

'I never implied I did!'

'I asked upfront how important your father's money was to you—whether it supported you—and you didn't correct me.'

Ella remembered that conversation the night they'd met. She'd been out of her depth, fighting not to show it. She'd been furious and combative. Later she'd revealed as little as possible about her life. It was her only defence against the feeling Donato was taking over her world.

'I'm a nurse.'

'Ah.' His slow exhalation of breath stirred her hair. 'Now, why doesn't that surprise me?'

*Here it comes.* She'd heard it all from her father. Everything from the dowdy uniform to the unglamorous nature of the job and the low pay.

'I have no idea. But I'm sure you're going to tell me.' Ella tried to pull away, but Donato's seemingly lazy hold kept her hard against him.

'Now, Ella, there's no need to get annoyed.' His lips brushed her hair. 'I hadn't guessed but it makes sense.'

'Do tell.' She gritted her teeth. In her family circle, nurses didn't exist. Careers were high profile or highly paid, preferably both. Emptying bedpans or cleaning wounds was just too nose-wrinklingly real.

'You're so assured. Nothing fazes you.' He stroked a finger along one bare arm, drawing her skin into feathery lines of goose bumps. 'You get angry and you're deeply passionate, but I can't imagine you panicking.'

'Assured?' Ella stared at the bright birds in the tree as if she'd never seen them before. She was competent and confident in her work but she didn't feel assured with Donato. He kept her off balance.

A chuckle rose in his deep chest and vibrated through

her. 'Absolutely. You put me in my place from the first. But you weren't patronising in that socially superior way. You weren't a snob. You just said it like it was.'

'I'm practical.' Her father had used that word like an insult.

'Just like every nurse I've met.'

'You've met a few?' She thought of that old scar on his cheek and the others on his ribs.

'Enough. You've got that same air of straight talking, but with all the aplomb of a duchess.' It didn't sound like criticism. It sounded like a compliment. Ella felt a little fizz of pleasure.

'Have you ever met a duchess?'

'I have, as it happens. She was more pleasant and down-to-earth than some of the snobby society types I've met.'

'I can imagine.' Her father was one such snob. He'd forgive you anything so long as you were rich or socially superior.

'So, what sort of nursing?' Donato sounded genuinely interested.

'Community care. I visit people in their homes, often the elderly or patients just released from hospital.'

'In their homes? Do you work in pairs?'

'I'm part of a team but I do my home visits solo.'

Donato's arms tightened. 'That's dangerous. You don't know what you could walk into.'

'We're fully trained. We have safety protocols in place. Anyway, most of my clients are frail.'

'It's not just your clients. *Anyone* could be there.'

'I can look after myself, Donato.' She turned in his arms and pressed a finger to his mouth before he could contradict her. 'But I appreciate your concern.'

In all her years of nursing none of her family or friends had expressed concern for her safety. That must explain the strange melting sensation in her chest as she met his stare.

She'd never had a protector. There'd been no one since her mother or Aunt Bea who worried about her. Fuzz and Rob saw her as capable and efficient, able to look after herself. And their father…he'd never cared enough to worry.

Crazy that the man logic told her not to trust was the one man who worried about her.

Crazier still that she liked it.

# CHAPTER ELEVEN

'WELL, YOU COULD have knocked me down with a feather. Really!' Samantha Raybourne's laugh tinkled melodiously, turning heads in the packed theatre lounge. 'I'd never thought of *you* marrying, Ella. Much less snaffling the most eligible man in the country.'

Ella's smile froze. Why had she told Donato she wanted to see this play? She should have known opening night would attract people like the dreadful Samantha, who'd once made her life hell. She hated that she'd put herself in this position, an unwilling partner in a public charade. But the constraints had been too great, despite her misgivings.

'What Sam means is congratulations.' Samantha's partner spoke. As compère of a reality television show he was adept at reading tension and knew when to intervene. 'We hope you'll both be very happy.'

Before Ella could respond Donato slipped his arm around her waist. His grip reminded her, *as if she could forget*, of the promise he'd extracted. He'd keep her father from badgering her daily about arrangements for the society wedding he planned and in return Ella would play along in public. Even though it meant maintaining the fiction that their relationship was permanent.

A wave of stifling warmth enfolded her. She and Donato wouldn't really marry and it drove her crazy trying to work out why he let her father peddle such a fantasy. What had he to gain? Surely this wasn't the behaviour of an honest man. Yet everything she'd learned of Donato testified that he was straight down the line, often brutally so. His refusal to explain, and to stop the charade, was a dark blot on a relationship that was otherwise almost too enticing.

'Thanks for the good wishes.' Donato's deep rumble sliced through the chatter around them.

Ella was tempted to blurt out the truth, that the engagement was a lie. But Donato had warned that without the 'engagement' he'd stop all involvement with her father. That wasn't an option, not while her siblings needed Reg Sanderson to repay the money he'd taken.

She'd grown tired of trying to force the issue. Whatever strange machinations went on between him and her father, ultimately neither could make her marry Donato. In the meantime she could only find relief in the fact that her real friends had no notion of the fake engagement. Only those in her father's set. Yet guilt and frustration gnawed at her.

'I had no idea the pair of you even knew each other,' Samantha purred, leaning forward to reveal even more pumped-up cleavage.

Anger pierced Ella. If she really were Donato's fiancée she'd take exception to the way the other woman pawed at him, chattering on about a party they'd both attended in Melbourne and giving him that intimate smile.

But Ella was just his temporary lover.

She hadn't let him encroach too far into her world. As for the time they spent on mutual interests, like antiques and art or activities new to her, like sailing and climbing, that didn't feel like encroachment. Those were pure pleasure.

In fact, she realised with a hitch to her breathing, *all* her time with Donato was pleasurable. Their sexual connection had grown into something more complex.

Ella blinked when Samantha leaned in and said with a saccharine smile, 'I get so bored when the men talk business, don't you? Media trends and market growth.' Beside them their companions were deep in discussion.

'No, I don't. I find it interesting.' When Donato spoke of his wide span of investments, she was fascinated.

'But then you've always been so serious, Ella. Serious and sturdy.' Samantha's violet eyes, their colour as artificial as her smile, swept Ella dismissively. 'That reminds me. Rumour has it your father's engaged Aurelio to design your wedding dress. Is it true?'

Ella shrugged, aiming for nonchalance despite her dismay. Surely her father hadn't gone as far as organising a dress and hiring the country's most exclusive designer! This was a nightmare. The sooner it ended the better.

*Except when it ends you and Donato will go your separate ways.*

Ella's stomach pinched. The thought of Donato moving on to another lover brought bile to her mouth.

She wanted what they had to last. She *enjoyed* being with him. No one else had ever made her feel like this.

The revelation knocked her for six, making her sway.

Instantly Donato's arm tightened around her. He looked down, flashing her a reassuring smile before turning back to his conversation, and her stupid heart kicked up pace.

*She wanted to be with him.*

'I'm amazed you've got Aurelio to agree to design your gown.' Samantha had taken her silence for assent. 'His work is exquisite but he prefers to work with *petite* clients to show off his amazing designs.' Again that sharp gaze, dismissing Ella's body as unfashionably rounded.

'Rake-thin women, you mean?' Ella didn't bother pretending to misunderstand. 'I wouldn't know. I'm not really familiar with his designs.' She knew the name, of course, but that was all.

'You're not familiar…?' The other woman delicately fanned herself. 'But why would you when you're not the *type* he normally dresses.' Again that horrified survey of Ella's height and hips.

Ella told herself to be grateful for the woman's cattiness. It distracted her from dismay over the revelation of her feelings for Donato.

Yet Samantha's words opened old wounds. She'd always made Ella feel like a galumphing elephant, reinforcing all her father's negativity. She was too big, too serious and dull to be pretty or exciting.

'But then, Donato's a force to be reckoned with, isn't he? What are artistic scruples compared with the chance to dress his bride, no matter what her size?'

Donato felt the shift of supple muscle under his arm as Ella straightened. More than straightened. A ruler could lie exactly along her taut spine as she gazed down at the woman before her.

His skin tightened in a familiar flurry of anticipation as he felt energy radiate off Ella. From the first he'd enjoyed sparring with her.

Only this time her focus wasn't on him.

He watched Samantha What's-her-name wave a languid hand as she spoke in that awful arch tone about dresses and Ella's size.

Understanding hit and with it came fury. Red-hot fingers of rage dug into his chest, squeezing his lungs. His hand clamped so hard at Ella's waist she swung round, looking up questioningly.

Was it imagination or did her eyes look bruised? The idea disturbed him. Then as he watched something in her expression changed and her lips tilted up in a smile.

Only he saw that it didn't reach her eyes.

'I don't care what some dressmaker thinks of my body,' Ella said, her gaze holding his so that his pulse grew heavy. 'But Donato likes it.' She leaned towards him, flagrantly ignoring the other woman. 'Don't you, Nato?'

For a split second shock grabbed him, because she'd

somehow chanced on the diminutive that only his mother had called him. Then a moment later came the stunned realisation that he liked the pet name on Ella's lips. He wanted to hear it again.

She blinked and he realised she was waiting for his response. Beyond her the hungry-looking woman with the blinding teeth and the bony collarbone watched avidly.

'You need to ask, *corazón*?' He let his hand slip down from the sweet incurve of Ella's waist to linger, circling at her hip. 'How could I look at another woman when I have you? You're the sexiest woman I know.'

'Even with my curves?' Her tinkle of laughter was a fair imitation of the woman standing before them, but Donato knew Ella well enough to hear the tightness in her voice. She did a good job of hiding it but, he realised, the other woman's words had struck home. He frowned, remembering so many times when Ella had tried to hide her body, as if uncomfortable with him seeing her naked.

'Your body,' he said deliberately, 'is a work of art.' He yanked her against him and her escaping breath puffed warm across his chin. 'Any designer would adore dressing you. You look like a woman, not a scrawny sack of bones.'

Dimly he was aware of a shocked hiss from the woman beside them, but his attention was on Ella's widening eyes.

Bending his head, he nipped the sensitive spot where her neck met her shoulder. She went limp, her head tipping back. Donato tasted summer fruit as he licked the spot then nuzzled his way up to her ear.

Ella gasped and clutched his shoulders and he scooped her closer, one hand at her hip, the other on the warm, smooth skin between her shoulder blades. Another kiss and she arched in silent invitation.

He needed to pull back. He'd made his point. They were in a public place.

But he didn't give a damn about creating a scene. Not

with Ella in his arms. Not when he wanted to erase the hint
of pain he'd read in her eyes. And forget the slash of guilt
that he, with his insistence on this farce of an engagement,
had made her a target for that witch's claws. But he couldn't
renege now. Not so close to bringing Sanderson to ruin.

Did guilt heighten his desire? Donato wanted to lose
himself in Ella. She was a drug in his blood, a pleasure
he'd grown addicted to.

*Carajo*, he was even hearing bells now. Kissing Ella,
holding her in his arms, made him forget where he was.

Her hands on his shoulders shifted, pushed, and she
pulled her head back. Dazed silver eyes met his, their
pupils huge and unfocused.

Donato leaned in to take her mouth again.

'No.' Her whisper came from lips now bare of make-
up but deliciously dark and plump from their kisses. 'In-
terval's over.'

Donato looked around the rapidly emptying space. What
had begun as a deliberate display had become something
else. The burn of rage and guilt in his belly and the indefinable emotions that stirred when Ella had turned to him,
looking proud yet so vulnerable, had torn away something
within him. He'd wanted to erase every vestige of hurt from
her face, but in the process he'd lost himself.

*Nato*, she'd called him. And it had felt right. So right he
hadn't wanted to draw back.

He'd wanted to help her but he'd also needed to tap into
that sense of well-being she always gave him. It was a feeling he'd come to crave.

And he'd wanted to possess her. Still he clutched her,
one hand anchored now in her honey-brown hair, making
a delectable mess of her upswept style.

She straightened, her hands going self-consciously to
her hair as her gaze slid to the last stragglers.

'Leave it,' Donato growled, his voice rough. 'I prefer it that way.'

'And that's all that matters, is it?' She tossed her head, pouting, and he smiled.

'No, but it's true. And surely I deserve some reward.'

Her eyes narrowed. 'Because you lied about my body to save my pride.'

'You really have no idea, do you, *cariño*?' She was a remarkable mix of savvy and innocent. 'I spoke nothing but the truth.'

Her beautiful mouth sagged and he smiled wryly.

'I deserve a reward because, despite my inclinations, I'm going to take you in to see the second half of the play. I'm not going to ravish you until we get home or at least to the car.' He drew in a breath that wasn't as steady as he'd like. 'You're going to show that witch and her ilk you don't give a damn for her empty insults because you're far superior to her in every way. Besides, you've got the most powerful, wealthy, scary man in Sydney wrapped around your little finger.'

'Donato?' She blinked and her mouth wobbled. 'Don't be kind to me. You don't need to pretend.'

The look on her face broke something Donato couldn't even name. He found himself hauling her in, kissing her, hard and thoroughly, on that ripe mouth till he felt her turn pliant. Then he made himself pull back, telling himself restraint was good for the soul.

'Our situation isn't simple, Ella.' Not for the first time he wished they'd met under different circumstances. 'But *this* is real. You're the woman I want.' He dragged in another breath and straightened his jacket, pretending the stark truth of those words didn't make his heart drum faster. 'Now come in before I change my mind and take you to the nearest bed.'

For a moment she said nothing, just stared, her head tilted to one side as the half-time bells fell silent.

Finally she slipped her arm through his. Donato was surprised at the rush of unfamiliar feeling that simple gesture evoked.

'You're wrong, you know,' she murmured as they entered the theatre side by side. 'You might be powerful but you're not really scary. Not when you can be so nice.'

Donato almost stumbled. *Nice!* If only she knew.

'You're sure you're okay, Ella? I know Dad when he wants something. I've never seen him so worked up as that last day I was in Sydney.'

Over the long-distance connection Ella heard the shudder in her sister's voice. Despite Fuzz's privileged position as their father's favourite, she'd suffered too, living with Reg Sanderson. They all had. But it was something the three siblings had learned to keep to themselves. Put on a public face and hide what you feel.

Ella looked across Donato's beautiful garden to the dark waters of the Pacific.

'He's not bothering me now.' Donato had seen to that and, despite her concerns about this sham engagement, it was wonderful not to have to deal with her father.

'You need to be careful. Dad's desperate. He couldn't be persuaded, and you know I can usually bring him around eventually.'

Ella had always envied Fuzz that ability. Ella had never been able to satisfy or soothe him.

'He was so set on marriage! I couldn't marry some stranger now I have Matthew.'

'You're really in love, then?' Even now, the idea of her sister committed to one man took some getting used to.

Fuzz laughed. Not her usual light laugh. This was husky and somehow more real. 'I am. Matthew's wonderful, so capable and practical. When there's a problem he doesn't shout, he just fixes it. He's kind and tender and...caring. And he thinks I've got *talent*, Ella. Real talent!'

'Of course you have. We all know that. You're a natural with colour and design.'

There was silence on the line. It lasted so long Ella wondered if the connection had dropped out. 'I should have stuck to that design course years ago, shouldn't I? Instead of taking off to the Caribbean for a couple of months.'

Ella shifted the phone, frowning. She'd never heard her sister regretful. She knew Fuzz had changed but hadn't expected this.

'There's nothing stopping you doing one now.'

'Ever the pragmatist, sis. I knew I could rely on you for a sensible response.'

Ella felt a pinprick of hurt. That was her. Always the pragmatic, mundane one who worried about consequences and responsibilities. Not the pretty, appealing one. Except when she was with Donato. He almost convinced her—

'I don't deserve you, sis. You're in this mess because I did a runner rather than face this Salazar guy.' Fuzz sighed. 'I wish I was as strong and sure as you. I always wanted to be...purposeful but I'm as weak as water. Even when we were kids you were the one with integrity and grit.'

'Fuzz?' Was this her nothing-can-faze-me sister?

'Don't sound surprised. You know it's true.'

Ella sank into a poolside chair, her legs unsteady. 'You're confusing mundane with strong. I just never lived up to expectations so I had to find my own way.'

'*Don't!* You've listened to Dad too much. He hated that you stood up to him. Why do you think he always found fault? Because you challenged him. I wish I'd learned to do that sooner. Getting away from him was the best thing I ever did.'

Ella brushed back the hair that had escaped her high

ponytail. Typically her attempt at casual chic was a disaster, with strands of hair dangling around her face.

'I'm glad you did, Fuzz. You deserve this chance. Rob too.'

'You think?' Her sister paused. 'I don't deserve to have you fighting my battles. But I won't give up Matthew for some ex-con Dad wants to impress.'

'He's more than an ex-con! Or one of Dad's usual business sharks.'

Silence followed Ella's words and she felt her heart thud against her ribs. Donato stood head and shoulders above her father and his sort. Despite the way he wielded his immense power, despite the threat he still represented to her family, he continually surprised her with his compassion and humour.

Then there was the way he made her feel—attractive, as if he saw something no one else saw. He challenged her and revelled in her response when she stood up to him.

'Are you *sure* you're okay, sis? If you need me, I'll come back. You're brave and beautiful and you always have an answer when things go wrong, but you don't have to do this alone.'

Ella blinked. Fuzz coming to her aid? Calling her beautiful? She swallowed hard. 'There's no need to butter me up. I know I'm not—'

'You *are*! The question is—do you want me there?'

'No. Stay there. Has the money come through? Dad promised he'd repay Rob's money.'

'Some of it. Enough to keep us at the renovations. But there's still a hefty chunk missing. Without that the resort's doomed.'

As Ella had suspected—their father was in no hurry to return all the funds he'd misappropriated. They could call in the police but that wouldn't help if Reg Sanderson was declared bankrupt.

'I'll find a way to make him pay it back.' Until she did she was caught, rejecting an arranged marriage but at the same time unable to walk away completely for fear Rob would never see his money.

And in the meantime she was enjoying the most intense, amazing relationship of her life with the man she refused to marry!

She'd never marry to grease the wheels of her father's schemes. Even if Donato was the only man she'd ever felt this way about. She was on the brink of giving in and moving in with him. Because she wanted him, not because of her father's schemes.

'Can you make Dad pay it back?' Hope and fear warred in her sister's voice.

'Don't worry, Fuzz. I'm his ace in the hole. He needs me for this deal. I'll sort it so Rob gets his money and you get to stay with Matthew.'

Footsteps sounded on the flagstones. It was Donato, watching her. How much had he heard?

'I have to go.' Ella turned away, lowering her voice. 'Thanks for calling, and for the offer to come back... That means a lot.' Her throat tightened. The Sanderson siblings had each found their own way of coping with their father. Fuzz's approach had been self-absorption.

'Okay. I should get back to this painting. I promised Matthew I'd finish this room today. But remember, if you need me, I can be there in a day.'

Fuzz, painting? When would wonders cease?

Ella pressed her lips together as she ended the call. She felt wobbly. Because of her sister's concern. Because of her offer to come back. Because Ella had felt a bond with Fuzz she hadn't experienced in years. With Rob, yes, but not with her sister. Ella had always lived in the shade cast by Fuzz's bright personality. It had never occurred to her that Fuzz wanted to be like *her*.

# CHAPTER TWELVE

'EVERYTHING ALL RIGHT?'

Donato stopped beside her and Ella had a disturbingly appealing view of powerful hands and muscled thighs in faded denim. She stood. Her sister's revelations had thrown her and she needed time to digest them, consider how to get the rest of Rob's money from their father.

But thinking clearly with Donato near was a big ask. Look what had happened at the theatre last night. He'd kissed her and she'd begun to believe...

'Of course. Everything's fine.'

One ebony eyebrow slanted up, reminding her of the superior way he'd regarded her that very first night. Before they'd become lovers.

A weight punched hard and low in her belly. Her conscience. She'd let him distract her from her purpose. She was supposed to be helping her siblings. Yet for weeks she'd been too busy discovering passion and pleasure with Donato. It was time she got back on track—faced down her father.

'Something's weighing on you.'

The gentle probing stiffened Ella's shoulders. She'd grown so close to Donato, her instinct was to share her problems with him.

Yet he was part of the problem!

This farcical situation was doing her head in. Her father insisted he couldn't repay the money till after the wedding. Meanwhile she was sleeping with Donato, not through coercion, but because she wanted him as she'd never wanted any man.

Ella rubbed her forehead. 'I have things to sort out.'

'Family things? To do with your brother?' Donato moved closer, his gaze intent. 'Something to do with money?'

Ella's head reared back. He *had* heard.

Again she felt that impulse to spill her worries. But if she revealed her father had stolen from his own son that would stymie his business deal with Donato, for how could Donato trust such a man? And if the deal didn't proceed, Rob wouldn't get his money.

'That was a private conversation.'

Donato's face changed. From concern his expression hardened, setting in severe lines. The spark vanished from his gaze, replaced by a coolness she felt like a blast of arctic air. She hadn't seen him look like that since the night they met.

'You don't trust me?' The words were silky smooth so she must have imagined the hint of hurt in them. Donato didn't do hurt. He was strong, always in control.

Ella breathed deep, torn between duty and desire.

And guilt. Last night he'd stood up for her and her heart had sung.

But she *couldn't* tell him, not if she was to help her siblings. 'You don't tell me everything about your life. You guard yourself so no one can get really close. But do I get upset when you don't let me in?'

He stepped near, engulfing her with his heat and his sheer presence. The delicious skin scent that was his alone filled her nostrils.

'I don't know? Do you?' The deep cadence of his voice mesmerised her. She wanted—

Sucking in a sharp breath, she moved back.

He moved with her.

'Do you, Ella? Is that what's bothering you? Because I

don't share every tiny detail of my life? You want my secrets and my soul as well as my body and my money?'

At the unexpected insult hurt crested. Unbelievably Ella
saw her hand rise with it.

Stunned, she felt juddering shock radiate through her
as Donato caught her wrist centimetres from his face. She
hadn't even registered the intention to strike him.

He held her hand high, drawing her closer, and she
planted her other palm on his chest for balance. Beneath
her touch his heart tapped an even rhythm, only fractionally quicker than usual. Nothing, it seemed, fazed Donato.
Meanwhile her heart slammed hard and fast. Her breath
came in uneven gasps.

'I don't want your money,' she whispered through
clenched teeth. 'You know that.' How could he *say* that
when last night he'd been so understanding, so wonderful?
She'd never felt more lost and confused.

'Are you sure?' Eyes like the sea, fathoms deep and
merciless, held hers.

Heat scored Ella's cheeks. He was right. She wanted
his funds to prop up her father's business so Reg Sanderson could repay the money he'd stolen. She looked away,
ashamed to be her father's advocate. It went against the
grain not to tell Donato the sort of man he did business
with. By keeping quiet surely she was culpable?

'Are you going to tell me, Ella?'

She shut her eyes against the temptation to spill everything, all her worries. But a lifetime's hard-won lessons
stiffened her spine. She shook her head.

'You don't trust me.'

Her eyes snapped open. Donato's face had softened. That
stark coldness was gone as he lowered their clasped hands.
He looked disappointed rather than angry.

'There are some things you can't fix so easily.'

She thought of the donation Donato had made to the

community centre her clients used. She'd mentioned its difficulty in getting funds to improve wheelchair access. The following day a donation had arrived, enough to upgrade the facilities and more. She'd traced the payment to Donato.

Then there was Binh, the gardener here. Ella had chatted with him about the beautiful landscaping and the flowers. He'd told her how, when his wife lost her job in a florist shop, Donato had given her an interest-free loan to start her own business when the banks wouldn't take the risk.

Donato quietly set about helping people, solving their problems.

He couldn't fix this.

'I'm sorry.' She swallowed hard. 'I shouldn't have lashed out. I don't know what's got into me.'

'You're upset.'

Ella shook her head. Why should her sister's call upset her? They were closer than they'd been in years. And yet she did feel...off balance. Because they'd dredged the depths of their dysfunctional family, stirring emotions she'd tried to put a lid on for years.

'Come on, Ella. Walk with me.' To her surprise Donato tucked her hand in his arm, drawing her close. She went with him. Her emotions might be a jumbled mess but she was honest enough to know it was what she wanted.

They'd reached the clifftop when he spoke. 'I shouldn't have reacted like that when you refused to tell me your problems. I apologise. That crack about you wanting my money was low.'

Ella's head snapped round. An apology? *She'd* been the one to take a swing at him! 'I shouldn't have lost my cool. I'm sorry. My behaviour was appalling. I just... I hate feeling I'm not in control.'

'That's how you feel?' No anger in his eyes now. *This* was the Donato she'd grown close to, so close it was tough remembering all that stood between them.

'I like to understand what's going on and make my own decisions. With you, with *us*, it's like I'm on a runaway train. It's racing ahead but I don't know where or why. All I can do is hold on and hope for the best.' The words spilled out. Ella hadn't meant to reveal so much. Yet increasingly she wanted to smash down all the barriers and...

What? Share everything with him? As if he wasn't just a temporary lover? As if they weren't on opposite sides because of her father's machinations?

As if she and Donato could be...important to each other?

'I understand. I used to hate feeling powerless. I was determined to take control of my life and shape it how I wanted.'

'I can't imagine you powerless.' Donato was purposeful, definite. That had appealed from the first.

His laugh was short and hard. 'You have no idea.'

'No, I don't.'

'But you want to know.' His gaze was needle-sharp. Ella nodded.

'It's not enough that we share our bodies and all our private time? That you know my politics and my taste in films and sport and anything else you want to talk about?'

Ella turned to brace her hands on the rock wall topping the cliff, searching for the right words. She shared more with Donato than she ever had with any man. Yet still she wanted...needed more.

'You know my father,' she said eventually. 'Where I grew up. Plus I tell you about my work.' Donato's interest had amazed her and his concern for her safety had been genuine. He rang every day after her last appointment to check she was okay. 'All I really know about your past is what I read in the press the night we met and the little you told me about Jack.'

His lips thinned. 'You want the story behind the headlines?' His tone was harsh, almost jeering, like his words just before she'd lashed out at him. What was it about his past that made him protect it so aggressively?

'Is it a crime to want to know you better?'

She looked up into that proud, scarred, implacable face, sensing turmoil. Was it really too much to ask? She couldn't shake the feeling that the real man remained hidden, despite the intimacies they shared.

'Everyone who's wanted to know more has only been after cheap thrills, mixing with the tame ex-con.' The words lashed her.

'I'm not everyone, Donato.'

Meeting his challenging stare, doubt assailed her. Was she wrong? Was she alone in thinking they shared something more than sex? Donato's eyes had that horrible blank look and she knew he deliberately shut her out.

So…he'd confirmed it. She was just a sexual diversion. There was nothing profound about what they shared. She'd been misled by her own silly yearnings.

Her stomach swooped and she turned away.

'Wait.' He threaded his fingers through hers.

Ella stiffened. His power over her was scary. He just had to touch her. And Fuzz called her the practical one! If she had any sense she'd run, not walk away from this man.

'I'm sorry, Ella.' His hand tightened on hers and he laughed, the sound strained rather than amused. 'There, two apologies in five minutes. I hope you realise that's a record.'

Ella turned. Donato's face was taut, his nostrils pinched and his mouth a harsh line that made something twist high in her chest. The sight of his pain did that to her. Her brain registered surprise that he let her read his feelings, but she was too caught up to think about that now. Impulsively she reached out, her palm cupping his jaw, sliding over his close-shaved chin.

Donato's hand closed on hers, dragging it to his mouth.

He kissed her palm and shivery sensations shot through her, making her tremble. The way he looked at her, the intensity of this connection, made her emotions well even higher.

'What am I going to do about you, Ella?' His voice was a low burr that furrowed through her insides.

She shook her head. 'I wonder the same about you, Donato. I knew you were trouble the first time I saw you.'

'That's nothing new.' His voice was harsh. 'I've been trouble all my life.' He smiled. 'You, on the other hand, have always been a good girl.'

Ella's chin jerked up. 'How do you know?'

'It's not an insult, you know.' Donato laughed. This time there was amusement in that dark-chocolate chuckle. 'How do I know? Because you're the Sanderson who works for a living instead of dabbling with other people's money.'

'My brother works.'

Donato shrugged. 'That remains to be seen. He's spent the last couple of years on your father's payroll. Besides, you're the one who's here, holding the fort. You're the one your father turned to. The one who's made a career caring for people.'

'That doesn't make me a saint.'

'Absolutely not. I'm not interested in saints.' Donato trailed a finger from her jaw, down her throat to her breast. Instantly Ella's breath stalled as her body softened, need rising.

It took far too long to break from his sensual spell and step away. Ella drew her hands from him so she could lean back against the clifftop wall.

'You're right. We need to talk.' Yet his eyes held that slumberous blue heat that was like an invitation to sin. An invitation she'd never yet been able to resist.

Finally Donato moved to lean on the wall, his gaze on the horizon. Ella stared at his strong profile, still dazed by the upsurge of hormones jangling in her body.

'You want to know about my past.'

'I'm not after cheap thrills.'

'I know. I shouldn't have said that. I realised from the first you were different from other women.'

*Different?* How? Immediately part of her brain started cataloguing all the ways she didn't measure up, with her less than svelte figure, her discomfort in society gatherings, her inability to charm—

Then Ella realised what she was doing. Fuzz was right. She'd listened to her father too much.

'I want to know you, Donato, and I believe that means understanding some of your past. But if you don't want to talk about it, I can respect that.' She *was* getting to know Donato in other ways.

'Didn't I say you were different?' But he didn't look at her, just drew a deep breath. 'I was born in inner city Melbourne. Our rooms were cramped and I played indoors or in back alleys. When I was tiny I always saw the sky in little slices between buildings. That's given me a love of wide-open spaces.'

Ella nodded. He'd said as much before.

'I lived with my mother. I never knew my father.'

'That must have been hard.' True, she'd have been happier without her father in her life, but that wasn't the case for everyone.

There was so much tension in the bunched muscles of Donato's shoulder and arm she almost reached out, but something held her back. Then he turned and the look in his eyes fixed her to the spot.

'Harder than you can imagine. My mother was a prostitute. She had no idea who my father was and didn't want to know.'

Ella blinked, shock blasting her.

'Apparently by the time the brothel owners found out she was pregnant it was too late for a safe abortion. She'd hidden it as long as possible because, strange as it seems, she wanted to keep me.' The shadow of a smile crossed his face. 'She believed a baby was a blessing. That's why she named me Donato—a gift. Luckily it turned out some of the punters liked pregnant woman so she got to keep me.'

'Your mother told you that?' Ella couldn't keep the horror from her voice.

Donato shook his head. 'I overheard her talking about it when I was older.'

Ella sagged against the waist-high wall. Was it her imagination or had he implied her mother might have been forced into an abortion otherwise?

'When I was six Jack took us away from the city. He was a client of my mother's and he fell in love with her, even agreed to take me on too. He smuggled us away and we lived with him for years in an old house with a vegetable garden out the back and a climbing tree at the front.'

Ella stared. 'Your mother fell in love with him?'

Donato's expression told her she was impossibly naïve. 'He had a steady job and he was never violent. He cared for her and he was willing to accept me as well.' He paused. 'If you'd known our lives before you'd know how precious that was.'

Silently Ella nodded. As a nurse, she knew how tough life was for many. Yet, despite his time in prison, she'd never expected something like this was hiding in Donato's past.

'Did you like him?'

'He protected my mother. And he gave us something like a normal life for years. I went to school, he worked and my mother cooked and cleaned. She smiled a lot too. Sometimes I even heard her sing.' His expression softened. 'She was beautiful, you know. Really beautiful. But life had worn her down. When we lived with Jack she blossomed.'

'He sounds like a good man.' At least Ella hoped he was.

Donato shrugged. 'He had a short temper and an old-fashioned approach to discipline, but he never laid a hand on her.' Something in his voice told Ella Donato would have put up with any amount of *discipline* if it meant keeping his mother happy.

'He died when I was twelve and everything changed.'

'What happened?'

'He hadn't left a will and his house went to a sister. My mother and I were out on the street and she took to prostitution again to support us. Social services found out and took me away.' A muscle in his jaw spasmed. 'I didn't like being in care. I kept running away to find her. I didn't last long in foster care. I got a reputation for being difficult.'

Ella tried to imagine Donato at twelve, parted from his mother for the first time. He was tenacious and strong and he obviously cared greatly for his mother. Of course he'd run away to look for her.

Her hand found his on the stone wall and he looked around, startled.

'It's too late for sympathy, Ella. I was a tough kid and it was a long time ago.' Yet he didn't move his hand.

'Where is she now? In Melbourne?' She'd bet one of the first things Donato had done when he became successful was provide for his mother.

'She's dead.' The bald words stunned her.

'Dead?'

He nodded. 'Battered by a client.' His voice dripped venom. 'She died later of her injuries.'

'Oh, Donato. I'm so sorry.' Ella squeezed his hand. She remembered how lost she'd felt when her mother died. She couldn't imagine the trauma of losing someone as a result of a violent crime. 'How old were you?'

'A teenager.' Beneath her touch his hand tightened. Energy vibrated through him. 'But I tracked him down when the police didn't have enough evidence to convict him. I made him pay.'

'That's why you went to prison? You found the man responsible for your mother's death?'

Donato nodded. 'There was a problem with the scientific evidence and the only witness was another prostitute. The lawyers made mincemeat of her evidence and he walked free.'

Ella struggled to absorb it all. She'd thought Donato might have tried to protect someone in that fight. Now she realised it hadn't been protection but vengeance that motivated him.

Or guilt because he hadn't been able to save his mother?

Ella exhaled. She thought she'd had a tough childhood!

'Heard enough of my disreputable past yet?'

'Did you find him again after you left prison?'

Donato shook his head. 'I learned a lot behind bars. Including that I didn't want to serve a life sentence for murder. Anyway, when I got out I heard he'd died in a car crash.'

Relief made Ella dizzy. 'Prison changed your life.'

'Definitely. I realised education was the key to turning myself around. That plus hard work and a willingness to take risks.'

'It's amazing what you've achieved.' Yet her mind wasn't on his commercial success. It was still boggling at his past.

'I was lucky. I was mentored when I left the justice system, part of a young-offenders programme. One mentor led to another and some opportunities opened up for me. I learned a lot and dedicated myself to taking charge of my life, getting some control.'

He made it sound easy. Ella could only guess at the struggle it must have been with a criminal record. 'You must have dreamed big.'

'Always.' His other hand covered hers. 'Have you heard

enough?' Despite his light tone, there was no mistaking the strain on his features.

'Thank you for telling me. I…' Ella shook her head. She felt overwhelmed, not only by what he'd revealed but by the fact he trusted her with such intimate details. 'I won't tell anyone.'

'You think I'm worried about that?' He looked big and bold and forbidding, as if the world could spit in his eye and he'd take it in his stride. Now she understood a little of what made him that way. 'Besides—' his voice lowered to something like a caress '—I know you, Ella. You've got too much integrity to gossip about my private life.'

*Integrity?*

Ella looked into those serious eyes and wondered. Was it integrity to keep her father's true character from Donato? Shouldn't she at least warn him that Reg Sanderson was as slimy as any sewer rat, and totally untrustworthy?

# CHAPTER THIRTEEN

ELLA'S DELIGHTED CHUCKLE took Donato by surprise.

'What are you laughing at?' Women didn't find him amusing in bed. Yet his mouth curved at the sound. Her delight was infectious.

An hour ago, telling Ella about his mother's death, he hadn't imagined laughing again so soon.

He'd laughed more these last two months than he had in years.

She traced her index finger over his chest, trawling down to circle his nipple. He sucked in his breath as desire shafted through him, tightening his groin and his muscles as he leaned over her.

'The fact we actually made it to your bed and we're naked. Usually we don't get this far the first time. Or if we do, we're still half dressed.' Ella's silver-blue eyes danced and Donato was as intrigued as ever by their beauty.

There wasn't one thing about Ella he didn't find intriguing. From her lush mouth to her delicious body and her tendency to cover it rather than flaunt it in revealing clothes. Then there were her smart tongue, her quick wit and her love of her career. The more he heard about her work, the more he realised it was part of her, caring for others. She took pride in what she did, yet was curiously defensive about it.

'I thought you'd appreciate the comfort of a mattress.' His smile widened as he lifted his hand to her breast, mirroring her movement against his body, watching her expression as he tweaked her nipple.

He loved the way she responded so honestly, giving freely even as she demanded everything from him.

Donato pushed her thighs further apart and sank between them.

'Don't get too used to the bed, *cariño*. I intend to take you in every room of this house, and there are parts of the garden we haven't explored.'

He took her nipple in his mouth and she arched high, gasping. She tasted of apricots, warm from the summer sun, and her skin's light floral scent was a heady draught for his senses.

Beneath him Ella shifted needily. 'I like the fact you're so...thorough.'

'Always, *cariño*.'

Except he'd never needed a woman as much and as often as he did Ella. He'd never known such unflagging desire.

He'd always been a discriminating lover—not surprising, given his mother's experiences. But this felt different to any previous sexual relationship. Nothing matched the pleasure he found with Ella. Whenever she gave herself to him it was so good.

Better than good.

The best he'd ever known.

That must explain why he took such inordinate care and time now. Why he concentrated as much energy and focus on pleasuring her as he did on finalising any of his multi-million-dollar deals. He wanted to fill Ella's senses till there was only him. He wanted her screaming his name as she flew apart beneath him, around him. He wanted her abandoned and sated.

Restless fingers burrowed through his hair. 'Kiss me, Donato. Please.'

He relinquished her breast with one final lingering lick and was rewarded with a sigh of delight. He lifted himself higher, looked down into her flushed face and stalled, his heart thumping.

Her eyes had lost that glimmer of humour. Even the desire he was accustomed to seeing had been eclipsed. Instead that diamond-bright glitter looked awash, glazed with tears, and her expression…he couldn't name it. It was more than arousal. More than sexual excitement. It was tender and sad and hopeful and a million things he couldn't name.

Because he'd never seen them in any woman's eyes before.

Except there was something there that reminded him of his mother when he'd been tiny and she'd cradled his skinny frame close, telling him everything would be all right, despite her bruises and his empty belly.

Emotion scoured him. His chest heaved and tightened.

How had sex morphed into *this*? Donato reared back, bracing himself on his arms above Ella.

She grabbed his shoulders, her legs lifting to wrap around his waist, stopping him when he would have moved further away.

He could have broken her hold, except, he realised, part of him wanted to stay. The part that was mesmerised by the tenderness in her expression.

Donato told himself it was the unfamiliarity of it. The novelty.

'Kiss me, Donato.'

'You're feeling *sorry* for me.' He couldn't believe it. Every instinct had warned against revealing so much of his past. But he hadn't expected *this*.

Everything rebelled at her pity. He'd looked after himself, and his mother, since he was a kid. He'd almost killed a man with his bare hands, before he learned to curb the anger inside. He'd survived prison, not unscathed, but stronger and in some ways more dangerous than before. He had the life he wanted, the power he desired. He bought and sold enterprises with ease. He was about to enjoy the biggest, most satisfying coup of his life.

'I don't want your sympathy.' The words emerged through gritted teeth. 'I refuse to accept it.'

Ella shook her head and shut her eyes. When she opened them again her expression was guarded and there was a wry twist to her lips.

'I'm sorry for the little boy you once were.' She lifted one hand to his face, her palm warm against his locked jaw. 'Sorry too for the lost teenager, trying to get back to his mother.'

'I was never lost. I knew exactly where I was.' Though, he admitted silently, he'd lost his way when grief and anger had erupted. When the keening sense of loss had been too much to bear.

Ella's hand shifted to stroke his scar. It wasn't the first time she'd touched it. But this time she did it with such deliberation his breath sucked in.

'Don't worry, Donato. I know you don't need my sympathy now. You're big and bold and formidable. You're dangerous in ways most men wouldn't dare to be, and most women dream of.' Her lips tilted in a tiny secret smile that made something flip and twist in his belly.

Her hand dropped and Donato swallowed hard rather than ask her to touch him again. The sensation of her light caress on his cheek lingered, as if she'd marked him.

'Good.' He nodded briskly. 'Just so you understand, I don't need pity. My needs are far simpler.' He lifted his hand to her breast again, his touch demanding, almost rough.

Inevitably, satisfyingly, Ella arched into his touch, her eyes alive with the same blaze of hunger consuming him.

Donato plundered her lips, taking her mouth in a kiss that held nothing tentative or gentle. It was a marauder's kiss. The kiss of a man taking what he wanted. A kiss that was hungry and not at all tender. A kiss to banish pity.

Yet, if he'd meant to frighten her into drawing away, he couldn't have been more mistaken. Ella matched him all the way, nipping at his bottom lip, grabbing at his hair, clinging with hands and hips and her lovely long legs wrapped tight around him.

His heart thundered as with one single thrust he entered her, anchoring her to the bed so she couldn't move unless he permitted it.

Triumph rose. He had her on his terms and it felt like heaven.

Except something had changed. Something about the way she accepted his weight, his hunger, his avoidance of anything like tenderness.

*Or was it something in him that had changed?*

Donato didn't know. But suddenly he was tearing his mouth away, lifting his head to stare down at her. He catalogued her swollen lips and the reddened marks where his unshaven chin had scraped her soft flesh. Shame hit. He'd been too rough.

Her chin lifted, daring him to read any sentiment in her expression. In that moment Donato understood that, despite what he'd implied, it wasn't just sex he wanted from Ella.

'Is there a problem?' Her eyebrows arched as if she were challenging him as she had that first night, instead of lying beneath him, her velvety warmth making it almost impossible to think.

'No problem at all, *mi preciosa niña.*'

He'd work out exactly what it was he wanted from Ella, given time. He'd find a way to deal with this sense of needing yet more. Didn't he conquer every challenge?

If he'd been thinking straight he'd have realised weeks ago that with Ella he wanted more than simple carnal satisfaction. He wanted her company, her mind, her humour and her infuriatingly independent attitude. And yes, even her tenderness.

'Donato?' She frowned and concern flickered across her face. She sank her teeth into her bottom lip as if to stop herself asking more.

Guilt smote. Was he really so insecure he couldn't cope with a little sympathy from a beautiful woman? From his lover? He'd behaved like a vulnerable kid, not the self-assured man he was.

'Tell me what you want, *cariño*.' He palmed her cheek, dragging his thumb over her reddened lips and planting a tiny kiss there. Instantly she kissed him back, the sweet caress of her mouth on his filling him with relief.

Had he really worried she wouldn't respond after his rough treatment?

*No,* he realised in a moment of blinding clarity, *he'd feared she'd stop caring.*

Donato's heart crashed against his ribs but he held himself still, forcing air through cramped lungs.

'You, Donato. That's what I want.' Ella kissed him again, then lay back waiting.

'That I can provide.' His voice was a rumble, gruff like distant thunder as he moved within her. Using iron willpower he kept his movements measured. He watched her face flush and her eyes shine as she moved with him, sinuous, sleek and mind-blowingly sexy.

Her sweet-nectar scent was rich in his nostrils. Her ripe body was everything he could desire. But even better was the expression in her eyes. Though she veiled it with a half-lidded look, he read tenderness there. Caring. And his heart swelled.

He cradled her face as he quickened his movements, feeling her ripple of arousal encompass him. She clasped her hands behind his neck, anchoring him. Her breath came in little quivering sighs, shorter and deeper the faster he moved.

'Like that?' He held her gaze, loving the way hers suddenly widened as he found that sweet spot and she convulsed around him, drawing him tight and hard.

As he watched, the blue-grey of her eyes morphed almost to pure silver, a burst of brightness that stole his breath. His name was a tender groan from those beautiful lips as she bucked high, her hands clutching as if scared he'd let her go.

Heat and light and wonder filled him as she drew him to the brink of ecstasy. He wanted her as he'd wanted no other woman. And he revelled in being wanted by her.

Then thought spiralled away, a fraying thread undone by white-hot pleasure as he fell into that silvery starburst and joined her in oblivion.

The sky had grown dark, the air sultry in anticipation of an evening thunderstorm, when they finally stirred. Ella was sprawled over him, her lips at his throat, her breasts against his chest. He wallowed in the skin to skin contact, the warm weight of her.

Desire stirred and with it something new.

He'd been wary of sharing his history because keeping his mouth shut was ingrained. His mother had spoken Spanish to him because it was her native language, but also to keep him apart from the people she mixed with. He hadn't been fluent in English till he went to school. They'd been a team, a pair against the world. Since losing her Donato had devoted his life to improving himself, building success upon success. That took dedication, single-mindedness and the ability not to be distracted by beautiful women.

Ella was the first to hear his story and he'd expected shock and disgust.

Yet she'd dumbfounded him. Instead of outrage he'd found understanding. Instead of disgust there'd been sympathy and support, and tears in her eyes as she'd held him. He'd felt her emotions rise—not excitement but tenderness and concern. Greedily he'd wanted to snatch it all for himself. Not because the past still pained him, but because he felt…different because of Ella's concern.

'We need to talk.' Her husky words surprised him. Usually the last thing Ella wanted in his bed was to talk.

Did she want to rehash his past? Delve into the nitty-gritty detail? Instantly his lassitude disintegrated.

'What do you want to talk about?'

Ella planted her hands on his chest and raised her head, looking down at him. Her hair was a froth of dark honey silk and her lips were the colour of crushed strawberries. She looked like a woman who'd been thoroughly bedded.

Donato's arms tightened as possessiveness sideswiped him. He didn't want any other man seeing her like this. Ever.

She smiled, that teasing tilt of the lips that he felt in the hollow place at the base of his belly.

'No need to be so wary. I wasn't going to pry.'

Was he that obvious? Donato frowned.

'Okay then. What is it?'

The smile slipped off her face and she looked away. 'My father.'

Now this *was* a first. Ella talking about her family, and especially her father, without prompting?

'You want to know how the business plans are proceeding?' That would be another first. As far as he could tell, Ella wasn't interested in her father's business. Originally he'd put that down to a sense of entitlement, thinking she lived off his money but didn't bother about how he got it. Now he knew the pair led separate lives.

'No. I wanted to tell you…' Her brow furrowed.

'Yes? Something about your father?'

She drew in a shuddering breath that rubbed her breasts

against his chest. Her face swung back and he saw the unhappy cast of her mouth, the tension in every feature.

'I can't give you any insights into his business. I know nothing about it, and I'm sure your investigators have been thorough tracking down his commercial interests.'

'They have.'

'I know you far outclass him in wealth and, I assume, business capability. But there's one thing you don't know. Something you need to know.'

'What is it, Ella?'

She met his eyes. Her own blazed. 'If there's a loophole he'll take it. If there's a way he can feather his nest at your expense he'll do it. Whatever the deal is on paper, whatever you've agreed, don't trust him.'

Donato stared up into her taut features, the twisting line of her mouth, as if she'd swallowed something foul, and began to understand.

'It's all right, Ella. I take precautions. He won't get the better of me. The contract will see to that.'

'You don't understand. I'm not talking about him jockeying for the best deal on paper.' Her gaze slid away. 'I'm talking about him breaking the rules, even the law. Don't trust him an inch. He uses people to get what he wants.'

Donato read her pain, felt the tension in her and wanted to smash Reg Sanderson's face.

'Ella?' He kept his voice soft as he brushed her shining hair back. 'What's he done to you?'

'This isn't about me. It's about you. You need to be prepared. I don't understand why you want to do business with my dad but you deserve to know he'll cheat and lie and use you any way he can. If I were you...' She looked away. 'If I were you I wouldn't do business with him at all.' The hoarse conviction in her voice told its own story.

'Why are you sharing this?'

She frowned. 'Don't you want to know what you're dealing with?'

*What.* As if Reg Sanderson were a thing not a person. Donato's pulse quickened. 'Has he hurt you?' He wrapped his arms around her, lashing her naked body to him.

'You think I'm telling you this out of spite?'

'Of course not.' He just wanted to know what else to add to Sanderson's account. He was sure there was something, probably many somethings. His jaw tightened. 'But I'd give a lot to know why you are telling me.'

Her brow wrinkled. 'You're not the man I believed. You're decent and real and... I care for you.'

It felt as if an unseen fist smashed through his ribs to pummel his lungs and heart.

How long since anyone had cared about him?

How long since anyone had looked out for him?

The rarity of it had to explain this overfull sensation.

'Can you give me an example?' He didn't need one but he wanted to know what Sanderson had done to Ella.

Her eyes when they locked with his were the colour of a stormy sky, her features pared back as if her flesh shrank on her bones. 'He stole from my brother. Rob inherited money from our grandfather which Reg invested for him. Now Rob needs his money for a project he's co-financing. But most of the funds have disappeared, stolen by our father. He says he can't pay it back till his deal with you is finalised.'

'Which is why you didn't tell me about this sooner.' Now the pieces fell into place. This explained Ella's willingness to play along with the wedding scheme, albeit under sufferance. 'He was holding it over your head.'

Ella shifted, trying to roll off him, but Donato held her close. Skin to skin, eye to eye, this was his chance to discover all he needed to know.

'At first I thought it didn't matter. I thought you were like him.'

Donato grimaced at the idea and Ella brushed her fingers across his mouth in a caress that made his heart leap.

'But you're not, are you?'

Before he could think of a response she went on. 'It's been eating at me. I've seen another side to you. The way you are with me, the things you do for other people.'

Donato frowned, wondering what she'd found out. Mostly he kept his charitable activities out of the limelight.

'I felt guilty, not telling you what he's really like. Today, when you told me about your mother...' Her mouth turned down. 'How could I ask you to share that and not warn you?'

'So this is quid pro quo?' His grating tone hid confusion. He'd been unsettled all day. Unsettled by Ella's sympathy and how, despite what he said, it warmed the dark places in his soul.

Ella stiffened, her chin jutting at a familiar angle. 'If you like.'

'I didn't mean it like that.' He ran the backs of his fingers down her peach-soft cheek. 'I appreciate you telling me. But it makes no difference. I knew already.'

He knew more about her father than he suspected Ella did. For the first time it hit him that revealing the enormity of Sanderson's crimes would have repercussions for Ella. How would she react?

'You're still going to do business with him?'

'Oh, yes.' Familiar satisfaction stirred. 'But with one change.' He palmed her hair from her face, feeling an unaccustomed protectiveness at the idea of Ella growing up under Sanderson's roof. He thought of her prickly defensiveness, her difficulty in believing she was attractive and knew he could lay that and more at Sanderson's door.

'What change?' Her eyes were wary, and why not? She'd been an unwilling pawn in his tactics.

Donato rolled over till she was beneath him, all that delicious femininity and warm silky skin.

'I'll make sure your brother gets his money.'

Watching the light in Ella's eyes was like watching dawn break over the ocean, except the warmth he felt was far more than skin-deep. She made him feel like a different man. A man who might believe in things he'd learned never to expect.

He felt her jolt of surprise. 'You will? But it's not your responsibility.' A smile hovered on her mouth but didn't quite settle, as if she feared to believe. It struck him how much stress she'd been under. From her father, and from him.

Something heavy dragged at his gut. Regret? Guilt?

'I'm making it my responsibility.'

Her smile broke wide then and its brilliance set off little tremors inside. Of pleasure, and relief.

See? He could make things okay for her. He could make her happy and still get the revenge he needed from her father.

'I don't know what to say.'

'Don't say anything.'

'Thank you, Donato.' Her hands cupped his jaw, her gaze met his. 'That means so much.'

'Good. Perhaps you can show me how much.' He basked in her approval, thrusting aside the knowledge he'd used Ella for his own ends. That she deserved to know the whole truth. He'd make it up to her. As for the truth, that would come soon enough. Probably too soon for Ella and her siblings.

He swept his hand down the sleek curve of her spine, desperation rising as he deliberately pushed aside the hovering shadow cast by his conscience.

It was far easier to lose himself in passion than to analyse these new troubling feelings.

# CHAPTER FOURTEEN

ELLA REREAD THE NOTE, not recognising her father's writing. He'd never written her birthday or Christmas cards, yet the slashing scribble could only be his.

*Urgent...designer insists you meet for a fitting but has sent this...only agreeing to work because of Salazar's high profile...demand you be there Friday three p.m...everything rides on this...no time for selfish games...*

The missive turned into a tirade and her empty stomach churned. She screwed up the paper and let it fall. Thanks to Donato's intervention she'd had no contact with her father for weeks and had almost forgotten how he made her feel. Now her flesh crawled as if someone had dropped a bucket of spiders onto her back.

Ella turned to the oversized garment bag the housekeeper had hung in Donato's dressing room. She didn't want to look. She knew it would be a mistake. There would be no wedding. Yet...how could she resist peeking at the dress created for her by one of the country's top designers?

She pulled off the protective covers and stood back.

*This* was the dress the renowned Aurelio had designed? He'd conceived *this* based on the clothes she'd left at her father's the night of his party?

Ella cringed when she thought of her uniform trousers and shirt being measured and assessed by someone who worked only with the finest materials, the most glamorous women.

This had to be a joke.

Yet the full-length, full-skirted wedding dress mesmerised her. Strapless, it was ruched to a point at one hip and fitted to reveal an hourglass figure. Feminine contours were accentuated by a dusting of glitter from breast to knee on one side. Despite being fitted, the dress featured a ballooning froth of satin skirt that turned the gown from sultry into sultry fairy tale princess.

Ella's breath sucked in, air lodging like a weight in her lungs.

This dress was *not* her. It was ostentatiously feminine and graceful. Alluring.

True, you'd need height to carry off a dress like this. She definitely had height, but that was all.

She'd never wear such a dress. Even if she were getting married, which she wasn't. Severely she squashed the *what if* in her head, the daydream of her and Donato as a real couple, not just short-term.

Atavistic warning flared as she lifted a hand. Surely it was unlucky to try on a bridal gown for a wedding that wouldn't take place?

Curiosity won out. She'd never again get to try a designer original.

Ten minutes later she stood, her hair pinned up off her shoulders, her arms extended from her body so as not to mar the lustrous satin, soft as butter, that draped her. The fabric was slippery and fine and if she didn't know better she'd think that was a starburst of diamonds, not rhinestones, rippling down from her breast.

The dress was too long when worn barefoot and a little big. She hitched it up to cover her breasts as it sagged, but still… Ella shook her head, disbelieving. She looked—

'You're gorgeous, *cariño*. Stunning.' The low voice wrapped around her, liquefying her knees.

In the mirror her eyes met Donato's and shock reverberated. The floor moved. Surely there was a seismic shift, not simply the impact of that fathomless indigo gaze.

Ella's pulse became a thud, her breathing shallow as her mouth dried and her mind struggled to believe her eyes.

She didn't want to turn because she knew in reality that look would be surprise and lust. Yet as she watched him in the mirror, her stupid heart imagined more than desire on Donato's face. It imagined tenderness, possessiveness and something yet more profound. Something that made her tremble from her knees to her knocking heart. Something like what *she* felt.

She'd fought it for weeks, the knowledge that she wanted far more than sex and companionship from Donato. That she cared for him more deeply than she should.

*That she'd fallen head over heels for him.*

Donato advanced slowly, his eyes eating her up. She didn't turn. Here, away from the window's bright light, the fantasy lingered that he felt the same as she did.

'It's just the dress,' she croaked.

She felt more vulnerable in this wedding dress than she ever had naked. The white satin, the embodiment of all those little-girl dreams she'd never allowed herself to harbour, had undone her. Her emotions were too close to the surface. It grew harder to hide her feelings.

Yet the way he treated her, the tenderness and joy, the way he'd begun to open himself to her...all had made her hope.

Donato stopped behind her. Had he read the yearning in her eyes? Her shiver of excitement?

'It's not the dress. It's you. You're beautiful.'

Finally Ella tore her gaze away. Enough was enough.

'I shouldn't have put it on. I don't want to damage it, but I was curious. I'll send it straight back.'

'No! Leave it.'

Ella's head jerked up, her gaze snagging on his in the mirror. 'Why? I can't keep it.' She brushed her palm down the petal-soft fabric. The dress was ridiculously unsuitable for her, even without the fact she had no occasion to wear it. 'I'll tell my father.'

'Don't.' Donato frowned, his expression so forbidding she swung around to face him, layers of material swishing and swaying around her. The soft, unfamiliar weight of it reminded her she had no business playing pretend.

Face to face she read tension in his features. Far more tension than the sight of her in a wedding gown warranted.

'I have to, Donato. Don't you see? He's still going ahead with these ridiculous wedding plans. Someone has to stop him.' She breathed deep. 'I will if you won't.'

But Donato shook his head. 'The wedding plans go ahead. Nothing is to be cancelled.'

Ella stared. Surely they'd got beyond this. Donato was going to help Rob. There was nothing to fear now. Surely there was no need to pretend any more.

*Unless it wasn't pretend.*

*What if he really wanted marriage?*

*What if, like her, Donato had fallen in love?*

The thought no sooner surfaced than she dashed it, telling herself flights of fancy wouldn't help, no matter how much she wanted them to be true.

Yet, peering up into Donato's shadowed face, Ella couldn't help but wonder.

A knock sounded at the bedroom door. 'Excuse me, sir.' It was Donato's housekeeper. 'There's an urgent call for you.'

'I'll be there in a moment.' Donato's eyes didn't leave Ella's. When the footsteps retreated he spoke again, his eyes pinning her to the spot. 'The marriage goes ahead, Ella. Don't say anything to your father.'

Donato paced the study, the phone to his ear. He should feel triumph at this latest news. Soon Sanderson's business, his finances and his reputation would be non-existent.

'Excellent. You've done well bringing it together.' Yet the words ground hoarsely from Donato's constricted larynx. He felt winded, like that time in prison when he'd been ambushed and only just deflected a lethal punch to the throat.

Gone was his laser-sharp focus on retribution and Sanderson's downfall. Only dimly did he hear the rest of his manager's report. Donato's mind was on Ella.

Beautiful, glowing Ella, breathtaking in that fairy tale dress. Like a princess waiting at the altar for Prince Charming to sweep her away to their happily ever after.

Donato yanked open another button on his shirt, trying to ease the tightness in his throat.

Seeing Ella in her finery, he'd been torn between wanting to claim her and the knowledge he couldn't be the man for her. The chasm between them had never been more obvious.

He'd never contemplated taking a bride. Those everyday dreams most of the population shared—someone to love, to build a life and family with—those had never been his. They had always been the stuff of fiction, far beyond the reach of someone like him. He'd never let himself expect anything so temptingly, wonderfully ordinary.

Oh, he could have taken a wife. But the women he'd known hadn't been the sort to spend a lifetime with.

Not like Ella.

His mind blurred as realisation hit.

With Ella he wanted things he'd never allowed himself to dream of.

He might have wealth and power and a driving purpose

that had kept him focused for years. But for the first time, on the brink of achieving the one goal that had kept him alive through prison and through every setback since, he wanted what he could never have.

Ella.

He scrubbed his hand over his face.

He could have her body.

He could have her company and her laughter and her smiles for a short time. But blood would out.

He was a loner, born not even of a dysfunctional relationship but of a commercial transaction. He knew more about the ways people hurt each other than anything else.

And Ella...she wanted him now. Wanted their passion. But eventually she'd also want marriage. The white dress. The family. The settled life. The loving husband.

*Love.*

All the things that were foreign to him. All the things his birth, breeding and experience cut him off from.

He huffed out a hollow laugh that scraped his ribs. The ex-con as the ideal husband? Hardly.

And when she found out what he was really doing to her father...

She disliked Sanderson but he was still her dad. She'd never forgive the man who took him down. And as for the fact he'd used her to further his revenge scheme...

'Sorry, Donato?' It was his second in charge on the other end of the line. 'I missed that.'

Donato stopped before the glass doors to the terrace, his jaw locked, his eyes on the horizon. Yet it was Ella's face he saw in his mind's eye.

'The plans have changed. We're bringing the date forward. Forget about waiting till the end of the month.' He inhaled slowly. Once he would have savoured the moment. Now he simply needed to get it over. 'I want everything finalised today. Yes, that's right. Today. I'll call later.' He ended the call.

Was this restlessness because triumph was so near? Surely he should feel satisfaction instead of this sense of anticlimax?

As for feeling empty—he could fix that with some new project. He'd driven himself so hard and long over this that it was just the prospect of having no purpose that was foreign.

Donato grimaced. Who was he fooling? The joke was on him. He'd always been the one on the outside, looking in.

He hadn't let it bother him—the raised brows and sudden silence when he walked into a room. The people who were scared by his past. The ones titillated by it.

It hadn't mattered because he'd never wanted to belong.

Until now. When finally, in the worst possible circumstances, he'd glimpsed the real thing—real passion with a woman who, for the first time in his life, made him feel *whole*.

'Donato!' He swung around to find Ella in the doorway, breathtaking in her finery. The sight of her punched emotion hard and low into his belly.

She was flushed and unhappy. One hand gripped the top of the low-cut dress that threatened to reveal too much pale honey flesh. The other held up the wide skirt as she negotiated her way into the room, past clustering sofas.

With her hair beginning to fall about her shoulders and her diamond eyes glittering, she looked like a bride who'd just been thoroughly, satisfyingly debauched.

Donato's body tightened as he fought the knowledge that he wanted to be the man to claim her. To scandalise the wedding guests by sweeping her away from the ceremony and making her his in the most intimate way he knew. He wanted to keep her with him, not just while he concluded his schemes for her father, but into a future he couldn't even imagine. A future where they were together and he'd never be alone again.

He breathed deep and reminded himself there'd never been a place for fantasy in his world.

'Aren't you going to say anything?'

'Sorry?'

'Sorry?' She stared at him as if he'd sprouted horns. 'Is that all you can say? This is beyond a joke. You calmly announce that the wedding is going ahead and then stalk off to take a call.' She gestured wide with one hand and her dress slipped lower. Donato's gaze followed, the part of him that was primitive, unthinking male delighted. Another inch or two and—

'Are you even listening to me?'

'Of course I am, *cariño*. But don't you think it better we have this conversation when you've changed?'

Her lips pursed. 'That's the problem. I can't get the zip down and I don't want to yank it. Can you?'

On the words she turned, presenting him with her pale slender shoulders. She was so alluring, even more so when she tilted her head forward and lifted her hair. The action revealed the sweet, slender curve of her neck.

Donato exhaled slowly, assuring himself he could unzip her dress and leave it at that. His conscience, or what passed for it, warned that seducing her in her wedding dress would be a mistake. One day she'd wear it, when she found the right man.

The trouble was, thoughts like that awoke the dark violence in him that he'd buried years ago. Donato wanted to throttle that *right man*, whoever he was. He wanted to beat away any man who dared look at her.

He wanted to muss up the pristine perfection of the dress she'd never wear for him. He wanted to wreck any chance she had of finding the groom she deserved because he wanted her for himself.

'Donato? I need help here. What are you doing?'

He stepped forward, sliding one arm around her waist and pulling her near.

With an *oof* of surprise she landed against him.

She felt different. The froth of skirt ballooning around his legs, the cinched-in waist emphasising her delicious shape and the soft pure fabric under his hand reminding him that she wasn't for him. Despite being his lover, Ella was unsullied by his world and that was the way she'd stay. Their time together had been delightful but it was an aberration.

Carefully, so as not to step on her long skirt, he made himself step back. He lifted his hands to the zip.

'Donato? We need to talk.'

'I know.' His voice was grim. This would be the end. As soon as she knew... 'There. That's it.' The zip slid down. Rather than stopping after an inch, he dragged it further, relishing the way it revealed the curve of her spine.

He bent and pressed his lips to the sliver of bare flesh, inhaling sweet summer flowers.

Ella pulled away in a rustle of offended satin. It took two hands now to keep the dress up and her chin lifted as she spun to watch him through suspicious eyes. 'Don't think you can distract me like that.'

Her breath came in choppy little bursts and Donato knew he'd already succeeded in distracting her. He was tempted to stride across the space separating them and tug the dress away. Give in one last time to temptation, before reality intervened.

'You can't just tell me there's going to be a wedding then waltz off like that. According to my father's note the date's set for a few *weeks* from now! He must have sent out invitations, booked caterers, the whole lot! I have to get him to cancel. This has gone on long enough.'

'You're right. It has.'

# CHAPTER FIFTEEN

ELLA LOOKED INTO Donato's stern face and cold shivered down her spine. Cold on the outside, overheated on the inside, she felt a wave of fear.

Donato had retreated behind that old stonewalling expression she hated. She hadn't seen it in ages and it filled her with dread.

'Why don't you want me to tell him there's no wedding? Surely this game of yours is over.' He'd even agreed to ensure Rob got his money back.

Donato stiffened, his jaw hardening. Before her eyes he turned into the man she'd met at her father's party.

No, not him. Then at least, despite his air of superiority, there'd been heat in his gaze and a flash of humour, even if it had been at her expense.

The man she surveyed looked dead on the inside. Ella swallowed and tasted ashes on her tongue.

'Donato, what's going on? You're frightening me.' Once she'd never have admitted it. But that was when he'd been her enemy. Now he was so much more.

'Why don't you get changed? We'll talk then.' He glanced across to the drinks trolley that he so rarely touched and Ella's heart dived. The truth was so bad he needed alcohol to deal with it?

'I prefer to talk now.'

'But your dress.' He gestured and she realised the bodice had sagged to the point of indecency.

Backing to a sofa, Ella subsided with a puff of satin skirts. 'That can wait. I want to know. *Now.*' The need to understand had become urgent. She'd told herself she didn't want to know about his business with her father, so long as her siblings were okay. She'd been a coward, sticking her head in the sand.

'You've been keeping something from me, haven't you?' She'd known it from the first but hadn't pushed. She'd been too caught up in dealing with her own feelings. Too busy enjoying her time with Donato.

Ella drew a fortifying breath and spread her fingers over the plush sofa. 'Come and tell me about it.'

Instantly his head reared back in rejection.

It was an instinctive movement, too quick to be deliberate, and it cut her to the core, as if he'd taken a blade to her heart.

Ella stiffened. She'd known this dress would bring bad luck. Oh, who was she fooling? This had nothing to do with the dress. Hadn't she known their relationship was on borrowed time? The mighty Donato Salazar with ordinary old Ella Sanderson!

'Just tell me, Donato! I can't stand the suspense.'

His gaze slewed to the drinks trolley then away. He ripped open a button on his shirt, shoving his palm under the collar and around the back of his neck. It was a sign of stress she'd never witnessed in him. Donato Salazar ruled his world, doing what he pleased. The idea of him stressed dried Ella's mouth.

'If you insist.' His tone was gravel. 'It's almost done anyway.'

'What's almost done?' Foreboding snaked through her.

'Your father's destruction.' Donato's gaze met hers. Those deep-set eyes looked more black than indigo. And cold. So cold Ella huddled against the cushions.

'Destruction?' The word wobbled on her tongue as her brain seized. 'No! You can't mean...' She didn't believe it.

Donato wasn't a violent man. Not any more. Passionate, yes. Strong-willed. But not violent. He'd learned from his past.

She snatched a quick breath, trying to slow her racing pulse.

'What have you done to him?' She met Donato's terrible blank look.

'I've arranged his just deserts.'

'Go on.'

'I've ruined him.'

Ella slumped back, one palm to her thudding heart. She'd known Donato wouldn't have harmed her father physically, yet relief pounded. Relief, she realised, as much for Donato as for her father.

The consequences for Donato if he'd… It didn't bear thinking about.

'Nothing to say, Ella?' He looked fierce, almost predatory with that harsh expression and his scar drawn tight down one clenched cheek. Yet there was something more too. Something that made her still.

'I'm waiting for you to explain.'

There it was again. A flicker of doubt. No, not doubt. Regret.

Ella's stomach bottomed. This was going to get worse.

'By the end of the day Reg Sanderson will have nothing. The project we were negotiating will go ahead without him.' Donato lifted his chin, daring her to protest. 'I've also acquired a number of other holdings where your father had interests or, more specifically, debts.'

'Let me guess. The debts have been called in?'

Donato nodded. 'He'll be declared bankrupt. His creditors and so-called friends won't forgive him that. He'll lose everything, including the house, the luxury cars and the cruiser.'

Strangely, Ella didn't feel as shocked as she might have done. Her father had always lived on the edge, investing in schemes other businessmen avoided. His recent desperation told its own story.

'You came to Sydney to destroy him.' It wasn't a question. It had been there for her to see from the first, if only she'd taken time to look. Donato's thinly veiled impatience with her father had obviously been more than a sense of smug superiority.

'I did.'

Ella swallowed, shifting in her seat, wondering what else she hadn't bothered to notice. 'And my brother... Rob's money? Were you genuine about getting that to him or is it gone for ever?'

Donato's eyebrows angled sharply down. 'I said I would. The money is already in his account.'

'I'm sorry.' Relief was a wave of lightness easing her tense frame. 'But I had to know.'

He lifted those impressive shoulders but there was nothing casual about his shrug. It spoke of leashed energies and raw tension. 'I understand. You grew up with a man who couldn't be relied on to keep his word.'

Ella stared, taking in the full measure of Donato's disapproval. He really...*hated* her father.

'What was I in all this?' She waved a hand at the magnificently over-the-top wedding gown spreading like a romantic dream around her. Her nipples scraped satin where she clutched the bodice tight. 'What was the wedding all about?'

For too long Donato held her gaze. Long enough for that little bubble of hope to surface again. The hope that what had obviously begun as a bad joke or part of a scheme had become something more. That Donato had come to care for her. That maybe he even wanted—

'Partly it was a diversion. It kept your father so distracted he wouldn't notice anything else.'

'And the other part?' Ella's flesh tightened across her nape. This was about *her*, not some financial scheme.

'It was the final touch that would seal his downfall.' Yet there was no satisfaction in Donato's eyes. 'I encouraged his schemes for the most grandiose society wedding. Any last cash or credit he might have had has gone on the preparations. His social standing will be destroyed when it's called off.'

'And so will the suppliers who'll be out of pocket!' The scheme was outrageous on so many levels.

Then she read Donato's expression. 'You had a plan for that, didn't you? What were you going to do? Pay them all when he couldn't?'

'Something like that.'

Ella supposed the cost was nothing to a man of his wealth. But this wasn't just about money. Her mind reeled. 'When was it going to be called off, Donato?'

He stared straight back. 'As late as possible.'

Ella nodded. 'For maximum impact.'

Finally she began to see. It wasn't just her father's money Donato wanted to take. It was his reputation, such as it was, his pride. She'd been caught up in a scheme far bigger than herself. She'd been...what was the saying?

Collateral damage.

Hurt scored deep, deeper than she'd imagined possible. Not even because of what he'd done to her father, but selfishly because of what he'd done to *her*.

She'd actually believed Donato wanted her for herself!

It wasn't easy dragging metres of ballooning satin up, especially with one hand clamped to her bodice. Ella managed it as if she'd been wrangling formal gowns all her life. Amazing what adrenalin could do.

'You used me!' She shot the words at him as she stalked forward. 'You made me a laughing stock.' And she'd let him. He'd barely had to make a move—she'd been so busy walking into his trap, falling for a man who saw her as a convenient tool. It wasn't the public humiliation that hurt, but the very private disappointment. She'd hoped—

Ella's stomach cramped and she slammed to a swaying halt as pain unravelled inside. Her eyes blurred as she realised how much she'd trusted him.

'Ella—'

'What was the plan, Donato?' Anger simmered like hot oil under her skin. 'To leave me at the altar? Would that have made you smile?'

'No!' He looked genuinely stunned. 'You weren't going to marry me. You always insisted you wouldn't.'

Ella drew a shuddery breath. The horror on Donato's face smashed the last of her stupid hopes.

*See, that's what he really thinks of us as a couple.*

The trouble was she'd begun to believe her own far-fetched dreams. She looked down at the bright glitter on the long gown. Not diamonds, of course, but cheap imitations.

'That doesn't excuse the fact you *used me*, Donato. Just as you planned to use Felicity.' Her voice shook and she snapped her mouth shut while she gathered herself. 'Whatever grudge you have against my father, did we really deserve that?'

She wanted to rage and howl. She wanted to demand he stop this pretence and become again the man she'd fallen in love with. The man who cared for her.

Except that had been a sham. An ache started in her chest, thrumming stronger with each pulse beat.

'I didn't want to hurt you, Ella.' Donato stood stiffly, his hands by his sides, keeping his distance. 'You know that. I was going to find a way to make it up to you.'

'And how, pray tell, were you going to do that?' Ella stood tall, every sinew and muscle taut with distress. 'With cash? Is that why you're paying back Rob's money? For services rendered?' The words stuck in her throat and for a frantic moment she thought they'd choke her.

'Ella.' Finally, finally, Donato moved towards her. But it was too late. She'd come to her senses. She shoved out her hand, stopping him.

'Why do you hate him so much? This isn't business... this is...'

'Retribution.'

'Sorry?'

'Retribution, for what he did to my mother.'

Ella gasped. 'You attacked the man who killed your mother. You're not saying—?'

'That Reg Sanderson had a hand in that?' Donato shook his head, his expression as grim as she'd ever seen it. 'No. Though he might just as well have.'

'I don't understand. Did my father know your mother?' Ella frowned. Was this some misunderstanding? Except Donato didn't make mistakes. Not when it mattered.

'Why don't you sit, Ella?' He moved as if to usher her to a chair.

'Just *tell* me, Donato!'

He sighed, his hand spearing through his hair. He didn't look like a man celebrating the success of his schemes. He looked like a man strung too taut.

'I doubt he ever met her. To him she was just merchandise.'

Something cold and hard slammed through Ella as Donato's words struck home. She had a bad, bad feeling.

'Go on.'

Donato turned towards the window. What did he see? The gorgeous gardens or something else?

'She didn't choose to be a prostitute, you know. She came to Australia thinking she'd be working as a chambermaid in a big hotel. The plan was to send money back to her family.'

Ella frowned. 'Your mother migrated here?' No wonder Salazar spoke Spanish fluently.

He laughed, the sound short and unamused. 'Not legally. She believed an immigration agent had sorted it before she left. She actually *paid* for the privilege. But that turned out to be a lie. She was trafficked into a brothel, brought in as a virtual slave.'

Ella put out a groping hand for support. Finding nothing she took a stumbling step to an armchair and leaned against it.

'A slave?' She'd read about such things but still it didn't seem real.

Donato's face, as stiff as cast bronze, convinced her. 'They took her passport, said she had to work for them to pay off her debt in coming to Australia.'

'Who were *they*?'

Eyes of polished stone met hers. 'Ah, that's the question. There was the man who ran the brothel, and his enforcers, but there were others behind the scheme. Others who made a fortune, exploiting women like my mother.'

Ella rubbed her hand over her breastbone to ease the painful thud of her heart. 'My father was one of them, is that what you're saying?'

She wanted to shout that it wasn't true. That he wouldn't stoop to that. But she couldn't. Everything she knew of her father pointed to the fact he'd use anyone. He had no conscience when it came to making the money he craved. Her stomach writhed.

Donato nodded. 'I'm sorry.' There was regret in his deep voice, as if he read her horror and shame.

Ella breathed hard, fighting dizziness. She felt lightheaded.

'Ella, sit down.'

He moved towards her and she shook her head. 'No. I'm all right. Tell me the rest.' She had to know it all.

'There's not much more to tell.' Yet the starkness imprinted on his features belied that. 'She was kept there for years, like many others, too scared to try going to the authorities, too ashamed to even dream about returning home.' He paused. When he spoke again his voice grated. 'I don't even know where she came from.' His gaze captured hers and the raw anguish in his eyes cut through her. 'Not even what country. She couldn't bring herself to talk of the past because she hated what she'd become. She couldn't face the thought of confronting her family with that.'

'Donato.' Ella reached out to him, but he didn't even notice. Her hand fell to her side.

What could she say? She could barely comprehend what his mother had gone through. Ella shuddered at the thought of being forced like that. No wonder Donato's mother had grabbed the chance for a 'normal' life with a man who had promised to take her away. No wonder the young Donato had been so desperate to do the right thing in their new home so they wouldn't be turned out.

Ella huddled down into the loose gown, seeking warmth yet knowing nothing could counter the chill in her bones.

'I made it my mission to find those responsible for the trafficking ring.' Once more Donato's voice was matter-of-fact, his tone clipped. 'It took years but eventually I narrowed it to two men. One had been under police investigation but died before he could be arrested. The other, your father, covered his tracks better. He was lucky too because several of the people who could testify against him died.'

'You're not saying—?'

'That he killed them? I doubt he gave them a thought. He'd moved on to build his prestigious business empire long ago.' Donato shook his head. 'No, life expectancy in that milieu isn't good. The final witness against him is an ex-prostitute, addicted to heroin. She'd be discredited in minutes in court. I've seen it before.'

Ella remembered that the case against the man who'd killed his mother had collapsed because of an unreliable witness.

'But you're *sure*?' Even as she asked, Ella knew it was fruitless. Donato wasn't the sort to leave anything to chance.

'I'm sorry, Ella.'

His gaze was steady, hiding nothing. She read sympathy and pain, and wondered if it was for her or himself.

What did it matter? This damaged them both. She wanted to go upstairs and scrub herself clean. Her father's actions tainted her.

'I can show you the evidence, if you like. It's been collected over years.'

'No. Thank you.' Ella didn't want to read the statements. She knew, deep inside, that it was true. She could ask her father, of course. He might not even deny it, might try to brazen it out.

She'd understood for years that Reg Sanderson wasn't a father to be proud of. What she knew of his business dealings didn't impress her, and then there was Rob's sudden decision not to work for him, and his absolute refusal to explain why. Ella knew he'd discovered something in their father's schemes he couldn't countenance.

'Ella, are you okay?'

It hurt to breathe. It hurt to think. It hurt, when she looked at Donato, to see that, despite his concern, he still stood aloof, keeping distance between them.

The truth lay between them. It was dark and abhorrent and it explained everything. Why he'd approached her. A distraction for her father.

An instrument of revenge.

Ella's breath seized as pain pierced her chest.

'Ella!' Donato moved towards her but she put her palm up.

'Don't,' she croaked. 'I'm fine.'

She was anything but. She doubted she'd be okay ever again. But she couldn't bear for him to touch her.

*Had* Donato seduced her just to turn the screws tighter on her father? To make his revenge sweeter?

Call her a fool, but she couldn't believe it. Donato was relentless and tough, but he wasn't cruel. Their passion had been real. After the way Donato's mother had been used by men, Ella couldn't imagine him using sex as a weapon in his schemes.

But Ella *had* been a convenient pawn in his plot. He'd kept her onside so as not to spoil the charade of a wedding. She looked at the white flounces trembling around her feet.

Whatever they'd shared was over now.

He had no need for her any more.

As for a future for them—her breath snared. How could there be? She was his enemy's daughter. That would always lie between them.

'You look like you need a drink.'

Still Donato kept his distance but Ella read the hollow look in his eyes. That was what finally stiffened her resolve.

'So do you.'

Donato shrugged. Facing Ella with the truth was every bit as bad as he'd feared. He couldn't drag his eyes from her, half-sitting on the wide arm of the chair. Her eyes looked bruised and the bright dress she clamped to her breast only emphasised the pain drawing her features tight.

Yet she kept her chin up, ready to deal with whatever else he might reveal. She really was something. Strong—unbelievably strong and decent and caring. Funny and gentle and passionate.

Her mother must have been an amazing woman to have produced a daughter like her despite Sanderson's influence.

'Can I get you something?'

She nodded. 'Something strong.'

'Whisky? Brandy?'

'Vodka. A double.'

Her chin rode even higher at his questioning look. Who was he to question? Wasn't he craving alcohol to deaden the feeling he'd destroyed something precious with his revelations?

Donato turned away, grateful for something to do. Behind him came the rustle of fabric. She must be getting more comfortable, sitting properly on that chair. Good.

His fingers didn't work properly and it took him a while to fumble the lid off the bottle and pour their drinks.

'I'm sorry to have shocked you.' The words sounded trite but it was true. He regretted causing her pain, even though she deserved to know the truth.

'Here. This should help.' He swung around, two glasses in his hands, then stopped, staring.

On the floor where Ella had been was a mound of white—her discarded dress. She must have stepped out of it and walked, naked from the room. Belatedly Donato registered the sound of movement overhead. She was in his bedroom.

His fingers tightened on the glasses.

He needed to talk with her, find out what, if anything, could be salvaged from the wreck of their relationship.

Except she'd made her feelings clear. She hadn't even wanted to share a drink with him. No doubt she couldn't bear the sight of him. He was the harbinger of doom, the man who'd destroyed her father and shattered any remaining illusions she might have had about Sanderson. He was the man who'd used her to further his schemes. He'd had no compunction about leading her on and making use of her.

No wonder she'd walked out on him.

And the dress on the floor?

He looked at the gleaming pile of pure white with its sprinkle of stardust. He'd seen Ella in it and his heart had shuddered to a stop. Not just because she was beautiful, but because he recognised how much he wanted her.

She was *his*. He felt it in the very marrow of his bones.

Donato lifted one glass and downed the double vodka, grimacing.

It took everything he had not to race up the stairs. She needed time. He owed her that at least.

His eyes turned back to the glimmering white dress on the floor, feeling as if one touch from him would mark its purity.

Ella was a world away from him. What could she possibly want with him now the truth was out?

Donato sank into a chair rather than follow his instinct and confront her. He had to allow her some privacy and dignity while she came to grips with what she'd learned.

He lifted the second glass and drank deeply. The neat alcohol burned his throat but didn't touch the arctic freeze at his heart.

He made himself sit for a long time, listening to the occasional faint sounds as Ella paced above him. Finally, when he could wait no longer, he put down the empty glasses and rose.

The empty bedroom surprised him, as did the leap of emotion in his chest. By the time he'd tried the bathroom and walk-in wardrobe and found them empty of Ella, not even a stray hairclip remaining, a clammy hand had closed around his hammering heart.

Fear. Not fear for his physical safety as he'd felt in prison, but fear like he'd known as a child. Fear that he'd lost the one person in the world who truly mattered.

# CHAPTER SIXTEEN

*Four months later*

THE DELIVERY CAME out of the blue. No note. No return address. The label was typed, impersonal.

But Donato knew.

It was from Ella. He sensed it.

Or was he kidding himself again? He'd put off leaving the Sydney house, even though he didn't have the stomach for a new project here. But he hadn't relocated back to Melbourne. Nor had he discovered anything to capture his interest.

Business didn't satisfy. Nor did any of the outdoor sports he usually revelled in.

His staff thought he was ill. But there was no medicine that could fix what ailed him.

More than once he'd picked up the phone to hire an investigator and locate Ella. It would be simple. He knew what part of Sydney she lived and worked in.

But then he'd remember her disapproval of such invasive tactics. He'd given his word he wouldn't do that to her. That promise chafed him now, when he needed so desperately to see her.

If she wanted to contact him she'd call. She had his numbers, and his address. After what he'd done it had to be her choice.

Her silence showed what choice she'd made.

Donato wrestled with the protective padding inside the delivery box and swore as he cut himself. He stopped and drew a breath. His hands were shaking. All because he imagined this was from her!

*Maldición!* What had he come to?

He grimaced and ripped the padding away. He stared. Pain banded his chest as he dragged in oxygen, then held it, shock making him forget to breathe.

Before him stood an ebony and walnut side table, subtly modern in its simplicity. Yet it gleamed with the patina only age and loving care could create.

Donato reached out to stroke the top, then the curve of one leg. The old wood was like satin. He shut his eyes and remembered the lush feel of that white bridal gown beneath his fingers and, even more exquisite, the softness of Ella's bare skin.

Had she worked on this table herself, polishing where he touched? Or had she sent it to a professional to restore? Opening his eyes, he peered at the inlaid top. There was no sign of the damage that had marred the table when Ella found it. He remembered it vividly, the day in the Blue Mountains she'd taken him antiques shopping. She'd been so happy, her eyes dancing with excitement. Her pleasure had been catching.

Donato's hand fell. He wanted that again. Ella happy. Ella with him. He *needed* it.

Revenge on Sanderson had turned to ashes in his mouth when he'd lost her. Sanderson was bankrupt, his reputation in tatters, and the police were investigating him, not for his role in people trafficking, but for fraud. But instead of completing Donato, his quest for justice and retribution made him realise how empty he was without her.

Yet he hesitated.

He didn't know if this gift was a sign she'd forgiven him or a farewell. Maybe she couldn't bear to see it and remember she'd been with him when she found it.

Nerves swarmed in his belly and his shoulders hunched tight.

Eyes on Ella's gift, he reached for the phone.

'Don't fidget or you'll spoil this make-up.' Fuzz tsked but didn't really sound annoyed. Ella had never seen her so happy.

Even tonight, before the lavish party to celebrate the opening of the tropical resort, Fuzz was relaxed, sure everything would work out. She wore a permanent smile and, for the first time, seemed utterly content. There were lots of reasons for that—having a purpose and an outlet for her creative talent, getting away from their father's influence. But, most of all, Ella put the change down to love.

She swallowed as her throat tightened. She was *not* jealous of her sister's happiness.

'I don't see why I need make-up. Or a new dress.' She fingered the dusky pink chiffon, delicate as fairy wings, fluttering around her legs as her sister fussed over Ella's hair and make-up.

'Because it's time to party.' Fuzz stood back, surveying her handiwork. 'I want you to look gorgeous.'

Ella snorted. 'Fat chance.' The closest she'd come to that had been in the ill-fated wedding dress. Instantly she clamped her mind shut against the memory.

That was over. It was time to move on. She couldn't hate Donato for bringing down her father. She'd tried for years to love Reg Sanderson but had never been able to. The news of his criminal past had been the final straw and she'd severed all ties. Bankrupt and bereft of friends, he'd slunk away from Sydney, she didn't know or care where.

As for Donato—he'd shattered her silly illusion that he really cared for her. She'd been just a convenient tool. She had no business pining for the man who'd taken advantage of her so ruthlessly. Surely she had more self-respect than that, even if she could understand his determination to ruin her father.

'Stop frowning! You'll scare the guests. There, that's better. No one can hold a candle to you when you smile.'

Ella looked up into the exquisitely delicate features of her sister and shook her head.

'It's true, Ella. You're the only person who doesn't re-alise it.' Fuzz reached for something. 'Here. One final thing to make the outfit complete. It sits high on your arm, not around your wrist.' She pressed a tissue-wrapped parcel into Ella's hand then swung away. 'Matthew will be won-dering where I am. See you soon.'

Ella unwrapped the paper and stared, agog, at the ob-ject in her hand. The light caught its facets, making it shine brilliantly. Ella's breath stopped. It couldn't be.

Of course it couldn't. It had to be a copy. The real piece, made by a world-renowned jeweller almost a century ago, featured platinum set with pink diamonds and onyx, and was forth a fortune. It had featured recently in an interna-tional sale catalogue.

Her insides squeezed as she thought of Donato and the fun they'd had poring over such catalogues.

Forcing her mind away from Donato, she pushed the bangle over her wrist and onto her upper arm. It fitted snugly.

Turning, she surveyed herself in the mirror. She looked different. Fuzz had hidden the shadows around her eyes from too many sleepless nights and the flash of the costume jewellery made her eyes sparkle. Her dress was sophisti-cated but subtle and feminine. She wished Donato could see her like this. Elegant. Happy. Getting on with her life.

For a second her lips threatened to crumple. Then she stiffened her shoulders and turned towards the door. She had a party to attend. Who knew, she might even meet some fascinating people who'd take her mind off what she'd lost.

She was halfway from her cabin to the main resort, following a path curving between lush palms, when a deep voice made her falter.

'Hello, Ella.'

Shock slammed into her. 'Donato?'

He stepped out of the shadows looking darkly charismatic and compelling. Her heart sprinted and she had to drag in a sustaining breath. Donato Salazar in a dinner jacket looked too good to be true.

'What are you doing here?'

'I was invited.'

'Invited? I didn't…' She frowned. No wonder Fuzz had raced off rather than waiting for her. When she got her hands on her sister—

'You look wonderful, *corazón.*'

'Don't.' She put out her hand to ward off his words. She didn't want those lilting Spanish endearments that turned her mind to mush and her knees to water.

Instantly the half smile curving his mouth disappeared. Tension replaced it.

'*Why* are you here?' She crossed her arms over her chest, holding in her galloping heart and the pain that welled there. Her fingers clamped on the new bangle, solid and cool against her overheated flesh.

'To talk. I needed to see you.' His deep voice wrapped around her like an embrace and she found herself leaning forward. With an effort she straightened.

'Why?' It was all she could manage. Excitement vied with nerves.

'Why did you send me the table?' he countered.

That was Donato. Straight to the point.

She swallowed. At the time it had seemed right. Yet now she was too scared to tell the truth. 'I knew you'd like it.' His gaze bored into her as if reading everything she couldn't say. 'And I've got a small flat. There wasn't room for it.'

'It's only a small table.'

She shrugged.

'Or was it because it evoked too many memories?'

'How did you—?' She clamped her lips shut. He didn't need to know she couldn't look at the table without remembering the fun they'd had together, their shared passion, the way he'd gently teased her then pleased her and always made her feel special. Until that last day when he'd shattered her illusions with the truth.

He stepped back, his eyes clouding. 'I see. It reminded you of unhappy things. Of the mistakes I made.'

Mistakes? Since when did Donato admit to mistakes? Everything he did fitted in his grand plan. Even being with her.

'Yet you accepted my gift.' He nodded to the bangle on her upper arm.

Ella started. '*Your* gift?'

'Your sister didn't tell you?'

Ella shook her head, her gaze going to the beautiful jewellery that even in this dim light managed to sparkle.

'I thought it was a copy. I had no idea!' She made to yank the armband off.

'Don't!' he barked. 'Leave it.' He drew himself up to his full height and she felt tension radiate off him, making her skin prickle. 'Think of it as a parting gift. An apology for the way I duped you. It was reprehensible of me.' He turned away, but the sight of him leaving broke her resolve.

'Wait! You can't just go like that.' Her fingers itched to reach for him but she forced her hands to her sides.

'Why not? You don't want me here.' There was something in his voice she couldn't identify. His profile was stony, his jaw tight, yet his words made her wonder.

Was she brave enough to find out?

'Donato.' She stepped closer, her breathing almost non-existent, her stomach churning. 'Tell me the truth. Why did you come?'

He tilted his head back, looking up at the darkening sky as if seeking guidance. When he swung his face towards her he'd lost that masked look. His expression was passionately alive, eyes gleaming and mouth twisted with pain.

Ella stared, shocked.

'To see you.'

'To apologise?' Donato took duty seriously. He'd used her and knew she deserved an apology. Stupidly her heart shrank at the idea of her being no more than a duty to be ticked off his list.

'That too. I should be on my knees grovelling, shouldn't I?'

'That too?' What else could there be? Her eyes grew rounder as he paced close, filling her vision.

'I came because I had to know how you feel about me.' He stopped and cleared his throat. His nostrils dilated as he dragged in a deep breath and it struck her he looked almost nervous. She must be projecting her own feelings.

'Everything is different without you. I can't—' He rubbed has hand across the back of his neck in a gesture of unease she'd seen him use only once before.

The butterflies in her belly became seagulls, whirling and swooping.

'What can't you do, Donato?' She clasped her hands tight together, barely noticing them tremble.

'I can't settle. I can't work.' With one more stride he was before her, taking her hands in his. They felt big and warm and tantalisingly familiar. An ache started up in the back of her throat and Ella told herself not to be foolish, but she couldn't help it. Hope was a tiny flame deep inside.

'I want you back, Ella. I need you.' He planted her palm

on his chest, his own hand covering it, pressing it down so she felt the quickened thud of his heart.

'I know you've no reason to want me after I destroyed your father and lied to you. I know you're going to send me away.' He paused and she saw his Adam's apple bob above his suave bow tie. 'But I had to be absolutely certain because I love you. And if there's one thing I know it's that love, true love, is a rare and precious thing. It shouldn't be ignored.'

Dumbfounded, Ella stared up into a face ravaged by emotion. The strong man she knew looked…unravelled.

'You can't love me.' It was a whisper of disbelief and awe.

The laugh that jerked out of him held no humour. 'Of course I can. Though I understand you hating me or believing a man like me can't love.' A frown ploughed his brow.

'A man like you?' She shook her head, still stuck on the word *love*. He loved *her*? Was it possible?

'A criminal. A man whose mother sold herself for money. Who grew up in places that would horrify you. Who—'

Ella's hand on his mouth stopped the dreadful words. His lips felt tantalisingly familiar on her sensitive palm. Slowly she pulled her hand away.

'Don't say such things. That's not who you are.' Her lungs felt too tight, clamped by unseen bands. 'It's not your past that defines you, Donato. You've made yourself the man you are today. You're respected and admired. You're generous and hardworking. And if it wasn't love you felt for your mother, I don't know what love is.'

It still broke her heart, thinking of him as a child, separated from his mother and running away to find her, again and again.

She blinked up into indigo eyes that shone with unabashed emotion. This close to him she felt the tremors running through his tall frame and the racing thud of his heart under her other hand.

'Everything you did, you did because you loved her. She must have been a special woman to inspire such devotion.'

Donato's eyes widened. To her amazement they looked over-bright. Then powerful arms scooped her against him, holding her to his heart. He planted his hand in her hair and Ella's eyes sank shut at the overload of pleasure: his fingers massaging her scalp, his body hard and strong against hers, the warm scent of his skin in her nostrils and the sound of his voice, rich and low, murmuring endearments in Spanish.

Ella couldn't help herself. She leaned into him, revelling in each sensation. In the tenderness of his embrace. In the love she heard in his voice.

*Love!* For her?

'You're an amazing woman, Ella. No other woman would think that way.'

She'd tried to hate him for the way he'd used her, but through the tearing pain, the anguish of discovering the truth, she'd found she couldn't. Her feelings for him couldn't be squashed, no matter how she tried, especially since she understood the darkness and pain that had driven him. How far would she have gone if she'd been in his shoes?

Now to discover Donato loved her, that he didn't believe himself worthy of her...

'No other woman loves you.' She wrapped her arms around him, hugging tight, trying to burrow as close as possible.

The big hand on her scalp stilled.

'What?' Beneath her cheek his heart hit a new beat.

Ella sucked in air scented with coffee and man and shivered at this intimacy she'd thought she'd never experience again. 'I love you, Donato. I—'

Her words cut off as he stepped back, cupping her cheeks in his hands and leaning down to watch her face.

'Say that again.'

Heat rose in her cheeks. 'I love—'

This time it was his lips that stopped her words. She didn't mind because he gathered her close, exactly where she wanted to be, his mouth working magic.

She strained up into him, pouring out all she felt, hoped and yearned for. And she was rewarded a thousandfold as Donato's kiss spoke of passion and tenderness and wonder. And love—the love she hadn't dared expect.

When they pulled apart enough to breathe Donato swiped the back of his hand across his eyes.

'You unman me, *preciosa*.'

Ella pressed closer against his aroused maleness. 'Of course I don't.'

He laughed and looked down at her with brilliant eyes. 'You make me *feel* things I'm not used to feeling. I haven't cried since I was a kid.'

Ella's heart turned over in her ribcage. Maybe if he'd learned earlier to cope with his emotions he would have found ways to deal with his anger and loss sooner. But he'd got there now.

'I like a man who's in touch with his feelings.' She gazed up at him, still unable to believe he was here and that he loved her. 'But are you sure?'

'About what, *cariño*?'

She closed her eyes as that liquid caress traced warmth across her bare arms and shoulders. She breathed deep then looked into his penetrating gaze.

'About loving me. I'm Reg Sanderson's daughter.'

'No one could blame you for your father's actions. You're as different from him as it's possible to be.' Donato's tender expression was balm to the soul. 'I've been falling for you since that first night. It confused me to want you so much, not just in my bed, but in every way. I've never wanted a woman like I want you, Ella. I want to be with you, grow old with you. Watch our children grow and have children of their own.'

'You do?' She blinked.

'Why do you think I'm here? It almost destroyed me when you walked out but I knew I'd hurt you. I didn't have the right to ask you to give me a second chance.'

'Yet you came.'

He nodded. 'When I got your gift I had to know.' He hefted in a deep breath, frowning. 'I haven't even apologised properly for what I did to you. I was selfish. I should never have—'

Ella stood on tiptoe and planted a kiss full on his mouth. With a groan he sank into her, hauling her close. Every nerve quivered with delight at being kissed by the man she loved. The man who loved her.

'There's time enough for apologies later,' she gasped when they finally broke apart. 'Apologies and explanations are important but right now I'm having trouble believing this is real. I forgive you, Donato, and I love you with all my heart. I just want to bask in happiness.'

Donato's smile transformed his face, banishing lingering shadows. He was the most breathtaking man she'd ever known and he held her heart in his hand.

'Don't worry, Ella. I have plans to make you happy for the rest of your life.' He hesitated. 'If you're sure...'

'I'm absolutely sure.' What she felt for Donato was unique. They were meant to be. 'I intend to work at making you happy too.'

'You already make me the happiest man alive.' His smile was the best thing she'd seen in her life. Yet his eyes were serious. 'You make me want to be a better man, Ella. To be someone you can be proud of.'

'You already are, Donato. I respect you more than any man I know.'

His eyes glowed. 'I've never known a woman of such

honesty and integrity, Ella. Or such passion. I never want to let you go.' He gathered her in and she sank against him, her soul soaring.

She sighed as the sound of music reached them. 'The others are expecting us. I promised I'd be there for their special night.'

'*Our* special night too.' Slowly he stepped back, lacing his fingers through hers. 'Come on, let's go and help your family celebrate. I have to thank them for trusting me enough to invite me here.'

'You want to spend the evening at a party?' Ella pouted and instantly Donato swooped down and claimed her lips in a kiss as brief and powerful as lightning. It left her quivering.

'I've booked the honeymoon suite,' he said in that rumbly deep voice that always turned her internal organs to mush. 'I thought we could make an appearance at the party then go back there. I still have those apologies to make. And after that I can begin.'

'Begin?' Ella was having trouble getting her brain to function after that devastating kiss.

'Courting you, Ms Sanderson. I want you to know my intentions are completely honourable.'

'Completely?' Her mouth turned down in mock disappointment, even as her blood fizzed with excitement.

Donato leaned closer. A smile lurked at the corner of his mouth but it was the love in his eyes that stole her breath. 'Almost completely.'

Then he kissed her again and she forgot all about talking.

\* \* \* \* \*

# SURRENDERING TO THE VENGEFUL ITALIAN

**ANGELA BISSELL**

*For Tony. Because you never stopped believing.*
*And you never let me quit.*
*Love you to infinity, Mr B.*


*And for Mum. The memories have left you but*
*our love never will.*
*You are, and always will be, our real-life*
*heroine.*

# CHAPTER ONE

HELENA SHAW HAD been sitting in the elegant marble foyer for the best part of two hours when the man she had trekked halfway across London to see finally strode into the exclusive Mayfair hotel.

She had almost given up. After all the effort she had devoted to tracking him down, she had almost lost her nerve. Had almost let cowardice—and the voice in her head crying *insanity*—drive her out of the plush upholstered chair and back into the blessed obscurity of the crowded rush-hour streets.

But she had not fled. She had sat and waited—and waited some more.

*And now he was here.*

Her stomach dropped, weightless for a moment as though she had stepped from a great height into nothingness, and then the fluttering started—a violent sensation that made her belly feel like a cage full of canaries into which a half-starved tomcat had been loosed.

*Breathe*, she instructed herself, and watched him stride across the foyer, tall and dark and striking in a charcoal-grey two-piece that screamed *power suit* even without the requisite tie around his bronzed throat.

Women stared.

Men stepped out of his way.

And he ignored them all, his big body moving with an air of intent until, for one heart-stopping moment, his footsteps slowed on the polished marble and he half turned in her direction, eyes narrowed under a sharp frown as he surveyed the hotel's expansive interior.

Helena froze. Shrouded in shadows cast by soft lighting and half hidden behind a giant spray of exotic honey-scented blooms, she was certain he couldn't see her, yet for one crazy moment she had the unnerving impression he could somehow sense her scrutiny. Her very presence. As if, after all these years, they were still tethered by an invisible thread of awareness.

A crack of thunder, courtesy of the storm the weathermen had been promising Londoners since yesterday, made Helena jump. She blinked, pulled in a sharp breath and let the air out with a derisive hiss. She had no connection with this man. Whatever bond had existed between them was long gone, destroyed by her father and buried for ever in the ashes of bitterness and hurt.

A hurt Leonardo Vincenti would soon revisit on her family if she failed to stop him seizing her father's company.

She grabbed her handbag and stood, her pulse picking up speed as she wondered if he would see her. But he had already resumed his long strides towards the bank of elevators. She hurried after him, craning her neck to keep his dark head and broad shoulders in her line of sight. Not that she'd easily lose him in a crowd. He stood out from the pack—that much hadn't changed—though he seemed even taller than she remembered, darker somehow, the aura he projected now one of command and power.

Her stomach muscles wound a little tighter.

Europe's business commentators had dubbed him the success of the decade: an entrepreneurial genius who'd turned a software start-up into a multi-million-dollar enterprise in less than ten years and earned a coveted spot on the rich list. The more reputable media sources called him single-minded and driven. Others dished up less flattering labels like hard-nosed and cut-throat.

Words that reminded Helena too much of her father. Yet even *hard-nosed* and *cut-throat* seemed too mild, too charitable, for a man like Douglas Shaw.

She shouldered her bag, clutched the strap over her chest.

Her father was a formidable man, but if the word *regret* existed in his vocabulary he must surely rue the day he'd aimed his crosshairs at Leonardo Vincenti. Now the young Italian he'd once decreed unsuitable for his daughter was back, seven years older, considerably wealthier and, by all accounts, still mad as hell at the man who'd run him out of town.

He stopped, pushed the button for an elevator and shoved his hands in his trouser pockets. Behind him, Helena hovered so close she could see the fine weave in the fabric of his jacket, the individual strands of black hair curling above his collar.

She sucked in a deep breath. 'Leo.'

He turned, his dark brows rising into an arch of enquiry that froze along with the rest of his face the instant their gazes collided. His hands jerked out of his pockets. His brows plunged back down.

'What the hell...?'

Those three words, issued in a low, guttural growl, raised the tiny hairs on her forearms and across her nape. *He'd recognised her, then.*

She tilted her head back. In her modest two-inch heels she stood almost five foot ten, but still she had to hike her chin to lock her gaze with his.

And oh, sweet mercy, what a gaze it was.

Dark. Hard. Glittering. Like polished obsidian and just as impenetrable. How had she forgotten the mind-numbing effect those midnight eyes could have on her?

*Concentrate.*

'I'd like to talk,' she said.

A muscle moved in his jaw, flexing twice before he spoke. 'You do not own a phone?'

'Would you have taken my call?'

He met her challenge with a smile—if the tight, humourless twist of his lips could be called a smile. 'Probably not. But then you and I have nothing to discuss. On the phone *or* in person.'

An elevator pinged and opened behind him. He inclined his head in a gesture she might have construed as polite if not for the arctic chill in his eyes.

'I am sorry you have wasted your time.' And with that he swung away and stepped into the elevator.

Helena hesitated, then quickly rallied and dashed in after him. 'You've turned up after seven years of silence and come after my father's company. I hardly think that qualifies as *nothing*.'

'Get out of the elevator, Helena.'

The soft warning made the skin across her scalp prickle. Or maybe it was hearing her name spoken in that deep, accented baritone that drove a wave of discomforting heat through her?

The elevator doors whispered closed, cocooning them in a space that felt too small and intimate despite the effect of mirrors on three walls.

She planted her feet. 'No.'

Colour slashed his cheekbones and his dark eyes locked with hers in a staring match that quickly tested the limits of her bravado. Just as she feared that lethal gaze would reduce her to a pile of cinders, he reached into the breast pocket of his jacket and pulled out an access card.

'As you wish,' he said, his tone mild—*too mild*, a voice warned. He flashed the card across a sensor and jabbed the button labelled 'Penthouse Suite'. With a soft whir, the elevator began its stomach-dropping ascent.

Helena groped for the steel handrail behind her, the rapid rising motion—or maybe the butterflies in her belly she couldn't quell—making her head swim.

It seemed her ex-lover could not only afford the finest digs in London…he could afford to stay in the hotel's most exclusive suite.

The knowledge made her heart beat faster.

The Leo she'd known had been a man of understated tastes, stylish in that effortless way of most Italian men but never flashy or overt. She'd liked that about him. Liked his grit and drive and passion. Liked that he was different from the lazy, spoilt rich set her parents wanted her to run with.

And now…?

Her hand tightened on the railing. Now it didn't matter what she felt about him. All that mattered was the havoc he'd soon unleash on her family. If he and her father went head to head in a corporate war and Douglas Shaw lost control of his precious empire the fallout for his wife and son would be dire. Her father didn't take kindly to losing; when he did, those closest to him suffered.

'Has your father sent you?' The way he ground out the word *father* conveyed a wealth of hatred—a sentiment Helena, too, wrestled with when it came to Daddy Dearest.

She studied Leo's face, leaner now, his features sharper, more angular than she remembered, but still incredibly handsome. Her fingers twitched with the memory of tracing those features while he slept, of familiarising herself with that long, proud nose and strong jaw, those sculpted male lips. Lips that once could have stopped her heart with a simple smile—or a kiss.

Emotion rose and swirled, unexpected, a poignant mix of regret and longing that made her chest ache and her breath hitch.

Did Leo smile much these days? Or did those lines either side of his mouth stem from harsher emotions like anger and hatred?

Instinctively Helena's hand went to her stomach. The void inside where life had once flourished was a stark reminder that she, too, had suffered. Leo, at least, had been spared that pain, and no good would come now of sharing hers.

Some burdens, she had decided, were better borne alone. She let her hand fall back to her side.

'I'm not my father's puppet, Leo. Whatever your misguided opinion of me.'

A harsh sound shot from his throat. 'The only one misguided is you, Helena. What part of "I never wish to see you again" did you not understand?'

She smothered the flash of hurt his words evoked. 'That was a long time ago. And I only want an opportunity to talk. Is that asking too much?'

A soft ping signalled the elevator's arrival. Before he could answer with a resounding *yes*, she stepped through the parting doors into a spacious vestibule. She stopped, the sensible heels of her court shoes sinking into thick carpet the colour of rich chocolate. Before her loomed an enormous set of double doors. It was private up here, she realised. Secluded. *Isolated.*

Her mouth went dry. 'Perhaps we should talk in the bar downstairs?'

He brushed past her and pushed open the heavy doors, his lips twisting into a tight smile that only made her heart pound harder.

'Afraid to be alone with me?'

Helena paused on the threshold. *Should* she be afraid of him? In spite of her jitters she balked at the idea. Leonardo Vincenti wasn't thrilled to see her—that was painfully clear—but she knew this man. Had spent time with him. Been intimate with him in ways that marked her soul like no other man ever had.

Yes, she could sense the anger vibrating beneath his cloak of civility, but he would never lose control and lash out at her. He would never hurt her the way her father hurt her mother.

She smoothed her palm down the leg of her black trouser suit and assumed a lofty air. 'Don't be ridiculous,' she said, and strode into the room.

Leo closed the penthouse doors, strode to the wet bar and splashed a large measure of whisky into a crystal tumbler. He knocked back the potent liquid, snapped the empty glass onto the bar and looked at the woman whose presence was like a blowtorch to his veneer of calm.

'Drink?'

'No.' She reinforced her refusal with a shake of her head that made her auburn curls bounce and sway. 'But... thank you.'

Shorter, he noted. Her hair was shorter, the dark silky ribbons that had once tumbled to her waist now cropped into a sophisticated cut above her shoulders. Her face, too, had changed—thinner like her body and more striking somehow, her cheekbones strong and elegant, her jaw line firm. Bluish crescents underscored her eyes, but the rest of her skin was toned and smooth and free of imperfections. It was a face no man, unless blind, would pass by without stopping for a second appreciative look.

Helena Shaw, he reluctantly acknowledged, was no longer a pretty girl. Helena Shaw was a stunningly attractive woman.

Scowling, he reminded himself he had no interest in this woman's attributes, physical or otherwise. He'd been blindsided by her beauty and guise of innocence once before—a grave error that had cost him infinitely more than his injured pride—and he'd vowed his mistake would not be repeated.

Not with any woman.

And especially not this one.

'So, you want to talk.' The *last* thing he wanted to do with this woman. *Dio.* He should have bodily removed her from the elevator downstairs and to hell with causing a scene. He banked the flare of anger in his gut and gestured towards a duo of deep leather sofas. 'Sit,' he instructed, then glanced at his watch. 'You have ten minutes.'

She frowned—a delicate pinch of that smooth brow—then put her bag on the glass coffee table and perched on the edge of a sofa. She drew an audible breath.

'The papers say you've launched a hostile takeover bid for my father's company.'

He dropped onto the opposite sofa. 'An accurate summary.' He paused. 'And...?'

She puffed out a sigh. 'You're not going to make this easy for me, are you?'

*Easy?* That simple four-letter word made him grind his molars. This girl's entire life had been easy. Her family's excessive wealth, her father's connections, had ensured she wanted for nothing. Unlike Leo and his sister who, after their mother's death, had survived childhood in a murky world of poverty and neglect. For them, nothing came easy.

'You want me to make this easy for you?'

*Like hell he would.*

She shook her head. 'I want to understand why you're doing this.'

So she could talk him out of it? Not a chance. He'd waited too many years to settle this score with her father. He returned her gaze for an extended beat. 'It's business.'

She laughed then: a short brittle sound, not the soft, sexy laughter that resided in his memory. 'Please—this isn't business. It's...payback.'

Her voice conveniently wobbled on that last word, but her ploy for sympathy, if that was her angle, failed to move him.

'And if I said this *is* payback, what would you say?'

'I'd say two wrongs don't make a right.'

He barked out a laugh. 'A quaint sentiment. Personally, I think "an eye for an eye" has a more appealing ring.'

She dropped her gaze to where her fingers fidgeted in her lap. Her voice was husky when she spoke again. 'People aren't perfect, Leo. Sometimes they make mistakes.'

His gut twisted. Was she talking about her father? Or herself? 'So you're here to apologise for your mistakes?'

She glanced up. 'I tried that once. You didn't want to listen. Would it make any difference now?'

'No.'

'I was trying to protect you.'

He bit back another laugh. By driving a blade through his heart? Leaving him no choice but to watch her walk away? A bitter lump rose in his throat and he swallowed back the acrid taste.

Seven years ago he'd come to London to collaborate with a young software whiz on a project that, if successful, would have guaranteed his business unprecedented success.

As always, he was focused, dedicated, disciplined.

And then he met a girl.

A girl so beautiful, so captivating, she might have been one of the sculptures on display at the art gallery opening they were both attending in the West End.

He tried to resist, of course. She was too young for him, too inexperienced. Too distracting when he should be focused on work.

But he was weak and temptation won out. And he fell— faster than he'd ever thought possible—for a girl who, five weeks later, tossed him aside as if he were a tiresome toy she no longer wanted or needed.

He curled his lip. 'Remind me not to come looking for you if I ever need protection.'

She had the good grace to squirm. 'I had no choice. You don't understand—'

'Then explain it to me.' Anger snapped in his gut, making him fight to stay calm. 'Explain why you walked away from our relationship instead of telling me the truth. Explain why you never bothered to mention that your father disapproved of us. Explain why, if ditching me was your idea of *protection*, I spent the next forty-eight hours watching every investor I'd painstakingly courted pull their backing from my project.'

He curled his fingers into his palms, tension arcing through his muscles. Douglas Shaw had dealt Leo's business a significant blow, yet his own losses had barely registered in comparison to the impact on his younger sister. Marietta's life, his hopes and dreams for her future, had suffered a setback the likes of which Helena could never appreciate.

*Sorry* didn't cut it.

'Perhaps you wanted an easy out all along—'

'No.'

'And Daddy simply gave you the perfect excuse.'

'No!'

There was more vehemence behind that second denial than he'd expected. She threw him a wounded look and he shifted slightly, an unexpected stab of remorse lancing through him. *Hell*. This was precisely why he'd had no desire to see her. Business demanded a cool head, a razor-sharp mind at all times. Distractions like the beautiful long-legged one sitting opposite him he could do without.

A lightning flash snapped his gaze towards the private terrace overlooking Hyde Park and the exclusive properties of Knightsbridge beyond. His right leg twitched with an urge to rise and test the French doors, check they were secure. He didn't fear nature's storms—on occasion could appreciate their power—but he didn't like them either.

Didn't like the ghosts they stirred from his childhood.

A burst of heavy rain lashed the glass, drowning out the city sounds far below. Distorting his view of the night. He waited for the rumble of thunder to pass, then turned his attention from the storm. 'How much has your father told you about the takeover?'

'Nothing. I only know what I've read in the papers.'

Another lie, probably. He let it slide. 'Then you are missing one important detail.'

Her fidgeting stilled. 'Which is…?'

'The word "successful". In fact…' He hooked back his shirt-cuff and consulted his watch. 'As of two hours and forty-five minutes ago my company is the official registered owner of seventy-five percent of ShawCorp.' He offered her a bland smile. 'Which means I am now the controlling shareholder of your father's company.'

He watched dispassionately as the colour receded from her cheeks, leaving her flawless skin as white as the thick-pile rug at her feet. She pressed her palm to her forehead, her upper body swaying slightly, and closed her eyes.

A little theatrical, he thought, the muscles around his mouth twitching. He shifted forward, planted his elbows on his knees. 'You look a touch pale, Helena. Would you like that drink now? A glass of water, perhaps. Some aspirin?'

Her lids snapped up and a spark of something—anger?—leapt in her eyes, causing them to shimmer at him like a pair of brilliant sapphires.

Leo sucked in his breath. The years might have wrought subtle differences in her face and figure, but those eyes... those eyes had not changed. They were still beautiful. Still captivating.

*Still dangerous.*

Eyes, he reminded himself, that could strip a man of his senses.

They glittered at him as she raised her chin.

'Water, please.' She gave him a tight smile. 'You can hold the aspirin.'

Helena reached for the glass Leo had placed on the table in front of her and sipped, focusing on the cold tickle of the carbonated water on her tongue and throat and nothing else. She would not faint. Not in front of this man. Shock on top of an empty stomach had left her woozy, that was all. She simply needed a moment to compose herself.

After a third careful sip she put the glass down and folded her hands in her lap. She mustn't reveal her turmoil. Mustn't show any hint of anxiety as her mind darted from one nauseating scenario to the next. Had her father hit the bottle in the wake of this news? Was her mother playing the devoted wife, trying to console him? And how long before the lethal combination of rage and drink turned him from man to monster? To a vile bully who could lavish his wife with expensive trinkets and luxuries one minute and victimise her the next?

Helena's insides trembled, but it wasn't only worry for her mother making her belly quiver. Making her pulse-rate kick up a notch. It was an acute awareness of the man sitting opposite. An unsettling realisation that, no matter how many days, weeks or years came between them, she would never be immune to this tall, breathtaking Italian. She would never look at him and not feel her blood surge. Her lungs seize. Her belly tighten.

No. Time had *not* rendered her immune to his particular potent brand of masculinity. But she would not let her body betray her awareness of him. If her father's endless criticisms and lack of compassion had taught her anything as a child it was never to appear weak.

She laced her fingers to keep them from fidgeting. 'What are your plans for my father's company?'

A muscle in his jaw bunched and released. Bunched again. He lounged back, stretched out his long legs, draped one arm across the top of the sofa. 'I haven't yet decided.'

She fought the urge to scowl. 'But you must have some idea.'

'Of course. Many, in fact. All of which I'll discuss with your father, once he overcomes his aversion to meeting with me.' He paused. 'Perhaps he's hoping his daughter will offer his new shareholder some…incentive to play nice?'

Heat rushed her cheeks, much to her annoyance. 'I don't know what you mean.'

'Oh, come now. There's no need to play the innocent for me.'

Leo's hand moved absently over the back of the sofa, his fingers stroking the soft black leather in slow, rhythmic patterns. Helena stared, transfixed, then hastily averted her eyes. Those long, tanned fingers had once stroked her flesh in a strikingly similar fashion, unleashing in her a passion no man had unleashed before or since.

She pulled in a breath, tried to focus on his voice.

'You needn't look so worried, Helena. You won't have to dirty your hands with the likes of me again.' His fingers stilled. 'I have no interest in anything you could offer.'

As though emphasising his point, his gaze travelled her length, from the summit of her blushing hairline to the tips of her inexpensive shoes. 'As for the company,' he went on, before she could muster an indignant response, 'if your father continues to decline my invitations to meet, my board will vote to sell off the company's subsidiaries and amalgamate the core business with my own. A merger will mean layoffs, of course, but your father's people will find I'm not an unreasonable man. Those without jobs can expect a fair severance settlement.'

Her jaw slackened. 'Dismantle the company?' The one thing guaranteed to bring her father to his knees. 'You would tear down everything my father has worked his entire life to build?'

He shrugged. 'As a minority shareholder he'll benefit financially from any asset sales. He'll lose his position at the head of the company, of course, but then your father's no longer a man in his prime. Perhaps he'll welcome the opportunity to retire?'

She shook her head. For Douglas Shaw it wasn't about the money. Or retirement. It was about pride and respect and status. About winning. *Control.*

'You don't understand.' Her voice trembled. 'This won't hurt only my father. It will hurt others, too—my family. Is that what you want, Leo? To see innocent people suffer?'

His eyes narrowed, his gaze hardening under his dark slanted brows. 'Do not talk to *me* about suffering. You and your family don't know the first meaning of the word.'

*Not true!* she wanted to shout, but she held her tongue. Another habit deeply ingrained from childhood, when she'd been taught to avoid such indiscretions—to lie, if necessary, about her less than perfect home life.

She stifled a frustrated sigh.

Why did people think growing up with money meant a life filled with sunshine and roses? That might have been the case for some of her friends, but for Helena it had been nothing more than a grand, sugar-coated illusion. An illusion her mother, the ever-dutiful society wife, still chose to hide behind.

Leo lunged his powerful shoulders forward, planted both feet firmly on the floor. 'This is business. Your father knows that. Better than most.'

He rose to his full impressive height: six feet four inches of lean, muscled Italian.

'I could have made things much worse for him. You might remind him of that fact.'

For a moment Helena considered telling him the truth—that she'd not seen or spoken with her father in years. That she worked as a secretary and lived in a rundown flat in North London and visited her family only when her father was absent on business. That Douglas Shaw was a domineering bully and she didn't care a jot for the man, but she did care for those who would suffer most from his downfall. That she held no sway with her father and could offer Leo nothing in return for leniency except her eternal gratitude.

But caution stopped her. The man who stood before her now was not the Leo she'd once known. He was a tough, shrewd businessman, bent on revenge, and he would use every weapon in his arsenal to achieve it. Knowledge was power, and he had plenty of that without her gifting him extra ammunition.

Besides, he'd already accused her of lying—why should he believe the truth?

She unlaced her hands and stood.

'There must be other options,' she blurted. 'Other possibilities that would satisfy your board and keep the company intact?'

'My board will make their decisions based on the best

interests of my business. Not your father's interests and not his family's.' He looked at his watch. 'Now, if you have nothing else to discuss, there are more important matters requiring my attention.'

She stared at him.

*More important matters?*

A bitter laugh rose and died in her throat.

Really, what had she expected? Understanding? Forgiveness? A friendly chat over a cup of tea?

Humiliation raged through her. She was a fool, wasting her time on a fool's errand. She snatched up her handbag. 'Next time you look in the mirror, Leo, remind yourself why you despise my father so much.' She returned his stony stare. 'Then take a hard look at your reflection. Because you might just find you have more in common with him than you think.'

His head snapped back, an indication that she'd hit her mark, but the knowledge did nothing to ease the pain knifing through her chest. Head high, she strode to the door.

The handle was only inches from her grasp when a large hand closed on her upper arm, swinging her around. She let out a yelp of surprise.

'I am *nothing* like your father,' he said, his jaw thrusting belligerently.

'Then prove it,' she fired back, conscious all at once of his vice-like grip, the arrows of heat penetrating her thin jacket-sleeve, the faint, woodsy tang of an expensive cologne that made her nostrils flare involuntarily. 'Give my father time to come to the table. Before your board makes any decisions.'

Leo released her, stepped back, and the tiny spark of hope in her chest fizzed like a dampened wick. God. She needed to get out. *Now.* Before she did something pathetic and weak—like cry. She pivoted and seized the door handle. At the same instant his palm landed on the door above her head, barring her escape.

'On one condition.'

His voice at her back was low, laced with something she couldn't decipher. She turned, pressed her back to the door and looked up. 'Yes?'

'Have dinner with me.'

She blinked, twice. Three times.

'Dinner?' she echoed stupidly.

'*Si.*' His hand dropped from the door. 'Tomorrow night.'

Her stomach did a funny little somersault. Was he fooling with her now? She narrowed her eyes at him. 'Is that an invitation or a demand?'

The shrug he gave was at once casual and arrogant. 'Call it what you like. That is my condition.'

'Tomorrow's Friday,' she said, as if that fact bore some vital significance. In truth, it was all she could think to say while her brain grappled with his proposition.

His nostrils flared. 'You have other plans?'

'Uh...no.' *Brilliant.* Now he'd think she had no social life. She levelled her shoulders. 'A minute ago you couldn't wait to get rid of me. Now you want us to have dinner?'

His lips pressed into a thin line. Impatience? Or, like most men, did he simply dislike having his motives questioned?

He jammed his hands in his trouser pockets. 'You wanted an opportunity to talk, Helena. Take it or leave it. It is my final offer. I return to Rome on Saturday.'

Helena hesitated, her mind spinning. This could be her one and only chance for a calm, rational conversation with him. An opportunity to appeal to his sense of reason and compassion—if either still existed. The takeover was beyond her control and, if he spoke the truth, a *fait accompli*, but if she had even a slim chance of dissuading him from stripping the company's assets, convincing him to settle on a strategy more palatable to her father, she had to take it. Had to try, no matter how daunting the prospect.

She nodded. 'All right. Dinner. Tomorrow night. Where shall I meet you?'

'I will send a car.'

Her stomach nose-dived. The thought of Leo or anyone in his employ seeing where she lived mortified her. Her neighbourhood was the best she could afford right now, but the area was far from salubrious.

She fished in her handbag for pen and paper, jotted down her work address and her mobile number. 'You can pick me up from here.' She handed him the slip of paper. 'And my number's there if you need to contact me.'

'Very well.' With scarcely a glance at it, he slipped the note into his trouser pocket and pulled open the door. 'Be ready for six-thirty.'

With a nod, she stepped into the vestibule and pressed the elevator call button, having briefly considered then dismissed the stairs.

She would *not* bolt like an intimidated child.

The man who'd stolen her heart and left behind a precious gift she'd treasured and lost might be gone, the stranger in his place more formidable than she'd imagined, but she would *not* be cowed.

Ignoring the compulsion to glance over her shoulder, she willed the elevator to hurry up and arrive. When it did, her knees almost buckled with relief. She started forward.

'Helena.'

Leo's voice snapped her to an involuntary halt. Without turning, she braced her arm against the elevator's door jamb and tilted her head fractionally. 'Yes?'

Silence yawned behind her, turning the air so thick it felt like treacle in her lungs.

'Wear something dressy,' he said at last.

And then he shut the door.

# CHAPTER TWO

Leo PICKED UP the half-empty water glass and studied the smudge of pink on its rim. *Had Douglas Shaw sent his daughter as a honey trap?* The idea was abhorrent, yet he wouldn't put it past the man. What Shaw lacked in scruples he more than made up for with sheer, bloody-minded gall.

He crossed to the bar, tossed out the water and shoved the glass out of sight along with the whisky bottle. Then he smashed his palms down on the counter and let out a curse.

He should have let her go. Should have let her walk out of here and slammed the door—physically and figuratively—on their brief, discomfiting reunion.

But standing there watching her strut away, after she'd stared him down with those cool sapphire eyes and likened him to her father; seeing the haughty defiance in every provocative line of her body...

Something inside him had snapped and he was twenty-five again, standing in a different room in a different hotel. Watching the girl who'd carved out a piece of his heart turn her back and walk out of his life.

Bitterness coated his mouth. He opened the bar fridge, reached past a black-labelled bottle of Dom Perignon and a selection of fine wines and beers and grabbed a can of soda.

At twenty-five he'd considered himself a good judge of character—a skill honed during his teens, when looking out for his sister, taking on the role of parent during their father's drink-fuelled absences, meant learning who he could trust and who he couldn't. Over the years he developed strong instincts, avoided his father's mistakes and weaknesses, but Helena remained his one glaring failure. For the first and last time in his life he'd let his feelings for a woman cloud his judgement.

He would not make the same mistake twice.

Just as he would not be swayed from his purpose.

Douglas Shaw was a bully who thought nothing of destroying people's lives and he deserved a lesson in humility. Leo didn't trust the man and he didn't trust his daughter.

He drained the soda and crumpled the can in his fist.

Shaw wanted to play games? Leo was ready. He'd been ready for seven years. And if the man chose to use his daughter as a pawn, so be it. Two could play at that game.

He threw the can in the wastebin, a slow smile curving his lips.

*Si*. This might be fun.

'Go home, Helena.'

Helena looked up from the papers on her desk. Her boss stood holding his briefcase, his suit jacket folded over one arm, a look of mock severity on his face. It was after six on Friday and their floor of the corporate bank was largely deserted.

'I'm leaving soon,' she assured him. 'I'm meeting someone at six-thirty.'

David gave an approving nod. 'Good. Enjoy your weekend.'

He started off, but paused after a step and turned back. 'Have you thought any more about taking some leave?' he said. 'HR is on the use-it-or-lose-it warpath again. And if you don't mind me saying…' he paused, his grey eyes intent '…you look like you could do with a break.'

She smiled, deflecting his concern. David might be one of the bank's longest-serving executives and knocking sixty, but the man rarely missed a beat. He was sharp, observant, and he cared about his staff.

She made a mental note to apply more concealer beneath

her eyes. 'I'm fine. It's been a long week. And the rain kept me awake last night.'

*Partly* true.

'Well, think about it. See you Monday.'

'Goodnight, David.'

She watched him go, then glanced at her watch.

She had to move.

The car Leo was sending was due in less than twenty minutes, and earning a black mark for running late was not the way she wanted to start the evening.

Shutting herself in David's office, she whipped off her trouser suit and slipped on the little black dress she'd pulled from the bowels of her wardrobe that morning, then turned to the full-length mirror on the back of the door and scanned her appearance.

She frowned at her cleavage.

*Good grief.*

Had the dress always been so revealing?

She couldn't remember—but then neither could she recall the last time she'd worn it. She seldom dressed up these days, even on the rare occasions she dated. She tugged the bodice up, yanked the sides of the V-neck together and grimaced at the marginal improvement.

It would have to do.

There was no time for a wardrobe-change—and besides, this was the dressiest thing she owned. She'd sold the last of her designer gowns years ago, when she'd had to stump up a deposit and a month's advance rent on her flat. Keeping the black dress had been a practical decision, though she could count on one hand the number of times it had ventured from her wardrobe.

She turned side-on to the mirror.

The dress hugged her from shoulder to mid-thigh, accentuating every dip and curve—including the gentle swell of her tummy. Holding her breath, she pulled in her stomach and smoothed her hand over the bump that no number of sit-ups and crunches could flatten.

Not that she resented the changes pregnancy had wrought on her body. They were a bittersweet reminder of joy and loss. Of lessons learnt and mistakes she would never make again.

She snatched her hand down and released her breath. Tonight she needed to focus on the present, not the past, and for that she would need every ounce of wit she could muster.

Outside the bank a sleek silver Mercedes waited in a 'No Parking' zone, its uniformed driver standing on the pavement. 'Ms Shaw?' he enquired, then opened a rear door so she could climb in.

Minutes later the car was slicing through London's chaotic evening traffic, the endless layers of city noise muted by tinted windows that transformed the plush, leather-lined interior into a private mini-oasis. Like the luxury suite at the hotel, the car's sumptuous interior epitomised the kind of lifestyle Helena had grown unused to in recent years—unlike her mother, who still enjoyed the baubles of wealth and couldn't understand her daughter's wish to live a modest life, independent of her family's money and influence.

She dropped her head back against the soft leather.

She loved her mother. Miriam Shaw was a classic blonde beauty who had moulded herself into the perfect society wife, but she was neither stupid nor selfish. She loved her children. Had raised them with all the luxuries her own upbringing in an overcrowded foster home had denied her. And when they'd been packed off to boarding school, at her husband's insistence, she'd filled her days by giving time and support to a long list of charities and fundraisers.

Yet where her husband was concerned Miriam was inexplicably weak. Too quick to forgive and too ready to offer excuses.

Like today, when she'd called to cancel their prearranged

lunch date. A migraine, she'd claimed, but Helena knew better. Knew her mother's excuse was nothing more than a flimsy veil for the truth, as ineffectual and see-through as the make-up she would use to try to hide the bruises.

*Denial.*

Her mother's greatest skill. Her greatest weakness. The impregnable wall Helena slammed into any time she dared to suggest that Miriam consider leaving her husband.

A burning sensation crawled from Helena's stomach into her throat—the same anger and despair she always felt when confronted by the grim reality of her parents' marriage.

She massaged the bridge of her nose. Over the years she'd read everything she could on domestic abuse, trying to understand why her mother stayed. Why she put up with the drinking, the vitriol, the occasional black eye. Invariably, when the latter occurred, a peace offering would ensue—usually some priceless piece of jewellery—and then Miriam would pretend everything was fine.

Until the next time.

Helena had seen it more times than she cared to count, but now the stakes were higher. Now her father stood to lose everything he held dear: his company, his reputation, his pride.

If Leo got his way the ShawCorp empire would be carved up like twigs beneath a chainsaw, and Helena had no doubt that if—*when*—her father went down, he would take her mother with him.

'Miss Shaw?'

She jolted out of her thoughts. The car had stopped in front of Leo's hotel and a young man in a porter's uniform had opened her door. Lanky and fresh-faced, he reminded Helena of her brother, prompting a silent prayer of gratitude that James was in boarding school, well away from all this ugly drama.

She slid out and the porter escorted her through the hotel

to a grand reception room with a high vaulted ceiling and decorative walls. The room was crowded, filled with tray-laden waiters and dozens of patrons in tailored tuxedos and long, elegant evening gowns.

'Have a good evening, miss.'

The young man turned to leave.

'Wait!' She clasped his arm, confusion descending. 'I think there's been some mistake.'

He shook his head, his smile polite. 'No mistake, miss. Mr Vincenti asked that you be brought here.'

Leo stood at the edge of the milling crowd, his gaze bouncing off one brunette after another until he spied the one he wanted, standing next to a wide marble pillar just inside the entrance. Weaving waiters, clusters of glittering guests and some twenty feet of floor space separated them, but still he saw the flicker of uncertainty in her eyes. The twin furrows of consternation marring her brow.

Satisfaction stirred. Last night the element of surprise had been hers. How would the minx cope when the tables were turned?

He lifted two champagne flutes from a passing silver tray and carved a path to her side.

'*Buona sera*, Helena.'

She spun, her startled gaze landing on the flutes in his hands, then the bow tie at his throat, before narrowed eyes snapped to his.

'*This* is dinner?'

*Score.*

He smiled. 'You look very…elegant.'

The look she gave him might have sliced a lesser man in half. 'I look underdressed.'

She smoothed an invisible wrinkle from the front of her short and exquisitely low-cut black dress.

'The other women are wearing ball gowns.'

'Your dress is fine,' he said—an understatement if ever

he'd uttered one. The dress wasn't fine. It was stunning. No eye-catching bling or fancy designer frills, but its simple lines showcased her lithe curves and long, toned legs better than any overblown creation could.

She stole his breath. As easily as she'd stolen his breath the first night he'd laid eyes on her. Her dress that night, however, aside from being a daring purple instead of black, had been less revealing, more…demure. By comparison, tonight's figure-hugging sheath was sultry, seductive, the tantalising flash of ivory breasts inside that V of black fabric enough to tempt any man into secret, lustful imaginings.

'It's a plain cocktail dress,' she said, fretting over her appearance as only a woman could. 'Not a gown for an event like this.' She pressed a hand to the neat chignon at her nape. 'And you're sidestepping the question.'

He extended a champagne flute, which she ignored. 'This—' he gestured with the glass at their lavish surroundings '—is not to your liking?'

'A charity dinner with five hundred other guests? No.'

He feigned surprise. 'You don't like charity?'

She glanced at a wall banner promoting the largest spinal injury association in Europe and its twentieth annual fundraiser. 'Of course I do.' Her eyebrows knitted. 'But I thought we'd be dining in a restaurant. Or at least somewhere…I don't know…a little more…'

'Intimate?'

Her eyes flashed. 'Private.'

'There's a difference?'

She glared at the flute in his hand, then took it from him. 'Do you make a habit of attending charity dinners at the hotels where you stay?'

'*Si.* When I'm invited to support a worthy cause.' He watched her eyebrows arch. 'There are better ways to spend an evening, admittedly, but this event has been a long-standing commitment in my diary. And it coincides with my need to do business in London.'

'Ah, well…' She paused and sipped her champagne. 'That's convenient for you. You get to mark off your social calendar *and* wreak revenge on my family—all in a week's work.' Her mouth curled into a little smile. 'There's nothing more satisfying than killing two birds with one stone. How eminently sensible for a busy man such as yourself.'

Leo tasted his bubbles, took his time considering his next words. Exert enough pressure, he mused, and a person's true colours would eventually surface. 'Revenge is a very strong word,' he said mildly.

Her eyes widened. 'Oh, I'm sorry. Do you have a different name for what you're doing?' She raised her palm. 'No, wait. I remember—"an eye for an eye", wasn't it?'

He studied the churlish set of her mouth, the dainty jut of her chin. 'I had not remembered your tongue being so sharp, Helena.'

Twin spots of colour bloomed on her cheekbones, but the glint of battle stayed in her eyes. 'This is retaliation for last night, isn't it? I turned up unannounced at the hotel and you didn't like it. Now you get to spring the surprise.' She raised her glass in a mock toast. 'Well-played, Leo. So… what now? You parade me on your arm at some high-profile fundraiser and hope it gets back to my father?'

He smiled—which only irritated her further if the flattening of her mouth was any indication. Her gaze darted towards the exit and the idea that she might bolt swiftly curbed his amusement.

Helena would *not* run from him.

Not this time.

Not until he was good and ready to let her go.

'Thinking of reneging on our deal?'

Her gaze narrowed. 'How do I know you'll keep your side of the bargain?'

'I've already spoken with your father's solicitor.'

'And?

'He has until Tuesday to get your father to the table.'

Her mouth fell open. 'My God…that's four days from now. Can you not give him longer?'

'Time is a commodity in business, not a luxury.' He didn't add that the solicitor's chance of success was slim, no matter the time allowed. Both men knew the invitation would be rejected. A great pity, in Leo's mind. He'd hoped to see for himself the look on Douglas Shaw's face when the man learnt the fate of his company. But Shaw's repeated refusals to turn up had denied Leo the final spoils of victory.

'He won't show.'

Her voice was so small he wasn't sure he'd heard correctly. '*Scusi?*'

'My father. He won't show. He won't meet with you, will he?'

He schooled his expression. Had she divined his thoughts? *Absurd.* He shook off the notion. 'You tell me. He's *your* father.'

'Leo, I haven't—'

'Leonardo!'

Leo heard his name boomed at the same time as Helena stopped talking and darted a startled look over his shoulder. He turned and saw a lanky, sandy-haired man striding forward with a petite blonde by his side.

Leo grinned. 'Hans.' He gripped the man's outstretched hand. 'I didn't know you'd be here. How are you? And Sabine.' He raised the woman's slender hand, planted a kiss on her knuckles. 'Beautiful, as always.'

She issued a throaty laugh. 'And you, my dear, are still the charmer.' Rising on tiptoes, she kissed him on both cheeks, then turned her sparkling eyes on Helena. 'Please, introduce us to your lovely companion.'

Leo shifted his weight, fielded a sidelong glance from Helena and sliced her a warning look. *Do not embarrass me.*

'Helena, this is Dr Hans Hetterich and his wife, Sabine. Hans, when he is not winning golf tournaments or sailing a yacht on the high seas, is one of the most prominent spinal surgeons in the world.'

'Nice to meet you, Helena.' Hans took her hand. 'And please pay my friend no attention. I am not nearly as impressive as he makes me sound.'

An unladylike snort came from beside him. 'I think my husband is not himself tonight.' Sabine commandeered Helena's hand. 'Normally he is not so modest.'

Hans guffawed and clutched his chest, earning him an eye-roll and a poke in the ribs from his wife. He winked at her, then turned a more sober face to Leo. 'Our new research unit in Berlin is exceptional, thanks to your support. Our stem cell procedures are attracting interest from some of the best surgeons in the world. You must come soon and see for yourself. And you are most welcome too, Helena. Have you visited Germany?'

Her hesitation was fleeting. 'Once, a long time ago. On a school trip.'

'Perhaps in a few months,' Leo intervened. 'When I get a break in my schedule.'

'How is Marietta?' Sabine said. 'We haven't seen her since her last surgery.'

His fingers tightened on his glass. 'She's fine,' he said, keeping his answer intentionally brief. He had no wish to discuss his sister in front of Helena. Proffering a smile, he gestured at the dwindling number of people around them. 'It appears the waiting staff would like us to be seated. Shall we…?'

With a promise to catch them later in the evening, Hans and Sabine joined the trail of diners drifting through to the ballroom. Leo turned to follow, but Helena hung back.

He stopped, raised an eyebrow. 'Are you coming?'

After a pause, she jammed her evening purse beneath her arm and shot him a baleful look. 'Do I have a choice?'

He gave her a silky smile—one designed to leave her in

no doubt as to his answer. But just to ensure she couldn't mistake his meaning he leaned in and said softly, 'You don't.'

Gorgeous. Devastating. *Lethal*.

Those were three of a dozen words Helena could think of to describe Leonardo Vincenti in a tuxedo. And, judging by the lascivious looks he was pulling from every corner of the ballroom, she wasn't the only female whose hormones had clocked into overdrive at the mere sight of all that dark, brooding masculinity.

He spoke from beside her. 'The fish is not to your taste?'

She cast him a look from under her lashes. 'It's fine. I'm not very hungry.'

The treacle-cured smoked salmon served as a starter was, in fact, superb, but the knots twisting her stomach made the food impossible to enjoy. Which really was a shame, some part of her brain registered, because she rarely had the opportunity these days to sample such exquisite cuisine.

She laid her fork alongside her abandoned knife and leaned back in her chair. So much for a quiet dinner *à deux* and the chance for a serious talk. She almost rubbed her forehead to see if the word *gullible* was carved there.

Surreptitiously she watched Leo speak with an older woman seated on his left. His tux jacket, removed prior to appetisers being served, hung from his chair, leaving his wide shoulders and lean torso sheathed in a white wing tip shirt that contrasted with his olive skin and black hair. He bowed his head, murmuring something that elicited a bright tinkle of laughter from the woman, and the sound scraped across Helena's nerves.

Age, evidently, was no barrier to his charms.

She averted her gaze, smothered the impulse to get up and flee. Like it or not, she'd agreed to be here and she would not scarper like a coward. If she was smart, bided her time, she might still persuade Leo to hold his plans for her father's company. A few weeks…that was all she needed. Time to make her mother see sense before—

'Bored?'

Leo's deep voice sliced across her thoughts.

She drummed up a smile. 'Of course not.'

'Good.' His long fingers toyed with the stem of his wine-glass. 'I would hate to bore you for a second time in your life.'

Helena's smile faltered. His casually delivered words carried a meaning she couldn't fail to comprehend. Not when her own words—words she'd bet every hard-earned penny in her bank account had hurt her more than they'd hurt him—were embedded like thorns in her memory. *I'm bored, Leo. Really. This relationship just isn't working for me.*

She shifted in her seat, her face heating. 'That's unfair.' She glanced around the table, pitching her voice for his ears alone. 'I tried once to explain why I said those things.'

After he'd left that awful message on her phone—telling her what her father had done, accusing her of betrayal and complicity—she'd gone to his hotel room and banged on his door until her hand throbbed and a man from a neighbouring room stepped out and shot her a filthy look.

'You didn't want to listen.'

He shrugged. 'I was angry,' he stated, as if he need offer no further excuse.

'You still are.'

'Perhaps. But now I'm listening.'

'I doubt that.'

'Try me.'

She arched an eyebrow. He wanted to do this *now*? *Here*? She cast another furtive glance around the table. *Fine.*

'I needed you to let me go without a fight,' she said, her voice a decibel above a whisper. 'And we both know you wouldn't have. Not without questions. Not unless I—' She stopped, a hot lump of regret lodging in her throat.

'Stamped on my pride?' he finished for her.

Her face flamed hotter. *Must* he make her sound so cruel? So heartless? She'd been nineteen, for pity's sake, staring down the barrel of her father's ultimatum. *Get rid of the damned foreigner, girl—or I will.* Naive. That was what she'd been. And unforgivably stupid, thinking she could live beyond the reach of her father's iron control.

She smoothed her napkin over her knees. 'I did what I thought was best at the time.'

'For you or for me?'

'For us both.'

'Ah. So you were being...how do you English like to say it...cruel to be kind?'

His eyes drilled into hers, but she refused to flinch from his cutting glare. She didn't need his bitter accusations. She, too, had paid a price, and however much she longed to turn back the clock, undo the damage, she could not relieve the pain of her past. Not when she'd worked so hard, sacrificed so much, to leave it behind.

She mustered another smile, this one urbane and slightly aloof—the kind her mother often wore in public. 'Hans and Sabine seem like a nice couple. Have you known them long?'

The change of subject earned her a piercing stare. She held her breath. Would he roll with it?

Then, 'Nine years.'

He spoke curtly, but still she breathed again, relaxed a little. Perhaps a normal conversation wasn't impossible? 'You never talked much about your sister,' she ventured. 'Sabine mentioned surgery. Is Marietta unwell?'

Long, silent seconds passed and Helena's stomach plunged as the dots she should have connected earlier—Leo's choice of fundraiser, Hans's reputation as a leading spinal surgeon, talk of the Berlin research unit followed by the mention of Marietta and surgery—belatedly joined in her head to create a complete picture.

A muscle jumped in Leo's cheek. 'My sister is a paraplegic.'

The blood that had heated Helena's cheeks minutes earlier rapidly fled. 'Oh, Leo. I'm... I'm so sorry.' She reached out—an impulsive gesture of comfort—but he shifted his arm before her hand could make contact. She withdrew, pretending his rebuff hadn't stung. 'I had no idea. How... how long?'

'Eleven years.'

Her throat constricted with sympathy and, though she knew it was silly, a tiny stab of hurt. Seven years ago they'd spent five intense, heady weeks together, and though he'd mentioned a sister, talked briefly about their difficult childhood, he'd omitted that significant piece of information.

Still, was that cause to feel miffed? She, too, had been selective in what she'd shared about *her* family.

'Did she have an...an accident?'

'Yes.' His tone was clipped.

'I'm sorry,' she said. 'I didn't mean to pry. I can see you don't want to talk about this.'

She lifted a pitcher of iced water in an effort to do something—anything—to dispel the growing tension. She'd half filled her glass when he spoke again.

'It was a car accident.'

Startled, she put the pitcher down and looked at him, but his head was angled down, his gaze fastened on the wineglass in his hand.

'She was seventeen and angry because we'd argued about her going to a party.' His black brows tugged into a deep frown. 'I didn't like the neighbourhood or the crowd, but she was stubborn. Headstrong. So she went anyway. Later, instead of calling me for a ride home, she climbed into a car with a drunk driver.' He drained his wine, dropped the glass on the table. 'The doctors said she was lucky to survive—if you can call a broken back "lucky". The driver and two other passengers weren't so fortunate.'

Helena tried to imagine the horror. Teenagers made bad decisions all the time, but few suffered such devastating, life-altering consequences. Few paid such an unimaginable price.

She struggled to keep her expression neutral, devoid of the wrenching pity it was impossible not to feel. 'Sabine mentioned surgery. Is there a chance...?'

Leo's gaze connected with hers, something harsh, almost hostile, flashing at the centre of those near-black irises. 'Let's drop it.'

Slightly taken aback, Helena opened her mouth to point out she *had* tried to drop the subject, but his dark expression killed that pert response. 'Fine,' she said, and for the next hour ignored him—which wasn't difficult because over the rest of their dinner another guest drew him into a lengthy debate on European politics, while the American couple to Helena's right quizzed her about the best places to visit during their six-month sabbatical in England.

When desserts began to arrive at the tables the compère tapped his microphone, waited for eyes to focus and chatter to cease, then invited one of the organisation's patrons, Leonardo Vincenti, to present the grand auction prize. After a brief hesitation Helena joined in the applause. In light of his sister's condition Leo's patronage came as no real surprise.

His mouth brushed her ear as he rose. 'Don't run away.'

And then he was striding to the podium, a tall, compelling figure that drew the attention of every person—male and female—in the room. On stage, he delivered a short but pertinent speech before presenting a gold envelope to the evening's highest bidder. People clapped again, finished their desserts, then got up to mingle while coffee was served.

Twenty minutes later Helena still sat alone.

Irritation sent a wave of prickly heat down her spine. *Don't run away.*

Ha! The man had a nerve.

She dumped sugar into her tea. Gave it a vigorous stir. Was he playing some kind of cat-and-mouse game? Or had he cut his losses and gone in search of a more agreeable companion for the evening?

Another ten minutes and finally he deigned to show. He dropped into his chair but she refused to look at him, concentrating instead on topping up her tea.

'You have no boyfriend to spend your Friday nights with, Helena?'

Her pulse skipped a beat. No apology, then. No excuse for his absence. Had his desertion been some kind of test? An experiment to see if she'd slink away the minute his back was turned? The idea did nothing to lessen her pique.

She piled more sugar in her tea. 'He's busy tonight.'

'Really?' His tone said he knew damn well she was lying. He lifted his hand and trailed a fingertip over the exposed curve of her shoulder. 'If you were mine I would not let you spend an evening with another man.' He paused a beat. 'Especially not in that dress.'

Carefully, she stirred her tea and laid the spoon in the saucer. He was trying to unsettle her, nothing more. She steeled herself not to flinch from his touch or, worse, tremble beneath it.

His hand dropped and she forced herself to meet his eye. 'You said my dress was fine.'

His gaze raked her. 'Oh, it's fine. Very fine, indeed. And I am sure not a man here tonight would disagree.'

Did she detect a note of censure in his voice? She stopped herself glancing down. She'd been conscious of her plunging neckline all evening, but there were dozens of cleavages here more exposed than her own. And, though the dress was more suited to a cocktail party or a private dinner than a glittering gala affair—cause at first for discomfort—there was nothing cheap or trashy about it.

She crossed her legs, allowing her hem to ride up, until

another inch of pale thigh defiantly showed. 'And you?' She watched his gaze flicker down. 'I wouldn't have thought a man like you would need a last-minute dinner date. Where's your regular plus-one tonight?'

His lips, far too sensual for a man's, twitched into a smile. 'A man like me?'

'Successful,' she said, inwardly cursing her choice of words. 'Money attracts, does it not? The world is full of women who find wealth and status powerful aphrodisiacs.'

One eyebrow quirked. 'When did you become a cynic?'

'Oh, I don't know.' She pursed her lips. 'Maybe around the time you were getting rich.'

He lounged back in his chair, the glint in his eye unmissable. 'In answer to your question, I'm between mistresses.'

'Oh...' She fiddled with the handle on her teacup.

Not girlfriends or partners. *Mistresses*. Why did that word make her heart shrink? So he enjoyed casual relationships. So what? His sex life was no business of hers.

She sat back, forced herself to focus. She couldn't afford to waste time. The evening was slipping away. If she didn't speak soon her chance would be lost. 'Leo, my father and I are estranged.'

In a flash, the teasing light was gone from his eyes. Her stomach pitched. Should she have blurted the words so abruptly? *Too bad*. They were out there now.

A vein pulsed in his right temple. 'Define "estranged".'

She hitched a shoulder, let it drop. 'We don't talk. We don't see each other. We're estranged in every sense of the word, if that's what you're asking.'

'Why?'

She hesitated. How much to tell? The bitter memory of that final violent confrontation with her father was too disturbing to recount even now.

'We fell out,' she said, her tongue dry despite the gallon of tea she'd consumed. 'Over you and what he did after we—after *I* broke things off. I walked out seven years ago and we haven't spoken since.' She paused and glanced down. Her hands were shaking. She lifted her gaze back to his. 'I dropped out of university and went to live in a rented flat. Father cut off my allowance, froze my trust, so I work at a full-time job. As a…a secretary. In a bank.'

Leo stared at her, his face so blank she wondered if he'd heard a single word she said. Her insides churned as if the tea had suddenly curdled in her belly. She wished she could read him better. Wished she could interpret the emotion in those dark, fathomless eyes.

And still the silence stretched.

*God, why didn't he say something?*

'You gave up your design studies?'

She blinked. *That* was his first question? 'Yes,' she said, frowning. 'I couldn't study full-time and support myself. The materials I needed were too expensive.'

Other students on her textile design course had juggled part-time jobs along with their studies, but they'd had only themselves to think about. They hadn't been facing the same dilemmas, the same fears. They hadn't been in Helena's position. Alone and pregnant.

*Careful.*

She shrugged. 'I might go back one day. But that's not important. Leo, what I'm trying to tell you is that I'm not here for my father.'

'Then why *are* you here?'

She leaned forward. 'Because what you're doing will hurt the people I *do* love. And before you remind me that my father—and thus his family—stands to gain financially from having his company torn apart, it's not about the money.'

Helena hesitated. She had to choose her words with care. Miriam Shaw might be too proud to admit to herself, let alone the world, that she was a victim, but she was none the less entitled to her privacy. Her dignity. She wouldn't want the painful truth about her marriage shared with a stranger. Who knew what Leo might do with such sensitive information?

'My father can be…difficult to live with,' she said. 'At the best of times.'

Leo sat so still he barely blinked. Seemed barely to breathe. 'So what exactly do you want?'

'I want you to reconsider your plans for ShawCorp.' The words tumbled out so fast her tongue almost tripped on them. 'At the very least give my father more time to come to the table. Offer him a chance to have a say in the company's future. Maybe keep his position on the board.'

He gave her a long, hard look. 'That's a lot of want, Helena. You do realise my company is overseen by a board of directors? I am not the sole decision-maker.'

'But you have influence, surely?'

'Of course. But I need good reason. Your concern for your family is admirable, but this is business. I cannot let a little family dysfunction dictate corporate strategy.'

'Can't you at least delay Tuesday's deadline by a few weeks?'

His eyebrows slammed down and he muttered something under his breath. Something not especially nice.

He rose. 'We will finish this talk later.'

Warmth leached from her face. Her hands. Had she pushed too hard? Said too much? 'Why can't we finish it now?'

He moved behind her chair, lowered his head to hers. The subtle scent of spice twined around her senses. 'Because we're about to have company.' His hot breath fanned her cheek. 'Important company. And if you want me to consider your request you will be very, *very* well behaved.'

# CHAPTER THREE

LEO STRAIGHTENED AND quelled the urge to mutter another oath.

Of all the damnable luck. This night was going from bad to worse. First a call on his mobile from a board member whose angst over a minor matter had required twenty minutes of placation, followed by his relief at finding Helena hadn't done a runner in his absence turning into stunned disbelief over her staggering revelations—revelations his reeling brain had yet to fully process.

And now Carlos Santino. Here in London. At this hotel. At *this* function.

Tension coiled in his gut as the older Italian approached. Santino stood a full head shorter than Leo, but the man's stocky build and confident gait more than made up for his lack of stature. Add to that hard, intelligent eyes above a beaked nose and a straight mouth, and you had the impression of a man who tolerated weakness in neither himself nor others.

Leo liked him. Respected him. Santino Shipping dominated the world's waterways, and in the last three years its cyber security needs had generated sizable revenue for Leo's company. The two men shared a business relationship based on mutual trust and respect.

But Leo had not seen Carlos Santino for several months.

Not since he'd rejected the man's daughter.

'Carlos.' He gripped Santino's hand. 'This is unexpected. What brings you to London? I thought few things could prise you away from Rome.'

His client grunted. 'Shopping. Shows. Anything my wife and daughter can spend my money on.' A chunky gold watch and a heavy signet ring flashed in the air. 'Nothing they cannot get in Rome, or Milan, but you know women—' he shrugged expressively '—they are easily bored.'

Leo fired a loaded glance at Helena, but she was already rising, gifting the newcomer a million-dollar smile that drove a spike of irrational jealousy through his chest because *he* wasn't the recipient.

'Helena, this is Carlos Santino, head of Santino Shipping.' A deliberate pause gave his next words emphasis. 'One of my company's largest clients.'

She extended a slim hand. 'A pleasure to meet you, Mr. Santino.'

'The pleasure is mine.' Santino's hand engulfed hers. 'And, please, call me Carlos.' For a long moment he studied her face in a frank appraisal that nearly but not quite overstepped the bounds of propriety. By the time he released her hand, her cheeks glowed a delicate pink. He turned to Leo. 'Business is not your only good reason for visiting London, *si*?'

Leo forced a smile that almost made his eyes water. 'This is a coincidence, running into you here.' He pulled out a vacated chair for his client. 'Maria and Anna are with you?'

Carlos waited for Helena to resume her seat before taking the proffered chair. 'This was Anna's idea. She remembered you were patron of this organisation and…well—' another very Italian shrug '—when my wife planned the weekend Anna called your office and asked if you would be in London.' His smile offered only the vaguest apology. 'You know my daughter. She is resourceful and persistent. And furious with her *papà* right now. She woke with a bad cold this morning and I forbade her to come out. The tickets were already purchased and Maria insisted she and I still come.' He waved his hand. 'My wife is here somewhere—no doubt talking with someone more interesting than her husband.'

Some of Leo's tension eased. The young, voluptuous Anna Santino was an irritation he'd spent several months trying hard to avoid. Running into her this evening, or rather running *from* her, would have turned the night into a complete disaster.

Carlos switched his attention to Helena. 'It is fortunate, I think, that my daughter could not be here tonight. I fear she would be jealous of such a beauty at Leo's side.'

The provocative compliment heightened her colour but her hesitation was brief. 'I'm so sorry to hear your daughter is too ill to come out, Mr San— Carlos. That really is most unfortunate.' Her voice sang with sympathy. 'I do hope she'll be back on her feet again soon. You must tell her she has missed a wonderful, wonderful evening.'

Leo fought back a smirk. She might blush like a novice in a convent, but there was backbone beneath that pseudo-innocent charm. He noted a quirk at the corner of Santino's mouth. A flash of approval in his eyes.

Carlos inclined his head. 'I will, my dear.' To Leo, he said, 'I owe you an apology, my friend. When you told my daughter you had someone special in your life I assumed you were letting her down gently with a lie. I see now I was mistaken. You do have a special lady, indeed. And I am pleased to make her acquaintance at last.'

Leo felt the flesh at his nape tighten. He'd known that small white lie would come back one day and bite him. But flat-out rejecting the daughter of a client as powerful as Santino had seemed as sensible as cementing his feet and jumping into the Tiber. Claiming he was committed to another woman had seemed a kinder, more effective solution.

Carlos's focus returned to Helena. 'How often are you in Rome, Helena?'

Her lips parted and Leo shot her a hard, silencing look. She closed her mouth and frowned at him.

'Not often,' he interceded. 'Business brings me to London on a regular basis.'

'Ah, shame. In that case you need a reason to bring her to our great city.' Carlos's sudden smile drove a shaft of alarm straight to the centre of Leo's gut. 'My wife and I are celebrating our twenty-fifth wedding anniversary next weekend. Maria has organised a party—something large and extravagant, knowing my wife. Please join us. We'd be delighted to welcome you both.'

In the fleeting moment of silence that followed Leo caught a movement from the corner of his eye, but not until he felt the press of her palm on his thigh did he get his first inkling of what Helena intended.

Too late, his brain flashed a warning.

'Thank you, Carlos,' she said, her voice as smooth and sweet as liquid honey. 'That's very kind of you. We'd love to come.' She turned her head and flashed him a dazzling smile. 'Wouldn't we, darling?'

She squeezed his leg and heat exploded in the muscle under her hand. He tensed, biting back an exclamation, the fire shooting straight from his thigh to his groin. *Madre di Dio*. If the vixen inched her fingers any higher he would not be responsible for his body's reaction. He gritted his teeth until pain arced through his jaw—a welcome distraction from the killer sensations stirring south of his waist.

'I will need to check my schedule.' He forced the words past the hot, viscous anger building in his throat. *What the hell was she doing?* 'I may have another commitment.'

'Of course.'

Carlos stood and Leo rose with him, unseating the hand that was dangerously close to setting his pants alight.

'My assistant will contact your office on Monday with the details.' Carlos inclined his head. 'I look forward to seeing you again, Helena. And now I must find my wife before my absence is noted. Leo—good to see you. It has been too long.'

Leo nodded and watched his client's retreating back, the

tension in his chest climbing into his throat until it threatened to choke off his air supply.

He turned, glared at her. 'Get your bag.'

'What?' She stared up at him, wide-eyed. 'Why?'

'Just do it.'

When she hesitated, he grabbed her bag and wrapped a
hand around her upper arm, hauled her to her feet.

She snatched her bag from him. 'Where are we going?'

'Somewhere private. To talk. Is that not what you
wanted?'

She didn't utter a single word as he marched her out of
the ballroom.

The instant the elevator doors closed Helena jerked her arm
out of Leo's grasp. 'There's no need to manhandle me.'

He punched the button for the top floor of the hotel and
threw her a look so thunderous a sliver of fear lodged in
her spine. She edged away, reminded herself with a hard
swallow that not all men were physically abusive. But if
he was planning to shout she wished to God he'd get on
with it. Anything had to be better than this…this tense,
oppressive silence.

Moments later he slammed the door of his suite closed
and rounded on her. 'What the *hell* was that?' His roar
rose to the ceiling, echoed off the walls and reverberated
through her chest like a boom of thunder.

She stood calm even as her insides quaked. 'I don't know
why you're so angry. I thought you'd be grateful.'

*'Grateful?'* The word barely escaped his clenched teeth.

'Yes.' She pulled her brows into a delicate frown. Ignored the jelly-like quiver in her knees. 'You were in a
sticky situation and I was being helpful.' Not to mention
reckless and impulsive and out of her mind crazy. *Lord
help her.* Whatever she'd done, it was either very clever or
very, *very* stupid. 'Or would you have preferred I set Carlos straight about us?'

'*Dio.*' He threw his tuxedo jacket over a lounge chair, ripped his bow tie from around his neck. 'I should have known you'd have another stunt up your sleeve.'

Oh, now, *that* was rich. 'You brought me here tonight,' she reminded him. 'Not the other way around. I couldn't have foreseen your client turning up.'

'But you didn't waste a second in twisting it to your advantage, did you?'

She let out a clipped laugh. 'And *you* made no effort to correct his notion that we're a couple. I'm not a mind-reader, Leo. How was I to know I shouldn't play along?'

'It was simple, Helena.' He enunciated each syllable as if she were missing a few critical brain cells. 'All you had to do was keep your mouth shut. Oh, but wait—' he flung his arms wide '—you're a woman. That would have been impossible!'

He tossed down the tie, tore loose the buttons at his throat, raked lean fingers through his thick black hair. Gone was the cool, suave businessman from the charity dinner. In his place stood a man who looked hard. Fierce. *Dangerous*.

Helena drew a calming breath. She couldn't bottle now. Not when she could see the future looming with such frightening clarity. The takeover was only the beginning. If her mother thought things were bad now, they were only going to get worse. Leo didn't want to own ShawCorp; he wanted to destroy it. And when he succeeded her father's rage would need an outlet. A victim. Helena could not sit on the sidelines. She couldn't stand idle while her mother became that victim.

'Look, I…I'm sorry if I made things worse.' She tried for a softer, more apologetic tone. 'But maybe we could turn this to our advantage? Come to some…arrangement that would benefit us both?'

He stalked towards her and stopped inches short of their bodies touching—so close she could feel the heat emanating from him. In sharp contrast, his dark eyes carried a chill that needled into her flesh like icy midwinter sleet.

'Newsflash, Helena. Mutual benefit works best when each party has something the other needs. And, like I told you last night, you don't have anything I want—or need.' He spun on his heel and strode to the bar, pulled a large bottle from a black lacquered cabinet.

For her own benefit, not his, she straightened her spine. 'You need a girlfriend for your client's party next weekend.'

'Wrong.' He fired the word over his shoulder as he uncapped the bottle. 'On Monday my assistant will advise Santino's office that I am, regrettably, unable to attend.'

'Carlos will be disappointed.'

Amber liquid sloshed into a crystal tumbler. 'He'll get over it.'

'And next time you see him? What if he asks about me? Will you pretend there's still *someone special* in your life?'

'That is not your concern.'

'It is if you pretend that someone is me.'

He turned, the whisky untouched on the counter beside him. 'I will tell him our relationship ended.'

She dropped her purse on the arm of a sofa and sauntered over. 'I'm sure his daughter—Anna, was it?—will be delighted by that news.'

Was that a growl in his throat? She lifted the tumbler of whisky, inhaled the eye-watering fumes and, before she could think twice, helped herself to a generous swallow. The fiery liquid shot down her throat and extinguished the air in her lungs, but the molten heat spreading through her innards fired her courage.

Frowning, he snatched the glass back. 'What exactly are you proposing?'

Hope flared. 'That I attend the party with you in Rome—at your expense, of course—and help you prove to Carlos and his daughter that you're a happily attached man.'

His brows sank lower. 'And in return?'

'In return you defer your divestment of ShawCorp's assets and keep any announcements under wraps until my father agrees to meet you. In the meantime the company operates as normal and my father retains his position on the board.' It would give her father a sense of security. A belief, albeit false, that he still wielded some control.

Leo fell silent for long seconds and she imagined his brain ticking through the options.

'What makes you think your father will come around?'

She hesitated. Chances were he wouldn't. He was too arrogant, too proud, and that was what she was counting on. Because she didn't want to *prevent* her father's downfall. She only wanted to delay it—long enough for Miriam Shaw to accept some hard truths, come to her senses.

'We can agree a time limit. Say…four weeks.'

In two smooth motions he downed the remaining whisky and set the glass on the counter. 'Let me get this straight. You want to play-act at being my mistress—'

'Girlfriend.'

He flicked a hand in the air. 'Same thing—in return for granting your father a grace period?'

'Of sorts. Yes.'

He closed his eyes. Ran a wide palm over his jaw. 'That's insane.'

*Totally.*

She hiked her chin, swatted away the inclination to agree with him. 'Why? We'd each be doing the other a favour. What's so insane about that?'

'Because I don't need—'

'I know. I know.' Her turn to flick a hand. 'You don't need or want anything from me.' She let that hang a moment. 'But Carlos has met me now, and you said yourself he's an important client. Why decline his invitation if you don't need to? And, assuming you do want Anna to get the message loud and clear that you're unavailable, why not make use of the opportunity?'

He folded his arms, his shirt stretching over biceps that bunched and flexed with what she guessed was a surge of testosterone-fuelled pride. 'I can handle Santino's daughter without your help.'

She let a knowing smile curve her mouth. 'I'm sure you can. And, let's face it, you've done a stellar job so far. So stellar, in fact, that she went to all the trouble of tracking your whereabouts and arranging to be at the same event as you—in a different city. A different *country*.' She shook her head, turned her smile into a pitying grimace. 'I hate to say this, Leo, but that's not a girl who's accepted no for an answer. That's a woman still hot for the chase.'

His muscles deflated slightly, though the arrogant set of his jaw remained. 'That's quite some proposition, Helena. You and I pretending to be lovers. How do you think your father would feel about that?'

Helena swallowed, or tried to, but her mouth had gone suddenly dry. *Lovers.* The word had skimmed off his tongue with such ease and yet it drove home the reality of what she'd suggested. Of precisely the kind of role-playing required to convince a crowd of partygoers that she and Leo were a committed couple. Her belly quivered with something much more unsettling than nerves, but she couldn't back down now.

She moistened her lips. 'I don't mix in my father's circles. Not any more. Few people of note would recognise me, and certainly not in Rome. And if they did, well…why would you care? Isn't that the reason I'm here tonight? Because you like the idea of getting under his skin?'

He frowned at that, eyes narrowed, his fingers yanking loose another button at his throat. He tugged at the collar and the shirt gaped, exposing the base of his strong neck and a triangle of chest deeply bronzed and dusted with fine whorls of dark hair.

Helena jerked her gaze north of his chin. *Focus.*

'There's no reason this can't work. If people in Rome

question why they haven't seen us together before we'll say we wanted to keep our relationship private until we'd figured out the long-distance thing. If we're convincing, Anna will back off and lose interest, and once she's moved on you can tell Carlos we broke up. That way he won't ever have to know you lied to his daughter—' she paused for a significant beat '—or to him.'

His jaw ground from side to side. 'You really think you could pull that off? Convince the Santinos and their hundreds of guests—and there *will* be hundreds—that we're a couple?'

'Sure.' She shrugged, strove for nonchalance. 'Why not? We were lovers once.'

Briefly, admittedly, and then only after she'd convinced him that at nineteen, besides being a legally consenting adult, she was a level-headed young woman who knew her own mind. He had been older, yes, but six years was hardly cradle-snatcher territory. She'd wanted it, wanted *him*, as she'd never wanted anything before. And not once had she regretted what they'd shared—even in the days and months of heartache that followed. Sex with Leo had been the most intense, most beautiful and physically liberating experience of her life.

Nothing, and no one, had come close since.

Drawing courage from the alcohol warming her blood, she stepped forward and cupped a hand around his jaw. 'It wouldn't be so difficult, would it? Pretending we're lovers? Pretending we're enamoured of each other?'

She swayed her hips—a gentle, seductive grind that bumped their bodies and sparked a slow blossoming of heat low in her pelvis.

Bone and muscle shifted under her palm. He ground out an oath, seized her wrist. 'What are you doing?'

'Proving I can play the part. I *can*, Leo, if that's what you're worried about.'

There was no mistaking the growl in his throat this time.

Or the sudden flash of heat in his eyes. His grip tightened and she thought for one heart-stopping moment he was going to kiss her—haul her against him, crash that harsh, beautiful mouth down on hers and kiss her. Her breath stalled. Her heartbeat hitched. A tiny, forbidden thrill of anticipation skimmed her spine.

Then his head was snapping back, his hand thrusting hers away as if he found her touch, her very proximity, repugnant. 'How do I know your father didn't put you up to this? That everything you've told me tonight isn't more lies? Tell me why I should trust you.'

Heat seared Helena's face even as the flare of desire in her belly iced over.

*Because I loved you once!* she almost shouted. *Broke my heart in two for you. And, by God, doesn't that make me the world's biggest fool?*

She bit the lining of her cheek. Distrust was written all over his face. In the hard, narrowed eyes, the implacable jaw. The contemptuous twist of his mouth.

She looked him in the eye and spoke with a quiet dignity that camouflaged the turmoil inside her. 'I lied to you once, Leo. I don't deny it and I'm not proud of it. I made up a weak, hurtful excuse to end our relationship because that was what my father wanted. *Demanded.*'

She passed a hand over her eyes, the strain of recent days coupled with sleepless nights taking its toll.

'My greatest mistake was believing that if I obeyed him, did what he wanted, that would be the end of it. Why he went after you I'll never know. Maybe he was punishing me. Maybe he did it simply because he *could*. Whatever his reasons, I can assure you this—I did *not* tell him anything about you or your project. Wherever he got his information, it wasn't from me.' She exhaled on a heavy sigh, the last of her energy rapidly waning. 'Is it really so hard for you to believe me now?'

His gaze held hers, no softening visible in those midnight depths. 'After the stunt you just pulled, what do you think?'

She backed up a step, the ice in her belly trickling into her veins. Astonishing that a man could nurse his anger, his resentment, his need for retribution for so many years. Pride, rage, distrust—whatever the emotions that drove him, they were too strong, too ingrained for her to fight against and win.

She collected her purse, turned to face him one last time. 'You really want to know what I think? I think you're right. This is insane, and I'm sorry I suggested it. Manipulation might be my father's forte, maybe even yours, but it's not mine.' She walked to the door and glanced back, her smile brittle. 'Good luck with taking my father down a peg or two.' She inclined her head. 'I believe he might have met his match.'

She opened the door and paused a moment, half expecting a presence to loom at her back, a hand to fall on her shoulder. But she heard no footfalls, no rustle of movement behind her. She stepped out, closed the door and rode the elevator down to the foyer.

Minutes later, striding through the brisk evening air to the nearest tube station, she angrily dashed the tears from her eyes.

She would *not* let them fall.

Leo didn't deserve her anguish.

Not seven years ago, and not now.

Leo stopped pacing just long enough to glare at the whisky bottle and dismiss the notion of refilling his glass.

Getting tanked so he could obliterate this evening from his memory held a certain appeal, but he'd cleaned up his father's drunken messes too often as a kid to condone such mindless excess. Not to mention he'd have one hell of a hangover. Besides, his pilot had scheduled an early-morning return to Rome, and a flight-change was out of the question. If he turned up to Marietta's first ever art exhibition a dishevelled, ill-tempered wreck he'd spend days, if not weeks, earning his little sister's forgiveness.

He flung his restless frame into a chair, his muscles stiff after the effort of holding his body in check. Of stopping himself from charging after Helena like some raging Neanderthal and forcing her to press those sultry curves against him one more time.

Scowling at the flash of heat in his groin, he got up to pace again. He was too wired to sit, his head too full of questions clamouring for answers. Answers he needed if he were to make any sense of Helena's actions. The idea that she'd come to him without her father's knowledge, that she and Shaw were estranged and had been for years, that she'd abandoned her studies, now lived alone in the city, worked nine-to-five as a secretary in a bank...

He shook his head as if he could clear the overload from his brain.

Truths, half-truths, or carefully constructed lies?

Whatever the answer, there were more layers to this situation than met the eye. And if his years of dealing with wily competitors and cut-throat corporates had hammered home any lessons, they were never to accept anything at face value, never to underestimate your opponent, and never to assume he'd go down without a fight.

Turning on his heel, he retrieved his tux jacket and pulled out his mobile. He placed a call and his friend Nicolas answered within two rings. Leo skipped the pleasantries—Nico didn't do small talk—and launched into his request.

'I need this ASAP,' he finished.

A short silence came down the line, then Nico's deep voice. 'No problem, *mon ami*. I will have something for you in forty-eight hours.'

Gratitude surged, even though Leo had known his friend would do him this favour, no questions asked. Nicolas

César ran a global security firm with an investigative arm reputed for its reach and discretion. He was a man with the resources to uncover the secrets of the world's most powerful and influential people. Confirming a few basic facts about an Englishwoman would amount to little more than child's play.

Leo tossed aside his phone, stripped off his clothes and headed for the en suite bathroom. He turned on the shower and let the steaming jets of water ease the tension from his muscles.

If Nico delivered with his trademark efficiency Leo would soon know if there was any truth to Helena's claims. And whatever his friend's probing unearthed, whatever truths—or lies—were revealed, she would soon discover this was far from over.

Whether she had planned to or not she'd started something tonight, and Leo intended to finish it.

The next time Helena Shaw walked out of his life it would be on *his* terms.

On Monday morning Helena stepped out of the elevator on the forty-second floor of the bank and knew at once something wasn't right. For a start the receptionist grinned at her, and prim, efficient, fifty-something Jill didn't grin. She smiled. Professionally. No grinning allowed.

'You're late,' Jill announced.

'I know,' Helena said, flustered enough without Jill stating the obvious. 'The Underground was a nightmare this morning.' And the last thing she'd needed on the heels of a long, sleepless weekend. All she wanted was to get to her desk and bury herself in work. 'Any mail for David?'

'He collected it ten minutes ago—along with your visitor.'

Helena stopped. 'My visitor?'

'A man.'

And there it was again. Not a smile. A *grin*. Helena

couldn't recall ever before seeing so many of her colleague's teeth.

'He said he was a friend, so once Security cleared him I had them send him up. When David arrived and I mentioned you had a visitor he took him through to your office. His name was…' She picked up a piece of notepaper. 'Yes, that's right. Mr Vincenz—no, Vincenti.'

Helena blinked. She wasn't at the office at all. She was still tucked up in bed. Dreaming about the infernal man who had single-handedly ruined her weekend.

Jill frowned. 'Helena? Are you okay?'

*No.* 'Yes,' she said, forcing herself to rally. To *think*. She managed a smile. 'Thanks.'

Before Jill could probe further, she pushed through the glass security doors and followed the executive corridor down to her workspace. With every step the tremor in her knees threatened to escalate into a full-blown quake.

At her desk, she dumped her bag, removed her blazer—the temperature in the office had soared suddenly—and glanced around. No tall, dark, brooding Italian in sight. She could, however, hear voices in David's office, and when a burst of laughter carried through the half-open door any lingering doubts were swiftly dispelled.

She clutched the edge of her desk, her stomach clenching in response to that rich, full-bodied sound and the confirmation that Leo was not only here, at her office, *in her boss's office,* he was having a nice little one-on-one with David while he waited for her to arrive.

Confusion followed by a spurt of alarm jolted her into action. Without knocking, she pushed open David's door and two heads swung in her direction. In a matter of seconds her brain registered two things.

First, David was not behind his desk but seated out front, beside his guest—a relaxed approach he only ever adopted with her or with people he especially liked. And second, though by no means less noteworthy, was the simple fact that Leonardo Vincenti looked just as mind-blowingly sexy in a silver suit, pale blue shirt and striped tie than he did in any formal tuxedo.

Helena's mouth went dry. No wonder Jill had been grinning like a schoolgirl.

'Ah, here she is,' said David, and then both men were on their feet, greeting her with smiles, the megawatt force of Leo's almost knocking her back on her heels.

He walked over, slipped his arm around her waist and dropped a featherlight kiss on her temple. Her knees nearly gave out.

'Morning, *cara*.' The firm press of his hand in her side sent a message—or was it a warning? 'My meeting was cancelled at the last minute and, since I was nearby, I thought I'd take the opportunity to see your offices.' He drew her into the room. 'And to meet David, of course.'

Her gaze darted to the older man, who now wore a grin to rival Jill's. She opened her mouth, but the dryness had crawled down her throat and no sound came out aside from a slight wheeze.

She gave herself a mental kick. 'Sorry I'm late, David. Problems on the tube…'

He waved off the apology. 'It's a nice change to beat you into the office for once. And I must say it's been an unexpected pleasure to chat with your man, here.'

*Her man.* The floor lurched and it was only Leo's grip that kept her steady, despite the unsettling effect his touch had on her insides. She wanted to swat his hand away, sink into a nearby chair. She forced herself to concentrate on David's voice.

'I was just telling Leo how seldom you take any leave, and he mentioned how keen he is to get you to Italy.'

He paused, rocked on his heels, looking immensely chuffed with himself all of a sudden. Helena felt faint.

'He also tells me you're off to Rome at the weekend and it would be the perfect chance for you to stay longer.' The men exchanged a glance. 'I think it's an excellent idea. Why don't you take a week?'

Helena couldn't help herself; she gaped at her boss. 'A…a *week*?'

Leo's fingers dug into her side but she refused to look at him. If he flashed her another of those devastating smiles she'd lose her ability to think, let alone remain upright.

She stared at David. 'I…I couldn't. Things are much too busy.'

'Nonsense. The office won't grind to a halt in your absence and neither will I. Hire me a temp who's half as efficient as you and I'll survive the week just fine.'

'Perhaps you should listen to your boss, *cara*,' came a silky voice in her ear, and she stifled the adolescent urge to stamp her heel onto his foot.

'I'll think about it,' she said to David. 'I promise. But right now we should get back to work. I'm sure Leo's taken enough of your time.'

A slight shift in her stance dislodged his hand from her hip. She turned, forced a smile onto her stiff lips.

'Shall we grab a quick coffee before you go?'

# CHAPTER FOUR

HELENA OPENED THE door to a vacant meeting room, stood to one side and waited for Leo to enter. He paused, gave the room a cursory once-over, then crossed to a large bank of windows overlooking the River Thames and the City of London's eclectic skyline of spires and towers.

'Not bad, Helena.' He turned his back to the view. 'You were a little stiff, but we can work on that.'

She closed the door, sucked in a deep breath and counted to twelve before the urge to shout had safely passed.

She expelled the air from her lungs. 'Why?'

'Why do we need to work on it?'

She made a ticking sound in her throat. 'Please don't play games with me.'

One eyebrow hooked up, as did one corner of his mouth—a subtle shift of facial muscles that barely qualified as a smile, yet Helena had the distinct impression he was enjoying himself.

'The only game I'm playing is the one you wanted to play, *cara.*'

'Stop calling me that.' She crossed her arms over her chest. 'And stop avoiding the question. I assume you've changed your mind about things since Friday? Why?'

Moving with more grace than a man of his height and size should possess, he propped his hip on the long conference table dominating the room. 'You're assuming my mind was made up.'

'Wasn't it?'

'No.'

'Then why did you let me leave?'

He shrugged. 'I wanted time to consider your proposal.'

She huffed out a breath. The possibility that in the interim *she* might change *her* mind clearly hadn't occurred to him. She changed tack. 'Why are you here?'

His brow furrowed. 'Did we not just establish that?'

'No, I mean why are you *here*? At my office. Talking to my boss.' She narrowed her eyes at him. 'How did you know where I work?'

'You gave me the address yourself.'

She thought about that, then bit her lip. He was right. She'd jotted down the address so he could send a car to collect her on Friday. A simple enquiry at the downstairs security desk would have filled in the rest. Still, it didn't excuse his turning up here with no warning. He had her mobile number. He could have phoned.

*Like you could have phoned him before turning up at the hotel?*

She slammed a lid on that voice. 'And your little *tête-à-tête* with David? What was that all about?'

His mouth quirked again. 'He invited me into his office. Refusing would have been rude, no?' The quirk lingered a few seconds more. 'Your boss seems a pleasant man—he speaks very highly of you, by the way. But tell me…' He paused, all trace of levity leaving his face. 'Why are you wasting your time in a job like this?'

His question stung. It shouldn't have, but it did. It reminded her of her father and all the hurtful criticisms she'd endured as a child. The small, painful barbs that pierced the protective wall her mother tried to erect between father and daughter. Her list of faults was exhaustive. And while being born a girl surely drove the first of many nails into her coffin, opting for design school over a law degree and dating a man not of her father's choosing certainly hammered in the last.

She lifted her chin. 'You're belittling my job now?'

'Not at all. I appreciate the value of a skilled assistant. I have an excellent one myself, and she is an asset to my office. But this—' he lifted a hand to indicate their surroundings '—is not the career you were planning seven years ago.'

Not the answer she'd expected. Still, she didn't need to justify her choices. Her job was *not* the dream career in design she'd once envisaged, but hopes and dreams, just like people—just like tiny, innocent, unborn babies—could unexpectedly die.

She dismissed his censure with a shrug. She worked hard, made an honest independent living, and no one— not her father and certainly not this man—had any right to judge her. 'Plans change. People change. And how I make a living is no business of yours.'

His black-lashed eyes treated her to a long, intense regard that made her tummy muscles tighten. 'You are right—it's not my business,' he said at last, though his tone wasn't in the least contrite. 'What you do in the coming weeks, however, *is*. Assuming you want to proceed with this little plan of yours?'

She stared at him, a prickle of unease tiptoeing down her spine. *Weeks?* Her arms fell to her sides. 'You're not serious about me spending a whole week in Italy?' Her stunned gaze met his cool, unwavering stare. She shook her head. 'Oh, no. That…that wasn't the agreement.'

His brows snapped together. 'We had no agreement, as I recall. You chose instead to put me in a difficult position with my client and then used it as a means of blackmail.'

*Blackmail?* 'I did no such thing!' Her face flamed. With indignation, she told herself. Not with guilt. Definitely not guilt. '*You* chose not to correct Carlos's assumption about us. I simply played along and then suggested we might come to some…some mutually beneficial arrangement.'

'Ah. Yes. The "mutually beneficial arrangement" in which I grant your father a grace period of four weeks, and in return you give me the pleasure of your company for—' his eyebrows rose '—one night?'

She smoothed her palms down the front of her black knee-length skirt. 'One *evening*,' she corrected, keeping her chin elevated. 'And, yes, that would be the arrangement to which I'm referring.'

He laughed—a deep, mellifluous sound that seemed to reach out and brush her skin like the rub of raw silk.

Her anger spiked. 'Is something amusing?'

'Only your ability to play naive when it suits you.'

'What is that supposed to mean?'

'It means you are well aware those terms are weighted in your favour and not mine.' He took his time adjusting a silver cufflink on his left sleeve. When he looked up, his expression had hardened. 'Did you think I would simply roll over for you, Helena?'

The undercurrent of menace in his voice made her knees quiver again. 'But why?' she blurted. 'What could you possibly want with me for a week?'

One side of his mouth kicked up. 'What, indeed?' he murmured, his gaze sweeping her length in an unhurried appraisal that set her teeth on edge—more so because she knew her clumsy question had invited it. 'Let's call it a balancing of the odds.' His eyes flicked back to hers. 'It would be a crime, would it not, if one of us were to feel…cheated?'

An enigmatic response at best. A deflection of her question as skilful as it was irritating.

She crossed to a window, leaned her hip against the metal sill and attempted nonchalance. 'So our pretence of being a couple—you're suggesting we keep that up for the entire week?'

'*Si.*'

'Why?'

'People will want to see us.'

'What people?'

'The people who have heard about you.' He tilted his head and smiled. 'Do not look so puzzled, Helena. You know how it is among the rich and privileged—the gossip mill is a voracious beast. And Rome is no different from London. Worse, in fact. We Italians love our drama.'

Her temples started to throb. 'But I met Carlos only three nights ago.'

He gave another of his maddening shrugs. 'Carlos tells his wife. His wife tells their daughter. Anna tells a friend… or twenty. News travels. You know how it works.'

Yes. She knew how it worked—that brittle, superficial world of the social elite. It had been her world once and she rarely missed it. Scratch the surface of gloss and glamour and every time you'd find a bitter core of hypocrisy and backstabbing.

She massaged the growing pressure in her temples. What madness had she started? 'What if we don't convince them?'

'That we are lovers?'

'Yes.' The word came out slightly strangled.

He straightened from the table. 'You assured me you could handle it. Are you getting cold feet already, Helena?'

She almost laughed at his choice of expression. Cold? Oh, no. No part of her felt cold right now. Not even close. Not when the prospect of their playing lovers for an entire week had her blood racing so hot and crazy she feared her veins might explode.

He stepped towards her. 'There *is* one way to ensure we're convincing.'

'Oh?' She tamped down the urge to scurry to the other side of the room. 'How?'

'Drop the pretence.'

Her brain took several seconds to register his meaning. She blinked, a bubble of incredulous laughter climbing her throat. 'You're kidding, right?'

'You find the prospect of sex with me abhorrent?'

The question—so explicit and yet so casually delivered—triggered a fresh wave of heat that burned from her hairline all the way down to the valley between her breasts. Abhorrent? No. Dangerous? Yes. Terrifying? *Utterly.* Though not for any reason she was fool enough to admit.

Her brain scrambled for a foothold. 'I don't understand.' That sounded lame. 'You said you didn't—that you weren't—that you no longer...' *Wanted me.* Were those the words he'd used? She squeezed her eyes shut. No. His exact words had been, *I'm not interested in anything you could offer.*

A shard of pain in the vicinity of her heart made her wince.

'What is there to understand?'

She opened her eyes to find him standing in front of her. Startled, she stepped back, the windowsill's sharp edge biting into her thighs.

'We know we're compatible in bed,' he said, his voice so calm, so matter-of-fact she wanted to scream. 'Why not make the most of our arrangement—throw some pleasure into the mix?'

Lightheaded suddenly, she gripped the ledge behind her, its hard metal surface cool and reassuringly solid beneath her palms. She breathed in. Out again. Summoned calm. He was toying with her...having fun at her expense. Needling for a reaction he wasn't going to get.

She tightened her fingers on the sill. 'I still don't believe you're serious.'

'And you still haven't answered my question.'

'What question?'

'Do you find the prospect of sleeping with me abhorrent?'

She looked him in the eye. She wouldn't lie.

'Of course not.'

But neither would she pander to his ego.

'But that doesn't mean I have any great desire to jump into your bed.'

He shifted closer and she shrank back—away from the

wall of masculine heat threatening to envelop her. A tell-tale pulse galloped at the base of her throat and she cursed her body's irrepressible responses. Why, oh, why could she not control her reactions to him?

'Is that so?' He lifted a finger and traced a fiery line from her jaw down to that delicate pulse-point in her neck. 'Then why do I make you nervous? Or is there another reason your heart is beating so wildly right now?'

She smacked his hand away and tried to straighten, barely daring to breathe. If she swayed the tiniest fraction their bodies would connect. Just the thought made her nipples peak hard and sensitive under the cotton layers of her bra and blouse.

'Don't flatter yourself,' she snapped, but his gaze was already dipping, taking in the evidence of her body's swift, mortifying arousal.

When his eyes reclaimed hers, the naked hunger in those inky depths nearly took her knees from under her.

'Your body betrays you, Helena.'

Before she could utter a denial his hands spanned her waist, his palms searing like hot iron through thin cotton as they slid upwards, coming to rest beneath the swell of her breasts. He dragged his thumbs up and outward, gliding them over taut, sensitive peaks. Her breath locked in her throat, a combination of panic and unbidden craving making her blood pulse at a dizzying speed.

'I think you are not as immune to me as you would like to believe,' he crooned in her ear.

And then he was setting her away from him. Stepping back. Giving her room to breathe.

Leaving her hot and flustered and confused.

He straightened his silver tiepin. 'Those are my terms.'

His tone had turned crisp, businesslike, his face impassive, and she wondered with a touch of hysteria if the lust she'd seen in his eyes had been imagined or real.

'Take it or leave it, Helena. But I need your answer—*now*.'

She hesitated, her thoughts splintering, scattering in too many directions. *Too unexpected...too overwhelming... too crazy...*

She drew a shaky breath and expelled it. 'I...I don't know...'

'In that case we have no deal.'

And just like that he turned to go.

Stunned, she stared after him, motionless at first, then with teeth clenched, hands fisting by her sides. She closed her eyes, the throb in her temples building to a painful crescendo. *What was she doing?* Was she really going to stand here and watch him leave? After he had, in essence, offered her what she wanted? He'd asked for one week in return—one week out of her life. Was that sacrifice so unthinkable?

*For her mother?*

She snapped open her eyes. 'Wait!'

He stopped, glanced back, one hand raised to the door. *'Si?'*

'Five days,' she croaked.

His arm lowered. *'Scusi?'*

She cleared her throat. 'Five days,' she repeated, certain he'd heard her well enough the first time. 'And my own room.'

'Seven.' He turned, his dark eyes glinting. 'And I can guarantee you'll find more satisfaction in my room.'

*Cocky bastard.* She smiled thinly. 'My own room.'

He shrugged, unconcerned. As if, for all his baiting, where she slept mattered to him not one way or the other.

'And my father gets six weeks.'

A mirthless laugh rumbled in his chest. 'Nice try.'

'Five, then.'

'Four.'

They stared at one another, eyes locked in challenge, each waiting for the other to concede. He wouldn't, she knew, but she needed this final moment of defiance.

Needed to savour these last precious seconds of sanity before she plunged off the edge into madness.

The prospect alone had fear clawing her insides, but it wasn't the promise of night-time pleasures with the man who had once owned her heart that frightened her beyond measure. It was the hot, delicious, burgeoning spark of desire in her belly she could neither extinguish nor control.

She squared her shoulders. Hiked up her chin. *Please don't let me regret this.*

'We have a deal.'

On Thursday, close to noon, Helena's mobile phone rang. She answered on the run, dashing out to collect a sandwich for David and a salad for herself prior to a lunch meeting.

'You're panting.'

*Leo.*

'I'm running.'

Well, almost. Walking briskly. She dodged a flying cycle courier, who in turn dodged a double-decker bus.

'Contrary to popular belief, secretaries don't spend all day sitting on their backsides.'

An unexpected chortle came down the line. A deep, sexy, gravel and velvet laugh that reminded her, fleetingly, of the old Leo. Her stomach flip-flopped.

'A car will pick you up tomorrow, at six p.m., to take you to the airport. Where do you wish to be collected?'

She jostled her way into a popular sandwich bar, wondered if he was still in London or back in Rome, then wondered why she cared.

She mimicked his cool, no-nonsense tone. 'From the office.'

'Fine. Six o'clock. Don't be late.' He ended the call as abruptly as he'd commenced it.

Helena frowned at her phone, then shoved it back in her blazer pocket and smothered a flash of annoyance. Letting his lack of geniality irritate her was silly—a waste of mental energy when she had none to spare. They weren't a couple, and nor were they friends. Out of the public eye there was no need for pleasantries or false sentiment. And as for his taunts about her sleeping in his room, sharing his bed—turning their ruse into reality—they had been nothing more than that.

*Taunts.*

Unfortunately that thought didn't placate her nerves later that evening as she stared at the neatly packed contents of her suitcase. Stomach churning, she ran through the list in her head one last time, confident she hadn't overlooked any essential items. Tomorrow the compact roller case would wheel easily on and off the train to work and her canvas carry-on, holding her passport, purse, and the jeans and tee she would change into for travelling, was light enough to hitch over one shoulder should she need a hand free.

Satisfied, she made some peppermint tea to pacify her tummy and settled on her sofa. It was late now—well after eleven—and her flat was silent, the tenants upstairs and the neighbourhood streets finally, blissfully quiet. She sipped her tea, let the fragrant brew circulate and soothe, then put down her cup and picked up the envelope she'd pulled from her nightstand drawer earlier in the evening.

She lifted the flap and pulled out a photograph—a picture of a tiny baby swaddled in the soft folds of a hospital-issue blanket. For long moments she studied the image, noting every detail even though she could close her eyes and still know every individual feature by heart. From the adorable tufts of jet-black hair to the miniature half-moons of delicate lashes and the sweetest little Cupid's bow mouth she'd ever seen on a child.

She'd named her son Lucas, and he would have been six now had he lived. She had other mementos of him, too. Small treasures. Keepsakes. Stored in the beautiful wooden memory box her mother had bought. But this image of her son—so tiny and precious, cradled in her arms as if he simply slept—was by far her favourite.

She swallowed and breathed through the dull, familiar ache that settled in her chest whenever she thought of her stillborn son.

Carefully, she slipped the photo back into the envelope.

Leo had been long gone by the time she had learnt she was pregnant, and though she'd known in her heart she had to tell him she hadn't found the courage to do so. He'd been so angry the last time they'd spoken, his declaration that he never wanted to see her again so adamant and final. Far easier, she had discovered, to let fear and hurt rule her head than to step back into the firing line.

And yet the day she gave birth to their son—the moment she cradled his tiny, silent, still warm body in her arms—all that fear and hurt became trivial. Irrelevant. Because she knew. Knew that if Lucas had been gifted life she could never have kept him from his father. Could never have denied Leo the chance to know he had created such a beautiful, perfect little boy.

She rose, went to her bedroom and slid the envelope back into her nightstand drawer.

Months of counselling had helped her to move on with her life, overcome her feelings of anger and guilt, but those dark, endless days of soul-destroying grief—she wouldn't wish those on anyone. Not her worst enemy and not Leo. What could be gained now by dredging up all that heartache and sorrow? Nothing. It was history. Water under the bridge. Whatever cliché one wanted to assign it.

Some burdens, she reminded herself, were better borne alone.

Leo stood at the head of the steps that scaled the private jet and checked his watch for the fifth time in as many minutes.

*Damn it.* Why did his shoulders feel as if they were

roped into knots the size of fists? And why couldn't he shake this weird, jittery feeling from the pit of his stomach?

Granted, he'd expected the car he'd sent for Helena to have arrived by now, but it was Friday rush hour and this was London. Traffic would be hitting its peak and a fifteen-minute delay was negligible. If the driver had encountered any serious hold-ups, or if Helena had failed to show, he'd have heard by now.

All of which meant he needed to kill this obsession with his watch and *relax*.

This arrangement of theirs might top the scale of hare-brained ideas, but his impromptu return to London on Monday had at least gained him an edge. In less than an hour he'd blindsided Helena at her office—fair payback for ambushing him at the hotel—tossed her firmly on to the back foot and enjoyed their verbal sparring to boot.

Though not nearly as much as he'd enjoyed putting his hands on her.

His fingers curled at the memory of her skin's heat penetrating his palms through her thin blouse and the way her nipples had pebbled in response to his touch. At some point the vibrant girl with her bold colours and creative ambitions had given way to a woman too content with mediocrity, yet he'd seen a spark of fire in her blue eyes that convinced him some remnant of that passionate, captivating girl still existed.

A flash of reflected sunlight at the edge of the Tarmac caught his eye and he squinted into the lowering sun. A silver SUV with tinted windows approached, cruising to a stop in the traffic safety zone alongside the aircraft hangar. The driver sprang from the vehicle and made for the other side, but his passenger had already climbed out. Smiling at the man, her loose curls tossed by the evening breeze, she spoke a few words Leo strained to hear but couldn't catch from where he stood.

He sucked in his breath, the edgy, irritable mood that

had plagued him all day dissipating beneath an entirely different kind of tension.

*Dio.*

Even casually attired, the woman was a breathtaking vision. A perfect combination of long, slender limbs and feminine curves in all the right places. An ache stirred deep in his groin as he watched her cross the Tarmac, her rounded breasts clearly outlined beneath her figure-hugging tee, the denim of her jeans stretched over shapely hips and slender thighs. In one hand she carried a jacket, in the other a small holdall.

He descended the steps. When she neared he took her bag, slipped an arm around her waist and pulled her flush against him. Her eyes widened, her mouth forming a perfect O of surprise.

'*Ciao*, Helena.' He lowered his head, intending to drop an experimental kiss on those sweet, inviting lips, but she averted her face and his mouth collided instead with her cheek.

Her body stiffened. 'People are watching,' she hissed.

He glanced at the men in overalls working around them, some engrossed in their tasks, others paused and openly staring.

'So they are.' He dragged her closer, some deep, primal instinct urging him to send a clear message to the onlookers. *Mine.* He turned his attention back to her mouth. 'Perhaps we should not disappoint them?'

Her eyes narrowed to pinpricks of sapphire and she pulled in a breath, but whatever retort hovered on that pretty pink tongue she chose not to share it. Instead she twisted from his grasp and started up the steps, the mesmerising roll and sway of her hips holding his gaze captive. He tightened his grip on her bag, his amusement tempered by a sting of annoyance.

Was this how she planned to fulfil her role as his mistress? By tolerating his touch only when it suited her?

*Think again,* cara.

'Drink?' he offered after he'd stashed her bag in an overhead locker and snapped the cover closed. For a woman she travelled exceptionally light. The carry-on he'd just stowed was small and compact, the single piece of luggage the driver had removed from the SUV not much larger.

The observation gave him pause. A week ago he'd have shrugged it off, assumed she planned to hit the shops in Rome and buy an extra case to carry home her purchases. Now, after Nico's report, he knew that scenario was unlikely. Despite her family's enviable wealth, Helena's lifestyle appeared modest, even frugal. A revelation he found oddly disturbing.

She tossed her jacket over a seat. 'Yes, please.'

He moved to a built-in bar where a bottle of champagne sat chilling on ice. He filled two long-stemmed flutes, handed one to Helena and raised the other in a toast. 'To our arrangement.'

She hesitated before touching her glass to his. The crystal sang sweetly as the rims clinked. 'To our arrangement.'

Her head arched back on her graceful neck as she took a surprisingly long swig of the effervescent liquid. She lowered the glass, gestured a hand at the cabin's interior.

'You travel in style.'

He considered the gleaming mahogany fixtures, fine Italian leather and thick cut pile carpet. The expansion of his business into Asia and North America over the last few years had demanded extensive travel, and his board had deemed the corporate jet a justifiable expense.

'You sound surprised.'

She shrugged. 'It's more luxurious than I'd expected.'

'And you disapprove?'

For a second the question seemed to throw her, then her features morphed back into an aloof, dignified mask. 'No. Of course not. It's just…not what I'm used to these days.'

'And what *are* you used to?'

Her eyebrows tugged together. 'I don't know. Things more…ordinary, I suppose.'

'In that case—' he took her glass, placed both flutes on the bar '—you will need to reacquaint yourself with things less…ordinary.'

He moved closer, enjoying the way her eyes flared wide, the titillating glimpse of her tongue as it darted across her lower lip. She was nervous, despite her cool, controlled demeanour. The skittering pulse at the base of her throat gave her away.

'And there is one more thing you must become accustomed to.'

She notched her chin. Quietly defiant. Utterly beautiful. 'And that is…?'

He captured her jaw between thumb and forefinger. 'Me.'

# CHAPTER FIVE

HELENA SWALLOWED. THE generous mouthful of bubbles she'd foolishly imbibed on an empty stomach was meant to give her sass and courage. Instead she felt lightheaded and shaky on her feet. She wanted to turn her head, tear her gaze from those mesmerising eyes, but his fingers held her captive.

'I don't know what you mean.'

'Then I will demonstrate.'

The instant his head lowered, panic seized her. 'Wait!' Her hands flew to his chest. 'What are you doing?'

He halted, his lips mere inches from hers, his black-fringed eyes glittering like a star-studded night. *With what? Amusement? Desire?*

'Demonstrating my point.'

She pushed harder, her fingers tingling, his warmth— his vitality—seeping through the fabric of his shirt and into her nerve-endings. 'What point?'

'That you seem to have developed an untimely aversion to me.'

He grasped her wrists, the latent strength in his long fingers making her bones feel small. Fragile.

'No one will believe we are lovers if you balk at my touch.'

She tried to free herself but he held fast, keeping her hands anchored to his chest. Under her palms his heart beat strong and steady, unlike hers, which had launched into the cardiac equivalent of a Fred and Ginger tap routine.

'We agreed to play lovers in public.' *Why did her voice sound so high and breathless?* 'Not in private. And I've proved to you I can do this.'

'Yet you stiffen in my arms like an innocent.'

He pulled her hands upward, linking them behind his neck. Dragging her body into agonising contact with his.

'It will not do, Helena. Carlos Santino is an astute man, his daughter no fool. If we are to convince them you must learn to relax with me.' His big hands circled her waist. 'And now is the perfect time for a lesson.'

Heat spiralled through her, but she fought the shiver of desire gathering momentum in her muscles. He was testing her boundaries, pushing her limits, and she would not give him the satisfaction of seeing her quiver. She dropped her arms and willed her body to go lax. Unresponsive. She could struggle, make it difficult for him, but he was strong. He'd kiss her anyway. Better to play it cool and aloof and retain at least some scrap of dignity.

She closed her eyes, pressed her lips together and waited, but the expected pressure of his mouth didn't come.

His hot breath skimmed her lips as he spoke. 'Your little martyr act doesn't wash with me, *cara*. Admit it. You want my kiss. My touch. Your body craves it—' his hand rose to the back of her head and closed around a fistful of curls '—just as mine does.'

She opened her eyes and shook her head—or tried to. Moving was difficult with his long fingers tangled in her hair. 'You're wrong.'

'Are you sure about that?' His teeth flashed, his quick smile too sharp. Too knowing. 'I remember the nights you begged for my touch…the nights you lay naked beneath me, panting and pleading—'

'Stop!' His brazen words evoked a hot rush of erotic memories. Fresh panic spurted in her chest. 'Maybe this was a…a mistake.'

His eyebrows hiked. 'This was your idea, remember? What are you afraid of?'

*Myself.*

'Nothing.'

Amusement rumbled deep in his chest. 'Liar.'

He tugged her head back, tilted her face to his, and she knew in the span of a single panicked heartbeat she was headed for trouble. Knew the instant his mouth covered hers this kiss would not be the hard, demanding, alpha-take-charge kiss she'd expected. No. This kiss was something altogether different. Something far more calculated and disturbing. A skilled, sensual assault that sent his mouth and tongue moving in long, lazy strokes over her tightly clamped lips.

Helena's nostrils flared, her sharp inhalation drawing in the heady spice of his cologne, and a whimper of protest caught in her throat. Or was it a moan? Either way, Leo showed no sign of relenting. His lips coaxed, his tongue teased, his teeth lightly grazed. And with every stroke, every nip and tug, her resolve to refuse him access suffered another crippling blow.

Ruthless, she thought, the floor tilting under her, the bones in her legs melting like heated wax. He was ruthless and she was drowning, oblivious to everything except the hard male body imprisoning hers and the sweet, blistering assault of his mouth.

Belatedly she registered a tugging at her waistband, a whisper of cool air on her midriff—and then the explosive charge of flesh against heated flesh. She jerked with surprise, but the hand behind her head held firm while the other rose to cup her breast. Deft fingers hooked aside cotton and lace and closed around one hard, almost painfully taut peak.

Helena arched her back and groaned. She couldn't help it. Her body was on fire and she couldn't douse the flames. Her lips parted, her lungs desperate for air, and she did nothing to resist when Leo's tongue swept in and tangled with her own. He growled—with satisfaction or triumph?— and then she was lost, unable to remember why she didn't want this. Didn't want *him*. With a moan of surrender, she wound her arms around his neck. Arched into his touch. Opened herself to his kiss.

'Ahem…'

Helena froze.

*Oh, no, no, no.*

That could *not* be the sound of a man clearing his throat inside the cabin. Heat of a different kind crawled up her neck as she realised that Leo, too, was motionless, his mouth locked on hers, one hand twined in her hair while the other cradled her breast beneath her tee.

Horrified, she wriggled to snap whatever spell held him frozen. Slowly his head lifted, his gaze blazing into hers with momentary intensity before shifting to the uniformed man standing near the entry to the cockpit. Her cheeks flamed. Why didn't Leo release her? Remove his hand from her breast? She squirmed, mortified.

'Five minutes to take-off, sir,' the attendant said, his voice neutral, his face devoid of expression.

Leo nodded. '*Grazie.*'

The man retreated behind a floor-length curtain and she dragged in a breath, waited for the curtain to fall, then shoved at Leo's chest. Her trembling arms possessed just enough strength to break his hold. Hastily she rearranged her bra and tee, conscious of her smarting cheeks. Her tingling lips.

*One kiss.*

And she'd lost herself completely. Been ready to give him whatever he wanted. Whatever he demanded. How could she be so weak? So pathetic?

Was this what her mother did every time she kissed and made up with her husband? Did she let herself get played? Sucked in by some practised seduction routine that made her forget all the hurt that had gone before? All the ugliness that would surely follow?

Anger flared, at herself. At him. 'Is this part of our

deal?' She yanked the hem of her tee into her jeans. 'That you get to maul me whenever you feel like it?'

He had the nerve to smile. A cool, sardonic smile that made her want to throw something—preferably at his head.

'You call that being mauled?'

'What would *you* call it when a man forces himself on a woman?'

His soft laugh jarred her nerves. 'Force?'

She would have spun away if his hand hadn't risen with startling speed to capture her jaw. Her pulse skittered.

'Don't fool yourself, *cara.*' He dragged his thumb over her mouth, parted her lips. Ran his tongue over his own as if recalling how she tasted. 'You enjoyed that as much as I did.'

A sharp denial danced on her tongue but she choked it back. His heated appraisal, the glitter in those dark eyes, told her he felt the pull of their physical attraction as surely and inexorably as she. Refusing to acknowledge what they both knew existed was futile. Dangerous. Instinct warned he'd take great pleasure in proving her wrong—again.

She jerked free of his grasp, moved to a window seat and strapped herself in. Outside, the ground crew completed their final safety checks and she stared out the window, feigned interest in their activity.

Leo made her feel vulnerable, exposed, and she hated it. Hated that her desire for him was so plain to see. Hated the ease with which he zeroed in on it, ruthlessly exploiting her weakness for him.

Her father did the same thing—found people's weaknesses, their soft spots and vulnerabilities. Was that why her mother stayed? Did he wield her fears and weaknesses against her? Use them as leverage so she didn't leave?

Helena blinked away the burn of tears. She'd never make her mother's mistake. She'd rather die a dried-up old spinster than tolerate a man who didn't treat her with respect.

If only Leo's kiss hadn't made her blood sing. Hadn't fired every dormant cell in her body to glorious life.

With a ragged sigh, she closed her eyes and let her head fall back against the seat.

*So much for cool and aloof.*

Leo closed his laptop as the pilot announced their descent into Rome's Fiumicino Airport. The flight had been uneventful and he'd passed the time with work, sifting through emails and reports while Helena had mostly slept. Or pretended to. He wasn't sure which. Either way, she'd avoided engaging with him, stirring only once in two hours to visit the restroom and accept refreshments.

He studied her in the seat opposite. Her eyes were closed, long lashes the same dark auburn as her hair fanned over ivory skin, and the slopes of her breasts rose and fell in time with the steady, hypnotic rhythm of her breathing. Her hair was shiny and tousled and the thick, lustrous curls he'd enjoyed twining his fingers through tumbled in soft waves to her shoulders.

His groin stirred, unbidden. She was a temptress. Beautiful as a mythical siren and twice as dangerous with those sweet, alluring lips that could test the restraint of any man with a libido and a heartbeat.

They had certainly tested his.

He let his gaze linger a few seconds longer, then dragged his focus to the window and the vast sprawl of lights in the blackness beyond.

This version of Helena was a mystery to him and he didn't like mysteries—or secrets. He liked staying one step ahead of the game. The takeover was a done deal, but writing off his opponent would be premature. Douglas Shaw would be seeking ways to retaliate, and the man had a reputation for playing dirty. The possibility that he'd reached out to his estranged daughter, manipulated her in an effort to undermine his adversary, was one Leo couldn't afford to ignore.

The jet's wheels hit the Tarmac and Helena stirred. She straightened, blinked, looked out the window, then peered at her watch.

'One hour,' he said.

She glanced up. 'Sorry?'

'Turn your watch forward one hour. It's just after ten.'

The plane taxied to a stop near a large hangar. Fifteen minutes later customs formalities had been completed and their luggage transferred to the trunk of a black Maserati convertible. He guided Helena into the front passenger seat, then slid behind the wheel, anticipating at once the dichotomous feelings of control and freedom he enjoyed whenever he took charge of the sleek, powerful machine.

'The Eternal City,' Helena murmured when, a short time later, he manoeuvred them into busier, more densely populated streets. She stared out her side window at the illuminated façades of elegant old buildings, towering columns and ancient timeworn structures.

'You've never visited Rome?'

She shook her head. 'I never got around to it.'

He glanced at her. Was that a wistful note in her voice? Seven years ago she had bubbled with excitement when he'd suggested bringing her to Rome. He didn't know why the fact she hadn't come with a boyfriend or lover in the years since should give him a small kick of satisfaction—but it did.

'I'd love to explore while I'm here.'

'You can sightsee during the days, while I'm working. I will arrange a driver and a guide.'

He sensed rather than saw her sharp look. 'I don't need a babysitter.'

'I am not suggesting you do.'

'But you'd be happier if someone kept an eye on me,

right?' Her sigh was loud. 'You really *do* have trust issues, don't you?'

A young couple on a red scooter swerved in front of the car, forcing him to brake. 'Meaning…?'

'Meaning I'm not going to run off the minute your back's turned. We made a deal and I don't plan to renege on it. I'm here, aren't I?'

The scooter sped off down an alley and he hit the accelerator again. 'Rome is a vast city, Helena. An experienced guide can ensure you see the best sights. Go to the right places. There are areas I would not like to see you, or any woman unfamiliar with the city, go to alone.'

'I can take care of myself.'

He smiled. Briefly. 'I have no doubt. But if you wish to sightsee you will have a guide. I will not debate with you on this,' he ended, injecting a note of finality into his voice.

Helena averted her face and he wondered if she would sulk. He didn't recall her being the petulant type, but then neither did he remember her being so argumentative. Perversely, he liked it.

'Are you always so over-protective?'

Her voice was soft, laced with curiosity rather than the irritation that had spiked her earlier words. He frowned, a ripple of discomfort sliding through him. The question felt intrusive, too personal, and for several awkward moments an answer eluded him.

'I do not consider the use of good sense to be over-protective,' he said at last.

Silence met his statement, and when he glanced over she was studying him intently. He tightened his grip on the steering wheel. Marietta, too, had accused him of being over-protective at times, but taking care of his sister was a responsibility he would never shirk—no matter how vociferously she objected. He knew the consequences of failing in that duty and he never wanted to feel the devastation of such failure again. Loving someone, being responsible for them, was no trifling task. Most days it scared the hell out of him.

Setting his jaw, he crunched the Maserati's gears and turned into the narrow lane that ran down the side of his apartment building. He pressed a key fob on his visor and a wrought-iron gate rattled open, granting access to the secure courtyard he shared with his tenants. He nosed the car past two others and stopped in a reserved space beneath the leafy branches of a mature orange tree.

Helena peered up at the building's ornate façade. 'You live right in the city?'

He shut off the engine. 'Apartments in central Rome with private parking are rare. When one of my clients put the building on the market last year I considered it a good investment.'

She gaped at him. 'You bought the entire building?'

He shrugged. 'It's convenient. My office is a few blocks from here.'

She shook her head and climbed out of the car, completely absorbed, it seemed, in her surroundings. Leo retrieved their luggage from the boot and hoped their previous discussion was over and forgotten. With any luck she'd realise the futility of defying him and accept his edict about the sightseeing.

If she didn't...?

Well, he could think of several ways to silence her arguments. And he wasn't above a few dirty tactics of his own.

Leo's penthouse apartment was spectacular.

Stylish modern furniture, richly textured rugs and great expanses of glass created a slick, contemporary oasis that floated in peaceful isolation above the heart of the ancient city.

Helena tried hard not to look impressed.

Tried harder still to calm the flutter in her belly as he took her to a bedroom with stunning views from a floor-to-ceiling window and an en suite bathroom so massive she could have swung a tiger. She slipped her holdall off her shoulder, her gaze landing on the gigantic bed with its big, plump pillows and soft ivory comforter.

A steady flush crept up her neck.

'Hungry?'

She darted him a look. 'A bit.' On the plane she'd snacked on biscuits and fruit between bouts of sleep. Now her stomach craved something more substantial. Not to mention her mouth. Dry as a sandpit. 'Thirsty more than anything.'

He laid her case on the upholstered ottoman at the end of the bed. 'Settle in, then come and find me in the kitchen when you're done. Back down the hall on the right.'

Left alone, and with a burst of energy born of nervous tension, Helena made short work of unpacking. Not that the task required much effort. Even with all her clothes arranged on individual hangers she'd utilised only a fraction of the gargantuan wardrobe. She straightened the skirt of the long black gown she'd bought on impulse from a store selling pre-loved designer fashion, stashed her case in the rear of the wardrobe, then checked her phone.

No messages, but she hadn't expected any. She'd told her mother she was going out of town, visiting a girlfriend in Devon and then attending a team-building course with colleagues during the week. Small, innocuous lies that had caused a pang of guilt, but there was no reason her mother should know about her arrangement with Leo.

She tucked her phone away. Recent conversations with her mother had been stilted, tense, but Miriam *had* agreed to meet and talk the following weekend, and that, if nothing else, was progress. In the meantime Douglas had run off to Scotland to shoot deer and no doubt seek solace in a bottle or two of single malt: typical behaviour for a man who thought himself untouchable. But on the upside her mother was safe. For now, at least. The coward couldn't lay hands on his wife while he wallowed in denial four hundred miles away.

Expelling her father from her thoughts, Helena ventured into the hall and followed the faint aroma of garlic and basil until she came to a big, stainless steel and black granite kitchen.

Leo stood behind a large central island, his hand wrapped around the handle of a sharp knife, a partially sliced tomato on the thick wooden board in front of him. An open can of soda sat on the granite. He appeared relaxed. At ease. And more achingly handsome than any man had a right to look, standing at a bench chopping vegetables.

She raised her eyebrows. 'You cook?'

He glanced up. 'Bruschetta is hardly cooking. But, yes, when I have the time. My housekeeper stocks the kitchen for me.'

A housekeeper. That explained the spotless floors and gleaming surfaces everywhere she looked.

'You said you were thirsty. Wine, juice or soda?'

Wine was tempting, but her lack of control after the bubbles on the plane made her shy away from that idea. 'Juice, thanks.' She raised a hand when he paused his work. 'I can help myself.' Better that than stand there gawking at him. She crossed to a stainless steel double-door refrigerator, surveyed its impressive contents, and selected a carton of apple juice. 'Glasses?'

'Cabinet on your left.'

After filling a tall glass and savouring her first thirst-quenching swallow, she hovered awkwardly. 'Anything I can do?'

He scooped the cut tomato onto a platter with thin strips of prosciutto, sliced mozzarella, fresh basil leaves and fat cloves of garlic. 'If you still like Cerignola olives, there's a jar in the fridge door. Small bowls are in the same cabinet as the glasses.'

Her mouth watered. Years ago he'd introduced her to the

large, sweet-flavoured Italian olives and she'd loved them. Still did. The fact he remembered that tiny detail made her heart clench in an unexpected way.

What else did he remember?

She found the jar and grabbed two ceramic bowls—one for the olives and one for discarded stones.

It didn't matter what he remembered. Or what he didn't. She wasn't here for a waltz down memory lane.

She hunted out a spoon and fished out the olives, putting them into a bowl, careful not to transfer too much of the oily brine.

She couldn't resist. The olives were plump and juicy and she was ravenous. She popped one straight from the jar into her mouth, paused a second to anticipate the burst of flavour on her tongue—then nearly inhaled the olive whole when two large hands circled her waist from behind. Her hand jerked and the spoon slipped, catapulting an olive over the benchtop like a miniature green missile. Helplessly she watched it shoot off the end and roll, leaving a wet, glistening trail over the limestone floor.

Leo pulled her against him. 'Relax,' he murmured in her ear, and she bit through the flesh of the olive.

The temptation to do exactly that—relax into him, let her shoulders and buttocks mould to his hard, muscular contours—was too strong. Too dangerous.

She gripped the edge of the bench.

*Oh, God.*

She wasn't ready for him to touch her like this, hold her like this, whisper in her ear like a sweet, familiar lover. No more than she'd been ready for the mind-blowing impact of his kiss. Yet in less than twenty-four hours she had to be ready. Tomorrow people would watch them closely. Especially the Santinos. And Italians were demonstrative people, unafraid to express themselves in front of others. She and Leo couldn't simply claim to be lovers. They must *behave* like lovers.

She forced her grip on the bench to loosen.

'I'm just getting in some practice.' His warm lips brushed the sensitive skin below her earlobe, inciting an involuntary shiver in her muscles. His arms tightened around her. 'You are cold?'

*Damn him.* She wasn't cold and he knew it. The evening was humid and sultry. She shook her head, not trusting herself to speak.

'So quiet, Helena…' His mouth trailed to the ultra-sensitive spot between her neck and shoulder. 'What are you thinking?'

*That I want this. I want you. I want you to stop and I want you never to stop.*

She removed the olive stone from her mouth and very carefully placed it in the empty bowl. 'I'm thinking I'd quite like that glass of wine now.'

He straightened. And chuckled? Yes, she could hear the gravelly purr in his throat. Feel the vibrations in his chest. His hands slid off her waist and she returned to her task. Focused on her breathing in an effort to slow her heartbeat.

He placed a glass of wine beside her.

'Thanks.' Somehow she managed to sound normal rather than breathless. Lifting the glass to her nose, she inhaled the spicy, berry-scented aroma. Did he also remember her preference for red wine?

Eager to avoid the onset of a tense, awkward silence, she sipped and said, 'Mmm…nice.'

'Vino Nobile di Montepulciano.'

She blinked. 'Pardon?'

'Noble Wine from Montepulciano. Not to be confused with the more commonly known wine derived from the Montepulciano grape in Abruzzo.' He extracted a tray of rustic-style bread slices from the oven's grill. 'Montepulciano is a hill town surrounded by vineyards in southern Tuscany. Vino Nobile di Montepulciano is one of Italy's oldest wines.'

'Tuscany?' Was he trying to put her at ease now with idle chitchat? Okay. Fine. It was safe ground—safer than where they were before. She'd go with it. She had to. She wouldn't survive the week if she couldn't handle a harmless conversation with him. 'I hear that part of Italy is beautiful.'

'*Si.* Very.' He transferred the platters to a slab of granite extending from the island and pulled out two high leather stools. 'I have a villa in the province of Siena, not far from Montepulciano.'

She sipped her wine, quietly digested that snippet of information. A villa in Tuscany. A penthouse in Rome. Exclusive hotel rooms in London. Not forgetting the house-keeper and, of course, his company jet. However severe his setback at the hands of her father, it hadn't stopped his meteoric rise to success.

She perched on a stool, decided that now was not the time to challenge him on that, and focused on the food. 'I'm hungry.' She studied the platters. 'Where do I start?'

'Here. Like this.' He rubbed a garlic clove on a piece of grilled bread, drizzled over olive oil, piled on tomato and mozzarella and topped it with basil leaves and a grind of salt and pepper. He handed it to her. 'Bruschetta—*tradizionale.*'

'Looks wonderful.'

And it tasted just as good.

They ate and drank and she asked him about Rome and Tuscany, quizzing him on the culture, history and climate of each region. He seemed content to keep their conversation light, the topics neutral, and gradually the pretence of normality eased her tension. Or was that thanks to the wine she'd consumed?

When Leo picked up the bottle again she covered her glass and shook her head. The wine had helped her relax, but too much would lull her into a false sense of comfort.

'We need a story about where and when we met,' he said,

his gaze fastening on her mouth as she fired in another olive. 'I suggest we use a version of the truth.'

Conscious of his scrutiny, she removed the olive stone as daintily as she could and washed the pulp down with a gulp of wine. 'The truth?'

'That we met at an art gallery in London some years ago and have recently become reacquainted.'

She nodded slowly. 'How recently?'

He sipped his wine, considered. 'Five months.'

Five months? Did that account for the time since he'd rejected Anna Santino and then some? Or had it been five months since his last mistress? Abruptly, she killed that line of thought. She didn't need to know. Didn't want to know.

'Okay. Five months.'

'Good.' He put his glass down, reached for an olive, the movement bringing his arm into contact with hers. The touch was fleeting, inadvertent, yet instant heat flared beneath her skin.

Without meaning to, she flinched.

His brows slammed down. '*Damn* it, Helena.'

'I'm sorry.'

'I don't bite.'

'I know.'

'Then why leap like a scalded cat every time I touch you?' Lines bracketed his mouth—deep grooves of displeasure that made her stomach lurch. 'Do you find my touch so repellent?'

Her eyes flared. 'No—'

'Perhaps you were right to have second thoughts.' He balled up his paper napkin and tossed it over the benchtop. 'We'll never pull this off. The whole thing is crazy. *Pazzo*.'

Panic surged up her throat. 'It's not. I *can* do this.'

'Can you?'

She pushed off her stool. 'Yes,' she said, her tone low and fierce, and before she could stifle the impulse she fisted her hands in his shirt, shoved him against the granite and slammed her mouth over his.

*Reckless!* a voice in her head screamed, but she silenced it. What better way to prove her ability to play his mistress than with a kiss? A kiss that had to knock him dead, she told herself, letting instinct and boldness take over as she flicked her tongue into his surprise-slackened mouth.

Heat combined with the taste of salt and red wine exploded on her tongue, and when he grunted she thrust deeper, a second time and a third, until his grunt became a low growl against her lips.

Leo moved, shifting his weight on the stool, and she felt the hot imprint of his big hands curving around her buttocks. Then he hauled her in close, his powerful thighs parting to accommodate her, and angled his head to give their mouths a better fit.

And, Lord, the man knew how to kiss. Knew how to use those sensual lips and that wicked tongue to devastating effect. He stroked into her mouth, his tongue hot, demanding, and she almost lost her grip on his shirt. Almost lost her grip on *herself.*

A warning shivered through her.

How easy it would be for her to let hunger overcome sense and give in to the hot need pulsing at her core. But this kiss wasn't about sating her needs, or his. It was about taking control. Proving a point. To herself as much as to him.

She wrenched her mouth away, stepped back and watched a range of expressions roll over his chiselled features. Her heart slammed against her ribs and she balled her hands, concentrated hard on calming her breathing.

Leo made no such effort. His breath fired from his chest in short, harsh bursts and a dark flush rode high on his cheekbones. She took in his bunched shirt, wet lips, stunned gaze. He looked like a man who had been thoroughly kissed.

*Please, voice, don't tremble.* 'I can handle this, Leo.'

She leaned in and rubbed her thumb over his mouth, wiping away the moisture from their kiss. His eyes darkened and his hands reached for her, but she backed off before he could touch her.

'Thanks for supper,' she said lightly. 'If you don't mind, I think I'll turn in. It's been a long day and I'm rather tired.' She paused in the doorway, forced a smile onto her lips. 'Goodnight.'

By the time Helena closed the door of the guest bedroom her heart was pounding so hard she felt short of breath and dizzy.

With swift, robotic movements that required blessedly little co-ordination, she brushed her teeth, shed her clothes and pulled on pyjama shorts and a matching cami. Then she crawled under the covers of the huge bed and groaned into a pillow.

These seven nights in Rome were going to be agony.

# CHAPTER SIX

LEO PUNCHED HIS pillow three times, and when that failed to appease him he sat up and hurled it across the room. The pillow sailed through the air, hit the far wall with a dull, satisfying thud, and slumped to the bedroom floor.

Juvenile behaviour, but it felt good.

He swung his legs off the bed, glanced at the digital clock telling him it was five minutes past six a.m.—ten minutes since he'd last glared at it—and pulled on some sweats. He needed to expend some energy, and since bed-wrecking sex with his house guest wasn't an option—not a wise one, at any rate—he'd have to settle for exercise.

Hard, punishing, sweat-drenching exercise.

*Damn the minx.*

He slung a towel over his shoulder, padded down his hallway to the small, well-equipped gym at the far end and set himself a gruelling pace on the treadmill.

Forty minutes later every muscle from his groin to his Achilles tendons strained and burned. Without slowing he swigged from his water bottle, yanked his tee shirt over his head and threw the sweat-soaked garment to the floor.

Perhaps if he'd made time for a mistress in recent months he wouldn't be struggling now to harness his libido. But his work in the lead-up to the takeover had consumed him day and night, leaving scant time for distractions of the female variety no matter how tempting or willing. A blonde, career-driven attorney in New York had been his one indulgence—a brief bedroom-only affair that ended by mutual agreement after his last visit eight, maybe nine weeks ago.

*Nine weeks.*

He cranked up the speed on the treadmill. No wonder he

was fit to explode after Helena's little sexpot performance in the kitchen last night. His memories of their lovemaking had remained vivid over the years—more so than he cared to admit—but he couldn't recall her ever having kissed him so senseless. Even now he could feel the imprint of her mouth, her tongue driving him wild, firing his body into a state of near-painful arousal.

With a grunt he stopped the treadmill, grabbed his towel and tee shirt and headed back to his room for a cold shower.

Helena was a paradox…a hotbed of unpredictability. Cool and flighty one minute, scorching the next. Estranged from her father yet willing to do almost anything, it seemed, to delay his day of reckoning. What game was she playing? So far nothing about her actions made sense. Nothing sat quite straight in his mind. And wasn't that the reason he'd brought her here? To keep her close until her true motives were revealed?

He snapped off the water, towelled himself dry and dressed in jeans and a button-down shirt. Feeling rejuvenated, he glanced at the clock. Still early, but he had emails to sift through, a mountain of paperwork to sort. He'd allow her another hour of beauty sleep. Two at the most.

*And then,* cara mia, *it's game on.*

'Morning, *cara.*'

Helena opened her eyes. Scowled. Shut them. She was dreaming again. Except this time Leo wasn't hot and naked and tangled in her sheets. He was sitting on the bed, fully clothed.

She threw her arm over her eyes.

*Get lost, Mr Sandman.*

'Your coffee is going cold.'

She snatched her arm down, blinked three times, then bolted upright so fast a galaxy of tiny stars danced in front of her eyes. 'Oh, my God!' *Not dreaming.* 'Wh…what are you doing here?'

'Breakfast.' He inclined his head towards a tray on the nightstand. 'Orange juice, *cornetti* and coffee. Unless you prefer tea in the morning?'

'I prefer *privacy* in the morning,' she snapped, to which he simply responded with a bone-melting smile.

Her heart tripped and fell and she swallowed a groan. Why must he look so crisp and gorgeous? She yanked the sheet to her chin, pushed a hand through her jungle of curls. 'What time is it?'

'Nine o'clock.'

'Oh…' She frowned, dismayed. 'I don't normally sleep so late.'

The tantalising smells of strong coffee and warm pastry wafted from the nightstand. She eyed the *cornetti*, all fresh and fluffy and tempting. Had he gone out especially for them?

She tried for a conciliatory smile. 'If you give me a few minutes I'll get up and dressed.' *In other words, get out. I can't breathe with you here.*

'Take your time.' He stood, and her shoulders sloped with relief—only to inch up again when he sauntered to the wardrobe. He flung open the doors. 'What are you wearing tonight?'

She blinked. 'I beg your pardon?'

He started riffling through her clothes and she leapt forward, one foot hitting the floor before she remembered her skimpy pyjama shorts. She sank back, frowning when he pulled out the long black dress.

He held it up. 'This?'

Her hands fisted in the sheet gathered against her chest. 'Yes. Does that meet with your approval?'

'It is black.'

'You're very observant.'

'And boring.'

She gritted her teeth. Okay, the high neckline and long

sleeves *were* a little conservative. But it was elegant and practical. 'I think the term you're looking for is classic.'

He tossed the dress onto the bed, flicked an imperious hand at the rest of her clothing. 'Where is the colour?'

She shrugged, but the tension in her shoulders made the gesture jerky. Where was he taking this? 'I'm a working girl now. Neutrals are more practical.'

He studied her intently. 'You used to like colour.'

His observation was hardly profound, yet all the same her insides twisted. 'Well, now I don't.' She reached for the orange juice, her throat suddenly parched, but her hand trembled and she put the glass down again.

She'd rather die of thirst than admit it, but he was right. Colour had been her passion. Her talent. Her joy. And her textile design degree, had she graduated, would have turned that passion into a career. But the day she buried her son—*their* son—the colour vanished from her world, and though she looked for it, tried desperately to reconnect with her passion, all she saw for the longest time were lifeless shades of grey. Bright colours had felt wrong. Artificial. Like painting the outside of a house to make it pretty while the inside remained neglected and rotten.

'I want to see you in something eye-catching tonight,' he said. 'Something more befitting my mistress.'

She stiffened. 'I don't measure up to your standards now?' An old familiar ache sparked in her chest. How many childhood years had she wasted, trying to live up to her father's impossible standards, knowing that no matter what she did it would never be good enough?

Leo's eyes narrowed. 'I'm talking about the dress. Not you.'

'Well.' She hiked her chin, tamped down her old insecurities. 'It will just have to do. It's the only gown I've brought.'

'Then we will shop today and buy you another.'

She shook her head. 'I can't afford anything new.'

'We agreed I would take care of expenses, *si*?'

'Travel costs. Not clothes. I don't need your charity.' *Or to be told what to wear.*

His eyebrows plunged into a dark V. 'Do not mistake my intent for charity, Helena. Outside of these walls you are my mistress, and tonight many eyes will be upon us. I will not have you fade into the background like an insipid wallflower.' He walked to the door, paused and glanced back. 'Enjoy your breakfast. We will leave as soon as you are ready.'

Helena sucked in her breath to hurl a refusal, but he was gone before the words could form on her tongue.

*Insipid?*

She glared at the closed door, seething for long minutes until a loud, insistent grumble from her stomach dragged her attention back to the pastries. Huffing out a resigned sigh, she picked up a fat *cornetto* and studied its golden crust. If she couldn't avoid the excursion, she could at least take her time getting ready.

Slightly mollified by the thought, she slouched against the pillows, bit off a chunk of pastry and chewed very, very slowly.

'Not this one.'

Helena dug her heels into the cobbled stones outside yet another exclusive boutique. She eyed the name etched in discreet letters above the door. If the prices in the last three stores had been outrageous—and they had—here they would surely qualify as scandalous.

Leo's grip on her hand firmed. 'It is not to your liking, *cara*?'

For what seemed like the hundredth time that day she let his endearment slide over her, forced a blithe smile and suppressed the inevitable shiver that single, huskily spoken word evoked. Like everything else, it was all part of their ruse—a ruse he had evidently decided to embrace today with unrestrained relish. Indeed, from the time they'd left his apartment scarcely a moment had passed without him touching her in some way: a hand at her waist, his thigh brushing hers, a random kiss on her mouth or temple.

And when, sitting at a quaint sidewalk café for lunch, he'd wiped a dash of cream from the corner of her mouth and sucked it off his thumb, her body had damn near dissolved into a puddle of liquid heat.

Worse—he *knew*. Knew that every touch, every lazy, lingering look from his hooded eyes, was making her quiver and burn.

She kept her voice low. 'It looks too expensive.'

His lips curved into the same tolerant smile he'd worn for much of the day, fuelling her suspicion that this exercise was less about buying a gown and more about some underlying battle of wills.

'I will decide what is too expensive.' He tugged her forward. 'Come.'

Inside, the routine was much the same as it had been at the other boutiques, only here the saleswoman was twice as elegant, the gowns four times more exquisite, and the proffered beverage not espresso or latte or tea, but sparkling wine served in tall, silver-rimmed flutes.

Helena pasted on a smile, as determined now as when they'd started out to find nothing she liked.

'I'm sorry,' she said to the tireless saleswoman four gowns later. 'It's just not my style.'

'Ah, pity…' The woman smiled, too professional to exhibit more than a glimmer of disappointment. 'The blue is perfect with your eyes.'

Helena carefully peeled away the layers of beaded chiffon and offered up an apologetic smile. 'It's beautiful, really, but the detailing is too fussy for me. I'd prefer something…plainer.'

A male cough, loud and lacking any kind of subtlety, came from beyond the mirrored screen.

Helena ground her teeth, then raised her voice. 'But nothing in black, please.'

Undeterred, the saleswoman tapped a red fingernail to her lips, then set off with a look of renewed focus.

As soon as she'd gone Helena pulled a silk robe over her bra and knickers, yanked the sash into a knot and stepped out from behind the screen. 'This is ridiculous.'

Leo sat—or rather, lounged—in a blue and gold brocade chair in the private sitting room, a half-consumed glass of champagne at his elbow, his long legs stretched out over a plush velvet rug.

He didn't bother glancing up from his phone. '*Scusi?*'

She scored her palms with the tips of her nails. 'Don't *scusi* me. You heard me perfectly well. This is pointless.'

He pocketed the phone and raised his head, his gaze travelling with a discernible lack of haste from her feet to her face. She squirmed, heat trailing over her skin in the wake of his indolent scrutiny. Teeth gritted, she fought the urge to adjust the robe over her breasts.

'Pointless only because you are being stubborn.'

She snorted. 'I'm not stubborn. I'm just…selective. I haven't seen anything I like, that's all.'

'You have tried on fourteen dresses.'

*He was counting?* She crossed her arms. 'And I told you—I haven't seen anything I like.'

'Then I suggest you find something you do.'

'And if I don't?'

'I will choose for you.'

The desire to stamp her foot was overwhelming. But no doubt he would enjoy her loss of composure. She settled for raising her chin. 'I don't know what type of relationships you have with the women in your life, and frankly I don't care. But I, for one, do *not* like to be bullied.'

In a single fluid movement of his powerful frame Leo surged off his chair. He prowled towards her and her nerves skittered, but she held her ground. He stopped just short of their bodies touching and locked his gaze on hers.

'My mother gave me three pieces of advice before she died.'

It wasn't remotely what she'd expected him to say. She frowned, uncertain. 'Did she?'

'*Si*.' His right index finger appeared in front of her face. 'One, to take my schooling seriously.' His middle finger rose beside the first. 'Two, to learn English and learn it well.' His third finger snapped up to join the others. 'And three, always to choose my battles wisely.'

Her frown deepened—a convulsive tug of the tiny muscles between her brows. During their brief time together he'd not spoken of his mother except to say that she'd died when he was eleven. Her heart squeezed now at the thought of a young boy grieving for his mother and it stirred a ridiculous urge to comfort him—this proud, infuriating man who wouldn't accept her comfort if they were the last two people on Earth.

'Your mother was a sensible woman,' she ventured, unsure how else to respond.

'*Si*.' He hooked his fingers under her chin. 'And her advice has served me well. As it will you, if you have the sense to heed it.'

She gave him a blank look. 'I was a straight A student, thank you very much. And I think you'll find my English is perfect.'

His teeth bared in a sharp smile that mocked her attempt to miss the point. 'Then you will have no trouble understanding this.' He lowered his mouth to her ear, his breath feathering over her skin in a hot, too-intimate caress. 'Wisdom is not only in choosing your battles with care, *cara*. It is knowing when to concede defeat. We will stay here until you choose a dress or I will choose one for you. Those are your options. Accept and decide.'

'I—'

He planted a brief, hard kiss on her mouth, stealing her breath along with any further attempt at protest, then held her gaze in mute challenge until she gave a grunt of anger and whirled away.

'Bully,' she muttered, but he either didn't hear or chose to ignore the slur, and by the time the saleswoman reappeared he was seated again, dark head bowed, his attention back on his phone.

With mammoth effort she mustered a smile and cast a critical eye over the two latest gowns, both backless halternecks with ankle-length skirts, one a bright turquoise, the other a deep, stunning claret. She ran an appreciative hand over the latter.

The saleswoman removed the dress from its hanger. 'Beautiful, *si*?'

Helena had to agree. 'How much?' she asked quietly.

The Italian woman quoted a number in euros that dropped the bottom out of Helena's stomach. The equivalent in pounds would pay the rent on her flat not for weeks, but for months.

She slipped into the gown and it was even more beautiful on, its weightless silk gliding like cool air over her body, the shimmering claret a striking contrast against her pale ivory skin. She performed a little pirouette in front of the mirror, her stomach fluttering with a burst of unexpected pleasure.

The saleswoman smiled. 'This is the one?'

Helena hesitated. Could she *really* allow Leo to buy her this dress? She studied her reflection. A lot of skin was exposed, and the style called for going braless, but he *had* said he wanted her in something more eye-catching. Something more *befitting his mistress*.

She chewed her lip. She could go out there, parade for his approval, but pride and some residual anger over his high-handedness stopped her. Maybe she lacked the glamour of his usual mistresses, and maybe her wardrobe was a little staid, but she still had enough feminine savvy to know when she looked good.

Confidence swelled. *Yes.* She could do this. She could play her part and convince the world—or at least the Santinos and their guests—that she and Leo were lovers. She had to. If she wanted to honour her end of their bargain—if she wanted Leo to honour *his*—there could be no half-hearted performances. She either did this properly or not at all.

She gave the ever-patient saleswoman a beatific smile. 'This is the one.'

Leo eased the Maserati to a stop in the gravel courtyard outside the Santinos' palatial mountainside villa. Behind him a long queue of taxis, luxury cars and black-windowed limousines stretched into the distance. Valets swarmed like worker ants on a sugar trail, keeping the line moving as guests poured from the vehicles and watchful dark-suited security men oversaw the hustle of activity.

He glanced at Helena, sitting silent in the passenger seat, but her face was angled away and he couldn't gauge her reaction.

He liked the way she'd styled her hair tonight, her glossy curls piled high on her head, a few random ringlets left loose to float around her face. He *didn't* like that all he could think about was how it would feel to pull out the pins and watch those silky tresses spill over his hands... his sheets...*his thighs*...

He killed the engine. 'Are you ready for this?'

Her head swung around, her blue eyes inscrutable under their canopy of dark lashes. 'Yes. Are you?'

He smiled at the challenge in her voice. 'Always.' He fired off a wink that earned him a frown, then climbed out, grabbed his suit jacket from the back seat and shrugged it on.

On the other side a valet opened Helena's door and she stepped out, a swathe of rich burgundy silk cascading like wine-infused water down her body. She smiled, and the kid's face split into a goofy grin that lasted all of three seconds—until he met Leo's dark stare.

'One scratch,' he warned in Italian, handing over his key, 'and I will find you.'

The young man nodded, his Adam's apple bobbing as if jerked by an unseen string, and Leo eyeballed him until he disappeared into the driver's seat.

The vehicle purred to life and Helena froze, her eyes widening. 'The gift!' She whirled and tapped on the side window as the car started to move. When it stopped she pulled open the back door and reached into the footwell.

Behind her Leo dug his fingers into his palms. Did his damnedest not to notice how the sheer dress clung to her hips and buttocks below her naked back. An exercise in futility, no less. He'd have to be blind not to notice all that smooth ivory skin. Those beautiful curves.

*Dio.*

He should have let her wear the black dress. It might remind him of a nun's habit, but at least his thoughts wouldn't be steeped in sin.

She turned and stilled, the gift-wrapped antique silver Tiffany bowl clutched in her hands. 'You can stop looking at me like that.'

*Like what?* Like he wanted to slide her dress up her thighs and bend her over the hood of his Maserati? He unfurled his hands. Tried to blank his expression. Hell, was he that transparent?

'I'm not going to screw this up, so you can wipe that frown off your face,' she said, her voice tinged with exasperation. 'Here—' she thrust the gift at him '—you take this. It's your gift.'

And a detail he'd have overlooked if she hadn't asked him earlier in the day what he'd bought the Santinos. Normally his PA took care of such things, but Gina had had a family emergency on Tuesday and he'd told her to take the rest of the week off work. He'd cursed at the over-sight, but Helena had promptly set about finding some-thing suitable—and pricey, he'd noted when handing over his credit card. Funny… Once she'd overcome her reluc-tance to choosing a dress she'd warmed noticeably to the idea of spending his money.

Inside, a waiter took the gift, offered them wine and guided them through a long piano hall doubling as a ball-room and outside to the uppermost of three sprawling ter-races. A floodlit swimming pool dominated the middle tier and in the distance, beyond the landscaped grounds, the lights of Rome winked like fallen stars under a purpling sky, painting a view of the ancient city that might have been impressive—breathtaking, even—had the flash and dazzle of the party guests crowding the travertine terraces not eclipsed the panorama beyond.

'Oh, my.' Helena stood beside him, one hand resting in the crook of his arm, the other cradling a glass of ruby-red wine. 'It's very…um…'

Leo dragged his gaze from the landscape back to the glittering assemblage before them. 'Flamboyant?' He didn't bother hushing his voice. The music piped into every corner of the grounds, mixed with the babble of a hundred con-versations and the chiming of crystal and laughter, made discretion unnecessary.

'That's one description.'

'You can think of others?'

'Mmm… Nothing as polite. You should have told me I'd need my sunglasses.'

Her wry humour extracted a grin from him. 'We Ital-ians know how to do bling, *si*?'

After a short silence she squeezed his arm. 'Thank you.'

He looked down at her. 'For what?'

'For not letting me wear that "boring" black dress.'

He shrugged. 'It wasn't—'

'Charity.' She looked him in the eye. 'Yes. I know. But thank you all the same.'

Her gratitude caused a ripple of guilt to radiate through him. The truth was she could have worn a sack and still outclassed every woman here—a fact he'd been confident of long before they'd arrived—but he had wanted to see her in something other than the nondescript black that seemed to have become her standard default. Had wanted, for reasons he refused to examine too closely, to see a glimpse of the old Helena.

She turned, lifted her face and broke into a smile that struck him square in the chest. 'Whisper in my ear and kiss me,' she said, her voice urgent, breathy. 'Carlos is on his way over. And he has company.'

*Well, hell...* That was an invitation he didn't need to hear twice. Without a beat of hesitation he put his lips to her ear, murmured a few words in Italian, then angled his mouth over hers.

And tried not to groan at the feel of her soft lips parting under his.

*Just for show*, he reminded himself, as the temptation to run his tongue into those warm, honeyed depths proved a true test of his restraint. Even knowing that his host approached and others looked on, he wanted to prolong the kiss into something far less chaste and fit for public display.

Helena, by contrast, appeared in full control, and by the time Carlos—and his daughter—reached their side she was rubbing the gloss off his lips and giggling as if they'd just shared some private joke.

Anna Santino glowered at them.

'Good to see you again, my friend.' Grinning, Carlos took Leo's hand in a strong grip. 'And Helena.' He turned, clasped her hands and kissed her on both cheeks. 'You look radiant, my dear. I am delighted you could make it.'

'Thank you, Carlos.'

Her voice was husky, her cheeks tinged a delicate shade

of pink. From the compliment? Or their kiss? The latter, he hoped.

'And congratulations on your wedding anniversary. What a wonderful party your wife has thrown. Thank you again for inviting us both.'

Carlos inclined his head towards the dark-haired girl by his side. 'May I introduce my daughter, Anna?'

Helena extended her hand, smiled warmly. 'It's a pleasure to meet you, Anna.'

'Likewise,' the younger woman said, her pretty face barely cracking a smile.

Had Leo been a betting man he'd have wagered that Carlos had dragged her over, told her to be polite, but the young socialite's pout said she was in no mood to be gracious.

She dropped Helena's hand and nodded at Leo, her brown eyes dark. Petulant. 'Leo.'

'Anna,' he said, and felt Helena's slender hand slide into his.

She pressed close and he caught a drift of the light, summery scent she wore on her skin. He tightened his hand over hers and she squeezed back, the contact spreading a peculiar warmth up his arm.

Smiling, she addressed Carlos. 'Leo has persuaded me to stay in Rome for an entire week. I'm planning to sightsee while he's working, but it's hard to know where to start. There's so much of your fabulous city to see.'

Smart girl. A safe, neutral topic and an irresistible opening to a man passionate about his city. Asking questions, listening intently, she kept the conversation alive until finally Carlos excused himself, invited them to a Sunday luncheon for their out-of-town guests, and moved on with his hosting duties. His sullen-faced daughter, who'd uttered not a word since the introductions, trailed away with him into the crowd.

Helena stared after them. 'She looks so miserable I almost feel sorry for her.'

He snorted. 'Don't.'

'Why not?'

'She's a pampered party girl with three priorities in life. Money, attention, and getting what she wants.'

Helena's expression was contemplative. 'She didn't get *you*.'

*Thank God.* He almost shuddered with relief. 'And see how she sulks.'

'Yes.' Helena sighed. 'A tragedy in the making, no doubt.' She hooked her arm through his. 'I dare say the poor girl's heart is ruined. You do realise she may never get over you?'

He narrowed his eyes. 'Are you mocking me, Helena?'

Her lashes swept down, but not before he'd caught the bright glitter of amusement in her eyes. He felt a thump under his ribs. A stirring of recognition in his blood. *There. That's her. That's the girl you remember.*

She signalled a passing waiter, swapped her empty wine-glass for a full one and turned her mischievous eyes back to him. 'Darling…' she cooed, loud enough for those nearby to overhear. 'Make fun of *you*?' She pursed her lips in mock reproach. 'Never. You're too sensitive. It's one of the things I adore about you. Come on.' She grabbed his hand. 'The night is young. Let's mingle.'

Letting her lead him into the crowd, Leo filed a mental note to teach her later about the perils of overacting. He could think of any number of activities he'd enjoy performing with her right now. Mingling wasn't one of them.

Yet mingle they did. For two endless hours. Hours during which his eyes glazed over and he repeatedly fought the urge to glance at his watch. Small talk was an art he'd mastered over the years out of necessity, not preference. Business dinners and charity events—the select few he supported—at least had a deeper purpose. But the kind of meaningless prattle that typified gatherings like this invariably wore at his patience.

'*Signor?*'

Assuming it was a waiter who had spoken behind him, Leo turned to say that he didn't want a drink or another damned canapé. What he wanted, he thought moodily, was Helena back by his side. How long did a woman need to powder her nose?

He frowned. The waiter was not bearing the usual tray of decadent offerings.

'Signor Vincenti?'

His frown sharpened. '*Si.*'

'Signorina Shaw would like you to know she is resting in the salon off the piano hall.'

*Resting?* 'Is she all right?'

The man hesitated. '*Si.* But there has been a small incident—'

Leo didn't wait for the man to finish. He powered up the steps of the terrace and into the hall, skirting the edge of the surging, overcrowded dance floor until he found the salon. He paused in the doorway. In the far corner Helena sat on a red velvet divan, and a kneeling waiter held a compress to the top of her left foot. Off to the side, a middle-aged couple hovered. As if intuiting his arrival, Helena glanced up and smiled and his chest flooded with relief.

He strode over.

'I'm fine, darling,' she said, her game face firmly in place. 'I just had a minor mishap.'

The middle-aged woman stepped forward. '*Je suis vraiment désolée*—I am so sorry,' she added in heavily French-accented English. 'I was clumsy. We were dancing and I did not see her walk past behind me.'

Leo took in the woman's solid frame and six-inch stilettos, then glanced at Helena's foot with renewed concern. '*Scusami,*' he said to the waiter, indicating that he should lift the compress, and then knelt on one knee to examine the damage.

'It's not serious,' Helena said quickly. She looked up to the woman. 'Please don't feel bad. It's just a scratch.'

More like a gouge and the promise of a decent bruise, but, no, it wasn't serious. He stood, picked up her purse and the high-heeled sandal she had removed and put them in her hands. Then he bent and hooked one arm around her back, the other under her knees, and lifted her against his chest.

'Oh!' Her exclamation came out on a gush of air. She frowned at him even as her arms looped around his neck. 'Really, darling.' She gave a little laugh. 'This isn't necessary. I can walk.'

He ignored her protest. 'Thank you for your concern,' he said to the couple. 'Please enjoy the rest of your evening.' He nodded to the waiter. '*Grazie.*'

Then he strode from the room and made for the nearest exit.

'We're leaving?' She stared at him, wide-eyed, her cheeks flushed, Her lips soft and pink. She looked sexy. Adorable. *Beddable.*

'*Si.*'

'But it's only ten-thirty.'

'You want to stay?'

She shook her head so quickly, so adamantly, a long auburn curl slipped its binding and bounced against her cheek.

His answering smile was swift. Satisfied.

'Good. Neither do I.'

# CHAPTER SEVEN

LEO CONTROLLED THE urge to floor the Maserati's accelerator until they'd cleared the mountain roads and had hit the expressway back to the city. Without traffic delays the journey time was forty minutes. He reckoned he could do it in thirty.

Helena leaned forward in the passenger seat, removed her other sandal and massaged her ankles. 'I swear high heels were invented by men as instruments of torture.'

She sighed—a soft, breathy sound that coiled through his insides like a ribbon of smoky heat.

'Could we have the air-con up a bit, please? It's awfully warm.'

Happy to oblige, he adjusted the controls and glanced over as she settled back in her seat. Her eyes were closed, her features smooth apart from a slight frown, and for a moment he was reminded of his sister. Of that intriguing combination of strength and vulnerability some women seemed naturally to possess.

A sudden tightness invaded his chest—the same suffocating sensation he always felt when he thought of Marietta and the battles she'd had to face. He gripped the steering wheel, his knuckles whitening. He had no business comparing Helena with his sister. They were poles apart. He loved Marietta. She was his blood, and he'd give his life for hers in a heartbeat. The feelings Helena stirred in him were rudimentary, nothing more than lust—a lust he intended to sate before this evening was out.

Thirty minutes later, in the courtyard of his apartment building, he pulled open the passenger door.

Helena glanced up. 'I can walk,' she said, gathering her shoes and purse before climbing out.

'We should see to that foot.'

She shook her head. 'It's fine. Really. It doesn't hurt all that much.'

Inside, he ushered her into the building's single elevator and watched her back into a corner, her belongings clutched in front of her like some sort of shield. Against what? Him? He thought of their too-fleeting kiss and all the little intimate touches and quips that had driven him slowly insane tonight. Anticipation spiralled in his blood.

'The skin's broken,' he said, looking at her foot. 'We should at least clean and dress the wound.'

They entered the apartment and he cupped her elbow, steered her towards the living room. Ignoring her mumbled protest, he sat her on the sofa and went to fetch the first aid kit from the kitchen. When he knelt in front of her she lifted her dress, obediently stuck out her foot and allowed him to clean the shallow gash. He finished by applying a neat dressing.

She offered up a smile. 'Thanks.'

He nodded, but didn't rise. Didn't speak. He held her gaze until her lashes fell and she shifted slightly.

'Leo...'

Liking the husky little catch in her voice, he sat back and hooked his hands behind her knees. Her teeth captured her lower lip and he held back a groan. The sight of her gently biting her own soft flesh was inordinately sexy. He pulled her to the edge of the sofa, spread her legs and moved between them.

Slim, toned muscles trembled under his hands. 'Leo, please... Don't do this.'

Undeterred by her soft plea, he cupped his hand under her left breast, cradling its fullness and weight in his palm. Only a sheer layer of silk separated his fingers from her flesh.

'This...?' He slid his thumb back and forth over the slippery fabric, teasing her nipple to a hard nub beneath the burgundy silk.

A tiny groan escaped her lips—a groan he might have mistaken for protest had she not arched into his touch.

'Yes.'

Her throat convulsed around that single word, drawing his gaze to the base of her neck where the skin looked so soft, so delicate, it begged to be kissed.

He leaned in and pressed his lips to the fluttering pulse there. *Oh, yes.* Soft. Warm. Sweet. He breathed in her summery scent, used the tip of his tongue to taste her skin.

'And this…?'

No words this time. No protest. Only a silent shudder that rode her body like the crest of a powerful fever. Satisfaction rippled through him. The message her body conveyed was unequivocal: she wanted him, hungered for him as fiercely as he hungered for her.

He shifted to cover her mouth with his, but she pulled back. Desire roughened his voice. 'Do not tell me you don't want this.'

'You know I do.'

Her candid, husky confession kicked his pulse up another notch.

'But that doesn't mean we should.'

'Tell me why not.'

'It will only complicate things.'

His laugh was short. '*Cara*, our physical attraction is the only thing between us that is *not* complicated. What could be more simple, more natural, than desire between a man and a woman?'

She shook her head. 'I didn't come here to sleep with you.'

'Yet you just admitted you want to.' More than anything else that frank admission fired his blood. Drowned out the rational part of his brain urging him to concede this was a bad idea.

She wedged her palms against his chest, shoved with surprising strength. Caught off guard, he rocked back on his heels.

'Is this how it works, Leo?' She shot to her feet and glared down at him, arms akimbo. 'You buy me a dress and expect me to demonstrate my gratitude with sex?'

For a second he stared at her. Then, as her words sank in, he launched himself up, his blood roaring in his ears like the bellow of a wounded bull. The idea that he would use material gifts as leverage for sex was galling. Distasteful. He balled his hands lest he do something foolish like grab her and shake her. Demand an apology.

She collected her purse and shoes. 'I'm tired,' she said, her gaze avoiding his. 'I'm going to bed.' *Alone.* She didn't need to say the word; it was implicit in her tone.

Hands fisted, heart thumping furiously, Leo stood silent and watched her stalk from the room. When he heard the closing snick of the guest room door he snatched up the first aid kit, strode into the kitchen and rammed it in a drawer.

He shoved his fingers through his hair.

Air. That was what he needed. And lots of it.

He shed his jacket, stepped onto the terrace and stared out over the endless tiled rooftops and church domes of Rome. He closed his eyes and breathed deeply, forcing his chest to expand and contract with each lungful of air. His anger slackened in a matter of minutes but his body stayed tense, trapped in a state of aching arousal he was powerless to quell.

*Powerless.*

He clenched his jaw. No. That wasn't right.

'Powerless' was holding on to his mother while the skies thundered and raged and the cancer stole the last of the light from her eyes. 'Powerless' was watching his father drown in the murky waters of addiction that had blinded him to his children and finally taken his life. 'Powerless' was walking into an ICU and seeing his sister's broken body, then turning around and walking out so she wouldn't see her big brother cry.

'Powerless' was *not*, by any stretch of its definition, some pathetic inability to bring his libido under control.

And yet this burning need Helena aroused in him, this inferno in his belly, would not be doused.

Turning on his heel, he marched inside and headed down the hall.

This night was not over.

Not by a long shot.

Helena stood barefoot in the en suite bathroom and stared at herself in the mirror. 'Congratulations,' her reflection sneered. 'You just earned the rank of first-class bitch.'

She laid her palms on the cold marble vanity unit and closed her eyes. Her body hummed with a current of sexual energy, her nipples felt exquisitely sensitive, and the wet heat of arousal lingered between her thighs.

*Dammit.* Why had he pushed? Why had she panicked? And why had she let that awful accusation fly from her mouth? His shocked face flashed into her mind and another burst of regret soured her tongue. She'd expected him to get angry with her; she hadn't expected him to look *hurt*.

She straightened and ran her hand over her stomach. If she and Leo *had* made love would he have noticed any changes in her body? Any subtle post-pregnancy differences?

She had no stretch marks, thanks to the diligent use of hydrating oils and the benefit of youth. And, while her mid-section was slightly more curvaceous than before, overall her body was thinner. No. She would not have needed to worry, she thought with an odd mix of certainty and regret. Her body would not have given up her secrets.

Heaving a sigh, she pulled the pins from her hair, undid the gown's halter neck and let the seamless fabric glide down her body. With a tiny pang of regret she went to the wardrobe and hung up the dress, well away from her own clothes. The stunning silk creation had made her feel sexy and confident, more feminine than she had in years, but she could not accept it as a gift.

Just as she could not fall into Leo's bed.

Oh, she would find a night in his arms explosive and unforgettable, of that she had no doubt. But they had a history of heartache and hurt, a past they couldn't erase, and there was no escaping the fact he still didn't trust her. Why would he? She was Douglas Shaw's daughter, guilty by association in Leo's eyes.

Perhaps seducing her and bedding her would have been no more than an opportune means of revenge?

Suppressing a shiver at the idea of such a callous motive, she closed the wardrobe door, pivoted on her heel—and screamed.

*Leo*.

Not inside the room, but standing in the doorway, his large frame silhouetted by the lighting from the hall. His hand rested on the handle of the door she knew she'd closed behind her. Had she been so lost in thought she hadn't heard the latch click? Or had he worked the handle with deliberate stealth?

He stared at her—silent, unsmiling—then stepped into the room and quietly closed the door.

Fright galvanised her. 'Get out!'

She hugged her arms over her breasts, glanced at the bed and considered diving for the safety of the covers. But he was already advancing.

'Leo, stop.' She was naked except for a thong! 'This isn't fair.' She backed up, felt the wardrobe door colliding with her bare buttocks and back. 'Get out,' she repeated, but this time her demand sounded weak. Unconvincing.

He stopped in front of her, leaned the underside of one forearm on the wood above her head. The suit jacket was gone, the black silk shirt unbuttoned to a point midway down his chest. She dropped her gaze and caught an eyeful of hard muscle under a dusting of fine hair. Before she could stop it, a groan rose in her throat. She wanted so very badly to slide her hands inside that shirt. To run her palms over his wide shoulders and thickly muscled chest.

'Tell me you are not a liar.'

She blinked up at him. 'Wh...what?'

'Tell me,' he barked, making her jump.

She scowled to let him know she didn't appreciate being shouted at—or being backed against a wardrobe naked, for that matter—but the set of his jaw told her he didn't give a damn what she did or didn't appreciate.

She found her voice. 'I'm not a liar.'

'Tell me I can trust you.'

She hesitated. *Test or trap?* Both, probably. She licked her dry lips. 'You can trust me.'

His gaze held hers. 'Now look me in the eye and tell me you do not want me, do not want *this*—' The fingers of his right hand skimmed down her stomach, slipped inside her thong and, before she could fully realise his intent, pushed into her slick folds. 'And then I will leave.'

Heat erupted between her thighs, flared like wildfire through her pelvis. Gasping, modesty forgotten, she dropped her arms and wrapped her hands around his wrist. 'Don't!' she croaked.

He thrust one finger upward, straight into her hot, moist core, then withdrew and circled his wet fingertip around her sensitised nub. Her legs nearly collapsed.

'Tell me, Helena.'

His rough command sent a hot shiver racing over her skin.

'Tell me exactly what you *don't* want.'

Convulsively her hands tightened on his wrist, his strong tendons flexing in her grip as his fingers stroked and teased. She bit her lip to keep from crying out, tensed her muscles to stop her body trembling. God help her. How could she tell him *no* when every inch of her flesh screamed *yes*?

'So wet,' he murmured, his other hand cupping the back of her head, his fingers tangling in her hair. 'So ready for me.'

He kissed her until her bottom lip came free of her teeth,

then sucked the tender flesh into his mouth. His tongue explored, invaded, as bold and shameless as his fingers—a dual assault that spun her senses until she couldn't tell which way was up.

He eased back enough to speak. 'Soon I won't be able to stop, so if you want me to leave—if you do not want this—you need to tell me now.'

She squeezed her eyes closed and prayed for sanity even as a part of her scoffed. *Sanity?* She'd forfeited that the moment she'd agreed to spend seven days with him in Rome. And no matter how many reasons she gave herself for why they shouldn't do this, why she shouldn't give in—why everything about this was wrong—one incontrovertible truth remained. She wanted this man, burned for him, and it really was that simple. That natural. Just as he'd said.

She let go of his wrist. 'Please...' she whispered, not caring how breathless and needy she sounded. 'Don't stop.'

He did stop, and she groaned, opened her eyes and frowned her dismay.

He gave a throaty laugh. 'Do not fret, *cara*.' He cupped his hands under her bottom, lifted her off her feet and headed for the bed. 'We are going somewhere more comfortable.' He started to walk and pressed an open-mouthed kiss to the base of her throat, his tongue dipping into the delicate hollow there.

She shivered with delight. If she came to her senses, told him to stop, would he honour his word and leave? She wrapped her legs around his torso, hooked her ankles behind his back. She didn't want the answer to that question. Didn't want to contemplate anything, *feel* anything, beyond the hot rush of anticipation in her veins. Surging her hands into his hair, she pushed his head back and covered his mouth with hers. He shuddered, growled something against her lips, and she sensed his control, like hers, was starting to slip.

When they reached the bed, her reluctance to unwrap

her legs had him overbalancing. He crashed down on top of her, crushing her breasts, spreading her thighs wide beneath his hips. Their mouths jerked apart and the air left Helena's lungs with a *whoomph*.

'*Dio!*' He levered his weight from her with one elbow. 'Are you hurt?'

She shook her head, too breathless for words, too aroused to care about anything other than getting her hands inside his shirt. His skin next to hers. She reached for a button, her fingers fumbling, shaking, until he closed a fist over her hands and stilled them.

'Soon,' he murmured, dropping a long, wet kiss on her mouth that made her forget what she was doing. 'First, I have something to finish.'

He lowered his head, closed his lips over one erect nipple and sucked the aching peak deep into his mouth. Then, when a shudder racked her body and she moaned, he turned his attention to the other.

Helena arched her back and dug her nails into the bedding. She couldn't decide which was more exquisite. More erotic. The graze of his teeth or the flick of his tongue. She writhed. 'Leo...'

As if responding to her strangled plea, he surged up, knelt between her thighs and slid his palms behind her knees. Their gazes locked and her breath hitched in her throat. She could see the intent in his smouldering eyes, knew that what he had in mind would drive her over the edge in seconds.

He spread her legs and stared down at her. 'I want to know if you taste the same, *cara*. If you are still sweet and hot.'

She rolled her head, tried to grasp his wrists. 'No... Wait...' *Too soon*. She would come apart too soon. And she wanted this to last. Wanted to savour every spark, every touch, every spine-tingling sensation. Wanted him to ride the swells of pleasure with her. *Inside* her. 'Not yet...'

He wasn't listening. Hands braced on her thighs, he

dropped to his stomach, hooked aside her thong, and used his mouth and tongue to take her to the crest of a swift, shattering climax. She bucked against his hands, cried out something—his name?—and then she was arching up, her thighs clenched, her fingers plunging into his hair, holding tight as each powerful wave of her orgasm rocketed through her.

Her blood pulsed. Her breath came in ragged little bursts. And through a dizzying haze of sensation she felt his hands release her thighs. Felt wet, searing kisses trailing across her hips and tummy, over her breasts and up her neck.

'Like honey,' he rasped. 'Hot liquid honey.'

He slid his mouth over hers, his kiss scorching, possessive, then pushed to his feet, tore off his shirt and tossed it to the floor. Shoes and socks next, then belt, trousers—a short pause to extract something from a pocket—and lastly his briefs. All removed in seconds.

He leaned down, hooked a finger in her thong. 'As sexy as this is, it needs to come off.' And with one yank it too was gone.

Her mouth dried. He was magnificent. Like a modern-day centurion with his wide shoulders and deep chest, his hard, flat stomach. A line of dark hair tapered south, drawing her gaze down until her eyes stopped at the sight of his impressive arousal. For a second she thought about reaching out, wrapping her hand around him, but a surge of belated shyness kept her hands by her sides, made her contemplate sliding under the covers so she didn't feel so exposed.

Leo didn't suffer the same affliction. He stood proud, unashamed of his arousal, his eyes trailing over her body like a starved man surveying a banquet, unsure which delicacy to devour first. The fierce glow in his eyes, the strength of his physical desire, told her he hadn't begun to sate his appetite.

He ripped open a condom packet, sheathed himself, and stretched out beside her on the bed.

'Beautiful.' His teeth nipped her earlobe, grazed her jaw, tugged at her lower lip. 'You are more beautiful than I remember.'

And as he kissed and nibbled and murmured words in Italian she didn't understand, his hands roamed and explored, rediscovering all the secret places from the backs of her knees to the delicate tips of her ears that he knew would drive her wild.

'And responsive,' he added, drawing one of her moans into his mouth. 'Still so responsive.'

'Leo?'

He nuzzled her neck. *'Si?'*

'Please shut up and make love to me.'

A brief moment of stillness, then a smile against her skin, a low, husky laugh that made her heart skip a beat. He moved over her, pushed his knee between hers, the chafe of his hair-roughened thigh exquisite on her sensitive skin.

He cupped her jaw with one hand, forced her to look at him. 'No regrets.'

She frowned. 'What—?'

'Say it,' he insisted.

'Okay.' *Whatever.* Whatever he wanted to hear. She needed him inside her. Now. She held his gaze. 'No regrets.'

The words had barely left her lips and he was poised for entry, braced above her, his hot tip pressed against her opening. She knew she was slick, ready to take him, yet still that first powerful thrust had her gasping aloud. She reached up and curled her fingers into his rippling shoulders. When it seemed he'd filled every inch of her he pulled out, the movement slow, torturous, then slid back in, setting a rhythm that started to build once more into that hot, sweet pressure deep inside her pelvis.

She closed her eyes, tipped her head back, let the feel of him, the scent of him, overtake her senses. For so long she'd gone without luxuries, denied herself pleasures, but tonight she would not deprive herself. Tonight she would indulge. Tonight she would take everything Leo wanted to give her and more. And tomorrow—or the next day, or the next—she would deal with the consequences.

'No regrets...' she whispered, and she moved her hips, matched his rhythm, urged him on faster and harder, until she flew apart a second time and Leo threw his head back and roared.

Leo kicked the sheets off his body, stared at the ceiling and listened to the sound of running water through the closed bathroom door.

After a long night of incredible sex he should be lying here feeling sated and spent. Instead he wanted more. More of the woman he was right now picturing in the shower, her long limbs and lush curves all soft and slippery and wet. His body stirred and yet as much as he ached to join her under the water, hoist her against the marble tiles and lose himself once more in her velvety heat, he needed to employ some restraint. Needed to bank his lust and make sure his head—the one on his shoulders, at least—was still on straight.

Anyway, she'd be too sore to take him a fourth time, and he already felt caddish on that front. Not that he hadn't tried to be the gentleman when, in the faint light of dawn, she'd winced as he'd entered her and clung to him when he'd tried to withdraw. He hadn't wanted to hurt her— had told her as much—but she'd wrapped her endless legs around him, sunk her fingernails into his buttocks and pulled him in deep, driving all thoughts of chivalry straight out of his head.

He expelled a breath, aimed another kick at the sheets.

Did her soreness mean she hadn't been sexually active for a while? In London she'd alluded to a boyfriend but he'd seen through that lie and he couldn't believe she'd be here now if she were in a relationship.

He scrubbed a hand over his bristled jaw.

Seven years ago he had taken her virginity, and though he'd been furious with her afterwards for not warning him, secretly he'd been flattered, his ego pumped by the fact she'd chosen *him* to be her first lover. In a primitive and yet deeply satisfying way he'd stamped his mark on her, and for the first time in his life he'd known the powerful pull of possessiveness—the fierce, unsettling desire to know that a woman was exclusively his.

He craned his head off the pillow and glared at the bathroom door. How many lovers had she taken since? One or two? A handful? Too many to keep count? A dark curiosity snaked through him. He should have given Nico a broader remit. Should have told him to look beyond her finances and living arrangements and dig a little deeper into her personal life: her friendships, her relationships. *Her lovers.*

He dropped his head back down and scowled.

*Dio.* What was wrong with him? Her liaisons with other men were no concern of his. Last night they'd indulged their mutual desire for one another—nothing more. A few hours of mind-blowing sex didn't change their past, and it sure as hell wouldn't change their future.

He swung off the bed, scooped his clothes off the floor and fired another look at the bathroom door. Either she'd managed to drown herself in three millimetres of water or she was taking her sweet time, hoping he'd give up waiting and leave.

Did she already regret their lovemaking?

The possibility turned his stomach to lead. He'd seen regret and something too much like pity in her eyes once before, the night she'd ended their relationship. He'd vowed he'd never let a woman look at him like that again.

As if he was a mistake she wanted to undo.

Naked, his chest tight, his shoes and clothes bunched in his fists, Leo turned on his heel and strode from the room.

# CHAPTER EIGHT

HELENA FLICKED A speck of lint off her black trousers and cast a sideways look at Leo. 'Lunch was nice,' she ventured, adjusting the car's seatbelt over her blouse. 'The hotel gardens were beautiful.'

His gaze remained on the road. '*Si.*'

Silence fell. She waited a moment. 'Anna was conspicuous by her absence, don't you think?'

He spared her a fleeting glance. '*Si.*'

'I didn't expect her mother to be so pleasant. We had a lovely chat over dessert. Do you know Maria well?'

'No.'

Helena sighed. *Excellent.* Three monosyllabic answers in a row. She sank down in her seat. This was not the man who'd sat by her side at the long luncheon table in the sun-drenched gardens of the Hotel de Russie. That man had been charming and attentive, playing the role of affectionate lover with such consummate ease she had, for a time, confused pretence with reality. Had actually indulged the notion their lovemaking might have meant something more to him than just a convenient lust-quenching tryst.

A wave of melancholy threatened but she fought it back.

*No regrets.* Wasn't that what she'd promised Leo? Promised herself?

She touched her mouth, tender still from his kisses, and conceded she'd allow herself one regret—that Leo hadn't joined her in the shower this morning. Her fault, she supposed, for being a coward. For letting her fear of what the morning might unveil in his eyes send her scurrying for the bathroom. What she'd really wanted to do was run her tongue over his salty skin, straddle his hips and take brazen advantage of his desire for her in spite of her body's tenderness.

When she'd finally emerged from the bathroom, her skin waterlogged from too long in the shower, Leo had been gone, the tangled sheets and the lingering smell of hot bodies and sex the only signs he'd been there.

She shifted in her seat, a sudden shiver cooling the warmth in her veins. Their lovemaking had been exquisite, everything she had expected, but in the sobering light of day nothing about their situation had changed. He was still a man driven by vengeance and she was still the daughter of the enemy he loathed.

Nothing would alter those facts.

*Nothing.*

Ten long, silent minutes later, they walked into Leo's apartment. Helena didn't bother opening her mouth. She turned down the hall and headed straight for the guest room.

'Where are you going?'

The question brought her up short. She whirled around. 'To my room. Is that all right with you?' She couldn't keep the pithiness out of her voice. His taciturn behaviour had bugged her and, dammit, it hurt. 'I'm going to change and go for a walk. Or do I need your permission for that, too?'

'Don't push my buttons, Helena.'

His deeply growled warning only fuelled her pique. 'And what buttons would they be? Clearly not the ones that control your power of speech, or I might have got more than three words out of you in the car.'

A deep frown puckered his brow. 'Why are you angry?'

She gave him an incredulous look. 'Why am *I* angry? That's a joke question, right?'

'I am not laughing.'

No, he wasn't. And neither was she. She stepped back, took a deep breath and tried for calm. Maybe they both needed some space. Maybe, after last night, she wasn't the only one feeling awkward and confused.

She retreated another step. 'I think we both need some breathing space,' she said, and turned.

'Do not walk away from me, Helena.'

Ignoring his grated command, she strode down the hall. She needed the refuge of her room. Needed to break the spell his presence cast over her. He looked so big and dark and formidable, and yet her pulse quickened not with anxiety or fear but with the vivid memory of all the ways his hands and mouth had explored her body last night.

She reached the bedroom doorway but he was right behind her, his arm bracing against the door before she could close it. 'Please go away,' she said, her voice steady even as her insides trembled.

He followed her into the room. 'Why? So you can have your "breathing space"? Is that what you need after a night in bed with me, Helena?'

She frowned at him, perplexed. 'I think *you* need some space, given your present mood.' Heart pounding, she put her purse on the dresser and removed the earrings that were starting to pinch. 'What is *wrong* with you, anyway?'

'I don't like being dismissed.'

She paused to stare at him. He looked utterly gorgeous in a light blue open-necked shirt and navy trousers, even with his features drawn into hard, intractable lines.

She put the earrings down. 'I have no idea what you're talking about.'

'No regrets. That is what we agreed, *si*? And yet this morning you could not face me. You hid in the bathroom until I gave up waiting and left.' He stalked forward. 'Why, Helena? Was the idea of waking up beside me so unpalatable?'

'Of course not!'

Her heart climbed into her throat. *Oh, God*. Had her act of cowardice unwittingly hurt him? As swiftly as the idea entered her head she rejected it. Leo wasn't the vulnerable type. Men like him were thick-skinned. Impervious. More likely his pride had suffered a blow. He probably wasn't used to women deserting his bed. Anyway, it wasn't even *his* bed she'd deserted.

'What is this really about, Leo?' She shored up her courage with a flash of anger. 'Your ego?'

Before he could answer she spun away, but he caught her wrist and swung her back to face him. The action was firm, not rough, and his grip didn't hurt, but still an ugly memory snapped in her mind. Reflexively she ducked her head, instinct driving her forearm up to protect her face.

A sharp, indistinct sound came from Leo's throat. He released her and she glanced up, saw the colour drain from his face.

'*Mio Dio.* Did you think I would strike you?'

Her chest squeezed. 'No, I… Of course I…I mean, you would never…' She bit her tongue and mentally cursed. Her babbled response had only worsened his pallor. She pulled in a deep breath. 'No,' she repeated, firmly this time. 'Of course I didn't.'

She reached out to touch him, to show she wasn't afraid, but this time he was the one who spun away.

'Leo, wait…'

But he didn't. And before she could find the right words to stop him, to erase that bleak look from his face, he was gone.

Leo stood on the terrace in the sultry afternoon heat and raked his fingers through his hair. His insides churned. The idea of Helena believing he would physically hurt her— despite her claim to the contrary—turned his stomach.

'Leo?'

He gripped the railing, loath to turn. Loath to look at her lest he see that flicker of fear on her face again.

'Leo, I…I'm sorry.' She appeared at the railing beside him. 'It was just a stupid reflex, that's all.'

He stared across the rows of tiled rooftops baking under the brilliant Roman sun. 'I would never harm you. I would never harm *any* woman.'

Her hand covered his, squeezed lightly, then slid away. 'Of course. I know that.'

*Did she?* Or was she offering words she thought would mollify him? The need to test that theory overtook him and he turned, lifted his hand and brushed the backs of his fingers down her cheek. She didn't flinch, and his relief was a balm more powerful than he could have imagined.

He dropped his hand. 'I am sorry. I scared you and that was not my intent.'

'I wasn't scared. Like I said, it was just a reflex.'

Leo studied her for a long moment. 'You assumed I would hit you, Helena.' Just saying the words made his stomach roil again. 'For most people that is *not* a natural reflex.'

'So I'm not "most people".' She shrugged, a smile flickering briefly on her lips. 'Really, it's no big deal. Let's forget about it.'

He wasn't fooled. Not by her dismissive tone nor by that brave attempt at a smile. Her determination to downplay the matter only sharpened his interest. He moved, putting Helena between him and the view and gripping the railing either side of her, hemming her in. He wouldn't touch her or frighten her again—not intentionally—but he would have the truth.

'Was it a boyfriend?' His gut burned, outrage simmering like a vat of hot oil beneath his calm.

Her lashes lowered. 'No.'

His hands flexed on the railing. 'Your father?'

She hesitated and the burn in his gut grew hotter. Thicker.

'You said he was difficult to live with,' he prompted, when the silence stretched.

Finally she looked up, her face pale even as a hint of defiance shimmered in her blue eyes. 'Must we have this conversation now?'

'*Si*,' he said. 'We must.'

Her gaze tangled with his for a long, taut moment, then she pulled in a deep breath and puffed it out. 'In that case I think I need to sit.'

Leo set two glass tumblers on the coffee table in the living room and poured a finger of whisky into each. He recapped the decanter, sat on the brown leather sofa and faced Helena. Inside him acid churned, along with a hefty dose of impatience, but pushing her would have the reverse effect. So he waited.

'My father's a consummate Jekyll and Hyde,' she said finally. She picked up her glass and stared into the pale bronze liquid. 'Charming when he chooses to be, lethal when he doesn't.'

'And he has struck you?'

Helena swirled the whisky, then sipped, grimacing a little as she swallowed. 'Twice.' She put the glass down, slipped off her shoes and curled her legs beneath her, favouring her bruised foot. 'The first time I was thirteen. My mother was good at running interference between Father and me, but I provoked him one day when she wasn't around. He backhanded me across the face.'

The acid rose into Leo's throat. A man could inflict pain on a woman or a child with an open-handed slap, but a backhand was a whole different level of vicious. He clenched his jaw.

'It hurt,' she went on, her gaze focused inward now, presumably on the past and whatever unpleasant images her memory had conjured. 'But the pain didn't make me cry nearly as much as the argument my parents had afterwards.'

Her chin quivered. The tiny movement was barely visible, yet still a deep-rooted instinct urged him to fold her in his arms.

He resisted.

Not only because he had told himself he wouldn't touch her unless invited, but because the compulsion stirred a dark, remembered sense of futility and loss. Of how he'd felt as a child, wanting to protect his mother, then his father, only to face the bitter reality that loving them, believing he could save them, had not been enough.

Loving them had only made his sense of inadequacy, of life's unfairness, more unbearable when they were gone.

Leo swallowed, tightened his jaw. He wouldn't let emotion distort his thoughts. Not now, in front of Helena—the woman for whom he'd once lowered his guard, opened himself to the possibility of love, only to have life serve him yet another reminder that love only ever led to disappointment and loss.

He dragged his hand over his face. Pieces of past conversations were slotting together, crystallising into a picture he didn't much like. *This won't hurt only my father. It will hurt others, too—my family.*

He refocused. 'This grace period for your father and his company—who are you really buying time for?'

She blinked, but didn't prevaricate. 'My mother.'

'Why?' He knew the answer—it had already settled like a cold, hard mass in his belly—but he wanted to hear her say it.

'When my father is angry or drunk or upset about something he can't control—like losing his company...' She paused, and the brief silence practically crackled with accusation. 'He lashes out at her.'

Leo pushed to his feet, his blood pounding too hard now for him to sit. He stared down at her. 'So you're telling me the takeover has put your mother at a greater risk of abuse?'

'Yes.'

He scraped his fingers through his hair. Frustration,

along with another, more disturbing emotion he didn't want to identify, sharpened his tone. 'Why did you not tell me this a week and a half ago?'

Her chin snapped up. 'I told you I was worried for my family.'

'But you didn't give me the whole story.' He paced away and back again. '*Dio*, Helena!'

Her posture stiffened, cords of tension visible in her slender neck. 'This is my mother's private life we're talking about—an issue that's sensitive and painful. Not to mention perfect fodder for the gossipmongers. I couldn't trust what you might do with the information.'

He bit back a mirthless laugh. *She* didn't trust *him*? He let his disbelief at that feed his anger, because the other emotion—the one that was feeling a lot like guilt—was burning a crater in his gut he'd prefer to ignore.

'Besides…' Accusation blazed in her eyes. 'Would you have reconsidered your plans if I'd told you everything then? Are you reconsidering them now?'

*Dammit*. Did he have an answer for that? He dragged in a deep breath, reminded himself that Douglas Shaw was the villain in all this. Not himself. 'Violent men can have many triggers, Helena. The takeover has clearly upset him—' *as intended* '—but any number of things could set him off. Changing my plans will not change the fact that your mother is in a volatile relationship and constantly at risk of abuse.'

'I understand that. But when my father learns that you plan to dismantle the company it isn't going to "trigger" a bad mood. It's going to trigger a major meltdown. I need more time before that happens—time to convince my mother to get out.'

'And our arrangement gives you that time, does it not?' Time he could extend, if he so chose. But not by much. Convincing his board to back the takeover hadn't been easy.

The buyout of shares had been costly, and divesting the company's assets would be critical for balancing the books.

Helena's shoulders suddenly lost their starch. Her gaze slid from his. 'Yes. It does. And hopefully it'll be enough.'

The resignation in her voice, the slope of her shoulders as she stared down at her hands, undid him.

His anger drained and he sat down.

'Your mother's never considered leaving?' He strove for neutrality but still the censure crept into his voice. He knew domestic violence was a complicated issue. Understood that fear and circumstance could deprive victims of freedom and choice. But surely Helena's mother had resources? Options? Why would she tolerate abuse?

'It's easy to judge from the outside looking in, Leo.'

The reproach in her tone made the tips of his ears uncomfortably warm.

'There's a hundred reasons women stay trapped in abusive relationships. Fear of reprisal. Fear of isolation from loved ones. Fear of being alone. Believe me, I've tried talking to her, but she shuts me down every time.'

He heard the tremor in her voice, saw the quiver in her lip she tried to suppress, and cursed.

*To hell with not touching.*

He shifted over and lifted her into his lap. She stiffened, surprise flitting over her pale features. But as he wrapped his arms around her, her body softened, acquiesced, and she dropped her head on his shoulder.

'I am sorry, *cara*,' he murmured against her hair. 'I know how painful it is to watch someone you love suffer.'

Everyone *he'd* loved had suffered. His mother with cancer. His father from grief and addiction. Marietta, whose life had been irreversibly altered by that one fateful decision.

Helena turned her face into his neck and he buried his fingers in her hair, the soft, peachy scent reminding him of the organic fruit orchards surrounding his villa in Tuscany.

He closed his eyes.

Five weeks they'd had together in London.

Five short, intense weeks. Barely enough time to get to know one another, and yet he'd fallen like a teenager on his first romantic crush.

*Hell.*

Had he really thought he could bring Helena to Rome for seven nights, keep her in his home, his bed, and not risk a return of the insanity that had proved his downfall the first time around? It was a colossal mistake—one he would no doubt regret. But not today. Not yet. Not until he had all the answers he needed.

'You said your father hit you twice.'

Instantly her body tensed. He waited until she relaxed, her breath warm on his neck as she released a pent-up breath.

'After that first time I'd never seen my mother more furious—or more willing to stand up to my father. It was the most violent argument I'd ever heard them have—and I'd heard a few.' She paused. 'I was in my room and couldn't hear it all, so I don't know everything she said to him, but I do know he didn't lay a hand on me again for six years.'

Swiftly Leo calculated that she'd have been nineteen when Shaw had next assaulted her. His brows sank. *Nineteen.* Her age when he'd met her. Coincidence? A sick feeling in his gut told him it wasn't.

'The night you wouldn't see me…after you sent me away from your hotel,' she said, her words segueing from his thoughts with uncanny accuracy, 'I went to confront him. I knew Mum was out at some charity thing but I was too angry for caution. Too upset to notice he'd been drinking.' A faint quiver undermined her voice. 'One minute he was cool and condescending, the next…he lashed out so quickly I never saw it coming.'

Leo gritted his teeth.

'My lip split,' she said before he could speak, 'and I fell, hit my head on the fireplace. When he came at me a second time I picked up the first thing within reach—an iron poker—and swung it at him.'

*'Dio!'* She'd fought back? Gutsy, but unwise if she'd had the safer option of fleeing. He smoothed her hair back, pulled her chin up so he could look at her. 'That could have been dangerous, *cara.'* He ran his thumb over the soft skin of her cheek, made the mistake of imagining that cheek bruised, her mouth bloodied. Tension coiled in his muscles. 'What happened?'

'I struck him,' she whispered, emotion creeping in now, her shoulders hunching forward. 'And he...he went down. I was horrified. I felt sick. There was a gash on his head and...and a lot of blood. I ran to help him, but he was already staggering to his feet and he shoved me away—so hard I fell again.' She shook her head, as if trying to dispel the ugly images. 'I got out as fast as I could and... Well, you know the rest. I haven't seen or spoken to him since.'

'And he cut you off?'

'He cut off my allowance, stopped paying my college fees, but *I* chose to make it on my own. As long as he supported me financially I was bound by his rules. His dictates. I wanted freedom, for myself and—' She stopped suddenly.

'Helena?'

She pulled her chin from his grasp, looked down. 'I... I wanted to live free of his control.'

Her fingers plucked at a button on his shirtfront and he covered her hand, stilled her fidgeting. 'Your father never met me, yet he took exception to our relationship. To me.' Even now, years later, that rankled deep. 'Why?'

Her hand curled into a delicate fist under his. 'Father had rules for everything—including who I dated. Boys who were wealthy, British and well-connected were the only ones deemed acceptable.' She emitted a soft snort. 'He never tried to hide his disappointment that his first-born wasn't a son. He once said my greatest worth was as marriage material, so I should at least choose someone he could benefit from.'

Leo's stomach clenched. He'd thought his loathing for the man couldn't deepen. He'd been wrong.

Helena shifted and he tensed. The glide of her soft, rounded buttocks over his groin was doing nothing to quell the desire he'd been struggling to subdue from the moment her backside had landed in his lap.

Her eyes rounded with comprehension. 'Sorry—'

'Sorry,' he said at the same time.

They both stopped, and half-laughed, half-groaned.

Before lust could incinerate his restraint, he gently moved her off him. Then rose and pulled her to her feet.

'Thank you.' He tipped up her chin. 'I know those weren't easy things to talk about.' He tucked a curl behind her ear, something tender, perplexing, moving inside him. 'Do you still want that walk?'

She stared up at him 'No,' she said.

And then she leaned in and pressed her lips to his—a move so entirely unexpected that for a moment he simply stood there, inert, caught by the sweetness of her breath and the subtle sizzle of promise in that tentative kiss.

Then her tongue darted out, stroked over his lips, and in one red-hot second her kiss had escalated from sweet to incendiary.

Leo groaned, hauled her against him and thrust into her mouth, needing to feel her, taste her, unable to get enough even when her fingers stabbed into his hair and pulled his head down for a deeper kiss. His clothes felt too tight, chafing his skin.

*Too many layers.*

Too much fabric between them.

He wanted the barriers gone.

Wanted her naked, laid bare—just for him.

His pulse firing with a flammable mix of impatience

and lust, he scooped her up, enjoying the warm nuzzle of her lips on his neck as he carried her to his bedroom. He lowered her feet to the rug beside his four-poster bed, satisfaction roaring when she tore at his shirt with an urgency that matched his own frantic need to get naked.

In seconds their clothes were shed and Helena was spreadeagled on his bed, her slender limbs pale against the dark cotton coverlet. He kissed her jaw, her collarbone, then sucked the hard, rosy peak of one breast into his mouth.

A low moan vibrated in her throat. When he slid his finger along her hot, wet seam her legs widened in a brazen invitation. Her fingers scraped over his scalp, her hips writhing as he circled her clitoris with his thumb and slid one finger, then two, deep inside her.

'Oh, yes...' Her moan fractured into soft little cries that stoked his desire. 'Please...I want you... Don't make me wait.'

*I want you.*

The words snapped his restraint. Shredded his intent to touch and taste and savour before burying himself inside her.

Hands unsteady, he pulled a condom from his nightstand and tore into the packet. Helena rose on her elbows and watched him roll on the sheath, her eyes glazed, her lips moist and slightly parted.

Leo moved between her thighs, positioned himself at her entry and began to nudge in. But she raised her knees, wedged her heels into his buttocks and tilted her hips so he slammed full-length into her searing heat.

*'Dio!'*

Stars exploded in front of his eyes and he squeezed them shut, opening them again when her hands framed his face and he heard his name whispered over her lips. He held himself rigid above her.

'You don't need to be gentle with me,' she said, and rocked her pelvis.

The sensual rhythm created an exquisite friction that forced another rough exclamation up his throat. He searched her face for any hint of the fear he'd seen earlier but saw only the flush of desire. The stark look of hunger in her eyes that mirrored his own.

He surrendered control and started to move, stroking his hard length in and out, building to a frenzied rhythm that she matched thrust for thrust until, a second before he climaxed, she sank her teeth into his shoulder and arched in violent orgasm beneath him.

A feral, utterly alien sound was torn from his throat, the intense pleasure of release amplified by the erotic pain of her bite and the feel of her internal muscles convulsing around him.

Moments later his strength gave out and he rolled onto his back, dragging Helena with him. Sensations came and went. Rapture. Languor. Satisfaction. But they were all fleeting. And as his heartbeat slowed and his breathing returned to normal Leo had the disquieting sense that *he*, not Helena, was the one laid bare by their lovemaking.

## CHAPTER NINE

THE TINY *TRATTORIA* tucked down a cobbled lane a few blocks from Leo's building was not what Helena had expected when, after a steamy afternoon in bed, he had declared they would go out to eat. From the moment the owner had greeted them with a broad smile and a back-slap for Leo, then ushered them into a cosy booth, however, everything about the place had charmed her.

She chased down her last bite of crispy Roman pizza with a large sip of Chianti. 'You were right.' She wiped the corners of her mouth with a red-and-white-checked napkin. 'That is quite possibly the best pizza in the world.'

He smiled, and her heart missed a beat even though she tried to be unaffected. Tried to wedge a solid wall between her head and her heart. Sitting here sharing a casual meal felt too…*ordinary*—and nothing about their contrived relationship or the things she had told him this afternoon was ordinary. Letting a few hours of phenomenal sex, a little easy talk over pizza and a disarming grin convince her otherwise was naive…and yet there was no harm in relaxing for a bit, surely?

She sipped her wine, savoured the intense flavour of ripe cherries on her tongue. She was pleasantly full, but the warm, contented feeling inside her wasn't only thanks to good food and wine. It was a carryover from earlier, when Leo had held her in his arms. When he'd listened to her talk about things she'd never talked about with anyone and made her feel safer, more secure, than she ever had in her life.

'You seem to know the owner well,' she remarked. 'Are you a regular?'

He leaned back, extended his long jean-clad legs under

the table. 'I worked here as a delivery boy during my first few semesters at university—one of three jobs that supported us while I studied.'

She couldn't hide her surprise. The man who ran a multi-million-dollar global business had delivered pizzas?

'Us?' she said.

'Marietta and me. My father was still alive then, but he was drunk most days and the people he mixed with were undesirable. My sister needed a better environment, so as soon as I could afford the rent I took her with me to a bed-sit in a safer neighbourhood. It was cramped, but clean—and secure.'

Helena frowned. 'Your father was an alcoholic?'

'He turned to drink after my mother's death. He never got over her loss.'

Sympathy bloomed. Leo and his sister had had such a traumatic childhood and then, as if they hadn't dealt with enough, Marietta's paralysing accident had happened. By contrast Helena's childhood, though far from perfect, had at least afforded material comforts, her father's wealth ensuring she'd wanted for nothing except the one thing money couldn't buy. The one thing she'd constantly craved as a child. His love.

'I'm so sorry,' she said, meaning it. 'I can't imagine the hardships you and your sister endured.'

He shrugged. 'We survived.'

She twirled the stem of her wineglass. They'd survived because Leo had made sacrifices, worked hard to keep his sister safe and create a better life for them both. Leo didn't trust or forgive easily, but he looked after his own. It was a quality in a man impossible not to admire.

'Does Marietta live in Rome?'

'*Si.* She has her own apartment and she's largely independent—both at home and at work.'

'What does she do?'

'She's curator at a contemporary art gallery—and an

artist in her own right. She recently had her first exhibition.' His voice resonated with pride. 'The landscape in my entry hall is her work.'

Helena's eyebrows shot up. 'Wow! I was admiring that just this morning. It's fabulous.'

'The accident quashed her ambition for a time, but with encouragement from her physical therapist she resumed painting a few years ago.'

'It would have been a shame if she hadn't. Talent like that shouldn't be wasted.'

'No,' he agreed, watching her intently. 'It shouldn't.'

Something in his tone made Helena's hand still on her glass. He wasn't talking about his sister now and they both knew it. She dropped her gaze, a flicker of unease chasing the warmth from her insides. She couldn't let the conversation go down this road. Couldn't explain the real reason she'd abandoned her textile design degree.

Desperately she cast around for a diversion, but only one sure-fire tactic sprang to mind.

Stifling a twinge of guilt, she reached under the table and slipped her palm over one muscle-packed thigh. 'So, are we staying for dessert…?' She glided her hand higher until, under cover of the table, she found the impressive bulge in his snug-fitting jeans. 'Or should we indulge at home?'

She ran the tip of her tongue over her lips and watched his pupils dilate, his throat muscles work around a deep, convulsive swallow.

He clamped his hand over her wandering fingers and leaned close, eyes glittering darkly. His voice, when he spoke, was a low, sexy rumble. 'You, *tesoro mio*, are insatiable.'

A breathless little laugh escaped her. The flash of raw hunger in his gaze—the knowledge that he wanted her even now, after hours of lovemaking—was a potent aphrodisiac in her blood.

Keeping pace with him on the walk back proved a challenge. By the time they tumbled through the front door of his apartment—hot, gasping for breath—his roving hands had already driven her mindless with need. He toed the door shut, backed her up against the hallway wall. For a long moment they stood panting, gazes locked, the heat of desire a living, pulsing thing in the air around them. Then his head came down, and his possession of her mouth was swift, almost brutal.

Helena's body responded with a powerful throb and she wrapped her arms around his neck, hungry for the crush of his mouth, the hot slide of his tongue against hers.

*Lord.*

He was right.

Her need for him was insatiable. Beyond her control.

Somehow they reached his bedroom, a haphazard trail of shoes, clothes and undergarments strewn in their wake. And then he was sheathed and inside her, filling her to the hilt with the hard, powerful thrusts of his possession.

Taking her to a place where there was only him.

Only her.

Only pleasure.

And then, too quickly, she was climaxing, her body arching wildly under him, multiple waves of pleasure radiating from her core as her internal muscles milked his simultaneous release. Her orgasm was so swift, the sensations flooding her so intense, she had to bury her face in his neck and hold back a sob of some inexplicable emotion as he rolled onto his side and cradled her into his chest.

When, a short while later, he carried her into his massive marble shower and started soaping the sweat from their bodies, she didn't have the energy to talk or move. She simply closed her eyes, clung to his wide shoulders and let the hot soapy water and his gentle touch prolong her bliss.

Back in bed, dry and cosy, snuggled into his side, she

drifted towards sleep. She was teetering on the edge of that sweet abyss when his fingers tilted up her chin. She kept her eyes closed, muttered a protest.

'Promise me something, *cara*.'

She frowned. They were doing *this* again? 'No regrets...' she mumbled, and tried to drop her head back onto his chest.

His grip firmed. 'A different promise.'

Sighing, she fluttered open her eyelids. 'Hmm...?'

'Promise me you'll never let your father—never let *any-one*—tell you you're worthless.'

She hesitated, her throat growing painfully tight. 'I promise,' she whispered, and *damn* if that warm glow from earlier hadn't flared back to life.

Leo emerged from the tendrils of a deep, dreamless sleep and sensed he was being watched. He opened his eyes and blinked, adjusting to the pale morning light slanting through the gaps in the blinds. Helena lay half atop him, her naked body warm and soft, her chin propped on the slim hand splayed over his chest.

His groin stirred.

'Morning, *cara*.'

Her smile held a hint of mischief, as if she knew how easily she aroused him and revelled in the knowledge.

'Morning.' She ran the tip of one finger down his jaw, her nail scraping through a thick layer of bristly stubble. 'Are you properly awake?'

He moved slightly, his erection nudging her hip. 'One hundred per cent.'

A pretty blush stole over her cheeks.

'Can I ask you a question?'

He crooked an eyebrow. An early morning Q&A session was not quite what he'd had in mind. *'Si,'* he said, gliding his hand over her satiny shoulder, down the back of her ribs to the dip of her waist and lower.

'Leo.' She smacked the fingers that had grabbed a hand-ful of soft, delectable buttock. 'I'm serious.'

Reluctantly, he moved his hand to her waist. Helena chewed her lip, her expression growing pensive, and a sud-den stab of instinct warned that he wouldn't like her ques-tion.

'Why do you need to do it?' Her voice was soft, curi-ous rather than accusatory. 'Why do you need to ruin my father after all these years?'

The heat of arousal in his veins instantly cooled. It was a candid question, one he had failed completely to antici-pate, and had she asked it twenty-four hours earlier he'd have refused to be drawn.

But that had been yesterday. Before she had opened up to him. Before she'd answered a few equally tough ques-tions with the kind of honesty his conscience was telling him he owed her in return.

*Hell.*

He expelled the air from his lungs. Gently he shifted her from him and climbed out of bed. 'Wait here.'

He scooped his briefs off the floor and pulled them on. Then he pushed a button on the wall to raise the blinds, padded down the hall to his study and riffled through a drawer till he found what he wanted.

When he returned Helena was sitting cross-legged on the bed, the top sheet tucked around her middle. The morn-ing sun fell across her bare shoulders and created a halo of rich amber in her tousled hair.

Her gaze went to the items in his hand. 'Photos?'

She took the two six-by-four snapshots he held out and studied the top one, an old shot of a tall, leggy girl mess-ing around on rollerblades.

'Your sister?' She glanced up for affirmation, then down again. 'Taken before her accident, obviously. She's abso-lutely stunning.' She studied the other photo, this one more recent. Her brow furrowed. When she looked up, her eyes were solemn. 'Still beautiful.'

'*Si*. Still beautiful.'

A familiar weight dragged at his insides. Even seated in a wheelchair, the lower half of her body visibly frail, Marietta Vincenti was a striking young woman. Nevertheless, the contrast between the photos was sobering.

Leo sat on the bed. 'Do you remember the Hetterichs from that charity dinner in London?'

'Of course.'

'Sabine mentioned Marietta and you asked me about her afterwards.' And he'd shut her down—hadn't wanted to discuss it.

'I remember.'

'For the last decade Hans has led the field in experimental stem cell surgery for spinal cord injuries and patients with varying degrees of paralysis.'

'Oh…I've read about that.' She sat forward, eyes bright with interest. 'It's a bit controversial, isn't it?'

'It's *very* controversial.' For a time he'd waged his own internal war over the ethics of it, but watching a loved one suffer did wonders for liberalising one's attitudes. 'After Marietta's accident I took an interest in Hans's work. I followed the early trials and eventually I contacted him. After reviewing Marietta's case he believed she'd be a good candidate for surgery.'

Helena frowned again. 'It wasn't successful?'

He took the photos and placed them on the nightstand. 'There is a window of time following the initial trauma during which the procedure has a greater chance of success. Marietta was already on the outer cusp of that time period.'

'So…it was too late?'

'*Si*. In the end.'

'In the end?'

'The surgery was delayed—by a year.'

Confusion clouded Helena's face. 'But…why?'

The old tightness invaded Leo's chest. Talking about this wasn't easy. The anger, the guilt, the gut-wrenching disappointment and the dark emotions he'd wrestled with had nearly destroyed him, and he had no desire to bring them to the fore again. Yet for some reason he couldn't define he felt it was important to make Helena understand.

'The surgery was only available privately, and it was expensive—beyond the means of most ordinary people. I had taken some aggressive risks to grow my business, tying up most of my assets and capital, but I had investors in the wings who were interested in a project with enormous potential. I knew if I could secure those investors I would be able to free up some of my own funds for the surgery.'

A stillness crept over Helena. 'How long ago was that?'

'Seven years.'

Her comprehension was instantaneous, the paling of her features swift. She placed her hand over her mouth and closed her eyes. When she opened them her lashes glistened with something he hadn't expected—tears.

'It was the project my father derailed?'

He nodded, his chest growing tighter. One by one his potential investors had backed off, suddenly claiming his project was too high-risk, too pie-in-the-sky for a young entrepreneur whose start-up was a tiny David in an industry full of Goliaths. When cornered and pressed, two of those men had let slip the name of Douglas Shaw. Somehow the man had used his power, his influence and connections, to identify Leo's investors and scatter them to the winds.

'Eventually I resurrected that project, but my business had taken a serious hit, and it was many months before I could reverse the damage—over a year before it was stable enough financially for me to reconsider the surgery.'

For that he'd wanted to hunt Shaw down and rip his head clean off. Instead he'd bided his time. Nursed his anger. Planned every detail of his retribution.

'Hans warned us that the chance of success was severely diminished, but I encouraged Marietta to have the procedure anyway.'

'And it was a failure?'

'She has some increased sensation and movement in her leg muscles, but nothing more significant. Barring a miracle, she will never walk again.'

Helena swiped a hand across damp cheeks. 'I…I had no idea,' she croaked. 'I'm so very sorry.'

He swore under his breath. 'Don't,' he said gruffly.

'Don't what?'

'Apologise for something that's not your fault.'

Her mouth twisted. 'But it *is* my fault, isn't it? I knew my father wouldn't approve of our relationship and I took the risk anyway. And in the end you paid the price for my stupidity. You…and Marietta.' She grimaced. 'No wonder you hate me.'

Leo rubbed a hand over his jaw. Of all the disturbing emotions that had churned through him these last forty-eight hours, hate had not been among them. 'I do not hate you, Helena.'

She gave him a look. 'You don't have to humour me. I know you think I walked away from you fully aware of what my father intended.'

An accusation he couldn't refute. Not with any degree of honesty. Seven years ago he had judged and condemned her, too blinded by ego to consider that her role in Shaw's machinations might have been as victim, not conspirator.

He tipped her chin up. 'Where you are concerned, *tesoro*, I am fast learning that what I think I know is more often than not incorrect.'

He leaned in and pressed a soft, lingering kiss to her lips. When he pulled back he noted the pulse beating at the base of her throat, the flush of colour down her neck and chest—sure signs he wasn't the only one so easily aroused. His body stirred again, his blood heating. Pooling. He trailed a fingertip over her collarbone down to the sheet covering her breasts.

*Enough talking.*

'We have one hour before I leave for work and your guide is due.'

She jerked back, frowning. 'My guide?'

*'Si.'* He curled his fingers into the sheet and yanked it down, exposing her lush breasts to his unabashed scrutiny. 'The guide who is taking you sightseeing today.'

Her mouth opened, no doubt to voice a protest, but Leo was already moving. With easy strength he tumbled her beneath him, pinned her to the mattress and smothered her squeal of outrage with a hard, ravenous kiss.

Six hours later, sitting on the Spanish Steps awaiting the return of the five-foot-two bundle of feminine energy that was her tour guide, Helena admitted that she'd have to eat every ungracious word of protest she had mumbled that morning.

She'd had fun—an absolute blast, in fact—and her guide, Pia, had been a delight: smart, funny, full of knowledge and, thanks to her local connections, able to leap even the longest tourist queue in a single bound.

In just a few hours Helena had counted the great marble columns of the Pantheon, shivered in the dungeons of the Colosseum, stood next to the towering four-thousand-year-old Egyptian obelisk in St Peter's Square, gazed in awe at Michelangelo's famous frescoes on the Sistine Chapel's ceiling, and performed the traditional right-handed coin-toss over her left shoulder into the beautiful Trevi Fountain.

*Phew!*

Now she basked in the sunshine of yet another glorious Roman afternoon, watching crowds of people mill about the Piazza di Spagna while she waited for Pia, who'd vanished on a one-woman mission for fresh lemon *gelato*.

She pushed her sunglasses up on her nose and smiled

at the antics of two young boys playing at the foot of the centuries-old steps. Both had dark hair and olive skin and didn't look dissimilar to how she imagined her son would have looked as an energetic boy of five or six.

Just like that her meandering thoughts caught her like a sucker punch, and she hugged her knees into her chest.

It had been impossible to sleep with Leo these last two nights and not think at least once about the life they'd inadvertently conceived. About the child she'd carried in her womb with such deep maternal love and the tiny grave where every year, on a frigid February morning, she would kneel on the cold, damp ground and mourn the loss of their son.

But she wasn't ready to tell Leo about Lucas. To inflict pain where so much hurt had gone before. Not when this truce between them was so new. So fragile.

Their revelations—hers yesterday and Leo's this morning—had caused a subtle shift in their understanding of each other. A sense of growing mutual respect. She couldn't bear it if they slipped backwards. Not now. Not when she had a tiny bubble of hope inside her. A blossoming belief that maybe—just maybe—once the dust had settled from the takeover, they could have something more. Something *real*.

'Helena!'

Pia called out from the foot of the steps and Helena rose, shelving her thoughts. This was not the time to sit and ruminate. Leo had no doubt paid good money for Pia's services. The best way Helena could show her gratitude was to enjoy the day.

Aware that eating on the steps was forbidden, she descended to the bottom. A minute later, around a mouthful of cold, creamy *gelato*, she said, 'Oh, Pia, this is divine!' And then muttered, 'Darn it...' when a muffled ringtone came from her bag.

'Here—let me.' Her ebullient, ever-present smile in

place, Pia relieved Helena of her cone so she could rummage for her mobile.

She checked the display and frowned. 'Mum?'

But it wasn't her mother on the line; it was her mother's housekeeper. And as the woman started to speak, her words rushed, the line scratchy in places, a chill that bore no relation to the cold *gelato* she'd eaten slid down Helena's spine.

She gripped the phone and stared at Pia, thinking dimly that the look on her face must be quite a sight. Because suddenly Pia's smile was gone.

Leo slouched in his office chair, threw his pen across his desk and scowled at the strategy paper he'd been attempting to red-pen for the last ninety minutes.

*Buono dio!* Had he ever had a day at the office this unproductive? And since when had a weekend of sex so completely annihilated his ability to focus?

He rolled his shoulders, twisted his head and felt a small pop of release in his neck.

Better. *Marginally.*

He blew out a heavy breath. Blaming his lack of concentration on the sex—no matter how spectacular—was a cop-out. It was the hot tangle of emotion in his gut that he couldn't unravel that had him distracted and on edge. He glared again at the papers on his desk and conceded he'd have to open his laptop and start from scratch.

He rubbed his eyelids, not thrilled by the prospect. His board of directors was expecting a detailed plan for divesting ShawCorp's assets. Instead he was drafting a recommendation for keeping the company intact—at least in the short term.

No doubt they'd all think he'd lost his mind.

Chances were they'd be right.

Aware of a dull ache taking root in his temples, he hit the button labelled 'Gina' on his phone and waited impatiently for his PA to pick up.

When she burst into his office moments later, a stricken-faced Helena hot on her heels, a jolt of surprise drove him to his feet. He strode around his desk, the pain in his head forgotten.

'*Cara*?'

She walked into his arms, her body trembling, her eyes enormous saucers of blue in a face as pale as porcelain.

'I need to go home,' she said, her grip on his arms verging on painful. 'My mother's had a fall. She's in Intensive Care—in an induced coma.'.

# CHAPTER TEN

MIRIAM SHAW REMAINED in a medically induced coma for two days.

Though her recollection of the incident was hazy, it was apparent she'd suffered a severe knock to the head that caused a swelling on her brain. Her sprained wrist, the bruising along her left hip and thigh, the presence of alcohol in her blood and the location in which the housekeeper had found her all pointed to an unfortunate and—though Helena balked at the idea—drunken tumble down the stairs.

'Helena?'

She jerked awake, lurched forward in her chair and reached on autopilot for the guardrail of the hospital bed. A second later her overtired mind registered the deep, rich timbre of the voice that had spoken.

She twisted round as Leo placed a plastic cup filled with black watery coffee on the small table beside her.

He grimaced. 'The best I could find, I'm afraid.'

She settled back in her chair—one of several in her mother's private room on the ward. 'It's fine. I'm used to it after four days.' She managed a smile. 'Thanks.'

He dropped into the seat beside her and reached for her hand, lacing his fingers through hers, his other hand loosening the tie at his throat. He'd swapped his jeans for a designer suit today, having gone to a business meeting in London, but the look of unease he wore every time he came to the hospital remained.

She met his gaze and her breath caught, her belly tugging with a deep awareness of him that was inappropriate for the time and place. *Incredible.* Even dulled by worry and fatigue, her senses reeled from his impact.

'Don't say it,' he said, his brows descending, his jaw, clean-shaven for the first time in three days, clenched in sudden warning.

'I wasn't going to say anything,' she lied, unnerved by his ability to read her. Somehow he'd known she was on the brink of telling him—for the hundredth time since they'd left Rome—that he didn't need to be here. That he shouldn't have come to London. That her mother's welfare wasn't his concern.

He felt responsible in some way. He hadn't said so—not in so many words—but every time Helena looked at him she sensed a storm of dark emotions swirling beneath his veneer of control.

'Has she been lucid today?'

She shifted her attention to her mother, restful in sleep and less fragile-looking now, without all the tubes and wires that had been attached to her in the ICU. She'd been brought out of her induced coma two nights ago. So far the doctors were pleased with her recovery.

'We've had a few brief chats. And she talked with James before he returned to boarding school this afternoon.'

The chance to spend a few hours with her brother had been bittersweet, in the circumstances. By contrast, coming face to face with her father in a packed ICU waiting room had just been…*bitter*. She was surprised he'd bothered returning from Scotland. Thank God he'd turned up when Leo wasn't there.

'Have you seen your father again?'

Helena shook her head. She didn't want to discuss her father with Leo. Not when she had the sneaking suspicion he was secretly hankering for an outright confrontation with the other man.

His hand squeezed hers. 'He cannot hurt you, *cara*. I won't let him.'

A lump rose in her throat. When he said things like that, looked at her the way he was looking at her now, she was filled with confusion. Torn between the cynical voice that said he was using the situation—using *her*—to get to her father, and the whisper of hope urging her to believe he truly cared.

'Helena?'

She started. The voice uttering her name this time was not deep and manly but soft and feminine. Her mother's. Pulling her hand free, she jumped to her feet.

Leo rose beside her. 'I'll take a walk,' he murmured, turning to go. 'Call me when you're ready to leave.'

'Or you could stay.' She touched his arm. 'You barely said more than hello to her yesterday.'

He rubbed the back of his neck. 'Another time. I have some calls to make.'

Helena didn't push. She understood his unease. Her mother was the wife of the man whose company he'd set out to destroy.

She dropped her hand and waited for the door to close behind him before moving to the bed. She pulled up a chair, took her mother's hand. 'How do you feel, Mum?'

'Fine, apart from this awful headache.' A weak smile formed on her pale lips. 'He's very handsome, isn't he?'

Helena looked down, frowned at the mottled purpling on the back of her mother's hand where an IV catheter—now gone—had ruptured a vein. Yesterday she had stretched the truth. Told her mother she and Leo were seeing each other, trying to work some things out. In reality she didn't have a clue *what* they were doing—and she didn't think he did either.

'I'm sorry he didn't stay.'

Miriam's smile vanished. 'You mustn't apologise, darling. For anything.' She closed her eyes, frowning, as if the pain in her head was suddenly too much to bear.

Alarmed, Helena sat forward. 'Mum?'

Miriam's eyes opened again. 'I've made choices,' she said, her blue eyes latching on to her daughter's. 'Choices

I know you don't understand. But I only wanted the best
for you, darling. And for James. Douglas is a difficult man,
a proud man, but he gave us the best of everything. You
can't argue with that.'

*Damned if she couldn't.* But she swallowed the bitter
retort. Now was not the time to catalogue Douglas Shaw's
many failings as a husband and father.

Miriam gripped Helena's hand. 'It wasn't all bad, was it?
We had some good times. After James came along things
were better, weren't they? Douglas was happy for a while.'

'Yes,' Helena agreed, reluctantly. 'I suppose he was.'

In fact the years following her brother's birth had been
the most harmonious she could remember, her father seemingly content for once—because, she supposed, he'd finally
got what he wanted. A son.

'But, Mum, that was a long time ago. And things…well,
they aren't fine now, are they?'

The proud, resolute look she knew so well came into
her mother's eyes. 'I can *make* them fine.'

Helena donned a dogged look of her own. 'For how long?
Until the next time he's angry and drunk?'

She reached out, gently touched the faint discoloration
under Miriam's left eye. Last week's bruise had faded, but
in time there'd be another. And another.

'Things are only going to get worse. *He's* only going to
get worse. You do see that, don't you?'

Miriam's mouth quivered, just for a second, before firm-
ing. 'I have to think of James.'

'Who's nearly sixteen,' Helena pointed out. 'Old enough
to understand that marriages can fail. Parents can separate. I love him, too, but you can't wrap him in cotton
wool for ever.'

Most of the year her brother was at boarding school,
limiting his exposure to the tensions at home. But he was
a smart boy, perceptive, and Helena suspected he already
knew more than he let on. To her knowledge their father

had never laid a hand on his precious son, but that could change. Violent men were unpredictable—especially when fuelled by rage and drink. She would sit James down and talk with him, make sure he understood his options. Ensure he was safe.

'It's a few weeks yet till the summer break,' she said. 'When he comes home he can decide who he stays with. Who he sees.'

A tiny tremor ran through her mother's hand. 'No. Your father won't let go that easily. He'll force James to choose between us.'

That was a possibility. One Helena couldn't deny. 'You're his mother,' she said gently. 'That will never change. He loves you.'

Miriam's throat worked for long seconds, then she whispered, 'I'm proud of you, darling. Do you know that? You had the courage to walk away when I didn't.' Her grip tightened on Helena's hand. 'I don't think I can be as brave.'

'Oh, Mum.' Helena hugged her, hiding the rush of moisture in her eyes.

*Brave?* The word seemed to hover in the air and mock her. Brave was not how she'd felt these last few nights, lying in Leo's arms as she searched in vain for the courage to talk about their son.

*Cowardly* was a more fitting word.

Maybe even *selfish*.

She pulled back and gave her mother a steady look. 'You can,' she said, the conviction in her voice as much for herself as for her mother.

She mightn't have a clue where she and Leo were headed but one thing she did know—she loved him now just as she had seven years ago. If they were to have any shot at a second chance she had to overcome her fear. Do the right thing and tell him about his son.

She squeezed her mother's hand. 'You *can*,' she repeated.

Miriam's eyes filled with tears. 'Your father will never agree to a divorce. And if he does where will I go? What will I do? I grew up with nothing, Helena. I can't go back to that. And I'm too old to start over on my own.'

'Mum, you're not even fifty! And you'll be entitled to a divorce settlement. We can find you a good lawyer.'

Somewhere in the distance a man raised his voice, the strident sound out of place in the quiet of the ward.

Helena tuned out the disturbance, her mind already too full of noise. 'Please, Mum,' she said. 'Let me help you.'

Miriam's tears spilled down her cheeks. She nodded and pulled her daughter into a tight hug.

'Miss Shaw?'

Helena straightened and turned. A nurse stood in the doorway.

'I'm sorry to interrupt,' the woman said, her tone brisk, her face serious. 'But could you come with me, please?'

Leo stood in the empty visitors' room at the end of the ward and stared out of the rain-spattered window. Outside, London was gearing up for another five o'clock rush hour and the frenzy of people and traffic on the wet streets below matched his edgy, restive mood. He swayed forward, letting his forehead bump the cool glass.

*Why was he still here?*

It was Thursday and he should be back in Rome, presenting his report on the ShawCorp takeover to his board—a task he had, until recently, anticipated with relish.

Now, not so much.

And wasn't that one hell of a kicker?

Seven years he'd planned this victory—*seven years*—and in a matter of days the taste of triumph had turned to ash in his mouth.

Footfalls echoed in the room and he straightened, pulled his hands from his pockets. Time to get some air, stretch his legs. Then he'd wait in the limo and clear his emails.

The hospital's sterile surroundings were closing in on him and, as mean-spirited as it sounded, he was in no mood for polite chitchat with the relative of a sick person.

The roar that rent the air before Leo had fully turned from the window gave him a split second to react. Even so, the fist flying towards him caught the left side of his jaw and sent a shard of pain ricocheting through his skull.

*'Bastard!'*

Douglas Shaw spat the word before lunging again, but Leo was ready this time. He dodged the blow and with a swift, well-timed manoeuvre seized Shaw's wrist and twisted his arm up his back.

'Calm down, you old fool,' he grated into the man's ear.

'Don't give me orders, Vincenti.'

Shaw struggled and Leo firmed his grip, inching the man's wrist higher up his back.

In a second, Shaw's voice went from gruff to reedy. 'You're breaking my arm.'

Making a noise of disgust, Leo let go with a shove, giving himself room to counter another attack if Shaw was stupid enough to try.

The older man wisely calmed down. He rubbed his arm. 'What the hell are *you* doing here?'

Leo returned his hands to his pockets, adopting a casual stance that belied the tension in his muscles, his readiness to act. He studied Shaw's hostile face—a face he had, until now, seen only in media clippings and corporate profiles. Hollows in the man's cheeks and a grey tinge to his skin made him look older in the flesh. Strong cologne and the waft of alcohol tainted the air.

Leo suppressed a grimace. 'I'm surprised you recognise me, Shaw. After all those declined invitations to meet I was beginning to think you had no interest in your new majority shareholder.'

'Is that why you're here?' Shaw snarled the question. 'Looking for a chance to gloat?'

Leo threw his head back and laughed. 'Don't flatter yourself, old man. I have better ways to spend my time.'

Shaw stepped forward, his sore arm and Leo's superiority in the strength department clearly forgotten. 'Maybe I should teach you another lesson—like the one I taught you seven years ago.'

Leo freed his fists, leaned his face close to Shaw's. 'You can try, but we both know your threats are empty. The truth is you're a coward and a bully. I know it. Your wife knows it. And your daughter knows it.'

A deep purple suffused Shaw's face. 'By God, I should—'

'Stop it! Both of you!'

A female voice sliced across the room, silencing whatever puerile threat Shaw had been about to deliver.

'This is not the time or place.'

Helena glared at each man before turning to murmur something to the nurse hovering in the doorway behind her. The woman muttered a reply, levelled a stern look at the men, then disappeared. Helena came into the room, her movements short, stiff, and stood shoulder to shoulder with Leo.

This time Shaw threw his head back and laughed. 'Of course!' he exclaimed to the ceiling. 'I should have guessed.' He snapped his chin down, pinned his daughter with a contemptuous stare. 'Some things never change— you're still a disloyal slut.'

Rage exploded in Leo's chest. Before his brain could intervene his muscles jolted into action. Within seconds his hands were twisted in the front of Shaw's shirt and he had the man pinned to a wall.

'Leo—stop!'

Helena's voice barely registered over the roar in his ears, but her firm touch on his arm dragged him back to his senses. Sucking in a deep breath, he dropped his hands, appalled by how swiftly the urge to do violence had overtaken him. That was Shaw's MO, he reminded himself with a flare of disgust, not his.

He stepped back and Shaw eyed him with a supercilious sneer that made Leo, for one tenth of a second, want to wipe the look off his face and to hell with being the better man.

Shaw straightened his attire and brushed himself off as if Leo's touch had left him soiled.

*Pompous ass.*

Helena turned to her father, her pale features set in the cool, dignified mask Leo had learnt to recognise as her protective armour. A week ago that very mask had bugged the hell out of him. Now her poise under pressure drew his unbridled respect.

'Leo's right,' she said, her voice as cold and sharp as a blade of ice. 'You're nothing but a coward and a bully.'

Shaw's face darkened, but Helena showed no fear. She stepped closer, and Leo braced himself to intervene if Shaw made any sudden moves.

'You tried so often to make me feel like a failure as a child. To make me feel worthless. But the truth is there's only one failure in this family and it's not me or Mum.' Her chin jutted up. 'It's *you*. It's *always* been you.' She pulled the strap of her handbag higher up her shoulder. 'Go home, Douglas,' she said, her voice quieter, weary now. 'My mother doesn't want to see you.'

And then she stepped back, looked at Leo.

'I'm ready to go whenever you are.'

Stiff and proud, she strode out of the room and Leo bolted after her, ignoring the man whose bluster had withered to a hard, brittle silence. A few days ago Leo would have sold his soul for a chance to face off with the man. Now there Shaw stood and Leo couldn't care less. The only face he wanted to see was Helena's.

He caught her in the corridor, pulled her gently to a stop. The tears on her cheeks caused a sharp burning sensation in his chest.

She swiped at her face with the heel of her hand. 'Please, just take me home.'

He frowned, picturing the cramped flat he'd cast an appalled eye over four days ago. He had announced with unequivocal authority that she would stay with him at the hotel.

'Home?' he echoed, his stomach pitching at the idea of taking her back there.

'I mean the hotel. Just anywhere that's not here.'

His innards levelled out. 'Si. Of course.' He cradled her damp face in his hands, pressed a kiss to her forehead. 'Will you wait here one minute for me?'

She nodded and he kissed her again—on the mouth this time—then released her and headed back to the visitors' room.

Shaw hadn't gone far. He stood by the window, much as Leo had earlier, staring down at the rain-soaked streets.

He glanced over his shoulder, his top lip curling. 'What do you want now, Vincenti?'

'To give you some advice.'

Shaw snorted. 'This should be good.'

Leo stood a few paces shy of the older man. 'Next time you feel the need to lash out,' he said, undaunted by the sudden fierce glower on Shaw's face, 'stay away from your wife. If you do not, and I hear that you have harmed her, know that I will come after you and do everything in my power to see you prosecuted in a court of law.'

He eyeballed Shaw just long enough to assure the man his threat was genuine, then started to leave, his thoughts already shifting back to Helena.

'Let me give *you* a piece of advice, son.'

Leo stopped, certain that whatever gem Shaw intended to impart wouldn't be worth a dime. He turned. 'What?'

'There are two kinds of women in this world. Those who understand their place and those who don't. Miriam always knew how to toe the line, but she coddled that girl far too much. If you want obedience in a woman you won't find it in Helena. She'll bring you nothing but trouble.'

*Dio.* The man was a raving misogynist. 'You don't know Helena.'

Shaw sneered. 'And you *do*?'

'Better than you.'

The sneer stretched into a bloodless smile that raised the hairs on Leo's forearms.

'In that case, since the two of you are so close, I assume you know about the baby?'

At that moment a grey-haired woman entered the room and headed for the kitchenette in the far corner.

Shaw stepped forward and Leo tensed, but the other man's hands remained by his sides.

He leaned in to deliver his parting shot. 'The one she buried nine months after you scarpered back to Italy.'

For a suspended moment Shaw's words hung in the air, devoid of meaning, and then, like guided missiles striking their target, they slammed into Leo's brain one after the other. His lungs locked. The skin at his nape tightened. And when Shaw walked away, his expression smug, Leo couldn't do a damn thing to stop him. Because his muscles—the ones that had been so swift to react earlier—had completely frozen.

Through a dark, suffocating mist, he registered a touch on his arm. He looked down.

'Are you all right, my dear?' The elderly woman peered up at him through round, wire-rimmed spectacles. 'You're as white as a ghost.'

'Tell me about the child.'

Helena stared at Leo's implacable face. 'Stop standing over me.'

She wished she hadn't sat down as soon as they'd entered the suite. She fought back a shiver. She'd thought his silence during the limo ride from the hospital had been unbearable. Having him tower over her now, like some big, surly interrogator, while she cowered on the sofa was ten times worse.

He gritted his teeth—she could tell by the way his jaw flexed—then visibly flinched.

'You should ice that,' she blurted, eyeing the livid bruise beneath his five o'clock shadow. She still couldn't believe her father had punched him.

'So help me, Helena, if you do not—'

'I wanted to tell you.' She jumped to her feet, unable to sit there a moment longer while he glowered down at her. She circled around the sofa, gripped the back for support. 'I was just…waiting for the right time.'

*Oh, God.* How weak that sounded—how very convenient and trite. He'd never believe it. Not now. Not in a million years.

She searched his face, desperate for a glimpse of the warmth and tenderness she'd grown accustomed to in recent days. But all she saw was anger. Disbelief. Hurt. She thought of her father and his smug expression as he'd passed her in the hospital corridor. A flash of hatred burned in her chest. He'd ruined everything. *Again.*

'You were waiting for *the right time*?' Leo plunged his fingers into his hair. 'Did you not think seven years ago that it was "the right time"?'

Her legs shook and she dug her nails into the sofa. 'You left,' she reminded him. 'You went back to Italy.'

'Because I had nothing to stay for. Your father had seen to that.'

'You said you never wanted to see me again.'

'I had no idea you were carrying my child.'

'Neither did I.'

Only once had they burst a condom, and she'd sensibly taken a morning-after pill. And since her cycle had always been erratic her overdue period hadn't, at first, been cause for concern.

'And when you *did* find out? Did it not occur to you *then* to find me and tell me I was going to be a father?'

'No—I mean...' She shook her head. '*Yes*. But I was confused. Frightened.'

'So you were thinking about yourself? Not me? Or what was best for our child?'

His words cut like the vicious lash of a whip. Smarting, she prised her hands from the back of the sofa then walked around it, her insides trembling.

'Be angry with me, Leo,' she said, stalking into his space. 'But don't judge me. Don't pretend you have *any* idea what it's like to be pregnant and scared and alone. I made some foolish decisions—some *bad* decisions—but don't think for a moment I didn't realise that. Don't think I didn't hold our son in my arms and regret, to the very bottom of my soul, that I had denied you that privilege.'

Leo's face suddenly paled and the flash of anguish in his eyes sliced through her heart.

'A son?' He dropped onto the sofa and bowed his head for a long moment. 'How...?'

He didn't finish the question. He didn't need to.

She sat beside him, close but not touching, and pulled in a deep breath. She spoke quietly. 'He was stillborn. He died in my womb two days before he was due.'

She stared at her hands, pale against the dark denim of her jeans. She didn't need to look at Leo to know his reaction. His shock was palpable.

'I knew something was wrong because I could no longer feel him kicking. I went straight to the hospital and they confirmed that he didn't have a heartbeat. The doctors couldn't tell me why it had happened. Apparently it just does sometimes.'

She curled her nails into her palms. Her memory of that day was still vivid: the horror, the pain. It was a dark stain on her soul she would never be able to erase.

'They offered an autopsy but I...I turned it down. I

didn't want our little boy cut open,' she said hurriedly, feeling she had to justify that decision. 'The results weren't guaranteed to be conclusive. And it wasn't going to bring him back.'

She looked up and Leo's expression was so stark she wanted to reach out and touch him. But there was no comfort she could offer him. No words of solace. Pain, she knew, eased with time. Nothing else.

'I'm so sorry,' she whispered.

Abruptly he stood, grabbed his jacket off the chair where he'd tossed it earlier and shrugged it on.

She swallowed, her heart plummeting. 'Where are you going?'

He looked at her, the emotion in those dark eyes impossible to fathom.

'Out. I need a drink.'

'You have a bar here.'

Ignoring that, he strode to the door.

Disbelief drove Helena to her feet. 'So you're just going to walk out? You don't even want to talk about it?' She blinked back tears.

*Damn him.* He was hurting. In shock. She got that. But he wasn't the only one who'd been through an emotional grinder today.

He stopped and turned. Several beats of silence pulsed between them, each one long and unbearably tense. For a moment she thought he would say something. He didn't. He spun on his heel and walked out through the door.

# CHAPTER ELEVEN

DARKNESS SHROUDED THE suite when Leo returned.

Had she gone? he wondered. Back to that grim flat of hers? Back to whatever bland, colourless life she'd consigned herself to since the death of their son?

He flicked on a light and blinked. He wasn't drunk. In fact he'd nursed a single Scotch in the hotel bar for over an hour before the need to move had overtaken him. And then he'd walked. From the streets of Mayfair to the teeming pavements of Soho and Piccadilly Circus and back to the tree-lined greens of Hyde Park. He'd walked until his feet burned and fatigue stripped away his anger, leaving in its wake the galling knowledge that he'd behaved appallingly.

He dumped his jacket and looked at his watch. Nine-thirty p.m. Three hours since he'd left—plenty of time for her to pack up and flee. But had she? He moved through the suite, a hard knot forming in his chest at the prospect that she really had gone.

But, no. Her clothes were still in the bedroom, her toiletries sitting in a neat row on the bathroom vanity.

So where the hell was she?

He went back to the lounge and found his phone. He'd switched it off earlier. Maybe she'd left a message? He powered it on and had his code half entered when he heard a noise at the door. A few seconds later it swung open and Helena walked in, carrying a bag and wearing a grey hooded jacket with damp patches on the shoulders.

He frowned, disguising his relief. 'You're wet,' he said. Inanely. Because it was better than shouting, *Where the hell have you been?*

'It's just started raining again.' She glanced at him, put

down the bag and took off her jacket. Her face was flushed, her breathing a little uneven. 'I only caught a few drops.'

'Where have you been?' He surprised himself with how reasonable he sounded. How *not* angry.

'I went home.'

He raised his eyebrows. 'How?'

'On the tube. You know…that thing called public transport—for common folk who can't afford limos.' Her sarcasm lacked any genuine bite.

He put his phone down. 'Why?'

'I needed to get something.'

She knelt by the bag and lifted out a wooden box, roughly the size of a document-carrier. It looked hand-crafted, its golden wood polished to a beautiful sheen, the lock and key and silver side-handles dainty and ornate. She placed it on the coffee table by the sofa and straightened, holding out her hand to him.

'I named our little boy Lucas,' she said, a smile trembling on her lips. 'And he was the most beautiful thing I had ever seen.'

Helena watched Leo's expression crumple in a way she'd never have imagined it could. He closed his eyes and turned away, his shoulders hunched, his head bowed.

'No. I can't.'

She walked over and touched his shoulder. 'You can,' she said, as firmly as she'd spoken those very same words to her mother. 'Our son was *real*, Leo. He didn't cry or open his eyes or take a breath, but he had ten fingers and ten toes and everything else a perfect baby should have.' She squeezed his shoulder, felt a tremor run through the hard muscle under her hand. 'Please,' she said, willing him to look at her. Willing him to trust her. 'Let me show you our little boy. I promise it will help.'

Endless seconds ticked by. Taut, silent seconds that stretched her nerves and amplified each painful beat of her heart. At the very moment her shoulders started to slump, weighted by defeat, he turned.

'*Si.*' He dragged a hand over his face. 'Show me, then.'

Relief—and a glimmer of hope—trickled through Helena's veins. She took his hand and led him to the sofa. He sat and she kicked off her shoes, knelt on the floor and opened the box. The first item made her heart give a painful squeeze.

Hands shaking, she passed it to him. 'I knitted it myself.'

Leo's big, masculine hands dwarfed the tiny purple beanie. He turned it over several times, his eyebrows inching up as he fingered the multi-coloured pompom. 'It is very…bright.'

She waggled a pair of fire-engine-red booties. 'I liked colour, remember? Pastels didn't get a look-in, I'm afraid.'

His soft grunt might or might not have been approval. Sitting forward, he peered into the box. 'Is this…?' He lifted out a small white plaster mould. '*Mio Dio.*' He ran his thumb over the tiny indentations created by his son's hand. His voice deepened. Thickened. 'So small…and perfect…'

'There are moulds of his feet, too,' she said, blinking away the sudden prickle of tears. 'And a lock of hair. Some outfits.' She delved into the box, removed more items, including an envelope. 'And I…I have photos.'

Leo shifted suddenly, sinking to the floor beside her, so close his warm, muscled thigh pressed against hers. He reached for the miniature mould of Lucas's foot, handling the tiny object with infinite care.

Helena watched, her throat growing hot, tight. Perhaps this hadn't been a crazy idea after all? If everything fell apart from here—if *they* fell apart—at least they would have shared this.

He put down the mould and turned his attention to the other items she'd laid out, taking his time to handle and examine each one in turn. When he eventually came to the photos he studied them for a long time in silence.

'He looks like he's sleeping,' he said at last.

'Yes.' The ache in her throat became a powerful throb. 'He does.'

She sat back on her heels. She could weep right now. For the son she had lost. For the strong, proud man sitting beside her. For the future for which she had dared to hope.

Instead she climbed to her feet and looked down on Leo's bowed head. 'I'm tired, and cold. I think I'll grab a shower before bed.' She hovered a moment, but his focus remained on the photo in his hand. 'Will you…be coming to bed?'

As she waited for his answer, her muscles tense, her body shivery from tiredness, she realised how much she wanted him to say yes. How badly she needed his arms around her tonight. How desperately she ached for his warmth, his touch, *his love*.

'Soon,' he said, and his eyes, when he glanced up, revealed nothing.

But when Leo finally came to bed, over two hours later, he didn't put his arms around her. He didn't touch her. He didn't even turn in her direction. And though it was only a matter of inches that separated their bodies, the gap might as well have been a chasm. A chasm Helena feared was too wide, too dark and too deep for either of them to bridge.

Leo stood at the French doors and watched lightning fork across the night sky, the jagged streaks of white light searing his retinas.

Or was it the tears making his eyes burn?

*Dammit.*

He hadn't cried since the night of Marietta's accident, but that box had been his undoing. Unravelling him in ways he hadn't thought possible. Flaying his emotions until his insides felt raw. And yet his pain must be nothing compared to what Helena had suffered. Helena had borne her loss alone, grieved for their son without him because she had been too afraid to tell him she was carrying their child. Too afraid because the last words he'd spoken to her—shouted through a closed hotel door, no less—had been hard, unforgiving words, fired without a care for how deeply they'd wound.

Thunder boomed, closer now, and he stepped back from the glass. *Idiota*, standing here watching the storm. Inviting memories of the night his mother had died.

As a child he'd thought thunder was a sign of God's anger. Had thought losing his mother was his punishment for boyhood sins: avoiding homework, skipping chores, cornering the big bully who'd pulled Marietta's hair and punching him in the nose—twice.

Since then he'd hated thunderstorms. Hated the idea of something so powerful and beyond his control.

Maybe God was punishing him now?

For his pride. His anger. His failure to forgive.

He had targeted one man with single-minded purpose and spared not a thought for collateral damage. Now a woman lay in hospital. Another in his bed.

*And what of her?* his conscience demanded. Would Helena, too, become collateral damage when all this was over? Or would the only damage where she was concerned be to his heart?

'Leo?'

He started, the soft voice behind him catching him by surprise. When he had thrown off the sheets and padded, naked, through to the lounge he had thought Helena asleep—undisturbed, it seemed, by the storm.

'What are you doing?' she said, drowsy. 'It's three a.m.'

He didn't turn. Didn't know what to say to her. What *could* he say? *I'm sorry?* No. Useless. Mere words couldn't express his regret for his behaviour today. His behaviour seven years ago.

He'd stormed back to Italy like an angry bear, licking

his wounds when he should have been here looking after her, sharing the burden of responsibility.

Of loss.

He glanced over his shoulder. Her form was a willowy outline in the glow of the single lamp he'd switched on in the corner of the room.

'I couldn't sleep,' he said.

'The storm?'

'I don't like them.' The words just spilled out. He didn't know why. He didn't make a habit of highlighting his weaknesses to people. But then, Helena wasn't *people*. She was… Hell, she was so many things—none of which he was in any mood to contemplate.

'Why?' She was right behind him now.

He shrugged. 'Bad memories.'

He could feel her breath on his shoulder, and the tantalising scent of warm, sleepy woman enveloped him. He scrunched his eyes closed, the rush of blood to his groin turning him hard against his will.

He wanted her.

Even with his gut in turmoil, tears drying on his cheeks, he wanted her.

He heard a rustling behind him and then her arms were slipping around his middle, her slender fingers splaying over his abs. Her heavy breasts pushed into his back, her hips against his buttocks, and his desire surged with the realisation that she'd shed her pyjamas and was now, like him, completely naked.

He groaned. 'Helena…'

'Shh.' She ducked under his arm and took his face in her hands.

When he drew breath to speak again she tugged his head down and silenced him with a long, drugging kiss.

Her taste exploded in his mouth, hot and sweet and undeniably erotic. He shuddered, closed his arms around her and surrendered to the burning need only she could assuage. The solace only she could offer. He hoisted her up and her legs hooked around his waist, their mouths continuing to meld and devour—until he started for the bedroom.

She wrenched her mouth away. 'No,' she whispered, lowering her legs, pulling him back to the French doors. She sank to her knees at his feet. 'Here. Take me here.'

He stared down at her, his blood pounding, his heart pumping so hard he feared it might punch from his chest.

This woman stripped him bare. Of his pride. His anger. His guilt. Everything but this deep, compelling need for her.

'Why?' he said, his throat raw.

She reached for his hands and dragged him down to the carpet, pushed him onto his back. 'To replace your bad memories with new ones,' she said, and mounted him so quickly he almost came the moment her slippery heat encased him.

He dug his heels into the carpet, seized her hips in an urgent bid to slow her. He wasn't wearing protection and she was hot and slick, her internal muscles a tight velvet sheath pulsing around him.

The sensation was exquisite.

'Condom...' he rasped.

'I'm on the pill.' She grabbed his wrists, guided his hands to her breasts and arched her back, taking him deeper. Her dark curls tumbled around her shoulders and her features were illuminated as another bright bolt of lightning tore the sky.

Leo stared up, captivated by the sight of her riding him, by the bold, sensual grind of her pelvis driving him to the brink faster than he'd have liked. Thunder rolled down from the heavens, loud and near, a boom so powerful it slammed into his body with an almighty thud.

'Come with me,' he ground out, grasping her waist, forcing her to still so he could satisfy his need to drive up into her.

'I…I'm close.' Her body flexed, her thighs squeezing his sides, a taut O of ecstasy shaping her mouth. 'Oh, yes… Now, Leo… *Now…*'

He plunged upward, penetrating deep, and she screamed at the same instant another flash lit up the sky. Her cry of release was all he needed and he let himself go, his orgasm thundering through him in a climax so intense it bordered the line between pleasure and pain and racked his entire body with a series of long, powerful shudders.

With a whimper Helena slumped onto his chest. She buried her face in his shoulder, made a soft mewling sound against his skin, and he stroked his hands up and down the graceful lines of her back.

He didn't deserve her compassion—didn't deserve *her*—but she felt so good nestled in his arms he didn't want to let her go.

He cradled her close.

He *would* let her go. It was the right thing to do. The only thing to do. And the sooner he did, the better.

Helena navigated the bedroom on autopilot as she packed up her things. The painkillers she'd forced down earlier hadn't worked and her temples throbbed, her eyes gritty from the crying jag she'd indulged in. Silly to have allowed emotion to overwhelm her simply because she'd woken to find Leo's side of the bed empty and cold. He'd left a note, at least. A bold, handwritten scrawl advising her that he'd gone to a meeting and would be back by noon.

She looked around for her pyjamas, frowned when she couldn't see them, then remembered and went through to the lounge.

Yes—there. On the floor by the sofa, where she had discarded them so brazenly in the night.

She reached for them and a sudden powerful sob of emotion rushed up her throat. On shaky legs she sank to the sofa, hating it that she felt so off-balance, so raw and exposed.

But how could she not?

She wasn't the same woman who had left London a week ago. She felt different—more aware of herself. As if someone—no, not 'someone', *Leo*—had shone a great floodlight inside her and illuminated all the parts of herself she'd ignored for too long.

He made her feel desired. Wanted.

*Worth* something.

Made her want to rip down the safe, boring black and white walls she'd erected like a concrete tower around herself.

She rubbed her chest as if she could banish the ache within.

She loved Leo, but what future could they hope for? One in which he spent his days trying to forgive her and she spent hers trying to earn back his trust?

A shudder rippled through her. Her mother had endured a miserable marriage and she didn't want that for herself. She wanted a partnership based on honesty and respect. On *love*. That last especially. Because if two people loved each other they could overcome anything, surely?

She forced herself to her feet, returned to the bedroom to finish her packing.

She didn't know if Leo loved her—didn't know if what he felt for her ran any deeper than lust—but she would not play the desperate, needy lover. She would not pout and demand that he declare his feelings for her. *No*. She would do this with dignity and strength. With self-respect. The kind she had often wished over the years her mother possessed.

And if Leo chose to let her walk away…if he was content to see the back of her…she would have her answer.

*Relief.* That was what Leo told himself he was feeling. When he walked into the suite and saw Helena sitting on the sofa, her bags packed beside her, he felt relief. She had come to her senses. Realised in the cold light of day that she could do better. Better than a man who had let her down when she'd needed him most.

'You're leaving.' He kept his voice flat. Neutral. As if those words *hadn't* stripped the lining from his stomach.

She rose, her expression serious and her eyes, he realised on closer inspection, bloodshot and puffy. Self-loathing roiled in his stomach. No doubt *he* was the cause of her misery. He thrust his hands into his trouser pockets before he did something selfish, like haul her into his arms and beg her not to leave.

'I think that's wise,' he said.

'Do you?' She looked at him, her gaze wide, unblinking.

'*Si*. Of course.'

He strode to the wet bar, pulled a soda from the fridge. Later he'd need something stronger. For now he just needed something to do—an excuse not to look at her. Not to drown in those enormous pools of blue.

'Our seven days are up, are they not?'

Silence behind him. He popped the tab on the can, quashed the temptation to crush the aluminium in his fist. Instead he took a casual swig and turned.

She took a step towards him, her clasped hands twisting in front of her. 'Yes,' she said. 'And I know you can't stay here for ever. Neither can I—which is why I'm going back to my flat...' Her voice trailed off, an awkward silence descending.

'I video-conferenced with my board this morning, regarding my acquisition of ShawCorp.' He kept his delivery brisk. Businesslike. 'They've agreed to a delay on the asset divestment.'

'Oh?' Her eyebrows lifted. 'How long?'

'Nine months, initially—provided costs can be restricted and profits improved.' He put the soda down. 'Time to see how the company performs and consider options for its future.'

She blinked. 'I...thank you.'

'Don't thank me, Helena.' A bitter edge crept into his voice. 'We both know you don't owe me any gratitude.'

Something flashed in her eyes. An emotion he couldn't decipher. Her hands continued to fidget and he fought not to reach out and still them.

'When will you return to Rome?'

'Tonight.' A decision he had just now made. Why stay? He couldn't sleep here. Not knowing she was in the same city, close and yet untouchable. He needed land, water, miles between them.

'I see. Will you—?'

His mobile chimed and he pulled it from his pocket, saw it was his PA calling and answered with a clipped greeting. He listened to Gina relay an urgent message from his second-in-command, then asked her to hold.

He glanced at Helena. 'I need to take this,' he said, and without waiting for an acknowledgement he moved through the French doors onto the balcony.

Ten minutes later Leo ended his call and turned away from the view. Instinctively, before he even stepped into the room, he knew Helena was gone.

Inside, the fragrance of her perfume lingered in the air—a bittersweet echo of her presence.

*Relief*, he reminded himself, but the cold, heavy weight pressing on his chest didn't feel like relief. Nor did the sudden insane urge to run after her.

He flung himself into a recliner and closed his eyes. When he opened them long minutes later his gaze landed on a small unsealed envelope on the coffee table. Frowning, he reached for it, lifted the flap and removed the single item from within.

A photo of their son.

The one he had studied so intently the night before.

He turned it over, and as he read the neat lines of hand-writing on the back his eyes started to burn.

*He was special because we made him.*
*Carry him in your heart, as I do in mine.*
*I love you—and I'm sorry.*
*H.*

# CHAPTER TWELVE

'LEONARDO VINCENTI, ARE you listening to me?'

Marietta's voice, sharp with exasperation, jerked Leo from his thoughts. He looked up from the dregs of his espresso, guilt pricking him. 'Sorry, *carina*.'

His sister's expression softened. 'You were miles away.'

He pushed his empty cup aside and cursed himself. This was Marietta's night. He'd brought her to her favourite restaurant in the upmarket Parioli district of Rome to celebrate the lucrative sale of two of her paintings, and yet all he'd managed to do was put a dampener on the occasion.

'What's wrong?' she said.

'Nothing is wrong.' If he didn't count the fact that he hadn't slept in weeks. Or eaten properly. Or achieved anything more productive than pushing paperwork from one side of his desk to the other.

'*Something* is going on with you.' She leaned in, elbows propped on the table, eyes searching his. 'Talk to me.'

Marietta's sweet-natured concern only amplified his guilt. He forced a smile. 'Tell me about this loft you found.'

She frowned at him, but she didn't push. Instead she said, 'It's perfect. Lots of natural light and open space.' A spark of excitement lit her eyes. 'And there's a car park and a lift, so access isn't a problem.'

His sister had searched for months for a space she could purchase and convert into a dedicated art studio. The need for wheelchair access had made the search more difficult, but she'd tackled the challenge with the same determination she applied to everything in her life.

Pride swelled. 'How much do you need for it?'

Her frown reappeared. She sat back. 'I have money saved for a deposit. I don't need a loan, Leo.'

'Of course not.' As if he'd ever *loan* his sister money and expect her to repay him. He could afford to buy her ten studios—one was hardly an imposition. 'You'll need a notary for the purchase contract. I'll call Alex in the morning.'

She threw her hands in the air. 'You're doing it *again*.'

'Doing what?'

'Taking over. Going all Big Brother on me. I can do this on my own—without your help.'

Leo stared at her, his jaw clenching, a stab of intense emotion—the kind he'd been feeling too much of lately—lancing his chest. He tried to smooth his expression, but Marietta knew him too well.

She reached for his hand. 'You know I love you?'

A fist-sized lump formed in his throat. '*Si*. I love you, too.'

'I know.' Her fingers squeezed his. 'And that's all I need.'

Leo swallowed. That damned lump was making it difficult to speak. 'It doesn't feel like enough,' he admitted, and realised he had never said those words out loud before.

Marietta's eyes grew misty. 'Enough for what? For this?' She tapped the arm of her wheelchair. When her question met with silence, she shook her head. 'Oh, Leo. This isn't your fault and you know it.'

'The surgery—'

'Wasn't successful,' she cut in. 'Maybe we waited too long, or maybe the delay made no difference—we'll never know for sure. But I've made peace with it and you must, too. My life is good. I have my job, my art, *you*.' She sat forward, her dark eyes glistening. 'I'm happy, Leo. Yes, my life has challenges, but I'm strong and I don't need you to prop me up or catch me every time I fall. All I need is for you to be the one person in the world I can rely on to love me—no matter what.'

Her fingers wrapped more tightly around his.

'There's one other thing I need, and that's to know my brother is happy, too.' She gave him a watery smile. 'Maybe you could start by sorting out whatever has turned you into such a grouch these last few weeks?'

Leo scowled, but underneath his mock affront his sister's words were looping on a fast-moving cycle through his head, their impact more profound than he cared to admit. He felt something loosen inside his chest. Felt the heavy shroud of darkness that had weighted his every thought and action for almost a month start to lift.

He reached across and tweaked her chin. 'I do love you, *piccola*. Even when you are giving me lip.'

She grinned. 'I know. Now, stop scowling. You're scaring off the waiter and I want my dessert.'

An hour later, after seeing Marietta safely home, Leo ignored the lift in his building and bounded up the seven flights of stairs, a burst of energy he hadn't experienced in weeks powering his legs.

*He loved Helena.* He had reached that conclusion within days of returning to Rome. Within minutes of walking into his apartment and realising how empty it felt—how empty *he* felt—with her gone.

For more than three weeks he'd clung to the belief that she deserved better than him.

But how could she do better than a man who would love her with everything he had for the rest of his life?

*Paris, eight days later...*

Helena pulled off her strappy sandals and took the stairs two at a time inside the old building near the bustling promenades of Les Grands Boulevards.

The apartment she and her mother had rented for the week was small but charming, with shiny wooden floors, decorative finishes, and a sunny balcony where each morning they soaked up the beauty of Paris over coffee and croissants.

It was a girls' holiday. A chance for mother and daughter to reconnect and a celebration of sorts. For Helena because she'd worked out her notice at the bank, and for Miriam because, following her discharge from hospital, she had walked out of the home she'd shared with her husband of twenty-nine years and retained one of London's most successful divorce lawyers.

The weeks since had been challenging—tongues had wagged and Douglas had refused to 'play nice'—but Miriam was holding strong and Helena was proud of her.

Warm from her stroll and the three-storey climb, she reached the landing, glad she'd worn her new dress today instead of shorts or jeans. With its camisole bodice and little flared skirt the yellow sundress was cute and bright, and she'd worn it to buoy her spirits as much as anything. She was doing her best to move on, to live the life she should have lived these last seven years, but still she had plenty of dark, desolate moments when all she wanted to do was curl into a ball and cry. When it seemed she would never excise Leo from her thoughts or her heart no matter how hard she tried.

It didn't help that he'd called her mobile several times this past week. She hadn't answered and he hadn't left any messages—which was good, because she wouldn't cope with hearing his voice. And, really, what could he say that she wanted to hear? Or vice versa? That last day at the hotel his lack of interest couldn't have been any clearer. The man who'd held her with such heartbreaking tenderness in the aftermath of their lovemaking had, in those final stilted moments, barely forced himself to look at her.

Sighing, she fished her key from her tote and ousted Leo from her thoughts. She was in Paris and the sun was shining—good reasons to smile. And she couldn't wait to tell her mother, who'd opted for an afternoon of lounging in the sun with a book, about the incredible street art she'd found nearby.

Helena pushed open the door. 'Mum!' she called. 'I found the most amazing—' She stopped short. Her mother had been outside on the balcony when she'd left but now Miriam sat in the cosy sun-filled lounge. And with her, looking utterly incongruous in an easy chair covered in pink floral upholstery, sat the man Helena decided some wistful part of her imagination must have conjured.

Her key and tote dangled from her fingers, forgotten. 'Leo?'

He rose and he looked…magnificent. Big and dark and sexy in faded jeans and a snug-fitting black tee shirt.

'*Ciao*, Helena.'

The deep baritone fired a zing of awareness through her she didn't welcome. Questions crowded her mind until one emerged from the jumble. 'How did you find me?'

His gaze roamed her face, her bare shoulders. For a second she thought she saw a flicker of heat in his eyes.

'When I couldn't reach you I contacted David. He told me you'd resigned.' His voice carried a note of surprise. 'He also said you'd planned a trip to Paris. The rest—' He shrugged. 'Let's just say I know someone who's good at tracking people down.'

She wanted to be annoyed. She wanted to be so very, *very* annoyed. But all she could focus on was fighting the desire to reach out and touch him.

She pulled in a breath and realised her mother was by her side, bag in hand.

'I want to check out that little bookstore and café we spotted yesterday.' Miriam touched Helena's cheek, her smile tender, then gave her daughter a quick hug. 'Hear him out,' she whispered, and then she was gone.

On rubbery legs, Helena went and perched her tote on the end of the small breakfast bar.

'I like this,' Leo said behind her, and she turned, ready to agree that the apartment was indeed likable.

But he wasn't looking at the chic decor, or the quintessentially Parisian views. He was staring at *her*—or, more specifically, at her dress.

He stepped closer and slid his finger under a thin daffodil-yellow strap. 'It's pretty.'

'And it's not black,' she quipped, nerves—and something else—jumping in her belly.

One corner of his mouth kicked up. 'It's certainly not that.' He fingered one of her curls, bleached amber by the sun, and let it spring free. 'So…no more black?'

'Well…*less* black.' She couldn't afford to ditch half her wardrobe. She'd made no definite decisions about her future, but whether she chose art school or simply a job that offered scope for creativity she'd need to stretch her savings. She shrugged. 'I guess I'm rediscovering my love of colour.'

'And what brought that about?'

'You did.' Her candour made her blush but she couldn't regret the words. She wanted to be truthful with him, even though it wouldn't change anything. 'You challenged me. Made me think twice about what I'd chosen to give up.'

He had reawakened her passion for art and life. For that, among other things, she would always love him.

She moved away, sat in a comfy chair, needing to escape the heat his close proximity generated.

'What do you want, Leo?' The question came out sharper than she intended, but that was all right. She needed to keep her barriers up. Already the sight of him was spreading unwanted warmth. Making her forget how cold and remote he'd been during their last encounter.

He reached for a jacket she hadn't noticed over the arm of a chair. He pulled an envelope from a pocket, tossed the jacket back down and dropped to his haunches in front of her. When he slid the photo out and handed it to her, back side up, a thick wad of emotion clogged her throat.

'Read it to me,' he said.

She glanced up, opened her mouth to refuse, but the firm set of his jaw made her reconsider. She looked down again, studying the words even though she didn't need to. They were carved for eternity on her heart.

She prayed her voice wouldn't wobble. '"He was special because we made him. Carry him in your heart...as I do in mine."'

The next line blurred in front of her eyes.

'Read the rest.'

Her throat thickened. 'Why?'

'Because I need to hear you say it.'

'Why?' she repeated, fighting back stupid tears. 'So you can watch me humiliate myself?'

He placed his hands on the arms of her chair. 'Why would those words humiliate you?'

*'Because!'*

She glared at him, discomfort turning to anger. Anger to resentment. He would do *this* to her? Make her pour out her wretched feelings? Confess her love in person to satisfy his ego? She should never have never written those words. *Never.*

'Because it *hurts*!' she cried, thumping the heel of her hand against his chest. 'It hurts to love someone and know they don't love you back.' She thumped again, her palm bouncing off a wall of immovable muscle. 'It hurts to know you've lost any chance with that person. It hurts, Leo—' She hiccupped on a stifled sob and whacked his chest a third time. 'Because I do, damn it. I love you!'

The silence that fell in the wake of her outburst threatened to suffocate her. As did her surge of outrage when she glimpsed the satisfaction on Leo's face. With a shriek of fury she shoved at his chest and tried to rise, but he seized her wrists, his grip strong. Unyielding. Instead of standing she fell on his lap, straddling his thighs, trapped against the chair with her dress hiked around her hips.

Her chest heaved, another mortifying sob rattling through her. She couldn't fight him any more than she could fight the hot stab of need in her belly. Being this close to his big, powerful body was agony. She writhed, helpless, conscious of her sprawled legs, her exposed panties.

'*Tesoro mio...*'

She stilled, but she had no time to wonder at the rawness in Leo's voice. He released her wrists, folded his arms around her and buried his face in her neck. His scent engulfed her. His body, so warm and strong, sent her pulse into overdrive. She couldn't move, could barely breathe he held her so tight.

'Leo...?'

Finally he pulled back. His hands cupped her face. 'I love you, *cara*,' he said, and Helena didn't know if it was the intensity in his dark eyes or his words that stole her breath. 'I loved you seven years ago and I love you now. And, like a fool, I let you get away from me—not once, or even twice, but three times. Believe me when I tell you—' his voice roughened '—it will not happen again.'

Shock. Disbelief. Hope. Too many emotions to process at once rushed through her. Her body shook. Her brain, too—or at least that was how it felt. As if her mind couldn't contain the enormity of what he'd just said.

She studied his face, unwilling to let hope take hold too soon. 'What makes you so sure you love me?'

Leo stared at the strong, stubborn, beautiful woman who had ignored every one of his calls these last eight days and driven him to the brink of despair. The smile he gave was tortured.

'Aside from spending every waking hour wanting to know where you are, who you're with, what you're doing... and whether or not you are thinking of me?' He brushed away the lone tear that rolled down her cheek. 'I've been a fool and a coward, *cara*. Paralysed by fear.'

'Fear?'

He touched his forehead to hers. 'Fear that I couldn't be the man you deserve. The kind of man you can depend on.' He lifted his head. 'I failed you, *cara*.'

Her brow pleated. 'How?'

'Seven years ago I sent you away because I was angry and hurt, my pride wounded. I refused to give you a second chance, and because of that I wasn't there when you needed me.'

'Oh, Leo…' She laid her palm along his jaw. 'That's not on you. I should have found you and told you I was pregnant but I wasn't brave enough—and that was *my* bad, not yours. You deserved to know and I denied you that.' Her mouth trembled, her eyes searching his. 'Can you ever forgive me?'

He shook his head. 'There is nothing to forgive. We have both made mistakes.' He offered up another smile, this one crooked. Rueful. 'I believe it is called being human.'

Two more tears slipped down her cheeks. He brushed each one away.

'We can't change our history,' she said. 'Undo our mistakes. What if you can't trust—?'

He laid his finger over her lips, then took her hand and pressed her palm to his chest. '*Il mio cuore è solo tuo.*' When she blinked, he translated. 'My heart is yours.' He punctuated the statement with a gentle kiss. 'There is nothing more valuable I can entrust to you. And I promise you this, *tesoro*. You will never have to fight for my love.'

*The way she'd had to fight for her father's.*

'It is yours. Unconditionally. Tell me it is enough,' he demanded. 'Tell me—'

His command went unfinished. Because Helena cut him off with a kiss. A sudden, fierce, full-on-the-mouth kiss that smashed the breath from his lungs and caused an explosion of heat in his blood. He groaned. She tasted of heaven. Warm, sweet—a taste he wouldn't tire of for as long as he lived.

When she finally pulled back they were both panting for breath. Her eyes were moist, her smile shaky but wide. 'It's enough, my darling,' she said. 'It's enough.'

She pressed her face into his throat and they stayed like that for long, contented minutes. Then he eased her back and let his gaze rove her face, her body. *Hell*. He loved the yellow dress. Bright. Bold. A little bit cheeky. It was the girl he remembered. The one he hoped was back for good. The one whose blue eyes sparkled now with a hint of mischief.

Her smile was coy. Sexy. 'I think my mother will be gone for at least an hour.'

Leo responded with a wolfish grin, sealed their future with a scorching kiss, and then set about demonstrating one of the many ways in which he planned to love his woman.

# EPILOGUE

*One year later...*

HELENA PRISED THE lids off the two test pots of paint and smiled at the colours. The first, Sugar and Spice, was a gorgeous lilac with a pretty shimmer. The second, Surf's Up, was a deep purple-blue.

Neither colour was the one she'd originally planned for this sunny room on the second floor of the Tuscan villa, but when she'd started her flurry of redecorating she'd imagined the room as a studio. A dedicated space where she could work on her projects for the interior design course she'd undertaken and, in her downtime, dabble in creative pursuits.

She'd even thought she might try her hand at painting some landscapes under Marietta's expert tutelage. The Tuscan countryside, with its sun-drenched hills, fragrant orchards and acres of lush vegetation, offered no shortage of inspiration.

She and Leo spent most of their weekends here, escaping the bustle of London or Rome. It was calming, rejuvenating, and she wondered how he would feel about the villa becoming their more permanent home.

Her mobile whistled, indicating a text message, and she rose from the canvas sheet on the floor. Leo was en route from Rome, and he'd already texted to say he wanted her naked when he arrived. They'd been apart only two nights, but according to her husband of six months that was two nights too long.

She rarely came to the villa by herself, but she'd needed to organise some tradesmen and their short separation had given her some time alone. Time to absorb the news that made her tummy flutter with a mix of excitement and nerves every time she anticipated the moment she would tell Leo.

She swiped the screen of her phone. His message said he was thirty minutes out and— Heat flooded her as she read the rest.

She grinned, shaking her head. Her husband was wicked. And sexy. And she loved him with every atom of her being.

Half an hour later the crunch of gravel and the low purr of the Maserati's engine heralded his arrival.

Pulse leaping, Helena put down her brush and leaned out of the open window. Leo climbed from the car and she waved to him.

'Up here!'

He looked up, late-afternoon sunlight bathing his bronzed features, and she knew she'd never get used to him smiling at her like that. As if she was his favourite person in the entire world.

He disappeared into the house and she heard his footsteps thunder up the curved staircase.

She barely had time to run her fingers through her dishevelled hair before she was in his arms, her legs wrapped around his waist, her breath stolen by his ferocious kiss.

'*Dio*,' he growled when he broke for air. 'You are beautiful.'

She laughed. 'Hardly.' Her curls were a wild mess, not a trace of make-up adorned her face, and she wore the old short denim dungarees she kept for painting and decorating.

'Do not argue, *tesoro*.' Still holding her high, he started out of the room. 'And—speaking of disobedience—did I not request my wife be naked when I arrived?'

She giggled and squirmed. 'Leo, wait. Put me down. I have something to show you first.'

He stopped and gave a pained sigh, but did as she'd bade him. Heart thudding, she led him by the hand to the section of wall where she'd painted a large square of Sugar and Spice and another of Surf's Up.

'What do you think of these colours?'

He shrugged. 'You know I trust your choices...' He glanced around the room and frowned. 'But this is to be your studio, *si*? Had you not decided on orange?'

'I thought we might use this room for something else,' she said, and moved closer to the wall. She pointed to the shimmery lilac. 'I was thinking this might be nice for a...a girl. And this one...' She pointed to the other square, her hand trembling, her throat tightening on the words. 'This would be good for...for a boy.'

Her breath stopped as she watched the rapidly changing expressions on Leo's face. From bemusement to confusion and finally a dawning comprehension.

He stared at her, his jaw gone slack. 'Are you telling me...? Do you mean...? Are you...?'

'I'm pregnant,' she blurted, taking pity on her gorgeous tongue-tied husband. She blinked, her eyes growing hot and prickly. 'Seven weeks—'

She didn't get to finish her sentence. Leo pulled her into a hug so tight, so engulfing, she couldn't draw breath to speak. He broke into a string of Italian she partly followed, thanks to months of lessons. Mentally, she translated the words she understood.

*Incredible...so happy... I love you.*

At last he pulled back, his hands curling gently over her shoulders—as if she might suddenly break.

'How do you feel? Do you need to rest instead of...?' His voice trailed off, a deep furrow creasing his brow.

'I'm good,' she assured him.

'Are you sure—?'

'Leo.' She took his strong, familiar jaw between her hands and gave him a reassuring smile. 'I promise you I'm one hundred per cent healthy.'

But she understood his sudden caution, the dark glimmer of anxiety in his eyes. Beneath her own excitement lay a shadow of apprehension. A fear that she would lose this child as she had lost Lucas.

But even that flicker of fear could not eclipse her joy or hope for the future.

Because this time she was not alone. This time she had Leo by her side. This time, whatever ups and downs life had in store, they would face them as one.

He was perfect. Ten fingers, ten toes, a fine thatch of black hair and the loudest, gustiest cry the nurses said they'd ever heard from a newborn.

Not for the first time since his son's miraculous arrival into the world two hours ago, Leo thought his chest might explode from the torrent of emotions coursing through him. Pride. Elation. Relief. And, of course, love. So much love it threatened to overwhelm him.

It had certainly stolen his ability to find words for such a momentous occasion. To tell his beautiful, incredible wife in the wake of her ten-hour labour how proud he was of her. Of their son.

He looked up from the tiny bundle in his arms. Despite the rings of exhaustion around her eyes Helena was radiant, her glow of happiness reflecting his own. He shifted on the edge of the hospital bed and gently laid their son in her arms.

For a long moment he stared at the woman and child he would spend the rest of his days loving, supporting, protecting. 'I love you.' He dropped a kiss on her mouth, another on his son's downy head. 'I love you both.'

'I love you, too.' She smiled at him through her tears. 'No regrets?'

He looked at his sleeping son—the most amazing sight in the world—then back to his beautiful wife.

He smiled. 'None.'

\* \* \* \* \*

# SOLDIER
# UNDER SIEGE

**ELLE KENNEDY**

To Danielle, Alex and the twins for their invaluable plotting help. Some of your ideas were…interesting, but the ones that made it into the book? Pure gold.

Also, special thanks to Keyren Gerlach and Patience Bloom for being so enthusiastic about this new miniseries!

# Prologue

*Eight Months Ago*
*Corazón, San Marquez*

The gunfire finally came to a deafening halt.

Silence.

Captain Robert Tate ignored the ringing in his ears and swept his gaze across the village. It was like looking through a gray haze. The smoke filled his nostrils and stung his eyes, the odor of burned flesh making his stomach roil. Orange flames continued to devour what used to be the church, the only structure left intact. Everything else had been reduced to ash—the ramshackle homes, the schoolhouse, the dusty village square…nothing but ashes.

He covered his mouth and nose with his sleeve and looked around, doing a quick head count. Sergeant Stone was bending over the bullet-ridden body of a rebel. Second Lieutenant Prescott was wiping sweat and soot from his brows. Lafayette, Rhodes, Diaz and Berkowski. Where was Timmins? There, maneuvering his way through heaps of charred flesh and mangled bodies.

Tate released a ragged breath. Miraculously, all of his men were accounted for. Despite the thick smoke choking the air, despite the stifling heat from the flames, despite the shootout with the rebels, they'd managed to— *Wait.* Where the hell was Will?

His shoulders stiffened. "Stone," he shouted. "Where's Will?"

Through the smoke, he made out the younger man's bewildered expression. "Haven't seen him, Captain. I think he—"

Tate held up a hand to quiet his men. Then he listened. The trees rustled and swayed. Flames crackled. Birds squawked. The wind hissed.

Footsteps. There. Through the brush.

Raising his assault rifle, he broke out in a run, nearly tripping over the body of a raven-haired woman burned beyond recognition. One of the villagers.

*Later. Think about the villagers later.*

As his heart drummed in his chest, he slowed his pace and moved stealthily through the canopy of smoke toward the tree line. His ears perked. Footsteps. He glimpsed a dark blond head, a flash of olive-green. The silver glint of a blade.

"Don't move," Tate ordered.

His prey froze.

With his finger hovering over the trigger, Tate took a few steps forward, just as the rebel holding the knife turned.

Tate's heart dropped to the pit of his stomach.

"Drop your weapon, amigo." Hector Cruz's voice was soft, soothing almost.

An uncharacteristic vise of terror clamped around his

throat. He couldn't tear his gaze from the knife. From the resigned expression in Will's green eyes.

The rebel tightened his grip on Will, digging the blade deeper into his prisoner's neck. "Drop the weapon," Cruz said again. "Drop it, and I'll let him go."

"Don't do it," Will burst out. "Don't do it, Captain."

"Shut up," Cruz barked at his hostage.

Tate swallowed. He stared into the black eyes of the rebel, seeing nothing but dead calm reflected back at him. The knife sliced deeper into Will's throat.

Fingers trembling, he lowered his rifle a fraction of an inch.

"That's it," Cruz said in encouragement.

"No!" Will shouted. "He'll kill me regardless."

The rifle dipped lower.

"For the love of God, shoot the bastard." Agony rang from Will's voice. "Forget about me, Robbie. Forget—"

Tate tossed the gun onto the warm brown earth.

Triumph streaked across Cruz's harsh features. Followed by a grin that lifted his lips. "Bad call," he said lightly.

And then the rebel slit Will's throat.

# Chapter 1

*Paraíso, Mexico*

*This is a mistake.*

Eva took one look around the dark, smoky bar and nearly sprinted right out the door. It took her a second to gather her composure, to force her feet to stay rooted to the dirty floor. She couldn't chicken out. She'd already come this far, traveled over seven thousand miles and crossed two continents to come here.

There was no turning back now.

Squaring her shoulders, she drew air into her lungs, only to inhale a cloud of cigar smoke that made her eyes water. She blinked rapidly, trying hard not to focus on the dozen pairs of eyes glued to her. Some were appreciative. Most were suspicious. It didn't surprise her—this place didn't seem as though it catered to many law-abiding citizens. She'd figured that out when she'd first spotted the dilapidated adobe exterior with its crooked wooden sign, the word *Cantina* chicken-scratched onto it.

The interior only confirmed her original assessment. The bar was small and cramped, boasting a wood counter that would probably give her splinters if she touched it, and a handful of little tables, most of them askew. Across the room was a narrow doorway shielded only by a curtain of red and yellow beads that clinked together. All the patrons were men; a few wore sombreros, several didn't have any shoes on, and all were looking at Eva as if she'd just gotten off a spaceship.

Ignoring the burning stares, she made her way to the counter, her sandals clicking against the floor. Her yellow sundress clung to her body like wet plastic wrap. It was nearly seven o'clock, and the humidity refused to cease, rolling in through the open front door like fake fog from a horror movie.

The bartender, a large man with a thick black beard, narrowed his eyes at her approach. "What can I do for you, señorita?" he asked.

He'd spoken in Spanish, and she answered in the same tongue. "I'm looking for someone."

He winked. "I see."

"I was told he's a regular here," she hurried on before the bartender misinterpreted her intentions. "I have business to discuss with him."

Gone was the playful twinkle in the man's eyes. He looked suspicious again, which made her wonder just how many times he'd heard this same old line before. Hundreds, probably. Paraíso wasn't the kind of town you visited on business, at least not the legitimate kind.

In her research, Eva had discovered that this little mountain town was a frequent stop for drug runners, arms dealers and men involved in all other sorts of nefarious activities. It was also the perfect place to hide. According to her sources, Mexican law enforcement turned the other cheek to what went on here, and with its mountainous landscape and neighboring rain forest, it was easy to disappear in a place like Paraíso. Its name translated to *paradise*. Irony at work.

"I'm afraid you'll need to be more specific," the bartender said curtly. He swept an arm out. "As you can see, there are many men here, almost all of them regulars."

She swallowed. "The one I want goes by the name Tate."

Silence descended over the room. The laughter of the patrons died. Even the music blaring out of the cheap stereo over the bar seemed to get quieter. From the corner of her eye, Eva noticed that the gray-haired man at the other end of the counter had blanched, his tanned leathery skin turning a shade paler.

So she'd come to the right place. These men knew Tate. And they feared him—she could feel that fear palpitating in the stuffy air.

"I take it you know him," she said to the bartender.

His dark eyes grew shuttered. "Actually, I can't say I've ever heard that name before."

She suppressed a sigh and reached into the green canvas purse slung over her bare shoulder. She fumbled around until her hand connected with the roll of American bills she'd secured with an elastic band. She peeled off four one-hundred-dollar bills and set them on the counter.

The man's jaw twitched at the sight of the cash—about five thousand pesos after the conversion.

"What about now?" she asked softly. "Have you heard of him now?"

Greed etched into his harsh features. "No, still doesn't ring a bell."

She added two more hundreds to the pile.

Smirking, the bartender pocketed the cash and hooked a thumb at the doorway in the back. "I believe you'll find Mr. Tate at his usual table, stealing money from poor, hard-working souls."

With a quiet thank-you, Eva headed for the doorway and slid through the string of beads.

The corridor was narrow, illuminated by an exposed lightbulb that dangled from the ceiling on a long piece of brown twine. Only one other door in the hall, all the way at the end, and she heard muffled male voices coming from behind it. A burst of laughter, a few Spanish curses and then…English. Someone was speaking English. She immediately picked up on a faint Boston inflection. Having spent her entire childhood and adolescence in New York, she knew an East Coast accent when she heard one.

Tate was definitely in Paraíso.

Eva's legs felt unusually weak as she made her way down the corridor. She instinctively reached into her purse, tempted to grab her cell phone and call the babysitter just to make sure Rafe was all right, but she resisted the impulse. The quicker she did this, the faster she could get back to her son.

Still, she hated leaving Rafe alone for even a few minutes, let alone the two hours she'd already been gone. She worried that if she let him out of her sight, she'd never see him again.

Lord knew her son's father was doing his damnedest to make that happen.

Her stomach clenched. God, what a fool she'd been. And as humiliating as it was to admit, she had nobody to blame but herself. *She* was the one who'd left New York to volunteer with the relief foundation in San Marquez. *She* was the young and idealistic fool who'd actually believed

in Hector's cause. *She* was the idiot who'd fallen in love
with an outlaw rebel.

But now she had the chance to be free of Hector Cruz.
After three years of running, after five close calls and half
a dozen fresh starts, she finally had the opportunity to van-
quish her personal demon once and for all.

Assuming Tate agreed to help her, of course.

Tucking an errant strand of hair behind her ear, she approached the door and knocked, then opened it without
waiting for invitation.

"Who the hell are you?" a rough male voice demanded
in Spanish.

Eva did her best not to gape. Her gaze collided with four
men sitting at a round table littered with colorful poker
chips and a pile of crumpled cash. A lone cigar sat in a
cracked plastic ashtray, sending a cloud of smoke curling
in the direction of the door. Two of the men were dark-
skinned, with matching shaved heads and menacing expressions. The third looked like a fat little character from
a Mexican cartoon, boasting bulging black eyes and a generous paunch.

But it was the fourth man who caught and held her attention. He was sitting down, but she could tell he was tall,
judging by the long legs encased in olive-colored camo
pants. A white T-shirt clung to a broad chest and washboard
stomach, the sleeves rolled up to reveal a pair of perfectly
sculpted biceps. His chocolate-brown hair was in a buzz
cut, and his face was ruggedly handsome, its most striking feature being eyes the color of dark moss.

This had to be Tate. The man had military written all
over that chiseled face and massive body.

"Tell Juan thanks, but we have no need for a whore,"
he said gruffly.

"I'm not a whore," she blurted out.

She'd spoken in English, and she noticed his eyes widen slightly, then narrow as he studied her. His gaze swept over her sweat-soaked sundress, resting on her bare legs and strappy brown sandals, then gliding up to her cleavage, which he assessed for an exasperatingly long time. She supposed she couldn't fault him for thinking she was a prostitute. In this heat, skimpy clothing was really one's only option.

"Who are you, then?" he demanded, switching to English. "And what do you want?"

She took a steadying breath. "Are you Tate?"

The room went silent, same way it had out in the bar. The two men with shaved heads exchanged a wary look, while the chubby one began to fidget with his hands. All three avoided glancing in the dark-haired man's direction.

"Who wants to know?" he finally asked.

"Me," she stammered. "I have something extremely urgent to discuss with Mr. Tate."

He slanted his head, a pensive glimmer entering those incredible green eyes.

To her shock, Eva's heart did a tiny little flip as he once again slid his sultry gaze over her. She hadn't expected him to be so good-looking. Her uncle had told her that Tate was rumored to be a deadly warrior, and granted, he sure did look the part, but the sexual magnetism rolling off his big body was something she hadn't counted on.

"Look," she went on, "my name is—"

He held up a hand to silence her. "Let us play out this hand." With the raise of his dark eyebrows, the man she'd traveled so far to see thoroughly dismissed her and turned to the fat man. "I call, amigo."

There was a beat of anticipation as both men prepared to reveal their cards. Tate went first, tossing a pair of aces directly on the pile of cash in the center of the table. With a resounding expletive, the Mexican threw down his cards and scraped back his chair.

"Tomorrow night, same time," the little man spat out.

Tate seemed to be fighting a grin. "Sure thing, Diego."

Eva resisted the urge to tap her foot as she watched Tate reach for the money he'd just liberated from his fellow card players. To her sheer impatience, he counted it. Then smoothed out each bill—one at a time.

Just as she was about to voice her frustration, he shoved the cash in his pocket, glanced at the other men and nodded at the door. At the unspoken demand, the trio shuffled out of their chairs and practically scurried out of the room.

Eva was unable to hide her amusement. "They're terrified of you, you know," she remarked.

The corners of his mouth lifted. "As they should be."

She suspected the warning had been aimed to unnerve her, but she received a strange sense of comfort from those four lethal words. Oh, yes. This man was exactly what she needed. Her uncle had been right about him. Then again, she really shouldn't have doubted Uncle Miguel. When a San Marquez army general warned you that you'd be getting tangled up with a ruthless warrior, he probably wasn't bluffing.

"So you are Tate, then," she said bluntly.

He nodded and gestured to one of the unoccupied chairs. "I am. Now why don't you have a seat and tell me what the hell it is you want from me."

Unfazed by his short tone, she sat down, crossed her ankles together and met his stormy gaze head-on. "I have a proposition for you."

He cut her off with a low rumble of a laugh. "Proposition, huh? Well, like I said, I'm not into whores. But—" he cocked his head "—maybe I'll make an exception for you. How much, sweetheart?"

Her skin prickled with offense. "I'm *not* a prostitute! My name is Eva. Eva Dolce. And I traveled a long way to find you, so please, quit calling me a whore."

Those green eyes twinkled for a second, then hardened into stone. "How *did* you find me, *Eva?* I'm not exactly listed in any phone books."

"I heard rumors about you." She rested her suddenly shaky hands on her knees. "Someone told me you might be able to help me, so I decided to track you down. I'm... Well, let's just say I'm very skilled when it comes to computers. I studied Computer Science at Columbia and—"

"You're from New York?"

"Yes. Well, I wasn't born there. My parents decided to move to the States when I was a baby. I was raised in Manhattan, we lived on the Upper East Side and—" She halted, realizing she was babbling. She hadn't come here to tell this man her life story, damn it. "Look, none of this is important. All that matters is that I found you."

"Yes, using your trusty computer," he said mockingly.

She bristled. "I'm good at what I do. I started the search at the military base in North Carolina."

His jaw tensed.

"You're good, too," she added with grudging appreciation. "You left so many false trails it made me dizzy. But you slipped up in Costa Rica. You used the same identity twice, and it led me here."

Tate let out a soft whistle. "I'm impressed. Very impressed, actually." He made a *tsk*ing sound. "You went to a lot of trouble to find me. Maybe it's time you tell me why."

"I told you—I need your help."

He raised one large hand and rubbed the razor-sharp stubble coating his strong chin.

A tiny thrill shot through her as she watched the oddly seductive gesture and imagined how it would feel to have those callused fingers stroking her own skin, but that thrill promptly fizzled when she realized her thoughts had drifted off course again. What was it about this man that made her so darn aware of his masculinity?

She shook her head, hoping to clear her foggy brain, and met Tate's expectant expression. "Your help," she repeated.

"Oh, really?" he drawled. "My help to do what?"

Her throat tightened. God, could she do this? How did one even begin to approach something like—

"For Chrissake, sweetheart, spit it out. I don't have all night."

She swallowed. Twice.

He started to push back his chair. "Screw it. I don't have time for—"

"I want you to kill Hector Cruz," she blurted out.

# Chapter 2

He was normally quite skilled at reading people, but for the life of him, Tate couldn't decide if the woman sitting across from him was for real. He also couldn't stop the blood in his veins from turning into pure ice the second she uttered those three pesky little syllables.

Hector Cruz.

Tate didn't bother interpreting the "I want you to kill" part. All it took was the sound of Cruz's name and a dose of bloodlust flooded his body, making him want to reach for the gun in his waistband and start shooting.

Before he could stop them, a barrage of grisly images burned a path across his brain. The charred woman in the brown dress. The heat of the fire. Dead rebels strewn on the ground. Cruz's coal-black glare. Will's eyes rolling to the back of his head.

*Bad call.*

Tate's hands curled into fists as rage consumed his body

like poison. He'd been agonizing about the botched mission for eight months now. He dreamed it. Breathed it. Fed off it. The one thing that kept him going was the thought of slashing a blade across Hector Cruz's throat and watching the bastard die.

And now this woman, this stranger who'd showed up out of the blue, was asking him to do just that.

But as tempting as it sounded, one look at Eva Dolce—if that was really her name—and all he could think was *trap*.

"I'm afraid you've been misinformed," he said, crossing his arms over his chest. "I'm not a hit man."

"I know that." Her voice wobbled. "But I also know that you want Cruz dead."

He shot her a bored look. "Says who?"

"You've been asking questions about Cruz for the past eight months, inquiring about his whereabouts, attempting to bribe the rebels who follow him. You've made no secret that you want to rid Cruz from this earth." She arched one eyebrow. "Do you deny that?"

Her matter-of-fact tone unnerved him a bit. Who the hell was this woman? And had she really tracked him down using nothing but a damn computer? She sure didn't *look* like some hacker extraordinaire. With her long black hair, sapphire-blue eyes and smooth golden skin, she belonged on the silver screen rather than in front of a computer screen. And that body… Forget movie star—those long legs and the firm breasts practically pouring out of the bodice of her yellow dress were better suited for a lingerie model.

*Who exactly are you, Eva Dolce?*

"I don't deny or confirm anything," Tate replied with a shrug.

She seemed annoyed. "You want Cruz eliminated, Tate. So do I."

All right. Now, *that* he might be able to believe. The

anger and disgust that entered her big blue eyes each time Cruz's name escaped her lush lips was unmistakable. But what was her connection to Cruz? Did she even have one?

Or perhaps she'd been sent here to lure Tate out of hiding. The people who were after him must be tired of slamming into the brick walls he kept placing in their paths, and he wouldn't put it past them to send in someone like Eva, a sexpot agent to seduce their favorite target into slipping up.

But…if they truly *had* found him, why send anyone at all? And one woman, to boot. Why not order an entire platoon to storm this craphole bar and riddle the place—and Tate—with bullets?

He pursed his lips, suddenly second-guessing every damn thought that fluttered into his head. Maybe they were toying with him? No, that seemed unlikely. If the people hunting him knew where he was, they'd have been here by now.

Which meant this raven-haired beauty might actually be telling the truth.

"Why do you want him dead?" Tate asked sharply.

A cloud floated across her expression. He saw more anger swirling there, but it was now mingled with…fear?

"You're scared," he said before he could stop it. He wrinkled his brow. "What are you scared of, Eva?"

"Hector," she whispered. Her chest heaved as she drew a deep breath. "That's why I want him dead. Because as long as he's alive, I'll be scared for the rest of my life." She exhaled in a rush. "He's hunting me, Tate. For three years now. I can't… God, I can't keep running anymore."

Her word choice—*hunting*—raised his hackles once more. Oh, he knew precisely what it felt like to be hunted. Was this a blatant attempt on her part to form some sort of camaraderie with him? To find common ground with the man she'd been ordered to…to what? Kill?

Battling his distrust, he pinned her down with a harsh glare. "Why don't you start from the beginning?"

She nodded, her delicate throat working as she swallowed. "Like I said, I was raised in New York, but I was actually born in San Marquez."

Tate swiftly masked his surprise. So she hailed from the same South American island nation as Cruz. Interesting.

"After I graduated from college, I decided to return to my birthplace and do some good."

When Tate laughed, her eyes narrowed. "My parents reacted the same way," she muttered. "They called me a bleeding heart. But they couldn't stop me from going. I kept seeing all this terrible stuff on the news—people dying, starving, suffering, and the government doing nothing to help them—so I joined a relief organization and began volunteering at a hospital in the mountains." She took another breath. "That's where I met Hector. Idiot that I was, I actually believed in his cause for a time."

Tate stifled a sigh. Yeah, no surprise there. According to his sources, a lot of folks had been—and were still being—duped by Hector Cruz and his ULF crazies. The United Liberty Fighters had been formed to fight the oppression of the strict San Marquez government, but over the years their freedom-fighting mentality had veered off into borderline terrorism. They were responsible for the bombing of government buildings, along with the deaths of countless politicians, and they'd even started robbing their own people—the people they claimed to be fighting for—in order to fund their activities.

"We were friends for a while," Eva went on, shamefaced, "but then he became obsessed with me. At the time, I was involved with another relief worker. John. We...we had a child together. Rafe—he's three. But Hector decided I belonged to him, and he—" she swallowed again "—he had John killed."

Tate stared at her thoughtfully.

"I ran away. I didn't want to have anything to do with that crazy son of a bitch, so I took Rafe and I ran. But Hector is always on my heels. When I found out he was thrown in prison two months ago, I thought it would finally be over, but then his men broke him out and..." She trailed off in frustration.

He could relate—that damn prison break had royally screwed things up for him, too. Two months ago, Cruz had been responsible for bombing the home of a well-known political figure in San Marquez. In a major feat for the military, Cruz had been caught and arrested, and he'd been awaiting trial when his fellow rebels orchestrated an escape and whisked their leader right out of jail.

Since then, Cruz had gone underground. Nobody had seen or heard from him in months, which made it annoyingly difficult for Tate to locate the bastard.

"For whatever messed-up reason, Hector believes that he owns me." Eva's voice jolted him from his thoughts. "Every time I think I'm safe, every time I settle down in one place, he finds me."

She grew quiet, her tale coming to a close, and an alarm went off in Tate's head. Something about that sob story didn't sit right with him. Something about it sounded... false.

"I'm tired of running," she blurted out when Tate didn't respond. "I just want that maniac to leave me alone."

As misgivings continued to course through his head, Tate met her gaze and saw that the fear had returned. Whatever lies she'd just told him, she definitely wasn't lying about her feelings for Cruz. She loathed the man. She was terrified of him.

Because he'd killed her lover? Because he'd developed a sick obsession that had sent her fleeing with her kid?

Raking a hand through his hair, Tate finally chuckled. "That was a nice story, Eva. I'm sure parts of it might even be true. But here's the thing—I don't trust you. I don't trust anyone, for that matter. So I think I'll pass on your proposition."

Desperation exploded in her eyes like a round of fireworks. "No! You can't. I *know* you're after him, too." Her features hardened in an expression that resembled defiance. "But you can't find him, can you? He's flown off the radar since he escaped from prison, and seeing as you're on the run, you can't exactly go traipsing around the globe looking for him, now, can you?"

He opened his mouth but she cut him off. "I don't know why you're hiding, and frankly, I don't care. I just want your help to get rid of Hector."

"Did it occur to you that I would need to come out of hiding in order to do that?" he said, rolling his eyes. "I've got my own problems, sweetheart. Like you said, I don't have the luxury of globe-trotting, and even if I did, I won't come along on a wild-goose chase for a man I may or may not want dead."

"But you *do* want him dead." Triumph crept into her voice. "And it won't be a wild-goose chase. I know where his hideout is."

Son of a bitch.

Tate faltered, unable to stop the rush of hope that swelled in his gut. She *knew* where Cruz was? He'd been trying for months to unearth the rebel's location, and he'd come up empty-handed each time.

If this woman truly knew where Cruz was holed up...

*He'll kill me regardless... Forget about me, Robbie.*

Like hell he would.

"And if you don't want to go to his hideout," Eva added, "all we have to do is find a way to contact him. Trust me, Hector will come to me if I make contact."

He didn't doubt her. With that gorgeous face and sexy-as-sin body, Tate couldn't see any man staying away from Eva Dolce. Hell, he was semihard just being in the same room as her. But common sense and honed instincts trumped the unfortunate desire she seemed to inspire in his body.

*Trust me.*

Yeah, right. He wasn't about to hand out his trust to a complete stranger. Especially not one as beautiful as her.

*Not even one who can lead you to Cruz?*

The nagging thought was the sole reason he didn't turn her down outright. He wasn't about to admit it, but she was right about one thing. He wanted Cruz dead. Annihilated. Wiped off the planet.

And he wanted it more than he wanted his next breath.

So…to trust, or not to trust.

Rubbing the stubble on his chin, he met Eva's pleading eyes, then rose from his chair. "Where are you staying?" he asked briskly.

She blinked. "Camino del Paraíso—it's that little motel on the east end of town. Room twelve."

"I'll contact you when I make a decision."

She shot to her feet, despair radiating from her petite, curvy body. "Please," she exclaimed. "Just give me an answer now. I *need* you, Tate."

Shrugging, he shot her a sardonic smile. "If you need me that bad, sweetheart, then you'll just have to wait." His smile transformed into a rogue smirk. "Besides, don't you know that anticipation is half the fun?"

As her eyes blazed with indignation, Tate strode out of the room without looking back.

* * *

"I don't like it," Sebastian Stone declared. "Are you sure she's not messing with you?"

Tate downed the rest of his beer and set the bottle down on the ledge. "I'm not sure of anything. That's why I'm running this by you boys."

"I think it's a trap," Sebastian said flatly. "They must have found us."

"Or they didn't," Nick Prescott chimed in. "And this chick really just wants Cruz dead."

Tate swallowed a groan. Nope, didn't surprise him that Stone and Prescott were yet again on opposite sides of an issue. Stone said up, Prescott said down. Stone wanted to go, Prescott wanted to stay. Out of all the men he'd commanded over the years, these two knuckleheads were the most difficult, stubborn and unbelievably exasperating.

But they were also loyal, intelligent and absolutely deadly when circumstances called for it.

He glanced from one man to the other, his chest going rigid with regret. Two men. Eight men had been with him on that extraction mission in San Marquez. Only two were still alive.

"Or she's dangling a carrot under the captain's nose," Sebastian grumbled in reply to Nick. "The jackasses after us have to know that Cruz is his weak spot. This is all just an elaborate trap."

"The captain's not an idiot. If it's a trap, he's not going to walk into it. But if there's a chance to get Cruz…"

With a snort, Tate held up his hand to silence them. "The *captain* is standing right here. Quit talking about me like I'm not."

They immediately went quiet, each one turning to gaze at the scenery below. Tate rubbed his temples and stared out as well, frustration gathering in his gut at the sight of the jagged brown peaks in the distance. The view, no matter how breathtaking, was just another reminder of how dire their situation was.

This isolated old fortress was nestled at the base of the mountain, and had stood abandoned for decades; apparently the Mexican government had no use for a crumbling pile of stone left over from the Mexican-American War of 1846. But it was the perfect place to lie low, and a decent stronghold with its tall watchtower and handy tunnel system. Ever since the shack in Costa Rica had been compromised, they'd been searching for a new hideaway, and this place had been a lucky find. They'd been holed up here for three weeks now, living on the mountain like a bunch of hermits.

Tate had thought the place to be safe, but clearly he'd been wrong. Because Eva Dolce had found them, and if she could, then so could the hunters.

"I think I might have to work with her," he spoke up, his voice thick with reluctance.

Sebastian's head swiveled around in surprise. "Are you nuts?"

"No, just practical." He shrugged. "I don't think she was sent here by our government, but if she was, then we can't afford to let her out of our sight. We need to find out who she is and why she's here."

Sebastian made a frustrated sound in the back of his throat. "No disrespect, sir, but...don't freaking patronize us. This has nothing to do with keeping an eye on that woman, and everything to do with avenging Will's death."

"What's wrong with that?" Nick interjected with a scowl. "Will was his *brother*. And he was my best friend. He deserves justice."

"He's dead," Sebastian said bluntly. "And wherever he

is, I doubt he's thinking about justice, and I seriously doubt he'd want us to risk our necks to get it for him."

Tate closed his eyes briefly, fighting a jolt of pain at the sound of Will's name. Had it already been eight months since he'd watched his little brother die? It felt like yesterday, damn it.

Sebastian was right. Will wouldn't have wanted them to seek revenge. The kid had always been too softhearted for his own good, constantly preaching forgiveness, even when the person in question didn't deserve a damn ounce of it. Like their old man. They'd endure a particularly brutal beating, and Will would wipe the blood off his face and say, *Don't be angry at him, Robbie. He just misses Mom.*

The memory had Tate gritting his teeth so hard his jaw twitched. Will might've been able to forgive their dad, but Tate hadn't. And he sure as hell wasn't going to let Will's murderer walk free, not if he had the chance to change that.

"You're right," he said, interrupting Sebastian and Nick's heated argument. "This isn't about Eva. It's about Cruz. Christ, Seb, I want him to die."

"What about the others who've died?" the younger man pointed out. His gray eyes blazed with anger. "What about Lafayette and Diaz? What about Rhodes and Timmins and Berk?"

An arrow of agony pierced Tate's chest. Just hearing those names made him want to pummel something.

"They were murdered, too," Sebastian went on. "Diaz and his mysterious drunk-driving accident—that kid never drank a day in his life! And Rhodes's *cancer.* Berk's *mugging.* Lafayette's—"

"Enough," Tate snapped. "I know how they died. Your constant reminders won't bring them back."

"No, but we still don't know *why* they died." Sebastian rested his fists against the dusty stone ledge ringing the watchtower. "That's what we need to be focusing on."

"The mission," Nick said wearily. "We know it has to do with the mission."

Always came back to that, didn't it? The mission that still made no sense to Tate. His orders had been to rescue an American doctor being held hostage by the rebels, but the doc was already dead when Tate's team swarmed Corazón, along with the hundred or so villagers living there, and before Tate could even begin to figure out what had gone wrong, the unit had been recalled back to the States for debriefing.

And, apparently, to systematically be killed off.

Rage and frustration coated his throat, thickening when he remembered his own close call with death. He'd been leaving his Richmond apartment at nine in the morning when a drive-by shooting had conveniently taken place out on the street. He'd escaped with a graze to the shoulder, ducking into a stairwell before the shooters could take aim again.

The police had attributed the event to a street gang who'd shot up the same area only a month before, but Tate knew better. A band of drugged-up teenagers hadn't been responsible for the attempt on his life. Oh, no, it had government-hit written all over it. Which hadn't exactly come as a shock, seeing as he'd already attended five funerals for members of his former unit.

Only Sebastian, Nick and himself were left, and the three of them had promptly disappeared after it became obvious they were being hunted down. They'd spent the past six months trying to figure out who was after them and why, but they'd struck out at every turn. Still knew squat, even after months of digging.

With so many unknowns hanging over their heads, Tate

had received great comfort from the one piece of knowledge he *did* possess.

Hector Cruz had killed his brother.

And Hector Cruz would pay for that.

"We'll figure out why they want us dead," he said, his voice low and even. "Will and I were related by blood, but make no mistake, *all* those men were my brothers. I won't rest until I know why they died."

Sebastian's silver eyes narrowed. "But…"

Tate released a breath. "But I can't let this opportunity pass me by. If Eva Dolce can lead me to Cruz, then I'll damn well be following her."

# Chapter 3

Tate wasn't going to help her. Eva forced herself to accept the cold hard truth as she stared at the angelic face of her sleeping son. It had been twenty-four hours since she'd met Tate at the cantina. No phone call, no knock on the door. She'd struck out. Failed.

*Back to square one.*

"Mommy, that hurts."

She nearly fell off the bed at the sound of her son's drowsy voice. When she glanced down, she realized she'd been squeezing his hand so hard she'd jolted him right out of a peaceful slumber.

As her chest tightened with the shame of knowing she'd brought him pain, she loosened her grip and moved her hand to his cheek.

"Sorry, little man, Mommy didn't mean to hurt you." She stroked his silky-soft skin. "Go back to sleep, baby."

His eyelids immediately drooped, his breathing growing slow and steady as he fell asleep again. She envied him sometimes—Rafe was out like a light the second his head hit the pillow, and he could sleep through a hurricane.

Eva, on the other hand... She couldn't even remember the last time she'd slept more than two or three hours a night. Maybe before she'd met Hector.

With a sigh, she stretched out next to her son, propping herself up on one elbow to gaze down at Rafe's sweet face. When she'd been in labor, she'd wondered how she would respond to him if he inherited Hector's harsh, dark eyes and angular features. Rafe was all her, though—the blue eyes, the black hair, his grandfather's dimples.

Still, she knew she would have loved him even if he *had* resembled his father. From the day he was born, Rafe had been his own little person—strong-willed, quick to laugh, unbelievably sweet.

"You're mine," she whispered fiercely, reaching out to smooth a lock of hair off his forehead. "I won't let him have you."

She suddenly had to wonder if maybe that was why Tate had decided to refuse her. Had he known she was lying about her true connection to Hector?

When she'd come to the bar, she'd had every intention of telling him the whole truth—her relationship with the ULF rebel, the pregnancy, Hector's single-minded desire to claim his son.

But her resolve had wavered when she'd glimpsed the look in Tate's hunter-green eyes after she'd said Hector's name. There had been murder in his expression. Murder and hatred and simmering rage.

She'd realized at that moment that if she told him she was the mother of Hector's child, he might very well wrap his strong hands around her throat and strangle the life right out of her—that was how volatile his emotions about Hector Cruz were.

So she'd lied. Glossed over certain facts, made up a fake lover. She'd hoped that it would be enough to convince Tate, that he'd see how genuine her terror was, how grave her situation, and agree to help.

Looked as if she'd hoped wrong.

With a heavy sigh, she rose from the bed and glanced around the seedy motel room, growing pale when she spotted a fat black cockroach scuttling across the linoleum floor. The roach disappeared behind the dresser, officially squashing any chance of Eva getting any sleep tonight. She was *not* a bug person.

She drifted to the tiny kitchenette and sat on one of the uncomfortable chairs around the white plastic table. "Please don't crawl up my leg," she muttered, shooting a paranoid look in the direction of the dresser.

Reaching for the laptop in front of her, she opened the computer and booted it up. The motel she'd chosen was the only one in the area with wireless access, and she immediately opened the internet browser and typed in the web address for the airline. She could book flights for her and Rafe under the current identities they were using, but once they reached their destination, she'd need to arrange for new papers.

But where to go? Europe again? Or maybe Australia this time. There were hundreds of places to hide down under.

*Lots of bugs, too.*

Shoot, that was true. She remembered hearing that the outback had some crazy bug statistic, something like more than two hundred thousand different species of insects…

Okay, no, thank you. She promptly decided to stay far away from that part of the world. Canada might be a better bet. Find a place out west, up in the mountains somewhere.

She was in the midst of doing a quick flight search when a sharp knock rapped against the door.

Eva felt all the color drain from her face. Her first thought was that Hector had found her again—until she remembered the way his men had kicked down the door in Istanbul. Right. Hector definitely wouldn't take the time to *knock*.

Drawing a deep breath, she reached for the .45 mm next to her laptop, gripped the weapon with both hands, and made her way to the door. She left the flimsy metal chain on as she inched open the door and peered out.

A pair of vivid green eyes glared back at her.

Relief flooded her belly. *Tate.* He'd come!

"You're here," she burst out, as she fumbled to unhook the chain. She opened the door and gestured for him to enter.

He stepped inside, his muscular body vibrating with reluctance and distrust. Eva's heart did a little somersault as his scent surrounded her—spicy, woodsy and male. When she noticed the way his pants clung to his rock-hard thighs, her pulse took off in a gallop. She didn't think she'd ever seen a more virile, sexier man, and her reaction to his maleness annoyed her.

Tate's hard gaze landed on the gun in her hands, and the corners of his mouth lifted. "Do you even know how to use that thing?"

She shrugged. "Point and shoot, right?"

"Something like that."

Unable to stop herself, she found herself staring at his mouth, which was far more sensual than she'd realized. His lips were surprisingly full, and the dark stubble above his upper lip and slashing across his strong jaw painted a blatantly masculine picture.

"You done gawking at me?"

His mocking voice brought the heat of embarrassment to her cheeks. He'd caught her checking him out, but he couldn't be a gentleman about it, could he? No, he just *had* to point it out.

*Gentleman? Look at him, dummy.*

Yeah, she really shouldn't expect any gentlemanly behavior from this man.

Swallowing, Eva hoped she wasn't blushing and locked her eyes with his. "So can I assume you're agreeing to help me?"

Rather than respond, he gestured to the two suitcases sitting beneath the painted-shut window. "Is that your stuff?"

"Who else's would it be?"

Ignoring her sarcasm, Tate reached into his back pocket and extracted a black gadget the size of a BlackBerry. He flicked a button, then strode across the room and swept the device over her bags. A steady beeping pierced the air. Eva realized he was checking for bugs and tracking devices.

When he finished with the suitcase, he glanced in the direction of the bed, shooting a frown at her sleeping son. "You've got your kid with you." He sounded annoyed.

The remark had her own irritation flaring. "Of course I do."

Tate's biceps flexed as he crossed his arms. "He can't come with us."

"He has to. I have nobody to leave him with."

He slanted his head. "What about your parents?"

"I haven't seen my parents in three years," she said in a dull voice.

Still looking irritated, Tate grumbled something unintelligible and marched toward her. "Spread your legs, arms out to the side."

Indignation seized her insides. "Pardon me?"

"I'm checking you for wires. Same goes for the kid."

Eva's eyebrows soared. "You honestly think I'd put a wire on my three-year-old child? Who would do that?"

"You'd be surprised." Those green eyes watched her expectantly, and when she didn't move a muscle, he gave a low chuckle. "You're not going anywhere with me unless I'm sure you're clean, so either you let me pat you down, or I walk right out the door, sweetheart."

Her cheeks grew hot again. Pat her down? God, she didn't want this man touching her. Not one bit.

But what other choice did she have?

Swallowing down her humiliation, she widened her stance and lifted her arms.

Two seconds later, Tate's big, rough-skinned hands were roaming her body as if they owned it.

He started from the south, gliding those callused palms up each of her legs, the heat of his touch searing through the fabric of her leggings and making her skin tingle. Her pulse quickened when his hands neared her midriff. He patted her belly, her back, her shoulders, while she stood there, cheeks scorching, heart pounding.

Why did this man affect her this way?

*Four years of celibacy will do that to a girl.*

Right, that had to be it. It wasn't Tate. Every human being had basic, carnal urges, and she'd been depriving her body for so long it was no wonder the mere proximity of a member of the opposite sex was getting it all excited.

Tate's hands suddenly cupped her breasts, and Eva squeaked in protest. The sudden contact confused her nipples as much as it confused her brain, because those two buds puckered at once and strained against the front of her T-shirt.

"No bra," Tate remarked, those green eyes glinting with approval. "Convenient."

Outrage and mortification mingled in her blood. "I'm

not wearing a bra because it's not comfortable to sleep in, not because I anticipated you taking it off me."

The corners of his mouth twitched as he dropped his hands from her chest. "I meant convenient in another sense, sweetheart. The best place for a woman to stash a wire is in her bra—either the straps or beneath the cups. Saves me time, not having to search your undergarments."

"Oh." She nearly apologized for assuming the worst but stopped herself at the last second. Why on earth should she apologize to this man? *He* was the one who'd just felt her up, for Pete's sake.

"That your laptop?" he asked, gesturing to the silver MacBook on the table.

She nodded.

"Unplug it, shut it down and take the battery out."

Her nostrils flared. "No."

"Do it or I walk out of here."

It was obvious he wasn't going to budge. Grumbling her displeasure under her breath, Eva followed his instructions. After she slid her computer into its plush case, she looked over at Tate with a frown. "What now?"

"Gather your stuff. We'll talk in the car."

Getting her things didn't take more than a minute. She hadn't bothered unpacking her bags—living out of a suitcase had become second nature after being on the run for three years. She collected a few of Rafe's toy trucks off the floor and threw them into one of the bags, then reached for the storybook on the nightstand, which she'd read only two lines of before her son had conked out.

She zipped up the suitcase and headed for the bed, tossing Tate a dark look over her shoulder. "Are you still intent on searching my son?"

"Sorry, but yes."

Eva bent down to scoop Rafe into her arms, then gritted her teeth as Tate stalked over and patted her son down with those rough, warrior hands. The little boy stirred, then burrowed his head against her breasts, made a snuffling sound and continued sleeping.

"Shocking," she muttered after Tate deduced her kid was "clean."

He ignored the barb. "Ready to go?"

Holding her son tight, she gestured to the suitcases and laptop case on the floor and shot Tate a pointed look. "Can you carry those?"

Without a word, he picked up the bags as if they weighed nothing, then marched toward the door.

The parking lot of the motel was dark and deserted when they stepped outside. Tate headed for a beat-up Jeep Cherokee that had more rust than paint and flung open the back door to toss the suitcases inside. While he slid into the driver's seat, Eva buckled Rafe in the backseat, then joined Tate up front.

After she was settled, the engine roared to life and then they were pulling out of the lot and heading for the main road. Eva briefly glanced out the window, watching the derelict buildings whiz by before turning to study her companion's hard profile.

He must have felt her gaze on him, because he gave the sharp swivel of his head and pinned her down with a scowl. "The kid's not coming with us," he muttered. "We'll have to leave him with my men."

Panic trickled through her. "I'm not going anywhere without him."

"And I won't take a child on a potentially dangerous op."

She chewed on her thumbnail, seeing his point. When she'd fled Istanbul and made the decision to find Tate, she hadn't exactly thought through all the logistics. The only thing on her mind had been getting rid of Hector once and for all, but now she realized they did indeed have a problem. They couldn't take Rafe to San Marquez.

But she couldn't leave her son in the hands of a stranger, either.

"Meet my guys and then decide," Tate added with a shrug.

"And if I don't trust them?"

Sarcasm dripped from his gruff voice. "I suppose we could research reputable day cares in the area."

Her nostrils flared. "Don't be a jerk." She tilted her head. "You don't have any children, do you?"

"None that I know of," he said with a crooked grin.

She rolled her eyes. "If you were a parent, you'd understand my apprehension about leaving my son."

"Well, I'm not a parent, and I don't give a damn what you do with the kid—but he's not coming with us."

His tone brooked no argument, so Eva smothered a sigh and fell silent. She would decide what to do with Rafe after she met Tate's "men." Until then, she would just have to be grateful that Tate was even helping her at all.

Twenty minutes later, Eva gulped as the Jeep ascended a dirt road that snaked its way up the mountain. It was pitch-black out. She couldn't see a thing, save for the two pale yellow beams provided by the headlights. Tate obviously knew where he was going, though. He sped along the barely visible road with confidence, not bothering to reduce his speed.

When he finally slowed down, she exhaled a rush of relief, then wrinkled her forehead when a foreboding gray fortress came into view, a structure she'd expect to see in a war documentary or history textbook. Shaped like a square, the fort looked old and unstable. Walls were crumbling away, and up above, the watchtower looked ready to tumble over, boasting several gaping holes where there should have been stone.

"Nice place," she murmured.

"Safe place," he corrected. He stopped in a small dusty courtyard and killed the engine. "It has a pretty complex tunnel system, leading out to various parts of the mountain. Lots of useful escape routes."

"Hector's hideout is in the mountains, too," she found herself saying. "The entrance is carved right in the rocks, almost completely hidden from sight."

His green eyes narrowed. "I see."

It took her a second to register the expression on his face as surprise. "You didn't believe me," she accused. "When I told you I knew where he was."

Tate shrugged. "I half believed you."

"And now?"

Another shrug. "Three-quarters."

Eva almost laughed. She couldn't quite figure out this man. One second he was as cold as ice, a lethal warrior who could probably kill her without breaking a sweat, and in the blink of an eye, he was a charming rogue, ready with a sarcastic remark, a mocking joke, a sensual grin. He completely unnerved her—yet at the same time, he made her feel oddly safe.

"I'll get your bags, you carry the kid," he barked, back to business.

She bristled. "His name is Rafe."

"Like I said, the kid."

As she hopped out of the Jeep to get Rafe, she ordered herself not to be annoyed that Tate viewed her son as a hindrance. What had she expected? That he'd welcome the idea of being saddled with a three-year-old? That he'd toss Rafe on his shoulders and parade him around with pride? Tate wasn't Rafe's father, for Pete's sake.

Oh, no. That honor belonged to a monster.

Holding Rafe tight, she stuck close to Tate as they approached the old fort. They paused in front of a narrow door, and Tate rapped his knuckles against the rusted metal in what sounded like a secret code. There was an identical resounding knock, then a grating sound, and the door swung open.

A shadow loomed in the doorway.

Eva instinctively recoiled when a man stepped out of the darkness, but she relaxed once she got a better look at him. He was in his late twenties, with a handsome face, shaggy brown hair and warm, amber-colored eyes.

"That was fast," the man remarked.

Tate gave that careless little shrug she was beginning to think of as his trademark. He gestured at Eva and said, "Eva, Nick. Nick, Eva."

Before she could greet the other man, Tate was ushering them all inside. She blinked a few times, trying to adjust to the dark as she followed the two men deeper into the fort. She stumbled after them toward the faint glow coming from the end of the corridor. A moment later, they entered a large chamber illuminated by dozens of candles that rested on the floor and various ledges.

She studied the room, taking in the squalor with a frown. There were makeshift tables, a couple of metal chairs, the skeleton of a couch. She spotted a few sleeping bags, along with several big black duffels and a crooked wooden table littered with canned food. Another table in the corner housed a whole lot of laptops. A tall man with dirty-blond hair was bending over one of the computers, and his shoulders stiffened at their entrance.

"This her?" the third man muttered, turning to examine Eva with a pair of suspicious gray eyes.

She nearly flinched under his impenetrable gaze. This

man couldn't be considered classically handsome like his cohorts, but there was something very magnetic about him. His features were hard, angular, and his nose wasn't quite straight, as if he'd broken it a time or two. He was sexy, though. Extremely sexy, in a stark, masculine kind of way.

"Eva, this is Sebastian," Tate told her.

Wary, she met the other man's angry eyes. "It's nice to meet you."

"So you want to kill Cruz," he said in lieu of a greeting.

She lifted her chin in resolve. "Yes."

Sebastian grumbled something under his breath, then cursed when he zeroed in on the bundle in her arms. "Is that a kid?"

Jeez, what was it with these men? Had they never seen a child before?

"Eva's son, Rafe," Tate filled in, sounding as disgruntled as Sebastian looked.

"Here, let me take him," Nick said with a genuine smile. He beckoned his arms at her. "He can sleep over here until we figure things out."

Warmth spread through her body. Finally. Someone who didn't act like Rafe had the Ebola virus.

"Thank you," she said gratefully. "He's getting a little too heavy for me to carry these days."

Smile widening, Nick plucked Rafe out of her arms and took him toward one of the sleeping bags. Eva watched in wonder as he tenderly smoothed out her son's hair before placing him down on the cushy bag.

"I love kids," Nick said over his shoulder, covering Rafe with a thin wool blanket.

"Do you have any?" she asked.

"No, but my older sister has three little ones. Her twin girls are two, and their big brother is five." He paused.

"They're probably enormous now—I haven't seen them in six months."

It was hard to miss the melancholy chord in his voice, which had her wondering, why were these men on the run? She hadn't given it much thought when she'd been tracking Tate—as far as she was concerned, his problems were none of her business. All she'd wanted from the man was his assistance in dealing with Hector, but now she couldn't fight her curiosity.

She swept her gaze from Nick, to Sebastian, to Tate. All three were clearly military, and all wore the same uneasy expressions, as if her presence had raised each of their guards.

"If we do this, we'll be leaving your son with Nick and Seb," Tate said. He glanced at her as if seeking her approval.

After a moment of hesitation, she nodded. "Okay. I think that could work."

Sebastian wouldn't have been her ideal choice of babysitter, but Nick had won her over. Anyone who looked at a child with such tenderness couldn't be a threat, right?

Still, her chest tightened at the thought of leaving Rafe behind.

"I'll take good care of him," Nick said, evidently sensing she needed the reassurance.

She nodded again, the thick emotion clogging her throat making it hard to speak.

"All right, so we've got babysitting duties out of the way," Sebastian said rudely. "Can we focus on more pressing matters now?" He threw Tate a pointed look. "Like why the hell are we working with this woman and how do we know she won't get us killed?"

Eva jerked as if she'd been struck. Sebastian's hostility rippled through the air like an invisible storm cloud. As indignation swirled in her belly, she shot a quick look at Tate in an unspoken request for backup.

To her dismay, he merely offered her a sardonic smile and said, "Yes, Eva, tell us why we can trust you." His smile went feral. "Tell us why I shouldn't kill you right where you stand."

# Chapter 4

The woman was fearless, Tate had to give her that. Rather than cower under his and Sebastian's deadly stares, Eva crossed her arms over her chest and scowled at them both.

"You shouldn't kill me because then you won't get Hector," she answered coolly. "And if you do kill me? With my three-year-old son sleeping less than ten feet away? Then you'd be the most coldhearted bastard on the planet."

Tate lifted a brow in challenge. "Who says I'm not?"

Those big blue eyes flashed with defiance. "Fine, you want me to call your bluff? Go ahead and kill me, then."

Their gazes locked for several long moments, and Tate couldn't help but chuckle. He didn't trust this woman, not in the slightest, but he did appreciate her steely fire.

"Sit down," he finally said. "Let's talk details."

Eva's shoulders remained stiff as she primly sank into a chair. Her black hair was twisted in a messy knot atop her head, and a few wispy strands slid out as she sat down, framing her beautiful face.

She crossed her ankles together, drawing his gaze to the shapely legs covered by tight black leggings. Her gray V-neck T-shirt was loose but couldn't hide the full, high breasts beneath it, and Tate's mouth went dry as he remembered how firm those breasts had felt when they'd filled his palms earlier. He almost wished she *had* been wearing a bra, just so he could've watched her remove it.

*Down, boy.*

Yeah, he definitely needed to control this rush of desire. For a man whose libido hadn't seen any action in eight months, a woman like Eva Dolce was the ultimate temptation. The perfect combination of vulnerable and gutsy, not to mention far too attractive for her own good. Sex appeal oozed from her pores, yet she seemed oblivious to it, which was either an act or she truly didn't know the effect she had on the males in her vicinity. Even Stone, who clearly didn't approve of Tate's decision to team up with the woman, kept eyeing her in a purely masculine way.

Ignoring the zip of heat moving through his veins, Tate lifted his gaze from Eva's chest and focused it on her cagey blue eyes.

"I suppose you want to talk money, right? I'll pay whatever you want. Well, within reason," she added hastily.

He waved a dismissive hand. "I don't want your money."

She looked surprised. "No?"

"No. But if we do this, I want to leave as soon as possible." He grabbed a chair, turned it around and straddled it. "Are you good to travel or do we need to set you up with documents?"

"I've got papers." She paused, her gaze drifting to the sleeping child across the room. "If you don't want me to go with you, I could always stay here with Rafe. I'll give you the exact location of Hector's camp, and you can—"

"No," he cut in. "You're coming with me."

Her dark eyebrows knitted in a frown. "No need to snap at me. I'm just thinking in practical terms—I don't want to slow you down."

He flashed her a cheerless smile. "I've got all the time in the world, sweetheart. If I'm going to San Marquez, you'll be coming with me. That's a deal breaker."

"Why is that— Oh, I get it," she said, understanding dawning on her face. "You still think I'm not being up-front with you."

"Do you blame me?"

"No, I guess not." She bit her plump bottom lip. "I'm not, by the way."

He arched his brows. "You're not being up-front with me?"

"I'm not leading you into a trap." Exhaustion lined her face as she released a sigh. "I want him dead, Tate. I can't keep running for the rest of my life."

Sebastian, who'd been leaning against the wall, stepped forward with a frown. "And why *are* you running?" he asked with a bite to his tone. "Are we seriously expected to believe that Cruz developed an obsession with you and is now spending his time and resources to locate you? That he's wasting his hard-earned money to track down a piece of ass?"

Eva didn't even flinch. Again, rather than back down, she met Sebastian's skeptical gaze head-on. "Are you friends with Hector?" she asked mildly.

Sebastian blinked. "What? Of course not."

"Did you spend a year working in San Marquez and talking to him nearly every day?"

"No," Sebastian said, his jaw going rigid.

"Did he ever share his hopes and dreams with you? Pursue you romantically? Call you his 'heart and soul'?" Eva's features hardened. "I'm going to assume the answer to those questions is also no. So, really, what makes you qualified to presume what Hector deems important enough to spend his time and money on?"

Seeing Sebastian's cloudy expression, Tate hid a grin, but Eva wasn't done.

"Maybe I *am* a piece of ass to Hector, but you know what? Clearly my ass is a big deal to him, because he's been after it for the past three years. He's hired investigators, sent men to tail me, has my parents watched, and every time I manage to disappear, he finds me." Her voice wobbled. "I'm sick of being on the defensive. I want him *dead,* goddamn it."

"Mommy?"

Eva's face went stricken. Cursing softly, she hopped off the chair just as her son stumbled groggily off the bed platform Nick had arranged for him, clutching a small stuffed elephant against his chest. Her outburst had woken the kid up, and Tate stifled a groan as he watched the little boy dash into her arms.

As Eva scooped the kid up, elephant and all, the boy peered past her shoulder, his blue eyes going as big as saucers when he spotted the three men.

"Mommy, who are *they?*" the kid whispered.

Eva's tone was unbelievably tender as she answered, "These are some friends of Mommy's. See the big one sitting over there? That's Tate." She crossed the room, stopping in front of Nick and Sebastian. "And this is Nick, and Sebastian."

"Hey, kiddo," Nick said warmly, leaning in to ruffle the boy's hair. "It's way past your bedtime, huh?"

"I had a scary dream."

Eva's expression strained as she carried her son to the chair and sat down again. The little boy instantly wrapped his arms around her neck and his legs around her waist, clinging to her like a monkey.

She rubbed his back in a soothing manner and planted a kiss on the top of his head. "You want to tell Mommy about it?"

Tate smothered a curse.

Jesus. What a messed-up situation. He wanted Cruz eviscerated, but saddling himself with this raven-haired sexpot and her snot-nosed kid? Not exactly his cup of tea.

Well, all right, Prescott and Stone would be the ones wiping the kid's snot, but Tate almost found that preferable to embarking on this journey with Eva Dolce.

He didn't trust her. It came back to that, and always would.

Did. Not. Trust. Her.

*She's going to lead you to Cruz.*

Tate held on to that reminder as he watched Eva kiss her son's forehead. "Come on," she coaxed when the boy didn't answer. "Tell me about your dream."

"The bad men were there and you were screaming and then the booms got really loud and…" The kid trailed off and snuggled deeper into Eva's breasts.

Tate frowned. Why did he get the feeling that was a lot more than a dream?

Over the top of her son's head, Eva sought out Tate's gaze and held it. "Cruz," she said, barely audibly. "His men came after us in Istanbul last month."

She rose from the chair and carried the kid back to the sleeping bag. "Give me a few minutes," she told the men.

As Eva tended to her son, Tate strode toward the table where Sebastian had set up the laptops. Both Stone and Prescott were damn good with computers, but so far, neither of them had managed to uncover why their own government was determined to kill them.

"I don't trust her," Sebastian muttered.

"Preaching to the choir," Tate mumbled back.

Nick spoke up in a quiet tone. "Her story checks out." He gestured to one of the laptops. "Orlando just got back to me about the info request we put in."

Tate leaned down and scrolled through the documents on the computer screen. His gaze flicked over the birth certificate, school transcripts, the application she'd filed with the Helping Hands relief foundation.

The documents backed up the story Eva had fed them, but then again, that meant absolutely nothing. Any agency worth its salt would produce the paperwork needed to corroborate an agent's cover story. *If* Eva Dolce was an agent.

"You're good," came her grudging voice.

He glanced over to see Eva standing next to Nick, peering at the screen. He shifted his gaze and saw that her kid was sound asleep again, curled up on the sleeping bag.

"I made contact twenty-four hours ago and you've already got your hands on my high school transcripts," she remarked.

"The credit's due elsewhere," Nick admitted sheepishly. "Our information dealer compiled all this."

"Information dealer, huh?" She sounded bemused. "Maybe I should've gone into that line of work." Her tone took on a cocky note. "Because I'm pretty sure I had *your* high school transcripts in much less than twenty-four hours."

It took Tate a second to realize she was talking to *him*. "Bull," he shot back.

The corners of her mouth lifted. "D-minus in tenth-grade English. What's the matter, Tate? Can't read? Were you one of those kids who slipped through the cracks?"

Nick snorted, and even Sebastian managed a reluctant smile.

"Funny," Tate grumbled.

Tenth-grade English... Yep, that was the year he'd missed three months of school after his old man broke both of Will's legs. Someone had needed to stay home and take care of his little brother.

He decided not to mention that. Let Eva think he was a dumbass. Playing stupid was never a bad strategy, and he could use it to his advantage if needed.

Eva's blue eyes abruptly turned somber. "But I can see from your expression that my background check doesn't convince you of anything, does it? You still don't trust me or believe I'm telling the truth."

He shrugged and moved away from the computer. "I'm more of a gotta-see-it-to-believe-it kind of man."

"So you won't believe I can lead you to Hector's camp until you see it with your own eyes?" Without waiting for his answer, Eva gave a determined nod. "Fine. Let's make you a believer, Tate. When do we leave?"

"Dawn," he said briskly.

"Are we flying direct?"

Scrubbing a hand over the stubble coating his jaw, Tate turned to Nick. "Air traffic's still being monitored by the San Marquez military, right?"

Nick nodded. "Ever since the ULF started running drugs using the relief foundation planes. If you don't have government clearance to land on the island, they'll shoot you right outta the sky."

"We could fly commercial," Eva pointed out.

Tate rolled his eyes. "Sure, sweetheart, why don't you go ahead and do that. I'll take the route that *doesn't* leave a trail, and we'll rendezvous later."

"No need to be snarky about it."

"We'll fly to Colombia," he decided, ignoring her muttered reply. "Hire a boat from Tumaco. Bribe someone at the port to look the other way."

Eva looked dismayed. "But the harbor is in the east. It'll be easier if we come in from the western mountains—that's where Hector is. Otherwise we'll have to trek through the jungle for days."

Tate once again ignored her. "Get in touch with Hastings," he told Sebastian. "Tell him we might need his cabin, depending on which route we take to the west."

"Who's Hastings?" Eva asked, her tone distrustful.

"An ally," Tate said vaguely.

He didn't elaborate, and wouldn't have even if she'd pushed. These days, allies were hard to come by, and Ben Hastings was too valuable an asset to lose. An expat living in San Marquez, Hastings was former military with a list of connections longer than the Nile. Tate had first met the man in basic training, and they'd kept in touch in the fifteen years since. Other than Stone and Prescott, Ben Hastings was the only other person in the world Tate trusted implicitly.

As his brain snapped into business mode, he barked out some more orders. "Prescott, grab Eva's gear from the Jeep. She and the kid can bunk in one of the cells tonight."

"*She* is standing right here," Eva announced. "And what the hell do you mean, one of the *cells*?"

"That's what we call the rooms in this place," Nick explained with a twinkle in his eyes. "Either that, or closets. They're all so small, which is why we usually just crash in this room." He swept his arm around the enormous chamber before ambling off to do what Tate ordered.

Sebastian drifted off, too, a satellite phone pressed to his ear. Once both men were gone, Eva turned to Tate. Her blue eyes flickered uneasily in the glow of the candles.

He couldn't help but notice that she looked annoyingly beautiful in candlelight, and he had to force his gaze away from all that smooth, honey-colored skin, the incredibly vivid eyes, the lush, sensual mouth.

Heat promptly flooded his groin, making him stifle a curse. Crap. He seriously needed to get a grip on this attraction. Lust had a way of fogging a man's brain, and foggy brains led to mistakes. He couldn't afford to make a single mistake around this woman.

"Is this fort really habitable?" she demanded, those big eyes narrowing as she examined her surroundings. "I don't know if I feel comfortable leaving Rafe here. What if the ceiling collapses or something?"

"We assessed the structural integrity before making this our base. The place is solid."

Her teeth dug into her bottom lip. "What about food? And, um, washroom facilities? And—"

Tate cut in. "We've got an outhouse, plenty of wild game in the mountain, a clean well, freshwater spring half a mile from here, and the town isn't far away if my men need more supplies."

"He'll have a blast," came Nick's reassuring voice. The younger man reappeared in the doorway, lugging Eva's two big suitcases, which raised a cloud of dust as he dropped them on the stone floor. "Seb and I will treat your son to a real wilderness adventure."

"What about security?" she asked in a sharp tone. "We just drove right up to the door, and a secret knock isn't much of a safety precaution."

"There are cameras and motion sensors all over the place," Tate said with a shrug.

She looked surprised. "Really?"

He gestured to the laptops scattered on the tables. "We'll see or hear anyone coming from a mile away. The tunnels provide half a dozen escape routes. Oh, and the whole mountain is rigged to explode. Anyone tries anything, Nick or Seb push a button and kaboom."

"Rafe will be safe here," Nick said gently.

To Tate's irritation, moisture welled up in Eva's eyes as her gaze drifted to her child. "I've never been away from him for more than a few hours."

Before Tate could make a quick escape—dealing with female tears were *not* his strong suit—Eva recovered from her emotional moment in an impressive display of self-control. "I guess I should get some sleep, then. You said you wanted to leave at dawn?"

He gave a brisk nod. "Oh-dark-hundred hours. That's the only way I operate."

Her lips twitched. "Fine. Wake me up when it's time to go. Now can someone show me and my son to our cell?"

A few hours later, a gruff voice jolted Eva awake. Her eyelids snapped open to find Tate's aggravated face staring down at her.

"We've got to move," he ordered.

She blinked a few times, oriented herself, then relaxed when she registered the heat of her son's body, snuggled close to her side. Careful not to wake Rafe, she slid out from beneath the scratchy wool blanket Nick Prescott had given her and stumbled to her feet.

The men hadn't been kidding about the size of the room. It couldn't have been more than eight by ten feet, with a dusty floor and oppressive stone walls that lent the space a claustrophobic feel. A tiny square window allowed a patch of moonlight inside; that silver light had been shining directly on her and Rafe, yet somehow she'd still managed to fall into surprisingly deep slumber.

"Now?" she said, wiping the sleep from her eyes.

Tate nodded. Shadows obscured his face, but that little shard of moonlight made his dark green eyes glitter like gems and emphasized the strong line of his jaw.

Her heart did an involuntary flip, and she hated herself for it. She couldn't remember the last time she'd responded to a man on such a primal, sexual level. The dark, heady scent of him stirred her senses, and his long, lean body brought prickles of feminine awareness to her skin.

This man was far too attractive for his own good.

And ruthless. Oh, yes, there was no doubt in her mind that he had a ruthless streak a mile long running through that warrior body of his. He wanted Hector dead, and he'd use anyone and anything at his disposal to make that happen. Including her.

But she'd known that going in. It was why she'd chosen Tate in the first place—that kind of single-minded determination was exactly what she needed if she wanted to get rid of her monster.

"Say goodbye to your kid," Tate said gruffly.

Her heart promptly sank to the pit of her stomach, and then she looked at her son and a jolt of panic blasted through her. Oh, God. She couldn't do it. She couldn't leave Rafe.

As her hands began to shake, she sucked in a deep breath and forced herself to calm down. No, it had to be done. She couldn't bring a toddler on a mission to kill his *father,* for God's sake. Rafe would be safer here, guarded by Tate's men.

*Men you don't even know.*

Her anxiety doubled.

"I don't know if I can do this," she blurted out.

At the shrill sound of her voice, Rafe stirred on the sleeping bag.

She quickly lowered her voice and shot Tate a miserable

look. "I don't trust you," she whispered. "I don't trust your men. How can... I... God, I can't leave him with strangers."

A muscle jumped in Tate's strong jaw. After a beat, he planted his hand on her arm. "Come into the hall."

The rusty iron door creaked as he pushed it open and led her into the corridor, which was lit by a single candle in a candelabra hanging on the wall.

"We both seem to be having trust issues," Tate said in a tone tinged with equal parts humor and aggravation. "I won't apologize for not trusting you, and I don't expect an apology from you, either. But your kid? He's an innocent. You understand what that means?"

She furrowed her brows.

"It means that my men and I don't use innocents as leverage, or pawns, or to further our agendas," he said roughly. "This world is a messed-up place, sweetheart. Bad people, bad situations. We've gotta preserve whatever innocence we have left, so trust me when I tell you that Prescott and Stone will protect him with their lives."

She certainly hadn't expected *that* from Tate, and some of the tightness in her throat eased. "Really?"

He nodded.

A wry smile played over her lips. "So I should trust you when it comes to my son, but not about anything else?"

"Pretty much." He tipped his head, a mocking glimmer entering his eyes. "Just like I won't trust anything but your desire to see Cruz dead."

"So that much you believe."

"Yes." He donned a contemplative look. "You want the man out of your life, but don't think for a second I bought the story you told me."

She worked hard to keep her face expressionless. He was absolutely right—she'd lied through her teeth about who Hector was to her and Rafe. But she didn't regret her decision to keep the truth from Tate. No way would he have agreed to help her if he knew she'd once been Hector's lover.

"You don't believe my story, yet you're still coming to San Marquez with me," she pointed out.

"Indeed I am."

She fixed him with a contemplative look of her own. "You'll take the risk that I'm playing you, all for a shot at Hector. Why is that, Tate? What did he do to you?"

A laugh escaped his lips, low and harsh. "Nice try, sweetheart. Now say goodbye to your kid. Come to the main room when you're done."

Eva watched as his tall, powerful body disappeared into the shadows. She wished she could figure him out. Rough, calculating, charming, indifferent, sensual—barely a day of knowing him and he'd shown her so many sides of himself she had no idea who he truly was.

*He's the man who's going to set you free, that's all you need to know.*

Wrenching her gaze off Tate, she walked back into the tiny room and knelt down beside her son. Hot emotion flooded her chest as she watched him sleep. When she noticed the way his bottom lip stuck out a little, she smiled and blinked back tears, wishing she didn't have to leave him.

It was funny how apprehensive she'd been about having Rafe. She'd been twenty-two years old and trying to find a way to escape the tyrant she'd foolishly gotten involved with, only to discover she was pregnant with the tyrant's child. She'd always wanted children, but not then, and certainly not with Hector.

Yet the moment she'd seen Rafe's sweet face, the moment she'd held that tiny infant in her arms, she'd fallen head over heels in love with her son—and she'd vowed to protect him at all costs. Theirs hadn't been an easy life so far—six moves in three years was exhausting—but Rafe was such a resilient child, well-adjusted, intelligent and with such a sweet disposition.

"Mommy has to go away for a few days," she whispered, gently stroking his silky hair.

She decided it was probably best not to wake him. It'd only upset and confuse him.

Then again, wasn't that precisely how he would react when he awoke to find her gone?

Guilt seized her insides. It was a good thing she'd already introduced him to Nick and Sebastian—Rafe would have been terrified to wake up and find himself with someone he didn't recognize.

"I promise you, I'll be back as soon as I can," she went on, her throat so tight it hurt. "I'm going to make sure that monster doesn't come anywhere near you. He'll never hurt us again, baby."

Blinking away the tears that welled up in her eyes, she planted a soft kiss on Rafe's forehead, breathing in his sweet, little-boy scent. It took all her willpower to force her legs to carry her out of the room.

Her heart throbbed with guilt and pain as she walked down the dark corridor in the direction of the main chamber. Angry voices wafted from the open doorway, and she instinctively ducked to the side, not feeling the slightest bit bad about eavesdropping. The more insight she had about these men, the better prepared she'd be.

"I won't stay behind."

She immediately recognized the gravelly voice as belonging to Sebastian.

"I'm giving you an order, Seb." Tate, sounding extremely irritated. "I need you here with Nick."

"You need me watching your six."

"Don't push this. You're not coming, Sergeant. That's an order." Tate paused. "I know you're out there, Eva. Get in here."

Eva's cheeks heated as she entered the room. "Wow. Do you have superhearing or something?"

"No, you're just very loud." Tate stalked toward her, stopping to swipe a pile of clothes from a nearby chair. "Change into these," he ordered, shoving the items into her hands.

She glanced down, and a frown marred her mouth. Jeans, T-shirt, socks, panties, bra and hiking boots—all belonging to her.

"Did you go through my suitcases?" she demanded.

Unfazed by the outraged expression on her face, he shrugged and reached for the black backpack sitting on the floor. "Yeah. I also took the liberty of packing you a bag. We only take what we can carry on our backs."

Although she was inwardly stewing over his presumptuous—and, frankly, nosy—behavior, she choked down her annoyance and stepped back into the hall to change her clothes. When she reentered the room a few minutes later, she headed for one of the tables and scrounged up a pen and scrap of paper. She scribbled down a few details before handing the paper to Nick Prescott, who raised his brows.

"What's this?" he asked.

"The address and phone number for my parents in New York." She swallowed. "If anything happens to me…if for some reason I don't come back…take Rafe to them, all right?"

Nick's brown eyes softened. "All right."

"And if you can, read to him before bedtime—his storybooks are in my suitcase. And don't give him too much sugar, he turns into a little terror if you do. Um, what else? He hates bath time. He can sleep through anything. He doesn't like to be yelled at, so quietly telling him he did something wrong is more effective than yelling. Um, he—"

"Any allergies or medical conditions we should be aware of?" Nick interrupted.

She shook her head.

He grinned. "Then that's all we need to know. Your son will be in good hands."

With an impatient breath, Tate strode across the room and picked up a nylon backpack, same style and color as the one he'd given her. He slid one strap over his shoulder, then bent down to retrieve a navy blue duffel bag from the floor.

"Eva and I'll take the Jeep," he told his men. "I'll stash it at the airfield. That leaves you the Rover and dirt bikes— you good with that?"

Sebastian still looked angry as hell, nodding stiffly to Tate's question. "We'll be fine."

Tate's gaze shifted to Eva. "You ready?"

She let out a shaky breath. "As I'll ever be."

Sebastian waited ten minutes after the captain left with Eva Dolce before springing to action. He stripped off his ratty jeans and threadbare T-shirt and replaced them with cargo pants and a muscle shirt made of lightweight, breathable fabric. Combat boots went on next, and then he shoved a handgun in his waistband and started putting together a go bag. Rifle, pistols, extra clips, grenades. Canteen, MREs, power bars, flashlight, poncho… He tossed in anything he might need for a potential trek, jungle or mountainous.

The entire time, Nick watched from the door. "Why am I not surprised that everything the captain said went in one ear and out the other?"

Sebastian ignored him. He swept his gaze over a table piled with enough weapons and gadgets to launch an assault on a small country, all courtesy of a black ops community that hadn't turned its backs on them even when their own government had.

"You actually think you can follow them without the captain making the tail?" Nick sounded highly amused.

He zipped up his bag and shot the other man an irritated look. "You saying I don't know how to be invisible?"

"No, I'm saying Tate's got superhuman senses. If you tail him, he'll know."

"That's a chance I'll have to take."

Nick ran a hand through his brown hair, suddenly looking very, very tired. "Maybe she can be trusted."

Sebastian snorted. "And maybe the Easter Bunny comes over for Sunday brunch every year."

"She might really lead him to Cruz."

"Or right into an ambush." He zipped up his bag. "Either way, I'll be around to make sure the captain walks out of this alive."

He slung the strap of the duffel over his shoulder and approached Prescott, extending a hand. He and the lieutenant might not always get along—fine, they argued like cats and dogs—but Sebastian had nothing but the utmost respect for Nick Prescott. They'd become brothers the moment they joined Captain Tate's command, and that bond had been tested and become stronger after years of death and bloodshed.

With six of their brothers already under six feet of dirt, Sebastian was even more determined to protect the two that remained. That meant Nick and Tate—no matter what his damn orders were.

"Contact me on the sat phone if you need me," he said gruffly, still holding out his hand.

After a moment, resignation settled in Nick's amber-colored eyes. He leaned in for the handshake. "Don't do anything reckless."

"Same goes for you." His lips twitched. "You just stay here and hold the fort. Literally."

Nick snickered. "I'll do that." His expression promptly sobered. "Be careful, Seb. I'm not in the mood to attend another funeral."

"Don't worry, Nicky. Nobody's dying."

Except for Eva Dolce, if she made even one wrong move toward the captain.

But Sebastian kept that thought to himself.

## Chapter 5

"Why didn't you want Sebastian to come with us?" Eva asked, as Tate steered the Jeep down the mountain.

*Because only one of us needs to die on this wild-goose chase.*

Rather than voice his dour thoughts, Tate just shrugged in response and focused on the road ahead. The sun had yet to set, but faint ripples of light hovered over the horizon line, hinting that dawn was near. Gomez was already waiting for them at the airfield, and Tate couldn't wait to get on the damn plane and get this over with.

Best-case scenario? Eva was telling the truth, they would infiltrate Cruz's hideout, and Tate would exact his revenge.

Worst case?

Jeez, there were so many of those he didn't even know where to start. Even if Eva was on the up-and-up, that didn't guarantee they'd make it in and out of Cruz's camp alive. Tate couldn't formulate a plan until he saw the place for himself, and who knew what he'd find in San Marquez? Cruz's lieutenants and followers continued to fight for the cause while Cruz was holed up underground, but for all Tate knew, the majority of Cruz's men were protecting that camp. An entire army might be waiting for him when he got there.

And if Eva *was* lying, Cruz might not be the pot of gold at the end of this messed-up rainbow. The people who wanted Tate dead might off him long before he even got close to the ULF leader.

That was why he didn't want Stone anywhere near this. Killing Cruz was *his* crusade, *his* albatross. If for some reason Tate didn't make it out of this alive, at least Stone and Prescott would survive and live another day to figure out why they'd become targets.

Twenty minutes later, he pulled up at the dusty airfield, which consisted of two dirt runways, a large hangar with a sagging tin roof, and two armed guards at the rusted gate out front.

The guards waved Tate through without batting an eye. No surprise. He was well-known here in Paraíso—and not for being an upstanding citizen.

His first night in town, he'd had a run-in with a lowlife drug dealer in the cantina, and it hadn't ended well for the dealer. That night he'd earned both the fear and respect of the townsfolk, most of whom were criminals or, like Tate, on the run for one reason or another.

"Is that even a real runway?"

Eva's uneasy voice jarred him back to the present. He glanced at the passenger seat and shot her a crooked grin. "Sweetheart, does this look like a real airport to you?"

"Can your pilot at least fly a plane?" she grumbled, tucking a strand of silky black hair behind her ear.

"Don't worry. He'll get us to Colombia safe and sound."

Tate parked the Jeep and hopped out without another word. He rounded the vehicle, grabbed his go bag and the two backpacks, then tossed one to Eva just as she jumped out of the Jeep. She caught it against her chest with a thud.

"Heads up," he said dryly.

She scowled at him. "You're supposed to say that *before* you throw something at someone."

"I wanted to see if you're quick on your feet. You passed. Come on, follow me."

He strode off, his tan-colored boots kicking up clouds of red dirt. Inside the dilapidated hangar, he found Manuel Gomez tinkering with the propeller of an older-model single-engine Cessna. The stocky bald man lifted his head at Tate's approach.

"Good. You're here," Gomez said in Spanish. His dark eyes flicked in Eva's direction. "Who's the woman?"

"Eva." Tate didn't elaborate, and Gomez didn't push, but the Mexican did arch his eyebrows knowingly before nodding hello at Eva.

"We all set?" Tate asked, gesturing to the plane.

"Good to go." Gomez tossed his wrench into the metal toolbox on the floor. "Throw your gear in the baggage hold."

As Gomez conducted his preflight check, Tate stowed their bags, then extended a hand to help Eva into the small plane.

She hesitated before accepting his hand, and the second his fingers made contact, a jolt of heat sizzled right down to his groin. Everything about this woman turned him on. Her silky jet-black hair, her centerfold body, the graceful curve of her neck. And her scent...talk about addictive. A flowery aroma, with a hint of orange blossoms and something uniquely feminine.

Damn, it had been way too long since he'd had a woman.

Eva was the first female he'd spent more than five minutes with since he'd fled Virginia. The whores at Juan's cantina didn't count—they held no appeal to him, and besides, Tate hadn't paid for sex a day in his life.

Then again, he could probably trust those prostitutes more than he could trust Eva Dolce. At least Juan's whores made their agendas clear.

He saw Eva's pulse throbbing in the hollow of her throat as she shrugged her palm out of his grip. She settled in one of the tattered seats in back of the plane, and he noticed her hands trembling as she buckled up.

"Everything okay?" Tate drawled.

Her jaw tightened. "I don't like the way you look at me."

A chuckle slid out. "And what way is that?"

"You know what I mean."

He pressed his lips together to keep from chuckling again, then climbed up beside her.

A moment later, Gomez slid into the cockpit, flicked some switches, and the little plane shuddered to life. As they taxied toward the makeshift runway, Gomez peered at Tate over his shoulder.

"Should be a smooth ride," the pilot said. "Flight will be a little over four hours."

He leaned back against the chair's headrest and shot Gomez grim look. "Did you file a flight plan?"

The man flashed a grin, revealing his crooked front teeth. "Why, of course, Mr. Tate. We're taking a day trip to Panama, remember?"

Tate grinned back. "Of course."

The engine hummed as the plane picked up speed, and five minutes later, they were in the air. Eva jumped when the landing gear retracted with a thump, but then she re-laxed and shifted her gaze out the window. She stared at the clouds for a long while before finally turning to shoot him a perplexed look.

"How do you have so many connections?" she asked. "When I tracked you down, I got the feeling the U.S. government isn't exactly looking out for you."

He shrugged. "Uncle Sam might have disowned us, but we've got a whole lotta cousins watching our backs."

She wrinkled her forehead. "Cousins?"

"Mercenaries, expats, active duty operatives, retired operatives, you name it. The spec-ops community looks out for its own. And when you work Special Forces, you develop a network of contacts that aren't always on the legitimate side."

"So you were Special Forces," she mused.

"You didn't already know that?" he said sardonically.

"No, I couldn't gain access to your military file. It was classified. But your status listed you as honorably discharged."

His shoulders tensed. "Are you telling me you actually managed to hack into the army database?"

Eva smirked. "Like I said, I'm good with computers. I had help with that one, though. I have this hacker friend— he can break into any system, and I mean *any* system. Anyway, we got off topic. How do you pay all these connections of yours?"

"Hasn't anyone ever told you it's rude to ask strangers about their finances?"

She rolled her eyes. "Seriously, how do you have enough money to sustain yourself on the run? I checked your financial statements, and no way was your military pension enough to pay for the kind of expenses you've got—the security measures, on-call pilots, all those weapons I saw back at the fort. When you cleaned out your savings account, it only had five grand in it, so how are you paying to stay hidden?"

He wanted to be insulted, but truth was, her tactics impressed him. It was exactly what he would do, research the hell out of a potential ally—or enemy. Still, it grated that this woman had been privy to the sorry state of his savings.

"All my funds were tied up in the house I bought a few years back," he admitted. "I didn't have time to sell it and cash out. We kind of skipped town without much warning." He smiled dryly. "But Seb and I had no idea how fat Prescott's wallet was. He cleaned out his savings account, too, and I'm talking seven figures here. Cash."

"You didn't know Nick was wealthy, even though you served in the same unit?"

"Another thing about us Special Forces guys—we don't like to talk about ourselves. I know Stone and Prescott better now than I did when they served under me." Tate narrowed his eyes. "What about you? You mentioned you've been running from Cruz for a while. How is it you can afford new identities each time you and your son haul ass? I saw your documents—they're flawless. Which means pricey."

"The first time we ran, my parents gave me money. Rafe was still a newborn, and I had just left San Marquez and moved back to New York. Hector showed up and demanded that I go back with him." Bitterness dripped from her tone. "It didn't seem to faze him that I kept saying no. He was determined to have me."

Rubbing her temples, Eva stretched her legs, drawing his attention to the way the faded blue denim hugged her firm thighs. He forced his gaze back to her face, ordering himself to concentrate on her words rather than her body.

"He got violent when I refused to leave with him. He told me he'd give me twenty-four hours to come to him willingly, and after that, he'd use extreme measures. So that night, my dad gave me fifty thousand dollars from his private safe. I said goodbye to my parents, took Rafe and disappeared. That fifty grand paid for our first identities and a house in Thailand."

"What happened when the money ran out?"

Her blue eyes grew veiled. "I became more resourceful."

He studied her, strands of suspicions coiling in his gut. "You stole what you needed," he said slowly. An alarm dinged in his head. "Oh, hell, you stole from *Cruz*." Now he felt a burst of triumph. "Is that why he's after you, Eva? Is that the real reason?"

"No. I told you why he's after me. He's obsessed." Her mouth relaxed as a smug little smile tugged at it. "He has no idea I stole money from him. There's no way he could ever trace it back to me."

"You sound certain of that."

"I am." She ran a hand through her hair, sending another wave of her intoxicating aroma his way. "The ULF stores their funds in dozens of bank accounts across the globe. Caymans, Switzerland, Dubai—name the country, and the ULF has a numbered account there."

He raised a brow. "And you managed to hack into all of these accounts?"

"Not all, but my friend helped me out and we managed to gain access to some of the accounts."

She proceeded to explain how she'd dipped into various accounts and transferred funds under the guise of commissions, banking fees and administrative charges; that way, if the ULF suspected or noticed something fishy, the wrongdoing would trace back to the person who oversaw that particular account, making it look as if that person had stolen the funds.

Tate let out a low whistle as he grasped what she'd

said. "You do realize that if Cruz or his lieutenants believe they're being cheated, these bankers will get their heads chopped off?"

There was zero remorse on Eva's beautiful face. "The men who cook the books for the ULF are not innocent. Accountant, banker, manager, I don't care who handles that money. They're as responsible for all the deaths the ULF causes as the rebels themselves. These people sit in their cushy offices and move blood money around and pocket it to look the other way. I have no sympathy for them. None."

He cocked his head. "Interesting."

"What?" she said defensively.

"You are far more ruthless than I would have imagined."

"Ruthless? No. Sick and tired of the corruption? Yes." Her expression grew stony. "I came to San Marquez four years ago to make a difference and all I got out of the experience was disillusionment. The ULF doesn't care about the country's people any more than the government. The only things anyone concerns themselves with are money and bloodshed."

"Says the woman who spent a considerable amount of time and energy to track me down—so I could kill a man for her."

"You're not killing Hector for me. You're killing him for *you*. I'm just giving you the means with which to do it."

"Win-win, then?"

"Murdering a man… Sure, Tate, it's win-win," she said flatly, and then she fixed her gaze out the window and promptly put an end to the conversation.

Eva was a bundle of nerves by the time they arrived in the small port city of Tumaco. Tate's pilot had taken them as far as Cali, Colombia, where they'd boarded another plane piloted by another nefarious-looking character from Tate's network of shady associates. Less than an hour later, they'd landed in Tumaco and taken a taxi to the harbor, where Tate was now haggling with the captain of a small cargo vessel.

It had only been six hours since they'd left Paraíso, but Eva was already exhausted. She felt as though she'd run a marathon followed by two triathlons and a decathlon thrown in for good measure. Probably the heat. March in South America could be brutal, and today was no exception. Only eleven in the morning, and the temperature must be nearing ninety-seven degrees already. The sun's merciless rays beat down on her head—her wide-brimmed straw hat was doing nothing to protect her scalp from the heat— and the air was so muggy it felt as if she was inhaling fire each time she took a breath.

She hoped it would be cooler on the water, but if the stifling breeze rolling off the ocean was any indication, the impending boat ride probably wouldn't offer much relief.

Her gaze moved in Tate's direction, and she couldn't help but notice the way his sweaty white T-shirt clung to every hard angle and corded muscle of his broad chest. With the brim of his baseball cap pulled low, she couldn't see his expression, but his body language displayed unmistakable irritation. He towered over the captain of the cargo ship, a slight, dark-skinned man who seemed determined to bleed Tate dry, judging by the second stack of bills he shoved in the man's palms.

A few moments later, Tate stalked over to where she waited, dodging dock workers on his way. "He'll take us. We leave port in thirty minutes."

"What did you tell him?"

"That we're American, here to volunteer with one of the relief foundations. I said we missed our flight and decided we wanted a nautical adventure rather than wait for the next plane."

"How long to San Marquez by boat?"

"Four, five hours. We'll get there late afternoon."

Eva glanced over at the fruit stands a hundred yards from the dock, a sight that elicited a grumble from her stomach and served as a reminder that she hadn't eaten a thing since last night.

"Do we have time to grab some food for the ride?" she asked.

Tate nodded and took her arm as they fell into step with one another. She didn't know if it was a protective gesture, or if he wanted to make sure she didn't run off, but the heat of his fingers as they curled lightly over her biceps made her heart to do a little flip.

Lord, her heart had to quit doing that. She had no business being attracted to this man. To any man, for that matter. After her experience with Hector, a result of her own naïveté, she had no desire to get burned by a man ever again. Her son was the only male she wanted—or needed—in her life now.

Banishing the awareness rippling over her hot skin, Eva filled a cloth sack with fresh mangoes and a bushel of bananas, paid the plump Colombian woman and then followed Tate back to the dock. At their approach, the captain impatiently gestured for them to come aboard, announcing in Spanish that it was time to go.

Lugging his duffel, Tate took the lead and strode up the gangplank, his boots thudding on the creaky main deck of the vessel. Eva scampered after him and accepted his hand as he helped her on board.

Not long after, they were heading due west, the balmy breeze slapping their faces and the salty ocean mist stinging their eyes. Thankfully, it *was* cooler on the water. As

Tate stood by the railing, watching the waves, Eva sank on a metal crate and gave her rumbling stomach some nourishment. She devoured two bananas, then cut open a mango with the small switchblade she found in her back-pack, unruffled by the sticky juices that stained her hands. Lord, she was hungry.

"Mango?" she asked Tate between mouthfuls.

His rugged profile shifted in her direction. "Toss one over."

She dug a mango out of the sack and lobbed it his way. He caught it easily, then slid a lethal-looking blade from the sheath on his hip and sliced a piece of the ripe fruit. He flicked it up to his mouth with the tip of his knife, bit and sucked the fruit, then tossed the peel into the water.

She was oddly fascinated as she watched him eat. His every movement was done with military precision, from the way he handled the knife to the way he threw away the peels. Even the way he chewed seemed carefully planned.

"Can I ask you something?" she asked, as she uncapped a bottle of water. It would probably be the last "luxury" drink she'd have in a while—once she and Tate reached the river, they'd only be able to drink water that they'd purified first.

"You can ask," he replied, "but there's no guarantee I'll answer."

She took a sip, then rested the bottle on her knee. "How come you don't go by the name Robert? At first I thought it was a military thing, using your last name, but Nick and Sebastian both used their first names when they introduced themselves."

His expression darkened. "I prefer Tate."

"Clearly. But why?"

"Robert was my old man's name," he said tightly. "I

didn't want to have anything in common with that man. Sharing a surname was bad enough."

An unwitting rush of sympathy filled her chest. "Bad childhood?"

"If you consider getting the crap kicked out of you on a daily basis for ten years *bad,* then yeah."

Her breath caught. She studied his harsh face, but there was no hint of humor, no sign that he was messing around with her. Instantly, her heart constricted with pain for everything he must have suffered growing up.

"I'm sorry," she said softly. "That must have been difficult."

"I survived."

She released a frustrated breath. "Do you always do that? Brush everything off like it's no big deal?"

"Only when it really *is* no big deal." He rolled his eyes. "Don't look at me like that, sweetheart, with those big pitying eyes. I dealt with my crap years ago. The past is the past."

God, she wished she could think like that. But for her, the past *wasn't* the past, not when it threatened her future. Her son's future. She'd made a mistake when she'd fallen for Hector four years ago, but Rafe didn't deserve to pay the price for it.

The wind picked up and snaked underneath her ponytail, blowing the ends of it into her mouth. She shoved the hair away and adjusted her hat, then glanced at Tate, still trying to make sense of him. "So your father, is he still alive?"

Tate moved his gaze back to the horizon line. "He died eleven years ago. DUI."

"I guess it would be too optimistic to think you mourned him."

He chuckled. "I was tempted to throw a damn parade."

"That's sad."

"What, that I didn't grieve for the bastard?"

"No, that you had him for a father in the first place," she said quietly.

He sliced off another chunk of mango and chewed slowly, shooting her a what-can-you-do look. "Luck of the draw. Some kids are just destined to have crappy parents, I guess."

Didn't she know it. Her son had drawn the short stick, too, when he'd gotten Hector Cruz for a father, but Eva was determined to protect Rafe from the man who'd sired him. Not only was Hector a violent, sadistic killer, but nothing was sacred to him, not even youth. The ULF frequently recruited child soldiers for its cause, a horrifying truth she hadn't realized until much later. Hector had even bragged to her that he'd personally trained some of the children in the movement.

Well, she refused to let Hector corrupt her little boy. Solving violence with violence had never been a philosophy she'd subscribed to, but in this case, she would make an exception. Hector had to die. It was the only way to keep her son safe, the only way to—how had Tate put it? Preserve innocence.

Eva rose from the crate and approached the railing. She gazed out at the greenish-brown dot in the distance. The island of San Marquez. Her birthplace, her son's birthplace. In a few short hours, she'd be back in the place she'd vowed never to return.

"You haven't been back since your kid was born?" Tate asked gruffly, following her gaze.

She shook her head.

"Where exactly does the name Dolce come from? I figured you'd have a Latin American name since you were born in San Marquez."

"My dad's Italian," she explained. "He met my mom

when she was vacationing in Italy as a teenager. She was from San Marquez, and Dad was too smitten to say good-bye to her, so he followed her all the way to another continent and they lived here for a couple of years. He worked in the capital, but then his firm transferred him to the States right after I was born, so we moved to America."

A cloud of smoke wafted in her direction, making her wrinkle her nose. Glancing over, she spotted a tanned deckhand standing by the stern, one arm resting on the steel railing ringing the deck, the other holding a hand-rolled cigarette. He inhaled again, then blew out another puff of the sweet, potent flavor unique to the tobacco produced on San Marquez.

The scent brought both a wave of nostalgia and a rush of dread to her belly. The latter feeling increased the closer they got to the island. Funny, how such a small, beautiful place could harbor so much ugliness.

San Marquez was smaller than the countries on the mainland but larger than most of the island nations dotting the continent. To the west sat the Marqueza Mountain range, looming over a coastline that offered nothing but boulder-ridden white sand and jagged cliffs with steep drops. Merido, the capital city, was centrally located, a crowded metropolis with a struggling tourism industry thanks to the strife with the ULF. The eastern region of the island featured an array of coastal towns and villages, along with a harbor that served as the base of the country's fishing and trade industry.

"Damn," Tate muttered, as the ship neared its destination.

Eva immediately understood the source of his unhappiness. The telltale navy-blue-and-gold uniforms stood out among the throng of people bustling in the harbor.

"I don't remember there being much of a military presence on the coast before," she remarked with a frown.

The deckhand she'd been eyeing ambled over, sucking hard on his cigarette. "Smuggling happen," he said in garbled English. "Drugs, weapons, hide on boats."

"ULF?" Tate said sharply.

The man nodded. "They be getting reckless lately. Cruz gone, rebels fighting each other."

Eva's frown deepened. Dissent within the ULF. Hector was probably fuming about that. Would he come out of hiding to take care of the problems? She prayed he wouldn't, at least not before she and Tate reached his hideout.

The closer the cargo vessel got, the more uneasy Eva felt. The port wasn't overflowing with soldiers, but she spotted at least a dozen posted at various points of the harbor, their hawklike eyes sweeping over the people milling the area.

By the time the ship reached the dock, her pulse was racing. She didn't want to attract any undue attention, but she might not be able to help it once they disembarked. The dockworkers were mostly male, and as a female, she'd stand out like a sore thumb.

Tate evidently concurred because he lowered his voice and said, "When we get off, keep your head down. I don't want anyone getting a good look at our faces."

She nearly said "mine more than yours" but quickly bit back the words. If anyone was the more recognizable of the two, it was her, the former lover of the ULF's *leader*.

Panic tugged on her belly as she realized that everything could go up in smoke if anyone connected to Hector recognized her. If Tate found out she'd been involved with his enemy, he'd either kill her or abandon her. Unfortunately, neither of those outcomes was desirable.

She nearly fell overboard when she heard a loud metallic thump. She relaxed when she realized it was the gangplank being lowered, but then she noticed Tate picking up his duffel bag and her anxiety returned. She didn't exactly know what was in that bag of his, but she had a pretty good idea that most of the contents weren't legal.

"What if we're searched?" she murmured.

"Taken care of," he murmured back.

She didn't have time to question that statement, but she found out soon enough. The customs official that greeted them on the walkway barely even glanced in their direction—or at the passports they handed him. He scribbled something on his clipboard, stamped their passports, then stalked off.

"How'd you manage that?" Eva asked as she watched the burly man's retreating back.

"All that cash I handed our captain in Tumaco? That was so he'd put in a good word for us with his brother." Tate hooked a thumb in the direction the customs clerk had gone in. "That was his brother."

She grinned. "How lucky for us."

After bidding goodbye to their captain, she and Tate maneuvered their way through the busy harbor, heading for the road several hundred yards away. The odor of fish, salt and earth hung in the air, along with that sweet tobacco that every male within ten feet seemed to be smoking.

Eva angled the brim of her hat and kept her head down as they walked, doing her best not to make eye contact with anyone. People jostled them, some pushing past using their hands, and she squeaked in objection when a particularly aggressive dockworker bulldozed past her, nearly clipping her in the side of the head with his elbow.

"You okay, baby?"

Tate's sandpaper-rough voice made her blink in surprise. *Baby?*

"Uh, I'm fine, he just bumped—"

She almost jumped out of her own skin when Tate slung an arm around her shoulder and dipped his head to nuzzle her neck. Despite the hundred-degree temperature, goose bumps rapidly rose on her skin.

What the hell was he—

His husky voice interrupted her thoughts. "I cannot wait to get you alone," he rasped. "Just you and me. On a bed. All night long."

# *Chapter 6*

Shock and arousal coursed through Eva's body like an electrical current. Her heart pounded, nipples puckered, core ached. She couldn't remember ever getting this turned on this fast.

Beside her, Tate seemed as cool as a cucumber. He rubbed his stubble-covered cheek on her neck, the prickly beard growth abrading her suddenly feverish skin. And he didn't even slow his pace—nope, just kept walking, practically dragging her beside him even as his lips closed over those sensitive tendons in her neck and sucked gently.

"What are you doing?" she stammered.

"You taste incredible." He swiped his tongue over her heated flesh then took a teasing nip with his teeth.

Before she could even attempt to figure out what had gotten into him, he abruptly straightened his shoulders and slid his hand to the small of her back, resting it there in a casual but possessive pose.

What on earth? Up until now, Tate hadn't shown an overt amount of sexual interest in her, but all of a sudden he was a different man. His smoldering green eyes, the sensual lift of his mouth, the dangerous seduction radiating from his masculine frame.

"Easy," he murmured, rubbing circles over her tailbone. His voice lowered to a scarcely audible pitch. "Play along, sweetheart."

Understanding dawned fast and hard, becoming clearer when she caught a flash of navy blue and gold in her peripheral vision. Soldiers. Two of them. They must have been walking directly behind her and Tate, but now they veered to the right and hurried off in a brisk march toward a group of unruly boys who looked to be in the middle of a full-out brawl.

As the soldiers shouted and raised their guns, the fighting boys broke apart and took off like bats out of a cave, disappearing in all directions.

Eva and Tate took full advantage of the soldiers' distraction, picking up their pace as they made their way to the road. It wasn't until they were out of sight that she allowed herself to dwell on the completely inappropriate response she'd experienced back there.

She'd wanted Tate.

In that moment, when his warm lips had met her skin and his big hand slid under the hem of her shirt to stroke her lower back, she'd wanted him more than she'd wanted her next breath.

His kiss. His touch. His powerful body crushing hers as he moved inside her. She'd wanted it all, damn it.

Even now, those wicked images caused that spot between her legs to tingle. God, this was wrong. Having sex with Tate would be a bad idea. A *terrible* idea.

And not even a viable idea, considering he'd faked that

entire flirty, seductive exchange. While she, idiot that she was, had believed every second of it.

"Sorry about that," he muttered. "They were staring at us too long for my liking."

She swallowed the embarrassment lining her throat. "How do you know they were staring? They were behind us. Do you have eyes in the back of your head or something?"

"Sensed it. Fifteen years in the military will do that to you." He shrugged. "I can sniff out a threat from miles away, even if it's behind me."

"Yeah? What kind of threats are around us right now?" she couldn't help but challenge.

"Other than the government soldiers crawling over every inch of the harbor? Well, there's the ULF rebel trying to blend in over there by the loading dock. The pickpocket that's already robbed two fishermen, which is damn impressive because the kid can't be older than five or six. That woman standing by the fruit cart is packing heat—AK, judging by the size and bulk, but I suppose it could be a lower-caliber ri—"

"I get the point," she cut in, unable to fight a smile. "You know your threats."

He tipped his head and shot her an ironic smile. "I sure do, Eva. And the biggest threat of all happens to be right beside me."

She bristled with insult, but she couldn't exactly fault him for being distrustful. This man was risking a lot to be here. He'd come out of hiding, and now he was taking a gamble that Eva could lead him to Cruz. Well, fortunately for him, the gamble would pay off because she planned on delivering Tate right to Hector's door.

And watching while he killed her son's father.

A shiver ran up her spine. Did it make her a coward, for

not doing the job herself? Or a monster, for actively seeking out a man's death? Maybe both. Maybe neither. All she knew was that her son would never have a normal life as long as Hector was alive.

"You'll realize soon enough that I'm not a threat," she said quietly. After a beat, she offered a dry smile. "Until then, try not to kill me in my sleep, okay?"

His lips twitched as if he were fighting laugher. "Deal."

"This is as far as I go."

The driver of the ancient truck they'd flagged down let the engine idle, which made the entire vehicle chug like a steam engine. Tate was happy to get out of the truck; he and Eva had been crammed in the front seat for the past three hours, and his body desperately needed a reprieve. Sitting there with Eva's firm thigh pressed against his had been pure torture.

He'd tried to distract himself by focusing on the scenery, but the green hills and soil-rich fields that made up the island's eastern landscape hadn't succeeded in making him any less aware of Eva Dolce. The woman smelled like temptation, all sweet and spicy and orange-blossomy, and she tasted like heaven—he knew that for a fact now, seeing as he'd had his lips buried in her neck earlier.

Christ, this unfortunate attraction to a woman he didn't trust was liable to drive him insane.

"Thank you so much for the ride."

Eva's melodic voice jolted him from his thoughts. As he pushed on the broken door handle of the passenger side, Eva leaned in to squeeze their driver's shoulder in thanks. Which was kind of impressive because Tate wouldn't have touched the man with a ten-foot pole. Long, greasy hair, bushy gray beard with what looked like pieces of food stuck in it, dirty fingernails and several missing teeth. The guy looked like a cartoon hobo, for Chrissake.

But hey, in the hobo's defense, he'd stopped to pick them up when he'd spotted them on the side of the road, and Tate was compelled to offer a thank-you of his own before he hopped out of the truck.

He rounded the vehicle and grabbed his duffel from the truck bed, which was piled high with wooden crates overflowing with oranges. The citrus scent filled his nostrils and made him think of Eva, who came up beside him, tightening the straps of her backpack. The moment he slung the duffel over his shoulder, the truck driver revved the engine and sped off in reverse, raising a cloud of moist brown dirt that nearly blinded them both.

Tate wiped the dust off his face, watching as the driver executed a rapid U-turn that made the vehicle lurch and chug harder. After the truck disappeared, he glanced at Eva. Her blue eyes were apprehensive as she gazed at the landscape up ahead, where the road became impassable.

Thick vegetation awaited them, and the scents emanating from the tangle of greenery were ones he'd recognize anywhere—damp earth and wildflowers and acrid rot. Even from where he stood, he heard the din of the jungle, the familiar noises of the wildlife, the buzzing of insects and rustling of trees, and he drew great comfort from it all. This was his element—out in the wild, hunting down his prey, a silent, shadowy predator. *This* was what he'd been trained for, not hiding away in a stone fortress like a coward.

"I hate the jungle," Eva remarked in a glum voice.

"Well, start loving it, because we've got a long walk ahead of us. Three days, barring any unforeseen complications, and that's factoring in only a few hours' sleep a night. If you want more sleep time, it'll take longer."

She made a grumbling sound. "Trust me, I won't be sleeping at all."

He had to grin. "Scared of what bumps in the night?"

"More like what *crawls*. I do not like bugs." Her tone was flat and emphatic. "At all."

"Then the jungle ain't gonna be your friend, sweetheart," Tate said with a chuckle.

They moved into the thick canopy of trees, and immediately, the temperature became more humid, the air muggy and moist. Clinging foliage and dense vegetation blocked the sun, but shafts of light found their way through gaps in the trees, making the dew sparkle on the colorful flora that cropped up all over the area.

And everything was so damn noisy. Mosquitoes buzzing past Tate's ears, a macaw squawking from somewhere high in the trees, the unmistakable bark of a spider monkey followed by a sudden rustling of branches. The jungle was a whole other world, a living, breathing entity pulsing with life and activity.

A sense of peace washed over Tate, ironic considering that danger lurked in every corner, from the decaying matter underfoot to the trees up above and everything in between.

He unzipped his duffel and grabbed a few necessities, including a razor-sharp machete, a handgun, his favorite Bowie knife and his trademark M-16 rifle.

"Planning for an assault?" Eva asked wryly.

"Always." After a beat, he removed a 9 mm from the bag and extended it to her. "Here. We might as well both be prepared."

She looked surprised, but handled the gun with ease as she checked the clip then stuck the weapon beneath her waistband at the small of her back.

Tate sheathed his knife, shoved the H&K in his belt and

slung the strap of his rifle over one shoulder. The machete he kept on hand.

"No mosquito netting," he muttered, as he peered into the duffel. Damn. Prescott must have forgotten to shove it into the go bag. Ah, well. He'd remembered the bug repellent, at least.

Tate quickly transferred the remaining contents of the duffel into his backpack, then shoved the duffel beneath a pile of rotting palm fronds; he'd only needed the bag to carry and conceal his weapons. Now it was time to travel light.

Palming the handle of his machete, he stood up and appraised Eva, pleased by what he saw. Her jeans would protect her from the bugs, and she could put on the white button-down tied around her waist if her arms started to get bitten. Her hiking boots were sturdy—he'd checked back at the fort—and that hat ought to protect her from the sun.

He gave a satisfied nod. "Ready?"

She nodded back.

"Good. We'll follow the river," he said briskly, his boots crunching over the dense undergrowth that made up the jungle floor.

Hope lit in her blue eyes. "If we're sticking to the river, why not just raft it?"

"Too risky. The river patrols have increased since Cruz went underground. Every member of the military is hunting him."

She sighed. "Fine. Then let's go. I want this to be over as soon as possible." As if to punctuate that, she slapped the mosquito that had the misfortune of landing on her neck and flicked the dead insect away with a grimace.

"Stay behind me," he ordered.

"I plan on it. In fact, if we get attacked by a crazed

monkey or something, I'm fully prepared to use you as a human shield."

A laugh escaped his mouth, and he quickly had to berate himself for it. Eva was gorgeous—no denying that. She was also far more intelligent than he'd previously thought, not to mention entertaining, thanks to that wry sense of humor.

But she was still a potential enemy.

He needed to remember that before he did something stupid—such as starting to actually *like* the woman.

They traveled at a vigorous pace for the next several hours. Tate used the machete to hack a crude path in the vegetation, while Eva trailed after him. To her credit, she didn't complain once during the trek, except to voice her annoyance with the relentless mosquitoes that refused to let up.

Tate could hear the river from the east, water gurgling and lapping the riverbank, but he didn't stick too close to it. He set a parallel course, one that kept them hidden in the event a river patrol cruised by. He and Eva stopped only to refill their canteens at a freshwater pool they happened upon, then scarfed down a couple of MREs while they waited for the purification tablets to do their job and make the water safe to drink.

By the time the sun dipped toward the horizon line, they'd made damn good time, and he was pleased with their progress. Eva didn't seem to be tiring, which impressed the hell out of him.

"You're in good shape," he remarked, as he hacked away at the low-hanging vines blocking his path.

"I work out at night when Rafe is asleep." She paused. "I don't sleep much. Especially not since Istanbul."

He used the blade of the machete to shove aside some moss-covered branches; you never used your hands if you knew what was good for you, as there were lots of nasty surprises in all that greenery.

"What happened in Istanbul?" he asked carefully.

"Two of Hector's men—"

The jungle drowned out the rest of her reply. Screaming monkeys, a breaking branch, the swoosh of wings as a macaw soared right above their heads.

Eva's soft laughter broke through the din. "Noisiest place on earth, huh? I can barely hear myself think. Anyway, as I was saying, two of Hector's men tracked me to the house I rented in Istanbul."

"Did they hurt you?"

"Almost. They broke down the door while I was feeding Rafe his dinner. They were armed, and they lunged at us. I grabbed Rafe and ran into the bedroom at the back of the house. I found my gun, and...and when they burst into the room, I fired." Her voice shook. "I unloaded the entire clip."

Tate halted, lowering his machete as he turned to face her. The torment in her eyes was hard to miss, and he noticed that her hands were trembling.

"I murdered two men," she said softly.

He let out a breath. "You were defending yourself and your son."

"But they weren't trying to kill us." Agony clung to her tone. "They were hired to bring me to Hector. They wouldn't have hurt me."

"Taking you somewhere against your will *is* hurting you. You did what you needed to do to survive."

Bitterness slashed across her face. "Is that how I should justify it?"

He shrugged. "Justify it however you like. All I'm saying is, you didn't murder two men in cold blood, Eva. You can let yourself off the hook."

"I've tried." Her teeth dug into her bottom lip. "He didn't

see it. Rafe, I mean. I shoved him under the bed just before the men burst into the room, but he heard the gunfire and…he must have heard their screams."

"He's three. I doubt he can truly grasp what happened that day."

"He has nightmares about it."

"They'll go away."

"You really believe that?"

*No.*

"Sure," he said lightly, before taking a step forward. "Let's keep moving."

She followed him without protest, sticking close as they forged a path through the jungle. "How come you don't have any kids?" she asked.

"Never wanted any."

"Why not?"

"Just not interested."

A branch snapped overhead, and Tate immediately looked up, seeking out the source of the disturbance. Critters had a habit of dropping right on top of your head out here. The way he saw it, if you weren't alert, you deserved whatever you got.

"Don't want the responsibility, huh?" Her voice held a note of amusement.

"I'm fine with responsibility, sweetheart." He paused. "I don't think I'd be much of a role model for a kid, okay?"

Now she sounded surprised. "Army captain, black ops supersoldier…you're like a real-life hero. Kids eat that stuff up."

Discomfort welled in his chest, and he was glad Eva was behind him so she couldn't see his face. He suspected his expression was as broken and empty as the rest of him. With Will gone, he had absolutely no reason to pretend anymore. Pretend to give a damn, pretend he had any humanity left.

Truth was, he'd shut down a long time ago, but he'd been putting up a pretense for his little brother's sake. Now there was nothing stopping him from embracing the anger burning inside him, nothing to stop him from giving the finger to a world that had constantly and unfailingly turned its back on him.

"I'm no hero," he said gruffly. "And I wouldn't wish my own company on any child."

Her tone softened. "I wasn't sure I'd be a good mother, either, but after I had Rafe, those maternal instincts just reared up out of nowhere. He's made me a better person, I think. He's my entire life now."

Tate chopped at some vines, then ducked through the opening he'd created. "Your entire life, huh? That can't possibly be healthy. No room for a man in your life?"

"Nope."

"What about in your bed?"

"What about it?"

He couldn't control the husky note in his voice. "You don't get lonely sometimes, Eva? Late at night, when you're lying alone in bed?"

"No." He couldn't see her face, but he felt the heat of her gaze on his back. "Why, you offering to relieve some of my loneliness?"

A bolt of arousal sizzled down his spine and settled in his groin. Damn, just the thought of burning the sheets with this woman got him harder than concrete.

"Because if so, I'd have to decline," she went on. "I kind of prefer it when the men in my bed actually like and trust me. Otherwise, it feels like—"

A high-pitched shriek sliced through the air.

"Holy hell, what was *that*?" Eva burst out. She slapped

her shoulder in a panic and proceeded to hop around as if the ground was on fire. "What was that *sound?* What the frickin' *hell?*"

Tate instantly drew her to his side and dragged her a few yards away. He ran his hands up and down her torso in a hurried inspection, then examined her shoulder, lifting up the sleeve of her T-shirt to take a look.

"Lucky girl," he told her. "You didn't get bitten."

"Bitten by what? What was that shrieking noise?"

She looked so utterly freaked out he stifled a laugh. "Bullet ants."

"That five-inch thing that pounced on my shoulder while screaming like a banshee was an *ant?*"

"Yes, and five inches is an overexaggeration—those things only grow about an inch or so. And for some messed-up reason, they make that noise when they attack you." Satisfied she'd been spared, he dropped his hands from her shoulders and took a step back. "You're damn lucky. Bullet ant bites are painful as hell."

She shuddered in revulsion. "Oh, my God. Why do insects like that exist? *Why?* And don't give me the whole food-chain, circle-of-life crap. I understand that everything needs to eat, okay?" Another shudder overtook her curvy frame. "Oh, man, I can't erase this creeped out goose-bumpy feeling."

This time he laughed out loud. "Wow. You weren't kidding about hating insects."

"I never kid about bugs. Ever." She sighed, then removed her hat so she could fix her ponytail, which had come undone during her meltdown.

As he watched her, Tate's hands tingled with the urge to slide through all that long black hair. To twine those silky strands around his fingers and angle her head so he could lean down and capture that lush mouth with his. A groan lodged in his throat as he imagined that moment when their tongues would meet, when Eva would arch her back and press her firm breasts against his chest while he kissed her, slowly, deeply, until she was begging him to take her.

"Why are you staring at me?"

He met her gaze. Noticed the knowing gleam in her blue eyes, mingled with the flicker of unease. "You know why," he said huskily.

Her lips parted in surprise. She swallowed, her delicate throat dipping.

Silence stretched between them, but their eyes stayed locked. His pulse kicked up a notch, and he cursed himself for it. What was he doing, standing there having eye sex with the woman?

Disgusted with himself, he broke the eye contact and shifted his grip on the machete. "It'll be dark soon," he muttered. "Let's find a place to set up camp."

She nodded a few times, as if trying to clear her head. "Sure."

They didn't say much as they resumed walking, and it was another mile or so before Tate found a suitable place to set up camp. Close enough to the river that he could hear its soft babbling, but far enough that they weren't in danger of being swept away in a flash flood. He cleared some of the undergrowth with the machete, probing beneath the snarled jungle floor with a branch to make sure the area was free of snakes and other menaces.

As he strung up the hammock, he felt Eva's blue-eyed gaze on him, and finally glanced over to frown at her. "What?"

"Did you only bring that one hammock?"

"Yes." He arched an eyebrow. "Something wrong with that?"

"So we're, um, sharing it?"

"Uh-huh. Unless you'd prefer to sleep on the ground with the snakes, ants, scorpions, termites and pretty much any other insect or reptile you can name."

Her cheeks took on a green tinge. "Oh. Well. Then I'd *love* to share the hammock with you, Tate."

He fought another burst of laughter. Damn it. This woman was testing his control—each time he raised his guard, she knocked it right down with her dry remarks, or her self-deprecating smiles, or her fear of bugs. She was not at all what he'd thought she was, and she'd been throwing him for a loop from the moment she'd walked into the back room of the cantina. A woman as gorgeous as this one often tended to be arrogant, strutting around with a pampered sense of entitlement. Either that, or ditzy and self-indulgent. But Eva was none of those things, which made it all the harder not to like her.

"I'm allotting us four hours of shut-eye," he said once the hammock was secured.

If it was up to him, they'd operate on less sleep than that, but Eva's fatigue was evident, even if she wouldn't admit it. She had dark circles under her eyes and smudges of dirt on her cheeks, and when she dropped her backpack on the ground and reached up to massage her shoulders, Tate knew the heavy load had gotten to her.

"I'm going to wash up in that stream we just passed." She tossed her hat on top of her bag, then lifted her arms over her head for a deep stretch. "I can't sleep if I feel grimy."

She bent down and rummaged through her pack, removing her canteen, a washcloth, and a fresh shirt and socks. "Also, would it have killed you to pack some tissues or something?" she asked. "I have to pee again and I really don't like using leaves."

He rolled his eyes. "The texture is too rough for your delicate parts?"

"No, I spend too much time examining the leaf to make sure there's no bugs on it."

He laughed and reached into his own bag for the package of tissues he'd noticed in the front zipper pocket. When he tossed the packet to Eva, she looked at him as if she'd won the lottery.

Then she scowled. "You had these the entire time? Holding out on me, were you?" She moved toward the trees before he could respond. "I'll just be a few minutes."

She'd just taken a step when Tate saw the flash of brownish-gold amid the greenery.

"Eva, stop," he hissed.

"But I want to wash up before it gets any darker—"

"Eva. *Don't move.*"

The lethal pitch to his voice didn't go unnoticed.

Eva froze on command, and her sharp intake of breath revealed the exact moment her gaze collided with the broad head and rounded snout of the pit viper dangling right in front of her face.

# Chapter 7

Eva was actually pretty proud of herself. She wasn't screaming her lungs out. Wasn't running for her life. Wasn't throwing up or passing out.

Then again, she wasn't doing any of those things because she was utterly and completely paralyzed with fear.

Her gaze locked with the hypnotic, catlike pupils of the deadly snake eyeing her down. The bushmaster—she recognized the species from the survival course she'd taken before joining the relief foundation five years ago. With its brownish-pink coloring and black diamond-shaped markings along its back, the deep pits on either side of its face and a terrifyingly long body, the snake was undeniably beautiful, in a predatory kind of way. The shape of the head gave its deadliness away—slightly triangular, a clear warning that this species was poisonous.

Her heartbeat accelerated, thudding out a frantic rhythm against her ribs. She was tempted to drop the canteen and clothes she was holding and run like hell, but she knew pit vipers were deceptively fast. And their bites were fatal. One wrong move and she'd be full of snake venom.

"Stay still, sweetheart."

Tate's voice was low, barely a whisper.

She opened the corner of her mouth a crack. "Should I try to grab it and whip it away?" she whispered back.

"God, no." She heard a soft rustling, and then, "I mean it, Eva. Don't move a goddamn muscle. If I miss…"

"Miss what? What are you—"

Something hissed right by her ear, slicing the air with a high-pitched whistling sound and ruffling the loose strands of hair at the side of her face.

A second later she heard a sharp smack and the viper was gone.

Shock, relief and adrenaline streamed through her blood, bringing a rush of light-headedness. Gaping, she stared at the wooden handle of the knife that had pinned the bushmaster to the tree—by its head. The snake was still alive, body undulating wildly and fangs exposed as it thrashed around, but the blade of Tate's knife made it impossible for it to escape.

"Go wash up." Tate came up beside her with another knife in his hand.

Her pulse continued to shriek in her ears. "Wh-what?"

"Wash up. I'll take care of this."

She felt dazed, unable to do more than just gawk at him. After a beat, he made a frustrated sound and forcibly moved her away from the tree. He cupped her chin with one strong hand, his thumb sweeping over the edge of her jaw. "Go to the stream and get cleaned up, Eva."

His rough command snapped her out of her fear-induced trance and suddenly she became aware of Tate's hand on her face. Her pulse raced, and this time it had nothing to do with fear or lingering adrenaline and everything to do with the sexy man standing so close to her. With his square jaw covered with dark stubble and his green eyes glittering with fortitude, he made a seriously imposing picture.

She sucked in a breath, only to inhale the spicy, masculine scent of Tate. Wow. Even after trekking through the jungle all day, the man smelled great.

*Uh, deadly poisonous snake pinned to a tree?*

The reminder nearly made her laugh. "Okay. Um. I'll be right back," she said, while the pit viper continued to thrash on the moss-covered tree bark.

Avoiding Tate's eyes, she stumbled through the trees toward the small freshwater pool ten yards away, where she stripped off her sweat-soaked tee and kicked off her boots. She quickly splashed water on her face, then washed her hands, feet and underarms before slipping into a loose long-sleeved shirt and fresh socks. She went to the loo with a tissue gratefully on hand, then filled up her canteen and dropped an iodine tablet inside to purify the water.

By the time she returned to the clearing, she felt calm and relaxed, her near-death experience with that pit viper nothing but an unpleasant memory. She glanced at the tree. No snake. Then she glanced warily at Tate, who was lying in the hammock with his arms propped behind his head.

"What'd you do to the snake?" she asked, as she shoved her things into her pack.

"Cut his head off and gave him a nice burial."

She blanched. So that was why he'd sent her away. He hadn't wanted her to see him brutally decapitate that poor fellow.

Tate gazed up at the green canopy high above their heads. Barely any light got through the trees, and everything around them was bathed in shadows now.

"No fire?" she said.

"No point. We'll be on the move again in a few hours." His voice became husky. "Better come up. It'll be pitch-black soon."

She knew he was right; it got dark scary-fast in the jungle.

She scampered over, then hesitated as she stared at the big body sprawled in the netting of the hammock.

With a knowing, slightly mocking smile, he shifted and held out his arm.

There was a lot of swaying and rustling as she climbed in next to him. The swinging motion had her falling against Tate's broad chest, and his arm quickly came out to steady her. His strong grip and warm touch caused her heart to do an annoying somersault.

It took a few moments to find a comfortable position—she ended up sandwiched next to Tate, her cheek pressed against one of his defined pecs, while his arm wrapped tightly around her.

By the time they were settled, darkness had completely fallen. She couldn't see a foot in front of her, and as Tate covered them with a thermal blanket, she was grateful to be above the treacherous ground and sheltered in Tate's arms.

After a moment's reluctance, she draped her arm over his chest and snuggled closer, taking advantage of his body heat and the comfort of his body. When her fingers brushed over something cold and hard, she lifted her head with a frown. "Are you holding your gun?"

"Yes. I never sleep without one."

His revelation was disconcerting, but oddly comforting at the same time.

"By the way, you did good today," he added.

She couldn't hide her surprise. "How so?"

"You kept up with my pace, you didn't complain, you wolfed down that MRE like it was a juicy steak."

She smiled in the darkness. "Eating it quickly was the only way not to focus on how bad it tasted."

"Regardless, you impressed me today. You didn't strike me as a fan of the outdoors."

The answering rush of warmth that rippled through her was unwelcome. She shouldn't care what this man thought of her. Yet…she did. For some reason, his approval and respect meant a lot.

"I love the outdoors," she confessed. "So do my parents. When I was growing up, we rented this cabin in Vermont every summer, right in the middle of nowhere, and we'd spend all day fishing and hiking and swimming. And Dad would take a few weeks off work every year so the two of us could go on an adventure together. An African safari, fishing trips, mountain climbing—pretty much whatever kept us outside." Her voice cracked. "When I was pregnant, Dad used to talk about all the adventures he wanted to have with his grandson…."

She trailed off, the lump in her throat making it difficult to continue. Lord, she missed her parents. She called or emailed them whenever she thought it was safe, but she hadn't seen them since Rafe was just a baby.

"What do your parents do?" Tate asked.

"Dad's a lawyer, he mostly does tax and estate stuff. Mom was an event planner, but she does volunteer work now, planning charity benefits, running committees, that sort of thing." She smiled in the darkness. "Neither of them was happy when I decided to help out with the San Marquez relief efforts after college. I'm an only child, so they've always been a tad overprotective."

"Must be nice," he murmured. "Having someone worry about you."

Eva saw right through the flippant response. The sad,

haunted note in his voice told her he was thinking about his own upbringing.

After a beat of hesitation, she said, "You told me about your father, but what about your mom? Why wasn't she around to stop your dad from…from hurting you?"

Now his voice dripped with bitterness. "My mother left when I was seven, but by then, we were all happy to see her go. She had a raging heroin problem, OD'd twice right in front of me and survived both times. I'm sure she's dead by now."

Each word was spoken in a flat monotone, and Eva's heart ached. She suddenly remembered a detail from the background search she'd conducted on him, but wasn't sure if she ought to bring it up. Tate hadn't volunteered that piece of information, after all.

Then again, he hadn't volunteered *any* information since she'd met him.

"Your basic file, the one I was able to access, mentioned you had a younger brother," she said carefully.

She immediately felt him stiffen.

When he didn't respond, she raised herself up again and studied his face. She couldn't make out his expression in the darkness, but the tight line of his mouth revealed a lot. "The file said he died."

A muscle in his jaw twitched. "Did it say how he died?"

"In the line of duty."

The low, cheerless laugh that slipped from his throat sent a cold shiver up her spine. "That's not true, is it?" she said.

"No, it's true. Technically."

"So he *did* die in the line of duty?"

"He was murdered." Three words, popping out in harsh bursts like bullets from a pistol.

Eva's breath caught. "Oh. How did—" Something suddenly clicked. "Hector. Hector killed your brother, didn't he, Tate?"

He didn't respond.

"That's why you're so set on killing him," she said slowly. "I knew your reasons for wanting Hector dead had to have been personal, but I wasn't able to find any connection between the two of you. I'm right, aren't I? He's responsible for murdering your brother."

"If you say so." His evasive tone gave nothing away, and yet told her everything.

"The American government was providing assistance to San Marquez in dealing with the ULF. Your unit was sent here, wasn't it? That's how you encountered Hector. It all makes sense now." She furrowed her brows. "Except for one thing—why are you in hiding now? What happened after you left the military? Or maybe I should be asking, what happened to *make* you leave the military?"

"Anyone ever tell you that you ask a lot of questions?"

Her eyes were beginning to adjust to the darkness, and she was able to make out the amused glimmer in his mossy-green gaze. "Anyone tell you that you don't provide a lot of answers?"

"I'm not in the habit of confiding in strangers."

"I don't think you confide in *anyone,* strangers *or* friends."

"True," he said, relenting.

A smile tickled her lips. "Well, I don't see the harm in telling me, considering you already think I'm here to lure you out of hiding."

His eyes narrowed. "Who says I think that?"

"Oh, come on, of course you do. That's why you don't trust me. A part of you suspects I'm an agent sent by the government to bring you in. Which is kind of absurd, because if I was supposed to arrest or kill you, wouldn't I have done it by now? And why would I bring my three-year-old son along on the assignment? Face it, Tate, your theory doesn't hold up. You have no reason to doubt me."

*Liar.*

All right, that wasn't entirely true. She'd kept a very huge detail from him when she'd solicited his help, but she refused to dwell on the lie she'd told. Besides, the fact that Hector was the father of her son had nothing to do with this mission. She and Tate *both* wanted Hector dead, and they each had their own reasons for it. So what if she'd given Tate a fake motive by claiming Hector had killed Rafe's father? As long as their endgames aligned, wasn't that all that mattered?

She'd never been a fan of the "ends justifies the means" mentality, but right now she was its biggest advocate. And no matter how guilty she felt about lying to the man who'd agreed to help her, she hadn't been able to take the risk that he'd turn her down, which he might've done if he'd known the truth.

Now, after realizing that Hector had killed Tate's brother, she was even more certain of her decision to tell that little white lie. She'd been romantically involved with the man who'd murdered Tate's brother. She'd given birth to that man's son, for Pete's sake.

Tate would probably kill *her* if he found out.

"You raise a good point." His grudging voice drew her from her thoughts.

"So you don't think I'm a government agent anymore?"

"I didn't say that." He shrugged, and the hammock swung a little. "But if you *are* government, my reasons for hiding out wouldn't be a surprise, so I guess there really ain't much harm in telling you."

With a pleased grin, she lay back down and settled her

cheek against his chest, but when Tate didn't speak immediately, she didn't push him.

She listened to the racket of the jungle instead. Even at night, the noise levels didn't abate by much. The clicking of insects as they scuttled along the jungle floor, the harmonic buzzing of cicadas, the drone of insect wings, the croaks and bellows of nearby amphibians. It was kind of peaceful, as long as she didn't focus too much on the bug noises, which reminded her that she was surrounded by, well, *bugs*.

"People want me dead."

His raspy confession brought a mock gasp to her lips. "No, really? Here I thought you were hiding out in Mexico for the fun of it."

"You know, your sarcasm doesn't make me want to confide in you."

"Sorry. Go on."

He let out a strangled laugh. "Anyway, for some reason I haven't been able to determine, my own government wants to kill me."

Her brows knitted in confusion. "You really have no clue why?"

"None. All I know is that it's related to the last op my unit was involved in."

"Which was?"

He hesitated for a long moment, then cursed under his breath. "Hell, no point in worrying about security clearance anymore, huh?" he said in a wry voice. "We went in to rescue a hostage. Richard Harrison, an American doctor who was doing research at a small medical clinic in the mountains. The ULF ambushed the village and kept the doc captive. They tried to negotiate with the U.S.—they'd release the doc if we called off the alliance between our governments."

Eva wasn't surprised—the ULF made no secret of the fact that they resented American interference in San Marquez's affairs. "But rather than negotiate, the States sent your unit instead," she guessed.

"We were ordered to extract the doc, but he was already dead when we got to the village. So were all the villagers."

Her lips tightened. "Hector?"

"Yep." He paused. "So we went home for debriefing, and a couple months later, nearly every man on my unit was dead, all from various bogus causes. When someone tried to blow my head off out on the street in broad daylight, I contacted Stone and Prescott and we got the hell out of Dodge."

As he went silent, Eva chewed on the inside of her cheek, trying to make sense of everything he'd told her. A monkey howled from somewhere in the tree tops, and its cry was answered by several matching wails.

"I don't get it," she finally said.

"Join the club."

"You have *no* idea why they want you guys dead?" She chewed on her bottom lip in thought. "Did you see something you weren't supposed to? Hear something?"

"I don't have a goddamn clue, Eva. All I saw in that village was a hundred dead bodies, burned to a crisp."

She flinched at the gruesome image he brought to mind. "Well, maybe—"

"Maybe it's time we go to sleep," he cut in, an edge to his voice.

She closed her mouth, then opened it to release a heavy sigh. "Fine."

She probably shouldn't push her luck, anyway. Tate had revealed more in the past five minutes than he had in the two days she'd known him. Might as well leave it at that and try again tomorrow.

*Try again?*

The puzzled voice in her head raised a good question. Why was she going out of her way to get to know Tate? Why did she care about his past or his motives or the reason he lived as if he had a target painted on his forehead?

All she needed to know about the man was that he was going to help her get rid of Hector.

Shifting, she tried to get comfortable again, but no matter where she put her head or arms or legs, she was still plastered against Tate like plastic wrap. His intoxicating scent, pure man, teased her senses, and the rock-hard chest beneath her palm was pretty much inviting her fingers to stroke it. Resisting the urge, she curled those fingers into a tight fist and slid her hand down to his belly so she wouldn't have to feel those defined pecs rippling beneath her fingers. But his washboard abs were just as tempting, and her hand being so close to his waistband meant her forearm now rested directly on his groin.

Which boasted the unmistakable bulge of arousal.

Heat scorched her face at the same time Tate's mocking voice broke the silence. "Are you finished feeling me up?"

"I wasn't feeling you up. I was just trying to get comfy," she sputtered.

"Uh-huh."

"I was," she insisted. Then she felt a spark of irritation. "And why am I the one defending myself? You're the one lying here with a *boner*. Jeez, Tate."

His husky laughter increased her annoyance. "Sweetheart, I'm a man. A man who's lying in a hammock with a beautiful woman—what else did you expect would happen?"

Eva swallowed. "You think I'm beautiful?"

He paused before releasing a ragged breath. "Yes. I think you're beautiful." His tone became sardonic once more. "So now, unless those busy hands of yours plan on unzipping my pants, let's get some damn sleep."

Desire pulsed between her legs, hot and persistent. His words were a challenge if she'd ever heard one, and for a moment, she almost did exactly what he'd taunted her about—unzipped his cargo pants, slid her hand inside and discovered if he was as big and hard down there as he was everywhere else.

But she fought the impulse, bringing her hand up and tucking it against her own belly.

"Good-night it is," he murmured wryly.

Gulping, Eva slammed her eyes shut and tried to pretend that she was alone. That she wasn't sharing a hammock with this sexy, magnetic man. That he didn't intrigue her. Didn't excite her. Didn't make her feel the first spark of attraction she'd felt in years.

She didn't want a man in her life, or her bed. Maybe someday, once she got the bitter taste of Hector out of her mouth, and only if she met someone worthy of her heart. Someone kind and gentle, someone she could trust with her son, someone who would *love* her son. Tate was neither kind nor gentle, and from the way he'd dismissed Rafe on sight, he would never be a part of her son's life.

As those thoughts cemented themselves in her head, the little pulses of lust shooting up and down her body dissipated, much to her relief. With Tate's steady heartbeat thudding against her ear, she fell into a soundless sleep.

He wanted Eva Dolce.
*No, you don't.*
Ah, hell. He did. He really, really wanted her.
*Dangerous thoughts, buddy.*
As one conflicting thought after the other wreaked havoc on his brain, Tate tried to focus on chopping a path

through the jungle. With all the voices throwing opinions around in his head, he was beginning to feel like a damn schizophrenic.

Not to mention that last night had done a real number on his groin—his entire lower body actually *ached,* though four hours in a hammock with a sexy woman plastered against him would do that to a man. He'd been lying with a hard-on the entire time, and it was a miracle he'd gotten any sleep at all.

When they'd woken up before dawn and set off, he'd hoped that the novelty of Eva would wear off on the second day of their journey, or that the attraction would taper to a level he might be able to tolerate, but that had been damn naïve thinking on his part.

As they walked at a brisk pace, he was painfully aware of Eva. The way she walked. The sound of her breathing. The squeaky little noise she made whenever a mosquito flew in her face.

Christ, he wanted her.

*No, you don't.*

Stifling a sigh, he hacked at a particularly annoying vine that refused to get out of his way. The machete finally sliced the thick diameter and the vine hit the jungle floor at the same time a flash of lightning lit up the sky.

"Oh, crap," Eva mumbled. "This is *not* gonna be fun."

Her words proved to be prophetic. Within seconds, the patches of sky that were visible through the trees turned black, a boom of thunder cracked in the air, and the rain began to fall in earnest.

It happened so fast neither of them had time to do anything but exchange rueful grins.

That reaction alone upped his opinion of the woman. Rather than shriek about getting soaked, Eva seemed completely unruffled. In fact, as sheets of rain drenched her clothes and plastered her hair to her head, she started to laugh, the melodic sound mingling with the loud pattering of the rain.

As the thunder rolled and the treetops shook, he grabbed her hand and pulled her toward a cluster of enormous banyan trees. They ducked beneath the dangling moss-covered branches and rootlike shoots, which provided instant shelter from the downpour.

Tate leaned his rifle against the tree trunk, stuck his machete in the dirt and wiped the moisture from his face with the back of his hand.

"Next time we decide to kill a man, let's do it during the dry season," Eva remarked in a facetious tone.

He had to chuckle. "Agreed."

She lifted her ponytail and wrung the water out of it, then shoved wet black strands off her forehead and tucked them behind her ears.

He couldn't help but admire her beautiful features, perfectly symmetrical, flawless, a touch exotic thanks to her olive coloring and sparkling cobalt-blue eyes.

"You're doing it again," she murmured.

"Doing what?"

"Staring at me. Every time we've taken a rest break today, you've been staring at me."

"Have I?" His voice came out hoarse, seductive, and he had to clear his throat before continuing. "Well, we already established that I think you're beautiful. I guess I like looking at you."

Surprise registered on her face. "I don't understand you."

"How so?"

"Since we met, you've made it clear you don't trust me. And yet…"

Her cheeks grew pink, but he couldn't be sure if it was

due to embarrassment or the humidity thickening the air. "And yet what?" he pressed, his voice low.

"You act like you want to go to bed with me," she murmured. "You would have done it last night, wouldn't you? If I'd given you the green light?"

Arousal, hot, thick and relentless, traveled down his body and hardened his cock. "Yes," he admitted.

"And that's what I don't get."

Her naïveté both surprised and appealed to him. "Oh, I see. You think sex and trust go hand in hand." When she nodded, he couldn't help but chuckle. "Oh, sweetheart, how wrong you are."

She frowned. "So you're saying you don't need to trust me in order to sleep with me?"

"That's exactly what I'm saying."

Eva fell silent, her gaze shifting from his face to the opening in the branches. She watched the rain hammer the vines and shrubs and decaying matter littering the jungle floor, looking perturbed as her teeth dug into her bottom lip.

"I couldn't do that," she said, her voice soft and distressed. "I can't sleep with a man I don't trust."

He took a step toward to her, bringing a wary glint to her eyes. "So if *I* gave *you* the green light, you would turn me away?"

Her breath hitched.

He moved even closer. Only a foot separated them. Her long-sleeved shirt was unbuttoned, so he had a clear view of the tight white tank top she wore beneath it. White wasn't a color you wanted to wear in the rain—in Eva's case, the wet fabric had become transparent, revealing her flesh-colored bra and the unmistakable puckering of her nipples.

"You're turned on," he said silkily, making no attempt to hide the focus of his gaze.

"I'm cold. From the rain."

"The rain is as hot as the air, sweetheart." Tate brought his hand to her cheek, enjoying the spark of heat that flared in her eyes.

His hand took on a life of its own. Even if he'd tried, he wouldn't have been able to stop himself from stroking Eva's smooth skin, from dragging his fingers to her mouth and tracing the seam of her lush lips. He didn't trust her, but damn, how he wanted her.

When he eliminated the final inches of distance between them and gripped her slender waist, her blue eyes widened.

"Tate." Her voice was throaty, lined with apprehension and…need.

It was that needy pitch that snapped the last thread of his control.

With a desperate growl, he took possession of her mouth and kissed her.

Christ, she tasted so damn good, and her body, lush and supple, felt like sheer heaven pressed against his. Curling one hand over her hip, he raked the other one up her body, grazing the side of one firm breast before traveling higher to cradle the back of her head.

He came up for air and searched her gaze, satisfied by the glaze of passion he glimpsed. Then he slanted his mouth over hers again and deepened the kiss, pushing his tongue inside without waiting for permission.

Eva's moan tickled his lips and quickened his pulse. Her hands clung to his shoulders, her blunt, unpolished fingernails digging into the fabric of his T-shirt and stinging his skin. When their tongues met, shock waves pounded into him, scorched his nerve endings and made him groan in desperation. Shoving his hands underneath her tank top, he stroked her flat belly, then moved higher to cup her breasts over her bra.

"Tate." His name left her lips, half a whimper, half a moan.

He couldn't remember ever being this hard. Ever wanting a woman this badly. Mindless with lust, he slid his hands out from under her shirt, brought them to her ass and hauled her up against him.

"Oh, *God,*" she choked out when her core came in contact with his unmistakable erection.

Her legs wrapped around his waist, hands clinging to his neck as Tate backed her into the trunk of the tree. Driving the kiss deeper, he rubbed his lower body into hers, thrusting his hips in time to the thrusts of his tongue in her mouth.

Screw it. Keeping his hands off this woman clearly wasn't gonna be an option. He craved her on a dark, primal level he couldn't explain, and nothing short of dying could stop him from claiming her.

No sooner had the last thought entered his head than his instincts began to hum.

Tate froze. His mouth lifted, hovering over Eva's lips.

"What's wrong?" she murmured. "Why did you—"

He pressed his index finger to her lips to silence her.

Cocking his head, he willed his heartbeat to steady, letting pure instinct take over. The rain had stopped—he'd been so consumed with lust he hadn't even noticed—but the abrupt silence wasn't the reason for his raised hackles.

Very slowly, he set Eva on her feet and peered through the tangled roots that surrounded them like a canopy. He didn't see anything out of sorts, but his ears compensated for what his eyes couldn't perceive.

He heard the same familiar noises that gave life to the jungle—monkeys and birds and insects, clicks and wails and hoots and squawks. Branches snapping and leaves rustling and wind blowing.

And footsteps.

"Son of a bitch," he hissed out, his arm snapping out to grab his rifle.

"What's going on?" Eva demanded.

"We've got company." With a grim look, he propped the rifle up on his shoulder. "Get down on the ground and stay here. Don't come out unless I tell you."

"Tate—"

Locked and loaded, he slid out and into the open—just as six armed men burst out of the brush.

They took one look at Tate and started shooting.

# *Chapter 8*

As a bullet missed his temple by an inch and a half, Tate hit the ground, rolled and took cover behind a gnarled tree trunk. The telltale *rat-tat-tat* of an assault rifle echoed in the air. Pieces of bark and branches flew over his head and landed on the ground with sharp smacks. The creatures that called this jungle their home didn't appreciate the sudden uproar—a chorus of bird cries joined the gunfire and created a deafening cacophony that made it hard for him to hear himself think.

His attackers were military. San Marquez military, to be precise, but not an elite unit, if their uncoordinated assault and disorganized formation were any indication. Bottom-of-the-totem-pole soldiers, then. Sent to…well, kill him, judging by the next round of bullets that slammed into the tree he'd taken cover behind.

Gritting his teeth, Tate raised his rifle and ducked out for a second, pulling the trigger to unload a round at his attackers. Two blue-and-gold uniforms went down, lifeless bodies tumbling to the twisted undergrowth. He didn't have time to high-five himself because the four men he *hadn't* hit were closing in on him.

He popped out again and sprayed bullets until his rifle clicked and emptied. Crap. Spare clips were in his backpack—which was sitting, oh, a yard away, with Eva, in the tree.

Looked as if he'd have to make do with the pistol. Dropping the rifle, he swiped the H&K from his waistband and took a steadying breath. Two more soldiers had gone down during his last sweep. Two remained, unless there was a second military unit somewhere, ready to attack on command.

Tate didn't question why these soldiers had been dispatched. All he knew was that they were a threat. To him. To Eva. And he'd be damned if a bunch of poorly trained grunts took him down before he got his shot at Cruz.

The gunfire had ceased. Only the sounds of the jungle remained now, to a civilian, anyway.

To Tate, the presence of the enemy was clear as a cloudless blue sky. Soft breathing, the swish of pant legs as the soldiers attempted to move soundlessly.

They were nearing the tree.

Adrenaline spiked in his veins. He tightened his grip on the pistol. Said a prayer. Then burst out from behind the tree—only to get his gun knocked right out of his hand by a soldier who turned out to be much closer than Tate had realized.

A gun fired, cracked in the air. He felt something hot whiz by his ear, which immediately began to ring, but despite the sudden loss of hearing, his equilibrium wasn't affected. Grunting, he brought his elbow to the jaw of the man who'd nearly shot his head off.

The soldier—lanky, black-haired and dark-skinned—made a guttural sound thick with pain and stumbled backward. Tate took advantage and did a leg sweep, knocking the soldier off balance. The man staggered, but before he could fall over, Tate grabbed him by the cuffs of his uniform shirt, spun him around and used him as a human shield.

The remaining soldier growled with fury as he watched his comrade absorb the impact of the bullets he'd been aiming at Tate.

*"Se va a morir!"* the man shouted. *You will die.*

Tate kept a steady grip on the dead soldier he still had in a chest lock. "I don't think so," he said coolly.

Before the enemy could react, he whipped the handgun from the holster secured to the lifeless man's hip and fired at the last surviving soldier.

He hit his intended mark—the soldier yelled in pain as the bullet sliced into his shoulder.

Tossing his human shield away, Tate lunged for the remaining man. He knocked the AK-47 out of the soldier's hand and tackled him to the ground. As the other man cursed and struggled, Tate pinned him down by jamming a knee into his chest and a forearm against his neck.

"Who sent you?" he demanded, speaking in Spanish so his demand didn't get lost in translation.

A pair of brown eyes shot daggers at him. "Screw you" was the harsh reply.

He bared his teeth in a mocking smile. "You want to live? Then you'd better answer the question."

This time he got a wad of spit that splashed his chin.

"Suit yourself." With a shrug, he pressed the barrel of his gun to the soldier's temple and pulled the trigger.

Silence.

For a split second, the jungle actually went eerily silent, as if someone had pressed Pause on a heavy-metal CD.

And then the play button clicked on, and the noise decibel returned to normal.

When he heard the unmistakable sound of leaves snapping beneath boots, he drew his weapon and bounced to his feet, but it was just Eva, stepping out from behind the long, dangling branches.

"That was…" Her gaze traveled over the six bodies strewn on the jungle floor. "Efficient."

Like Eva, he swept his gaze over the dead soldiers littering the ground. Taking them out had been no difficult feat; military training in San Marquez was far inferior to the rigorous training endured by members of the American armed forces, which was probably why the ULF rebels continued to wreak such havoc on the country—and why the San Marquez government had been relying more and more on its Western allies to help them contain this revolution.

Tate eyed the dead men again, one by one. Mediocre soldiers, sure, but damn good trackers. Not a surprise, seeing as this jungle was their native turf; they knew every square inch of the place, every leaf, every tree, every vine and speck of dirt.

"Were they following us the whole time?" Eva asked, her face going pale.

"They probably picked up our trail back at the road, but they were smart. They must have hung back and covered ground when we camped for the night." His jaw tensed. "They knew I'd sense them if they got too close, so they waited for a distraction, the right moment to close in."

"The rainstorm," Eva mumbled.

Suspicion clouded his face as he met her blue eyes. "How did they find us?" he asked in a low voice.

She blinked. "What? You just said—"

"I mean, how did they know we were on this island to begin with?"

Her dark brows drew together. "I don't know. Maybe someone spotted us at the port."

"That's what I suspect, but that means someone was on the lookout for us. *Expecting* us to show up." His eyes narrowed. "Why would anyone be expecting us, sweetheart?"

Exhaustion washed over her beautiful face. She'd been hugging her own chest since she'd stepped out of the tree, and her hands seemed to curl tighter over her upper arms.

"Who knew we were coming?" he demanded.

Her cheeks took on an ashen hue, and she began swallowing repeatedly. "Tate…"

He fixed her with a deadly glare. "Why were we expected?"

"I don't know," she stammered. Gulp. Gulp.

He moved even closer. "What's the matter, Eva? Why do you suddenly look so nervous?"

"I…"

Another gulp. Her cheeks grew paler. And then her hands dropped from her chest and he saw the bright spot of crimson on her left sleeve.

Blood.

She'd been shot.

"Tate, I don't feel—"

Her sentence died abruptly, and Tate lunged forward just in time to catch her as she fainted.

Someone was holding an open flame to her flesh.

Or at least, that was the only explanation Eva had for the excruciating burning sensation in her upper arm, for the pulses of hot agony and the feeling that someone was poking a knife underneath her skin.

When her eyelids fluttered open, she realized that was *exactly* what was happening.

Tate was *literally* digging through her flesh with a pair of tweezers.

As a wave of nausea scampered up her throat, she passed out like a light.

When she came to the next time, she got the foggy impression that Tate was threading a needle.

Cue the black dots flashing in front of her eyes.

The third time, she managed to stay conscious, which earned her a rueful smile from Tate. "See if you can pass out again, sweetheart. This is gonna hurt."

He was right. It did. In fact, it hurt so much she was actually quite stunned that she *didn't* pass out. Getting stitched up without a numbing agent was no picnic. Each time the needle sliced into her skin, she experienced a sharp throb and fiery pinch. Tears sprang to her eyes, but she didn't scream in pain. She bit her bottom lip instead, until she tasted the coppery flavor of blood in her mouth.

Unhinging her jaw, she glanced at Tate's intense green eyes and croaked out, "Am I going to live?"

"Yes. Doesn't seem to be any arterial damage. I got the bullet out and gave you a shot of antibiotics. You'll have to take a dose every six hours if you want to ward off infection."

She felt another painful pinch in her arm, and her stomach rolled.

Gulping down the rising queasiness, she shifted her gaze skyward and tried to distract herself by counting the veins on a leaf above her head. Tate cleaned and dressed the wound, taped the stark white bandage down with clear tape, and by the time he muttered a quick "All done," she was close to throwing up.

Stumbling to her feet only increased the nausea; pins

and needles pricked her hands, and her vision grew so blurry she had to blink several times before everything came back into focus.

"Sit down," Tate said roughly.

She drew in a slow breath, not answering him until she managed to fight the overwhelming need to empty the contents of her stomach.

"No. We should go," she insisted once the nausea passed. "We don't know if those soldiers called for backup before—"

She halted when she noticed that the six bodies were gone. For a second she wondered if she'd imagined the whole thing. Maybe nobody had rushed out of the trees. Maybe the bullet that had slammed into her upper arm while she'd been hiding had come from a rare breed of bullet-shooting monkey or something.

But no, Tate must have carried her away from the scene of the assault, because the tree they'd sought shelter under was gone, too, and that cluster of sweet-smelling orchids definitely hadn't been here before.

"Thank you," she said quietly. "I know the only reason you didn't leave me to die back there was because you need my help to find Hector, but I still appreciate it."

"That's not the only reason I didn't leave you."

For a second she thought he was implying it had something to do with the kiss. That hot, explosive kiss that had set fire to her body and robbed her of all common sense.

But the edge to his voice spoke otherwise. As did the suspicion clouding his green eyes.

Confused, Eva met his gaze head-on. "What is it?" she asked warily.

He hooked his thumbs in the belt loops of his cargo pants. "It's time we finished our conversation."

"And what conversation is that?"

"The one in which you explain why anyone would be expecting me to show my face in San Marquez." His jaw moved as if he were grinding his teeth together. "Who've you been in contact with?"

Shock traveled up her spine and slackened her jaw. "Nobody."

"Oh, sweetheart, please don't give me the wide-eyed innocence routine right now. I just killed six men and then performed jungle surgery on your damn arm when I could've just let you die."

"Then why didn't you?" she snapped. "Clearly you think I'm responsible for those soldiers ambushing us."

"Aren't you?"

Anger skidded up her spine. "No, I'm not. Obviously someone recognized one of us at the port and tipped off the military. Which makes no sense, because why would the San Marquez military be after either of us? You're being hunted by *our* government, and me? I've done nothing to piss off San Marquez. Besides, my uncle would never—"

He cut in sharply. "Your uncle? What are you talking about?"

"My uncle Miguel. He's the one who suggested I track you down."

The expression on Tate's face frightened her. So did the way he began pacing in front of her, one fist clenched to his side, the other hovering over the butt of the gun poking out of his waistband. He could draw that weapon in a nanosecond and blow her brains out, and from the rage burning in his eyes, she got the feeling that outcome wasn't so farfetched.

"You never told me about this *uncle*." He strode toward her, assuming an aggressive stance.

"It wasn't important," she said defensively. "Miguel is my mom's older brother. He lives in Merido. He had heard the rumors about a man asking about Hector, and he's the one who told me your name."

"Why would your uncle know my name?" Tate demanded, his voice colder than an Arctic ice cap.

She swallowed. The menace rolling off his big body sent a shiver up her spine. "Because he knows pretty much everything that goes on in his country." She licked her dry lips. "He's a general with the San Marquez army."

If the jungle weren't so damn loud, the silence that followed would have been of the hear-a-pin-drop variety.

A combative gleam ignited Tate's eyes, along with a dose of ire and a splash of betrayal. And then, before she could blink, he whipped up his gun and aimed it directly at her chest.

# *Chapter 9*

"What are you going to do, Tate? Shoot me?" Eva's blue eyes were heavy with resignation.

Tate clenched his teeth so hard his jaw hurt. Damn it. Goddamn it. This entire op had turned into one giant, screwed-up mess. The ambush, Eva getting shot, finding out her frickin' uncle was a frickin' *general*.

He knew without a shred of doubt that Eva's uncle had used her to lure Tate out of hiding. The only question was, why?

He had no beef with the San Marquez government, no connection to this godforsaken country aside from one botched mission that went down eight months ago. He'd been back to San Marquez a few times since, talking to rebels, asking around about Cruz, but that was no reason for the military to target him. If anything, the government ought to be *happy* he was here—they wanted the leader of the ULF dead as much as Tate did.

Really, giving Tate free rein to kill Cruz was probably this country's best course of action.

So why try to kill him just now? It made no sense. Unless...

"Well, are you going to shoot or what?" came Eva's flat voice.

His gun was still aimed at her heart, but after a second, he lowered the weapon and let out a savage expletive. Frustration punched him like a pair of fists. Nothing made sense. Absolutely *nothing* made sense.

In front of him, Eva's scowl faded, her expression taking on a sympathetic light. "Talk to me, Tate," she said softly. "Tell me what you're thinking."

He scrubbed a hand over the thick stubble darkening his jaw, unable to put a single thought into words. He walked over to his pack and grabbed the canteen, then took a long swig of water.

Eva's sigh hung in the late afternoon air. "My uncle couldn't have sent that unit after us. Well, technically he *could* have, but I don't think he did."

He raised his eyebrows in challenge. "Yeah, and why not?"

"Because I could have been killed, too. He knew that if you showed up in San Marquez, I would be traveling with you. Miguel would *never* put me in harm's way."

"You weren't," Tate said darkly. "Not a single one of those soldiers pointed their weapons at the tree where you were hiding, or made an attempt to go after you."

"Uh, hello?" She gestured to her bandaged arm. "I was *shot*."

"By accident," he replied with confidence. "I think you got hit by a stray bullet."

She huffed out a breath. "So what are you saying? That

my uncle *did* send that unit and ordered them not to hurt me, but to kill *you?*"

"That's exactly what I'm saying." He took another sip of water, then reached up to pinch the bridge of his nose, hoping to ward off an oncoming headache.

None of this made sense. If Eva's uncle, the *general,* had indeed dispatched the attack squad, then that could mean two things—either someone in San Marquez also wanted Tate dead, or the U.S. had enlisted San Marquez's help in tracking Tate down.

"The government here hates the ULF," he spoke up thoughtfully.

Eva looked confused. "Yes. They do. Hector has been on the most-wanted list for years now." She tilted her head. "Where are you going with this?"

"Your uncle, I assume he knows what happened to your kid's father?"

For a second, she looked even more confused, but then she gave a quick nod. "Right. Yes, Miguel knows about Rafe's dad."

"And he knows you want Cruz dead?"

Another nod, and then she offered a triumphant look. "See, that's another reason why Miguel couldn't have ordered that ambush. He knew I was going to you for help in getting rid of Hector, and Miguel hates the ULF as much as everyone else. He wouldn't have tried to stop us from killing Hector, which means he couldn't have tried to kill you just now."

Tate didn't share her conviction. "Are you sure old Uncle Miguel isn't playing you, sweetheart? That he's not on Cruz's take?"

Her blue eyes flickered with indignation. "No way. Miguel can't be bought."

Again, he didn't feel much conviction about that, but

he dropped the subject. Truth was, he didn't care if Eva's uncle was in cahoots with Cruz. He was more concerned about the notion that San Marquez was in cahoots with the Americans, and the ramifications of that.

"Damn it," he mumbled, so frustrated he felt like tearing his own hair out. "What the *hell* happened on that mission?"

He suddenly wished that Sebastian or Nick were here so they could talk this out, but they weren't, and his only sounding board was a woman he didn't trust.

At the thought of Seb and Nick, he muttered another curse, realizing it was now imperative he check in to make sure they hadn't had to deal with an ambush of their own.

Bending down, he rummaged through his pack until he found the satellite phone.

Eva immediately dashed to his side. "Are you calling Nick?" she demanded.

He nodded, dialing.

"I want to talk to my son."

Ignoring the request, he listened to the dial tone, growing uneasy the longer he waited. When Nick finally picked up with a quick "Prescott," Tate experienced a burst of relief.

"It's me," he said brusquely. "Checking in."

Nick sounded as relieved as Tate felt. "Is it done?"

"Not even close. Still making our way there. We hit a snag a while ago."

"What kind of snag?"

"The easily taken-care-of kind. Just wanted to make sure everything is all right on the home front."

"Everything's good here, Captain. Don't worry about us. Rafe is having a blast."

"And let me guess, Stone dumped all the babysitting duties on you."

"Something like that," Nick said in a rueful tone.

He chuckled before going somber. "Stay alert, Prescott. If you catch even a whiff of trouble, get yourselves and the kid outta there."

"Yes, sir."

"Now put the kid on the line. Eva wants to talk to him."

As a shuffling sound came over the extension, Tate handed the phone to Eva, who grabbed it as if it were a winning lottery ticket. She lifted the phone to her ear, and a moment later, absolute joy flooded her eyes.

"Hey, little man," she said, her voice softer and warmer than Tate had ever heard it. "Are you having fun?"

Keeping his ear on the one-sided conversation, he began gathering up the supplies he'd used to tend to Eva's arm and shoving them back in the first aid kit.

"Mommy misses you, too....I know, baby, I know.... You *did?*" Her tone grew incredibly amused. "Well, that's amazing! Maybe if you ask Nick very, very nicely, he'll take you again tomorrow."

Zipping up their packs, Tate stood up and headed over to Eva. He handed her the backpack, then made a gesture for her to wrap up the call.

"I've got to go now, little man." Her voice wobbled a little. "I'll be home soon, okay? And when I come back, I'll take you out for ice cream and then—" Now that voice downright cracked. "And then we'll go to New York to see your grandparents....Uh-huh....Yep....I promise. Love you, baby."

A moment later, she hung up and handed him the sat phone. He didn't miss the moisture that sparkled in her eyes and clung to her long, sooty eyelashes.

"The kid's doing good?" he said gruffly.

She reached up to wipe her eyes. "He sounds like he's having a lot of fun. Nick took him on a hike this morning, and apparently last night they ate hot dogs." A fresh batch of tears welled up. "I miss him."

Uncomfortable, he slid his arms into the straps of his backpack, then made sure all his weapons were secure. "We should go," he said.

Surprise flickered across her face. "You mean you want to go on?"

"As opposed to what?" he cracked. "Turn back, thus making these past few days a total waste?"

Without waiting for a response, he shifted his rifle to his other arm and found a more comfortable grip on the machete handle. Then he headed toward the trees.

"You can trust me, you know."

Soft and even, Eva's voice rang with confidence.

Slowly, Tate turned to face her. "Whatever you say, sweetheart."

"You can," she insisted.

Tightening the straps of her pack, she strode toward him, and he couldn't help but notice the way her firm breasts swayed beneath that tight white tank top. Her long-sleeved shirt was tied around her waist, and when he caught sight of the bloodstained sleeve, he bit back another string of obscenities, knowing he was reaching the end of his rope.

He had no frickin' idea what to make of this woman. An hour ago, he'd dug a *bullet* out of her flesh, then stitched her up while she'd been conscious, and now here she was, standing in front of him with her shoulders set high and her eyes glittering with conviction. He didn't doubt she was in pain—he could see it in her eyes, in the way she'd flinched when she'd slid her arm through the backpack strap. Yet she refused to give up or slow down, and that impressed the hell out of him.

"When I tracked you down, I knew you were hiding from something," Eva went on, "but I promise you, I had no idea what it was. I don't know why people want you dead, I don't know if my uncle used me to lure you out of hiding—but I highly doubt that—and I don't know who's working with who."

He rolled his eyes. "Sounds like you don't know much of anything."

"At the moment, no." Steel hardened her blue eyes, making them glint like cobalt. "But I'll find out."

He arched a brow. "Oh, really."

"I'm making you a promise right now, Tate. See this through with me, kill Hector for me, and in return, I'll do everything in my power to figure out why you're being hunted."

Doubt washed over him. "What, you think you'll hack into some magical spec-ops system and find a file labeled Why We Want to Kill Tate?"

She scowled at him. "Obviously it won't be that easy. And I can't promise that I'll be able to find the truth all wrapped up in a tidy little bow, but I will try."

Her assurances didn't do much to appease him. Eva might have tracked him to Mexico, but that didn't mean she was a miracle worker.

"So what do you say?" she asked. "Can we agree to trust each other, at least until we see this through? Like, 'no more pointing guns at me' kind of trust?"

An unwitting smile tugged at his mouth. "I'll see what I can do."

Swiveling on his heel, he started to set out once more, only for Eva's voice to stop him again.

"And, Tate?"

He half turned. "Yeah?"

"That kiss…" Her cheeks turned pink. "I'm not sure why you kissed me, but I don't want to play games."

Games? He decided not to mention that kissing her had

been the furthest thing from a game. He hadn't been trying to unnerve her, hadn't been manipulating her, hadn't been doing a damn thing but satisfying the craving that been plaguing him from the moment they'd met.

"So." She cleared her throat. "It can't happen again. I don't *want* it to. Okay?"

He swept his gaze over her tousled black hair, rumpled clothing and bandaged arm, and decided that he'd never seen a sexier sight.

But she was right.

That one kiss had distracted him to the point where he'd nearly allowed a military unit to blow his head off. No matter how much he craved Eva, it was time to drag his head out of the gutter. Focus on revenge rather than sex.

And keep his hands—and lips—to himself.

Twenty-four hours later, Eva exhaled with relief as she and Tate finally put the jungle behind them.

The little community they stumbled into was a welcome sight. A small marketplace took residence in the center of the village, and the smell of cooking meat and rich coffee wafted through the air. Everywhere she looked, she saw people milling around, talking, laughing, haggling.

A group of tanned, dark-haired women stood by a booth offering brightly colored scarves, holding plump, toothless-grinning babies in their arms. The sight evoked a pang of longing. Hearing Rafe's voice yesterday had been pure torture. She'd wanted so badly to abandon this mission and go home to her son, and it had taken all her willpower to refrain from doing that.

Rafe would never be safe as long as Hector lived. She simply had to remind herself of that every time she missed him.

Lifting the tin cup to her lips, Eva swallowed her coffee, enjoying the way the rich flavor teased her taste buds. Coffee was one of San Marquez's main exports; it was in high demand, in fact, which didn't surprise her one bit. The coffee here was to die for.

She would've liked to spend a few more hours in the village to rest, wash up, call her son again. But Tate wasn't having it. For the past twenty minutes, he'd been in deep conversation with one of the male villagers who owned the rusted pickup truck Tate had been eyeballing ever since they'd arrived.

Ten minutes later, when he strode over with a set of keys in his hand, she didn't even raise an eyebrow. Given his penchant for pushing people around, it wasn't at all surprising that he'd persuaded the driver to part with the truck. With his big, hard body and that intense glare he'd perfected, you felt compelled to give the man anything he wanted.

*Anything?*

The inner taunt made her frown. It also brought a jolt of heat straight to her core.

No, darn it. She had to quit thinking about that kiss. How firm his lips had been, the seductive swirl of his tongue, the strength of his arms as he'd lifted her up and rubbed his lower body all over her aching core.

A groan lodged in her throat. God, this was *not* the time to be lusting over a man. Especially one as ruthless and enigmatic as Robert Tate.

"Let's go," Mr. Ruthless and Enigmatic ordered. "I want to make it to Valero before nightfall."

Taking one last swig of coffee, she rose from the splintered wooden bench and followed Tate toward the pickup truck parked on the dirt several yards away.

"Why Valero?" she asked, wrinkling her forehead as she pictured the rustic mountain town. She'd spent some time in that area when she'd worked with the relief foundation, and she remembered all the towns around there being rather isolated.

"The associate I mentioned, Hastings, has a cabin there."

"So?"

"So we'll bunk there until I figure out the best way to infiltrate Cruz's camp. I won't go into this half-cocked."

Of course he wouldn't. Sliding into the passenger seat of the truck, she resigned herself to the possibility that it could still be days before they closed in on Hector. Tate would probably plan this attack to the last detail.

He turned the key in the ignition, and the truck's engine chugged to life. Since her seat belt was broken, Eva ended up bouncing and sliding in the front seat as Tate sped down the bumpy dirt road leading out of the village. Both the windows were rolled down, and the air was cooler here near the mountains. Still humid, but not as suffocating, and the breeze that met her face when she peered out the window was quite refreshing.

Tate expertly shifted gears as the manual transmission truck traveled along the two-lane road that eventually turned from dirt to gravel. "How's the arm?" he asked, shooting her a sidelong look.

She gingerly touched the bandage covering her upper arm, a tad impressed that she'd completely forgotten all about her bullet wound. She'd been diligently changing the dressing, shooting herself up with antibiotics and popping Tylenol every few hours to alleviate the pain, and the dull throb was nothing more than background noise now. She felt the pain only when Tate reminded her of it.

"It's fine," she replied. Then she grinned. "I've never been shot before. Now I'll have a cool story to tell Rafe." She paused. "When he turns eighteen, maybe."

Tate chuckled.

The husky sound made her heart skip a beat, a reaction for which she quickly berated herself. "I assume you've been shot before," she said wryly.

He shrugged. "A few times."

Shifting her gaze, she focused on his chiseled profile. "What made you decide to enlist in the army?"

"It was my ticket out."

She didn't have to ask *out of what.* "What about your brother?" she said carefully. "He was, what? Five years younger than you?"

The air in the pickup cab grew cold, something she hadn't thought possible in this sweltering South American climate. From the way Tate's stubble-covered jaw went tighter than a drum, he clearly didn't appreciate the mention of his younger brother.

"Yes," he said stiffly.

"So he would have been thirteen when you enlisted." She frowned. "Did you leave him behind?"

His head swiveled, and the look of revulsion on his handsome face caught her off guard. "You honestly think I'd leave my kid brother in the clutches of our abusive bastard of a father?"

Eva faltered. "I don't know what to think. I have no idea what you're capable of, Tate."

And yet she *didn't* believe he'd do that to his brother, which he confirmed with his next words. "He came with me when I left Boston," Tate muttered. "We had an aunt in North Carolina, and I convinced her to let Will stay with her while I went through basic training."

"That was nice of her."

He snorted. "Sure, Auntie Carol was a real saint. That arrangement cost me every penny I had."

Sorrow thickened her throat. "Your aunt demanded you pay her to take care of her own nephew?"

"Yep."

"What happened when Will came of age?"

"He enlisted, too." Tate's voice went hoarse. "When I was asked to head up a spec-op unit, I requested that Will be assigned to my team."

"So the two of you stayed close over the years."

"He's—*was*—the only person I've ever been close to."

She choked down a lump of sadness. "I'm sorry for your loss, Tate."

He offered another one of those careless shrugs, which she was beginning to see right through. "S'all good, sweetheart. I've made my peace with it."

An incredulous laugh slipped out. "No, you haven't. You're currently risking your neck just to exact revenge on the man who killed your brother."

He laughed right back. "Talk about the pot and kettle. You're here for revenge, too."

"Maybe," she agreed, "but I'm not pretending to be at peace with what I've lost."

"My brother's dead, Eva. I *have* made peace with that."

"Okay." She tilted her head. "What happens after you avenge Will? You go back to hiding?"

"Yes. At least until I figure out why I'm a wanted man."

The reminder had her biting her lip in thought. "I still don't get it," she murmured, her brain kicking up a gear. "You *must* have seen something during that mission. It's the only thing that makes sense."

"Nothing makes sense," he grumbled. "And I didn't see a damn thing."

"Tell me again what happened."

He released a sigh, his green eyes focusing on the road ahead. The brown peaks of the mountains loomed in the horizon, making a seriously pretty picture against the cloudless blue sky and shining yellow sun. But there was nothing pretty about any of this. What awaited them in those mountains was ugly. Very, very ugly.

"Tate?" she prompted when he still didn't answer.

"I already told you," he said in a tone overloaded with frustration. "When we infiltrated the camp, the doctor was dead and—"

"How did he die?"

"Bullet between the eyes, courtesy of Cruz's rifle."

She flinched. "Okay. And the villagers?"

"The rebels burned the bodies." His jaw set in a grim line. "Hopefully they all got bullets between their eyes, too. I'd hate to think that son of a bitch burned them alive."

Queasiness churned in her belly. Banishing the horrifying images Tate had brought to mind, she gulped down the acid lining her throat and said, "Why?"

"Why what?"

"Why would Hector kill the doctor and burn the villagers?"

"Who knows. Maybe he knew the U.S. would never negotiate with him and decided to cut his losses. Or maybe someone alerted him that a military force was closing in on him, so again, he decided to cut his losses. Trust me, I plan on asking Cruz the very same questions before I slit his throat."

A chill skidded up her spine. God, that cold, blunt statement terrified her, and as much as she hated doing it, she couldn't help but compare Tate to the very man he was itching to kill. Hector had no qualms about slitting throats, either, and just like Tate, he considered it his duty to exact revenge on his enemies.

The sad truth caused a sense of weariness to wash over her. Men were ruthless creatures. Honor, loyalty, vengeance, justice—sometimes she wondered if the male sex just used those concepts as excuses to be violent, tried to give some legitimacy to their primal desire to kill and destroy.

"And afterward?" she said quietly. "After you kill Hector and confront the people who want you dead, what will you do then?"

"Disappear."

"And live the rest of your life alone?"

"Yes."

"That's very sad, Tate."

He went quiet for a beat before letting out a husky laugh. "Don't waste your sympathy on me, Eva. I want to be alone. I prefer it. Hell, if it weren't for Will, I would have waved goodbye to the world a long time ago."

She gasped. "You mean, *killed* yourself?"

He laughed again, sounding far more amused this time. "Of course not. I definitely would've left civilization behind, though. Built a cabin in the woods or a shack on the beach, and lived the rest of my life in peace and quiet. On second thought, I still might do that."

"That's…sad," she said again.

"You know what they say, one man's hell is another man's heaven."

The cabin was actually cozier than Eva expected it to be. Made of weathered logs, the A-frame structure was nestled in the trees, almost entirely hidden from view, and a good ten miles outside of Valero, the little town where Tate had stashed their pickup truck. They'd trekked it to the cabin on foot, reaching it just as the sun set and the air grew considerably cooler.

Eva sighed in relief as she followed Tate toward the front door. The past four days had been nonstop walking, and though she was in good shape, she looked forward to the rest. Tate had said the cabin even had indoor plumbing, and she could not wait to take a shower.

"Stay out here," he ordered, swiftly bringing his rifle up as he approached the door.

Although she was dying to immerse herself in some semblance of civilization, she patiently waited for Tate to assess the interior of the cabin. A few minutes later, she heard a soft whistle, then his gruff voice saying, "We're good, sweetheart. Come in."

*Sweetheart.* She didn't know why, but her heart did a dumb little flip whenever the endearment left that man's lips.

Make that *mocking* endearment, she had to amend. But still, even knowing that those two syllables were most likely a taunt didn't squash the desire that hearing them inspired.

As they entered the small main room, Eva dropped her backpack on the hardwood floor and glanced around. Her gaze encountered sparse furnishings, bare walls and no personal touches—the place looked uninhabited, which apparently wasn't the case since Tate said his former army buddy had been living here for years.

"Where is this Hastings?" she asked warily, continuing to inspect her surroundings. A minuscule kitchen took up the other side of the room, and she deduced that the narrow corridor behind her led to the bedrooms.

"Picking up some supplies for us," Tate replied.

*Right.* She remembered something of that nature being discussed when Tate contacted his buddy via the sat phone. Nevertheless, she didn't particularly trust Tate's mysterious colleague. All she knew was that he was a former Green Beret turned expatriate who now lived in a cabin in the middle of the wilderness. Needless to say, she wasn't sure how comfortable she felt about any of this.

Tate must have sensed her hesitation. "Relax. Ben is a good guy. He can be trusted."

"I'll decide that for myself, if you don't mind."

"Not at all." He shot her a crooked grin. "The jury's still out on how much *we* trust each other, so what's one more untrustworthy companion?"

"I'm really starting to hate that word," she grumbled. *"Trust."*

"Deadliest word in the English language," he said with a shrug.

Tate leaned his rifle against the back of the ratty polyester couch, then slid his pistol from his waistband, and he made such a sexy, imposing sight that Eva couldn't tear her gaze off him. Everything about him excited her—the muscular body, clad in cargo pants and a snug white T-shirt streaked with dirt. The thick beard growth covering his strong jaw, lending him a lethal air. The ease with which he held his weapon, the soundless way he moved despite the heavy boots on his feet.

The dark, seductive smile he flashed when he caught her eyeing him...

"Oh, sweetheart, if you keep looking at me like that, I *will* kiss you again. You know that, right?"

Heat danced through her body, bringing a flush to her cheeks and an ache to her core. "We already agreed that wasn't going to happen," she reminded him.

He set his pistol on the uneven table next to the sofa, his eyes downright predatory as he made his way toward her. "We agreed to no such thing," he said, that hot gaze glued to her mouth.

Eva's pulse raced. "I told you I didn't want it."

"You lied," he countered.

She gulped. Hard.

Tate's gaze continued to eat her up as if she were a juicy

steak he couldn't wait to dig his teeth into. "I have no idea what to do with you, Eva," he said after a moment.

His voice came out rough and rueful, and the odd glimmer of apprehension she saw in his gorgeous green eyes was absolutely puzzling.

"What do you mean?" *Her* voice came out as a squeak, which was super annoying.

"I mean… Ah, hell, I don't know *what* I mean." His massive chest heaved as he released a breath. "All I know is that I'm going to kiss you again."

Her words came out squeaky again. "I don't want that."

"Liar."

And then he called her bluff and slanted his mouth over hers in a deep, unapologetic kiss.

Yep, she'd lied. She *did* want this. She wanted it desperately, and as his sensual mouth coaxed and teased and kissed her into oblivion, she realized she'd never, ever wanted to kiss anyone more than she wanted to kiss Tate.

His spicy, intoxicating scent enveloped her senses, and the persistent strokes of his tongue unleashed a rush of pleasure that heated every erogenous zone in her body. With one strong hand, Tate yanked at the elastic band holding her ponytail and let her hair loose, tangling his fingers in her long tresses and angling her head so he could kiss her deeper, harder, more possessively.

He slid one hand to her throat, swept his thumb over the pulse point there, then chuckled.

"Your heart's beating fast," he murmured, his warm breath tickling her lips. Both his hands traveled down to her chest. "And your nipples are hard."

Eva gasped as he squeezed her breasts. When he toyed with her nipples over her shirt and bra, she nearly passed out from the wild pleasure that rocketed through her.

"So who's playing games now?" he rasped. "You want this as badly as I do. At least have the guts to admit it."

He was right.

She wanted him.

She *craved* him. Like heroin. Or something equally addictive.

"Fine," she choked out. "I want this. I want you. God, I want—"

*Click.*

She froze midsentence, as the unmistakable sound of a gun being cocked echoed in the room.

Battling the tingle of fear, she shifted her gaze to the door and found herself staring down the barrel of the gun.

## Chapter 10

Despite the fact that a gun was currently being aimed at him, Tate didn't feel threatened in the slightest. If anything, he was just annoyed by the interruption.

"Nice to see you, too, Ben," he grumbled without turning around. "And your timing sucks."

"Gee," came the deep, sarcastic voice, "sorry to interrupt, Robert. Next time I'll be more considerate in my own home."

Chuckling, Tate stepped away from Eva and strode over to his old friend. He'd seen Ben a few months ago when he'd come to San Marquez to do some digging about Cruz's whereabouts. Ben had taken him in without question then, just as he did now.

"It's good to see you," Tate said, holding out his hand.

Ignoring the hand being extended to him, the beefy African-American pulled Tate in for a hearty hug, then slapped his shoulder and released him.

"Still alive, I see," Ben remarked, sounding pleased. "How're the boys?"

Tate hid a smile. Stone and Prescott hated being called "boys," but neither of them had voiced a single complaint when Ben had referred to them as such during that last visit. With his shaved head, harsh features and black goatee, not to mention the roped muscles and barrel chest, Ben Hastings was one mean-looking SOB. And it wasn't all for show—the man really was as lethal as they came.

"The boys are also alive," Tate answered.

Ben's dark eyes drifted to Eva. "This her?"

Tate nodded. "Ben, Eva. Eva, Ben."

With visible wariness, Eva walked over to shake Ben's hand. At six-five, Ben towered over her petite frame, and for some reason Tate felt the oddest urge to move to her side in a gesture of protectiveness.

Brushing off the strange thought, he glanced at Ben and said, "Mind if Eva uses your shower?"

The request brought a blush to Eva's cheeks, which made him roll his eyes. "You keep longingly looking at the corridor, as if you're dying to find out if there's a bathroom there."

"There is," Ben confirmed. "And it's yours for the taking. Spare towels in the cabinet below the sink. Soap in the medicine cabinet."

Although Eva's expression perked up, she didn't make a move to go. Rather, she looked from one man to the other, then frowned. "You're trying to get rid of me, aren't you?"

"Yep," Tate confirmed.

After a second, the frown faded. "Fine. Whatever. Talk behind my back all you want. As long as I get to shower, I'm cool with that."

Tate noticed Ben's lips twitching as Eva dashed off toward the hallway. Once she disappeared from view, his buddy let the grin show. "That is one fine woman."

Tate couldn't disagree.

"But, dude, is it really a good idea for you to be hitting that?" Ben continued, heading to the kitchen. "Or have we decided she's trustworthy?"

"We haven't decided a damn thing," he admitted.

"Beer?"

Before he could answer, a longneck bottle sailed in his direction. He caught it with ease, making a face as he studied the label. The local beer sucked, but for some reason, Hastings seemed to love it. Whatever. After three days of traveling through the jungle with the ultimate temptation by his side, he deserved a reward, even if it came in the form of watery beer.

Twisting off the cap, he brought the bottle to his lips and took a long swig. "Thanks." He arched a brow. "What's for dinner?"

"If you think I'm gonna cook for you, you're seriously delusional."

Tate stared at his buddy.

"Fine. We're having lamb stew," Ben said grudgingly.

He barked out a laugh. Ben Hastings might be strong, dangerous and downright frightening, but the man did love to cook. And he was damn good at it, too.

The sound of creaking pipes wafted from the corridor, followed by rushing water, and the second Tate pictured Eva stepping under the shower spray and getting all nice and wet, his mouth went utterly dry. Christ. She would look spectacular naked. No doubt about that.

Pushing aside the wicked images, he took another sip of beer, then said, "So tell me what's been going on around here. ULF seems to be causing even more trouble since Cruz went underground."

Ben's expression darkened. "Let's talk outside." The silver dog tags hanging around his neck clinked together as he headed toward a door off to the right.

Tate followed the other man to the back porch. The wooden slats beneath their boots creaked as they walked to the pine railing, where both men set their beers. The back of the cabin offered a view of the mountains in the distance, as well as the narrow creek visible through the trees.

"There's been more riots," Ben began, as he tapped his long fingers on the railing. "A couple of assassination attempts on high-ranking officials. Cruz's second in command, Luego, is flashier than his boss—he goes for shock and awe, big explosions and loud noises to get his point across."

"Always an effective strategy."

Ben snickered. "Yeah, well, it's not working. Military presence has gone up a hundred percent—"

"I noticed that at the harbor. There were a lot more soldiers compared to only a few months ago."

"Like I said, Luego has been causing some trouble."

"So Cruz still hasn't shown his face," Tate mused.

"Nope. Ever since he pulled off the Great Escape, he's been MIA."

Tate stifled a curse. Crap. That meant he had no choice but to go forward with this potentially suicidal mission. Cruz sure as hell wasn't going to come to *him*.

"Your girl really knows where Cruz's hideout is?" Ben asked, reading his mind.

He made a gesture of frustration. "She claims to, but who the hell knows if she's telling the truth?"

"I *am*," came Eva's sharp, yet earnest, voice.

Both men turned to see her standing in the open doorway. She wore a fresh pair of jeans and a tight black T-shirt. With her black hair loose, feet bare, and face pink and glowing from the shower, she looked absolutely incredible, and as usual, Tate's body responded to her nearness.

As his groin stirred, he banished the rising arousal and focused on Eva's blue eyes. "So you keep saying," he said vaguely.

A sigh left her lips. "I thought we agreed to the whole trust thing." Without letting him answer, she turned to Ben. "Do you have a computer I can use?"

Ben arched one bushy black eyebrow. "And what do you need a computer for?"

"I made our friend *Robert* a promise," she replied, shooting Tate a pointed look. "You still want to figure out why you're being hunted, right?"

As much as he didn't enjoy giving Eva the upper hand, he couldn't deny how tempting her offer was. If she could truly discover the truth behind the past eight months from a few keystrokes, he'd be a fool to stop her.

With a resigned breath, he turned to Ben and said, "If you've got one, give it to the lady."

Looking intrigued, Ben nodded and headed back to the door. Tate trailed after him, beer bottle in hand, as he watched the bulky African-American stride toward the tall wooden cabinet in the corner of the living room. Ben unlocked the cabinet with a set of keys he unclipped from his belt, opened the doors and removed an older-model Dell that he placed on the coffee table.

It was hard to miss the way Eva's entire face lit up at the sight of that laptop. The resulting rush of jealousy that burned his gut was downright laughable. Jeez. He was jealous of a damn *computer*? Because it had put that look of rapture on her face?

Wow. Clearly he had some problems.

Eva flopped down on the shabby sofa and opened the laptop. "Password?" she asked Ben.

"No password. I hardly ever use that thing."

A perplexed groove dug into her forehead. "You don't? Where do you store all your personal information?"

Ben tapped his temple with his index finger. "Everything I need is right in here."

She grinned. "You're an old-school kinda guy, huh?"

"You know it, baby-cakes."

*Baby-cakes?*

Tate resisted the urge to shake his head in bewilderment as he listened to their exchange. Ten minutes ago, Ben had been eyeing Eva like she was a threat to national security, and then one good-natured wisecrack on her part and they were best buds?

Yet somehow that didn't surprise him one damned bit. Eva Dolce, he'd come to learn, was incredibly easy to be around. Too damn likable for her own good.

"I can't believe you get wireless here," she commented, as her fingers moved over the laptop's track pad.

"San Marquez isn't a total failure in the technology department," Ben agreed.

Eva's face set in intense concentration as she studied the screen, her long, delicate fingers flying over the keyboard. "Mind if I explore your hard drive? I need to get a sense of what I'm working with here."

"Explore away."

It didn't take long before Eva mumbled a string of aggravated curses that had Tate and Ben exchanging a look.

"This computer sucks," she announced, lifting her head with an expression of disgust.

Ben held up his meaty hands in surrender. "Like I said, I'm old-school."

"I'm serious. I cannot emphasize how much this computer *sucks*. Not enough RAM to run any of my software.

Hell, even the internet browser takes an eternity to load."
She huffed out a breath. "It's not fast enough."

Ben didn't look at all bothered. "I told you, I barely use
that thing. Only to check my email every now and then."

Tate noticed that Eva now looked distraught. Catching
his eye, she bit her bottom lip, then said, "I can't help you.
At least not using this system."

He shrugged. "It's fine, Eva." He neglected to add that
he hadn't expected her to find anything of use anyway.

"No, it's not. I promised I'd find out why people want
you dead." Her mouth tightened in determination and when
she looked at him again, he glimpsed that same fortitude in
her big blue eyes. "Let me contact my friend, Tate."

"No way," he said instantly.

"I promise you, he's discreet. And he's good, even better than I am. He can hack into any system without being
detected."

Tate remained doubtful.

"I'm serious," she insisted. "He's the one who helped me
get into the army database, and so far, the military police
haven't come knocking on either of our doors, so clearly
nobody knew we got in."

"And how *do* you get in?" Ben spoke up, sounding intrigued.

"Depends on what we're trying to do."

She ran a hand through her hair, and Tate's fingers itched
to slide through those long, damp tresses. And the way
she kept chewing on her bottom lip…it made his own lips
tingle with the urge to kiss her again. Christ. Why the hell
couldn't he stop thinking about kissing this woman?

Shaking the cobwebs from his head, he tried to focus on
the words coming out of Eva's mouth rather than on that
sensual mouth itself.

"Most people think hackers are evil, looking to stick it

to 'the man' and infect the world with virtual viruses, or to steal from corporations and hardworking folks, or simply to cause trouble for the hell of it. But that's not what hacker culture is about," she said, sounding so animated Tate fought a smile.

Ben looked equally amused. "So what *is* it about?"

"Challenge. Curiosity. We're visionaries. Pioneers. Sure, there are some hackers who have malicious intentions, but the majority of us don't do what we do to hurt anyone. We embrace the challenge of getting into a system nobody else can, or one that programmers brag can't be breached."

"Doesn't make it any less illegal," Ben quipped.

"No," she agreed, "but sometimes it ends up helping the people whose privacy we violated. Like my friend, for example, he breaks into systems and then creates programs that implement better security measures, which he sells to the companies that utilize the vulnerable security pathways he breached in the first place."

Ben grinned. "But I bet he doesn't tell them that."

She grinned back. "No, not usually." The smile faded and her features grew serious again as she glanced at Tate. "If I had my computer with me, I could run my own software, but you made me leave my laptop behind." She punctuated that with a scowl. "But if you let me contact my friend, he can do the grunt work for us."

"Let me guess, for a price," he said sardonically.

"Actually, no. He owes me one." That sassy grin played over her lips again. "He owes me tens of thousands, in fact."

Because she'd stolen from the ULF, Tate remembered. With the help of this "friend," whom she'd no doubt monetarily rewarded for his troubles. From what he was starting to know of Eva, she was all about returning favors. He got the feeling she didn't like owing anyone anything, and that was a mindset he totally understood. Outstanding debts had no place in his life, either.

"He can be trusted, Tate. Just say the word, and I'll contact him and get the ball rolling."

Indecision washed over him, but he couldn't bring himself to turn down the offer. Nick and Sebastian were good with computers, but they weren't first-class hackers or anything. That honor had gone to Berkowski, the tech specialist of their unit.

Bitterness clogged his throat. Unfortunately, Berk was dead, and unless Tate got some answers, he'd never be able to know why Berkowski had died.

"Fine," he said gruffly. "Contact your friend."

When her features brightened, he held up his hand and fixed her with a toxic look. "But if this *friend* doublecrosses me, make no mistake, I'll be holding *you* responsible, sweetheart."

She rolled those beautiful blue eyes. "Shocking. Just add it to the list of all the other negatives you attribute to me— I'm a secret government agent, I'm a liar, I'm in cahoots with my uncle…anything else I'm forgetting?"

Tate's only response was a hard frown.

Next to him, Ben chuckled. "I think I like her."

Dinner consisted of a lamb stew prepared by Ben, and after three days of eating Meals Ready to Eat, Eva devoured the delicious home-cooked meal like a starving woman. As the trio sat around the lopsided table in Ben's small kitchen, she surreptitiously studied the men and tried to make sense of their unlikely friendship.

Ironically, neither man behaved in a way that corresponded to his appearance. While Tate was ruggedly handsome and sinfully sexy, his personality was thorny, brooding and sarcastic—which was what she'd have expected from Ben, whose harsh features and enormous body were incongruous with his laid-back charm and easy laughter.

Ben had explained that the two of them had struck up a friendship during basic training in the army, but while Tate had remained in the military, Ben only completed one tour before moving to South America to "retire." Eva suspected Tate's friend was involved in shady enterprises, but she'd yet to figure out what he actually did for a living.

After dinner, she helped Ben clear the table, then accepted the beer he handed her. Once again, the two men drifted onto the back terrace. This time she joined them, refusing to let them shut her out again. She knew they intended to discuss the plan for taking out Hector, and she'd be damned if she didn't have a say in how it went down.

Tate frowned as she leaned against the wooden railing, but he didn't order her to leave, a fact for which she was grateful.

"I can't see you walking out of this alive. Either one of you."

Ben's frank remark brought a spark of panic to Eva's gut. She met the man's dark eyes, then turned to Tate. "Do you think he's right?"

"Probably." He shrugged. "But I knew from the start that there'd be a fifty-fifty chance I'd end up dead."

She was not expecting to hear *that*.

"Then why did you agree to come with me?" she demanded, baffled.

Although he didn't respond, his silence spoke volumes.

He'd agreed to this mission because he didn't *care* if he died. As long as he got to kill Hector, Captain Robert Tate was perfectly willing to give up his life.

The realization intensified her panic. No. This couldn't

be a suicide mission. Tate might be okay with dying, but she refused to die. She had a three-year-old son to live for.

"I get it," she said evenly. "You want Hector eliminated and you don't care if you die trying. But *I* care. I will do anything in my power to go home to my son, which means you can't half-ass any of the planning for this."

Ben grinned at her. "You tell him, honey."

Without cracking a smile, she lifted her beer to her lips and took a long sip. When she felt a little calmer, she glanced at Tate again. "So how are we going to do this?"

"You tell me." His green eyes twinkled briefly with amusement before going hard. "You're the one who's familiar with Hector's camp."

"Should I draw you a map of everything I remember?" She was already moving to put down her beer, but Tate waved a hand. "Later. Right now I just want a general overview. You said he's hiding out in the mountains?"

Eva nodded. "In an underground bunker. The entrance is carved right into the rocks. You'd walk right past it if you're not looking for it."

"Only one entrance?" He sounded dubious.

"Two that I know of. The main one in the rocks, and another way out through the western foothills. There's one tunnel running beneath the bunker, leading out to the hills."

She halted, noticing that both men were staring at her. "What?" she said defensively.

"How exactly are you privy to these details?" Ben asked before exchanging a look with Tate.

"You never said you've been *inside*," Tate added, a suspicious cloud traveling over his face.

She gulped. "I told you, I supported the ULF cause at one time."

"Enough for Cruz to bring you to his secret lair?"

"I—*we*, Rafe's father and I—were close with Hector.

We were attempting to find a way to move supplies to the needy areas of the region using the relief foundation's resources. We held a lot of strategy sessions in that bunker."

The lies slid from her mouth, smooth as cream, but she couldn't afford to feel guilty about it. Besides, the fiction sounded so much nicer than the reality of it all. Strategy sessions in Hector's bunker? She *wished* their association had been that benign.

She spoke before the men could question her previous remarks. "The main entrance is guarded, but the one in the hills isn't."

"You sure about that?" Tate said sharply.

"It's Hector's secret escape route. He doesn't draw attention to it. Inside the tunnel is another story—there's a guard posted at the exit door, and a couple more by the ladder that leads up to the bunker."

Tate glanced at Ben. "Thoughts?"

The African-American looked pensive. "Clearly the entry point will be the foothills. Getting in will be easy, Robert, you know that. It's getting out that'll be the problem."

"I know," Tate said grimly. "What if we create some chaos? Draw the guards to one entrance and make sure they stay there, giving me enough time to sneak in through the tunnel, take out Hector and then get out the way I came."

"What do you mean, *you?*" Eva said in confusion.

He spared her a brief look. "Once we reach the camp, you're out of this, sweetheart. I go in and take care of Hector alone."

Surprise spiraled through her. "But why?"

"You said it, Eva. You have a son to go home to. I don't." He met her eyes, looking vaguely embarrassed before he wrenched his gaze away. "Once I'm convinced you've led me to the right place—and that I'm not walking into an ambush—Ben and I will handle it from there."

She turned to Ben. "Wait—you're coming, too?"

"Of course. Who else is gonna create the chaos? Speaking of which, I should head out." The big man polished off the rest of his beer before tossing the empty bottle into the plastic bucket by the door. "There are a few more items I need to procure. It might take all night, so don't wait up."

As Ben lumbered off, Eva furrowed her brows. "What exactly does he *do?*" she blurted out. "What items is he *procuring* and why will it take all night to get them?"

Tate chuckled. "Ben's what you'd call a middleman. If you need something, he hooks you up with someone who can provide it for you."

"Something?" she echoed warily. "Like weapons? Drugs?"

"He has the strings to get you anything you want, but weapons and information are his specialties."

Again with the whole information-as-a-commodity thing. Eva made a mental note to look into that when all this was over. With her skill on a computer, she might actually be able to make a darn good living selling information, but that was an idea for another day. Right now, she had to focus on the task at hand.

"Why don't I draw that map now?" she suggested. "Maybe if you see what the interior of the bunker looks like, it'll help you come up with a plan."

Tate nodded in agreement. He threw his head back and drained his beer, then followed her inside and watched as she rummaged around in the kitchen for some scrap paper and a pencil.

Rather than join her at the table, he edged toward the doorway. "I'm gonna hop in the shower while you do that," he said, scrubbing a hand over the beard covering his jaw.

"Okay," she said absently, already sketching the basic outline of the bunker.

After Tate left the room, she tried to focus on constructing a detailed map for him, but it wasn't long before the sound of the shower distracted her.

Eva lifted the pencil from the page, feeling her cheeks go hot as she listened to the water running. She couldn't help herself—she pictured Tate, big and hard and naked beneath the spray, soapy water coursing in rivulets down his broad chest, gliding over rippled muscles and hard sinew.

*I knew from the start that there'd be a fifty-fifty chance I'd end up dead.*

His words continued to haunt her. Did he really not care if he died? Because if that was the case, why was he bothering to hide out at all? Why not just let himself be killed by the people who were after him?

*For his men.*

The answer flew into her head, making her sigh. Of course. Tate wasn't trying to figure out the truth about that failed mission for *his* sake. He was doing it for Nick Prescott and Sebastian Stone.

Chewing on the inside of her cheek, Eva set down the pencil and stood up, too wound up to focus on the map. She knew Tate and Ben wouldn't leave this cabin until they had a solid plan in place, but she wished they could just go after Hector tonight. Now, even. She missed her son, and she was tired of feeling so…edgy.

Tate made her feel hot and uncomfortable and…well, *edgy,* damn it. The sexual awareness she felt in his presence was beginning to drive her nuts, though in her defense, maybe she'd be able to ignore it if he didn't keep kissing her every five minutes.

Okay, fine. He'd only kissed her twice.

But those two kisses had packed a *hell* of a punch.

Her ears perked at the sound of pipes groaning, and then the water stopped.

Somehow, she found herself making her way to the corridor. She heard quiet noises from behind the bathroom door—footsteps, the squeak of the faucet, running water, a toilet flushing. When she saw the doorknob twist, she ordered herself to dash back to the living room, but her feet stayed rooted in place.

She was standing right outside the door when it opened.

Tate frowned the second he saw her. "What's going on?" he asked instantly.

Eva couldn't answer. Her vocal cords had stopped working the second she laid eyes on his bare chest. Hard pecs and washboard abs and sleek, golden skin assaulted her vision. He wore a towel that rode precariously low on his hips, a sight that made her entire mouth go drier than sawdust.

"What do you want, Eva?" he asked in a tight voice.

She met his green eyes and saw unmistakable arousal flashing back at her. The smart thing to do would be to walk away, but her feet refused to comply.

Tate waited a few seconds, then sighed when she still didn't answer. "Fine. We'll deal with this later. I'm getting dressed."

She blocked his path. Her gaze dropped to his towel, then moved back to his face. A wry note entered her voice. "Don't bother."

His eyes narrowed. "Don't bother what?"

"Getting dressed." She brought her hand to his chest and stroked the spot between his pecs. "We both know any clothes you put on will come right off, anyway."

Tate inhaled sharply and she felt his pectoral muscles quiver beneath her fingers. "You're playing with fire, sweetheart."

She tickled his flat, brown nipples with the pads of her

fingers. "We've both been playing with fire since the moment we met," she corrected.

Licking her lips, she reached for his hand. After a moment, he intertwined their fingers and studied her face one last time, his green eyes blazing with passion. "You sure about this?"

She stared at their joined hands, then met his gaze. "Who knows what tomorrow will bring, right?"

His voice came out gruff. "Meaning?"

"Meaning we may as well enjoy ourselves tonight."

# *Chapter 11*

The bedroom was dark when they entered it. Eva paused at the foot of the twin bed and studied their darkened surroundings, baffled by the total lack of furnishings. Ben's room consisted of nothing but the bed, a table littered with books, and half a dozen duffel bags on the floor. No dresser, no desk, not even a closet.

Which was fine. Because all they really needed was that bed.

Her pulse sped up as Tate reached for the knot on his towel. Despite the surge of excitement, she also experienced a flicker of apprehension. Was she really going to do this? Sleep with a man she still barely knew?

Tate's towel hit the floor, officially making the answer to both those questions a big, resounding *yes*. He was the most incredible-looking man she'd ever seen. A warrior to the core, with long limbs, roped muscles and various scars marring his golden skin.

Her heart screeched to a stop, then took off full speed ahead as she watched his arousal grow before her eyes. Her mouth watered, and without any conscious thought, she found herself standing in front of him and wrapping her fingers around his erect shaft.

A low groan rumbled out of his chest. "Are you sure?" he asked again.

She nodded. "I'm tired of fighting this attraction." To prove it, she eased her hand along the hard length of him, then released him so she could reach for the hem of her T-shirt.

"We still don't trust each other," he reminded her, his dark green eyes locking with hers.

"Well, as someone once told me, sex and trust don't necessarily go hand in hand."

She took off her shirt and sports bra, and tossed them on the floor.

Tate's gaze instantly homed in on her bare breasts. Her nipples puckered in response, hard and tingly, and an answering flash of lust and appreciation lit his face.

But then he seemed to notice the bandage on her arm. "You're hurt," he mumbled. "You're not up to this."

She smiled faintly. "Says who?"

Without breaking eye contact, Eva unbuttoned her jeans and wiggled out of them, then peeled her panties down her legs. She straightened up and stood there fully naked, every inch of her skin burning as Tate devoured her with his eyes.

Three feet of distance stood between them, between their respectively naked bodies, between their mouths and their hands, but she refused to bridge that distance. She'd already made this first move, and now she wanted Tate to come to her. She wanted to watch *him* fall apart, to give in to the attraction that had been tormenting her hormones for days now.

It didn't take long before she got her wish. Tate raked his hot gaze over her one final time, then let out a growl that startled her, and the next thing she knew, she was flat on her back with his big warrior body crushing her on the bed.

He captured her mouth in a toe-curling kiss, stealing the breath right out of her lungs. As his tongue plundered and possessed, he rocked his hips, his heavy erection pulsing against her belly and making her moan with abandon.

"You taste so good," he muttered before kissing her again.

Long, deep and passionate. His drugging kisses had her head spinning, and when his hands began a slow exploration of her body, she nearly passed out from the incredible sensations. His callused palms scraped her hypersensitive skin. Teased, caressed, tickled. He cupped her breasts, feathering his fingertips over her rigid nipples and summoning another moan from her lips.

"You like this?" he murmured, and then he gently pinched her nipples.

"Yes." Her head flopped to the side, her arms coming around his broad shoulders, clinging to him, needing to steady herself. She was lying down, but she feared if she didn't have something to hold on to, she might actually be swept away by the unbelievable waves of pleasure coursing through her.

Planting a quick kiss on her lips, Tate dipped his head and inched his body lower, so that his mouth was level with her breasts. Without hesitation, he took possession of a nipple, flicking his hot, wet tongue over it before suckling. A bolt of heat sizzled from her nipple right down to the juncture of her thighs, and her hips shot off the bed, her aching core seeking relief.

Tate chuckled. He gripped her waist to steady her, then

shifted his attention to her other breast, getting the exact same reaction out of her.

"Please, I need more," she choked out. "I need you."

"Don't worry, sweetheart, you'll get me."

Amusement rang from his husky voice, but though his words were meant to reassure, his teasing didn't subside. While his mouth continued tending to her breasts, he glided one hand down her body and brought it between her legs, stroking her damp folds with barely there caresses that caused frustration to build in her body.

The tension between her legs was liable to kill her. And the heat. God, her skin was on fire, humming, crackling, threatening to burn her alive.

Sweat broke out on her forehead. *"More,"* she pleaded, her hand desperately moving between their bodies in search of his erection.

A strangled groan left Tate's lips, and when she focused her eyes, she realized that he was not as calm and blasé as she'd thought he was. His facial muscles were taut, green eyes glittering with dark hunger that would've scared her if she weren't feeling the same damn thing.

His voice was hoarse, strained, as if he were speaking through clenched teeth. "I'm trying to make this last, sweetheart." The tendons in his neck tightened as he forcibly moved her hand off his arousal. "It's been too long for me."

"For me, too," she mumbled. "Which is why I don't want to be teased right now. I want…" She moved her hand right back to his hard length and squeezed. "I want you. *Now,* Tate."

With a groan, he removed her hand again, and she nearly slugged him out of sheer frustration, but fortunately, he was simply donning a condom.

Anticipation gathered as she waited for him to sheathe himself. Her nipples tingled, her thighs clenched, her sex throbbed. She'd never felt this way before. Hot, needy, as if she'd actually die if she didn't have this man inside her.

And when he gave her what she craved and drove his cock deep, the anticipation transformed into an explosion of heat and ecstasy that made her cry out and convulse.

Waves of release shuddered through her from that very first stroke. She hadn't realized how badly her body had needed this, and as her climax skyrocketed into her and sent her soaring, Eva wrapped her legs around Tate's trim hips and rode out the release.

Her climax ebbed, leaving her feeling warm and sated and unbelievably contented. She watched Tate's face, floored by the passion she saw there, the naked need, the softness that she'd never seen before and probably wouldn't see again, at least not outside the bedroom. Watching this big, strong man come apart triggered another rush of pleasure, another tiny orgasm that skipped along her nerve endings and made her gasp with surprised delight.

*"Eva."* He said her name on a groan, and his thrusts quickened, shortened, then stopped altogether as he buried himself deep and jerked with release.

Running her hands along his muscular back, she smiled in the darkness and waited for him to catch his breath. She felt his heartbeat hammering against her breasts, and her smile widened at the knowledge that she'd put him in this state of frantic excitement.

When he rolled off her, she experienced a pang of disappointment, but to her surprise, he didn't get up and walk away. Rather, he slung his arm around her and pulled her close, and although his motions had a slightly awkward feel to them, Eva didn't complain.

"How's the arm?" he asked, his voice gruff.

"It's fine." She rested her cheek against his damp chest,

inhaling the clean, soapy smell of him, enjoying the way his light dusting of chest hair abraded her cheek.

After a moment, he idly began stroking the small of her back, the awkwardness in the gesture evident once more. Clearly he wasn't a cuddler, and a strange sense of joy tickled her chest over the fact that he was still here, snuggling in bed with her. She'd needed the sex, but she suspected she needed *this* more—nestling next to a warm male body that wasn't her son's, feeling sheltered in a pair of strong arms.

"What was your brother like?" she whispered.

His chest stiffened beneath her cheek. "Why do you ask?"

"I'm just curious. It's clear you loved him very much. I mean, you're willing to give up your own life just to avenge him." She paused, a faint smile tugging on her lips. "Was he a thorny, grumpy pain in the ass, too?"

She could practically feel Tate rolling his eyes. "No. He wasn't any of those things."

"Then what was he like?"

It took several seconds before he replied, and when he did, his voice was thick with grief. "An optimist. Will was the eternal optimist. He always looked for the best in people, gave you the benefit of the doubt even when you didn't deserve it. He was a damn good soldier, but he lacked that killer instinct. Don't get me wrong, he was tough as nails, and he could kill without batting an eye just like all the other men on the unit, but he didn't have that ruthlessness that a lot of us Special Forces guys have, and he definitely wasn't jaded, which is something that happens real fast in our line of work."

"So he was a glass-half-full kinda man."

"More like glass-is-overflowing-it's-so-full," Tate said, sounding wistful. "I never understood how he could be so damn happy all the damn time. I used to think it had to be an act, but Christ, it *wasn't*. My brother was actually one of those rare people who was completely happy with every aspect of his life."

Eva smiled in the darkness. "That's what I want for Rafe," she confessed. "I want him to grow up happy and positive. I don't ever want him to have that ruthlessness you just talked about."

Her heart began to weep as she realized it might already be too late. Rafe was only three, and his life was anything but normal. Moving around from place to place, no real family except for her, no friends, no house or picket fence or drooling golden retriever to toss a stick to. And being ambushed by Hector's men in Istanbul had scared him, enough to give him recurring nightmares. How could she ever hope for her son to be happy and positive when all she'd shown him so far was sad and negative?

"Hector needs to die." The lump in her throat was so enormous, she could barely keep talking. She gulped once, twice, blinking back tears. "Rafe won't be able to lead a normal life until that maniac is out of our lives."

Tate's touch was warm and surprisingly protective as he dragged his hand over her bare shoulder. "Cruz won't come after you or your kid again. I'll make sure of it, Eva."

Despite her rapid blinking, two tears slid out from the corners of her eyes and streamed down her cheeks. Before she could stop it, a rush of shame flooded her, and though she quickly tried to tamp it down, she wasn't fast enough. As a result, shivers racked her body and the tears fell a little bit faster.

Tate, of course, didn't miss either reaction. "What's wrong?" he demanded, tightening his grip on her.

"I'm the one who did this to my son." Her voice shook. "I'm the reason he doesn't have a normal life, Tate."

"Eva—"

"You know it's true," she cut in, unable to curb the bitterness that climbed up her throat. "If I hadn't been so caught up in saving the world I wouldn't have supported the ULF. I wouldn't have met Hector. Rafe would have a father who wasn't—" She halted abruptly, a vise of fear squeezing her gut at her slip-up.

"A father who wasn't what?"

"Dead," she finished. "A father who wasn't dead."

For the first time since she'd met Tate, the lie got stuck in her throat like a clump of hair in the drain. Maybe it was because they were naked in bed together. Lies seemed so out of place in such an intimate setting.

"You loved him? Rafe's old man?" Tate sounded oddly annoyed, as if he didn't want to ask but curiosity had gotten the best of him.

She wiped her eyes with the back of her hand, managing a quick nod. "I did. I loved him a lot."

For all of twenty minutes, she failed to add. It was true, though—she *had* loved Hector at the beginning. He'd been larger than life. A true rebel *with* a cause, and it was a cause she'd truly believed in: freeing the people of San Marquez from a government that was oppressing, starving and killing them. But when the ULF's methods had gone from peaceful to violent in the blink of an eye, Eva had realized that the "cause" had never been about saving anyone, only about fattening up Hector's wallet.

But she couldn't say any of this to Tate, not without the risk of revealing details she couldn't afford to reveal.

"Rafe will never know his father," she said sadly. "Hector made sure of that."

"Fathers are overrated," Tate quipped.

Biting her lip, she propped herself up on one elbow and studied his face. "Do you really never plan on having kids?"

"Nope."

"Is it a fear thing? You think you might end up like your dad?"

He chuckled. "You're reading far too much into it. I'm not afraid I'll end up beating my kids—trust me, that'll never frickin' happen. I just don't want to be responsible for another human being. Now that Will is gone, I don't owe anything to anyone. Only myself."

"Must be nice," she murmured, though she was only being half-serious. Truth was, she wouldn't trade Rafe for the world. She'd rather be overburdened with responsibility and have her son in her life than be worry free without him.

"You know what would be nicer?" He rolled her over without warning, his lips hovering over hers. "This."

He kissed her, softly at first, then with more urgency, until she was gasping for air and clinging to his sculpted shoulders. "Tate—"

"No more talking," he said hoarsely. "We already established that we might die tomorrow. Wouldn't we rather spend tonight doing more interesting things than talking?"

He had a point.

With a contented sigh, she closed her eyes and relinquished control, letting Tate bring her to new levels of passion, losing herself in the delicious sensation of him moving inside her, the release that sent her soaring to dazzling heights and reduced her to a hot, boneless mess when it finally receded.

Later, when they were once again sated, Tate pulled her into his arms and tucked her into his bare chest. With his big, warm body spooning her from behind, Eva fell asleep feeling safer than she'd felt in a long, long time.

Tate had just poured himself some coffee the next morning when Eva's voice wafted from the living room. "Tate, get in here. My friend just got back to me."

His shoulders went rigid. Gripping the tin cup, he stalked out of the kitchen. Rather than join Eva on the couch, he loomed over her, his tension levels at an all-time high.

"What did he find?" Tate demanded.

Ignoring him, Eva continued to peer at the computer screen with a look of extreme concentration. As she read, his impatience climbed higher and higher, until he finally put down his cup and crossed his arms over his chest before he gave in to the urge and snatched the laptop from her hands.

"Okay, this isn't much," she announced. "He couldn't find any record of that last mission, and all the files on you and the members of your unit have officially been locked. Only the highest security clearance can access them, and he didn't want to trigger any red flags by trying to infiltrate those restricted areas."

Tate fought a burst of disappointment. Granted, he hadn't expected some computer hacker to be able to solve this mystery in twenty-four hours when he himself hadn't learned diddly-squat in eight months, but he couldn't deny that Eva's confidence had gotten some of his hopes up.

"Oh, well. You tried," he said with a shrug, as he handed her back the laptop.

Her teeth dug into her bottom lip for a moment, while her gaze scanned the screen. "He found quite a lot of background information on that doctor, though. You said his name was Richard Harrison, right?"

Tate furrowed his brows. "Yeah."

"Is this him?" She angled the laptop so he could see the screen.

Squatting down, he studied the photograph and gave a brisk nod. The salt-and-pepper hair, ruddy cheeks and deep brackets around a thin mouth definitely belonged to Dr.

Harrison. The man looked the same as Tate remembered, minus the bullet between the eyes, of course.

Eva turned the laptop back, her sharp blue eyes narrowing the more she read. "Huh. That's weird."

Tate's instincts kicked into gear. "What's weird?"

"What do you know about Dr. Harrison?"

He searched his brain, trying to remember the details he'd been provided eight months ago. "Harrison worked for a medical research lab. I was told he was involved in developing vaccines and he came here to test the water in the towns and villages that were affected by that cholera outbreak a few years back."

Eva nodded absently. "Right, I remember that. Hurricane Isabella did a number on the water systems. More than a hundred thousand people died during that outbreak."

"Well, apparently Harrison was collecting samples—I guess he was trying to develop a more effective vaccination for cholera. He was working out of a small field hospital in Corazón to do his research. I think he brought a couple of assistants with him."

"Okay. But…" She drifted off, her tone distracted.

"But what?"

She wrinkled her forehead. "But Harrison didn't develop vaccinations. According to this, he was the department head for the lab's biological development unit."

Tate stiffened. "What?"

"It says so right in the file. Harrison worked for D&M Initiative, one of the biggest private research labs in the country. The world, actually. They work closely with the government, the WHO, CDC, pretty much all the big players in the health sphere. Like I said, Harrison's specialty was biological development."

Alarm bells went off in his head. "What the hell does that mean?"

"I'm guessing it's a euphemism for biological weapons," she said with a wry look. "The U.S. supposedly shut down its biological weapons program a long time ago, but the government still provides funding for medical defense. Private labs and government agencies are continually conducting research on how to defend against potential bio attacks." She shrugged. "Call me a cynic, but personally I think our government focuses on more than just defense. I think offensive programs are still going on, whether the White House admits it or not."

"Wouldn't surprise me," he agreed.

Eva turned back to the screen and bit her lip again, a gesture he was beginning to associate with puzzlement. "There's absolutely nothing here about Harrison being sent to San Marquez in relation to the cholera outbreak." Her breath hitched. "Wait a minute. It says he was there to coordinate with his lab's field researchers about something called Project Aries."

"Project Aries? What's that?"

"I have no idea. My friend couldn't gain access to the project file. He made a note saying it was *beyond classified.*" She scrolled down. "Yeah, apparently none of the databases would let him in. The firewalls were insane, which means someone really doesn't want unauthorized eyes seeing that file."

"So Harrison was in Corazón conducting some top secret project that had nothing to do with vaccination shots," Tate said slowly.

"That's what it looks like."

Frustration jammed in his throat. "That doesn't shed light on anything, Eva. In the end, Harrison was still taken hostage by Cruz and his men, who killed him before we could extract him. None of that explains why my unit was hunted down."

"I stand by my original suggestion—you must have seen something in the village."

Stifling a groan, Tate resisted the impulse to slam his fist into the nearest wall. He'd gone over the events of that op a thousand times already, and nothing, *nothing,* stood out as not ordinary. Dead doctor, dead villagers, rebels swarming the area, Will's throat slashed. That was all there was to it. Except evidently it wasn't that cut-and-dried.

So what the *hell* was he missing?

Eva must have picked up on his turbulent state of mind because she stood up and approached him. Her sweet, feminine scent floated toward him and his pulse immediately kicked up a notch.

At five-six, she wasn't a tiny thing, but she still had to tilt her head to look up at him, and when her blue eyes locked with his, he was reminded of the way those eyes had shone with passion last night.

The sex had been good. Really frickin' good. In fact, he'd been having trouble getting it off his mind all morning. And earlier, when he'd opened his eyes and found Eva's lush body curled into his, he'd nearly caved in and given her a wake-up call she would never have forgotten.

Instead, he'd quietly sneaked out of bed, knowing that what happened last night needed to remain a onetime occurrence. Sex had no place on this mission. Besides, with Ben accompanying them on this final leg of the journey, there wouldn't be many opportunities to get naked anyway.

And Tate was just fine with that, because as mind-blowing as it had been, he couldn't do it again. Sex was one thing, but cuddling the way they'd done last night? Totally uncool. He didn't want Eva getting any ideas about them—mainly, that they could have any sort of future, which was an absolute impossibility.

"Where did you find Harrison's body?" she asked, her

businesslike tone revealing she was oblivious to where his thoughts had drifted.

Tate forced himself to focus on the more pressing matters. "In the makeshift clinic in the village. The whole building was engulfed in flames, but the fire hadn't reached the office yet. Harrison was sitting behind the desk with a bullet in his head."

She grimaced. "Okay. Well, was there anything unusual about the office? Papers in disarray? Weird medical vials or something else that stood out to you?"

"There was a lot of smoke, so I can't be sure, but nothing stood out. The only thing that looked out of order to me was the dead man at the desk."

"And outside? What did you see outside?"

"Not much," he admitted. "The smoke was thick as hell. And the smell—" a cold shiver ran up his spine "—the smell made your eyes water as much as the smoke did. Have you ever smelled burned flesh, Eva?"

Her face paled. "No."

He swallowed. "It's not an odor you're likely to forget."

She faltered for a moment, as if trying to absorb that. "So Hector's men killed the villagers and burned the bodies and the buildings to the ground. Was there anything about the bodies that seemed suspicious?"

His frustration returned, eating a hole in his gut. "All I saw was charred corpses."

"Okay. What about…" She hesitated. "What about your brother's death? How did that happen?"

Pain jolted through him. "Cruz wasn't expecting to be ambushed by my unit. There was a lot of gunfire, rebels coming after us, flames everywhere. In the chaos, Cruz managed to escape into the brush. Will went after him."

"And you found Will's body later," she finished softly.

His heart constricted. "No. Will was alive when I found

him. Cruz took my brother hostage. He told me to lay down my weapon, and that if I let him go, he'd release Will."

"You believed him?"

"Pretty frickin' foolish of me, huh?" Sarcasm dripped from his tone.

"Tate—"

"Yes, Eva, foolish, moronic me put down my gun—and Cruz sliced Will's throat anyway."

She gasped.

Anger bubbled in his blood. "And instead of going after Cruz, I tried to help Will. I thought there might actually be a chance I could save him, but I couldn't, and so there you go. Another act of foolishness and Cruz got away."

"Trying to save your brother wasn't foolish," she said firmly. "You made the right choice."

"If you say so," he said dully.

Eva cupped his chin with her delicate hands, her grip surprisingly strong. "I do say so. You chose to help your brother rather than go after Hector. That *was* the right decision, and if you hadn't done it, and there was a chance that Will could've been saved? You would have never forgiven yourself."

"I don't forgive myself now." His voice came out harsher than he intended. The confession was unintended, too.

Christ, what was he doing, opening himself up to this woman?

Sure enough, his rough admission made those big blue eyes soften. She stroked the stubble coating his jaw, and though her touch was meant to be gentle and reassuring, it sent a bolt of heat right down to his groin and stirred his cock.

Gritting his teeth against the onslaught of desire, Tate stepped out of her touch, trying to steer his thoughts back to safe territory. But there was nothing safe about any of this, especially when the front door of the cabin suddenly flew open and Ben burst into the room as though his ass was on fire.

"They're on their way," Ben boomed at them. "You need to go. Now."

## Chapter 12

Everything happened so fast Eva had no time to react. One minute she and Tate were talking in the living room, the next, Ben was flying through the door with a hard expression and tense demands.

"Get your pack," Tate barked at her when he noticed she was still rooted in place.

Snapping out of her bewilderment, she sprinted toward the bedroom where she'd left her backpack. She jammed yesterday's clothes into the bag and grabbed the handgun she'd left on the pile of books by the table beneath the window. She idled only long enough to pull her hair into a tight ponytail and shove the gun in her waistband, then hurried back to the main room, where she found Ben zipping up a duffel and Tate shoving a clip into his rifle.

"Who exactly is on their way here?" she demanded when neither man so much as glanced her way.

Tate checked his extra magazines before shoving them

in his pack. "Military. They were asking about us around town."

She swore. "How did they know we were here?"

Slinging his rifle over one shoulder, and the strap of his backpack over the other, Tate shot her a hard look. "Someone must have tipped them off."

The implication hit her hard. "You think it was *me?*"

"You were on the computer all morning..." He let the remark hang.

Indignation ripped through her. "Yeah, helping *you!* I didn't tell anyone where we were, Tate."

Even though they'd already determined that sex had nothing to do with trust, his lack of faith in her was still upsetting. And yet it wasn't surprising in the slightest.

What *did* surprise her were his next words.

"I believe you."

"You do?" she said warily.

He shrugged. "You've got nothing to gain by tipping off the military. Not when we're this close to getting Cruz."

It wasn't a declaration of trust, but she'd take it. "So then how did they find us?" she asked again.

"It's not improbable that they tracked us down. The unit in the jungle was tracking us for a while before they attacked—they must have reported our general movements to whoever they were checking in with, and you've got to assume reinforcements were dispatched after that unit went AWOL."

"So someone else picked up our trail?" she said, feeling queasy as she followed Tate to the door. "And tracked us here?"

"I wasn't making much of an effort to cover our tracks. Besides, it's common sense we'd end up here. Valero is the first town you hit once you reach the end of the river."

"And I'm the only American living in these parts," Ben

added in a grim voice. "If Tate was turning to anyone for help, it'd be me, and these men know that."

All talk ended, leaving Eva to panic in silence as she followed the men out the door. Outside, Tate shouldered the duffel bag Ben had brought back from town, the contents of which had yet to be divulged to her.

Ben tossed Tate a set of keys before stepping up to bestow his buddy with one of those macho-man side hugs. "ATV's stashed beyond those trees. You remember the coordinates I gave you?"

Tate nodded. "We'll see you there in two hours."

Eva swiveled her head to Ben. "You're not coming with us?"

"We'll rendezvous later. I've gotta deal with the soldiers."

She felt even queasier. "Deal with them how?"

The big African-American smiled, his white teeth gleaming in the morning sunlight. "I'm not gonna off them, if that's what you're afraid of. Don't worry, baby-cakes, I'll just send them on their merry way—and far away from you and Robert."

Relief trickled through her. "Okay." On impulse, she bounded over to Ben and threw her arms around him in a tight hug. "Be safe, okay?"

Surprise and unease flickered in his brown eyes, but after a moment of stiffness, he returned the embrace. "You, too, Eva."

Five minutes later, she and Tate were on an ATV, bouncing through the woods and putting miles behind them and Ben's cabin.

Though not as noisy and treacherous as the jungle, the mountainous terrain offered its fair share of obstacles. Thick brush, rotting logs and grand trees limited their path options, and the bugs were as plentiful and relentless as in the jungle, slapping Eva's face and hissing by her ears as Tate kept a solid foot on the gas and sped them to safety.

Each bump in the trail sent a throb of pain to her bandaged arm, and she readjusted her grip around Tate's waist, pressing her face between his shoulder blades and holding on tight. As they cut a path through the brush, the duffel bag he'd strapped to the back of the ATV kept jostling her knee. She wondered what was in it. Something important obviously, seeing as it had taken Ben all night to "procure" it.

At the thought of Ben, another tremor of panic skittered up her spine. "Do you think he'll be okay?" She shouted over the wind so Tate could hear her.

He didn't respond, but she felt his back stiffen against her breasts. He would probably never say it out loud, but she knew he hadn't liked leaving his friend behind to deal with the impending arrival of those soldiers.

She didn't doubt that Ben Hastings could handle himself—*look* at the guy, for Pete's sake—but she also couldn't help but remember the way that last military unit had pounced on them in the jungle. No hesitation, no attempt at civilized talk; those soldiers had been sent to kill Tate, and most likely her, too. What if the men who arrived to question Ben were of that same mentality?

She said a quick prayer for Ben's safety, knowing there was no point in worrying. At least not until they reached those coordinates. The two men must have arranged the meeting place when she'd been gathering her gear.

Nearly an hour later, Tate finally slowed the ATV, and Eva lifted her head to examine their surroundings. They were still amid the forested landscape, sheltered by a canopy of green, but the path was nearly impassable now. They'd been deeper inland before, but now they hugged the edge of the mountain, traveling alongside a steep, rocky slope where the foliage was sparser. Soon the ATV wouldn't be able to fit on any trail, and she wasn't surprised when Tate killed the ignition and told her to hop off.

"What'll we do with the ATV?" she asked as he unloaded their packs and Ben's duffel. "We can't just leave it on the side of the mountain."

"We won't." He swept his gaze around, squinting in the bright sun. After a moment, he cursed, dug his aviator sunglasses from his backpack and shoved them on the bridge of his nose. "Okay, check the GPS while I stash the ATV."

He rattled off the coordinates, which Eva had to memorize quickly because he only recited them once, and then he was gone, reversing the vehicle the way they'd come and disappearing into the brush.

She rummaged in Tate's pack until she found the portable GPS device she'd seen him use when they'd been in the jungle. She typed in the longitude and latitude he'd given her, and a moment later, the location appeared in the form of a red dot on the small digital screen. The green dot was their current location, and she gave a pleased nod at how close the two dots were to one another.

"We're two miles away," she told Tate when he reemerged from the brush ten minutes later.

He took the GPS, studied the display and offered a nod of his own. "Good. Let's book it, then. Won't take long to get there."

Eva fell in line behind him, not voicing a single protest about the two-mile walk. It was blistering hot out, but she wasn't going to complain about that, either, not when they were so close to Hector she could practically taste the freedom.

With the rugged terrain, it took them twenty-five minutes at a steady walk to reach the coordinates. At first sight, there was nothing special about the area, just a bunch of boulders and grass, hilly slopes marked by thorny shrubs and colorful wildflowers, but Tate seemed pleased with what he saw.

It wasn't until he pointed it out that Eva discerned the mouth of the cave hidden on a rocky incline ten yards away.

Taking out his pistol, Tate took a step toward the slope, glancing at her over his shoulder. "Wait here. Let me check it out."

She nodded, busying herself by sipping from her canteen while Tate ascended the hill to investigate. A few moments later, he let out a sharp whistle, which she took as her cue to join him.

Pebbles and twigs crunched beneath her hiking boots as she climbed up to the cave. Tate appeared at the top of the hill and extended his hand to help her up, and the moment their fingers touched, warmth seeped into her hand and spread in every direction.

Her heart skipped a beat when his mossy-green eyes landed on her mouth. She knew he was contemplating kissing her, and she nearly opened her mouth to blurt out the words *do it*. But at the last second, she bit back the demand. A good thing, too, because Tate's gaze abruptly shifted and his hand dropped from hers.

*Message received.*

Didn't mean she wasn't disappointed, though. In fact, disappointment had pretty much been her mood of the day, ever since she'd woken up to find Tate sneaking out of the room without so much as a good-morning kiss.

But what had she really expected? That one night of sex would lead to something long lasting? That they now shared a deep, meaningful connection? Of course it wouldn't, and of course they didn't. They'd given in to their carnal urges, enjoyed each other's bodies, and now it was business as usual: two people with a common goal, zero mutual trust and no future.

The cave's entrance was only four feet high or so, and Tate had to duck in order to walk inside. Eva trailed after him, cautious as she stepped into the shadows. Rays of sunlight sliced into the mouth of the cave, casting a weak glow over the rocky walls and dirt floor.

Fortunately, it didn't look as though they were sharing the space with any other living creatures, though the musky scent of dung in the air increased her wariness.

"Mountain lion," Tate supplied. "But the droppings are old. Ditto on the tracks, so you don't need to worry about any surprise visitors. We won't be here long, anyway."

The reminder made her glance at her watch, which showed that an hour and a half had passed since they'd left the cabin. Ben would be here soon, and then they'd need to be on the move again. And fast, depending on what happened with those soldiers back there.

"Are you hungry?" Tate asked, bending down to unzip his pack.

"Not really." They'd split a loaf of bread and a brick of soft Brie for breakfast, and though several hours had passed since, the excitement of the past couple hours had stolen any appetite she might have had.

Tate pulled out a package of beef jerky, tore off a strip and popped it in his mouth. He slid down the cave wall and sat on the ground, stretching his long muscular legs in front of him.

After a beat, she sat on the wall across from him and searched his face through the shadows. "Ben will be okay, right?" she said, trying to ignore the wave of anxiety that refused to subside.

His expression revealed nothing, but he sounded confident as he replied, "Ben can take care of himself."

"But what do you think the soldiers will do to him?"

"They'll ask a bunch of questions, maybe hurl out some threats." Tate shrugged. "They want me, not Ben, and once they confirm that I'm not at the cabin, they'll move on."

A cloud of annoyance and frustration swirled through her. "Doesn't it drive you crazy, not knowing why people are after you?"

"Yep."

"Can't you just…I don't know, call your former commander and demand an explanation?"

"You think I didn't already do that?" he answered dryly. "Once the third member of my unit was found dead—a mugging gone awry, of course—I put two and two together and started to see the pattern. I called my former CO with my concerns, which he brushed off."

"So you think he's in on it?"

"He's gotta be. I contacted him again after Berk died—Stephen Berkowski, a damn good soldier, the fifth and final one to die. My CO told me to quit asking questions and accused me of being paranoid. A few days later, someone nearly blew my head off on the street. So yeah, I think Commander Hahn is absolutely aware of what's happening and why."

Eva frowned, feeling angry on Tate's behalf. "Have you considered kidnapping this Hahn and torturing him until he tells you what the heck is going on?"

Tate laughed. "I'd considered it, yes, but Nick and Seb talked me out of it."

At the mention of Tate's men, a pang of longing tugged at her heart, and the image of her little boy's blue eyes and mischievous grin flashed across her brain.

"When can we call Nick again?" she asked. "I haven't spoken to my son in two days."

"Nick would've contacted us if anything was wrong."

"I know that, but I still want to hear Rafe's voice and tell him that his mother loves him." Her lips tightened. "Is that too much to ask?"

Tate arched his brows. "I didn't force you to leave your son behind, Eva. Going after Cruz was your idea, remember?"

Her shoulder sagged. "I know. I'm sorry. I just miss my son, that's all." Before she could stop them, tears pricked her eyes. "He's all I have, Tate. For the past three years, he's been the only constant in my life. I can't see my parents, my family, my friends." A laugh popped out. "I'm twenty-five years old, and my only friend and confidant is a three-year-old boy. How sad is that?"

"You're still young," he said roughly. "You've got a lot of time, Eva. Once you get Cruz off your back, you can start over. You'll have your family and friends back in your life, and you'll make new friends, fall in love, you know, all that stuff normal people do."

His last comment brought a smile to her lips. "Let me guess, you don't consider yourself one of those normal people, do you?"

"Me? Normal?" He shot her a self-deprecating grin. "Baby, I'm thirty-four years old, on the run from my own government, living in a fortress in Mexico and trekking across this godforsaken country to murder a man. Tell me, is that normal?"

Despite the dismal facts he'd recited, she had to giggle. "Definitely not."

They both fell silent after that and Eva used the time to mull over everything Tate had said, coming to the conclusion that it probably *was* for the best if they didn't sleep together again. His life was even more complicated than hers, and he was right—*nothing* was normal about his situation.

But for her, normalcy was almost within her grasp. Once

Hector was gone, Rafe would be safe. She would be safe. And the two of them could start over, just like Tate said.

The longer the silence dragged on, the sleepier Eva became. The darkness of the cave made her eyelids droop and her limbs loosen, and she must have fallen asleep, because the next thing she knew, someone was shaking her shoulders.

Blinking in disorientation, her eyes focused to find Tate bending over her, a grave look on his handsome face.

"Did I fall asleep?" she mumbled, sitting up straighter and rubbing her eyes. "Is something wrong?"

"Yes, and I don't know." His voice sounded grim. "I'm heading back to the cabin."

His announcement snapped her into a state of full alertness. "What? Why?"

"Because Ben still hasn't shown up. It's an hour past the time we were supposed to meet."

"Maybe he's just late," she said feebly.

"Maybe." Tate rose to his full height, and his head was inches from bumping the ceiling. "I want you to stay here while I find out what the holdup is."

She hopped to her feet, panicked. "You're leaving me?"

"Only for an hour or two. I'm going to do some recon on the cabin and see what's up."

"Then I'm coming with you."

"No." His tone brooked no argument. "You're staying here. You'll only slow me down."

Indignation hardened her jaw. "Have I slowed you down so far?"

He ignored the question. "You're not coming." He abruptly turned away from her and grabbed his rifle. "I'm leaving the packs and duffel here. If you get hungry, there's a ton of MREs in my pack. Beef teriyaki or veggie bean-and-rice burritos—take your pick. But don't start a fire."

Eva knew there was no protesting or changing his mind. He was a man on a mission—his broad shoulders set high, his jaw tight, green eyes gleaming with fortitude. Yet beneath the commanding demeanor, she sensed something else. Desperation? Fear? She couldn't put her finger on it, but she knew without a doubt that Tate was not as calm and composed as he was acting.

He was worried about his friend, and frankly, as she glanced at her watch and noted the time, she was getting pretty worried, too. She hadn't known Ben for very long, but she liked the man, and he wouldn't even be involved in any of this in the first place if it weren't for her.

As she watched Tate go, she bit her lip and prayed that Ben was all right.

Because if he wasn't, she knew Tate would hold her responsible for it.

Hell, she'd hold *herself* responsible.

Death was in the air.

Tate couldn't explain it, but the moment he neared the woods behind the cabin, his heart sank to the pit of his stomach like a cement block and he knew he was too late.

Maybe it was the silence—the forest was too damn quiet for his liking—or it could be the coppery scent in the breeze, though he suspected he wasn't actually smelling blood.

Just anticipating it.

Keeping a solid grip on his rifle, he positioned himself at the edge of the rocky slope that would provide him with a better view of the cabin. The rear of the structure looked innocuous. No soldiers, no Ben, no sign of foul play, yet Tate's instincts continued to buzz, persistent and ominous.

Moving soundlessly, he crept through the trees and headed for the front of the cabin. His breathing was steady, his pulse regular—neither of those vitals changed, not even when the gruesome sight assaulted his vision.

But a part of him died. Right there, on the spot.

"Goddamn it, Ben," he mumbled, as hot agony streaked up his throat to choke him.

Ben's body was sprawled on the bottom steps of the porch, one lifeless arm flung out, stiff fingers still wrapped around a 9 mm that he probably hadn't even had a chance to use. Blood from the bullet hole in Ben's forehead continued to drip onto the dirt, forming a crimson puddle that made Tate see red. Literally and figuratively.

But he wasn't surprised. Oh, no. There had only been one possible explanation for Ben being a no-show at the rendezvous point. But hell, those soldiers hadn't even given him a chance. They must have stalked up to the cabin and shot him point-blank. Had they even asked him about Tate's whereabouts before they blew his brains out?

A fire of rage scorched a path through his veins. His gaze stayed glued to his friend's dead body. Damn it. God-frickin-*damn* it. He'd known Ben since they were eighteen years old, for Chrissake. Other than Will, Ben was the only person Tate had trusted implicitly and without question, and now he was gone. All because Tate had involved him in this foolish quest to kill Hector Cruz.

He wanted to go to his friend. Give him a proper burial, touch his hand, try to express how much Ben had meant to him all these years. But he couldn't. His gut told him the soldiers who'd killed Ben were long gone, but from his vantage point, he couldn't get a good look at the cabin's windows. For all he knew, those bastards were lying in wait inside, hoping Tate would walk right into an ambush like some kind of novice.

*Ben will understand.*

Right. Ben would understand that his only friend had

no choice but to leave his dead body lying there to rot in the sun.

Fury skyrocketed through him.

"No," he said through clenched teeth. "No frickin' way."

He couldn't just leave his buddy there, couldn't let him become food for scavengers. If an ambush awaited him, then so be it. He refused to disrespect Ben, not after everything the man had done for him.

Raising his rifle, Tate emerged from the brush, hyper-aware that he was out in the open and that any amateur with a sniper rifle could pick him off. To his relief, no bullets plowed him down as he made his way toward his friend's body.

He was ten yards away when he noticed another pool of blood on the dirt, and a wave of satisfaction swelled in his gut. Ben *had* managed to fire a shot before he'd died. The size of the puddle hinted that the recipient of Ben's bullet had lost a decent amount of blood. Good.

Tire tracks also streaked the dirt, which told him that the soldiers had come and gone in a military-issued jeep. It was a reassuring sign—perhaps nobody was waiting for him in the cabin after all.

When he neared his fallen comrade, he found himself unable to keep it together. His pulse suddenly went off-kilter, his throat tightened to the point of suffocation, and it felt as if someone was pinching his chest with rusty pliers.

Ben's dark brown eyes were open. Expressionless, and yet Tate could swear his friend was glaring at him in accusation.

The only way to get through the next ten minutes was to shut down. Mentally. Emotionally. Moving on autopilot, he carefully dragged Ben's massive body around the side of the cabin, toward the edge of the woods where the dirt wasn't as compact.

He didn't breathe, barely blinked, just located the shovel from the tin shed behind the house and dug a grave for his friend as if it were something he did every day. The whole process took an hour. One hour for four feet of earth to dislodge from the ground, for Ben's body to slide into that hole, for that dirt to cover it, for Tate to construct a cross from two branches.

One last thing before he could walk away. He dug a hand in his pocket and fished out the silver chain he'd removed from Ben's beefy neck. Dog tags, remnants of Ben's army days.

Looping the tags around the makeshift cross, Tate stared at the grave for several long moments before finally wrenching his gaze away.

His friend was dead. Another casualty of the war he'd found himself fighting. A war he didn't even know *why* he was fighting.

But he knew one thing, and that was that Ben Hastings was not going to die in vain.

The San Marquez military was clearly in cahoots with the United States in tracking Tate and his men down, but a bunch of soldier grunts weren't calling the shots. Someone with more clout, someone of importance, was giving the orders. That someone had ordered the unit in the jungle to shoot first and ask questions later, and now they'd done the same thing again with Ben.

Well, Tate was going to track that someone down, and when he did, maybe he'd take a page out of these bastards' book and do the exact same thing.

Don't ask questions.

Just shoot to kill.

## *Chapter 13*

Eva was waiting outside for him when Tate strode back to the cave hours later. He'd taken his time walking back because he'd wanted to avoid the questions Eva would surely have, and he'd needed to say goodbye to his friend in private.

Ironically, the weather had decided to match his mood. It was only four in the afternoon, but the sky had turned gray sometime during the walk from the cabin to the cave. Black thunderclouds loomed overhead. The temperature had grown cooler, and the wind picked up, rustling the tails of his olive-green long-sleeved shirt.

"Hey," Eva called tentatively when he ascended the slope.

"Hey," he said, keeping his tone neutral.

After almost a week with Eva, he'd learned that she was too damn caring for her own good, and he had no doubt that she would shed tears for Ben, despite the fact that she'd hardly known him at all. A part of him was tempted to withhold Ben's death from her just to avoid an emotional situation, but not telling her wasn't even an option, because she took one look at his face and seemed to know exactly what happened.

And sure enough, tears filled her eyes.

"Oh. Oh, God, Tate. Is he dead?"

He swallowed.

"Is he?" she said, her voice wobbling.

After a second, he finally nodded. "Shot to death. I...I buried him."

His voice wobbled, too, and the evidence of his shaken composure annoyed the hell out of him. He didn't want this woman to know how much Ben's death had torn him apart. Keeping his emotions hidden was a skill he'd mastered at a young age; it had been the only way to gain the upper hand with his old man. His father could smell weakness and vulnerability from miles away, and if Tate revealed either shortcoming, the beatings would be substantially worse. Needless to say, he'd quickly learned to bury his emotions.

He didn't like giving Eva a glimpse of what lay beyond the composed, indifferent mask he usually wore, and when she did precisely what he'd expected and stared at him with those big, sympathetic eyes, tears clinging to her sooty lashes, anger replaced his irritation.

"Why are you crying?" he muttered. "You didn't even know him, for Chrissake."

Two strands of tears slid down her cheeks, and she reached up to wipe them away with her sleeve, shooting him a scowl as she responded with, "Are you seriously telling me I'm not allowed to cry for him? Because too bad. I *liked* Ben, and his death saddens me, so if I want to cry about it, I damn well will. And FYI, he's not the only one I'm crying for."

Tate frowned.

"That's right, I'm crying for *you,* too. You lost your friend, Tate. It must be tearing you apart, but we both know you're not going to admit it. You'll just pretend it's no big deal. You know, because you're a big, tough military man who doesn't let his emotions get the best of him."

"Save your tears," he snapped. "I don't need you or anyone else crying on my behalf, sweetheart."

No sooner than the words left his mouth than the sky cracked with thunder and the clouds released sheets of rain that fell so hard they nearly knocked him over. The downpour was so violent he and Eva were drenched in a matter of seconds.

Cursing, he grabbed her arm and herded her into the cave, where total darkness enveloped them. He couldn't see a thing, but he sure as hell felt it when Eva pressed her lips to his.

Although he'd promised himself he wouldn't sleep with Eva again, Tate couldn't resist parting his lips to grant her tongue access to his mouth. Here in the dark, he didn't have to see the compassion in her eyes, or risk her seeing the absolute agony in his, and he knew the kiss was Eva's way of offering comfort.

"Make love to me again." Her voice came out throaty, her breath warm against his lips.

Groaning, Tate ran his hands down the sleeves of her wet shirt before peeling the garment off her slender shoulders and tossing it aside. He couldn't have stopped this even if he'd tried. He was too pissed off right now, too wrecked and too broken to care about anything other than getting Eva naked and losing himself in the pleasure she had to offer.

After their damp clothing was tossed aside, he yanked her against him, and naked flesh met naked flesh. He was mindful of her injured arm, but it didn't seem to be bothering her because she raised both arms and tightly twined them around his neck, forcing his head down for another kiss.

There was something desperate about the entire encounter. He found that his hands were shaking as he roamed her endless supply of curves, squeezing her perfect breasts, skimming his fingers over her hips, cupping her firm bottom.

Each breath came out ragged, each beat of his heart sending a jolt of pain through his body. He couldn't stop thinking about Ben's empty eyes. Ben's lifeless body.

Damn it. He'd gotten Ben killed by involving him in this mess. How many more people had to die because of him before he learned his damn lesson?

"Don't think about it."

Eva's soft voice cut into his dark thoughts. Her hands gripped his jaw, forcing him to look at her. Her face was cloaked in shadows, but he saw the intensity in those blue eyes, the firm set of her sexy lips.

"Put the pain away," she whispered, dragging her thumb along the line of his jaw. "Let me help you forget, at least for a little bit."

As his shoulders sagged in defeat, Tate allowed her to guide him into the cave wall. Cold stone chilled his bare back, but the rest of his body was on fire, the flames growing stronger as Eva sank to her knees in front of him and took his erection in her hands.

Somehow he managed to do what she'd asked. He put the pain away. Cleared his mind of the unwanted images and incensed thoughts. Closed his eyes. Tangled one hand in Eva's silky hair.

At the first brush of her lips over his cock, a moan slipped out of his mouth. His hips thrust of their own volition, seeking Eva, seeking relief. She didn't hesitate. She took him in the warm, wet recess of her mouth and sucked him so delicately that shivers skated up his spine.

A part of him felt unworthy of the worship she bestowed him with. She teased him with her fingers and lips and tongue, until the pressure in his groin was too much to bear.

"I'm too close," he murmured, stilling her loving movements by cradling her head. "Come up here."

She rose without a word, her arms coming up to loop around his neck, her head tilting and lips parting in anticipation of his kiss. Taking possession of her mouth, he kissed her roughly, that thread of desperation once again coiling inside him, threatening to snap at any moment.

He left her only to grab a condom from the kit in his pack, and then he was sheathed and ready and lifting her up. She wrapped her legs around him as he took her right there, standing up against the wall. They both groaned at that first upward thrust.

Pressure built in his groin, in his throat, his heart, and he couldn't have controlled his rough, hurried thrusts even if he'd tried. He wanted her too badly, needed this too greatly, and so he closed his eyes and lost himself in Eva. Each stroke sent him careening closer to the edge, and he slammed into her, over and over again, latching his mouth to her neck and sucking on her hot flesh as his body drove them straight to paradise.

When he felt her inner muscles clamp over him and heard her cry out in release, he let himself go. The climax shook through his body with the force of a hurricane. His heart thundered and his knees almost buckled, and as he struggled to catch his breath, he was vaguely aware of something wet tickling his shoulder.

Breathing hard, he glanced down to see Eva's eyes sparkling with tears. She was crying again, but before he could question her, she let out a shaky breath and said, "Don't tell me I can't cry for you. Because I can."

He didn't argue. Instead, he just stood there, still lodged deep inside her warmth, holding her tightly against him as she cried the tears that he couldn't.

Three hours later, the rain hadn't let up. If anything, it only got worse, the wind increasing in velocity and gusting into the opening of the cave, bringing a chill into the dank, shadowy space. Eva snuggled closer to Tate, who was lying on his back with one arm wrapped around her. They'd gotten dressed after the intense encounter against the wall, but rather than putting distance between them once their clothes were back on, Tate had surprised her by creating a makeshift bed for them on the cold ground and pulling her down beside him.

They lay under a thermal blanket, but even without it, she would have been toasty warm. Tate's body was like a furnace, radiating heat even while a torrential storm raged outside the cave.

"I didn't think tropical storms reached this far inland," she mused in the darkness, listening to the shriek of the wind.

"Me, either." He jostled her by giving his trademark shrug. "But hopefully it'll stop raining soon so we can get moving."

Uneasiness crawled up her throat like a colony of ants. "Tonight? You want to leave tonight?"

"I want this over as soon as possible," he replied in a flat tone. "The faster I slit that bastard's throat, the faster I get back to my men, and you get back to your son."

His brutal words painted a grisly picture, but Eva didn't begrudge him his bloodlust. Hector had brutally murdered Tate's brother, after all. And the more she got to know Tate, the more she realized he wasn't the indifferent, ruthless warrior he made himself out to be. He cared about people a whole lot more than he let on. The ravaged look in his eyes when he'd come back from burying Ben had said more than Tate's gruff words ever could.

He'd lost a friend tonight. He'd lost a brother. He'd lost his team.

And all that loss ate him up inside, no matter how much he pretended it didn't.

"You really just want to be alone?" she heard herself asking. "You want to live your life without letting a single person in?"

He stayed quiet, and she could feel the discomfort rolling off him in waves. "Why does it bother you so much?" he finally muttered. "There are worse things than solitude, Eva."

"I know. It's just…don't you ever get tired of your own company? Don't you feel the need to get close to someone else?"

"Getting close always ends in one thing—misery." A tiny note of bitterness hung on his words. "One day you'll learn that the only person you can trust is yourself, sweetheart."

"So you didn't trust your brother?" she challenged.

"I trusted Will as much as I could. But one hundred percent pure, blind trust? Nobody will ever get that from me."

"That's sad."

His harsh laughter echoed in the darkness. "You want sad? I trusted the woman who gave birth to me to take care of me, and she chose to take care of herself instead, by pumping poison into her veins. I trusted the man who sired me to step in and fix things, and he decided to use me as a punching bag instead. I trusted my government to protect me, and now I'm being hunted like a dog." His ragged breathing heated her forehead. "How's that for sad, baby?"

Her heart wept for him. "Tate—"

"No pity, Eva. No sympathy, no reassurances. I've accepted the cold hard reality of it—you get close, you get betrayed. That's the running motif of my life, and that's why I'm not just okay with being alone, I *embrace* it."

"I guess I understand that," she conceded. "But me? I don't think I'd want to be alone."

He chuckled. "One thing I've discovered over the years is that not a lot of people can stand their own company. In fact, they're so uncomfortable with themselves and out of touch with who they are that they surround themselves with other people in order to define themselves."

"Oh, I know who I am, and trust me, I'm fine with it. I can be alone if I need to be, but like I said, I wouldn't *want* to. I like having someone else to talk to, someone to share my thoughts and feelings with." Her throat closed up. "I've been lonely the past three years. Do you ever get lonely, Tate?"

To her surprise, he caressed her shoulder, his rough-skinned fingers tickling her skin. "Yeah," he admitted. "I do."

"What's your coping strategy? How do you cheer up when you feel lonely?"

"I remind myself of all the crap that's happened in my life. I remind myself why I chose to be alone."

"That's…depressing."

He hesitated. "What do *you* do?"

"I think of my son. Everything I've done these past three years, all the new houses and new names and new places—they were all to protect Rafe. So it doesn't matter if I feel happy and fulfilled, all that matters is that Rafe is, and it doesn't matter if I'm sad or lonely, as long as he *isn't*. That little boy is my entire life. He's the only thing that matters."

Tate fell silent again. She felt his heart beating beneath

her ear, a steady, comforting rhythm that brought a sense of peace she hadn't felt in years. Tate might be rough around the edges, cold at times, arrogant at others, but she couldn't deny that he made her feel protected. She'd actually managed to get some real, satisfying sleep since she'd teamed up with him. She could close her eyes and let her guard down because she knew that Tate would keep her safe, and the realization brought prickles of discomfort to her skin.

She trusted him. Somehow, during this past week, she'd come to trust Tate.

"Let's get some shut-eye." His raspy voice broke through her disconcerting thoughts. "I want to head out the moment the rain stops."

"Okay," she murmured, snuggling closer.

But she was still thinking about what it all meant—trusting Tate—as she drifted off to sleep.

When two days passed and the storm showed no indications of abating, Tate was beginning to think he and Eva would never be on the move again. Outside, the slope had turned into an ocean of mud, making it difficult to leave the cave without the risk of being carried away by a mudslide. He and Eva only ventured out to use nature's bathroom, and each time they did, the rain and wind nearly knocked them off their feet.

Fortunately, they had plenty of food in the form of the MREs, beef jerky, crackers and bottled water Tate had shoved into Ben's duffel before they'd left the cabin. They couldn't start a fire because the cave didn't offer much in terms of a chimney, but they had a blanket, and they could share body heat—which they did. A lot. With nothing to do but sit and wait out the storm, getting naked had become the best way to pass the time.

And though he'd never say it out loud, he'd enjoyed

being with Eva these past two days. He'd enjoyed it immensely.

"Why don't you believe me?" she demanded.

Her annoyed tone made him chuckle. So did the way she scowled at him, as if he'd accused her of committing a major crime when all he'd done was express a teeny bit of doubt about her response to his question. Out of sheer boredom, they'd started talking about what they envisioned to be the perfect life, and Eva's description had definitely triggered his skepticism.

"Because it doesn't seem like something you'd be into," he replied, rolling his eyes. "You want to live out in the boonies, have a bunch of dogs, let your kid run wild and pretty much isolate yourself from society."

Her scowl deepened. "What's wrong with that?"

"Nothing's wrong with it. In fact, it's exactly..."

Exactly what he wanted for himself. Minus the kid part, of course.

But he didn't finish that thought. Instead, he trailed off, and searched her gorgeous blue eyes for a sign that she was joking around.

Her expression remained dead serious. "I hate cities," she said frankly. "I grew up in Manhattan and hated every second of it. The crowds, the traffic, the pollution, the noise. I told you how every summer my parents would rent a cabin in Vermont, right? Well, it was all I looked forward to all year. That's when I knew I belonged in the boonies."

"Yeah, and what about your trusty computer?" he countered. "Seems like your love for technology doesn't mesh with the country life."

She shrugged, causing several strands of black hair to fall over one of her bare shoulders. The only light came from the flashlight resting on a ledge above Eva's head, and the yellow glow created a halo effect and made her blue eyes sparkle.

She was sitting cross-legged beside him, while he was sprawled on his back, and he reached out to tuck her silky hair behind her ear. For some reason, he'd been touching her far too frequently during this forced confinement, and not just during the sex. Stroking her hair, rubbing her back, brushing his fingers over her slender arm. He couldn't seem to stop himself, and damn, but it felt nice touching Eva. She was so soft and warm and womanly that he simply couldn't resist.

"All I need is an internet connection," she said. "I already told you, I want to design software, maybe contract myself out to companies who are worried about the security of their websites and databases. I can do that from anywhere."

"True," he agreed. "But I still can't picture you living in the middle of nowhere."

"I'm a simple girl, Tate. I like the outdoors, I love big, open spaces, and I hate all the superficial stuff that so many people are obsessed with." Her perfect lips quirked in a smile. "I don't want my son to be superficial, either. I want him to run around outside and have fun adventures and discover new things, not sit inside playing video games all day. It's important for him to learn how to use technology, but I don't want that to define him, you know?"

Tate had already lost count of how many times he'd had to hide his deep approval for this woman. Eva continued to surprise him—she was far more intelligent than he ever would have guessed, had a sensible head on her shoulders, fiercely spoke her mind, was quick to laugh, easy to talk to.

He couldn't remember ever liking or respecting a woman this much, and it troubled the hell out of him that his guard was slowly lowering in her company. He wasn't supposed to trust or care about her, yet the longer this storm raged on, the more his defenses began to crumble. He couldn't even believe half the stuff he'd told her—about his family, his brother, his need for solitude. He always tried to keep a distance from other people, but with Eva…damn it, with Eva, he only seemed to pull her closer and closer.

"Oh, no." She suddenly grimaced. "I have to pee."

Tate had to grin. "I already told you, it's fine if you want to go in the corner. I'll close my eyes."

She looked horrified. "I refuse to do my business in this cave. I'd rather get wet and muddy."

He laughed as he watched her stumble to her feet. She wore nothing but a white button-down shirt and black bikini panties, and her legs were long and smooth, her delicate feet bare. With her hair loose and her cheeks flushed, she made a truly spectacular picture. His body, of course, immediately responded to her, which wasn't a surprise seeing as getting hard for this woman had become a habit he couldn't kick.

"I'll be right back," she said, reaching for the second flashlight sitting on top of her pack.

She switched it on and pointed the shaft of light at the entrance of the cave. The rain was still pouring, a constant stream of water that didn't seem at all interested in easing up. The only upside was that the air itself remained hot and humid, so when you stepped into the rain, it was like entering a warm bath.

After Eva left the cave, Tate sat up and rummaged around for his T-shirt, which he pulled over his head before searching for his pants. Once he was dressed, he did a quick inventory of his pack, made sure their food and water supply wasn't dwindling, checked his ammo situation and examined the contents of the first-aid kit. That final task had his eyebrows shooting up. He'd lost track of the number of times he and Eva had wound up naked over the past forty-eight hours, but judging by the solitary condom left in the plastic pouch, they'd clearly reached nymphomaniac status.

Zipping up the bag, he stood up and headed to the cave's entrance, swallowing his rising frustration as he gazed out at the relentless rain. They'd already been delayed two days, and he didn't like it one damn bit. The only saving grace was that the soldiers who'd ambushed Ben at the cabin were probably grounded, too. This area was notorious for mud- and landslides—nobody would be stupid enough to be on the mountain in this weather. Nevertheless, he'd feel better once they were no longer sitting ducks, and on the move.

"Eeeek!"

The shrill female cry interrupted the steady pounding of the rain and made Tate's stomach go rigid.

"Eva?" he shouted.

When there was no answer, he sprang to action, a rush of adrenaline whipping through his veins and making his pulse speed up.

He didn't bother putting on his boots, just tore out of the cave barefoot, cringing when his feet sank into a thick layer of slimy brown mud. It was late morning, but the sky was so overcast it looked more like twilight. Running wasn't an option, not unless he wanted to slide down the slope and break both his legs, and panic hammered a reckless beat in his chest as he moved as fast as he could in the direction Eva usually went to take care of business.

"Eva!" he yelled again.

No answer.

His panic intensified. Christ, why wasn't she answering?

He followed the muddy terrain toward a set of huge jagged boulders in the distance, unable to control the frantic thumping of his heart. What if the soldiers had grabbed her, or an animal attacked her, or—

He staggered to a stop when he rounded the boulders and spotted her.

"Thank God," he blurted out.

Then he noticed her predicament and burst out laughing.

"Don't you dare laugh at me," she ordered, her jaw so tight he knew she was grinding her teeth.

"You okay?" he asked between chuckles.

Looking pissed off and mortified, Eva lay on her back, covered from head to toe in mud. Her shirt was no longer white but brown, and the mud and rain had caked her hair to her head and was dripping down her face, making her look like a creature out of a horror movie.

"I tripped," she grumbled. "Got the wind knocked out of me. Tried to get up and tripped again."

Tate stifled another laugh and managed a supportive nod. "I can see that." He tilted his head. "You need a hand, or are you just going to lie there in the mud for the rest of the day?"

Her bottom lip stuck out in defeat. "I need a hand."

Lips twitching with amusement, he carefully walked over to her and extended his hand. The second their fingers touched, he realized her evil intentions, but by then it was too damn late.

Eva tugged on his hand and he came crashing down on top of her, sending wet muck sailing in all directions.

"You little…" He spat mud from his mouth, then tried to wipe his face only to make it worse.

"That's what you get for laughing at me," she said, wiggling beneath him. "A true gentleman politely keeps his mouth shut in the face of a lady's humiliation."

"I'm no gentleman, sweetheart." And then he proceeded

to prove it by sliding his wet, dirty hands beneath her wet, dirty shirt.

She squeaked in surprise, then moaned and arched her spine, pushing her breasts into his palms. Her enthusiasm made him groan. She was always so eager for him, so ready and willing and welcoming, no matter when he reached for her, no matter how rough he was.

He hated to admit it, but he didn't have the upper hand anymore. He'd lost that sometime over the past two days, when his desire for Eva had reached a new level of desperation that both shamed and thrilled him.

"I love it when you touch me like this." She sighed happily as he gently squeezed her breasts.

"I love touching you like this," he answered gruffly.

He swept his thumbs over her distended nipples, and she moaned again. The husky sound teased his senses and stirred his cock, which grew hard, heavy, pulsing with need.

Neither of them seemed to care that they were lying on the wet, muddy ground. In fact, Tate was completely oblivious to his surroundings as he captured her mouth with his and kissed her, long, deep and thorough. The rain continued to fall, soaking them both as they lay there kissing, drowning out all sound and reason.

"I didn't bring a condom out," he murmured.

"That's probably a good thing, because I don't think I want mud getting all over my delicate parts," she said wryly. She slid her hand between their bodies and rubbed her palm over the bulge in his pants. "But I think we can arrange something for you."

"You don't have—"

But she wasn't listening. She'd already unbuttoned his pants and reached inside.

Tate's head lolled to the side as she tormented him with

her hand. When he could barely support his own weight, he rolled onto his back. The raindrops felt like little needles as they fell into his face, but he barely noticed the downpour. With Eva curled up at his side, her hand wrapped around his shaft as she pumped him in fast, sensual strokes, the rain was the last thing on his mind.

"Oh, sweetheart, I'm close," he rasped.

She increased her speed, tightened her suction, and within seconds, he lost himself in a mind-shattering release that made him gasp for air. When he regained his faculties, he found Eva watching him with a satisfied gleam in her blue eyes.

"Do you forgive me for pushing you down in the mud?" she teased.

It took him a moment to find his voice. "I forgive you."

"Good." She bent her head to plant a kiss on his lips, then carefully got to her feet.

Tate watched as she tipped her head up to the sky and let the rain wash the brown streaks from her face. In fact, within seconds, her face and bare legs were totally clean, but her white shirt was beyond saving.

His heart rate had just steadied after that explosive climax, but it quickly sped right back up when Eva began unbuttoning her shirt. She peeled it off her slender shoulders, and then she was gloriously naked save for her bikini panties. Her gorgeous, golden limbs assaulted his vision and made his mouth go dry. Everything about her reignited his arousal—her bare breasts, round and full, the raindrops clinging to her pebbled nipples and sluicing over her flat belly, the sexy curve of her buttocks.

His gaze landed on the dirty bandage covering her upper arm, and he stumbled to his feet with a frown. "We need to change your dressing," he said firmly. "And you should take another antibiotics shot."

"Later," she answered, and then she continued to wash up, running her hands over her breasts and belly.

Trying to ignore the sexy sight, he followed her lead and let the rain wash him clean. The faster he got this mud off him, the faster he could be back in the cave with Eva, making use of that last condom in his pack.

She must have read his mind, because she shot him a broad smile. "You're totally going to have your way with me, aren't you?"

He responded with a rogue smirk. "You complaining?"

"No." She donned a thoughtful pose. "But you've got to do one thing for me before I give you free rein of my body."

"Yeah, and what's that?"

"Admit you like me."

His jaw tensed, just for a second, but he quickly forced it to relax. The playful look in Eva's eyes told him she wasn't making demands of him, but he knew there was a lot more to that lighthearted request.

He was perfectly aware that he hadn't given her any indication of what he felt for her. She must know he was wildly attracted to her—fat chance of him hiding *that*—but in terms of where his head was at? His heart? He understood her need to figure that out, and he didn't blame her; he'd learned a long time ago that the women in your bed sometimes needed a little reassurance.

So he opened his mouth and told her what she wanted to hear.

"I like you." He shrugged awkwardly. "I like you a helluva lot, Eva."

Except then something strange happened, something that almost made him topple right back into the mud.

He realized that he'd meant every damn word.

# Chapter 14

"Okay, so what's the plan?" Eva asked the next morning.

Tate's green-eyed gaze swept over the piece of paper he'd spread out on the boulder near the cave. The rain had ceased right after dawn, almost as quickly as it had started, and Eva was still having trouble adjusting to the blinding sunlight beating down on her head. Although some parts of the area were still wet and muddy, most of the earth had dried up, leaving streaks of brown clay on the soles of their boots.

She and Tate had eaten breakfast outside, both of them needing the fresh air after being cooped up in the cave for forty-eight hours, and now Tate was all business as he examined the drawing she'd made of Hector's bunker. She'd included every detail she could remember, which Tate seemed to appreciate, but she still had no idea how the two of them would manage to sneak in and out without being shot on sight.

"Ben and I came up with something before, but…" Tate drifted off, his expression strained.

Knowing how difficult it was for him to talk about his friend, she reached out and took his hand, squeezing it gently. "What did you come up with?"

"He would provide a distraction while I went in from the tunnel over here." He pointed to the exit she'd labeled on her map, the one located in the foothills that the bunker's tunnel led out to.

"Okay. What kind of distraction?"

"A full-on assault. Rig the area over here—" he pointed again "—with explosives, and take out the entrance with an RPG."

Her eyebrows flew north. "A rocket launcher? You've got one of those?"

Tate's mouth quirked. "That was one of the supplies Ben went to get."

"Oh. Okay. So what was supposed to happen after he took out the entrance?"

"The camp would be in chaos. All the guards would be drawn to the explosion. They'd try to make sense of the commotion, Cruz would most likely send a team out to investigate. Ben would've strategically detonated explosives and lured any rebels away from the camp, while I went in from the foothills, took out Hector and snuck back out."

"Wow. All right. Well." She pursed her lips. "Why can't I be the one in charge of the distraction? I'm sure I could handle a rocket launcher without screwing it up too badly. It's just point and shoot, right?"

His expression hardened. "No way."

"I can do it," she insisted. "I'll hide out in the trees over here—" she jammed a finger at the map "—and when you give me the go-ahead, I'll take out the entrance. And I can work a remote detonator. When the rebels come out to investigate, I'll make them all go boom."

He didn't look the slightest bit amused by her attempt at humor. "No. Way."

His tone invited absolutely no argument, and it elicited a burst of irritation.

"I won't screw it up," she muttered. "And I take direction really well. All you have to do is tell me how to—" She stopped abruptly as it dawned on her. "It's not that you think I can't handle it, is it? You don't *trust* me to do it. You think I'll screw you over or something."

Pain squeezed her throat, but really, why did that surprise her? Tate had made it clear from day one that he didn't trust her, and their sleeping together didn't change that. Heck, that was *another* thing he'd made clear—sex and trust were one hundred percent mutually exclusive.

Yet his lack of faith brought a dull ache to her heart. She might have lied to him about her relationship with Hector, but she hadn't lied about anything else. Her life story, her love for her son, her thoughts and fears and hopes. There had been nothing false about any of that, and it troubled her how willingly she'd confided in Tate about those things.

She wasn't supposed to let another man in. After her disastrous and reckless involvement with Hector, she'd promised herself to be warier around men. Not to give her trust so easily, and yet here she was, putting all her faith in another soldier. Another ruthless alpha male who didn't care about her at all.

"Forget it," she mumbled when he didn't respond. She averted her eyes, pretending to study the map. "If you don't trust me to be part of this mission, then fine. We'll do it your way."

Her peripheral vision caught a flash of movement, and she jumped when Tate's rough hand gripped her jaw. His touch was surprisingly tender, his gaze even more so as he forced eye contact.

"That's not it," he said gruffly.

She swallowed. "What are you talking about?"

"I won't let you play Rambo and blow things up, and that's not because I think you're going to screw me over." A strangled breath flew out of his mouth. "It's because it's too damn dangerous and I refuse to let you get hurt."

Astonishment rippled through her. "What?"

"Once things go to hell, all those rebels will be running out to find the source of the chaos. They'll be pissed off and trigger-happy and gunning for the person who had the nerve to blow up their lair."

His hand dropped from her chin and curled into a fist that he slammed on the dirt. "You're not dying on my watch, Eva. I refuse to let you die. You understand?"

Her shock only deepened. "Why?"

"Why what?" He sounded—and looked—embarrassed.

"Why don't you want me to die, Tate?" She softened her tone. "Yesterday you told me you liked me, but I think you were saying that more for my sake than anything. You've made it clear from the beginning that you don't particularly care about my wellbeing, so what's changed? Why do you suddenly care whether I live or die?"

His silence dragged on and on, and she'd just given up on ever receiving an answer when he cleared his throat and offered an awkward shrug. "Your kid. I want you to live so your kid can grow up with his mother."

Before she could question—or challenge—that statement, Tate stood up. "I'm gonna grab some water and then we can talk this through some more. Want anything from the cave?"

She shook her head, then watched him stride off, feeling incredibly perturbed.

*I want you to live so your kid can grow up with his mother.*

She had to wonder, was that really it?

Or was it possible that maybe, just maybe, Tate was actually starting to care about her?

It took twelve hours to reach their destination, but Tate didn't feel the slightest bit winded. If anything, he was riddled with adrenaline, fraught with tension and champing at the bit. Hector Cruz was less than a mile away. One measly mile. For the first time in eight months, the man who'd murdered his brother was within his grasp.

Although he preferred to travel at night, impatience and eagerness had overruled his need for caution, and so he and Eva had navigated the mountainous terrain while the sun beat down on their heads, leaving them hot and sweaty. They'd discussed their options during the trek, but Tate hadn't come up with a workable plan of action yet.

Eva insisted that she should be in charge of causing a distraction, but he was loath to put her in the line of fire like that. Ben would've easily been able to disappear in the woods and evade the men who would no doubt be dispatched to comb the mountainside. But Eva? She was no soldier, and he'd be damned if someone else died under his watch.

*Right, that's why you're so concerned.*

The nagging voice brought a frown to his lips. He'd been battling those same doubts all frickin' morning, and he'd yet to make a single lick of sense about the strange emotions swirling through his chest. He didn't want Eva to die. That much he knew, but…but why the hell should he care if she did?

Because they were sleeping together?

Because her kid would be orphaned?

Because he'd be losing something…*worthwhile* if she wasn't in his life?

Ridiculous. All those options were utterly ridiculous, and only increased his annoyance. He'd be just fine if Eva was no longer warming his bed. He didn't care about her kid. And he certainly didn't need or want her in his life.

"The sun will set soon," she remarked, coming up beside him. "What's our plan, Tate?"

Other women would probably look exhausted and disheveled after a twelve-hour hike, yet Eva seemed downright cheery. Her eyes flickered with determination, and she held her shoulders high, despite the fact that a backpack had been weighing those shoulders down all day long.

"When it gets dark, I'll go on ahead and do some recon," he replied.

Her eyes narrowed. "Alone?"

"Yes, alone." He arched a brow. "Will I get an argument from you?"

"No, but…" Her teeth nibbled on her bottom lip. "But what if something happens? What if the guards spot you?"

"They won't." Confidence lined his tone. "I'm black ops, sweetheart. I'm invisible."

"Somehow that doesn't reassure me."

Sighing, he moved closer and rested a hand on her shoulder. "It'll be fine. I was trained for this kind of thing, Eva. And I work better alone, so you're going to stay here like I ordered and let me do my thing, okay?"

"Okay," she said in a grudging tone.

He dipped his head, brushed his lips over hers and forced himself not to question this need to reassure her. The two days in the cave had created an intimacy between them that made him unbelievably uncomfortable, yet at the same time, he found himself almost soothed by it.

Oh, brother. He was in deep trouble.

Stepping backward, he headed over to their gear and unzipped Ben's duffel. Along with the aluminum case containing the RPG-7, there were also a handful of grenades, trip wires and enough C4 to blow up a small country. He was pleased to discover that Ben had even done most of the prep work—the explosives just needed to be rigged and armed, and then Tate could detonate them remotely if need be. As far as strategies went, this one was flimsy at best, but without Ben, there weren't many other options.

Tate gathered up the supplies he needed and stowed them in his pack, then grabbed his rifle and glanced over at Eva. Overhead, the sky had darkened, the sun steadily dipping toward the horizon line.

"Stay out of sight," he told her, gesturing to the crude blind he'd constructed for her in a cluster of dense shrubbery.

Her expression was resigned. "I will." Then she bent down, picked up her backpack and dutifully ducked into the hiding spot he'd fashioned.

Fighting the stupid urge to yank her out of the tree and kiss her goodbye, Tate dragged the heavy duffel into the brush and covered it with fallen branches and dead leaves. A moment later, he slung his rifle over his shoulder and took off walking.

It was the first time he'd been alone in days, and he welcomed the respite, the silence. He moved through the wilderness without making a sound, and this time, he made an effort to cover his tracks. He hadn't bothered in the jungle or on the way here, because, frankly, he didn't give a damn if anyone knew where he was going. Let the hunters follow him—as long as he killed Will's murderer before they caught up to him, he'd die happy.

Yet he couldn't seem to maintain that careless indifference any longer. He might not care whether he lived or died, but he sure as hell cared if Eva did. For some reason, protecting her had become a priority for him, and if that meant covering his tracks so that his enemies didn't stumble across her, then so be it.

Tate's instincts began to hum as he maneuvered the foothills that made up the base of the small mountain range spanning San Marquez's western coast. The sun had set completely by then, shrouding the entire area in darkness. Since he couldn't afford to make a single wrong move, he stopped only to remove his night-vision goggles from his pack. He slipped them on, and his surroundings immediately came alive again.

He kept walking. The trees thinned as rocky slopes and craggy hills appeared, making it all the more important to stay invisible. The enemy was close. He felt it with a bone-deep certainty, and the conviction was validated when he finally laid eyes on the prize he'd been seeking for months.

*Hello, Cruz.*

Eva hadn't lied. At first glance, one would think they were looking at a wall of solid rock surrounded by heavy shrubbery. In the distance, the jagged peaks of the mountains seemed to glow thanks to his goggles, but they weren't the only things glowing. In the daylight, the copper-colored door built right into the rock formation up ahead would probably be mistaken for dirt and rock, but the night-vision goggles picked up on the inconsistency, making that particular feature glint like the metal it was.

Like Eva had said, the entrance was guarded, but there weren't as many men as Tate had expected. He counted ten. Two at the door, four stationed higher in the hills, armed with rifles and binoculars. Four more walking the perimeter.

All were rebels, which was clear thanks to the unkempt brown uniforms and the potluck collection of weaponry—

AKs, M-16s, handguns, a shotgun or two. The ULF rebels were organized for the most part, but when it came to supplies, they took what they could get. Rumor had it Cruz had deals in place with several major arms dealers, but it also wasn't uncommon for the rebels to raid military camps or villages to steal weapons.

Since he needed to get a sense of the perimeter guards' movements before he did anything, he hunkered down behind a couple of boulders and spent the next two hours watching and learning.

It turned out the guards didn't travel far. They simply circled the compound every ten minutes in teams of two, following the same path each time. Every now and then, they'd light up a cigarette and stop to chat near the half-dozen Jeeps and pickup trucks littering the base of the slope.

Cruz's hideout was no maximum-security prison. More like the place you sent perpetrators of tax fraud or petty crime, but then again, that made total sense. Cruz wouldn't want to advertise his presence, and making this particular camp seem unimportant was a nice touch. Anyone who caught wind of this place would never dream to think that the leader of the ULF was hiding here, out in the open with barely any protection.

It took Tate no time at all to set up a few strategically placed explosives, and then he was heading back the way he came, putting distance between himself and the rebels who'd been oblivious to his presence.

He was halfway back to Eva when his body started humming again. His back stiffened and the hairs on his nape stood on end. His rifle snapped up instinctively as he slid behind a gnarled tree trunk, where he stayed out of sight. Waiting. Listening.

Nothing sounded out of place. Just the night noises of the creatures that inhabited these woodlands.

So why couldn't he shake the feeling that he was being watched?

One minute passed. Two. Five. Ten. By the time the fifteen-minute mark crept up, Tate was wondering if his intuition was on the fritz or something. Whatever danger he'd sensed was gone. If the threat had even existed in the first place.

Reluctant, he stepped out and continued making his way back to camp, but the hairs on the back of his neck tingled the entire damn time.


"That is a *terrible* idea!" Eva hissed a few hours later, after Tate divulged the details of his plan.

The moonlight cast a glow over his handsome face, emphasizing the determined line of his mouth. "It's the best one I've got," he said in a low voice.

She shook her head, unable to fathom how he could sit there so calmly after outlining the flimsiest, most suicidal plan she'd ever heard in her life.

To make matters worse, he'd completely misled her. The two of them were ducked behind a cluster of thick shrubs about twenty yards from the rusted metal hatch that was barely visible through the brush. That hatch led to the tunnel, which in turn led to Hector's bunker, and by bringing her here, Tate had made her believe he needed her help with this mission.

Apparently that wasn't at all the case.

"I'm going in alone." His tone was firm, his expression inflexible. "I already told you that a dozen times before."

"But that was when Ben had your back. Now you're on your own." She frowned. "What happened to the rocket launcher plan? The big distraction?"

"That was when Ben had my back," he mimicked. "With Ben watching the front and me here in the rear, there would have been no chance of Cruz getting away, but now, Cruz could flee the bunker while I'm blowing the main entrance to smithereens, and I won't be here to stop him."

"I could watch this exit while you blow things up," she offered.

"No."

"Fine, then let *me* blow things up."

"No."

Frustration spiraled through her. "Stop saying no to everything. This plan of yours sucks. You're just going to waltz through that hatch without trying to distract any of the guards standing right on the other side of that hill? And then you're going to shoot your way to Hector, kill him and shoot your way back out?" An amazed laugh popped out of her mouth. "You're nuts, you know that?"

He merely shrugged.

"And let's not forget about *my* part in all this. What's my part again?" She faked an epiphany. "Oh, right, *nothing*."

Tate ignored the sarcasm. "Same deal as before, Eva. Get yourself to the coordinates I gave you. Take the sat phone, and if I'm not there at the arranged time, call Gomez and he'll come pick you up."

She scowled. "Just like that, huh? What happened to what you said about the government shooting unauthorized aircraft out of the sky?"

"Gomez won't be flying you off the island, just taking you to the coast. You can make your way to Tumaco from there, and then Gomez will rendezvous with you in Cali and bring you back to Mexico. Back to your kid."

The thought of seeing Rafe brought a rush of longing to her chest, but the fear and concern already swimming there overpowered the new addition. No matter how much she wanted to be reunited with her son, she couldn't let Tate undertake this crusade alone. Walking into Hector's hideout like he owned the place? With no contingency plans in place? No backup? No guaranteed way out?

The stubborn fool was going to get himself killed, damn it.

Her gaze drifted toward the unguarded hatch in the distance. Tate had said there were nearly a dozen rebels on the other side of the rocks, but back here, the hills were dark and deserted at four in the morning.

She understood his point about not wanting to risk Hector escaping, which was a real possibility if Tate was forced to take out the front entrance and then rush all the way over here. By then, Hector could already be halfway down the mountain in one of those off-road vehicles Tate had seen.

"I'm coming with you," she announced.

"No."

She lifted her brows in defiance. "Say no all you want. It won't change a damn thing."

Reaching around, she pulled her gun from the waistband of her jeans, ignoring the way Tate's green eyes smoldered with menace. In the darkness, with his angry expression and thick beard, he looked deadlier than usual, but Eva wasn't about to let him push her around.

Somehow during the past week, she'd come to care about this man, and she refused to let him die, especially not when she was the one who'd dragged him to San Marquez in the first place.

"Eva…" His voice thickened with annoyance.

"Tate," she replied, her voice calm.

"You're not coming."

"Like hell I'm not."

"Eva."

Now she rolled her eyes. "Quit saying my name. And

quit arguing with me. I'm going into that tunnel with you, whether you like it or not."

He let out an exasperated breath. "I won't let you."

"You don't have a choice." She removed the magazine of her gun and checked to make sure she had a full clip, then shoved it back in and cocked the weapon. "I'm coming."

"Why, damn it?"

*Because I'm in love with you and I don't want you to die!*

The thoughts whizzed to the forefront of her mind so fast that her brain nearly shorted out. Shock slammed into her, but she scrambled to maintain her composure, to remain expressionless.

God. It couldn't be true. She couldn't have fallen in love with Tate.

Right?

As her throat became dry and tight, she gulped a few times, searching for an excuse, an excuse Tate would believe. Because no way could she tell him the truth. He wouldn't be comfortable with the idea that she wanted to help him because she cared, and as that notion settled in, she realized the best answer she could give him was the one that catered to his natural cynicism.

"Because I want to see Hector's dead body with my own eyes," she said with a shrug.

A deep crease dug in his forehead. "I see."

"I thought you would. Trust, remember? You don't trust me, and I don't trust you. How am I supposed to know you'll actually kill Hector?"

"Oh, I'll kill him," Tate declared, a fierce look entering his eyes.

"Well, forgive me if I can't take you at your word. I'm coming with you, Tate."

His head tilted pensively as he appraised her. "To make sure that I actually kill Cruz."

"Yes."

For a moment, she thought he'd continue to argue, but apparently her appeal to his cynical side had worked.

It was pretty damn sad that he couldn't accept worry or affection as a reason for her to offer backup on a mission, but fear of betrayal? He had no problem buying that.

Even sadder? That she might actually be in love with a man who, given the choice, would probably prefer her distrust to her love.

Tate was acutely aware of Eva as the two of them moved through the shadows toward the unmanned hatch. He wanted to throw her over his shoulder in a fireman's carry and cart her back to safety, but after days of traveling with the woman, he knew she wouldn't take too kindly to being pushed around. She'd made up her mind about coming along, and nothing he said or did would change that.

*I want to see Hector's dead body with my own eyes.*

Her words continued to float through his head, bringing a multitude of emotions he couldn't quite get a handle on. On one hand, he absolutely understood her need to ensure that Cruz truly met his demise. He wouldn't be satisfied with secondhand confirmation, either—oh, no, he'd need to see that bastard's head on a spike before he believed Cruz was dead.

On the other hand...well, he supposed it shouldn't bother him that Eva had so little faith in his ability—and his promise—to follow through and kill Hector.

But it did bother him. It bothered him a helluva lot.

It shouldn't, though, seeing as he didn't trust her, either.

*Yes, you do.*

He nearly froze in his tracks. Had to force himself to keep moving, even as that alarming revelation continued to flash through his head like a strobe light. Was it true? Did he trust Eva?

Christ, did he *care* for Eva?

Stricken, he forcibly banished each and every disturbing thought from his mind. Now was *not* the time to ponder any of it. Maybe after he killed Cruz. Or after he managed to get him and Eva out of this alive. Maybe *then* he'd let himself think about the answers to those terrifying questions.

"Stay behind me." His voice was barely a whisper as they came upon the entrance of the tunnel.

Raising his rifle, he reached for one of the rusted handles on the two halves that made up the metal hatch. The opening was low to the ground and on an angle, which meant Tate would be looking down at whoever happened to be behind those doors.

"Ready?" he murmured.

As Eva offered a soft assent, he said a quick prayer, then yanked open the door. Despite the thick layer of rust on it, the hatch didn't make a single sound as it opened. No creak or groan or croak. Someone must have been oiling the hinges regularly, a fact that Tate was incredibly grateful for at the moment.

When they didn't encounter a single guard behind that door, however, his gratitude transformed into suspicion. He stared at the three concrete steps leading to the gaping opening, then glanced at Eva. "You said there should be a guard here."

She looked confused. "There was the last time I was here."

Frowning, he carefully descended the steps and entered the tunnel. The overhead lights flickered incessantly, humming like insects in the musty-smelling space and bringing a throb to his temples.

He turned at the sound of Eva's quiet footsteps and

raised his finger to his lips to signal her silence. She nodded slightly, falling behind him once more as they made their way down the narrow tunnel. It was only fifty yards or so before the tunnel ended in front of a metal ladder built into the wall.

Tate glanced up and spotted yet another hatch at the top of the ladder. Eva had mentioned there'd be guards up there, too, but considering they hadn't encountered a single man in the tunnel, he was beginning to question everything she'd told him.

Sure enough, they didn't run into any trouble once they slid through the second hatch. This one led to a small room with cinder-block walls and no furniture, and as he crept to the door, rifle in hand, Tate's uneasiness continued to grow, until his gut was damn near overflowing with it.

Nothing about this seemed right.

Battling his rising apprehension, he slowly pushed on the door handle and peered out into the corridor. Empty. Why wasn't he surprised?

He replaced his rifle with his pistol, which was affixed with a silencer, then gestured for Eva to follow him. He'd memorized her drawing, and knew exactly where to go, provided her intel was solid.

The bunker was deceptively larger than it seemed from the outside, and Tate felt far too exposed as he and Eva moved deeper into the enemy's domain. The lack of security continued to unnerve him—not only the absence of guards, but he didn't see a single camera mounted on any of the walls, either. Maybe Cruz didn't deem it necessary. Maybe Cruz was so arrogant that he believed himself to be untouchable.

Wouldn't surprise him. He'd witnessed that same arrogance eight months ago when Cruz had nonchalantly murdered Will. The rebel had considered himself untouchable then, too.

On the other hand, maybe the lack of precaution had nothing to do with arrogance, Tate decided as he noted the bad lighting and poor ventilation, the cracked cinderblock walls and dirty cement floor. The ULF wasn't as well funded as other "freedom" groups, and he doubted Cruz had specifically built this bunker for the purpose of having a secret hideout. The rebel leader had probably just stumbled upon this lair and knew a good thing when he saw one.

"Hector's quarters are this way." Eva's voice was barely over a whisper.

Tate still wished she'd agreed to stay behind, but it was too late to second-guess his decision to let her come. He just hoped this all didn't blow up in his face.

After rounding another corner, they descended a set of low stairs and crept down another hallway, this one narrower than the others. They took a left, then a right—and suddenly found themselves face-to-face with the startled eyes of a dark-skinned guard.

Odd as it was, the notion that they weren't alone brought a blast of relief to Tate's gut. He'd been starting to think this damn bunker was abandoned, and he was happy for some proof that it wasn't.

Still, that didn't mean he enjoyed the killing the man.

He had no other choice, though. He pulled the trigger and shot the guard between the eyes, then darted forward to catch the limp body before it toppled to the floor. The suppressor screwed to the barrel of his pistol ensured that the kill had been soundless, and nobody came running to the guard's rescue.

As he lowered the dead man's weight to the floor, his peripheral vision caught Eva flinching.

Without remorse, he offered a dry look and murmured, "You have something to say?"

She slowly shook her head, but her cheeks were pale.

Tate got to his feet and stared at the wooden door the dead man had been guarding, then glanced at Eva in an unspoken question.

When she nodded, he gestured for her to move behind him. She did, all the while holding her gun in a two-handed pose, her breathing soft and steady.

Taking a steadying breath of his own, he tucked his pistol in his belt and raised his rifle instead.

*You ready for me, Cruz?*

The notion that his brother's murderer was right behind that door flooded his mouth with saliva. As bloodlust ripped into him, he aimed at the doorknob, pulled the trigger and let the bullets spray. The deafening sound of gunfire reverberated in the corridor, making his ears ring and Eva yelp.

Adrenaline burned a path through his veins, giving him a boost of energy as he kicked open the bullet-ridden door and bounded into the room that lay behind it.

A yellow glow filled a room that turned out to be half a bedroom, half a library. But it wasn't the abundance of books stacked on every available inch of the small space that triggered Tate's bewilderment. Nor was it the futon across the room, or the laptop blinking on a round metal table, or the wine bottles sitting on the floor.

No, what had him gaping in disbelief was the man on the ratty beige couch that spanned one cinder-block wall. Hector Cruz. Sitting there with a semiautomatic Ruger resting on his knee as if he had no care in the world. In fact, he looked downright bored as his gaze collided with Tate's.

"Hello again," Cruz said with a pleasant smile.

White-hot rage funneled through his body and lodged

in his throat like a piece of spoiled food. The son of a bitch looked the same as he remembered: curly black hair, mocking eyes, unkempt goatee. Only his attire was different—he didn't wear a brown uniform, but a pair of black cargo pants and a threadbare gray tank top that revealed the tattoos covering both his biceps.

*Bad call.*

Tate couldn't get the taunt out of his head. It repeated in his mind like a continuous loop, until all he could hear were those two teasing words and all he could see was the blood gushing from Will's throat as—

Sucking in a breath, Tate blinked once. Twice. And then he pointed his rifle at Cruz and finally found his voice. "Anything you want to say before I kill you?"

Cruz's smile widened. "I suppose a thank-you would be in order."

He faltered. "What?"

"Thank you." The rebel leader shrugged. "For bringing my woman back." He craned his neck, peering past Tate's shoulders. "Where is she, by the way? Eva, are you out there in the corridor?"

His jaw stiffened. He opened his mouth to tell Cruz to shut up, but the rebel kept talking—and his next words made Tate's blood run cold.

"Eva, *mi amor,* did you bring our son?"

# Chapter 15

*Our son.*

Those two words left Tate momentarily frozen. Just for a second, but it took only one second of hesitation to send everything to hell, and that was exactly what happened.

Before he could blink, something hit him from behind with the force of a Mack track. His rifle clattered out of his hands as he went sailing forward. A female scream registered, but he couldn't move, couldn't look in Eva's direction, because now there was a five-hundred-pound weight crushing his back.

Pain jolted through him as his arms were yanked violently behind him. He felt himself being disarmed—guns, knives, all gone—and then his wrists were twisted and tied together, and his equilibrium abandoned him once again as he was hauled to his feet.

It happened so damn fast Tate didn't know what hit him,

and he bit back a string of expletives for allowing himself to be caught off guard like that.

A quick assessment of the situation he'd found himself in, and Tate realized he was out of luck. Four more rebels with assault rifles had entered the room, joining the one who'd tackled him, a beefy man with the shoulders of a linebacker. With all those AKs pointed at him, he had no chance in hell of fighting his way out.

And where was Eva? He shifted his gaze, then stiffened when he saw her standing in the doorway. Her blue eyes were glued to Cruz, her cheeks paler than snow and her slender shoulders trembling like leaves in the wind.

There were no guns pointed at Eva. *That* he didn't miss.

*Our son.*

"Don't worry, *mi amor*," Cruz spoke up, his voice strangely somber. "I understand why you didn't bring our *hijo*. There are probably some matters to straighten out before we involve our boy."

Tate's jaw tightened further, a response that Cruz noticed, because those black eyes focused on him. "Judging from the look on your face, I gather she didn't fill you in on our history, did she, *amigo*?"

A shaky breath sounded from the doorway. "Tate—" Eva stammered.

Cruz interrupted her. "Quiet, Eva. I can handle this." With a jovial smile, the rebel rose from the sofa and strode toward Tate.

It took all his willpower not to launch himself at the other man, but he knew he'd be shot down like a dog if he did. He couldn't afford to be stupid about this. He'd already made a grave error by letting Cruz's revelation distract him, and if he wanted to get out of this mess alive, he had to play it cool from this point on.

"I don't know what she told you," Cruz began, "but I

suppose she said whatever was necessary to get you here."
Those black eyes moved to Eva. "It's all right. I don't hold
it against you. I treated you very badly, didn't I?"

Eva said nothing.

From the corner of his eye, Tate saw her mouth set in
an angry line. *Ha*. He doubted she was as angry as he was.

He still wasn't a hundred percent on what the hell was
going on, but one thing remained clear: Eva had lied to him.

Cruz was the *father* of her kid.

The resulting rush of rage, combined with an unwelcome burst of jealousy, set his insides on fire. Just picturing Eva in Hector Cruz's bed brought bile to his mouth.
And the memory of her kid…Christ, he'd left his men behind to protect *Cruz's son*.

Goddamn it.

"I'm afraid I wasn't very good to our Eva," Cruz told
Tate, his tone rueful. "But you know how it is, right, Captain? Love drives people to behave in crazy, irrational ways.
So does stress. And I'll admit, times were stressful then,
more so than they are now."

The rebel's eyes softened as he looked at Eva. "I don't
blame you for running away. I behaved very, very badly,
*mi amor,* and I truly regret that."

Tate couldn't stop himself for turning his head to study
Eva's expression. Her face was a mask of disbelief. "You
behaved badly?" she blurted out. "You turned me into a
prisoner in my own life!"

Cruz recoiled. His strained gaze darted to the five rifle-
wielding rebels in the room, as if it pained him to have
this dirty laundry aired in front of them, and then his eyes
flashed and he shot Eva a hard look. "Let's not trouble everyone with the boring details. We'll continue this discussion in private."

Cruz cocked his head at one of his men. "Take my

woman to the room we prepared." He spared Eva a pithy glance. "I'll be there shortly."

A yelp of protest flew out of her mouth as a rebel grabbed her arm and began leading her to the doorway.

"Tate!" Her voice was thick with anguish. "Don't believe anything he says, Tate. Don't trust—"

He didn't hear the rest of that sentence. Didn't really care to, either. The word *trust* hung in the air, making him want to laugh uncontrollably.

She was actually talking to him about trust? The woman had been lying to him from day one. Which didn't surprise him in the slightest, did it? He'd known all along that she hadn't told him the entire truth, but this? Covering up the fact that Hector Cruz was the father of her child? That she'd had a relationship with the man?

Anger and disgust burned a path down to his gut and seized his insides. He'd slept with the woman who'd once shared Cruz's bed.

The man who'd murdered his brother.

Jesus.

As he choked down his revulsion, he was tempted to throw smarts into the wind and do something foolish, like rush at the rebels holding guns on him. That'd probably earn him a tidy little bullet in the head, but at this point, did he really care? He wasn't getting out of this alive anyway. Might as well take out a few sons of bitches before he met his maker.

"Don't." Cruz's voice was deceptively soft, his gaze knowing as he glanced at Tate. "They'll shoot. And that would be a shame, wouldn't it?"

"Right," Tate said sardonically. "Because you're really going to let me walk out of this alive."

"I am. I have no intention of killing you, Captain Tate."

Cruz's tone or expression didn't reveal any mistruth, but Tate didn't buy it. Not one damn bit.

He feigned a bored look. "Oh, really?"

"Really. You don't know how impressed I am that you made it here alive. I heard about the ambush in the jungle, and it seems you evaded another attack a couple of days ago, too." The rebel chuckled. "The Americans are desperate, no?"

Tate narrowed his eyes. "Why do you say that?"

"Because they've teamed up with my military to hunt you down, and we both know your government likes to clean up its messes on its own. They'd probably be better off, too. I'm afraid the military in my country is nothing but a joke. But you already know this, since you made it here in one piece."

"And I'm supposed to believe you want me to stay in one piece, huh?"

"I do," Cruz confirmed.

"Yeah, and why is that?"

"Because I'm going to put you to use instead."

The laugh he'd been holding earlier slipped out, a harsh, bitter sound that resonated in the air. "Sorry to disappoint, but that's not going to happen. I'd rather let your men shoot me."

Cruz gave a chuckle of his own before nodding at his men. "Leave us," he told them. "But stay close."

After the rebels shuffled out of the room, Cruz gestured to the sofa. "Sit."

Tate didn't move. He stared down the ULF leader, feeling the odds return once more in his favor. Even with his wrists tied behind his back, he could disarm Cruz and snap the bastard's neck with his legs if he got him on the ground and in a good lock.

"Oh, Captain, you are so very predictable," Cruz said

with a sigh. "You could at least try to hide your desire to kill me."

"Why should I?" He offered another callous laugh. "You slit my brother's throat, you son of a bitch."

Surprise flickered across the other man's face. "Your fellow soldier, you mean?"

*"My brother."* Fury constricted his throat. "So you might as well kill me now, Cruz, because the two of us? We won't be reaching any goddamn agreements, not unless they involve me slitting *your* throat, amigo."

The rebel's answering sigh was heavy with annoyance. "My condolences about your brother, Captain, but it wasn't personal. I did what I had to do to save myself, so I could live another day to fight."

"Fight? All you do is rob and cheat and kill, under the guise of freeing your people from oppression. But all that money you squirrel away, where does it go, Cruz? To buy food and medicine and clothes for the people you're pretending to care about? Or does it go directly into your wallet?" He laughed again. "Don't bother responding—we both know the answer to that."

"Your arrogance astounds me, Captain, and I'd prefer if you didn't speak of things you know absolutely nothing about. I *protect* my people—"

"Protect them? Is that what you did in Corazón when you murdered hundreds of innocent people? You *protected* them?"

"My men and I did not harm those villagers."

"No, you just burned them to death."

Sarcasm dripped from Tate's voice, and he nearly launched himself at Cruz out of sheer anger and frustration. He couldn't believe they were standing around talking about that day as if it were a normal topic of conversation.

Burning villagers. Slitting throats. Just another day in the life of Hector frickin' Cruz, huh?

As his bound hands curled into fists and bloodlust flooded his mouth, Tate's gaze flicked to the Ruger dangling idly from Cruz's hand. Five steps and he could tackle the son of a bitch to the ground before the man even raised that gun.

"I'm sorry to burst your bubble, but those people were dead before my men and I even got there," Cruz informed him.

Tate raised his eyebrows. "And the doctor? I suppose he was dead, too?"

A dark smile graced the man's mouth. "Oh, no, he was very much alive, at least before I had the pleasure of putting a bullet in his brain."

"And why would you do that?" Tate said sarcastically.

Just like that, for the second time in less than thirty minutes, Cruz threw him for another loop.

"Because the bastard is the one who killed all those innocent villagers you're so concerned about."

Eva was numb. She couldn't move a muscle, couldn't form a coherent thought, couldn't even breathe properly. Her reaction back in that room shamed her. She was the *worst* backup on the planet. A cataclysmic failure. She hadn't even managed to get a shot off before one of Hector's men had ripped her gun from her hand. And she hadn't even *tried* to give Tate an explanation after Hector dropped that bomb on him.

In her defense, she'd been too damn shaken. She hadn't heard Hector's voice in three years, hadn't seen his face since the day he showed up at her parents' Manhattan co-op and demanded that she and Rafe return to San Marquez with him. Seeing him again had knocked her off balance.

She'd frozen in place like a deer in the headlights, seeing that car careening in her direction and unable to do a thing but let it slam into her.

And by the time she'd regained her composure, Tate had already been restrained by Hector's men and was looking at her as though she'd committed the ultimate betrayal.

*You did. You had a child with his brother's murderer.*

The mature, rational part of her pointed out that she'd had that child long before Tate's brother had died, but she knew that wouldn't make a difference to him. In his eyes, she'd become the woman who'd warmed a murderer's bed, and she knew nothing she did or said would change that.

Damn it. Why had she insisted on coming with him? She should've known that a confrontation with Hector would lead to the truth coming out. If she'd let Tate go alone, her name probably wouldn't have even come up, Tate would've killed Hector, and her secret would've been safe. But she hadn't been able to stomach the thought of Tate doing this alone. Of Tate getting hurt.

Except now he *would* get hurt. Who knew what Hector would do to him, and it was all thanks to her.

As agony ripped her heart to shreds, Eva rose from the four-poster bed that didn't belong in a room made up of cement walls.

Hector hadn't been kidding when he'd said he'd "prepared" a room for her. It wasn't the same one she'd occupied the last time she'd been here. No, that room had been more like a nursery, with a crib and rocking chair and changing table, items that were gruesomely out of place in this dark bunker. But Hector had insisted she spend her pregnancy in a safe place. He'd allowed her to go outside—under a watchful guard, of course—but every night, he'd make sure she was back in her room, locked up nice and safe for the night.

Her lips curled in a frown as she looked around. Along with the elaborate bed, which featured a mountain of pillows and a soft burgundy comforter, there was a small bookshelf crammed with all her favorite novels and an antique armoire filled with clothes that were her exact size. The one thing that was conspicuously absent? A computer, which told her Hector was as smart as she remembered. No way would he leave her alone with a computer; even if this bunker didn't have an internet connection, she'd still find a way to contact the outside world.

She started to pace, wondering what the hell Hector was expecting to happen. His reaction to seeing her had not been what she'd expected. He'd seemed happy. And *regretful*.

"He's playing you," she muttered to herself.

Yeah, he had to be. His apologetic admission about treating her badly was nothing but a ploy. She might be locked up in this room, but she still had the upper hand thanks to Rafe. Hector would never dream of hurting her as long as their son was still out there somewhere and she was the only person who knew where.

A sharp knock sounded on the door, putting a stop to her pacing. "Are you decent, *mi amor?*" came Hector's voice.

She experienced another burst of surprise. Since when would her state of undress deter him from marching into a room?

When she didn't respond, the lock creaked and then the door opened. Stepping into the room, Hector swept his dark eyes over her and frowned. "You're still wearing those filthy clothes. I had thought you'd want to be more comfortable. Didn't you see all the things I bought for you?"

"I saw them," she said stiffly. "They just didn't interest me."

When his eyes blazed, she instinctively moved backward, anticipating an outburst. Hector wasn't known for his restraint. If you angered him, you were punished, and nobody was immune to his wrath.

Or at least that was how he'd behaved in the past. Now, the rage in his eyes burned hot for only a few seconds before dimming into resignation. "I won't hurt you," he said in a quiet voice. "I already did enough of that three years ago."

Eva clenched her teeth. "Stop it. Just stop it already. I don't buy this remorseful act of yours. I don't know what game you're playing, but—"

"No games."

He didn't make a single move toward her. Just stood there with his hands dangling at his sides. He wasn't even holding a weapon, she realized.

"I mean it, Eva," Hector went on, his voice heavy with regret. "I was out of control back then. I was reckless and desperate for change, and nothing was happening. The cause was stalled, those bastards in our 'government' were refusing to hear our demands. Our people were dying at the hands of our military, dying from disease and starvation."

She stifled an irritated groan. She'd heard this all before, many, many times. Four years ago, his "dedication" to the cause had been inspiring, but he no longer fooled her. Hector was a tyrant who used violence to advance his cause, who used children to fight his wars, and she refused to believe he had anything good inside him.

"I took my frustration out on you," he said, gazing at her with earnest eyes. "And when you got pregnant, I was angry. Angry that yet another child would have to be born in this miserable country, a dictatorship operating under the guise of democracy. I kept asking myself, how could we bring a child into the world when every day children in San Marquez are dying?"

"Spare me the idealistic crap," she retorted. "I don't care

how angry or frustrated or scared you were. You had no right to *hit* me. No right to become my warden and control every aspect of my life." She shook her head angrily. "For God's sake, I had to *beg* you for *permission* to take our new-born son to New York so he could meet his *grandparents*."

His black eyes blazed with belligerence. "And I was right to deny you, was I not? You used that trip as a ruse to run away from me!"

"You made my life a living hell for eighteen months," she said coolly. "Nine of which I spent pregnant, right here in this dark, horrible bunker."

"I brought you here to keep you safe," he insisted.

"You brought me here to keep me under your thumb."

A frustrated growl left his mouth, and then he marched toward her, not stopping until his hands were gripping her waist like a vise. "I'm sorry. Is that what you want to hear, Eva?"

"I don't want to hear anything from you," she said bitterly. "All I want to know is what you did with Tate."

Something dark and sinister flickered in his eyes. "You're sleeping with him."

Her lips tightened. "What did you do with Tate?"

"Answer the question."

"You didn't ask one. But I did. So tell me what you did with him."

They stared at each other for several long moments, and then Hector's expression relaxed once more. She had no idea how to handle this new side to him. She was used to the volatile Hector, the one who exploded at the slightest provocation, who solved problems with his fists and cared for nobody but himself. This new Hector was calmer, more analytical, more restrained.

"The good captain is in a quiet place, where he can think about everything we talked about," Hector finally revealed.

"What the hell does that mean?"

"It means Captain Tate and I share a common goal. I made him an offer and now he must ponder it."

Both confusion and relief swept through her. She had no clue why Hector was keeping Tate alive, but she wasn't one to look a gift horse in the mouth. Tate was safe. For now, anyway.

And now she had to figure out a way to get them both out of this mess.

She shot Hector a wary look. "Why didn't you kill him?"

"Because he's of more use to me alive than dead." Hector waved a dismissive hand. "Why do you think it was so easy for the two of you to get in here, Eva? I've been expecting you both, and the guards were ordered to stay out of your way."

Surprise jolted through her. "Why were you expecting us?"

"Well, more you than the captain," Hector conceded. "I figured your uncle would take care of Captain Tate. That was our compromise, after all."

"My uncle? What are you talking about—" Her surprise transformed into a rush of hot outrage. "Miguel told you I was coming after you?"

"Of course he did. Miguel has been aiding the ULF agenda for years, *mi amor*."

She blinked in horror. "You're lying."

But all she had to do was look into his eyes to know that he was telling the truth. Her uncle, a military *general,* was on the ULF's payroll.

She'd gone to him for *help,* damn it. Miguel had been the one to tell her about Tate, the one to voice his agreement that her son couldn't live a normal life as long as Hector was still alive. God, her uncle had all but encouraged her to hire Tate to kill Hector.

"Miguel called me the moment he knew you were on your way here. He's the one who told me you'd be bringing Captain Tate along."

"What was the compromise?" she demanded.

"I'm afraid the Americans really want Captain Tate dead, so Miguel had no choice but to send a unit to eliminate the man. He has a pretense to put up, after all, as a loyal member of the military. As much as I wanted to use the captain, I agreed to let him be killed, as long as you were brought to me, safe and sound."

Eva gaped at him. "So my uncle agreed to *bring* me to you?"

"Yes, but it was unnecessary. The captain managed to stay alive. He's good, I'll give him that." Hector offered a self-deprecating smile. "Miguel didn't warn me that you were sleeping with the man, though." He held up his hand before she could speak. "It's all right, Eva. I forgive you. I drove you away and I accept responsibility for anything you've done during our separation."

Disbelief sent her eyebrows soaring.

"But although I've developed a new appreciation for patience and restraint, I won't tolerate my woman screwing around on me. Like I said, I need Captain Tate's assistance, but you're to stay away from him, Eva. I don't want my son near that man, either, once we bring him here. Now that you're back, I expect you to—"

"Back?" she cut in, her jaw falling open. "God, Hector! You're completely delusional. I'm not *back*. I don't love you anymore, I don't want to be with you, and I'm not letting you anywhere near my son!"

A short silence ensued.

For the first time since this sick reunion, Eva caught a glimpse of the Hector she remembered. The cold, cruel Hector who killed anyone who got in his way, who trained children to murder and steal, who orchestrated a prison break rather than pay for his crimes.

As his rugged features twisted in rage and his black eyes glittered like burning coal, Eva saw the man she'd run away from, and fear trickled down her spine like water from a leaky tap.

"My son belongs with me," he said, his voice so soft it sent a chill through her body.

"*My* son will never get anywhere near you."

A second silence hung over the room. Hector took a step back, crossing his arms over his chest. His biceps flexed, causing the tattoos on his skin to ripple ominously. His left arm boasted a tattoo of a red snake coiled around a machete—the ULF's symbol—while the right arm was completely covered with text. The cause's mission statement.

However, when Eva peered closer, she noticed a new line of text near his wrist.

RAFAEL.

Lord, he'd inked Rafe's name and birth date on his skin.

"My son belongs with me." Hector repeated himself in a lower, deadlier tone. "He needs to be groomed to lead the people once I'm no longer able to."

Terror erupted in her belly.

"Hopefully by then, there will be no need for rebellion—the country will be what we desire it to be," Hector went on, oblivious to her stunned expression, "but if not, my son will possess the skills necessary to lead. Now, I'd prefer if the three of us could be a family, the way it was intended, but if you choose to opt out of that arrangement, that's your decision. But Rafael—"

"Don't you dare say his name!"

"—will grow up with his father. Where is my son, Eva?"

A hysterical laugh lodged in her throat. "Somewhere you'll never find him."

Hector merely shrugged. "I'm afraid you're wrong about that. I have no doubt that our son is safely hidden at the moment, but it's not difficult to figure out where he'll be after I kill you."

Her heart lurched with horror.

"You would've named your parents as his guardian in the event of your death, isn't that right?" Hector smiled. "So really, all I have to do is put a bullet in your head and then send someone to New York to fetch my boy. I met your parents, Eva. They're not equipped to protect Rafael from the likes of me."

Anger swirled through her like a tornado. "I won't let you near him, Hector. I won't let you corrupt him."

"Corrupt him?" He sounded irritated. "That's rather melodramatic, don't you think?"

"What I think is that you're poison," she shot back. "You kill and destroy anything and anyone that stands in your way. Rafe is an innocent little boy—I refuse to let you—"

Pain stung her cheek as Hector backhanded her, stunning her into silence.

"You refuse?" he echoed. "You *refuse?* You have no say in this, Eva! That boy is mine! Not yours, but *mine.* Mine to do whatever I damn well please with."

She tasted the coppery flavor of blood in her mouth and realized that he'd split her lip. Wiping the corner of her mouth with her sleeve, she stared at the father of her child with undisguised bitterness.

"You're a different man, huh?" she mocked. "Because you seem like the same volatile, spoiled, angry man that I remember, a man who strikes out first and thinks about it later."

Ragged breaths flew out of Hector's chest, and she could

see him struggling to maintain control. Both his hands were curled into fists, and she instinctively moved back, anticipating an attack.

To her surprise, it didn't come.

"I think we both need some time to calm down," he said wearily. He took a step to the door, then stopped, turning to face her with a glint of humor in his eyes. "I've missed you, Eva. Your fire, your strength and determination. I don't want to have to kill you."

She barked out a laugh. "Gee, thanks."

"I want you to consider my offer. You, me, our son. A real family."

Another laugh, this time loaded with incredulity. "You escaped from prison and you're living in a bunker. What kind of life is that for a little boy?"

Annoyance crossed his expression but it faded quickly. "I mean it, Eva. I want to make this work." He paused. "In fact, as a show of good faith, I'll even do you a small kindness."

Her eyes narrowed. "What are you talking about?"

He extended his hand. "Come here."

She stayed rooted in place.

Hector's mouth tightened. "Come. Here."

With the taste of blood lingering on her tongue, she reluctantly approached him, but she didn't take his hand, much to his obvious displeasure. Yet again, he displayed that newfound sense of restraint, because he didn't react to the rejection.

She followed him out of the room, flinching when he rested his hand on her upper arm, and this time he *did* react.

"It would behoove you to be a little nicer to me, Eva. Keep being rude and maybe I'll change my mind and take you back to your room."

She ignored the threat. "Where are we going?"

"You'll find out soon enough."

They turned the corner and followed the hallway until its end, pausing in front of a solid steel door.

"See if you can persuade him to my way of thinking," Hector said as he stuck a metal key into the lock.

"What? Who are—"

Her words died as Hector pushed open the door and she found herself staring at Tate.

# Chapter 16

Tate lifted his head as the door creaked open. Hector Cruz's mocking face entered his line of vision, but it wasn't the sight of the rebel leader that quickened his pulse. It was Eva, who apprehensively appeared at Cruz's side.

He didn't want to look at her, but his gaze refused to comply despite his brain's command to look away. When he spotted the blood dripping down her chin, he had to forcibly stop himself from jumping to his feet and pulling her into his arms.

That he could still feel concern for her sent anger shooting up his chest, and he quickly armored himself with that rage, refusing to let Eva see that he still gave a damn about her.

Sitting on the floor, with his legs stretched in front of him and his wrists tied behind his back, Tate watched as Cruz stepped into the room, a semiautomatic dangling loosely from his grip.

"I thought you two might like to chat," Cruz said, sounding both amused and annoyed. Those black eyes pierced Tate's face. "Have you given any more thought to my proposition?"

Tate didn't reply.

Cruz sighed. "I see you need more time to consider it. Fine. Maybe Eva will have more luck." Now he gave her a pointed stare. "Knock on the door when you're ready to return to your room. Javier is right outside."

Cruz took a step to the door, then stopped and tossed a casual glance at the security camera mounted in the corner of the ceiling. "Feel free to untie him, but don't do anything foolish, *mi amor*. I'll be watching you." He smirked, then marched out of the room and closed the door behind him.

Once the lock clicked into place, Eva dashed across the room, her expression awash with concern. "Are you okay?" she asked in an urgent tone.

Tate shrugged.

She dropped to her knees, leaning behind him to tug at the restraints binding his wrists. Her hair got in his face, tickling his nose and making him want to throw his fist into something. Why did she have to smell so good? And why the hell was he reacting to her nearness? Didn't his traitorous body know that this woman was nothing but a liar?

Her breathing was shaky and irregular as she untied the knots, her fingers cold as they brushed his skin. When the ropes finally came free, Tate brought his arms back to his front and rubbed his chafed wrists.

Noticing that Eva was still half-draped over him, he shot her a hard look and said, "Thanks. You can move now."

She didn't say a word as she crawled away from him. She ended up stumbling to the other side of the small space and settling in a sitting position on the cold cement floor.

Although Tate didn't make eye contact, he felt her gaze on him, felt the desperation radiating from her slender body.

"Tate. Look at me."

He spared her a terse look.

"I'm sorry I lied. I should have told you that Hector was Rafe's father, but I knew that if I did, you wouldn't agree to help me."

A groan lodged in his throat. He wanted to block out the sound of her voice, but clearly he was a masochist, because he found himself hanging on to her every word. He gave her no sign of it, though, maintaining a cool, indifferent mask even while fighting the insane urge to go to her and wrap his arms around her.

What the hell was the matter with him?

This woman had *lied*. She'd *slept* with Cruz, had a child with that monster. She didn't deserve Tate's sympathy or concern, and certainly not his forgiveness.

"Everything I told you about my past was true," she said softly. "My reasons for coming to San Marquez, my support of the ULF. The only thing I lied about was Rafe's true father. I…" Her voice cracked. "I was in love with Hector. Stupidly in love with him."

The streak of jealousy that soared up his spine irked the hell out of him. He wisely kept his mouth shut, knowing that if he said something, Eva might see through his uninterested façade. But hell, why *was* he interested? He shouldn't want to know the unholy details of that unholy union, and yet the need for details, the need to make sense of it all, gnawed at his gut like a hungry scavenger.

"It only took six months before he showed his true colors," Eva went on, sounding ashamed. "He was cold, violent, had a hair-trigger temper. Things weren't going well for the cause at that point, a lot of arrests and strife, no money coming in. Hector was furious about everything, and he took it out on me."

"And yet you stayed with him," Tate couldn't help but snipe. He immediately regretted that show of emotion, but added, "What, was the violence a turn-on?"

Her blue eyes flooded with sadness. "No, it wasn't a turn-on. I decided to leave him after the first time he hit me, but then I found out I was pregnant. I made the mistake of telling him, and he refused to let me go. I wasn't kidding about being a prisoner—I had guards on me at all times. I couldn't go anywhere alone, couldn't talk to my parents without Hector being in the room. He hovered over me during the entire pregnancy, and eventually I played along. I made him think that I'd calmed down, that I wasn't planning on leaving him once the baby was born."

Tate raised his eyebrows. "And he believed it?"

"I'm very convincing," she said dully.

Oh, he didn't doubt that. Not one bit. Another rush of jealousy filled his gut at the notion that Eva might have used her sexuality to convince Cruz of her sincerity.

"I made him believe I was still in love with him and that I wanted us to be a family. He bought it, and eventually he stopped keeping such close tabs on me. After Rafe was born—" her smile was dry and bitter "—he was born here, actually, in this bunker. And after his birth, I convinced Hector to let me fly to New York so my parents could meet their grandson. He agreed, as long as I took a couple of guards with me."

She uncrossed her legs, stretching them out in front of her, and Tate couldn't help but remember how amazing those shapely legs felt wrapped around his waist as he moved inside her.

The memory brought a silent curse to his lips. Christ. What was *wrong* with him?

"The moment the plane touched down on American soil, I knew I was free. Hector tried to bring me back, but my parents helped me leave town, and, well, you know the rest of the story," she finished. "Three years of running, and then I found my way to you."

"And conned me into helping the mother of Hector's child," he muttered.

Her tone grew chilly. "Rafe is *my* child. It's not my son's fault that his father is a monster. I've spent three years trying to keep Rafe away from that man. Everything I've done has been to protect my little boy."

Tate frowned. "You should have told me the truth."

"Would you have teamed up with me if you knew?"

"No."

"Then I'm glad I didn't tell you," she said bluntly. "Because the only way to keep Rafe safe is to remove Hector from his life, and I needed you in order for that to happen."

Tate snorted, gesturing around the cramped, windowless room. "How'd that turn out for you, Eva?" Now he chuckled. "You know, you would have had a better shot of me killing Hector if you'd stayed behind like I wanted you to. I would've killed the SOB in a heartbeat, instead of hesitating because I was too damn shocked to hear that he's your *lover*."

"Was," she corrected, her voice stiff. "The only thing I feel for that man now is loathing and disgust."

"Oh, I know all about disgust, sweetheart. I'm feeling quite a bit of it right now."

She flinched as if he'd struck her. "That's not fair."

"You really wanna talk about fair when we're locked up in a room by the father of your kid?"

Even from six feet away, he could see her pulse vibrating in her delicate throat. Panic moved over her face as she studied their surroundings, and he saw exactly what she was seeing—no furniture, no windows, no weapons. A locked door with a guard behind it, and a slim-to-none chance of escape, leaning closer to *none*.

*You had your shot and you didn't take it.*

The reminder only deepened his foul mood. Yeah, he'd had his chance to kill Cruz, hadn't he, but he'd let the bastard blindside him with that baby-daddy bullcrap. Now he had to pay the price for that asinine move.

The silence dragged as each of them sat in their respective corners. Tate kept his gaze on his feet, but he felt Eva watching him intently. Sure enough, when he tipped his head up, he noticed her astute blue eyes focused on him.

"What?" he muttered.

"Before he brought me in here..." She visibly swallowed. "He told me he doesn't plan on killing you. He said the two of you share a common goal. What did he mean by that?"

As much as he wanted to be juvenile about this and give her the silent treatment, Tate couldn't fight the need to talk this entire baffling development through. He still couldn't believe everything Cruz had told him, and now that he was reminded of it, the perplexing details began flashing through his head again.

Torn between making sense of it and shutting out a woman he clearly couldn't trust, he drummed his fingertips on the cement floor, feeling Eva's curious eyes on him.

"Tate?" she said quietly.

He released a long breath. "Cruz claims the villagers in Corazón were dead before the rebels even got there."

She looked dubious. "That sounds suspect. And how did they supposedly die?"

"From the virus that Richard Harrison tested on them."

Her breath hitched. "What?"

"Project Aries," Tate said. "Cruz says Harrison's lab

manufactured a biological weapon that was being tested in remote villages throughout the country."

"And how on earth does Hector know this?" she demanded, sounding skeptical.

"That's what Harrison supposedly told him before Cruz killed the guy. It was all the information Cruz managed to get—he claims to have no idea who gave the green light for Harrison's project, or if either of our governments is even aware of it. All he knows is that when he and his men showed up at the village, everyone was already dead."

"So why did they burn the bodies?"

"To control the infection," he said grimly. "They weren't sure if the virus was contagious."

"Hector isn't a doctor," Eva muttered. "How does he know those people were even infected with something?"

"He says the only visible symptoms were nosebleeds, and that it looked like some of the villagers had foamed at the mouth. But he was pretty much convinced of foul play when he discovered Harrison and his staff examining the bodies and taking notes."

Eva's blue eyes blazed. "Harrison was still in the village, *cataloging* the dead bodies?"

"According to Cruz, yes. Supposedly the village was a test site for this disease."

Eva went quiet for a moment. "Then it must have been approved by the American government," she said steadfastly. "And now they're trying to cover up what happened in the village. That's why they're trying to kill you, Tate."

"Then why send my team to begin with?" he pointed out. "Why put us in the position to discover what Harrison was up to?"

She shrugged. "They needed Harrison. Hector took him hostage, right?"

"He denies that. Says that he and his men interrogated

Harrison for six hours, seven hours tops, before my unit showed up. Which makes no sense," Tate said in frustration, "because we were told that Harrison had already been a captive for twenty-four hours at that point."

"I think it's safe to assume that everything you were told was a lie," she replied. "And it doesn't matter what the details are. Maybe Hector is lying and he *was* holding the doctor hostage and trying to negotiate with the U.S., or maybe Harrison managed to get an SOS out before the rebels swarmed the village. Maybe he contacted someone in the government and asked to be extracted. Like I said, doesn't matter."

"And why not?"

"Because either way, Harrison was still the head of that project, and our government couldn't afford to lose him. They probably thought, hey, we'll send in a team to see what's going on and try to bring the doc home if he's alive. Tell them it's an extraction and then deal with shutting their mouths once they come home." Her mouth set in a grim line. "The second your team was exposed to that village, someone was already planning on making sure you couldn't talk, regardless of whether you figured out the truth while you were there."

It made sense. It also grated, how levelheaded Eva was about this all, and how quickly he'd confided in her when he shouldn't be saying a damn word to her.

"What exactly does Hector expect you to do for him?" she suddenly asked, sounding uneasy.

"Help him take down his government."

Her jaw fell open. "Are you serious?"

"Yep. He wants me to go back to the States and expose what happened in Corazón. He'll offer me money and protection, and give me a fleet of guards if necessary, as long as I take this all the way to White House."

Now she laughed. "And do what?"

"He wants the American alliance with his country severed. He wants our troops and our relief workers and our doctors out of San Marquez."

"That's...ambitious."

Tate rolled his eyes. "Apparently I'm the man to make that happen. His reasoning is that if we threaten to expose that the U.S. government is actively developing biological weapons while telling the world it isn't, they'd happily cut ties with San Marquez in order to cover that up."

"Does he not know our policy of not negotiating with terrorists?"

"I didn't say his reasoning made sense."

Sense? It suddenly occurred to him that maybe what didn't make *sense* was the way he was sitting here and chatting with Eva as if nothing had changed between them.

The absurdity of his actions settled over him like a black cloud, but what infuriated him even more was the awareness that picking Eva's brain had become so natural he didn't even question it anymore. He hadn't realized how much he'd come to enjoy having her around, talking to her, bouncing ideas off her, sharing his frustration about that mission-gone-awry that he still didn't understand. Somehow, this woman had sneaked through his defenses, and that pissed him off beyond belief.

"Don't shut down on me."

Her strained voice jerked him back to the present. "What are you talking about?"

"You're about to shut down. I can see it in your eyes." She sighed. "For a moment you forgot that I lied, and you were talking to me like everything was normal, but now you're going to shut down again and pretend I don't matter to you."

"News flash, sweetheart—you don't." He didn't regret

the callous words, not even when he saw the flash of pain in her eyes.

Pain that quickly transformed into steely fortitude. "You're lying," she retorted. "You care about me. If you didn't, you wouldn't have freaked out at the thought of putting me in harm's way, or tried so hard to make me stay behind outside the tunnel."

"Maybe I didn't want you in my way—did you ever think of that?"

"You care about me," she repeated. "You like me and you respect me and you wouldn't be so angry with me right now if I didn't matter to you. I'm sure people lie to you all the time, Tate—do you react this way every time it happens? I doubt it."

"Eva—"

"Tell me I matter," she interrupted. "Stop patronizing me and tell me I matter to you, damn it."

*You matter.*

"You don't" was what he said, and as a result, her beautiful face collapsed. "Don't fool yourself, Eva. The only thing between us was sex. No relationship, no hope for a future. It was just sex."

"Just sex," she echoed, her voice laced with sadness.

"That's right. All I ever wanted from you was your body. I never made any promises or led you on. I never made you think it would be all rainbows and sunshine and happily-ever-after for us."

But a part of him *had* secretly wondered if it was possible, hadn't it?

That cold, embarrassing truth burned a hole in his gut. Christ, he *had* considered it. A lot, in fact, during those two days they'd been stuck in the cave. Holding Eva, talking to her, laughing with her—for a few brief moments, he'd gotten caught up in the foolish notion that he and Eva might be able to keep this going after Cruz was dead.

But who the hell was he kidding? He knew better than that. Getting close to people only resulted in heartache. And Eva in particular? The woman was no good for him. She was nine years younger, and she had a *kid*. Make that *Cruz's* kid, for Chrissake.

"You never made me any promises," she agreed. "I didn't make any, either. But I'm promising you something right now—I didn't lie because of some secret plot to lure you out of hiding or to bring you to Hector, or whatever other suspicions are running through your head. I lied because I was scared. I needed you, and I was scared you wouldn't help me if you knew the truth about my relationship with Hector."

She slid up to her feet and crossed the room, kneeling before him once more. When her hands came out to cup his chin, Tate stiffened, but he didn't have the strength to push her away.

"Maybe I don't matter to you, but *you* matter to *me*," she said fiercely. "You know why I fought to confront Hector with you? It wasn't because I didn't trust that you'd kill him, it was because I didn't want you to get *hurt*. I wanted to have your back just in case you ran into trouble—because I care about you and because the thought of losing you was too much to bear."

He swallowed, hoping she couldn't see the rapid hammering of his pulse in his throat.

"I trust you, Tate, and I care about you. All this time we've spent together has taught me that not all men are like Hector. You've treated me like an equal on this entire journey. And yeah, you're ruthless and grumpy and cold at times, but you're also sweet and tender and funny—" her breath caught "—and I'm falling for you."

As her confession hung in the musty air, it took several moments for it to register in Tate's brain. When he absorbed what she'd said, his initial reaction was unexpected—his heart did a pathetic flip, his breath hitched the slightest bit, and he experienced a hot, unfamiliar emotion that was akin to...*joy?*

Just as quickly, that feeling faded, replaced by something equally hot but this time familiar: anger. Directed at Eva. Directed at himself.

*Especially* at himself, because what the hell was the matter with him? He shouldn't feel joy over the fact that this woman might love him. He didn't want or need her love.

Suddenly he couldn't even look at her. His body was overcome by a heap of volatile emotions he couldn't define, and his anger intensified, so powerful he could swear he felt the walls move from the force of it.

It wasn't until he saw the look of shock and fear on Eva's face that he realized his fury wasn't manifesting itself in this room.

The bunker was under attack.

As a deafening boom reverberated in the air, the walls literally shuddered, pieces of cement breaking off from the ceiling and fluttering down to the floor like confetti.

Tate shot to his feet just as he heard a second blast. Muffled, as if it had happened far above them. Without questioning his actions, he launched himself on Eva and shielded her with his body, keeping his head down as he anticipated another explosion.

It didn't come. Other than a slight ringing in his ears and Eva's shallow breathing, everything had gone silent.

He awkwardly shifted his weight, annoyed that his first instinct in the face of danger had been to protect Eva, but before he could question the impulse, gunfire erupted beyond the door. There was a startled cry, another gunshot, and then footsteps approached the room.

Just as the door swung open, Tate stood up and pushed Eva behind him.

And came face-to-face with a pair of familiar gray eyes.

"Are you frickin' kidding me?" he demanded.

Sebastian Stone flashed a rogue grin. "Mornin', Captain. Fancy meeting you here."

Eva blinked a few times to make sure that was actually Sebastian standing there in the doorway. Short blond hair, mocking gray eyes, rugged features. Yep, that was him. He was the last person she'd expected to walk in, but boy, was she happy to see his face.

She had no clue what was going on beyond this room, but it didn't sound pretty. Gunshots, explosions, tremors. Was someone waging a small war out there?

"What the hell are you doing here?" Tate barked, scowling at the sandy-haired man who'd waltzed in as if he owned the place.

In his dirt-streaked T-shirt, army fatigues and military-issued boots, with an assault rifle in his hands, Sebastian looked every bit the warrior he was. Only the smirk on his face seemed out of place.

"Saving your ass," he replied. "So come on, let's not waste time. Cruz's sorry excuses for soldiers are up there scrambling to figure out why they're under attack, but they won't stay confused for long."

"What exactly did you do?" Tate asked, as Sebastian tossed him the rifle.

The other man pulled a handgun from his waistband and cocked the weapon. "I blew up the entrance, and most of their vehicles."

Eva didn't miss the amusement on Tate's face. "How'd you swing that?" he asked.

"Note to Tate—don't leave a rocket launcher lying around in the shrubs," Sebastian replied with the roll of his eyes. "Someone else might come across it and blow up a rebel leader's secret lair."

Tate snorted.

"Those explosives you set all over the perimeter didn't hurt, either," Sebastian added. He grinned and held up a small silver device that Eva guessed to be a detonator. "I figured you wouldn't mind if I hijacked your bombs."

"Not at all," Tate said solemnly. He adjusted his grip on the rifle. "Come on. Let's beat it."

Sebastian's gray eyes flicked in Eva's direction. "She coming with us?"

Tate hesitated.

Eva's heart dropped to the pit of her stomach.

He'd hesitated.

He'd actually *hesitated*.

But before she could fully absorb the implications behind that one little beat of silence, Tate was already nodding. "Yeah," he said gruffly. "She's coming with us."

Without checking to see if she was following, the two men bounded out the door, leaving Eva to tail after them while continuing to battle that frigid burst of clarity.

Her heart felt as if someone had pummeled it with a baseball bat, and the hot tears stinging her eyes made her vision go cloudy. She was vaguely aware of two dead rebels sprawled on the corridor floor. Sebastian's doing, most likely.

They moved at a breakneck speed, navigating hallways that were surprisingly quiet and threat free. Why weren't rebels popping out and trying to shoot them? Where was Hector? He'd had a camera in that room, for Pete's sake.

He had to know that she and Tate had escaped, so where the hell was he?

"There's just one more thing I need to do before we blow this joint."

Tate's low voice jerked her from her troubled thoughts.

"Already way ahead of you," Sebastian said, as they turned another corner.

"Obviously not, or you'd know we have to go *this* way," Tate replied, his green eyes flashing with irritation as he took a step back toward the opposite end of the hall.

Sebastian grinned. "Just trust me. We're going this way."

Reluctance creased Tate's features, just for a moment, but then he nodded and allowed the other man to take the lead.

Eva tried not to feel upset in the face of Tate's easy acceptance of Sebastian's "trust me." It shouldn't have bothered her, or hurt her, that he trusted the other man. After all, they'd known each for years.

Yet it *did* hurt, how readily he trusted Sebastian when he'd viewed her with nothing but distrust since the day they'd met—even after spending hours naked in each other's arms.

And he'd *hesitated* when Sebastian asked whether to take her with them.

Ignoring the pain squeezing her heart like a boa constrictor, she forced herself to match the men's swift pace. The cinder-block walls whizzed past; overhead lights hummed and flickered as they raced through the bunker toward the room that led to the tunnel entrance.

Five minutes later, they'd ducked down the hatch and were hurrying toward the end of the tunnel, and when they finally emerged from the second hatch, Eva blinked wildly as bright light assaulted her. They'd entered the bunker when it was still dark out, but now the sun sat high in the morning sky, shining down and marring her vision with sunspots.

When the scent of smoke wafted toward them, she turned her head and saw thick black plumes rising from the other side of the rock face. Muffled shouts could be heard in the distance. Then Sebastian clicked the silver device in his hand, and suddenly the ground beneath their feet shook. Another column of smoke swiftly rose from beyond one of the craggy hills.

"This way," Sebastian said, leading them in the direction of a rock-strewn slope a couple of yards away.

Eva noticed Tate frowning as they trailed after the other man. Her own brows knit together, then soared when she spotted the dead man lying at the top of the slope. The man was sprawled on his back, and the front of his brown ULF uniform boasted a dark stain. Blood.

She'd barely absorbed the sight when she noticed the Jeep parked ten feet away. And the other two bodies. The pools of blood spreading beneath the rebels' heads made her blanch.

"You've been busy," Tate murmured.

Sebastian shrugged. "Like I said, saving your ass. Come on. Got a surprise for you."

Eva felt unbelievably uneasy as Sebastian gestured to the Jeep. She hung back, unsure she wanted to see this "surprise." Instead, she watched as the two men stalked off, with Sebastian in the lead. The Jeep's top was down, so she could still see both men as they rounded the vehicle.

Tate's green eyes dropped to the ground, focusing on something out of her line of vision, and when she heard him mutter a savage curse laced with satisfaction, Eva knew exactly what was back there.

Swallowing hard, she staggered toward the Jeep and peered around it.

Lying on the dirt, tied up and gagged, was the father of her child.

# *Chapter 17*

The bittersweet taste of satisfaction filled Eva's mouth
as she stared at Hector's immobilized figure. He wasn't
blindfolded, and his eyes snapped open when she walked
up, oozing with betrayal as they locked with hers. But he
didn't make a single sound. He just stared at her with those
burning eyes, his face an angry accusation.

"Caught him trying to flee after I blew up the entrance,"
Sebastian explained with a smirk. "Figured you'd want the
honor of ridding the earth of this bastard."

For a second, Eva thought he was talking to *her,* but
when Tate let out a growl of approval, she realized the
comment had been directed elsewhere.

"We don't have a lot of time," Sebastian added, taking
a step back. "I'll give you some privacy."

Eva scarcely noticed the man walk away. She was too
focused on Hector's outraged black eyes and Tate's strained
profile.

Her hands started to shake, her heart beating irregularly as she waited for Tate to do something. Anything. And yet when he finally made a move, slowly lifting his rifle, she nearly yelled, "Stop!"

Could she really stand here and let him kill a man in cold blood?

*This is the man who terrorized you!*

The internal reminder didn't ease the sudden tightness of her throat.

"I would have preferred to end it with a knife," Tate said in a calm voice, his green eyes fixed on Hector, "but you disarmed me back there, so I'm afraid I'll have to make do with this." He waved the barrel from side to side, just in case Hector hadn't noticed the rifle pointed at him.

Eva's entire body went cold with fear and indecision. "Tate, maybe—"

"Maybe what?" he cut in. "Maybe I should spare this bastard's life?"

She gulped down the lump wedged in her throat. "I...I don't know."

"I should have known you didn't have the stomach for this. Go wait with Sebastian, Eva. You shouldn't be here."

He was right. She shouldn't be. She also shouldn't stand by and watch him murder an unarmed man, yet she couldn't move a muscle. She was frozen. Numb. Unable to think clearly.

"I want to ask him something first," she blurted out.

Irritation flickered in Tate's gaze. He lowered the rifle. "Is that really necessary? Everything he'll tell you will be a lie."

"I don't care." She stubbornly lifted her chin. "I want to ask him anyway."

She failed to add that whatever she did next depended on the answer Hector gave her. Wholly depended on it, in fact.

Because she could fight Tate. She could demand he spare Hector. She could throw herself in front of that rifle if need be, as long as it meant living the rest of her life with a clean conscience, one that didn't harbor the burden of knowing she was a murderer.

The irony didn't escape her. She'd *asked* Tate to kill Hector for her. She'd brought him here for that exact purpose, and now that the opportunity was here, now that the only thing standing between herself and her freedom was Hector, she couldn't in good conscience let it happen.

"Take off his gag," she said softly.

With a sigh, Tate bent down and grabbed Hector by the armpits, yanking the man up into a sitting position, with his back against the rear wheel of the Jeep and his bound wrists resting in his lap.

Tate pulled the rag out of Hector's mouth, and immediately, the rebel spat at him. Unperturbed, Tate wiped the spittle off his chin, stood up and glanced at Eva.

She stepped forward and peered down at Hector, whose eyes took on a calculating gleam. "You know you don't have it in you, Eva," the man she'd once loved accused. "If you let him kill me, you'll live with it for the rest of your life."

She drew in a slow breath. "I want to ask you something. And I want an honest answer."

Hector's lips set in a wary line, but the suspicious expression faded fast, replaced by a soft look that reminded her of the day they'd met. The day they'd spent hours passionately talking about what they wanted for their country.

"Ask me anything, *mi amor*," he said, his voice gentle yet seductive. "I'll answer honestly."

She exhaled in a rush. "What does Rafe mean to you?"

His proud forehead furrowed in puzzlement. "I don't understand."

With a burst of frustration, she sank to her knees in front of him. "What does he mean to you?" she repeated. "Why do you want him in your life? What do you want for his future? Why do you love him, Hector?"

Now he seemed incredibly frazzled. "Because he's my son! He's my blood, and he belongs with me."

"Why?" she pressed.

"Because I need him to lead when I can't! Because I want him to be a symbol for hope, a symbol for this revolution! His future is here in San Marquez and I'm going to raise him to appreciate his roots, to fight for them, to—"

She was done listening.

*My son. My blood.*

Hector didn't love his son. No, Rafe was just a pawn in his power play, a *symbol,* and Hector would eventually destroy that little boy. Raise him to fight and revolt and do his bidding.

That was the difference between her and Hector. He didn't care about Rafe's future, only his own, while she… well, she'd gladly give up her life if that ensured Rafe would have a safe and happy future.

And she'd also sacrifice her conscience.

She glanced over her shoulder, her gaze locking with Tate's. "You're right," she whispered. "This needs to happ—"

Before she could finish her sentence, she was yanked backward as Hector looped his arms around her neck and jammed his forearm into her throat.

She gasped for air, her windpipe burning, her heart pounding.

Hector's wrists were restrained, but that didn't take away from his strength. "Put the rifle down," he hissed, "or I break her neck."

Eva looked up at Tate, whose green eyes had gone cold

with fury. Rather than lower his weapon, he continued to aim it at Hector.

"Lay down your weapon," Hector demanded. "We'll go our separate ways, amigo, and Eva lives." His spittle splashed the side of Eva's cheek, the scent of sweat, anger and desperation filling her nostrils.

Tate still didn't make a single move.

Her pulse raced with panic. Oh, God. What if he stood by and let Hector snap her neck?

But the fear was unwarranted. With a harsh chuckle, Tate took a small step forward. "You honestly think I'm going to fall for that line of bullcrap again?"

And then he pulled the trigger.

The gunshot was deafening. It exploded in her ear, making her head ring like a carnival game. The pressure on her windpipe eased, and Eva stumbled forward, sucking in deep gulps of oxygen. Something warm and sticky stained her cheek.

Hector's blood. Hector's brains.

The nausea hit her hard and fast. Crawling away from Hector's lifeless body, she threw up, unable to control the horror that continued to spiral through her. When she had nothing left in her stomach, she crouched in the dirt dry-heaving, until she finally felt a hand on her shoulder.

She looked up and saw Sebastian looming over her, his gray eyes gleaming with impatience. In her peripheral vision, she caught sight of Tate dragging Hector's body away from the Jeep. The blood oozing from the bullet hole in Hector's forehead brought a fresh wave of queasiness.

Numb. She felt numb. And so very cold, but she got the feeling the chill wouldn't go away for a long, long time.

She might not have pulled the trigger, but she was as guilty of killing Hector as Tate was.

*He would've killed you. He would've destroyed your son.*

She clung to that reminder, knowing with bone-deep certainty that Hector's death was the only guarantee of her son's safety.

"Let's get outta here."

She turned at the sound of Tate's gruff voice. Their gazes collided and held. He'd saved her life. She knew without a doubt that Hector would have snapped her neck if Tate hadn't pulled that trigger.

"Thank you," she whispered.

He remained expressionless. "I didn't do it for you. I did it for Will."

Her throat tightened. Of course. This had always been about avenging his brother, the only person he'd ever cared about. She was an idiot to think that Tate might actually care about her wellbeing, that he'd been protecting *her* when he'd shot Hector. He would've killed Hector regardless.

Lord, maybe Tate really *was* the heartless bastard she'd thought he was when they'd first met. Maybe she'd been fooling herself by believing they could have something real.

Collecting her composure, she staggered to her feet and headed for the Jeep. Without a word, she slid into the backseat, while Sebastian took the wheel and Tate got in the passenger seat.

Before Sebastian could step on the gas, she leaned forward and gripped Tate's shoulder.

He turned around, his face expectant. "What?"

"You were considering it," she said dully.

His eyebrows lifted.

"Leaving me in the bunker," she clarified. "You hesitated. Like you were actually considering leaving me."

He was quiet for a moment, and then he offered that careless shrug she was beginning to loathe. "That's because I was," he said coolly, and then he turned around and banged on the dashboard, a signal for Sebastian to go.

Agony punched her in the gut. Her hand dropped from his shoulder, and she sagged backward into her seat, working valiantly to control the tears threatening to break free.

Heartless bastard, indeed.

*Paraíso, Mexico*

Tate had never glimpsed a more beautiful sight than the crumbling exterior of the stone fortress. It still astounded him that only six hours ago they were running out of a bunker in the Marqueza Mountains. Even more astounding was that the three of them had made it back here in one piece. They hadn't encountered a single hiccup, not during the chopper ride to the harbor, the boat to Ecuador, the private plane to Tijuana. Somehow, not a single thing had gone wrong, and Tate was starting to believe a higher power was looking out for them.

During the entire trip home, Eva hadn't said a solitary word to him. Sebastian hadn't spoken much, either, despite the fact that the man clearly had *a lot* on his mind.

Tate would never say it out loud, but he was damn proud of the sergeant. Aside from that one moment in the woods, when Tate's instincts had screamed that he was being watched, he hadn't picked up on Sebastian's presence in the slightest, despite the fact that Sebastian had tailed them all the way to Hector's hideout.

He'd trained the other man well, that was for sure. Maybe a little *too* well.

Didn't mean he was happy about the way Sebastian had blatantly disregarded his orders, though. He'd already verbally assaulted him for it, which was probably why the man was acting so moody.

"Mommy!"

The high-pitched voice drew their gazes to the door beneath the watchtower, which burst open as Eva's son dashed out of the fort, with Nick hot on his heels. For a toddler, the kid could sure move, but Prescott scooped the boy up before he got close to the Jeep. The little boy proceeded to wiggle like an eel in Nick's arms, crying out for his mom, who didn't even wait for the Jeep to come to a complete stop before she dove out.

As Eva made a beeline for her kid, Tate couldn't help but watch the reunion. An odd lump of emotion rose in his throat. He choked it down, disgusted with himself. So what if she was hugging that kid as if she never wanted to let him go? So what if her eyes sparkled with tears and her voice overflowed with pure love as she spoke to her child?

*Cruz's child.*

Then again, did that even matter anymore now that Cruz was dead?

The reminder brought a rush of saliva to Tate's mouth, a sense of deep satisfaction. He'd fantasized about this for eight months, and now it had finally become reality. The man who'd murdered his brother was dead.

"Good to have you back, Captain."

Tate tore his gaze from Eva and Rafe, and leaned in to give Nick a quick side hug and back slap. "Good to be back." He arched a brow. "Not happy that you kept me in the dark, though. You could've given me the heads up that Stone went AWOL."

Nick looked sheepish. "I figured you'd make the tail within two minutes."

He let out a breath. "I was a bit distracted."

Fortunately, Prescott had the good sense not to hazard a guess about the source of that distraction. The guy already knew, anyway, judging by the way his amber-colored eyes gleamed knowingly when Eva made her way over to them.

The kid was clinging to her like a monkey, but he lifted his head when Eva came to a stop, and peered at Tate with big curious eyes.

"Thank you for taking care of my son," Eva said quietly, her eyes shining with gratitude as she looked at Nick.

"It was my pleasure. He's a great kid." Nick reached out and ruffled the little boy's hair, eliciting a peal of laughter from the boy.

Tate experienced a burst of discomfort. He wasn't great with children, and he didn't like the way the kid kept staring at him. As though he was an alien from another planet or something.

"What?" he grumbled when the kid refused to quit it.

Rafe's bottom lip dropped out for a moment, a shy expression playing over his face, and then he grinned, pointed at Tate's face and said, "You're hairy!"

Despite himself, Tate cracked a smile, which earned him surprised looks from both Nick and Eva.

"Yeah, kid, I guess I am," he answered, dragging one hand over the thick beard covering his jaw. The thing was starting to itch, too. He definitely needed to shave.

Eva turned to Nick. "Do you mind giving us a moment?"

The other man nodded. "No problem."

As Nick drifted off toward Sebastian, who was loitering near the Jeep, Eva shifted Rafe to her other hip. "What now?" she asked softly.

"Mommy, I want down," her son whined. "Wanna go to Nick!"

She gave the boy an indulgent smile before setting him on the ground. He barreled off toward Nick, giggling in an easy, carefree way that brought another wave of discomfort to Tate's gut and had him wincing.

Eva didn't miss his reaction. "You don't like him."

Her blunt tone made him scowl. "I don't even know him."

"And you don't want to, right?"

His jaw tensed. "What the hell are you really asking me, Eva?"

Sadness washed over her beautiful face. "Do you want me to stay, Tate?"

He had no idea what to say to that.

"Because if you say the word, I'll stay." Her voice grew husky, thick with emotion. "I wasn't lying in the bunker. I'm in love with you."

Something hot and painful pinched his heart. "Eva—"

She didn't let him finish. "I don't know what kind of future we can have, but I'm willing to find out. I could stay. *We* can stay, me and Rafe." Hope burned in her blue eyes. "I know you're still angry I didn't tell you that Hector was Rafe's father, but I didn't keep the truth from you out of malice. And now Hector is no longer a threat. He's gone. My son is safe. And I'd like for Rafe and me to stay here. With you." She searched his face intently. "Ask us to stay, Tate."

Indecision burned a path up to his throat, nearly choking him. Was it that easy? Just ask her to stay?

But what was even the point? What kind of relationship could they have with him living in hiding? And would she expect him to be a father to that kid?

How could he be? He wasn't fatherhood material, wasn't interested in love or commitment or any of that emotional garbage.

So then why did his heart constrict at the thought of letting Eva go? And why did his gaze keep drifting toward that little boy happily playing with Nick ten feet away?

His silence stretched on and on. He couldn't seem to

get a solitary word out, and the longer he stayed quiet, the sadder Eva looked.

"Okay." She cleared her throat. "Okay, I get it. I'll…ah, I'll just go inside and pack up our stuff and, um, I'll ask Nick to drive us into town. Rafe and I can stay in the motel there until I book a flight back to the States."

His chest ached so badly it felt like a thousand-pound Sumo wrestler was sitting on the damn thing, but he still couldn't seem to utter a word.

"Um, well, then, I guess I'll just say goodbye now." Her throat worked as she swallowed. "So…goodbye, Tate."

## Chapter 18

"I love you, too, Mom, and I can't wait to see you guys," Eva murmured into the phone. "You still there, Dad?"

"I'm here, sweetheart." Her dad's warm baritone voice emerged from the speaker, and he sounded as choked up as she felt. "I'm dying to see that grandson of mine! The pictures you've been emailing aren't nearly enough."

Eva smiled through her tears, her gaze drifting toward the bed in the center of the motel room, where Rafe was sleeping soundly. "You'll see him soon enough, Daddy."

In fact, she would've preferred to be on her way to the airport already, but all the evening flights had been canceled thanks to a hurricane bearing down on them from the Gulf, so there was no point in hanging around the Tijuana airport waiting for the storm to pass. Might as well stay warm and cozy in this motel, and hope that the planes were back in the air tomorrow morning.

"Will Miguel be taking you to the airport?" Her mother

didn't sound thrilled by the idea, which wasn't surprising. Miguel LaGuerta was a nationalist to the core, and he made no secret of the fact that he disapproved of his younger sister's marriage to an Italian, and subsequent move to America. They'd been estranged for as long as Eva could remember.

But at the mention of her uncle, Eva's shoulders stiffened. Hector's accusation flashed in her mind, reminding her that she'd eventually need to confront Miguel about his part in all this. Someone had warned Hector that she and Tate were coming to him, and the only person who'd known about her plan was Miguel.

At this point, though, she didn't give a damn if Miguel was on the ULF take or if Hector had been lying. She was done with San Marquez. She didn't care what her uncle did or who he may or may not have betrayed. Now that Hector was gone, she had no reason to ever return to that godforsaken country.

"Miguel didn't come with us to Mexico," she told her mother.

*Because I couldn't risk telling him where we were,* she almost added, but stopped herself at the last second.

"So we'll take a cab to the airport," she finished.

"Okay, well, get some sleep, honey," her mother replied.

"That way you'll feel fresh and energetic tomorrow when you come home to us," her dad piped up.

She blinked back another rush of tears. It was so nice to hear her parents' voices. Even nicer to know that she'd be coming home to them so very soon.

"I will," she promised. "I'll call you guys tomorrow with my flight details, okay?"

After she hung up, she stared at the prepaid cell phone for a few seconds, tempted to dial another number. The number Nick had slipped in her hand earlier, the one for the men's satellite phone.

But she resisted the urge, knowing there was no point.

Tate hadn't asked her to stay.

He hadn't *wanted* her to stay.

She shouldn't be surprised, shouldn't allow it to hurt her, but she was, and it did. Despite the callous way he'd treated her back at the bunker, she understood where his anger had stemmed from—she'd kept something important from him, after all—but she also knew it was about more than one little lie. Tate had opened up to her during their time together, and that had scared him to death.

His bleak childhood had hardened him. He'd shut down, convinced himself that he preferred a life of solitude to a life filled with love. By letting her in and letting himself care for her, he'd probably broken the number-one rule in his emotionless warrior code.

*You're better off.*

Was she? In one sense, she supposed she was. Tate was a difficult man. Ruthless, dominating, prickly. And if they got together, she'd have to sacrifice her and Rafe's freedom once again, at least until Tate came out of hiding, and who knew when that would happen?

On the other hand, was anyone *really* better off without love in their life?

She hadn't planned it, hadn't wanted it even, but somehow, she'd fallen for the man. She'd glimpsed past his gruff exterior and discovered a man who could be sweet and tender, a man who'd protect her with his dying breath, who treated her like an equal and made her body burn with the simplest touch.

So no, she didn't feel better off.

Not by a long shot.

* * *

"A virus," Nick muttered, shaking his head for the hundredth time. "That's all Cruz said?"

"That's all he said," Tate confirmed.

The trio was up on the watchtower again, safe from the downpour thanks to the stone overhang above their heads. Tate had already filled them in earlier about everything Cruz had told him, but Nick and Sebastian were still visibly bewildered by it all.

"So the doctor we were ordered to rescue released some killer virus in Corazón," Sebastian said, shaking *his* head for the hundredth time.

"According to Cruz," Tate emphasized. "But I'm inclined to believe it might be true, especially since Eva came across that mysterious project Harrison was working on. Project Aries."

He was rather proud of himself—his voice didn't crack at all when he said Eva's name. And his heart had ached only a little, as opposed to the excruciating sense of being sledgehammered in the chest, which he'd felt earlier as he'd watched Nick drive away in that Jeep with Eva and Rafe.

"They're trying to shut us up then," Sebastian said, sounding confident. "Our government is experimenting with biological weapons and testing them on *human beings*. When they sent us to the village, they probably knew all along that we'd have to die, just in case."

"That's what Eva suspects," Tate admitted.

Sebastian got a funny look on his face, but it disappeared fast. "They can't be sure what we saw in the village, or whether we had contact with the doctor before he died. Either way, they need to silence us."

"So what's our next move?" Nick asked. "Find out who authorized Harrison's project? Maybe take this to the White House? Alert the media?"

He rubbed his hand over his freshly shaved chin. "I don't know yet. Let's sit on this for a while, let it settle, before we figure out a plan."

Nick nodded. "Sounds good."

Sebastian offered a nod of his own. "Agreed."

A flash of lightning lit the sky, drawing his gaze back to the steadily falling rain. The wind continued to pick up speed, and the sky was so black and cloudy you couldn't even see the moon.

*No flights will be leaving here tonight.*

Tate swallowed. He had no idea why that thought had crept into head.

Okay, fine. He knew exactly why he'd thought it.

"Hey, Prescott, give us a minute, will ya?" Sebastian said lightly.

Although his brows furrowed, Nick didn't object. "Yeah. Sure. I'll head inside and see if the wireless is working. I wouldn't mind doing a little online digging about that lab Harrison worked for."

After Nick disappeared, Sebastian didn't pull any punches. He simply crossed his arms over his broad chest and said, "Why the hell did you let her go?"

Tate blinked. "Pardon me?"

"Don't play dumb, Captain. Why did you let Eva go?"

"Because there was no reason for her to stay," he muttered. "We both got what we wanted. Cruz is dead. She and her kid can go back to New York now."

Sebastian's gray eyes flickered with irritation. "She doesn't want to go back to New York. She wants to stay here with you."

"Yeah, what makes you say that?"

"The woman is in love with you. Any idiot can see that."

Tate stared out at the rain sliding down the crumbling stone walls of the fort. Ignoring Sebastian's frank words, he shrugged and said, "We were right, by the way. She was lying right from the start. Cruz was her kid's father."

"I kind of gathered that. I heard what she said to him." Sebastian cocked his head. "Is that why you told her to get lost? You can't stomach the idea of raising Cruz's kid? Because if that's the case, shame on you, Captain."

He gaped at his fellow soldier.

"I'm serious," Sebastian said angrily. "I'm not much of a kid person myself—they're bratty and annoying and grubby—but even I know better than to blame an innocent child for his father's sins."

"I'm not blaming anyone for anything," Tate grumbled.

"So it's not that you can't raise Cruz's kid?"

"I can't raise *any* kid, Seb. I'm not father material."

"Bull." Sebastian actually had the nerve to laugh. "You'd make a good father. You wanna know why? Because you're a good man. Any kid would be lucky to have you as their old man, Captain."

He arched a brow. "What's with all the compliments? This is unlike you."

The other man shifted in embarrassment. "Look, I was following you and Eva for days. I couldn't risk getting too close, but sometimes, well, sometimes it couldn't be helped. And sound carries in the jungle and in the woods, so I'd hear things, whether I wanted to or not. But there was one thing in particular that I kept hearing, something I couldn't wrap my head around."

"What?" Tate said gruffly.

"Laughter." Sebastian grinned, and his white teeth gleamed in the darkness. "She made you laugh. A lot."

Gnawing on the inside of his cheek, Tate stepped toward the edge of the tower. Instantly, a gust of wind blew rain into his face, but he didn't bother wiping it off. He welcomed the cool drops, wishing the rain would wash away all the confusion plaguing him at the moment.

"That's when I knew that she was good for you," Sebastian went on. "The woman challenges you. She makes you come alive."

Tate gritted his teeth. "Where are you going with all this?"

"Will's dead, Tate."

A jolt of pain smacked him square in the chest. "I know that."

"He was the only person in your life that you opened yourself up to. I'd like to think that me and Nicky are important to you, too—"

"You are," he said roughly.

"But we both know you've always held a part of yourself back." Sebastian shrugged. "I get it, and I know why you do, but face it, it's not healthy. You can't close yourself off to people, otherwise you're in for a damn lonely life."

"Maybe it's the life I want."

"No, you don't. Nobody does." Sebastian blew out a frustrated breath. "Let's say you let her in, man. What's the worst that could happen?"

Uncomfortable, Tate shifted his gaze back to the rain, but Sebastian didn't take the hint and drop the subject.

"If you feel something for Eva, don't ignore it. Don't shove it aside and pretend she doesn't matter."

Tate sighed. "What's your point, Seb?"

"All I'm saying is…if you wanna go after Eva, and bring her and the kid back here, I wouldn't stand in your way. And if you want my opinion? I think that's exactly what you should do."

With that, the other man drifted toward the door, disappearing through the threshold and leaving Tate alone with his thoughts.

*What's the worst that could happen?*

Sebastian's question continued to float through his head, and the answers came in the form of images.

His mother's bluish skin as she lay OD'd on the floor.

His father's meaty knuckles coming toward his face.

When you let people in, they either betrayed you or abandoned you. People were selfish. They pretended to care, pretended to love you, but in reality, they only loved themselves. Selfish.

*Not Will,* a little voice pointed out. *Not Ben.*

And not Eva.

His breath caught as he glimpsed the truth in that. Eva wasn't selfish. She'd lied to him, yes. Convinced him to help her kill Cruz, yes. But not for her own self-interests. She'd done it for her kid. Ever since her son was born, she'd put that little boy first, which was something neither of his no-good parents had ever done.

Eva wasn't selfish. She was smart. Sassy. Determined. Courageous.

Not only that, but she was in love with him. For some asinine reason, that woman actually *loved* him.

And he was just going to let her walk out of his life?

*Idiot.*

Eva smoothed a lock of hair off Rafe's forehead and smiled at her sleeping son, who'd conked out the second she'd put him down and hadn't stirred since. Apparently he'd had the "bestest time ever" with Nick this past week, though he'd admitted to having a few nightmares and wetting the bed twice. Hearing that absolutely killed her—it broke her heart that she hadn't been there to comfort her son.

Because she'd been too busy *killing his father.*

God, what would she do when Rafe asked her about his

father? Surely he would, at least when he got older. What on earth was she going to tell him?

Her heart pounded as she imagined that inevitable conversation. She definitely needed to decide how much to tell Rafe, but she knew one thing for sure, she would never, ever tell him that she'd played a part in killing his father.

Swallowing, she stroked Rafe's cheek one last time, then stood up and headed for the kitchenette. She doubted she'd get any sleep tonight, not with the windows rattling and the walls shaking from the wind and rain, but maybe a cup of decaf tea would make her drowsy.

The motel had an electric kettle in the cabinet beneath the sink. She filled it with water and plugged it in, clicking the button just as a sharp knock sounded on the door.

Her pulse immediately sped up, her first instinct to grab the gun sitting on the table, but she quickly berated herself for it. Hector was dead, damn it. His men weren't behind that door. Neither was his ghost.

Only one person could be out there, and Eva's heart raced even faster as she hurried to the door. She undid the chain and threw open the door, and sure enough, there he was. Soaking wet, his black Windbreaker plastered to his chest, droplets clinging to his clean-shaven face. He was ruggedly handsome, undeniably sexy, blatantly masculine.

"What are you doing here?" she said, having to raise her voice over the din of the wind.

"Asking you to stay," Tate answered sheepishly.

She stared at him in surprise. "What?"

"You heard me." His voice came out gruff. "Now, are you going to invite me in or should I grovel out here in the rain?"

Overcome with both shock and amusement, she opened the door wider so he could step inside. As he entered, he unzipped his jacket and carefully draped it on one of the kitchen chairs, then turned to shoot her an apologetic look. "Sorry, I'm dripping all over the place."

"It's okay." She smiled. "So, what was it you were saying about groveling?"

Remorse flickered in his green eyes. "I shouldn't have let you go like that. Without telling you that…uh…" He exhaled shakily. "You matter, okay? You matter to me, Eva."

Her heart somersaulted. "Really?"

Tate nodded in earnest. "My whole life, I've tried to keep my distance from people. It was the only way to guarantee I wouldn't get hurt, but over the years, I've let a few people in. My brother. Ben. Sebastian and Nick. And you. I let you in, Eva, and now that you're under my skin, I can't get you out."

When she narrowed her eyes, he held up his hand. "I don't *want* to get you out. My entire life has been one bleak, miserable mess. I'm surrounded by violence and death and darkness, and I was okay with that, at least before I met you."

He offered his trademark shrug, which brought a smile to her lips and tears to her eyes.

"You brightened everything up for a short while, and then you left and the darkness was back, and I realized I didn't want to live like that anymore." He shifted awkwardly. "I'm in love with you, and I don't want you to go."

Tate's sandpaper-rough voice made her heart skip a beat. She wanted so badly to throw her arms around him and tell him she wasn't going anywhere, but one thing held her back. Her gaze shifted to the little boy sleeping on the bed. *Her* little boy. The only person who mattered more than Tate, more than life itself.

Tate followed her gaze, and his green eyes softened. "I know it's a package deal, sweetheart. If you'll let me, I want to be a father to your son."

Astonishment slammed into her. "Are you serious?"

He offered another nod. "I don't know if I could ever be a good role model for a kid, but I'll try to be the best man I can be, for you, and for your son."

Before she could answer, Rafe chose that exact moment to wake up. With a loud, childlike yawn, her son sat up like a light, rubbed his eyes and said, "Mommy, I'm thirsty." Then he noticed Tate and wariness widened his eyes. "Mommy?"

"It's okay, little man. This is Tate. You remember him, right? Tate's the one who took me on that trip."

Wrong thing to say, she realized, as Rafe's expression turned cloudier than the sky outside.

As Rafe glared at the man responsible for taking his mother away from him for so long, Eva suppressed a sigh and took a step toward the bed, but Tate swiftly moved in her path.

"Let me?" he murmured.

Intrigued, she hung back and let him approach her son, watching in bewilderment as he lowered his big body on the edge of the mattress. Rafe stared at the intruder with suspicious blue eyes, but Tate wasn't perturbed.

"You're mad at me because I took your mom away, aren't you?" he said gruffly.

After a second of reluctance, Rafe nodded.

"Yeah, I kinda figured. I'm sorry I did that. I guess I was a little greedy, huh? I just wanted your mom all to myself, but that wasn't cool at all, was it?"

Tate flashed that crooked grin of his, and Eva hid a smile when she noticed her son fighting hard not to grin back.

"Well, I promise you right here and now that next time your mom and I want to go on a trip, we'll bring you with us. Your mom said you like adventures, so what kind of adventure should we pick? River rafting? Rock climbing?"

And just like that, Tate won her son over.

"I wanna see giraffes," Rafe blurted out. "And a big castle. And a dragon. And snow."

As her smile reached the surface, Eva drifted toward the kitchenette to get Rafe a cup of water. He was still babbling a mile a minute, reciting everything he'd ever wanted to see or do, but he stopped talking to gulp down the water.

"All right, we'll continue thinking of adventure ideas tomorrow," she said firmly as Rafe handed her the empty cup. "Right now, you're going to bed, little man. Say goodnight to Tate."

"G'night, Tate."

Rafe didn't give her any arguments as she tucked him back in and read him a quick story. As usual, he passed out the second his head hit the pillow, which earned her a mystified look from Tate. He'd been sitting at the table while she'd put Rafe to bed, but now he stood up and quietly approached her.

"Your kid doesn't put up a fight at bedtime?"

She grinned. "Never. I must be the only mother in the world whose kid *loves* bedtime. I'm lucky."

Tate's sensual mouth curved in a smile. "I think I'm the lucky one."

Their eyes held for a moment, and then his expression turned serious again. "Do you forgive me for the way I acted at the bunker?" He swallowed. "When I hesitated about leaving you behind, it was my anger talking. I felt—"

"Betrayed. I know. And I forgive you." She searched his face. "Do you forgive me for not telling you the truth about Hector?"

"Yes."

Their gazes locked again.

"So what now?" she asked softly. "How will this work?"

Unhappiness creased his features. "I want to make you

so many promises, Eva, but I can't. Not while I've still got a target painted on my back. I need to find a way out of this mess, figure out who ordered the hits on me and my men."

"I can help," she said immediately.

"I'd appreciate that. But I'd also understand if you want to go. You've been running for three years, sweetheart, and now you don't have to anymore. You can go to New York, reunite with your family, build a life for yourself and Rafe." His voice grew hoarse. "It's not fair of me to ask you to hide out with me, because that's what I'm going to keep doing, at least until I can be sure my life is no longer in danger."

She gave him a gentle smile. "I'm not going anywhere, Tate."

Frustration crossed his face. "I have no right to ask you to stay. I'm a total ass for doing it."

"Like you said, I've been running and hiding for three years. What's a few more months?"

He stepped closer and stroked his knuckles over her cheek. "Are you sure?"

"I'm not going anywhere," she repeated. "You helped me get rid of my demon—it's only fair that I help you get rid of yours."

His hand continued to caress her face, and she covered it with hers, running her fingers over his rough-skinned knuckles. She lifted her other hand to his chest and placed it directly over his heart, feeling it beating beneath her palm. Strong and steady, just like Tate.

They stared at each other for a moment, and then he lowered his head ever so slowly and kissed her. Their mouths fused, lips parted, tongues explored. Tate drove the kiss deeper, fueling the fire building in her core, and she was gasping by the time they broke apart.

"Are you sure?" he asked again.

"I'm sure. I love you, and I want to be with you, even if

it means hiding out for a while longer." She leaned on her tiptoes and brushed her lips over his smooth jaw. "I just have one requirement."

"What's that?"

"We relocate to a better hideout. I love the outdoors, but I also love indoor plumbing. And real beds." She flashed an impish grin. "With that said, I've still got a lot of money."

"Stolen money," he said dryly.

She shrugged. "I like to think that I earned it, after everything Hector put me through. And I can think of nothing better than using Hector's money to find the five of us a secure place to lie low until we get you out of this mess."

"The five of us?"

She shot him a "duh" look. "Rafe and I are a package deal. Nick and Sebastian are *your* package. We're not leaving them behind."

The emotion shining in his green eyes took her breath away. "You're an amazing woman, Eva Dolce." His voice roughened. "And I promise you, I'll protect you and Rafe with my life."

"I don't need your protection," she murmured. "Just your love."

His mouth curved in a smile. "Well, that you've got. Anything else?"

"Yes, actually. One more thing."

Tate arched one dark brow. "Which is?"

"Your trust."

He reached for her hand. "Remember when I said that trust and sex don't have to go hand in hand?"

She nodded.

"Well, trust and *love*? Now, that's a whole different story, sweetheart." He slowly brought her hand back to his heart and held it there, flattening his palm over her knuckles. "You've got my heart, Eva. You've got my love. And you've got my trust."

Emotion clogged her throat, making it difficult to say a single word. But she managed four. "Right back at you."

# Epilogue

*Two Months Later*

"Seb, get in here."

Halfway to the kitchen, Sebastian detoured and ducked into the living room of the beach house, where Nick was peering at one of the laptop screens.

"What's up?" he asked.

"Come read this."

Furrowing his brow, he came up beside Nick and studied the medical report on the monitor. Key phrases stood out: *Malaria. Possible outbreak. Six dead. Containment. Valero, San Marquez.*

Sebastian hissed out a breath. Thanks to Eva's not-so-legal software, they'd been keeping tabs on any unusual medical emergencies in San Marquez, monitoring every hospital and clinic on the island. They'd yet to determine whether Hector Cruz had been telling the truth about a virus killing the people of Corazón, but they couldn't afford to ignore the potential lead, even if it had come from a dead rebel leader.

"Should we check it out?" Nick asked, his expression conveying his lack of enthusiasm.

"I don't think we have a choice, but let me go ask Tate what he thinks."

His gaze drifted to the window, which provided a view of the turquoise ocean and endless stretch of white sand. At the water's edge, Tate was crouched next to Rafe, pointing at the waves as he explained something to the little boy. Eva stood a few feet away, her black hair loose and ruffling in the warm breeze as she watched the two males with a smile.

Sebastian moved his gaze from the happy family and squared his shoulders. Forget *asking* Tate. No, he'd *tell* the captain that someone needed to check out this San Marquez outbreak situation. And that someone was not going to be Tate. The captain had a lot more to lose these days. A woman he loved. A kid he adored.

Sebastian, on the other hand, had absolutely nothing to lose.

"Call the airfield," he barked at Nick. "I want to leave for San Marquez. Tonight."

\* \* \* \* \*

# LET'S TALK

## *Romance*

For exclusive extracts, competitions
and special offers, find us online:

**f** facebook.com/millsandboon

**⊙** @millsandboonuk

**𝕐** @millsandboon

Or get in touch on 0844 844 1351*

For all the latest titles coming soon, visit
millsandboon.co.uk/nextmonth

# Want even more
# ROMANCE?

## Join our bookclub today!

'Mills & Boon books, the perfect way to escape for an hour or so.'

Miss W. Dyer

'Excellent service, promptly delivered and very good subscription choices.'

Miss A. Pearson

'You get fantastic special offers and the chance to get books before they hit the shops'

Mrs V. Hall

**Visit millsandbook.co.uk/Bookclub
and save on brand new books.**

## MILLS & BOON